STAR
BRINGER

STAR
BRINGER

TRACY WOLFF
AND NINA CROFT

PIATKUS

PIATKUS

First published in the US in 2023 by Entangled Teen,
an imprint of Entangled Publishing LLC
Published in Great Britain in 2023 by Piatkus
This paperback edition published in Great Britain in 2024 by Piatkus

1 3 5 7 9 10 8 6 4 2

Copyright © 2023 by Tracy Deebs-Elkenaney and Nina Croft

Cover art and design by
LJ Anderson, Mayhem Cover Creations and Bree Archer
Stock art by Nadezhda_Shuparskaia/Gettyimages and
xyligan_987/Depositphotos
Interior design by Toni Kerr

The moral right of the author has been asserted

A CIP catalogue record for this book
is available from the British Library.

PB ISBN: 978-0-349-43997-6

Printed and bound in Great Britain by Clays Ltd, Elcograf S.p.A.

Papers used by Piatkus are from well-managed forests
and other responsible sources.

Piatkus
An imprint of
Little, Brown Book Group
Carmelite House
50 Victoria Embankment
London EC4Y 0DZ

An Hachette UK Company
www.hachette.co.uk

www.littlebrown.co.uk

ALSO BY NINA CROFT

To my boys, who are my everything.
—Tracy

To Rob, who has promised to explore space with me
should the opportunity ever arise!
—Nina

Star Bringer is a thrilling sci-fi adventure romance with a heartstopping twist. However, the story includes elements that might not be suitable for all readers. Violence, alcohol use, sexual activity, graphic language, shootouts, hand-to-hand combat, perilous situations, blood, human trafficking, imprisonment, gunshot wounds, human experiments, and bombings are shown in the novel. Readers who may be sensitive to these elements, please take note.

CHAPTER 1

Kalinda, Crown Princess of the Nine Planets

"That's it. Your privileges as companion-in-waiting have been officially revoked."

Lara lays out the giant purple monstrosity she's selected for me to wear, undeterred. But I see the tiniest hint of a grin start to slip onto her lips. "And what privileges would those be, Your Highness?"

"You don't think you've got privileges?" I send her an arch look from where I'm sitting on the bed, but she's already returned to smoothing out my dress. "So ungrateful."

One of the best parts of having your best friend also be your companion-in-waiting is that you can give her shit. Sure, Lara tends to stick to propriety even when it's just the two of us, but our best moments are when I can get her veneer of decorum to crack. And the full-on grin she's giving me now warms me up from the inside out.

Of course, when your best friend is also your companion-in-waiting, she can talk you into *doing* shit you don't want to do—like wearing giant purple dresses that make you look like a Kridacan desert slogg with a nasty case of space pox.

"If by privileges, you mean the honor of waking up before five every morning, then may the Ancients bless you for the honor." Lara continues unbuttoning the ugliest dress in existence before retrieving a matching pair of high-heeled shoes.

I bat my eyes. "Admit it. You love our early-morning swims."

"Oh, absolutely, Your Highness." She shoves her long brown hair out of her face, then picks up one of the heels and undoes its delicate jeweled clasp. "Almost as much as you love dates with ambassadors' sons. Maybe I should mention to the Empress how much you miss Jorathon."

I narrow my eyes at her. "You wouldn't dare."

Before she can answer, the pod we are traveling in comes to a stop. We have officially docked on the Imperial Space Station *Caelestis*.

My stomach twists with a combination of nerves and excitement. I've been dying to get a look at the crown jewel of the Empire's science program since the spacebreaking ceremony several years ago. But this is the first time I've actually gotten near her, and I'm practically coming undone with excitement.

The fact that it's also my first official duty away from the palace negates some of that excitement—as does the fact that I have to tour it in full Imperial Regalia while doing my level best not to screw anything up. If I make one mistake, the Council's doubts will be confirmed, and I'll be stuck in the palace for the next fifty years.

Which is why I have no intention of messing up. The consequences don't bear thinking about.

"Give me your leg." When I continue to scowl at her, Lara grabs my leg herself and starts shoving my foot into the shoe. She snaps the clasp shut hard enough to have me yelping, then reaches for the second one.

"I keep telling you—I can do that myself." I try to take the purple heel away and get a hand slapped for the effort.

"Companion. In. Waiting," is all she says as she starts slipping on the second shoe, albeit much more gently than the first.

"Exactly. Waiting, not dressing."

"It's the same thing, and it's my job." She snaps the second heel into place, and her expression softens. "You're going to look gorgeous in this dress, Your Highness."

I sigh. "So gorgeous I might even find some hot Corporation guard or science nerd to show me a *good* time?" I waggle my eyebrows, just in case she didn't get my emphasis on the word "good."

Her firm mask of propriety is back in place, her russet skin smooth and unmarred by so much as the tiniest grin. "Absolutely not. For so many reasons."

Lara holds the dress out for me to slip on feet first—less chance of me messing up the elaborate hairstyle she spent the last hour twisting my long hair into.

"Kidding. I haven't forgotten we're here to talk about saving the entire system from total annihilation. I feel like that's more important than me getting laid."

Lara mutters something that sounds a lot like, "Debatable," but it's so fast that I can't call her on it.

"Plus," I add, "my mother went against the Council to send me on this trip. She's trusting me to do a good job and not screw anything up. Sleeping with some random in a space lab seems like the definition of screwing things up."

I try to take a deep breath, the weight of everything I'm about to do suddenly way more substantial than it was a second before, but Lara is already buttoning me into a dress so heavy and jewel-encrusted, it might as well be body armor. There's no longer room for movement of my diaphragm, which means joking around is definitely out. Unfortunately, so is breathing.

"You look so beautiful, Your Highness." Lara steps back as she finishes with the last of the tiny jeweled buttons. "What do you think?"

"Are there any sloggs bigger than the ones from Kridacus? Because if there are, I definitely look like one of those."

"Nope," she replies as she turns me to face the full-length mirror that runs along the wall. "Kridacans are definitely the largest."

I sigh glumly as I survey my reflection. "Then I'm definitely a new species. Hopefully of the nonpoisonous variety."

She takes the dress's cape out of the closet and wraps it around my shoulders. Because, obviously, a giant purple cape is what it was missing.

I glare at her, which she completely ignores as she fastens it with a brooch in the shape of a starburst just beneath my neck.

Before I can try to talk her into leaving the cape off—overkill is an actual thing—the comms beep. Lara and I exchange a look, and I sigh heavily. Only one person would be calling the comms link right now, and her title begins with E and ends with double S. Lucky me.

"What does she want now?" I mutter as I slide into the seat in front of the screen. Or, more accurately, try to slide. The dress makes it impossible, so I end up moving the chair aside and just standing.

"To wish you luck, I'm sure." Lara's answer is circumspect—exactly how a companion-in-waiting should answer. Her expression, however, falls for a second into total annoyance.

I snicker as I answer the call.

The Empress narrows her eyes on me from the viewscreen. "I hope you don't plan on laughing like that when you get off the ship, Kalinda. What is it I always tell you?"

"A royal's mask never falters," I recite for the millionth time.

"That's right. I know you have this, Kalinda." She sends me a smile that, for just a second, actually appears indulgent. But then naturally, she follows it up with, "Don't make me regret sending you off-planet. Do I need to go over how important this is?"

I mentally roll my eyes. "I know how important it is, Mother. And I've wanted to come aboard the *Caelestis* since before she became operational. I promise I won't embarrass you or the Empire."

"See that you don't. Also, make sure Ambassador Holdren doesn't get you alone. He has an agenda that doesn't coincide with ours, and I don't want you making any promises to him. And avoid the delegate from Glacea. From what I understand, he tends toward inappropriate conversation, and I would prefer to avoid any more *unfortunate incidents*."

She gives me a look that I know is supposed to shame me. But I stand behind my decision to push Councilor Samalani into my mother's Verbosnia bushes. Well, except for the fact that my hands had to actually come in contact with him to do it.

On the plus side, he hasn't said a single thing about my breasts since.

A knock sounds on the door. "Sorry, Mother, but Arik is here. I have to go."

"He'll wait until our conversation is through, I assure you." But she relents. "Don't overpromise. Don't ask too many questions. Don't forget the Imperial face, and you'll do great."

As if I could ever forget the Imperial face. Don't smile. Don't frown. Look interested but bored at the same time—all without actually moving a facial muscle. She's had me practicing since I was five.

"I won't. Thank you for this opportunity, Mother." I sign off before she can say anything else. I'm nervous enough already without any more of her awesome pep talk.

"We're so lucky to have her," Lara says. Again, totally circumspect. But also totally not.

There's another knock.

"Coming, Arik," I call.

Lara opens the door for me, then steps back to let me precede her into the main section of the pod—which is about half the size of the royal quarters I was just in.

"I'm sorry to rush you, Your Highness," Arik says with a respectful bow of his head. His green eyes glow with amusement.

"Not at all," I tell him. "I was just speaking with the Empress."

He gives me a sympathetic wink. Like Lara, he's been with me all my life and was a friend of my father's. I trust him implicitly.

My other bodyguard, Vance, is a new member of my entourage, and I'm pretty sure he's reporting to my mother. I'd trust him with my life but not my secrets—if I had any.

A sudden, sharp beeping splits the air. I jump, and both Arik and Vance look concerned. I mentally roll my eyes again—like they're the only ones who are allowed to be a little on edge? This is my first time representing the Empire. Surely I'm allowed a few nerves.

I'll be fine once I'm out there.

The pilot must have noticed my reaction, because he smiles at me before continuing to press a bunch of buttons that all look exactly the same to me. "It's just the final system-check indicator, Your Highness," he says. "We're cleared to disembark."

"Thank you."

Lara reaches a comforting hand toward me, then stops at the last second. From now on, we're on strict royal protocols, and a person doesn't just reach out in public and touch a Princess of the Senestris System—even if that person happens to *dress that same princess every day*. Just another of my mom's bizarre rules, and I add it to my mental list of things to change when I'm Empress.

I take another deep breath and give Lara my cockiest I've-got-this smile. She returns it with a little head tilt that tells me to get moving.

But as the shuttle's disembarkment ramp extends, my stomach flips with nerves. I ignore it and focus on my job instead. Toe the line. Deliver the message. Don't shame the Empire.

I straighten my spine and settle my best regal, I'm-so-bored look on my face. Then turn to Lara for an inspection.

She looks concerned.

Less grimace, more grin, then. Got it.

"Ready?" she asks.

"More than," I answer.

I'm ready to step onto the ramp, but Vance and Arik beat me to it. One quiet look from Vance's steel-gray eyes has me standing down despite the impatience gurgling inside of me. It's his job to make sure no one gets a clear shot at me. Except, of course, the Empress...

While I wait, I study the docking bay further—a huge, cavernous room with silver walls and a curved ceiling high above us. It's crowded with sleek and shiny shuttles of various designs. They all look new and impressive—even the patched ones—like every delegate is determined to put their best foot forward.

Then my gaze snags on something that doesn't quite fit in. It's dry docked in the far corner of the bay. I presume it's a ship, much bigger than the shuttles, but it's hard to tell anything else as it's covered by some sort of dark cloth.

To protect it or to hide it?

I love a mystery, and I itch to head over there and take a peek. But at that moment, Arik gives the all-clear from below and we're ready for business. My heart rate jumps. I'm trying to be cool, but this is a huge deal. And not just for me.

Because the reason we're here is to find out exactly where the oh-so-brilliant Dr. Veragelen is with her very important and very expensive research.

Is the massive amount of money poured into this research station going to save us all from a fiery and very imminent death?

Or to put it frankly—are we all going to die?

CHAPTER 2

Rain, High Priestess of the Sisterhood of the Light

"Oh, Merrick, look. There she is. She's so perfect. She looks just like a…" My mind goes blank, the way it does when I'm excited. Thankfully, that doesn't happen very often: the blankness *or* the excitement.

Maybe it's due to the drugs they gave me to help my body adjust to the much higher gravity here on the *Caelestis*. The space station is set to Askkandian gravity, which is more than twice that of my home planet, Serati. All I know is I've never felt this heavy before, like I'm fighting through mud with every step I take.

Then again, that could just be my nerves. Of all the places I'd ever imagined standing, here on this space station isn't one of them. Not just because its mission—stopping the sun from exploding—goes against everything it's pretty much my job to help bring about, but because high priestesses don't usually do this sort of thing.

"I think the word you're looking for is 'princess,' High Priestess." Merrick's tone is dry, but then, it's always dry. I think sarcasm is his second calling, right behind being my bodyguard.

"Maybe so, but how am I supposed to know that? It's not like I've ever seen a real live princess before." It's not like I've seen much of anything before. But that's not Merrick's fault.

It's no one's fault, really. It just is.

The princess glides to the top of the ramp, and I push up on my tiptoes to get a better look at her. She's tall, really tall, and though I tell myself that it doesn't matter, I can't help being a little jealous.

Not of her tiara or her amazing dress but of her long, willowy height.

I know high priestesses aren't supposed to care about their looks, and most of the time I don't. But every once in a while, being the shortest person in any room I'm in really stinks.

Today it stinks more than usual. Partly because I'm lost in the crowd and partly because in every glimpse I manage to get of her, the princess looks perfect. Regal. Serene. Confident.

I'd really like some of that serenity—and that confidence. Both are hallmarks of every high priestess the Sisterhood has ever had. Until me.

The princess floats toward the dais, her feet barely touching the ground. As people lean forward, eager to get a glimpse of her, I realize Merrick and I will soon be face-to-face with her. "Merrick?"

"Yes, High Priestess?"

"What do I call her again?"

He sighs, and in it I hear all the disappointment he doesn't voice. But he doesn't have to. I get that I'm a trial and a tribulation to him most days, but I also suspect that deep down, he cares about me. "If she addresses you directly—and let's all send up a special prayer that *doesn't* happen—then you must call her Your Highness."

His words momentarily quash my excitement at being here. In the same room as the princess, yes, but also here on the space station, so far from the only place I've ever lived. Home.

But then the energy of this place—of these people—has my blood fizzing in my veins. "Got it. And, Merrick—?"

Another sigh. "We went through all of this on the flight. You should have been paying attention."

"I know. But I was in space, Merrick. In *actual* space." And I wanted to know how everything worked. I think I annoyed the poor pilot with my incessant questions.

But what does Merrick expect? I've spent my entire nineteen years of existence in the monastery on Serati. And except for this one trip, it's likely where I'll spend the rest of my life—as all the high priestesses do. So I intend to make the most of it.

"Don't curtsy," he tells me, and I glance over at him as he smooths a large hand down the front of his white robes. "It's not required of an ambassador, and for the love of the Dying Sun, do not touch her. That's punishable by death. Just remember you're representing not only the Sisterhood but the planet of Serati."

How could I possibly forget? My own importance has been drilled into me every day of my life.

Though I'm honestly still scrambling to believe that I'm here. I shouldn't be. But at dinner four nights ago, the ambassador who was supposed to go— I cut off the thought before the picture of her choking and foaming at the mouth forms in my brain yet again.

She was poisoned, Merrick says. By someone who hates the Sisterhood, obviously. And someone who wanted her to suffer.

Even after what happened to that poor woman, I didn't think I'd be selected for this trip. As high priestess and the second-ranking person in the Sisterhood's hierarchy, I know I'm important—to the Sisterhood and my planet. But I don't normally play an active role in anything. I just…wait. And have faith. And when the time is right, I'll… Well, no one actually knows that bit. Or if they do, they haven't shared it with me yet.

Still, all will eventually be revealed.

Or not.

Like each of the high priestesses before me, I'll likely die not knowing, then be reborn to live this life again.

Except, for the first time, that might not be true.

Merrick says we're in unprecedented times. My spiritual advisors tell me everything is different now.

Because the time of the Dying Sun is upon us. It began nearly twenty years ago. At first there were only a few signs of instability, mainly solar flares, but as the years passed, our sun began changing color—first orange, now tinged with red. Plus, it's expanding, causing system warming that is—at the moment, anyway—mainly affecting the inner planets. Serati was always hot, but now it's *seriously* hot.

Despite the downsides, it's been an exciting time for the Sisterhood, with a record number of new members. Unfortunately for me, that excitement hasn't managed to extend to the monastery.

But thoughts of rebirth remind me of something. "Did you know we're both from Askkandia?" I ask Merrick.

It's unusual for a high priestess to come from anywhere but Serati. I'm apparently an anomaly, but the portents were all in place. When the old high priestess dies, another is reborn. And there are all sorts of signs and precursors that guide the Sisterhood to the new priestess. In this case, those signs guided the Sisterhood to me.

"Me and the princess," I clarify.

"Yes," Merrick replies shortly. But then, Merrick knows everything.

"And we're both nineteen?"

"I'm aware of that as well." He jerks his chin toward the princess. "Now pay attention."

Merrick's watching everyone carefully. He's a warrior priest and has been my bodyguard for the last four years. Though honestly, it's a pretty cushy job. He's trained to fight, but it's not like there are a lot of threats in a monastery. Except poison, but that's a very new development. A four-day-old development, to be exact.

Ever since that night, he's been eating a bite of my food and drinking a sip of my drink before I ever get to touch it. Bodyguard *and* poison tester now.

No wonder he's in a bad mood.

Plus, this gathering is a whole different situation, and he's been distracted since we got the news. I can't decide if it's because he's worried about protecting me or if he's just wondering why I, of all people, was chosen to be the ambassador from Serati.

Of all the people on our planet, how could the Sisterhood really think I should be the one to replace Ambassador Frellen when she died? Surely there was someone more suitable for the job. Someone who was actually trained in the protocols of the Ruling Families.

I don't even look Seratian.

The people from Serati, where Merrick was born, are unique—they've adapted over the generations to cope with the planet's less-than-ideal conditions of high heat and low gravity, not to mention off-the-charts levels of radiation. While I'm short, with pasty white skin, Merrick is tall and quite thin. His skin is tanner than mine because he's outside more, but it also has faint silver lines in a beautiful swirling pattern that is common to all people of Serati, as it helps keep them cool in the brutal temperatures. He has narrow, slightly tilted eyes with dark black irises to cope with the radiation, and his hair is platinum blond.

He's very striking, and I always feel insipid standing next to him.

At least our trip has taken his mind off his other issues. Merrick's father died recently, and it hit him very hard. I sense they were close, though he's never spoken to me about his family.

I turn my attention back to the side of the dais just as the princess is ascending. She doesn't even climb stairs like a normal person — she seems to float majestically up them.

I think I have a crush.

As she moves closer to us, I glance around at the other delegates. They're so colorful, like the exotic flying creatures from the rain forests of Ellindan. I sigh and peer down at my ugly white robes. I know it's beneath me — my mind is obviously meant for higher things — but the fact is, I long for color.

Plus, it's just one more thing that separates me from them, as if our belief systems weren't enough.

I know from my reading — I read a lot; there's not much else to do in the monastery — that each delegation is decked out in a different color, as dictated by tradition. Blue, green, purple, red, yellow, orange, and white. Of course, only members of the Ruling Families are allowed to wear these colors. The workers' guild wears browns and grays. The technicians who work for the Corporation wear black.

Mingled with all the color are the black-and-gray uniforms of what I presume are the station's security officers. There are a lot of them about. Are they expecting trouble? Maybe that's why Merrick is so tense.

We've all been standing on this dais in the center of the docking bay for an hour now, lined up in order of the farthest to the nearest planet from Serai, our sun. First, the outer planets of Glacea, the farthest, then

Vistenia, Askkandia, Ellindan. Then the inner planets: Permuna, Kridacus, and finally, Serati—where I live. Serati is the only planet not governed by one of the Ruling Families. It's run by the Sisterhood. Obviously there's no one here from the outermost "dead" planets of Tybris and Nabroch—they're too cold and inhospitable to support human life.

At the very end of the line, dressed in a long blue coat trimmed with fur, is the delegate from Glacea. He's short, even shorter than me, like most Glaceans, and has a lot of hair to protect him from the cold. He smiles, showing really sharp teeth, and his taupe skin is chapped and peeling from the wind and freezing weather. The princess nods back and speaks briefly, then moves on.

See, Rain, not so scary. You can do this.

For a second, I imagine how our exchange will go. She'll smile at me, her eyes a kindly silver—I love silver—warming as they meet my plain brown ones. She'll ask me a question about Serati, and I'll dazzle her with an answer that makes those same eyes widen in surprise. Her smile, already more than polite, will grow more interested and—

"Pay attention," Merrick hisses again.

I sigh, but to show that I heard him, I stand up so straight that my back muscles hurt a little bit in all this dense gravity. It's not nearly as much fun as my imaginary life, but I'll admit, finally getting to see people from all across the seven inhabited planets is pretty fascinating.

The next in line is the delegate from Vistenia, Glacea's nearest neighbor and the main grain producer in the system. The ambassador is a tall, blond woman with pearlescent skin and the large eyes with big pupils so common on her often dark planet. She's dressed all in green and reminds me of the graceful gala lilies that bloom on Vistenia only one month of the year.

"Your Highness," she murmurs.

The princess nods more warmly this time. "Ambassador Terra, I hope you had a pleasant journey."

Then Askkandia, in purple like the princess.

And so it goes.

She greets the ambassador from Ellindan, who's dressed in a tight-fitting red jump suit only a few shades darker than her copper skin.

The ambassador flashes a showy smile—I've heard that everyone from Ellindan has red teeth, stained from drinking too much akara juice, and it's fascinating to see that's true. To me, it's not exactly a good look, but apparently everyone on Ellindan is super proud of it. Plus, the juice is addictive enough that they'd probably deal with it regardless.

The princess is getting closer, and I can feel my muscles tensing up. It will be my turn soon.

Don't touch her. No matter how kind her silver eyes look smiling into yours, don't so much as skim a finger along her cape. Princesses aren't to be touched.

Although the closer she gets to me, the more I wonder if she really will be kind. Or if she'll be upset that I'm here because of who I am and what my religion believes.

The fifth delegate is from Permuna, the first of the inner planets. He has a barrel chest and large ears like most Permunians and is dressed in long robes the yellow of the desert sands of his planet. The skin around his eyes is darker than the rest of his face. I glance down and see his hands are the same color.

Apparently, from an early age, they dye those exposed areas to avoid sunburn, until the dye becomes a permanent mark. It looks like he's wearing a mask, and it makes his yellow eyes stand out even more. They seem like the eyes of a predator, but I read that the color is a side effect of a diet rich in starburst cactus, one of the only plants that grow prolifically on Permuna.

The ambassador doesn't look happy. His eyes are narrowed, his lips pinched, and his hands clench into fists as he steps forward to meet the princess. In a blink, a huge man with sepia skin and close-cropped gray hair in purple-and-black body armor moves between them—the princess's bodyguard, presumably—and I feel Merrick tense beside me.

"Stand down!" The princess's command is nearly inaudible, but it freezes her bodyguard in his tracks. It's a neat trick—one I wish I had in my repertoire. Then again, bodyguard or not, Merrick doesn't listen to anyone but himself.

"Speak, Ambassador Holdren," the princess says.

"Your Highness, I wish to ask, on behalf of the people of Permuna, why the last two grain deliveries have been rescheduled. My planet is running short; people are going hungry. I—"

The ambassador from Vistenia steps forward. "I hardly think this is the time or the place, Holdren."

"I think it's exactly the time and the place. We were promised the deliveries would not be interrupted. And now—"

I watch, fascinated, but the princess holds up her hand and the ambassador stops speaking immediately. "I'm sorry for your hardship, Ambassador. I will bring this matter to the Empress's attention when I return."

"You think she doesn't know?" His voice is bitter, irreverent, and an answering murmur runs through the increasingly tense crowd. It also causes the princess to raise her brows, but in surprise or arrogance, I can't quite tell.

Merrick moves in front of me, and though I want to push him out of the way, I understand why he's nervous. While Serati is tightly controlled by the Sisterhood and we hold ourselves separate from the other planets, even in the monastery, I've heard rumors of unrest among our neighbors. For decades now, the temperatures in the system have been rising and the agricultural productivity declining. Frequent solar flares are wreaking havoc with communications, and the exponential warming is making parts of the inner planets completely unlivable.

Our scriptures tell us that it will be okay, that a period of great joy will follow the upheaval. I know I just need to have faith. But it's hard when so many people are suffering.

As the sounds of dissent grow louder, the princess's eyes sweep the crowd. "Silence, please," she starts. "Let's not forget why we are here today. I'm sure Dr. Veragelen will have news of a solution to all our problems." She turns back to the ambassador. "I promise I will look into this matter."

He looks doubtful but bends his head nonetheless. "Thank you, Your Highness."

I half expect the same sort of comments from the ambassador

from Kridacus, a shrewd-looking woman in an orange gown, but the expression on her sun-lined, white face seems purposefully blank.

And then it's my turn. Princess Kalinda shifts her stern face and kind—I knew they'd be kind—eyes to me.

"Be calm. You can do this." Merrick's hand touches my shoulder, and immediately my racing heart slows as I feel his strength, both mental and physical. He might find me a trial, but for the last few years, he's been family, teacher, friend, protector, all rolled into one.

If he says it will be okay, then it will be okay.

The princess is even more beautiful close up, with the same light golden-brown skin and dark red hair of the Empress. But her skin has the same swirling silver pattern that Merrick's does, and in this light it's like she almost glows. Standing next to her makes me feel drab and young, despite the fact that we're the same age.

"Ambassador Fr—" A frown flickers across her face. "You're not Ambassador Frellen."

It sounds like an accusation, and I wonder if she recognizes me and if that's why she's frowning. Because she is here for a solution to the Dying Sun and I exist because there is none.

For a second, I can do nothing but blink up at her and wait for her to say something to me about our beliefs. When she doesn't, and instead just continues to frown at me, instinct takes over, and—even as I'm thinking *don't bow*—I do it anyway. I drop into a low, deep curtsy that has Merrick's hand tightening on my shoulder as though he can stop my descent.

Too late, Merrick. Way too late.

I'm nearly to the floor before he pulls me up like a puppet. But the damage has been done. Everyone saw what I did—most especially the princess.

I'm expecting the worst when I finally work up the nerve to glance at her face. But she's actually smiling, amusement flickering in her eyes.

"I don't think I know your name," she murmurs.

"I'm Rain," I say. "It's an honor to meet you, Princess."

I hear Merrick's indrawn breath behind me, because, of course, I've made another mistake. Flustered, my face burning with mortification,

I do the only thing I can think of to make this better. I reach out to touch her…and… Yes, it's official. I am a total and complete disaster.

Thankfully, Merrick yanks me backward before my hand can connect. At the same time, the big man in the body armor pushes himself between the princess and me. As he does, he reaches for the weapon at his side.

"For goodness' sake, Vance," the princess mutters. "Stand down."

Vance looks like he wants to argue, but eventually he steps back. And I don't blame him, which is why I do my best to look harmless. It's not hard, considering I'm 1.6 meters tall with a total baby face. But still, after the mess I just made, I'm not taking anything for granted.

Except the princess's lips are twitching. I'm a source of amusement, which is completely humiliating.

"I think proper introductions might be in order," she says.

Merrick steps forward. "Your Highness. May I introduce Rain, High Priestess of the Sisterhood of the Light and *temporary* ambassador of Serati."

"High Priestess?" Her eyes widen, and I wonder what her feelings are toward the Sisterhood. Our relationship with the Ruling Families has often been a little…fraught. "Well, I'm glad I didn't allow Vance to shoot you. It would definitely have caused a diplomatic incident."

"Yes, Prin—" I suck in my breath. "Yes, *Your Highness*," I say. "I'm glad as well. Very glad."

She laughs then, holding my gaze as she does. For a second, I think I see wariness, or maybe pity, in her eyes. But then she reaches out and touches a finger to the emblem of the second sun on the upper left lapel of my robe. As she does, a murmur goes up around us and Merrick stiffens beside me.

But before anyone else can throw a fit, a loud buzzer goes off. The blaring shifts the tension as across the docking bay, a light flashes above a set of double doors.

The princess drops her hand and steps back. "It looks like something is finally happening." Then, just like that, she turns and walks away as the sound continues.

Something *is* finally happening. Seems it's time to shift focus from the disaster that I am to the disaster that I'm supposed to save us all from.

CHAPTER 3

Ian, Mercenary and Smuggler and (Very) Occasional Good Guy

The incessant buzzing sound of yet another ship's approach blares over the speakers, and I glance at the fancy clock above the door.

Twenty-two hours and approximately seventeen minutes until I get off this flying bucket of bolts. Not that I'm counting or anything.

Then again, it's hard not to count when we've been stuck on this shithole twice as long as Max and I originally planned.

Sure, most people consider the *Caelestis* the crown jewel in the Empire's *very impressive* fleet. And maybe she is—she's definitely shiny as all fuck—but I've been on board long enough to know she's also a goddamn cesspit of evil. One I'll be more than happy to see the back of. The prison ship, the *Reformer*, arrives tomorrow, and Max and I will be on her.

The *Reformer* will lead us to Milla. She has to—otherwise, we've hit a dead end.

I grit my jaw as I stride down the narrow corridor. I could have done without the extra shift today—I have things to do. But everyone is on duty. There's something big going on, some sort of important presentation Dr. Veragelen, aka Dr. Wicked, is giving to some visiting bigwigs. I have no clue what, and to be honest, I don't give a shit.

I just need to get through this extra shift—and the ceremony Dr. Veragelen has been surreptitiously planning for weeks now. She may be walking around acting like she doesn't care about today, like it's some giant inconvenience or something, but anyone who works closely with her knows it's all she's been thinking about.

Since I have the misfortune of working more closely with her than most—bodyguard to the head doc in charge comes with a lot of downsides—I know exactly how on edge she's been about today's presentation. After all, it's hard to conquer the known universe if you're on the Empress's bad side. And if there's anything the doc wants more than to make this bizarre experiment of hers work, it's access to all the secrets of the universe. And the power that comes with it.

That's probably why she's dressed in style today. She's in her usual black lab suit, but she's added a fancy black cloak. She looks goddamn ridiculous. Who the hell wears a cloak, anyway?

Rumor has it that the not-so-good doc is over three hundred years old and that the Corporation—founded by the seven Ruling Families and the ones in charge of all the tech around here—has found ways to extend their lifespans. If so, they're not sharing the secret with the rest of us.

But that's the Corporation for you. Secretive bastards.

Regardless, ever since Doc V laid eyes on me when I arrived two months ago, I've been on permanent personal bodyguard duty. I think she has a thing for me, but *never going to happen*. I'd rather fuck a slogg.

Apart from the fact that she gives me the creeps, I hold her personally responsible for whatever happened to Milla. I've seen a little of what goes on in the labs here—and the thought of that being done to one of the most important people in the system to me makes my blood boil. I'm thinking, once Milla is safe, I'll make that personal visit to the doc and pay a few overdue debts.

Although not the way she's expecting.

The docking bay doors slide open as we approach, and she walks inside. I follow two steps behind, exactly how she likes me. I'm hyperalert— also how she likes me—eyes scanning the crowd for any semblance of a threat. It's no skin off my ass if someone kills her, but I don't need any excuse for the prison ship not to land tomorrow as planned.

There are a lot of visiting shuttles in the bay—more than I expected—and a dais has been set up in the center of the room. A bunch of brightly dressed assholes are lined up along it.

My gaze is drawn to a woman in the center of the group and slightly in front, and my lips twitch. Another grandiose know-it-all who doesn't actually know anything, only this one's in a purple cloak instead of a black one.

She's tall, maybe the tallest woman in the room, and beneath the cloak, she's wearing a skintight, floor-length dress of a deep purple, which hugs her—admittedly—impressive curves. I'm guessing it would be a pain in the ass to get her out of all those shiny little buttons. But I'd be up for trying.

We're nearly to the dais as I lift my gaze to her face. Her mouth is wide and lush, her cheekbones high. She's watching me out of strange silver eyes, and something about the way she's looking at me makes me think she definitely likes what she sees.

I raise an eyebrow in response, my lips twisting into a smirk I don't even try to hide. Her eyes widen, and then she sniffs and gives me a haughty look in return. It's pretty hot—and so is she, despite the cape.

Too bad I can't stick around.

The doc climbs the steps to the podium and comes to stand in front of her, blocking my view, and I shift to the side.

"Your Highness," Doc V says with a cursory bow of her head.

Your what the fuck now?

I've been eye-fucking a goddamn princess. That's a first.

But eye-fucking is all I'll be doing, because I fucking hate the Ruling Families. They're a load of parasitic assholes who look after themselves and don't give a shit about the rest of us. And I'm sure, if that stick-up-her-ass look is anything to go by, this princess is no better than the rest of them.

"It's an honor to have you with us on the ISS *Caelestis* today," the doc continues in her rapid-fire way. She's never been one to waste time on pleasantries.

"It's an honor to be here, Dr. Veragelen," Princess Stick-Up-Her-Ass answers in a voice as cool and classy as the rest of her. "I'm excited to tour the laboratories. And hear what progress is being made."

I can't help wondering if she plans on checking out *all* the laboratories—or just the ones Dr. Veragelen doesn't hide behind Top Secret signs. Then again, she's probably got more than top-secret clearance—which means she already knows exactly what the good doctor gets up to behind locked doors.

After all, the Ruling Families founded and essentially run the Corporation, which essentially has a monopoly on tech in the Senestris System. I didn't know much about it until recently. In general, the people on my planet stay the hell away from the Corporation, like any sensible person does. But we're here now, and it's best to know your enemy.

This guy, Gage, who's a technician on board, has been helping us out—for a price—and he's told us some stuff about the Corporation that makes even *this* hardened criminal feel like a Sister of the Light.

"I look forward to showing you around," Doc V manages with a small curve of her lips that makes me wonder if her face is about to crack.

I've been here for nearly two months, and I've never seen her smile. I didn't think she knew how.

"All in good time," she continues before turning to address the rest of the people on the dais. "As you are probably aware, the *Caelestis* is the most sophisticated science vessel in the system. We have twenty-seven laboratories on board, as well as the fastest, most advanced computers ever designed. Today, we will be—"

She breaks off as a green light flashes above the doors to the airlock. That ship that buzzed the alarm earlier must have landed, and when the doc frowns as a crew member approaches, I go on full alert, my right hand flexing beside the laser pistol strapped to my thigh.

"Ma'am, the *Reformer* is asking for permission to dock."

Well, fuck. That's not good news. Max and I aren't ready.

"They're not expected until tomorrow. I *specifically* arranged for them to come tomorrow." The doc's nostrils flare, but it's the only outward sign of her annoyance.

Apparently, having a princess around puts her on surprisingly good behavior.

She purses her lips as she thinks it through, then says, "Make sure she's loaded and leaves before the tour is over."

More bad news. This is a fucking disaster—at least for me. Because, tour or not, princess or not, there is no way I'm waiting around until the next time the *Reformer* docks. Not when it could be months. And not when those months mean Milla is on her own, who the fuck knows where, suffering who the fuck knows what.

No fucking way.

"*Max!*" I call out for him in my head, the way we've been doing since we were kids. For a moment, I don't get a response.

"*What is it? I'm busy.*"

But he doesn't sound pissed to be interrupted. Of course, that's Max—cheerful in the face of all adversity. Honestly, I get exhausted just thinking about how he maintains it, but his unwavering positivity might be what I like most about the guy. Well, that and his chobwa chip pancakes.

"*The* Reformer *is docking right now. We need to move up the plan,*" I tell him.

"*What do you need?*" Before I can even reply, he says, "*I'll get Gage.*"

"*Agreed. About time he earned the outrageous amount we've been paying him. Meet me in the docking bay. I'll get back here as soon as I can give Dr. Wicked the slip. Maybe see if you can cause a diversion. You know what to do.*"

"*Got it.*"

Doc V takes a deep breath, plasters on a totally fake smile, and turns her attention to the princess. "Let's begin the tour." Whirling around, she heads off in the direction we came from, and I fall into place behind her.

I can almost feel Purple Cape's royal eyes on me as I walk away, and I can't help thinking that for her, I might just have lowered my standards.

Too bad I've only got about twenty minutes to get the hell off this boat and onto the *Reformer*—or lose my chance to save Milla, maybe forever.

CHAPTER 4

Kali

Don't ogle the sexy bodyguard's ass. Don't do it—especially on your first trip representing the Empress. I need to behave with proper royal comportment at all times, no matter how hot Dr. Veragelen's bodyguard is.

And make no mistake. He is hot. Smoking hot.

Thick black hair that shows off his high cheekbones.

Velvety dark-brown skin.

A jaw sharp enough to use as a blade.

Tall and broad-shouldered, despite being from Kridacus, based on the insignia on his uniform—I've never heard of anyone that big coming from the high gravity of Kridacus. He must be extremely strong at this lower gravity.

Dark, intense eyes—framed by the longest, thickest lashes I've ever seen—that seem to cut through all the royal pretense and see everything I'm trying to hide from the world.

Too bad I don't know if that's a good thing or a bad thing. And since he's walking away, I'll probably never find out. Which, I decide, is a very good thing. Because such things just aren't done...no matter how good his broad shoulders and muscled chest look in his black guard's uniform.

And they look very, very good.

Lara tugs at my cloak, and I glance at her.

"You might want to get that look off your face," she murmurs in a voice that's as amused as it is concerned.

"What look?"

"The I-want-to-get-into-that-guard's-pants-and-have-a-party look."

Sadly, she's probably right, even though he looks as good from the back as he did from the front. He also looks like trouble with a capital T. For a moment, I have a longing for all the things I can't have.

Then he glances over his shoulder at me, the smirk still in place, like he knows exactly what I'm thinking, and the longing gives way to annoyance. In response, I give him my best bored regal stare—the one I learned from my mother even before I learned the different gravities on the nine planets.

He doesn't crumble like most men do. Maybe because I'm doing it wrong. Or maybe because he's made of sterner stuff. Either way, I ignore the smirk and force my mind to other things.

I wonder what the *Reformer* is—I've never heard of a ship by that name, and I consider myself a bit of an expert on our fleet. Whatever it is, it's got the doctor flustered, and that intrigues me even more.

From everything I know about Dr. Veragelen—which is a lot, as science has always fascinated me and I'm a huge fan of hers— she's seen and done it all in her career. Though she started off on an exploratory vessel all those years ago, she's steadily been working her way up until she's not only the head scientist on the *Caelestis* but director of the whole Corporation, answering only to the board controlled by the Ruling Families.

Is it any wonder everyone is here to meet the doctor and see what she's managed to accomplish in the last four years? Dr. Veragelen eats problems for breakfast, which is why my mother put her in charge of the biggest problem we've got—saving Senestris from total annihilation.

As I follow her, the other diplomats keeping pace behind me, I can't help thinking the doctor is everything and nothing like what I expected. Tall and almost emaciated, with short, sensibly cut gray hair, she looks exactly like every picture I've ever seen of her.

I force down my disappointment at her initial brusqueness and follow her through a large set of double doors. On the plus side, my nerves have settled and all that's left is excitement.

I can't wait to see this ship.

It's rumored there are alien artifacts on board, and I've always been fascinated by anything to do with the Ancients—the name we gave whoever must have lived here long before us. Of course, some people don't believe there was ever an ancient alien race on any planet in the system, but there's evidence of their existence all over Senestris, though mainly on Serati. I guess for some, it's more comforting to believe we're the first than that any civilization could end—especially given our current looming demise.

The doors lead into a corridor with a curved ceiling and walls made of some sort of silver metal. The light illuminating the hallway is soft and orange, and though I look for where it's coming from, I can't find an energy source.

As we continue down the hallway, questions bubble up in my mind—so many that it's hard to keep them all straight. How is the ship powered? How many people are currently on board? What are they working on? Where are the Ancient artifacts? And most importantly: Have they found a way to save our sun?

I want to ask her, but Dr. Veragelen is striding off at a brisk speed, and it's all I can do to keep up in my ridiculous dress.

She finally stops at what I presume is some sort of safety door and presses her palm to the biometric scanner. I take the opportunity to move closer.

"Dr. Veragelen, can you tell me a little about the work the Corporation is doing here? Have you had any breakthroughs?"

She turns to me with a glint in her eyes that makes me just a tiny bit uncomfortable. "I can confirm that we are well on our way to finding the solution to the accelerated degeneration of our sun. We believe we have the means in our hands to not only stop that degeneration but to reverse the effects. Rest assured, your lives are in our hands, and we will save you all."

Her voice rings with conviction, but I don't know—there's something about that one brief look that makes me think there's more here than what she's saying. Also, it's hard to ignore the fact that she hasn't exactly answered my question.

I open my mouth to come at it another way, but we're already moving again, and it takes all my concentration not to trip over my cape. Royal protocol or no, I'm never wearing this thing again.

As we continue racing through the same corridor, which I'm guessing runs a loop parallel to the ship's perimeter, it's just more of the same. Numerous doors that line both sides. All closed with complicated security panels. All labeled CLASSIFIED and AUTHORIZED PERSONNEL ONLY.

The more secured doors we pass and the less Dr. Veragelen says, the more curious I get. What happened to her giving us a "tour"?

Yes, the doors are marked CLASSIFIED, but we're delegates from each of the planets' governments. We have top security clearance. And we're with the woman who runs this entire ship and who presumably has access to everything on it.

So what is she waiting for?

This meeting is supposed to give the delegates good news they can take back to their people, settle the unrest, and give them hope for the future. We all need to believe that the Empress, together with the Corporation, is working on a solution, which will be impossible if we never get to see evidence that the solution exists.

"Dr. Veragelen," I finally say as we pass yet *another* RESTRICTED sign at top speed. I'm beginning to think she's training for next year's interplanetary games. There's no other reason for her to be rushing us past these laboratories so fast. "Are we actually going to be entering any of the labs," I ask, "or are you just planning on walking us past them all?"

I hear a low snigger and turn slightly to peer at the guard at her shoulder, but his face is expressionless. Maybe I imagined it.

"We're almost there," Dr. Veragelen assures me, then smiles in a way that looks like it hurts more than a little.

"Almost where?" demands Ambassador Terra. "We've been walking for ten minutes and haven't seen anything but doors we aren't allowed through."

The others grumble their agreement. Obviously, I'm not the only one irritated with what's beginning to feel like a waste of time.

The high priestess from earlier is the only one who doesn't look like they want to skin Dr. Veragelen alive—and me along with her. But she doesn't look exactly happy, either. More like befuddled, which still isn't what we need people to take away from this trip.

Which means I'm going to have to say something else. Even though I don't have a clue what that something is yet.

Still, I clear my throat and give it my best shot. "Dr. Veragelen."

This time, the look she gives me is less thoughtful and more annoyed, but I'm determined now.

"Can you at least tell us what experiments you're conducting in each of these labs?"

We stare at each other for several long seconds, and I can see the moment she finally remembers who I am. She blows a long, slow breath out through her nose, and her tight mouth unpinches just a little.

"I'm sorry, Your Highness," she tells me, though she sounds anything but sorry. "I'm afraid it's for your own good. These areas are off-limits because of the chemicals we use in them. They're hazardous to anyone not wearing the appropriate protective clothing."

She gives me another forced smile—and this one looks like a full-on grimace. Probably because she's managed to speak *and* "smile" and still hasn't relaxed her mouth at all. "I'd hate to send you back to your mother...damaged in any way."

That sounds more like a threat than actual concern, but I've spent all nineteen years of my life living under the Empress's special brand of passive-aggressiveness. The doctor is going to have to work much harder if she wants to send me running away with my tail between my legs.

"That may be true of the Authorized Personnel doors, but what experiments are you running behind the Classified doors?" I counter.

"And why are they even classified on a vessel that's meant to be working to solve problems that aren't classified? Problems that affect us all."

Her bodyguard turns to stare at me, and when we make eye contact, it causes little shivers to skate down my spine. Somehow, he manages to look both impressed and bored by my questions, but I'll take it.

My attention is brought back to Dr. Veragelen when she glances at the nearest locked door, then sighs and rubs a hand over her forehead like I'm causing her a great amount of trouble. Good. It's fair to say that my childhood crush on Dr. Veragelen is dying a rapid death.

She must catch on to the fact that I'm not backing down until I get some answers, because she cuts the act and says, "I promise you, Princess, if you rein in your…impatience a little while longer, you will be more than satisfied." Then she deliberately moves away before I can ask her anything else.

We finally stop in front of a set of wide double doors. Like the others we've passed, they have a CLASSIFIED sign right across the middle of them. But unlike the others, it looks like we might actually have a snowflake's chance on Serai of getting through them.

Dr. Veragelen claps her hands like a schoolteacher trying to get the attention of her recalcitrant pupils. Brilliant or not, the woman obviously has pretty major control issues—something else I recognize after spending the last two decades with my mom.

"Now, I'm about to show you our most important laboratory"— she glances directly at me, one eyebrow raised—"which has the added benefit of being unclassified for your visit today."

She says the last with a definite bite in her tone. My mother would call her on it—in fact, she would probably eviscerate her for it—but I choose to let it go, at least for now, because maybe I'm going to see something interesting at last.

I only hope that whatever she's got here is as good as she thinks it is. Because all of our lives depend on it.

The small crowd behind me starts to shift restlessly.

Dr. Veragelen must feel it, too, because suddenly she cuts to the chase of what I get the impression was supposed to be a pretty lengthy speech. "What I have in here," she says, gesturing to the doors behind her, "is far beyond any technology currently in use in the Empire of the Senestris System. What I have in here will awe you. It will inspire you. And it will prove to you, once and for all, that I am capable of doing more than averting disaster. I am capable—*we* are capable—of nothing short of absolute salvation.

"Salvation for your families. Salvation for your planets. Salvation"— her voice drops to a whisper that echoes throughout the now silent corridor—"for the entire system."

Well, this sounds more like what we've been waiting for. My heart is beating fast and hard as she presses a palm to the biometric scanner.

This is it. This is it. Please let this be it.

"Ambassadors." Dr. Veragelen looks at each of us in turn. "I give you what I am certain is the answer to all of your questions. And your prayers."

Then she throws open the doors to the laboratory with a flourish.

My mouth drops open.

Hot steaming drokaray droppings.

CHAPTER 5

Kali

For a moment, nobody moves. Or says a word.

I stand in the hallway, staring through the wide-open doors with my mouth agape as I try to figure out exactly what I'm looking at. The room beyond is huge—even bigger than the docking bay. It must take up the entire height of the center of the ship. And filling most of the space is a black sphere hovering without any visible means of support about three feet above the floor.

I swallow hard.

For her part, Dr. Veragelen looks like the bamiling that ate the varmak. Then again, she more than deserves the self-satisfaction. When else has an entire group of politicians actually been struck speechless?

"Can we go in?" Rain asks, and there's an eagerness in her voice that's unmistakable. She's the closest delegate to me, separated by Arik, who makes sure no one gets too near, but that doesn't stop her from peering around him, looking more like an excitable young girl than the High Priestess of the Sisterhood.

It makes me like her more than I expected to—and probably more than I should.

"Of course. Of course," Dr. Veragelen says as she strides through the open door. "After all, *this* is what I invited you all here to see."

I don't miss her subtle emphasis on the word "this" or the fulminating glare she shoots in my direction when she thinks I'm not looking.

Rain bounces forward, but her escort touches her arm before she can take more than one step. She glances up at him questioningly, and he nods subtly toward me. As soon as he does, she gasps in horror, ducks her head again, and mutters something under her breath.

I want to tell her that it doesn't matter—that I don't care who goes in first. But my mother lives for pomp and circumstance, and as long as I'm here, representing her, I need to as well—or I'll never be allowed off-planet again.

And there are a whole lot of places I want to see. And maybe, just maybe, if Dr. Veragelen can do what she thinks she can, I'll finally have time to do them.

But this second gaffe—or is it the third?—of Rain's does beg the question: Why would Serati send an ambassador with absolutely no formal training in royal protocols to an important event like this? It makes no sense for *any* planet to do that, let alone one whose code of law is so elaborate and extensive it makes the Empress look like an anarchist. I try to remember what I've heard about the high priestess. Not much—the Sisterhood are a secretive lot—but I do know that high priestesses don't usually take an active role in politics.

Still, their mistake isn't her fault, so I give Rain an encouraging nod as I walk into the room, then fix my attention on the black sphere. What is it? A memory niggles at my brain—I know I've seen something similar before. But in a dream.

When I was thirteen, I started having strange dreams. Dreams of the dying sun and of artifacts I somehow knew had never been made by humans. Of flying through space when I'd never been on a spaceship. I told my father, and he told *me* to keep the dreams to myself. I'm not sure why; maybe he thought my mom wouldn't like it. She can be a little strange about me on my good days—the last thing she needed was a reminder that I'm less than perfect.

My father was assassinated two years later—the worst day of my life—and I've still never told anyone else about the dreams.

The sphere is about the height of a three-story building, and not opaque, as I first thought, but vaguely translucent, though I can't see inside. There's a motif right in the center facing me—it looks like a star surrounded by a circle. I've dreamed of that image before as well, and a shiver of something ripples through me.

The laboratory is filled with technicians in form-fitting black lab suits, all moving purposefully around the sphere. Guards are stationed at regular points at the periphery of the room, and they all have laser pistols and electric batons—is the doctor expecting trouble?

Scaffolding has been set up beside the sphere. Technicians swarm over it, taking readings from various points of the surface. Others are moving around it with equipment and HUDs. More techs bearing the insignia of the Corporation work at consoles around the room.

It's the most intense laboratory I've ever been inside, and I can't help wondering what exactly it is Dr. Veragelen thinks she has here. Or, more important—what she thinks it does.

Is that why all the guards are so heavily armed? Because she thinks it's valuable enough to be *dangerous*?

A combination of fear and excitement skates along my spine, has my breath catching in my throat. Is this it? Is this sphere, or whatever it is, what we've been looking for all along?

Lara must be thinking the same thing, because she leans close to my ear and whispers, "What do you think it is?"

"I have no clue." But that's not entirely true. It's an alien artifact. A big one.

This is freaking amazing. And suddenly, my fingers itch with an almost overwhelming urge to move closer. To touch it.

"Well, it's clearly very impressive," Ambassador Kellarp says, smiling to show her red-stained teeth. "But what is it?"

"It's a heptosphere," the man accompanying the high priestess answers in a voice devoid of emotion. "It's from the Ancients."

I've never heard the term *heptosphere* before, but hearing him confirm what I already suspected about the Ancients has me turning to study him. And I'm not the only one. For the first time since we got to the *Caelestis*, Dr. Veragelen looks almost…pleased.

"It is, indeed." She beams at the man like he's her star pupil. "And you are?"

"I'm Merrick, ma'am. Of the Sisterhood of the Light. Secondary delegate from Serati."

I cast him a quick glance. Up to now, I've avoided looking at him too closely, scared I'll end up staring. Because with his tall, lean body, tan skin, and platinum hair, he reminds me so much of my father that it makes my heart ache. My father was the best person I've ever known, and I still miss him every single day.

I push the memories to the back of my mind and drag myself into the present. "Where did you find it?" I ask.

And why haven't I heard of it before? Surely my mother would have told me about something as amazing as the heptosphere if she'd known about it. And if she doesn't know that it exists, then Dr. Veragelen is about to have a lot of very uncomfortable questions to answer.

"It was discovered on Askkandia nearly twenty years ago," she answers me. "Deep in the Rodos Mountains. For some reason, after what we believe is centuries—if not longer—hidden underground, it started emitting some sort of signal, which we picked up. Excavating it and getting it off-planet was quite the challenge. The Empress had to send in her best research and construction teams to help us. The *Caelestis* was designed and built specifically to conduct research into the heptosphere."

So my mother does know about it. But why wouldn't she tell me before now? She knows how interested I am in the Ancients—and in finding a way to save our system.

Then again, the Empress does whatever the hell the Empress wants to do. Maybe she had a reason for not telling me, or maybe she didn't. All I know is that this trip is raising a lot more questions than it's giving answers.

"But what does it do?" Ambassador Terra demands.

The entire room seems to hold its breath as we wait for the scientist to answer.

For the first time, she looks a little unsure. "We don't actually know." She holds up a hand as murmurs of disappointment ripple through the lab. "But our research has strongly suggested that it holds the key to revitalizing our dying sun."

"So this is it?" Ambassador Kellarp says. "This is what you'll use to save us?"

"It is," Dr. Veragelen confirms, her tone confident. "We are at the point of uncovering all its secrets, and soon we'll be in control of its formidable powers."

"Good luck with that," Merrick mutters.

His voice is emotionless, but his hands are fisted at his sides, and I sense he's more shocked than he wants to give away. Of course he's upset. The Sisterhood of the Light has spent the last several millennia praying for nothing more than the dying of the sun...so they can save us all. Now everyone else is trying to stop it first.

It's the central tenet of their religion—the welcoming of the Dying Sun—derived from the civilization that seems to have inhabited this system before us. The Ancients, as the Sisterhood calls them, left remnants of an advanced civilization across the nine planets, though mainly concentrated on Serati, the closest planet to the sun and the one most...uncomfortable for human life.

From their studies of that alien civilization, early Seratians deduced that the Ancients were the creators of the system, and they came to believe that at some point, the sun would fail but the Ancients would return to our system in order to bring it back to life and save us all. A religious group developed, the Sisterhood of the Light, claiming the Dying Sun would bring a time of great change and enlightenment, even foretelling the return of the Ancients.

Of course, no one actually knew when the sun was supposed to die—but no time soon. And so, not worth worrying about. In truth, many planets—especially the ones more hospitable to human life, like Askkandia—didn't have much of a Sisterhood presence at all. While Askkandian children grew up with legends of the Dying Sun, they were considered more fantasy than prophecy. Then, two decades ago, everything changed. *Was this around the time the heptosphere turned up?* I wonder.

Even though the consequences were immediate and dire, like destruction of ecosystems, declining agriculture, and increasing solar flares, the Sisterhood proclaimed it a miracle, the answer to their prayers, and that we needed to have faith and all would be revealed. People from across the seven inhabited planets started converting in droves.

The Sisterhood isn't commenting on that.

I guess they think some sort of miracle is going to happen. Unfortunately, the rest of us—the Empress included—just want to stop us from going up in smoke.

As kind as this high priestess seems, right now, we don't need faith. We need science.

I glance at Rain, expecting to see the same anger on her face that's on her escort's. But she just looks curious, her gaze fixed on the heptosphere as though she wants to touch it as much as I do.

"Can we touch it?" I ask. Why not?

But as I move closer, Dr. Veragelen's guard—he of the tight ass and razor-sharp jaw—steps forward, blocking my way. And he's big enough to stop me in my tracks. I can almost feel Arik and Vance bristling behind me. Even Lara tenses up, like she's ready to throw herself between the hottie and me.

I raise my hand to hold them off and turn my focus to the guard. It's pretty rare for someone to challenge a member of the Ruling Families, and on the odd occasions it has happened, the person usually trips over themselves as they backpedal from their mistake.

This guy isn't backpedaling, though. Nope. Instead, he's standing his ground, his dark-brown eyes staring into mine with an insolence that feels very much like a challenge.

That insolence is unwarranted—I'm sure we've never met. I don't remember ever seeing him on Askkandia, and he's *definitely* someone I would remember. After all, it's pretty hard to forget the most striking guy I've ever seen—especially when he clearly has the personality of a rabid drokaray.

Maybe he didn't like me ogling him earlier.

"Step back," Arik orders in a voice that brooks no disagreement.

The guy doesn't budge, though he does cock his head in a way that almost seems like he's listening to some music only he can hear. And while there's a part of me that wants nothing more than to stand here trading glares with him, I'm painfully aware that we're drawing a lot of attention right now. Attention that should be on Dr. Veragelen and the heptosphere and not on a pissing contest between some guard and me.

So I step back instead, ignoring the triumph that briefly flares in the depths of his eyes. I have better things to worry about than some arrogant jerk on a power trip. The fate of our world—our entire solar system—hangs in the balance.

"Of course you can touch it," Dr. Veragelen tells me as I turn back toward her. She shoots the guard an annoyed look, which he returns with an expression so bland it has to be manufactured. "I apologize if there was ever any doubt about that. Private Ian, like the rest of us, is just very protective of the heptosphere."

"It's fine," I tell her, because it is. Scientific discovery—especially of the magnitude she's attempting—is way more important than indulging my curiosity. To prove it, I deliberately stick my hands in my cloak's pockets as I resume walking around the sphere. "I'm good with just looking."

She still seems concerned. "No, really. It's more than okay if you want to touch it. It's an interesting experience." She turns to the rest of the delegates. "In fact, any of you can feel free to touch the sphere while you're here. It's made of a very unusual material, and, as far as we can tell, it's impervious to damage."

She barely finishes her sentence before there's a mad rush for the sphere. Everyone is reaching out a hand to touch it and exclaiming about how strange it feels. Cool, hot. Smooth, bumpy. Substantial, intangible. Everyone seems to experience something different, and now I want to touch it more than ever, just to see what it feels like to me.

But a glance back at Private Ian only strengthens my resolve not to show how interested I am. He's watching me with an expression that reminds me of my mother's when she's just waiting for me to mess something up so she can jump down my throat.

I'm not about to give him the satisfaction—any more than I give it to her these days.

I don't have a clue who pissed in this guy's Moon Mallows or why he's decided to take it out on *me*, but he has. And that annoys me enough that I return his glare with interest before deliberately walking one hundred and eighty degrees around the heptosphere so that I don't have to put up with him watching every move I make.

Of course, I can't get near the thing, considering how many members of the delegation are currently crowded around it. I could force my way in—princess trumps ambassador any day—but that's not the kind of ruler I want to be.

So instead of focusing on the heptosphere like the others, I turn toward the console that runs along the wall behind me. It appears different from the other computer equipment in the lab, and I'm guessing it must be some sort of control panel to correlate all the information about the sphere. The board is elaborate and complicated, and I can't help but feel a small thrill. I'm actually in a room with something that was made by an ancient race so many years ago that their history is more hypothesis than fact.

I can't even begin to guess what all the various controls do, but presumably Dr. Veragelen must have some idea by now, considering she's been working with this thing for nearly five years, or perhaps longer, if study began before completion of the *Caelestis*.

Above the board is a mass of screens. There are dozens of them— some small, some big, some giant—and all of them receiving a constant influx of information, judging by the rate data are scrolling across the screens.

Are these real-time results from the lab techs who are taking readings from the heptosphere? Just the thought of being able to pull this much information from an ancient artifact is fascinating.

I lean closer to investigate just as a rumble fills the air and a powerful tremor runs through the ship. The disruption is followed by a moment of absolute silence, right before an explosion rips through the laboratory.

I have one moment to think, *What the fuck?* and then I'm flying backward.

Pain courses through me as I crash into something hard. Then everything goes black.

CHAPTER 6

Kali

What the fuck just happened?

I'm lying on my side, and a wave of heat sears my cheek. A crackle fills my ears. Not good.

I've got to get out of here.

I blink my eyes open to chaos.

The air is thick with smoke, screams fill the room, and for a moment the world makes no sense. I shake my head and push myself up. I must have hit something.

At least I'm alive, but for how long? The screen I'd been staring at is on fire, and I scoot backward.

Was it an assassination attempt? I swallow as I think of my father, then push the thought away.

More likely, it was someone after the heptosphere, though if that's the case, why risk blowing it up? Unless that was the purpose. If so, it failed. The sphere is still floating gently in the center of the room while the ceiling falls around it. Beyond that, I can see what I presume is the outer hull of the space station. At least it's still intact—otherwise, we'd all be space debris.

The lab is filled with the screams and moans of the injured and dying, and my stomach churns.

Get a grip.

I need to help.

But as I scramble to my feet, another explosion rocks the ship and sends me careening into the heptosphere.

As my palms touch the surface briefly, a shudder runs through me. Then another explosion, and I'm hurled backward, slamming into someone behind me. It's High Priestess Rain, and she appears unhurt. I start to turn but then look back, stopping and staring. The heptosphere is no longer translucent black.

Instead, it's lit up inside with multicolored rings spinning like a gyroscope that can't find its orientation. Was it damaged in the explosion?

I'm spellbound, the colors filling my mind so I can't drag my gaze away. Then another scream rends the air, and I'm back in motion, racing toward the injured.

I drop to the ground beside Ambassador Terra. She's silently weeping, her hands fisted at her stomach, blood oozing between her fingers and turning her green dress brown. Her blond hair has come loose from its bun, and terror fills her large eyes.

"It's okay," I tell her as I reach down and rip off a large piece of my tattered ceremonial cloak. "Let me help you." I fold it several times, then gently move her hands. I go still, despair filling me—the wound is deep and jagged, way beyond my skills—but I try not to let that show as I firmly press the material against her stomach.

A tremor runs through her, and her spine arches. She cries out, a garbled sound of agony, and I glance around for help, for a medic, for something, but find only Dr. Veragelen standing there, seemingly uninjured, staring at me with a look in her black eyes that chills me to the bone.

What the hell is going on inside that brilliant head of hers? Whatever it is, I don't want any part of it, so I look away.

Lara drops to her knees beside me as yet another explosion rocks the laboratory and sends me tumbling forward. I catch myself.

"Are you all right?" she demands. Her voice is raspy, as if she's been knocked breathless, though I don't see any visible wounds.

"None of this is all right," I answer. Ambassador Terra moans again, and I touch her cheek, trying to comfort her. She stares up at me with the knowledge of her own death in her eyes.

"I meant—"

"I'm fine." I cut Lara off abruptly, because if I think about how I really am right now, I'll fall apart.

Ambassador Terra exhales long and low. And then…nothing.

"Goddamn it, no!" I curl my hand into a fist and punch her chest, trying to remember my never-before-used CPR lessons.

Lara tugs at me, yelling something in my ear, but I fight her off and continue the CPR.

"She's dead, Kali, and we have to get out of here or we'll be dead, too."

"We can't just leave her like—"

"We've no choice. She's beyond care. And we've got to get you somewhere safe."

New explosions shake the ship until she's shuddering and buckling all around us. I put my hands over my head as debris crashes to the floor, narrowly missing us. Lara throws herself over me so hard and fast that it knocks the wind out of me. Then she's up and dragging me to my feet—protocols forgotten. With one last look at the dead ambassador, I allow her to pull me toward the wide double doors. For a second, the lights go out and the room is lit by the whirling illumination inside the heptosphere, a disorienting kaleidoscope of color. I stumble over another body, but they're not moving.

Then the lights flash on again and we're out the door.

I glance back and spot Arik racing toward us. "Princess Kalinda!" he shouts just as an automated voice calls over the ship's internal communication system.

"Decontamination system activated. You have ten seconds to vacate area 27."

I have no clue what that involves, but it doesn't sound good. "Hurry," I yell.

Arik is almost up to us as loud sirens blare and a metal bulkhead slams down between us, cutting me off from Arik and the others still inside the lab.

"No!" I thump on the metal, desperate not to leave all those people behind. But Lara is pulling me again, and I can't fight her. Not when I can't even breathe.

My lungs hurt. I'm guessing the decontamination system is sucking up all the oxygen, leaving us gasping for breath.

I grab her hand and search frantically for a way out. But we're on a fucking space station—where could we even go?

I don't want to think about what's happening inside the lab. But at least others got out as well. I spot Ambassador Holdren, High Priestess Rain, and Secondary Delegate Merrick. Around us, people are crashing to their knees. My own breathing is growing even more labored, and I know I don't have long. I need to find the control panel and switch off the decontamination system, but I don't know how. We need to evacuate.

If we make it to the docking bay, hopefully we can take off on one of the shuttles. I look around through the swirling gray smoke. Which way? I have no idea, but to the right, the corridor is blocked by a security door, so I pull Lara with me and head left.

Out of nowhere, a hand grabs my elbow and I'm being propelled along the corridor. I have one second to register that someone is actually *touching* me before it also registers that I'm being pulled in a direction I don't want to go.

I whirl around, prepared to fight. Then freeze when I realize just who was brave enough to risk a death penalty and put his hand on me.

CHAPTER 7

Ian

The princess is staring at the spot where my hand touches her bare arm like I'm committing some sort of sacrilege.

Maybe I am.

How the hell would I know? Fucking etiquette lessons weren't on the agenda where I grew up.

"You," she wheezes, and the way she says it doesn't sound complimentary.

I should just let her go. This is wasting time I don't have.

The princess can look after herself. She was probably trained from birth in the art of self-preservation. And I have to get to the docking bay anyway—if there's even a docking bay left after whatever the fuck just happened. If that was Max's idea of a diversion, we'll be having words later.

As for the princess—she's a problem I don't need right now. I tell myself to let her go, but somehow, I can't seem to do that. In fact, my grip tightens.

It's just another bad decision in the string of bad decisions I've been making today. I'm supposed to be keeping a low profile. So what was I doing in there, warning her away from that damn weird sphere that Dr. Wicked is so obsessed with?

I don't have a fucking clue, and Max wasn't exactly thrilled about it, either. All I know is I didn't want her touching it. I've heard rumors of people—prisoners—burned to a crisp by that thing, but still, I acted without thinking. Never a good idea, but especially not today.

Yet here I am again. Going on instinct instead of thinking shit through.

I try to tell myself that it's because she might come in handy as a hostage or something, but the fact is my brain isn't functioning right now. Probably due to lack of oxygen. The edges of my vision are blurring, which seems to prove my point. We have to get out of here like, yesterday.

I drag the princess toward the security door, but she's fighting me every step of the way, punching and kicking.

"Quit with the goddamn wriggling," I snarl just as someone leaps on my back and starts thumping me on the head. "What the hell? Get the fuck off me."

"Don't touch the princess!" she screams back at me.

Which just goes to prove that nothing good ever comes from trying to help someone else, especially not someone like her.

Lesson fucking learned.

I reach behind me and peel whoever the hell is hitting me off my back before dropping her to the floor. I have no clue who this woman is, but she's slowing me down, and *that* I'm not having. While saving the princess could be a smart bet for me later on, this other one gets me nothing. So she can go down with this flying fucking torture chamber.

But before that happens, I plan to be long gone.

I continue dragging Princess Pain-in-the-Ass, my lungs screaming for oxygen.

At the security door, I release my grip on her arm and plug in the only security code I know for these things.

The door doesn't budge. Big fucking surprise.

Our rogue technician, Gage, memorized every code to every door in this place, and now that everything is going to shit, I wish I had, too. But wishes won't get me much, and they sure as fuck won't get me out of here. So I reach for my hip and pull out the one thing that will.

The princess backs away, staring at me with those strange silver eyes of hers, like she's afraid I'm about to shoot her.

I probably should—something tells me my escape would go a lot smoother.

Instead, I shoot a blast at the scanner. Nothing happens.

"Fuck," I growl and shoot again. This time the scanner bursts into flames, but at least the door slides open.

I turn to the princess and wave at the door in the closest thing to a gentlemanly move I've got. For a moment, she doesn't look like she's going to budge. But then the ship shimmies around us hard enough to have her careening into the wall. Which is all that needs to happen for her to make a dive for it, with the other girl close behind.

I follow right after them, and as soon as I'm through the door, oxygen floods my system, filling my lungs, spreading through my body.

Fuck, that feels good.

I take a couple of deep breaths before looking around to get my bearings. The princess glares at me like I just stole her favorite tiara or something. Again, typical. The Ruling Families aren't exactly known for saying *thank you*.

"Don't touch me!" she yells.

What is it with the touching thing? I hold up my hands. "Believe me, I wasn't planning to." But I'm starting to get a little pissed off. "I did just save your life, though, so a thank-you would be nice. Not to mention—"

Two more people burst through the security door, both dressed in these weird white robes that make them look fucking creepy. At the rate things are going, who knows who could appear next? An Ancient?

Either way, these two can take care of the princess from here. I've done my good deed for the day—probably for the century. I've got to go.

As I turn away, another explosion shakes the ship. Alarms are shrieking nonstop now, blaring up and down the corridor as the comms system crackles to life.

"Evacuation protocols have been instigated. Please go to your

designated evacuation point."

"What about everyone in the lab?" the princess asks. "We can't just leave them. What if something happens?"

"In case you haven't noticed, Princess, something *is* happening," I tell her.

"My name is Kali," she snarls. "Not Princess. Or, if you insist on formality, the correct address is *Your Highness*."

"Because formality is what I'm worried about right now. *Princess*." I start to move down the corridor. Then, because the lack of oxygen obviously did something to my own self-preservation instinct, I call over my shoulder, "You can stay here and blow up with the rest of the ship, or you can come with me and try to get the hell off this thing."

Why did I say that? I don't need her trailing me.

She stares down the corridor where the two in the robes have disappeared. Then at the girl beside her, whose face is ashen, her eyes wide and panicked. The princess gives a curt nod. "Let's go."

She tries to run but, two steps in, trips over the tight skirt of the dress she's wearing and lands on her ass, muttering something about sloggs under her breath.

I pull my knife from the scabbard at the small of my back—it's not standard issue, but it's gotten me out of a lot of jams in my life, and I don't go anywhere without it. Her expression goes scarily blank, and she shimmies away from me.

Why the fuck am I wasting my time again? I start to say to hell with it, but once again something prevents me from leaving her.

Instead, I point out, "You can't run in that."

I see the moment she gets it, because she scrambles to her feet and gives another quick nod. "Do it."

It sounds enough like an order that it gets my back way the hell up, but I let it go as I kneel beside her.

Her friend gives a horrified gasp, but I ignore her, too, as I grab the heavy, stone-encrusted material. *Are the jewels real?* I wonder as I try to figure out the best way to cut the damn thing. If they are, she's walking around wearing enough wealth to feed a good portion of my home planet for a month.

Fucking Ruling Families.

A slit up the front would be easiest, but it's so long she'll likely still trip and break her royal neck. So, I hack away at it just above her knees. Beneath it, her long legs are bare and she's wearing *very* high heels.

She follows my gaze, then kicks them off with a scowl. "Are we going? Or waiting around here all day?"

"Going." I drag my gaze from her bare legs by reminding myself they belong to a princess. Then I'm off and running.

I hear them behind me but don't slow. I've already gone fucking way beyond the call of duty.

I'm racing toward the open docking-bay doors up ahead, determined to make it before shit goes any more sideways. I'm almost there, but then another explosion rips through the ship, and I go careening into the wall.

"What the fuck is happening on this fucking piece of shit?" I roar.

I push off the wall and dive for the door as behind me, I hear someone stumble and fall.

Don't look back. It's not your problem. None of this is your fucking problem.

They're words to live by—literally—but I whirl around anyway, just in time to see the princess running back toward her fallen friend. But she only makes it a few steps before another blast hits us and she crashes to the floor just as a bulkhead slams down between them.

"No!" the princess screams, scrambling to her feet and banging her fists on the metal. "Lara? Lara!"

"It's too late," I tell her. "She's gone."

She ignores me, running her hands along the edges of the metal door as though she can find a way through. Not going to happen. Max and I have studied all the plans of this station, and once that particular fucker closes, nothing is opening it until the state of emergency is over. And judging from the way the ship is bucking like a pissed-off ocewallen, that's not happening anytime soon.

"You can't open it," I point out in my most reasonable tone.

"But I can't leave her. I just can't." She pounds on the door.

"Damn it," I growl. "We don't have time for this. The ship—"

"Princess Kalinda." Someone speaks from behind me, and I glance around. It's one of the people in the weird white robes—a girl with long braided blond hair and a sweet face. "It's not safe. You have more people depending on you than are on this ship. And your duty is to the many, not the one. You have to come away from there."

I can see from the expression on the princess's face that she doesn't want to listen—not to the advice and not to the speaker giving it. But the girl lays a hand on her shoulder, and the princess's whole body seems to sag.

She turns her head, and their eyes meet in some kind of communication I just don't get. The princess blinks, and I think she's about to cry. I'm not sure I want to be around if she does. But her back stiffens before she sheds a tear, and instead, she reaches out, touching her fingers briefly to the metal bulkhead before turning away.

Thank God. I turn as well and feel relief tug at my shoulders because Max is standing there, one eyebrow raised. He tosses me a bag—my kit—and I snag it out of the air one-handed.

He lifts a brow, and though he doesn't say it in my mind, I know he's calling me a show-off.

"*Nice catch*," is what he says instead.

I ignore it. "*About fucking time.*"

"*Hey, I've been waiting for you as instructed. You're the one who's late.*"

"*I've been saving damsels in distress.*"

He frowns. "*That doesn't sound like you.*"

I wave a hand to encompass the little group. Along with the princess and the blonde, there's a big dude in a long white robe—Seratian from the look of him. He seems about as happy as I feel.

"Meet Princess Kalinda," I tell Max.

I can see her looking back and forth between the two of us, taking in the similarities. Max is dressed in the same black-and-gray guard uniform as me, but it goes further than that. We look pretty similar, though Max is a little shorter, a little wider, and smiles a hell of a lot more than I do.

Fucking candy-ass.

"*No shit.*" He looks incredulous. "*A princess? Really?*"

"*Really.*"

The grin is back. He steps forward and holds out his hand. She eyes it like it might bite but then takes it briefly—no screaming at *him* not to touch her, I notice.

"I'm Max," he says. "Nice to meet you, Princess Kalinda."

He glances at the other two and then at me.

"No fucking clue," I respond.

The blonde steps forward. "I'm Rain," she says, holding out her hand. Max shakes it. "And this is Merrick, my...friend." She turns to me. "Thank you for what you did back there. I think we would have died if you hadn't shot out the door."

The dude in the robe says something in a language I don't understand, presumably Seratian. That's the only planet with its own language, likely because they were cut off from the rest of us for so long. Or maybe because they just like to be different—the Sisterhood thing they've got going definitely attests to that.

The girl gives a solemn nod before turning to the rest of us. "Merrick says if we're going to leave, we need to do it now. This place is unstable."

Too right. I'm ready to go—the ship is juddering beneath and around us, and the air is thick with smoke. I don't know how many more explosions the *Caelestis* can take before she implodes, but I do know that I don't want to be here when it happens.

I glance around and go still. The docking bay has been reduced to carnage. "Shit."

"Yeah," Max mutters, "*shit* just about covers it."

The place is in ruins, littered with the corpses of all the bright, shiny shuttles. Gone is the neat semicircle of parked ships. In its place is a disaster zone. But over at the far end, near the airlock doors, stands a dilapidated ship, seemingly undamaged.

"*The* Reformer, *huh?*" I ask Max in my head.

He nods.

Finally something's going our way. "*Gage?*"

"*Fuck knows. But he did his bit—paid off whoever needs paying. All we have to do is get on board, and the crew will pretend they never saw us.*"

"*Good riddance to him, then. Let's go*," I tell him.

He glances toward the others, but before he can say anything asinine, the princess asks, "So, what do we do now?"

"Our shuttle looks like it's the last one still intact." The Merrick guy nods toward the shuttle at the other end of the group of burned-out wrecks. He's right—she looks in way better shape than the others.

"Well, have a good trip," I say, because I certainly can't take her on the *Reformer.*

Strangely, I feel a flicker of what I'm guessing is guilt. It's not an emotion I'm overly familiar with, though, so maybe it's something else. Indigestion?

"You're not coming?" the princess asks, and there's something in her voice, too, that has me glancing at her sharply. Does she sound *disappointed*? But then her eyes narrow on my uniform. "Isn't it your job to keep us safe?"

Nope, not disappointment; just more of the Ruling Families' arrogance. Good fucking riddance. My regret—scratch that, my *indigestion*—probably came from Max's look...and what I knew he was going to suggest. He's always been the kinder man.

Then again, he hasn't spent the last few minutes with the princess snarling at him.

"Not anymore. I guess this is goodbye, Princess." I send her a last smirk and turn away, then start to move through the scattered debris in the direction of the *Reformer.* Max is close behind me.

"Wait! You can't go. I demand you—" She breaks off, and I glance back to see what's stopped her. She's staring aghast at the last remaining shuttle. Flames are flickering from the rear engine.

Suddenly, there's an ominous crack.

"Get down!" someone yells.

Too late. The whole shuttle explodes. The force knocks me off my feet, and I'm flying backward through the air. I crash into something behind me, the air leaving my lungs in a whoosh.

"Fuck."

CHAPTER 8

Rain

"High Priestess? Rain. Rain! Talk to me."

I blink my eyes open at the sound of Merrick's panicked voice and immediately see stars. Am I floating in space? Panic starts to take me over, too, but then I realize I'm breathing. Which means my space hypothesis is pretty unlikely.

I blink again, and the stars clear. I blink once more and realize I'm lying on my back, staring up through thick black smoke at the high curved ceiling of the *Caelestis*' landing bay. My nose hurts, my throat is raw, and my ears are ringing—I'm pretty sure I hit my head—but underneath all that, I can hear screams from somewhere far away.

"Rain? Are you okay?" Merrick asks again.

Okay seems like it's asking a bit much, considering everything hurts. But I'm hanging in there.

I sit up slowly, shaking my head to clear it, and the screaming becomes louder and not so far away. My whole body is trembling, and my heart feels like a trapped faconal trying to pry its way out of my chest.

Life in the monastery did not prepare me for this.

Merrick is looming over me, face concerned, a large, rough hand held out to me. I grasp it, and he pulls me to my feet.

"Are *you* all right?" I ask because he still doesn't look well.

"Of course. I was just worried about you. You were out cold."

"I hit my head, I think. But it's fine." I pat his arm to reassure him. "You won't have to go back to Sister Grinor and tell her you've failed and she has to wait for the next high priestess to awaken." At least not just yet.

He shudders, his tan skin going sallow. "Don't even think that."

See, he cares, even if it is just about keeping the high priestess safe. I know it's not exactly the same thing as caring about me, Rain the person, but at least it's more than the nothing I used to have.

I peer through the smoke and spot the princess. She's with the guard who helped us—Ian—and they seem to be having a... contentious conversation. "Come on," I say to Merrick, "let's join the others." Before the two of them kill each other.

"Just keep your hands to yourself," I hear the princess snap as we draw closer. She's looking a little frayed at the edges. Literally and figuratively.

Ian snarls. "I was just helping you. *Again*."

"I never asked for your help." She draws herself up, then catches sight of us and neutralizes her expression. "Rain, I'm so glad you're okay."

"Thank you, Your Highness." I smile as I realize I got it right.

I glance at Merrick to see if he noticed, but he just shakes his head at me, which makes me smile more. We've been together long enough that I even know why he's shaking his head—high priestesses are supposed to be concerned with *less* worldly things.

But then my short-lived pride in myself dies because there are people *screaming* somewhere, and they clearly need help, and the space station is collapsing around us, and there's a very good chance we're all going to *die*.

And despite the reassurances that, according to the scriptures, I'll be reborn, I *really, really* don't want to die. Especially not here on some cold space station in the middle of nowhere.

"Where's that screaming coming from?" the princess asks, beating me to it.

Ian gives a jerky nod toward the end of the docking bay. "From there."

"Where?" I frown as I look around. There's a ship parked at the far end of the docking bay, close to the airlock. It's considerably bigger than the shuttles, and—at least for now—it's in one piece. It is lying on its side, though, and doesn't look like it's going anywhere anytime soon.

"There are people in that big ship all the way at the end?" the princess asks. "Why?"

He gives her an incredulous look. "It's a prison ship. I doubt anyone's there by choice."

"A prison ship?" she repeats slowly, like she's really thinking about his answer. "But that doesn't make sense. This is a research facility. Why would Dr. Veragelen okay a prison ship to land here?"

"I guess she's just taking out the trash," Ian answers, voice dripping with disdain.

Her eyes narrow on him. "What does that even mean?"

"She brings people here. For her experiments." Ian is speaking slowly, enunciating each word. "And she has to do something with them when they're no longer of any use. Don't tell me you don't know about the experiments?"

Shock flares on her face. Clearly, she didn't. Neither did I—I haven't heard so much as a hint of such a thing. I glance at Merrick, and he shakes his head. He doesn't know, either. But there's a ring of truth in Ian's voice that makes it hard to doubt what he's saying.

I wish my ears would stop ringing long enough for me to make sense of any of this.

Ian lifts a brow. "Nothing to say to that, Princess?"

"Stop messing with her," Max says as he runs up. He's bleeding from a gash on his arm, but he doesn't seem to notice. Neither does Ian. "We need to go."

"I was just waiting for you."

Max frowns. "I was looking for Gage, but he's nowhere."

"Probably ran for cover at the first big bang. He's not exactly the kind to care about anyone's ass but his own."

Max smirks. "I don't know. From what I've heard, he likes all kinds of bangs. And all kinds of asses."

"Shut the fuck up." Ian shakes his head. "You're shocking the princess. Not to mention the other one."

Other one? Does he mean me? "I'm...not shocked." I actually really want to know more about the different kind of bangs this Gage person likes.

Ian raises a brow but doesn't say anything else to me. "We don't have time for this."

He takes off toward the so-called prison ship without another word.

"Come on, Princess Kalinda," Max tells her, waving a hand to encompass Merrick and me, too. "We'd better get on that ship."

"It's Kali," she murmurs. "And what—"

"Leave her," Ian tosses over his shoulder. "We don't need her."

"You don't know that," Max calls after him. "What about an insurance policy?"

What does he mean by that? I glance at Merrick, but his face is deliberately blank, a definite tip-off that he and I are on the same page. Who exactly are these men? Not who they appear to be, I'm beginning to think. They definitely seem to know more about things than the rest of us. Does that mean they also have a different agenda?

Merrick touches my arm and leans close. "I don't think we should have anything to do with these people," he says quietly in Seratian. "We'll find another way."

I want to agree with him—something definitely seems off here. Trouble is, I don't think there *is* another way.

"That ship is headed where we need to go," Ian is telling the princess. "That's all you need to know."

"Not to be a killjoy," the princess retorts, "but that ship is not going anywhere. Look at it. It's dead."

"We'll get it moving," Ian replies.

"How can you be so sure?" I ask.

He shrugs. "Because we have to."

Max gives us a rueful smile and hurries after Ian. The princess looks at me, a definite question in her eyes—one I don't have an answer to.

At least not until the *Caelestis* gives a particularly violent shudder, like the death throes of some great beast. Without a word or another thought, we take off running after them.

We're halfway across the space when the ship's doors open and a flood of people clamber out. They're all in gray jumpsuits. Are these the prisoners, then?

Before I can ask, another explosion tears through the station, and the interruption of gravity on the *Caelestis* makes it feel like we rise several feet. I throw my arms out to steady myself as the shrill shriek of a new alarm fills the docking bay. It's so loud it freezes all of us in place, and I clap my hands over my ears in a desperate attempt to shut out the noise.

I'm afraid I know what's coming next. There's a definite pattern of explosions and then—

Before I can even form the thought, a huge bulkhead slams shut in front of us, cutting us off from the prison ship—and what's likely our only possible escape route—for good.

"No, no, no, no, no!" Ian yells as he sprints the remaining distance. "That's our last shot at finding Milla!" he yells again, kicking viciously at the bulkhead like he thinks that will get it to open.

When it doesn't, he pulls out the pistol he's so fond of and shoots at it. When it still doesn't move, he lets out a roar of frustration nearly as loud as the alarm still pealing around us.

This Milla person must be very important to him.

I glance at the princess, who shrugs like it's not a big deal. But I can see the panic in her eyes, know the same fear is probably reflected in mine. Ian doesn't exactly seem like the most trustworthy sort, but at least he had a plan. Now, he's losing it, and the rest of us don't have any idea where to begin.

"What do we do now?" Merrick echoes my thoughts, shouting to be heard over the blaring alarm and Ian's very loud, very inventive, stream of curses. I've never heard most of them before, and I commit them to memory, just in case they're ever needed back at the monastery.

"Wait it out?" the princess suggests, but she doesn't sound convinced.

I shake my head. "I don't think it would be a long wait, Your Highness." It's getting uncomfortably hot in here, and the smoke is still hanging in the air, making my eyes smart. Sweat slides down my spine beneath the heavy robes. Ian has gone mostly quiet; he's holding a whispered conversation with Max, who seems to be trying to calm him down.

For a second, I imagine a different outcome for us. Me throwing myself at the bulkhead and lifting it up with my bare hands, clearing the path to the prison ship and saving us all. Merrick would be proud of me for once, and Princess Kali would be so grateful that she might actually give me a hug. Ian and Max would—

"No, I guess not," the princess says, interrupting the daydream that's so much better than our current reality. "And please, call me Kali."

It's not a hug, but I'll take it.

I search the docking bay, and my eyes settle on a bulky object over on the far side. It appears untouched by the chaos, but it's covered by some sort of dark tarpaulin so I can't see what it is. It looks big enough to be a ship—bigger than the shuttles, at least.

"What's that?" I ask, pointing.

Ian stops cursing long enough to look. "Well, I suppose if we're desperate," he says, eyes narrowing. "And I think we can all admit that we are."

"Oh, hell no." Max looks horrified. "That's not going to happen."

"Come on. I know you have no better ideas," Ian says, lifting a brow.

"What is—" Princess Kalinda starts, but Ian is already striding away. She looks at me, and this time *I* shrug. They clearly know what's under the tarp, but whatever it is, Max doesn't think it's the answer to our salvation.

All the same, we're running out of options.

Ian stops beside the tarp-covered object, then grabs onto the cover and starts dragging it off to reveal the sorriest-looking spaceship I have ever seen. Not that I've seen many, but I don't need to have to know that this thing is a heap of junk that looks like it hasn't flown in a millennium. The *Caelestis* is in better shape—in its current state.

"Oh, you have *got* to be kidding," Kali snaps, looking at Ian like he's some kind of particularly gross breed of slogg.

"What's the matter?" Ian taunts. "Not good enough for you, Princess?"

"That flying death trap isn't good enough for any sentient being," she answers coldly. "No wonder it seems like such a good idea to you."

I'd be devastated if someone said that to me, but Ian just cups a hand to his ear, pretending he can't hear her. Then he heads around the front of the ship.

Max follows. And—after giving her an apologetic shrug, since apparently that's how we talk to each other—so do I.

The ship is bigger than a shuttle but smaller than the prison ship, maybe about forty meters in length. The body is triangular, and it sits on landing gear that looks like a tripod and holds it about six meters off the ground. It's hard to tell what color it is under all the grime—I'm guessing rust-colored. There's a door close to the pointed end of the triangle. Ian stops beneath it and hits the button on the landing gear, presumably meant to lower the entrance ramp.

Nothing happens.

"Big surprise," Kali mutters from behind me. Looks like she decided it's worth checking out after all.

Ian ignores her and punches the button again. Not surprisingly, nothing happens *again*. Except the *Caelestis* chooses that moment to groan and lurch sickly to the side.

"Maybe we need to rethink this," Max comments.

"There's nothing to rethink. We're out of options." Ian glances at me. "Now might be a good time to pray."

Sadly, our religion doesn't work that way. What will happen will happen as the Light wills. The monastery gets pilgrims every year from all over the system, begging priestesses—especially the high priestess—to pray to the Light to intercede on their behalf, but they're misguided. I can't do anything to change the world. I'm just ready to save it when the Light shows the path.

But I don't have to get started with that complicated explanation, because at that moment, a man peers over the top of the ship. He's wearing a black lab suit, so he must work for the Corporation. He's also got silky black hair with a bright purple streak, sallow white skin, and narrow dark-brown eyes. I love the hair—I really hope there's nothing in the Book of the Dying Light that says a high priestess can't have purple hair, because I think it's going to be my next fashion choice.

"Gage," Ian yells up at him. "So that's where you've been hiding, you tricky bastard. Let us in."

Gage grimaces as he leans over the edge of the ship and shouts something unintelligible. Ian raises his arms in a what-did-you-say kind of gesture, so Gage tries again. And again. Finally, he rolls his eyes and holds up a finger. Seconds later, a ladder drops down the side of the ship.

"A fucking ladder?" Kali mutters with a disbelieving shake of her head. "This just gets better and better."

I kind of agree with her, but I'm not brave enough to say so. Especially since Ian clearly has no concerns about the primitive method of entry. He's already halfway up, with Max right behind him.

I edge closer, but Merrick stops me with a hand on my arm and says, "I don't think this is a good idea. We have a better chance staying on the space station. They're probably getting everything under control right now."

"It *is* the most sophisticated space station ever built," Kali puts in. But despite her serene expression, she sounds unsure.

"The most important thing is to get you home," Merrick says.

I think about being back in the monastery and wait for happy thoughts to fill my mind. It's the smart choice, the *good* choice. But there is no happiness inside me at the prospect of making it. Instead, just considering it feels like a full-grown narthompalus is sitting on my chest, getting heavier and heavier until I can't so much as draw a breath.

I stare up at the ladder leading who knows where, with people whom I suspect are not particularly good. Still, the pressure eases. And just like that, I know what I'm going to do.

When the ship issues a particularly loud groan, I take it as a personal message.

"It's not safe here," I say. "I think we should leave. Now."

Without waiting for Merrick to come up with any more perfectly logical reasons why we should stay, I grab the first rung of the ladder. I start to climb, and I don't look back.

Maybe it's the wrong choice, but surely these feelings are the Light guiding me on the path. Is it really so bad to just want a little more time to be free?

Just a tiny bit more, then I'll go back, and I'll do my duty without complaint.

I swear.

CHAPTER 9

Kali

I s it just me, or is my first official duty going really, really well?
Sure, I'm about to throw out the rulebook once and for all because
not only am I *not* calm, but judging from the look on Merrick's face,
I'm also doing a terrible job at not appearing panic-stricken.

Of course, that's probably because I *am* panic-stricken, but it's
all fine, right? Just another day in my life. Everything is totally and
completely under control right now. Dear old Mom would be so
proud.

As if to underscore my thoughts, the *Caelestis* gives another loud,
shuddering groan that has chills skating down my spine. Because
state-of-the-art space stations always sound like that when things are
running perfectly. Obviously.

It's just Merrick and me now, standing in the docking bay, staring
up at Rain's bottom half as she disappears up the ladder. And while
I'm still not certain staying on board is the way to go, I'm also not
ready to commit to climbing into the bucket of misplaced bolts in
front of us, either.

Surely there's another option. I just haven't thought of it yet.

The ship shimmies again just as Rain vanishes over the top of
the spaceship, and my heart jumps to my throat before sliding right

back down my esophagus into my stomach. Her making it on board is clearly the call to action Merrick needs, because he's suddenly racing up the ladder like her life depends on him getting to the top.

Of course, that leaves me on the ground *alone*, staring up at *his* bottom half and wondering what I'm supposed to do now.

I really don't want to get on this broken-down piece of space detritus. I really, really don't want to.

But then the alarms stop. And though I try to take it as a good sign, I suspect it's because even the emergency systems are breaking down. All around me, the station is creaking and shifting, and the common sense I've worked so hard to ignore is telling me it's only a matter of time—very limited time—before she falls apart completely.

I'm between a disaster and a hard place, and neither seems like the way to go.

But standing here isn't going to get me anywhere but dead, so I make the only decision I can.

I climb the ladder.

It leads to the top of the ship, and there's an open hatchway in the center. I peer down but can't see anything, so with a last look at the chaos surrounding me, I lower myself inside.

Once my bare feet touch the metal floor, I look around and try to get my bearings. I presume I'm in what passed for an airlock thousands of years ago. There's an open door to the left of me, so I go through it. There's no one in sight, but I can hear voices, so I follow them and find myself on what must be the bridge at the front of the ship. It's a triangular space about twelve meters long. There's a seat right at the front, then three seats down each side, and another, bigger one with an impressive array of controls on the arms right in the center of the room.

Looks like it's calling my name.

Viewing screens stretch the full length of each of the side walls, but they're covered with some sort of shields right now. Probably because this thing has been in dry dock *forever*.

On the plus side, the inside of the ship looks like it's in a lot better condition than the outside, as though she's been protected from the vagaries of space. But the layout is unfamiliar, some sort of antiquated setup that's different from anything I've seen before.

Rain, Merrick, and Max are standing along the right wall near a row of seats. Ian is messing with some sort of control panel at the back, while the purple-haired guy—who looks to be around my age and is wearing a black lab suit, so he certainly works on the *Caelestis*— leans around him with a screwdriver in one hand and a giant wrench in the other.

"I'm telling you she doesn't work," he says. "I don't care how many buttons you push or how many times you push them; the ship isn't going to magically activate. I've been trying to get her to start since I ducked in here, and nothing."

"Yeah, well, Gage, maybe you're not as clever as everyone says you are," Ian snarks as he crouches down to look underneath the console, like he's going to find some magic button Gage missed.

"I'm a fucking tech genius," Gage retorts with a roll of his eyes. "And you know it, or you wouldn't keep coming to me to fix shit for you. Right, Max?" He glances over his shoulder with a smile—then freezes when he locks eyes with me. A slight choking noise comes from his throat, and before I can so much as blink, he bows. Really low. His hair falls to the side, revealing the *CT* tattoo on his neck— definitely Corporation—and a long, dangly rondolinite earring. Then he peers up at me with a cocky grin. "Your Very Royal Highness. I am a big fan."

It's the first time I've heard it put like that, but after the day I've had, I'll take it. "If you can get this thing flying, the feeling will definitely be mutual."

Ian glances up at Gage, a scowl on his face. "If you could stop the royal ass-kissing for a moment, I could use some help here."

"And I've already told you there's no help to be had. This ship isn't flying." But Gage finally straightens from his bow and heads back over to the control panel beneath the console. "Get out of there, will you, before you break something worse than it's already broken."

I'm really starting to like his style.

"Can I help?" I ask.

"No!" Ian pounds his fist against the control panel a few times before crawling out from under the console so fast he nearly takes his own head off. "For fuck's sake, the last thing we need is you poking around down here."

"Why? Because you're doing such a bang-up job of it?" I ask archly. "Emphasis on the bang?"

"How about both of you take your seats and let me have another go at this?" Gage asks. "It won't work, but, what the fuck."

"I've always said your optimism is the best part of you," Max calls from where he's now seated against the wall.

"That's because you haven't actually *seen* the best part of me," Gage retorts as he ducks under the console.

I'm too wired to sit down, though. In here, we seem cut off from the chaos surrounding us, but I can't help wondering what's going on outside and how long we've got before this whole thing comes tumbling down. I don't want to die, and I don't want any of my subjects to die, either.

But I'm deathly afraid it's too late for that. What about Vance and Arik? Lara? Dr. Veragelen? Are they still alive? Am I just leaving them here to perish?

And what about the heptosphere? Will it survive the certain destruction of the *Caelestis*? If it doesn't, what will that mean for the system? It was our only hope.

Which leads me to wonder if this was deliberate sabotage. Maybe the rebels? They hate the Ruling Families, blame us for everything that's wrong with the system. But destroying the *Caelestis* hurts them as much as it does us. It doesn't make sense.

There's nothing I can do about it right now, so I try to shake away the thoughts. Some might say I'm borrowing trouble, but a lifetime surrounded by palace intrigue has taught me to trust my gut...and not to trust people who seem to have their own agendas. Ian and Max are not behaving like legitimate members of the security forces—I'd know; I've been around them my entire life. And while I instinctively like Rain, even if she is a part of the misguided Sisterhood, it's very obvious that she has no training in being an ambassador...which means that she's here for some other reason. And that her bodyguard is, too. The only one who might actually be genuine is Gage, who seems like a nice guy. But that could just be because it's what he wants me to see…

Right now, he's busy working away under the console, trading jokes with Max while Ian paces back and forth and curses under his breath. Rain and Merrick are in their seats, talking quietly in Seratian.

Restless, I wander up to the console, more out of curiosity than because I think I can actually help. But I'm guessing this ship is old—really old—and the history buff in me can't help but be a little interested. At least it takes my mind off my imminent death.

Will it hurt?

Don't think about it.

I peer at the console. It's just a smooth black surface, except for what looks like some sort of bio-scanner on the top. But as I bend down to get a closer look, a loud crash sounds outside the room. I whirl around so fast that I lose my balance and stumble into the console.

A woman suddenly appears in the open doorway. Maybe a year or two older than me, she's medium height, with olive skin and curly black hair. The skin around her yellow eyes is stained darker than the rest, and I recognize the telltale signs of a native of the desert planet Permuna.

There's a scar running down her neck, the black ink of a tattoo snakes down her bare arm, and I'm pretty sure that's blood staining the front of her ripped gray jumpsuit. One look into her face has me straightening up—and then going still. She's staring back at me out of cold, flat yellow eyes, and I catch something dark and twisted flickering behind them.

But then she blinks and it's gone.

"Holy shit! I really am a genius!" Gage's enthusiastic shout breaks the tension in the air as he scoots out from under the control panel. I drag my gaze from the newcomer and focus on the front of the ship, only to realize that he's right. The console is glowing.

"You did it?" Ian asks, sounding doubtful. It might just be the first thing we've ever agreed on.

"I did it!" Gage confirms, his smile quickly giving way to a frown. "I have no clue how I did it, but she's coming online. Whether or not we can fly her is something else entirely."

"I can fly," comments the woman who just appeared from nowhere.

"And you are?" demands a very suspicious-looking Ian.

Okay, make that two things we can agree on.

The woman blinks a couple of times as if she's not sure what the answer is. "Beckett," she finally says, but she sounds uncertain.

I tell myself it's because she got hit in the head during the explosions, but my gut is working overtime telling me not to trust her.

"How did you get up here?" I ask, because her name tells us absolutely nothing. "I thought we were cut off from the rest of the space station."

Her gaze shifts back to me, and she frowns. "I was on the other ship."

"The other—" I break off as I realize what she's talking about. She came from the *Reformer*, what Ian called the prison ship. I didn't realize any of the prisoners made it to our side of the docking bay before the bulkhead dropped.

She could be a pirate. Or a murderer. Or any number of other types that shouldn't be left to run free around the system. Not that any of that matters right now. It's not like we're about to leave her behind on a space station that's going to crash at any moment.

One more thing Ian and I must agree on, because instead of wasting time on a bunch of useless questions, he says, "Then take a seat. You can be my copilot."

Then he turns to me. "You plan on standing there all night, Princess, or are you going to buckle up?"

"Oh, I'll definitely buckle up. I'll need to, if your flying is as good as your engineering skills."

I eye the big chair in the center of the room, but Ian beats me to it, and I'm too exhausted to fight for what my mother would call my royal privileges. Instead, I sink into the nearest seat, next to Max.

Buckling up isn't that easy, however. The seat restraint is so old that it takes me a couple of minutes to figure out how to work it. I don't feel too bad, though; everyone else is doing the exact same thing. And it occurs to me that if the controls are just as archaic, then we might be jumping from one kind of trouble to another.

"Please tell me you know how to fly this thing?" I ask, sounding a little desperate even to my own ears. "You do, don't you?"

"Not a clue," Ian replies.

At that moment, the station rocks as a giant explosion tears through the docking bay, and Ian grabs onto the controls. "But I'm about to take a crash course." He flashes me a grin. "Having fun yet, Princess?"

"You know it. So much fun."

Ian slams his hand down on the control panel. Nothing happens.

Another shock rips through the *Caelestis*.

Don't puke, don't puke. Don't fucking puke.

He beats his fist against it again, just as I wrap my hands around the armrests and squeeze for all I'm worth. The hit must be what the ship needs, because it gives a little shake, and then the console flashes with colorful lights. The shields covering the screens lift, and all of a sudden I can see out into the chaos of the docking bay of the ISS *Caelestis*. The somewhat tarnished and rapidly crumbling jewel in the Empire's crown.

The ship we're on starts rising, hovering above the floor, and I hold onto the armrests even tighter. Beside me, Max smiles.

"Ian has got this," he reassures me.

Then we're moving, weaving around the detritus of the crumbling docking bay.

"Hey, you're doing great, Ian," Max calls after a few seconds.

"Actually, I'm doing fuck all." He sounds bewildered. "I think I must have switched on the autopilot. She's doing it all on her own."

I'm not sure if that's a good thing or a bad one, but it's too late to do anything but hold my breath and pray, considering we're aiming for the airlock but the doors are tightly closed.

That doesn't stop Ian—or the autopilot he says is controlling the ship. In fact, she just keeps speeding up, even though we're heading straight for the toughest, most crash-proof metal in the Senestris System.

Apparently we're going to put that assertion to the test.

Fear turns my insides to mush, and to keep from screaming I bite my lip until it bleeds. One of the many rules of being a princess? Never, ever scream in a spaceship crash. Instead, die with dignity.

Too bad I feel anything *but* dignified right now.

Beside me, Max mutters something vile beneath his breath. Rain gasps. Merrick merely looks ill. Gage covers his eyes with his hands while Beckett laughs, a high-pitched, wild sound that has every hair on my body standing straight up. And through it all, Ian looks straight ahead, face grim and jaw locked as if willing the doors to open through sheer grit alone.

I'm not sure if it works or if something else happens. But at the last second, the doors miraculously slide open, and we glide straight through into the airlock.

I have one second of relief before they close behind us, leaving us in total darkness.

"Come on, you son of a varnook," Gage growls. "Open sesame."

A few more seconds of darkness. A few more seconds of holding my breath. And then the outer doors slide open, the light of a thousand stars burning away the darkness.

For a second, we hover; then the ship shoots out into the vastness of space, leaving the burning hulk of the *Caelestis* behind on its path to who knows where.

CHAPTER 10

Kali

My mother says, *To get what you want, smile until it's time not to.* And as we cruise through space with absolutely no destination in mind, I'd like to think that I've legitimately reached the "time not to smile" part, but I don't think that's how it actually works. Mom taught me smiling has nothing to do with being happy—it's a way to elicit a desired response. And not smiling is exactly the same.

She's had me practicing my regal smile—not to mention my regal bored expression—in the mirror since I was four, and sometime around age ten it became second nature. She used to tell me it was building my armor because we need to be strong for the good of the system.

Except it doesn't feel like second nature right now.

I'm trying to smile—really, I am—but my lower lip refuses to stop wobbling. I clamp it steady with my teeth and blink against the sudden, suspicious prickling behind my eyes. If emotions are off-limits, then tears are a fate worse than death.

In the rear-view screen, I can see the *Caelestis* implode, smooth outer shell folding in, as all imperial space stations are set to do in case of critical error so we don't cover the system in deadly debris. And I'm trying hard not to let my imagination loose on what must have happened to Lara and Arik and Vance and all those other poor people still on board. Maybe they all got away after we did. But I know that's wishful thinking—which is just escapism for the masses, according to my mother, and not to be indulged. We have a responsibility to think ahead.

I guess it doesn't matter that Lara and the others died on the ship—maybe it was actually a blessing, considering the rest of us are going to burn in the not-too-distant future. The *Caelestis* was our hope for salvation, and now she's turning to ash.

And me? I had such high hopes that I would finally be able to be useful. To do some good.

Ha.

The Empress's minions will all no doubt say "I told you so" as soon as they hear about what happened. More than likely, they'll also find a way to heap all the blame for this disaster on me.

I can hear them now, whispering to my mother that I blew the *Caelestis* up out of pure incompetence. Or worse, out of spite.

I've never been popular with the Council—or any of the upper echelon of the Ruling Families, and not just because they're hoping to take my family's place in the hierarchy. Most of them were against my mother's marriage to my father because he wasn't one of them. He was a priest from Serati—part of a delegation to Askkandia—when he met my mom and fell in love. My father used to tell the story to me when I couldn't sleep, and I always adored it.

Of course, that was before I realized that their love was one-sided and that my mother hid her true contempt from him for the years she needed him, and not for one second longer. She smiled until it was time not to smile…and my father and I are the ones who paid the price.

Most of the minions believe I have weak blood because my father was not from Askkandia or even from one of the Ruling Families. I don't care. I wouldn't swap his blood for anything.

An abyss of sadness beckons—like it has every day since his death—but I ignore it…as I have every day since his death. Time to take stock and decide where to go from here, literally and figuratively.

If I'd wanted to drift aimlessly around space, I could have just leaped off the *Caelestis* in a space suit and hoped for the best.

Reaching down, I tug at a loose strand of cloth from the frayed hem of my Imperial Regalia. The dress is hacked off just above the knee, revealing more bare leg than I've ever shown before. And bare feet, *dirty* bare feet. I lost the cloak somewhere on the run from the lab to the docking bay—though that's definitely not a loss. Good riddance to bad fashion, if you ask me, but Lara would have a fit if she saw me right now. All her hard work reduced to *this*.

At the thought of her, my lower lip starts to wobble again, so I shut it down, banishing her from my mind even as I press my lips together so tightly that my jaw aches. What would my mother tell me?

One day, I'll be able to think of Lara, when I can do something positive with the memory. Just not now.

And maybe not ever, considering I'm stuck on a piece of space junk that will likely disintegrate around us any second, leaving us floating in space for eternity. Add in the company I'm presently keeping, and what happens next is anyone's guess. Especially considering everyone in this group seems to be looking out for number one and no one else—except maybe Ian, who's looking out for Milla, whoever that is.

All I know is he was ready to hop aboard this thing without a second thought just for the chance at saving her.

I'd like to think that makes him honorable, but the truth is, it just makes him even more dangerous.

I can sense someone staring at me, and I raise my gaze to find Beckett, the escaped prisoner from the *Reformer*. She's leaning against the console, and she has that look in her eyes again—the one I can't quite decipher but I'm pretty sure means nothing good. When she sees me watching, her lips curve into a small smile and she waggles her fingers at me in a way that sends shivers of unease prickling along my spine.

I tell myself it's because she could have done anything to earn her spot on that ship. For all I know, she could be a murderer of prupples and kanadoos and baby varlens and deserves everything that happens to her.

Or maybe she was planted on the *Caelestis* to sabotage her. She could even be part of the Rebellion. I grit my teeth at the thought—I hate the rebels and everything they stand for. They killed my dad. Blew him into so many pieces that there wasn't even a body left to bury.

But when I look at Beckett again, both her hands are twitching. They're hanging at her sides and bear the same dark stain as around her eyes. As though she senses my gaze, she screws her left hand into a fist. It hides the stain but doesn't stop it from trembling.

I remember Ian's comment that they were carrying out what surely must be illegal experiments on the *Caelestis*. To be fair, they'd have to be illegal—my mother may be a stone-cold political operative, but there's no way she'd countenance experiments on her citizens.

But that doesn't mean Dr. Veragelen didn't take things into her own hands. Maybe she did something to Beckett that did more than scar her skin. Maybe she damaged her mind. Which means I can't just presume she's a bad person thinking horrible thoughts about me. Maybe she's just…broken. If that's the case, I have to at least try to be kind to her.

I smile back, trying to think of something to say. But she meets my smile with a look of total and complete contempt before deliberately turning her back on me. I start to get angry, but then I see the writing on the back of Beckett's jumpsuit. *Prisoner 826.*

Maybe her contempt is justified.

I shift my gaze to where Max has just stood up from the seat beside me. He's still in his guard's uniform, but I'm doubling down on my previous impression that neither he nor Ian are actually guards. Now that I can think a little clearer, it's obvious they were only on the *Caelestis* to track down this Milla person.

Part of me wonders if *they* blew up the *Caelestis* to hide their escape on the prison ship. If so, they messed up, as the *Reformer* was destroyed as well…which makes them incompetent as well as armed, dangerous liars. Though it's hard to think of Max that way when he

glances up and gives me a grin and a very mischievous wink—one I
internally fight not to return.

Despite everything I'm figuring out, I can't help liking him.

Also out of his seat now, Gage is fiddling with one of the control
panels on the back wall. Of everyone on the ship, he seems the nicest
and the most uncomplicated. Then again, I gather he's been working
with Max and Ian all along, so maybe he's not as uncomplicated as
he seems.

On the other side of the triangular bridge are Rain and Merrick,
their heads close together. I really like Rain, but Merrick I'm not so
sure of—despite the fact that he reminds me of my dad. There's a
reserve to him that makes me suspect we've yet to see the real man.
Despite pledging his life to the Sisterhood, he moves like a fighter,
and he looks a little bit older than the rest of us—maybe in his mid-
twenties.

But, while I like Rain, they're still officials of the Sisterhood, which
means their agenda—worshipping the Dying Sun, even hastening its
demise—will always be in opposition to the rest of ours—to save it
by any means possible. So can any of us truly trust them? Rain is
the most unlikely ambassador I have ever come across—and I know
what politicians are like—so did the Sisterhood somehow learn about
the heptosphere and Dr. Veragelen's work and decide to destroy it?
They nearly died themselves, but martyrs are hardly unheard of in
religious organizations.

And then there's Ian—I've saved the worst and most obnoxious
for last. Right now, his long, lean body is sprawled in the captain's
seat, even though he's given up all pretense that he's actually flying
this piece of junk. His eyes are half closed, and he has a brooding
look on his handsome face that makes me wonder what he's thinking
about. Milla, maybe? Or how catastrophically wrong his plan has
gone? Does he feel responsible for what happened to the *Caelestis*
and the mess we're currently in?

I have to remind myself that he did in fact save my life—I
think I would have passed out if he hadn't gotten me out of the
decontamination zone when he did. Then I also remind myself that

he likely had an ulterior motive. That he was just thinking of his getaway and how he could use me as a hostage.

Truth be told, it seems like just about everyone on this ship could have had a reason to blow up the *Caelestis*. Which means I need to keep my wits about me. I need to get the rest of us somewhere safe. And I'm the only one with the plan to do so.

I glance around at the others and decide it's time to inform the rest of them of my plan. And more than time to prove what a formidable leader I can be. Because if the person who blew up the *Caelestis* is on this ship, I'm not going to let them get away with it.

CHAPTER 11

Ian

I can feel the princess's eyes on me again, but I don't bother to look. There's nothing there but trouble, and I've got more than enough of that in my life right now.

Yeah, we escaped the fiery pit of doom that was the *Caelestis*, but the *Reformer* is going down with it. And with it our best—and possibly last—chance to find Milla.

My hand curls into a fist of its own volition, and I force myself to uncurl my fingers one by one. It's hard, though, when all I want to do is punch something. We were so fucking close, right fucking there. Right up until the princess showed up and everything went straight to shit.

Maybe it's unfair of me to blame her for this disaster, but I don't give a fuck. Those explosions weren't accidents—they were murder attempts at worst, sabotage at best. And while there were a lot of diplomats on board the *Caelestis*, common sense tells me all that force was meant for the pretty, pretty princess over there.

Having spent the better half of the last hour with her myself, I can't say I blame whoever tried to blow her up. I just wish to shit they'd done it after Max and I made it onto that prison ship and got the hell out of there. If they had, we might be halfway to Milla by now instead of flying this piece of shit to who the fuck knows where and hoping we don't die.

It's a clusterfuck, all right, and one I'm more than happy to lay at the princess's door.

Even before she jumps to her feet and claps her hands. Not surprisingly, nobody takes the slightest bit of notice of her except me. I'm not about to give her the satisfaction of knowing I'm looking at her, but I do turn my head a little so I can watch her out of half-closed eyes. And I've got to say, at least in the looks department, she's a far cry from the all-decked-out ambassadors who came aboard the *Caelestis* a couple hours ago.

She looks bedraggled, for lack of a better word, in her cut-off dress and bare feet. Strands of all that dark-red hair of hers have come loose from the elaborate style she started the visit with, and her makeup has long since worn off. Plus, she's got a streak of grime running down her left cheek that would be laughable on anyone else.

But strangely, despite the mess, she still looks like a princess. There's an innate sense of...confidence about her that no amount of dishevelment can hide, like she just has to open that lush little mouth and we'll all fall to our knees and follow whatever commands she issues.

Fuck that.

It's going to be amusing to watch her try, though.

Sure enough, a frown flickers across her face when no one so much as looks at her, but it's quickly replaced by a smile. Like a mask has fallen over her features—which immediately ups my already high level of suspicion. Experience has taught me that people who can hide their emotions like that usually have a lot more to hide, none of it good. Plus, it's just really fucking creepy.

"Excuse me, everyone," she says in that cut-glass accent of hers. "Could I have your attention for a moment, please?"

Still not much of a response.

Max and Gage are talking about something—their voices are low, so I can't hear what they're saying, but judging by the look on Max's face, it's about Milla. I get that he's worried about her—I'm going out of my fucking mind trying to figure out what to do now—but I'm not thrilled with the fact that he's confiding in Gage. We may still need him to find Milla, but we can't trust the guy. He's the most mercenary person I've ever come across, and I've come across a few. He betrayed his own people to us for a payout—and not even a big one. While it was useful for us, my motto is if he'll betray one person, there's a good chance he'd betray a lot of others. Hell, right now, he's probably working out exactly how he can make a few more planeta credits out of this whole fuck-up.

"I said, can I have your attention."

No "please" this time, and her voice has gotten louder. Sounds to me like the princess is a little put out, and I sort of expect her to start stamping her feet at any moment. Her bare feet.

I barely resist the urge to laugh.

From her spot near the console, Beckett turns around, a slight smile on her face as she looks at the princess. But it's not a nice smile, and it doesn't reach those cold yellow eyes of hers.

She may have been a prisoner, but there's a good chance she could be completely innocent. While she doesn't look innocent, I know that along with political prisoners, some of the "experimental subjects" on the *Caelestis* were bought from the raiders. The raiders are illegal, at least officially, but as far as I can tell, they move around the system unhampered. I'm guessing they serve a useful purpose doing anything that the Ruling Families or the Corporation want done but don't want to be seen doing themselves.

Anyway, a lot of the prisoners have committed no crimes, have done nothing at all other than being in the wrong place at the wrong time. I should know. That was Milla, Max, and me ten years ago. Eventually we got away, but not everyone is so lucky.

And now Milla is a prisoner again.

But we will get her back. Anything else is unacceptable. We just need a new plan—one that doesn't involve Princess Stick-Up-Her-Ass calling all the shots. Or any shots, for that matter.

But the longer I sit here, the itchier this uniform gets. I hate the damn thing anyway—not only is it made of the worst material, it's also a mark of subservience to a regime I despise. It's long past time I got rid of it.

I do a quick scan of the panel on the arm of my chair. There's nothing buzzing or flashing, so I presume everything is working as it should. I get to my feet and grab my bag from the floor, considering changing in here, but I don't want my princess to get too excited—or to give the little girl in white a heart attack—so I head for the exit.

"Hey, I was talking!" the princess exclaims as I walk right by her into the corridor. "Where are you—"

The door slides closed, cutting her off mid-word—which isn't satisfying at all.

Now that I'm alone, I quickly strip off my weapons and uniform. I pull my own clothes out of the bag and am dressed again in minutes. I slip the knife into the sheath at the small of my back, another into my left boot, one under my jacket, and then strap the laser pistol back around my waist and tie it at my thigh.

I feel better once I'm in my own clothes. More like myself.

When I stroll back into the room, the princess does a double take, her eyes widening. She clearly still likes what she sees, though you wouldn't know it from the scowl on her face. It's a subtle thing.

Surprisingly, it looks like she somehow managed to get everyone else's attention when I was changing. Nice of her to save me the trouble.

But before I can say anything, she clears her throat. "I was just telling everyone that we need to head directly to Askkandia."

"That's one idea," I say conversationally as I give her a deliberately slow smile, just because I know it will piss her off. She's a lot easier to argue with—and get the better of—when she's angry. "Too bad it's not happening, Princess."

"What do you mean? Of course it's happening. What else would happen?" She pauses for a moment, studying me like she's trying to figure me out. It's all I can do not to laugh and tell her that's not going to happen, either.

But then she gives another one of those scary smiles of hers and continues. "I can assure you that you will be compensated for taking me home. My mother will pay very generously for my return."

This time, I do laugh. Max and I are wanted on every planet in Senestris—probably even the dead ones. The second we step foot on Askkandia—especially with the Empress's daughter—we'll get tossed in a cell. Which will be followed by a very rapid execution, I'm sure. And that's only *if* the Empress is in a generous mood because we returned her baby girl to her.

If she's not…well, if she's not, we'll probably get handed over to Doc V's minions for her experiments. I know a good captain's supposed to go down with the ship, but there's nothing good about her. Besides, people like her don't die that easily. I'd bet a lot of planetas she'll be back in business in no time, trying to save Senestris by making sure no one who isn't part of the Ruling Families is actually safe.

It's total fucking garbage, but I don't bother sharing this with the princess when she probably knows it all already. Instead, I settle for, "I've got other plans."

"You mean this friend of yours? Milla?" She takes a deep breath, and her smile is more genuine this time. "I promise you, if you get me back safely, my mother will help you find your friend."

Beckett snorts. "Is she for fucking real?" she asks the ship in general before looking straight at the princess. "Are you for fucking real? I mean, do you actually believe the shit you're spouting, or is this all part of the good-little-princess act you've got going on?"

The princess's mouth gapes open like she's a fishgalen in search of a hook, but I'm not paying her all that much attention right now. No, I'm more focused on Beckett, who suddenly seems a lot more lucid than she did when she first arrived. Sure, she's got a twitch in her left hand she can't control and a weird-ass way of blinking that freaks me out, but she's calling the princess on her shit, and that is something I can definitely get behind.

"You really think your mummy won't kill us because she's such a nice, kind lady who likes to help people in need?"

"I know exactly who and what my mother is," the princess answers, which isn't an answer at all. "And she will take care of all of you if you bring me home."

Beckett snarls, leaning forward like she's ready to tangle with the princess. But then she winces.

She rubs the back of her skull and closes her eyes for a moment. Then she shakes her head and turns away. She walks to the nearest seat and lowers herself into it, once again closing her eyes like it hurts too much to keep them open.

I don't know what to make of it—or her. Either she was hurt in the explosions or—and this seems more likely—she's suffering the aftereffects of one of Doc V's experiments. I almost feel sorry for her. Doesn't mean I'll take any shit from her if she decides to direct it at me instead of the princess over there, though.

Speaking of which, the princess is staring at Beckett with her mouth hanging open. Has she been rendered speechless? I somehow doubt it, but I suspect she's led a sheltered life and probably thinks everyone loves her because she's a fucking princess. Now, she's coming face to face with the real world. And guess what—I don't feel even vaguely sorry for her.

The guy in the white robe stands up. "I think we should head to Serati. We need to return the high priestess to the safety of the monastery."

"High Priestess?" I ask, focusing on the girl with him for the first time.

She grins. "I know, I know. You expected a high priestess to be taller, right?"

I didn't expect her to be anything at all. I can honestly say that the words "High Priestess" have never even passed through my mind before.

"But honestly, you don't need to worry about getting me back to Serati right now. There's absolutely no rush."

"I wasn't worried," I tell her.

"Oh, good. The last thing Merrick and I want is to be an inconvenience when you all have far more important things to do." She takes a deep breath and then, very deliberately not looking at Merrick or me, she suggests, "Maybe we *should* take Kali to

Askkandia. I was born there, but I haven't been back since I was a baby and I'd love to visit the capital. Everyone should visit at least once, don't you think?"

Not even a little bit. The capital can get fucked for all I care, along with the Empress and every member of the Council.

I start to say that, but in the end I just shake my head. Rain is a lot for such a little person, but I sort of like her. There's a sweetness there you don't see very often, and an enthusiasm for life that I suspect the rest of us lost a long time ago. If we ever had it.

"There will be a reward," Merrick tells the rest of us. "You'll be heavily compensated for returning us to Serati."

The way the rich think their money will buy them anything and everything they want has always been the thing that disgusts me most about them. The fact that they're usually right is the thing that has always disgusted me most about the world we live in.

Max and I exchange a look, and he doesn't have to say anything for me to know he feels exactly the same way.

"Hush, Merrick," the little high priestess says. "They're not going to want a reward. They're nice people. You're forgetting, Mr. Ian saved all our lives back there."

Merrick shakes his head, I'm guessing because he's as bewildered by her outlook as I am. But he continues like she hadn't interrupted. "And we can see that Princess Kalinda gets home safely afterward."

The princess frowns. "Except I can't go to Serati. I have to go to Askkandia. Right now."

"And no doubt what the princess wants, the princess gets," Beckett mutters. "Why? Are you more important than the rest of us?"

That silences the princess, but there's a furrow between her eyes as though she doesn't quite understand the question. Finally, she clears her throat and says, "Not more important."

The way she says it tells the rest of us that yes, she does think she's more important. Even before she adds, "I'm a princess. And you're…"

She seems so bewildered that it's all I can do not to laugh.

Beckett doesn't even bother to try. When she laughs, it's not a pleasant sound. "I don't think that will get you very far on this ship, *Princess*."

I straighten up a little at Beckett's tone—I don't actually like her calling Kali *Princess* in that way. I reserve that little pleasure for myself.

I look around to see if anyone else has got anything to add, any suggestions as to where we should go and what we should do before I tell them exactly what's going to happen. But everyone has gone quiet. Even the princess. *Especially* the princess. I think it's finally dawning on her that she's not in charge here.

It's about fucking time. And while I don't like my idea much more than anybody else's, it's the only way to get the information we need now that we lost the *Reformer* when the station went down. Yeah, it's a long shot, but when it comes to Milla, I'll take any shot I get. Even ones that might—and by *might* I mean *probably will*—get me killed.

With that thought in mind, I break the now awkward silence. "We're heading for Vistenia."

At first, no one says anything; then: "Vistenia? Why?" This from the Merrick guy.

I normally don't like being questioned, but I'll give a little leeway this once, because they don't know me yet and likely everything will go more smoothly with a little cooperation.

"The *Reformer*'s home port is on Vistenia. We're going to get access to the records and see if we can find out where she was heading."

"*You make it sound so easy*," Max says in my mind, his tone rife with amusement.

"*Just greasing the wheels*," I respond.

"*Since when do you bother with grease? Usually you just shoot anything that opposes you.*"

"*I'm practicing my diplomatic skills*," I answer with a shrug. "*Plenty of time to shoot something—or someone—later.*"

He laughs but gets serious fast. "*You know those records were probably doctored—if they even exist. It's not like what the* Reformer *was doing is exactly legal.*"

"*A reason to keep Gage around for a little while longer.*" A very little while. "*He may be an asshole, but he's skilled as shit. He can track any abnormalities. Plus he's Corporation—once we find the ship, he can get us the info we need to find Milla."*

"True." Max pauses to consider for several seconds. *"Vistenia's not the worst place to hide out."*

"Not even close." That honor is reserved for Askkandia herself, with all her politicians and "very important people."

Vistenia doesn't have anyone important, at least not by Council standards.

It's mostly farmers, and they're a pretty placid bunch, most of whom have never gone hungry, so they don't get all defensive the way people from other planets tend to. And since security is almost nonexistent there, it's a better place than most to hole up while we decide what to do next.

"What do you care about where the *Reformer* was heading?" Beckett asks.

"It's that Milla person, isn't it?" the princess says. "You're still looking for her."

Of course I'm still fucking looking for her. It's not like I'm going to stop. I couldn't even if I wanted to, and neither could Max.

I don't answer, but that doesn't mean she stops pushing.

"Just who is she to you? I know she's someone important."

Suddenly, I'm furiously angry. This woman doesn't know anything. Fuck all. I take a step closer, and she starts to back away but holds her ground. Looks like she's braver than I thought.

"I told you my mother will help," she says in a voice that wavers more than a little. Maybe not so brave, then. And definitely more than a little brainwashed.

"Princess, your mother will toss us in a cell and shut off the oxygen—if we're lucky."

"You don't have any—"

"Give it up, Princess," I snarl as my temper gets the best of me. "We are *not* going to fucking Askkandia."

She looks around the room, maybe expecting some support, but everyone glances away. Except for Beckett, who gives her an obnoxious smile. Definitely no love lost there.

"I think we should take a vote," Merrick says.

"*Keep your cool*," Max urges me.

I do my best. I even take a deep breath and count to ten in my head like Milla always reminds me to. But then I draw my pistol and point it straight at Merrick's head. "Like everything else in this fucking system, this is not a democratic process."

He stares at me, and if he had a gun, I'm pretty sure he'd be using it. He's definitely got attitude for a religious type. But I learned a long time ago that attitude only gets you so far in this system—a gun gets you the rest of the way.

And he doesn't have one. I do. So he can shut the fuck up.

"Cool gun," Beckett interrupts like she's discussing the weather, not watching a mercenary menace a priest. "How long's it hold a charge?"

Really? Right now? "Around two months," I tell her. Her interest is kind of undercutting the mood.

"Nice," she says. "Really nice."

"Okay," I say, sliding the pistol back into the holster. I've made my point. "Looks like it's decided. We're going to Vistenia."

CHAPTER 12

Kali

So...formidable I definitely was not.

Like so many of my mother's other arcane rules, the smiling thing didn't do nearly as much good as I'd hoped. Big surprise.

Then again, when has a smile ever trumped a gun?

Never, especially not when that gun is wielded by a guy like Ian. All of which means we're definitely going to Vistenia.

On a more positive note — and by more positive I mean less likely to end in death than getting into a gunfight with an arrogant, draw-first-and-think-later kind of prick — I've never been to Vistenia, and after the complete mess of my first official duty, I'm likely never going to get another chance.

Then again, Ian can demand that we go to Vistenia all he wants — that doesn't mean we'll make it. Especially since no one actually knows how to fly this ship.

Sure, at the moment she's doing it all on her own, but who knows how long that will last? Plus, if we don't work out how to communicate with her soon, this thing is going to take us wherever she wants. Even if where she wants to take us is the surface of Serai.

Honestly, at this point, I wouldn't even be surprised.

Now that we're away from the immediate danger, the effects are hitting me. My feet are battered and bruised, my throat is sore from the smoke, and I'm thirsty. Really, really thirsty. I'm just about to ask someone to find me a glass of water when Gage speaks up.

"Don't pull the gun back out, Ian, but I think we may have a problem with that plan."

"You've got a lot of problems," Ian shoots back without so much as looking his way. "Doesn't mean I want to hear about any of them."

"Yeah, but that doesn't mean we *shouldn't* hear about them," Max tells him with a sigh. "Go ahead, Gage."

"Thanks for the permission." Gage makes a face at him before continuing. "I had a little time to poke around before you guys came on board, and I'm pretty sure there's no food or drink on this ship. I just got the moisture-collection system working, so eventually we'll get purified water from that—with the fun bonus of not drowning in our own sweat—but that won't exactly keep us fed short-term."

"Is that supposed to be a surprise?" Beckett asks. "This thing is so old it was in dry dock. Why would there be food or drink on board?"

The fact that she's right doesn't stop my stomach from rumbling. I just hope none of the others heard it—it's not what I'd call a good look right now.

"Not that big a deal," Ian tells them. "We can go a couple of days without."

Gage gives a long-suffering sigh. "It's more than a couple of days, and you know it."

"Exactly how many more?" I ask, because the difference suddenly seems very important.

"How long will it take to get to Vistenia?" Gage looks to Ian.

"With current planetary alignments, it would take fourteen Askkandian days on a mid-level freighter to travel from Askkandia to Vistenia. I'm not sure how long it will take on this ship." Ian's voice is completely devoid of emotion—a surefire sign that he's starting to come to grips with just how screwed we are.

"So what you're saying is we'll all be dead by the time we hit Vistenia." Max looks frustrated for the first time.

My stomach rumbles again, and judging from the sympathetic

look Rain shoots me, it's definitely loud enough to be noticed. I deliberately don't look at Beckett, but that doesn't mean I can't feel her malicious gaze on me as I watch Ian plop back into the captain's chair.

"Shit," he mutters as he turns to look at Max and silence stretches uncomfortably between the lot of us. Max holds his gaze, then a few seconds later shakes his head with a definite frown. Ian responds with a roll of his eyes...and a reluctant nod that makes me wonder just how these two can communicate so clearly without words. Because they are very definitely communicating, even if they don't want the rest of us to know it.

"Ian and I have enough food and water to last the two of us five days," Max says finally. "But it isn't enough to get us all to Vistenia alive."

He reaches down to the bag at his feet and pulls out some bottles of water. I lick my lips, so thirsty now that I can almost taste it.

"I've got five bottles," Max continues. "And Ian has the same. But I doubt that will last us more than a day."

"So, we need to head to the nearest port." Merrick speaks up for the first time since Ian pulled a gun on him.

"Which is Askkandia," I point out. Looks like I'm going home after all.

"Don't look so relieved, Princess," Ian sneers. "You won't be leaving us just yet."

"You can't actually believe that you'll be able to keep me hidden on my home planet, do you?"

He shrugs. "Askkandia's a big place. I don't see any reason why we have to get you within a kilometer of the palace."

A combination of alarm and outrage jangles through me—along with a third emotion I'm afraid to acknowledge, let alone name. Which is why I focus on the outrage when I open my mouth to argue—no matter what he thinks, he's not actually in charge here. But when he glares at me the same way he glared at Merrick when he pulled the gun, I shut it again. At least for now.

"There is the other little problem," Gage says.

Ian blows out his breath. "And that is?"

"We have no clue how to fly this thing. No way to steer. Right now, we could be heading anywhere, and I, for one, have no idea how to change that."

"So, we could keep going right past Glacea and crash into the asteroid field?" Max says.

"Yup. Or we could be going in the opposite direction, and we'll dive headfirst into the sun." Gage shoves a hand through his hair, making his purple stripe stand straight up. "Hell, at the moment we don't even have any of the instruments or comms online. So never mind where we're going, where the fuck are we right now?"

"I'm not sure what you're all so worried about," Beckett comments with a yawn. "We'll all die of thirst long before we dive into the sun."

And on that cheery note…I smooth my expression. I don't know about anyone else, but I'm really starting to not like Beckett. "This is all probably a moot point," I say after a second. "There are probably people out searching for us right now."

"Fantastic," Beckett mutters.

I ignore her. "In the meantime, why don't we keep busy and search the ship? Maybe we'll find something that can help us navigate."

"Of course we will, because the last people to fly this thing obviously kept their navigation tools in the cargo bay," she answers.

And yep, it's official. I don't like her. I suspect the feeling is mutual.

Ian gets up and stretches, and I find myself staring at him as he rolls his shoulders. Not because he's hot—though he's definitely that, and he knows it—but because he looks…lawless. In the guard uniform, he had a veneer of legitimacy. He looked like he belonged, like he fit in. In what I presume are his own clothes, he definitely doesn't. More, he looks like he doesn't want to.

For someone who's always had to act and speak and be exactly how her mother—and her people—expected her to be, his freedom to just exist as he is is strangely enticing.

He's strangely enticing.

In Senestris, people are what they are born to be. If you're born a farmer, you're a farmer for life. If you're a merchant, you're a merchant for life. And if you're a princess, the same goes.

With almost no exceptions, it's the same for where you're born. If you're born on Kridacus, that's where you live and where you die. The only people outside that system are the Corporation, who live off-planet, mainly on space stations. And outlaws.

It's pretty obvious by now that Ian is not working legitimately for the Corporation. Which leaves outlaw.

He certainly looks the part. Dressed in black leather pants that fit him like a second skin, long boots, a dark red shirt, and a black jacket, he looks lean, mean, and dangerous, between the pistol on his hip and the fuck-everything look in his dark-brown eyes. He's also sexier than he has any right to be, but maybe that's just me. My attraction to bad boys is my deepest, darkest secret, even more so than my strange dreams. Not even the Council's truth seekers have been able to get me to admit it.

Not that I'm attracted to Ian. No way. Bad boys are one thing. Homicidal assholes are another.

But then he turns and our eyes meet as he watches me watching him.

Shit. Could I be more obvious?

He raises a brow as if inviting me to engage.

But princesses don't do that—*I* don't do that. Instead, I look away, despite the tiny part of me that wants to take Ian up on his offer, no matter how dangerous—how foolhardy—it might be.

"Okay, then," he says after a too-long pause. "Gage, you and Max stay here and see if you can figure out how this thing works and how to get us to Askkandia. The rest of us will scour the ship for anything that might be of use, especially anything to drink or eat. We'll meet back here afterward and work out what to do next."

As soon as he mentions food and drink, my stomach grumbles a third time and my mouth feels like a desert has taken up residence in it. But the discomfort doesn't stop me from realizing that, in this one thing, Ian has taken my side—and my suggestion.

It's not a big deal. Any normal person would want to inventory the ship they're flying through space in at an alarming speed, but still.

Considering my trying to take charge didn't go well, it still feels good to know my suggestion had some value to him—to all of these people. My mother's way didn't work. They despise me. So maybe this is a chance to become a leader my way, a different way.

It almost makes me want to do it again, to be valuable to them. Almost.

I drag my gaze from the beautiful little bottles, because staring at them is only making my thirst stronger. But when I glance behind me, it's to find Rain watching me with thoughtful eyes.

She gives me a small smile, then steps toward Max and says, "Could I have a drink, please? I'm feeling a little…faint. And my throat hurts from all the smoke."

"Of course."

"I think we should be rationing it," Ian warns. Just because he's right doesn't mean he isn't also a control freak.

"A little sip now won't hurt anyone. Here." Max hands a bottle to Rain, who takes a small drink before holding it out to me.

I hesitate a second but then can't resist. *Thank you.* I mouth the words because I know what she did. She saw my need and recognized that I was too proud to act on it. She's a good person, even if she is part of the Sisterhood.

I lift the bottle to my lips, and the water tastes like the finest alcohol I've ever drunk. Better, even. I want to guzzle it down, but I force myself to stop at one mouthful. Because Ian is right. We need to be careful with the meager resources we have.

"All right, then. Let's get to work." Ian whirls around and heads out the door, which slides open as he approaches. I hurry to catch up. It probably won't work, but I want to have another go at persuading him that it's a good idea to take me home.

Outside the bridge, the lighting is a dim warm glow, almost nonexistent. To the left is what looks like a double door—I'm presuming the main exit, the one that didn't work. Through a door right ahead is the airlock where we entered, and then beyond that, two corridors head left and right, curving around a closed-in central area. Drawn by something I don't understand, I press my palm to the wall. It's warm, and there's a faint vibration. There's a smooth black door, but it's firmly locked—I can't help but wonder what's inside. But Ian is disappearing down the corridor to the right, and I set off after him.

I can see the outlines of a number of doors on the outer wall, but Ian passes them, and I follow him down what must be the length of the ship, maybe about twenty meters altogether. I catch up as we reach a door that I presume leads to the rear section of the ship. It slides open as Ian comes to a halt in front of it. He disappears inside. So far, he's made no indication that he knows I'm here, though I'm pretty sure he does and he's just ignoring me.

"You might as well come in and stop hovering," he says all of a sudden.

I step into the room. "What is this place?" I ask, determined to gloss over the fact that I obviously followed him here.

"I think it's the engine room, though I've never seen one like it. I'm not even sure what's powering this thing, to be honest. I just know it doesn't feel like the same as the thrusters on the ships I've been on."

"Have you been on a lot of ships?" I ask, suddenly curious about him. But why shouldn't I be? My life is in his hands, which is pretty scary considering his proclivity for weapons.

Ian raises his brow at the question but eventually shrugs. "I've been on a few, Princess. How about you?"

"The flight to the *Caelestis* was my first."

Shock flares in his eyes at that. "I somehow thought you royals would be flitting all over the place, having fun."

"Which just goes to show what you know about the Ruling Families. All space travel is controlled by the Corporation, and we don't have fun. We do our duty."

"Of course you do."

I ignore the sarcasm and look around. We're in the broadest part of the triangle that makes up the ship, and the room is long and narrow but with sections extending into the ship's tail. The walls and ceiling are made up of the same dark matte metal as the corridors, and the floor is remarkably dust-free for such an old ship. There are lots of consoles, but all of them are blank right now, and there aren't even any flashing lights. I trail my finger over the nearest, and a tingle runs through me, almost like static.

"It's completely dead," Ian tells me.

I frown as I look around. "What I don't understand is, what was it even doing on the *Caelestis*? An obsolete ship like this?"

"I have no fucking clue." Ian reaches out and thumps it hard with his fist, just like he did with the control panel upstairs. "Fucking start, you bastard."

"You really think that's going to—" I break off as a strange whirring noise fills my ears, a sort of soft buzzing.

"See." He smirks. "Sometimes violence works."

"And sometimes it doesn't." I gesture to the now silent engine. "I don't see anything actually *working*. But maybe if I take a closer look, I can—"

"Don't touch anything." He cuts me off, but it's with a quick wink. "Let's get out of here. Go look at the rest of the ship."

I follow him, trying to figure out what's going on. He seems a lot friendlier now than he did on the bridge, but that doesn't mean he won't be back to being a jerk three seconds from now. He's such a contradiction that it's hard to catch up.

But as we walk silently through the ship, I remember something I've been meaning to ask him. I quicken my pace, wanting to see his face when I do.

"Why didn't you want me to touch the heptosphere?" I ask. "Back in the lab—why did you stop me?"

Ian looks at me, calculation in his eyes. His expression doesn't change. He pauses, gives a shrug, and for a moment I'm sure he's not going to answer, but then he says, "That thing is dangerous. I haven't seen it in action, but I've heard rumors of people burned to a crisp by it."

So he was trying to keep me from getting hurt? It's not the answer I was expecting, and it makes me feel a little funny inside. Probably just a side effect of the hunger. "But Dr. Veragelen told us it was safe to touch."

He gives me a look—a sort of are-you-really-that-naive look. "Yeah, well, Doc V isn't exactly known for her sweet nature. You know what her nickname was among the crew?"

"No idea."

"Dr. Wicked. Those prisoners being shipped off in the *Reformer*? They were the lucky ones who survived the experiments. There were a lot who didn't." He pauses for a second, like he's trying to decide how much to say. "Though I'm not sure 'lucky' is the right word to describe the survivors. We don't actually know where they were being taken."

"I agree that Dr. Veragelen seemed problematic, but I still don't believe she would do something like that. Use people in that way. My mother would never permit such a thing."

He gives me a look I can't begin to decipher. But I know it's not good, and that infuriates me.

"My mom may be a lot of things," I tell him with a scowl, "but she wouldn't condone human experiments of the kind you're talking about. And she definitely wouldn't condone some prison ship taking people off to be tortured, as you're implying. She's tough, but she's not cruel."

Yet, even as I say the last, I'm not so sure. Years of being a disappointment to her have proven that my mother has the capacity for cruelty, even if I don't know how much she actually indulges that capacity. Or in what way, if it doesn't have to do with me. My stomach churns at the thought.

I expect Ian to argue with me, but all he says is, "Maybe you should have a chat with Beckett about that."

I don't want to. Maybe I'm scared of what I'll hear. I power forward. "I'll do that. But even if Dr. Veragelen was doing experiments on the *Caelestis*, it doesn't mean my mother knew about them or authorized them."

"Yeah, you cling to that, Princess, if it helps you sleep at night."

I start to say something, but he's opening another door and peering inside before I can formulate a thought. "Sleeping cabin," he tells me before moving on to the next door. "Bathroom."

He steps inside and does something I can't see. "No water.

What a surprise."

The rest of the doors lead to more cabins and another bathroom. "Looks like there are three cabins," Ian says. "Some of us will be sharing."

I push past him to get a look at the room myself. It's quite small, and there are three narrow beds, one along each wall. All are bare of bedding, but at least it's warm on the ship and we won't freeze when we try to sleep.

And just that easily, a wave of exhaustion washes over me. It's been a long day. But it's not time to sleep yet. We still have decisions to make.

"So, who will you be sharing with, Princess?" His voice is teasing, but the look on his face is anything but. It makes me uncomfortable, but in a good way, if that makes sense.

"I—I can't share. I need a room to myself."

"I don't think that's going to happen." He studies me like I'm some sort of interesting specimen. "Are you always this selfish? Is that just part of being who you are?"

I start to tell him that it's not selfishness, that I need a room to myself because a princess can't be seen in moments of weakness or vulnerability. I can't change clothes in front of anyone but my companion-in-waiting. Grief threatens to swamp me again at the thought of Lara, but I beat it back down. I certainly can't cry in front of someone.

And I can't sleep in front of anyone, either. What if one of my dreams—or worse, my nightmares—has me crying out?

I can't tell him that, though. Just wanting that privacy makes me sound weak or needy, neither of which is acceptable.

When I remain silent, just staring at him with what I'm sure are confused eyes, Ian shakes his head in annoyance. "Whatever you're used to back home, on this ship you're just another person, like anyone else—except, I suspect, a little more useless."

The words are more painful than they have any right to be. I want to argue, to say I'll do what it takes to pull my weight on this ship, but he barrels on and doesn't give me a chance.

"You can share with Max and Gage. Max would never do anything to hurt you. And Gage—" He shakes his head in obvious annoyance. "Gage may be an untrustworthy fuck, but you won't have to worry about him crawling into bed with you in the middle of the night. You're not his type."

"I never presumed I was. But how do you know that?"

"Gage is into guys, and you are most definitely not a guy." He shrugs. "But, hey. If you want to room with Beckett instead—"

"Max and Gage will be fine," I tell him hastily. Because I definitely don't trust her not to hurt me the second I close my eyes.

"That's what I thought," he smirks. "But I'll warn you—Max snores."

I couldn't care less about Max snoring, but I file away the information that Ian doesn't trust Gage, despite the fact that he obviously hired him for something back on the *Caelestis*. Maybe if he's for hire, I could persuade him to help me get home—in exchange for a hefty reward, of course.

I glance up at Ian, who has a small smile on his face as if he knows exactly what I'm thinking. Abruptly, I realize how close he is—way less than a meter away. His dark eyes are gleaming in the dim half-light, and I'm suddenly a little lightheaded.

"What about you?" I ask, and my voice is slightly hoarse—probably from all the smoke I inhaled earlier. Still, there's something inside me urging me to take a risk for once, to be just a bit reckless. I listen to it, even though I know I shouldn't, and ask, "How do you like your guys?"

"I don't, normally." He takes a step closer, and my breath catches in my dry throat. "Do you really want to know what I like, Princess?"

I swallow and shake my head, adding a little disdainful sniff for good measure. "Why would I?"

He ignores the comment. "Right now, I seem to like stuck-up princesses who think they're better than everyone else. I have an overwhelming urge to find out just what makes you so special."

I consider backing away, but I've done that more than I ought to in the past day. So I stand my ground and square my shoulders even as I try to ignore the warmth that's settling low in my belly. "Then why don't you come over here and find out?"

He moves toward me a little bit at a time. "Here I come, Princess. Better brace yourself." He's leaning in slowly. Steadily. Closer and closer until the very air between us is filled with the warm coffee-and-leather scent of him.

It's a good scent—an arousing one—and I find myself drawing it deep inside my lungs as I wait and wait and wait.

"It doesn't matter one bit to me what you do." I try for a superior air, but did my voice just tremble?

Honestly, in this moment, I don't give a shit, because Ian is right here, big and strong and so, so dangerous, and all I can think about is the way he's looking at me. And the way I am the worst of liars, because nothing has mattered more than what he plans to do next—

There's a sudden thump behind us, like someone's just dropped something or run into a wall.

I jump back, heart in my throat. Then stare up at Ian, wide- and wild-eyed as I realize what just almost happened here. And that someone else on board saw the whole thing.

CHAPTER 13

Beckett, Newly Escaped Prisoner 826

My head hurts. A lot. And not because I just almost walked in on the ship's self-appointed captain and the princess doing… whatever it is they were doing, though what I did see was more than enough to turn my stomach. I thought Ian would have better taste.

No, the ache in my head is different. I've had it for days. Weeks. I've got no idea where it came from and even less of an idea when it started. I just know that one day I woke up and my head felt like it was being split straight down the middle — by a crowbar. Slowly.

No matter how many times I try to think it through, I come up blank. I remember lots of small moments from my childhood. I remember Jarved. I remember my mom. I remember joining the rebels, then getting captured. I remember being taken to the *Caelestis*. I even remember some of the "experiments" they did on me. But then…nothing. One minute I was strapped to a chair while they asked me questions, and the next I was curled in a ball in the corner of my cell, crying.

Except weeks passed in between, weeks I have absolutely no recollection of. It's maddening. And terrifying. I can't help wondering if the same thing happened to Jarved when they took him.

I really hope not. It's one thing for me to be going through the confusion and the pain. It's another thinking about my little brother suffering the same agony.

I just wish I could remember exactly what—

A sharp pain slices through my head, putting my brain in a vise and nearly bringing me to my knees. I cry out, reaching for the wall to steady myself as I try to breathe through the pain.

It's harder than it sounds. When the pain finally passes, it's all I can do to remain upright.

I don't have a choice, though. I don't know any of the people on this ship, and I sure as shit don't trust them. There's no way I'm going to lower my guard with them for a second. Especially not when the crown princess herself is on board.

When the nausea finally passes, I start walking again. This isn't a big ship, but it's not tiny, either. And if my stay on the little space station of horrors taught me anything, it's to know your environment. If I hadn't paid attention—at least while I was lucid—to all the places they took me and all the codes they entered when they thought I wasn't looking, there's no way I would have gotten off the *Reformer*. And no way that I'd be here now.

I'm not sure *here* is a particularly good place to be, but it's better than not being alive at all, which is what likely happened to everyone else on that ship, and right now, that's good enough. I'm going to know every nook and cranny of this ship before the night is over.

As I pass a hallway, I glance down it and see the little one—Rain, I think her name is—sneaking out of one of the rooms that run along the corridor. She's not overtly doing anything to make me think she's sneaking—no tiptoeing, no glancing over her shoulder or up and down the hallway—but I hold to my first impression. There's something about the way she's moving, so carefully and quietly, like she's afraid to attract any attention, that intrigues me. And has me altering my plans and turning down the hallway to follow her.

Now both of us are sneaking down the hallway, which doesn't make me feel ridiculous at all. But I'm too intrigued to turn back. I want to know where she's going and why she feels the need to be stealthy as she does it.

And maybe—probably—this isn't what I should be doing when I still have so much more of the ship to learn. But in times of crisis, you're supposed to know your enemies so you can understand them. Surely I can chalk this little detour up to getting to know how Rain thinks. The fact that she didn't feel like an enemy when I met her on the bridge only makes it more important that I figure her out.

After all, what's more suspicious than someone who doesn't seem suspicious at all?

CHAPTER 14

Rain

From the moment Ian and the princess left, Merrick didn't look happy. I understood why—being trapped on this ship with a guy who just pulled a gun on him, who is also telling us what to do, is probably his worst nightmare. Especially since I'm fairly certain the ship is taking us *away* from Serati, where he really, really wants to go.

I tried to copy his disgruntled expression—I'm definitely supposed to be as upset as he is—but it was hard to do because inside, I was fizzing with excitement.

"Arrogant bastard," he muttered after Ian disappeared out of the room, closely followed by Princess Kalinda.

"I know," I said, trying to inject my voice with an annoyance I definitely didn't feel. "Come on," I added in an effort to divert his attention. "Let's go look around."

I didn't wait for him, instead heading straight out into the corridor. It runs in two directions around a solid section that takes up the middle of the ship. There's a door, but it won't budge. Maybe it's some sort of power supply?

I could hear Ian up ahead to the right, and, since Merrick was right behind me, I took the other corridor. The first door led into some sort of storage bay with lots of containers. I opened up one of them and peered inside.

It was full of what looked like bedding. Not very exciting. Merrick was dug in, though, methodically going through each of the other containers.

I wanted to see the rest of the ship, so I slid toward the door. But as soon as I was within a few feet of it, Merrick said, "Rain," in the warning tone I know all too well.

I sighed and started looking in a second box. *It's not his fault he's so boring*, I reminded myself as I pawed through a bunch of pillows. He just takes his duty to protect me a little too seriously.

As I moved onto a third box, I imagined slipping out of the room and continuing to search the ship on my own. It would probably creak a little bit—not surprising, considering how old it is—but that wouldn't scare me at all. Nothing would.

I'd cross paths with everyone else as I explored. Princess Kali, Beckett—a strange shiver runs through me at the thought of the mysterious woman—Max, Gage. They'd all tell me to go back to the bridge, but I'd be undaunted—

"I'm pretty certain there's no water hidden in those pillowcases, Rain." Merrick's carefully regulated voice chased away my daydream and dropped me right back into the dismal little room packed with boxes full of things we didn't actually need, like a weird amount of blank paper and blue ink. "Why don't you check those boxes on the other side of the door?"

It was the last thing I wanted to do, but it wasn't like I had a choice. I never do.

Merrick and I worked in (semi) companionable silence for a few minutes. But when he walked behind a giant pile of boxes nearly as high as the doorway, I seized the opportunity and slipped out of the room and back into the corridor.

So now here I am, following the hallway to the next door, which takes me into what I assume is the kitchen—or galley, as we're on a ship. This room is wider than the previous one; there's a table in the middle with ten seats around it and some sort of sink-type thing on the side, but when I turn the tap, nothing comes out. I guess Gage was right and there really is no water on the ship. There are also some tall cabinet structures. I open one, and it's cold inside but there's no food. There's nothing in any of the other cabinets, either, and my stomach rumbles. I've never actually been hungry before—it's a new experience, one I try to accept for what it is. A chance provided to me by the universe and the Light to feel more connected with so many of the less-privileged citizens of Senestris.

I know it's not the same—I'll be hungry for a few days while many of them have been hungry for their entire lives—but it's a start. And something I won't forget, even when I'm safely back at the monastery.

Footsteps sound behind me. Merrick, of course. He probably panicked when he realized I was gone and came looking for me. "There's nothing to eat here," I say without turning around. "Looks like no supper for us tonight."

"Fuck. I'm starving."

I whirl around at the voice, because it definitely doesn't belong to Merrick. It turns out it's the woman. Beckett.

I smile.

She doesn't smile back.

But that doesn't deter me. Honestly, I'm not sure anything could. I've never met anyone like Beckett before, and she fascinates me.

There's an edge of danger to her, but Ian has it as well, and so does Merrick, when he lets it show. But I'm not fascinated by them. Maybe it's because I've never seen it in a woman before—the sisters at the monastery aren't exactly the dangerous sort—but, honestly, I think it's more than that.

I just don't know what.

She's a good fifteen to twenty centimeters taller than I am. Her curly black hair is cut off at her chin, like someone hacked away at it with a pair of kitchen shears, and her full mouth is drawn tight like she's in pain.

Instinctively, I move closer—if there's anything I can do to ease her pain, I would like to—and her eyes follow my every move. They're huge and the same yellow as the early-morning sun over Serati, with the longest lashes I've ever seen. She's probably from

Permuna—lashes like that are apparently good for keeping sand out of your eyes. But they're also really pretty, especially when they frame those striking eyes of hers.

As I get closer, I notice that she's got a little bit of blood crusted under her nose—it stands out in stark definition against her olive skin—and there's a lot more on the front of her gray jumpsuit.

"You're hurt," I tell her, waving a hand toward her face.

She frowns, then reaches up and wipes a finger under her nose before looking at it. "It's nothing."

"Was it in the explosion?"

Her face goes blank for a moment, like she's having trouble remembering. Then she blinks and shakes her head. "Nah."

As she does, I can't help but notice the jagged scar on her neck. It's healed, but badly, and it makes me sad when I think about what might have caused it.

Then again, a lot of things make me sad when I look at her.

I want to ask what caused the blood, but then she winces, pain flashing in her topaz-colored eyes. Then she raises her hand and rubs the back of her neck, just like she did earlier.

"Are you okay?" I ask.

"Shit, no," she answers with a sardonic little laugh.

"Let me have a look." Without waiting for a reply, I move around behind her. She goes very still but doesn't say anything as I hop up on a counter and run my hands through her tangled curls.

Some of the stiffness goes out of her, and her shoulders sag. I raise her hair and stare at the ugly scar that runs the length of the back of her skull and down her neck to her spine.

It's an angry red line—not new, but, like the one under her ear, not something she got today. "There's a scar here," I tell her.

"Yeah."

I wait for her to say something else, but when she doesn't, I prompt, "What happened?"

"They did…something. I just don't know what."

An unfamiliar feeling starts burning low in my belly, but I ignore it as I try to piece together what she's saying—and what she's not.

"Who did something?"

"On that station."

"The *Caelestis*?" I ask, trying to keep the shock from my voice.

She frowns. "I suppose. If that's where we've just come from."

"You don't know?"

"No. I was…" She shakes her head like she's trying to clear it. "I think I was drugged when they took me on board. I don't remember much from my time there—just a cell and the lab where they…" She waves a hand at the back of her neck and the scar.

"Where they did this to you." I remember Ian saying something about experiments. I'd thought he was exaggerating or making stuff up to annoy the princess, but it sounds like he was telling the truth.

I hop down to stand in front of her again. Just the idea that someone could do such a thing is a revelation to me.

"That's evil."

She lets out a short laugh. "That's the Corporation, baby."

"They're doing experiments on innocent people?" The feeling in my stomach is getting hotter, harder to ignore.

She looks away for a second. "Not innocent."

"It doesn't matter what you did! They had no right to use you like this! No right to do any of this to you!"

Her brows draw together, and she studies me as though she can't figure me out any more than I can figure her out. I start to think she's going to say something more—something important. But then she gives a shrug and waves her hand up and down in front of me. "That's a fancy robe."

Hardly fancy. "Not really. I always dress like this."

Her brows hit her hairline. "Hard luck. I thought I had it bad."

She gestures toward her own gray prisoner jumpsuit. It's ripped, one of the missing sleeves revealing a slender arm, the skin smooth and tattooed, and suddenly I itch to touch it.

"So, what did you do to deserve that?" she asks.

"Nothing. It's an honor to wear the robes. I'm the High Priestess of the Sisterhood of the Light."

She stares at me for several seconds, then throws her head back and laughs.

Huh. Not the response I usually get to that statement. I purse my lips and try not to feel offended.

"You're not serious?" she says when I don't say anything.

I wait another beat. "Well, I'm certainly not kidding."

"I've never met a high priestess before."

It's not like there are a bunch of us to go around. I don't say that, though. It sounds elitist, even in my head, though I don't mean it that way. "Well, I've never met a…" I trail off as I realize I have no clue what she is or what I should call her. I don't want to offend her. And I definitely don't want her to leave.

"A criminal?" she suggests.

I blink a couple of times. "Is that what you are?" I whisper.

She gives a shrug, then rubs her forehead. "Probably. It's all a little…blurry, but I'm pretty sure I was with the Rebellion."

"Oh. Wow. Even in the monastery, I've heard of the rebels." They use terror techniques to try to bring down the legal government of Senestris. Violent. Dangerous. Despicable. Certainly not working in the interest of the holy Light.

I never thought I'd ever meet one—or that I would like her when I did. But Beckett draws me in. More than she should, considering who she used to be. Maybe even who she still is.

"Aren't you scared, little priestess?" Her tone is mocking now. "Don't you want to run away?"

Not even a little bit. I don't say that, though; I just shake my head.

Which has her eyes narrowing. She takes a step closer, and I don't move a muscle. I'm not sure I could even if I wanted to. But I don't. I *really* don't, especially when she reaches out and takes hold of the end of my long braid. Her calloused fingers stroke back and forth over the wispy ends of my hair for a moment before she tugs me closer.

"Pretty," she murmurs.

I'm not sure if she's talking about my hair or me. I don't suppose it really matters, considering a shiver runs through me either way. I feel quite strange, sort of hot and cold and really aware of my own skin all of a sudden.

"You interest me," she murmurs, head cocked to one side as she studies me. "Why do you interest me so much, little priestess?"

"I—" My voice breaks, and I have to clear my throat, try again. Except my mouth is suddenly as dry as any desert in the galaxy, and something tells me it doesn't have anything to do with the strict water rationing we're currently experiencing. "You interest me, too."

She laughs a little at that. "Now you're just being nice."

I want to argue that I'm *not* nice. How can I be, when I'm always having the most wicked thoughts?

"Tell me something," she murmurs, and her fingers go from stroking my hair to stroking my cheek.

A strange, devastating heat flares inside me. "What do you want to know?" I whisper, afraid to speak too loud in case she moves her hand.

But she doesn't stop. In fact, her fingers keep moving, sliding along the sensitive skin of my jaw until they're dancing along the nape of my neck. "Have you ever been kissed?"

I gasp as shock runs through me, along with another delicious flare of heat.

She laughs in response, then licks her lips. And just like that, my gaze is glued to her mouth. I couldn't look away if the fate of Senestris rested on it.

I swallow hard but don't answer her. I can't.

Which I'm fairly certain is an answer in and of itself, even before she murmurs, "I'll take that as a no."

I shake my head vehemently.

"Well, I guess that leaves me with just one more question."

I wait for her to ask it, and when she doesn't, a low, keening sound works its way up my throat. It echoes in the silent room, and I'd be embarrassed if I wasn't so…*hot*.

She laughs again, a low, wicked sound that makes my stomach flip even as it slides along my every nerve ending. But she still doesn't speak.

"What—" My voice cracks again. "What do you want to ask me?" I finally manage to get out.

"That's easy." She smiles even as she leans closer to me. "Do you want to be?"

Oh my goodness.

It's not easy. It's not easy at all. In fact, the answer to that question is the very opposite of easy.

I know what it should be. What it has to be. I really, really do. But for some reason I can't make my mouth form the word. Instead, all I can do is *nod*.

Beckett seems as surprised by my answer as I am. But she doesn't let her surprise stop her. Instead, her direct yellow gaze holds mine as she moves closer, her hand cupping around my neck. And then slowly — so slowly that it barely appears she's moving at all — she leans forward and brushes her lips against my own.

I can't breathe. I can't move. I'm burning up.

"More?" she whispers against my lips.

My head nods without any command from my brain. And she presses her lips to mine just as the lights flash bright, an alarm rings out, and someone calls my name.

It looks like Merrick has found me.

CHAPTER 15

Ian

What the fuck was I thinking? Kissing Kali? What a disaster that would have been.

I didn't see who was watching us, but the alarm that started ringing not long after was a much-needed wake-up call. For me, not her, considering I've got absolutely no idea why she'd suddenly want to kiss me anyway. I know she thinks I'm hot, but I have a hard time believing this has anything to do with that. More than likely she's just trying to get on my good side so I'll take her back to Mommy like she wants. Too bad that's not happening—no matter what she says, the Empress would have her entire fleet on our asses within minutes of getting her baby back.

I don't plan on keeping her forever—who the fuck wants that kind of complication?—but until Max and I find Milla and the three of us can disappear on one of the outer planets and stay completely out of the Empress's orbit, the princess stays where I can keep an eye on her.

An eye, not a mouth, I tell myself as I race back to the bridge. No matter how sexy—how tempting—that plum-colored mouth of hers might be.

Max hasn't shut up about my sudden determination to keep her with us since I told her she wasn't going anywhere near the palace *or* her mother. He thinks it's a mistake, but what the fuck else is new? We've been doing things differently our entire lives. Yeah, we're both determined to do whatever it takes to get to Milla—it's just that our whatevers almost always vary.

The alarm is still ringing—in fact, it seems to be getting louder—and I expect us to crash at any moment. It's been that sort of day.

That sort of year, actually.

But as I finally make it to the bridge, I skid to a halt. Because Gage and Max are just sitting there, talking loudly. Completely ignoring the blaring alarm. "What the fuck is going on?" I yell to be heard over the noise.

Gage shrugs. "Everything came to life about five minutes ago. I pressed that big red button over there—" He waves a hand at the big red button in question.

"Why?" I demand. Did the asshole think we didn't have enough problems? He needed to create more?

"Because it's big and red and I wanted to see what it would do." He says it like it's the most obvious thing in the world.

And, okay. Sure. What else are big red buttons for if not for morons to press? But I still need to know: "What did it do?"

"Nothing. But the alarm started about thirty seconds later."

"Well, did you push it again?"

"Didn't seem like the best idea, considering who knows what it did the first time."

I look at Max. "*Is this guy for real?*"

He gives me an amused look. "*Apparently.*"

"*Next time, remind me to spring for the top-of-the-line rogue technician, because this bargain-basement version doesn't seem worth the planetas we paid for him.*"

Then I walk over and push the big red button for what is apparently the second time. Because it's big and red and how much worse can we be fucked than we are already?

"Hey, don't—" Gage starts but breaks off when the alarm stops. "Oh. Okay, then." He grins like he's the cleverest guy ever created.

"I'm guessing the big red button is a manually activated alarm."

"*How can someone that smart with technology also be this ridiculous about everything else?*" I mentally roll my eyes.

"*Is there a word for below bargain basement?*" Max asks dryly.

"*If there isn't, there should be.*" I turn to Gage. "Don't press any buttons unless you know what they do."

"Well, that's no fun."

"Because everything else about this day has been a real party," I growl.

"Emergency over?" a voice asks from the doorway. I turn to see Beckett standing in the doorway to the bridge. Seconds later, the high priestess and Merrick appear behind her. The little blonde looks flustered, her cheeks pink. It's a good look for her.

The scowl on her big friend's face, not so much. Which makes me think it wasn't him who put the color in her cheeks.

There's still no sign of the princess—not that it matters to me. No skin off my ass what she's doing, as long as it isn't sabotaging this ship. Still, it pisses me off that I even noticed.

"There was no emergency," I answer. "Just a jerk pressing buttons."

"You shouldn't talk about yourself like that," Gage tells me. "Hasn't anyone ever told you to love yourself?"

And people wonder why I claimed control of this little shit show. The only person on this ship I trust besides myself is Max. And he sure as fuck doesn't want to be in charge.

I flip Gage off as I settle into the captain's chair I claimed earlier.

Beckett strolls across the floor, taking in the array of flashing lights and lit screens on the forward console. "So, she's finally up and running?"

"For all the good it does us," I answer with a shrug. "We still have no idea how to fly her."

She looks at Max. "Move."

He lifts his brows as he stares back at her. But he moves, because he's Max and he tends not to make a fuss. At least not until he decides it's time to make a fuss.

He's in the seat right at the nose of the ship, and Beckett slides into it like she owns the thing.

"What are you doing?" I ask, 'cause I sure as shit don't trust her to have her own best interests at heart, let alone anyone else's.

"Flying." She glances over her shoulder. "Don't get your feelings hurt, big boy. You can still keep the fancy chair and call yourself captain."

I think about arguing with her on general principle—I *am* the captain—but if Beckett wants to be in charge of figuring out the flying thing, who am I to get in her way? Sure, I'm an okay pilot, but Milla was the flier of our group. She was the one who kept our ship in the air and the one who solved the problems when it broke down—which was often.

No telling what she's going to say when we finally get her back and she realizes we sold her baby to compile enough money for all the bribes we've had to pay out to get us this far. But I'd give up a hell of a lot more than a spaceship if it means getting Milla back.

I'd give up everything, and that, I know, she'll understand.

But all I say to Beckett is, "I plan to."

"Hey, looks like he *can* be reasonable." She gives me a mock-impressed look. "Wonders will never cease."

She's in a better mood than I've ever seen her—which makes me wonder if *she's* the one who ruffled little Miss High Priestess's feathers. If so, I hope it's not a one-off, because this Beckett is a lot easier to deal with. Even if she is a shit talker.

"I'd wait until you prove that you're not all talk before you start messing with the rest of us," Max tells her.

"Watch and learn." She turns to the dash and starts running her hand over the various screens, buttons, and otherwise indecipherable shit.

Nothing happens.

"It's not—"

"Hush," she snaps at me.

A second later, the screen directly in front of her lights up. There's a little red dot in the middle but nothing else. "That's us," she says.

"Yeah, but that doesn't tell us anything. Where the hell are we?" I ask. I stand to get a better look.

"Wait." She moves her hand again, and the image zooms out. A blue-green planet with a single moon appears on the edge of the screen. Askkandia. And it looks like we're heading away from it.

"What's going on?" a very recognizable voice says from behind me. Looks like the princess has decided to make an appearance at last.

I glance over my shoulder and give her a smirk.

She scowls.

"Beckett is learning to fly the ship," Rain tells her.

"Impressive," the princess answers, I assume just to piss me off. But I'm too glad that we finally know where we are to take offense.

But I do point out that, "We're going in the wrong direction."

Beckett zooms out some more, and a second planet appears, a lot farther away than Askkandia. Permuna, I think, and we're heading straight for it. But unless my knowledge of the planets' current orbital positions is off—which it's not—it's almost as far away as Vistenia.

"You need to turn around," I tell her.

She actually snarls at me in response. "Shut up and let me fucking concentrate for one second, will you?"

And yup, looks like the old Beckett is back and worse than ever.

Beckett leans back and studies the console in front of her. "Accelerator," she says, pointing to a part of the console that looks exactly the same as all the rest to me.

I don't say anything, though I can feel Kali over my shoulder, watching Beckett's lesson. I just wait to see what goes down. Beckett touches a finger to it, but nothing happens.

"I don't think—" Gage starts, then breaks off when she presses her palm down and we shoot forward so fast that Kali tumbles against me.

I grab the back of Beckett's chair, then wrap my arm around Kali's waist to stop us both from falling. I have a second to register that she feels good against me—really good—as I wait for Beckett to slow us down.

It doesn't happen. Instead, we keep going faster and faster, until I can feel my vision blurring. Around us, the others are calling out. Groaning.

"*Fucking stop her!*" Max says in my head.

But I'm already trying. It's just taking a while—and all the effort I've got—to force my hand forward, grab her arm, and pull it from the console.

We slow immediately—but not before Rain pukes at the back of the bridge.

"What the hell were you doing?" I demand, furious at Beckett and myself as I look around fruitlessly for some kind of towel. This is what a little bit of trust gets you—an acceleration headache and vomit on your bridge.

I definitely should have known better.

Beckett just grins at me, her eyes wild and laser bright. "Just seeing how fast she can go."

"The answer's pretty fucking fast," I growl.

"I think you mean *really* fucking fast," she corrects. "Why? Were you scared, *Captain*?"

The emphasis she puts on Captain turns it into an insult, but I don't give a shit.

"We were all fucking scared. The question is—why weren't you?" I ask. But she's still grinning, and the weird light still shines in her eyes. "You're really messed up, you know that? You could have killed us."

"*Well, she did just spend who knows how long as the subject of one of Dr. Wicked's experiments*," Max reminds me.

Which is his not-so-subtle way of getting me to lay off her—not to mention reminding me that we don't have a fucking clue what shape Milla will be in when we finally get her back.

When someone starts shoving against my chest, I realize I still have my arm around Kali—and she's not entirely happy about it.

"Let go of me," she snaps.

"Hey, I was helping you, *Princess*," I snap back. "And what is it with you and the touching thing, anyway?"

"It's punishable by death," Rain says as she picks herself up off the floor and brushes her hand down her now dirty white robe.

"Death? For touching you?" I shoot Kali an incredulous look even before she nods. "That's seriously fucked."

"It's the law," she says. "I didn't make it, and it goes back a long, long time. But it's never actually been enforced."

"You sure about that, Princess?" Beckett says without taking her eyes from the viewing screens in front of her.

"Yes," Kali snaps back, though she suddenly looks a little uncertain. I think this trip may be an eye-opener for the princess, and she's not liking what she sees.

"I'm sorry I threw up," Rain says quietly.

If it was Kali apologizing, I'd make some kind of sarcastic comment—but this is Rain, so I shrug it off. Even I'm not that big a shithead.

"It's just a little water," I tell her, handing over a towel from my bag. Which reminds me that a sip of water is all she—or any of us— has had for more hours than I want to think about.

"Did anyone find any food or drink on their search?"

The others shake their heads—except Kali, who moves to the chair farthest away from Beckett and sits down in it, hugging her knees to her chest.

Fuck. We probably have enough for a couple of days *if* we're careful. Not nearly enough to get us to Vistenia, just like Gage said earlier.

"Looks like we're going to make a detour to Askkandia. If Beckett can get us there, that is."

"I'll get us there," she says grimly. She leans toward the accelerator, but I put a hand in front of it before she can touch it.

"Why don't you concentrate on figuring out how to turn us around for now?" I suggest. "At a normal speed?"

"You're as boring as you look," she tells me. But she keeps the ship at a normal speed.

I reach for my bag again and rummage inside. The rations Max and I packed consist of protein bars filched from the *Caelestis*'s commissary. I grab a handful and drop one in front of Beckett before tossing another to the princess.

She catches it, then looks at it as if she doesn't quite know what it is—or what to do with it. By the time I hand the rest around, Beckett has already finished hers, so I give her mine. I'm thinking she likely hasn't been eating too well.

She glances up, surprised. But I don't want to get into a thing with her, so I just lean against the front console and look out at the others.

Kali is staring at her bare feet, her bar in her hands. Rain munches on her rations as she watches Beckett while Merrick watches her. Max is dozing in one of the chairs, his legs kicked out in front of him while Gage watches him.

As crews go, we're a goddamn disaster. A princess, a priestess, a bodyguard, a prisoner, a con artist, a goofball, and me, self-appointed asshole in charge of them all.

It's a recipe for catastrophe, but we're just going to have to figure out how to make it work. Because I'm not walking away from this ship until we've rescued my best friend.

"I think I figured it out, Ian," Beckett says to me from the pilot's chair. "Get ready to turn."

Instinct has me grabbing hold of the nearest chair, and it's a fucking good thing because the next minute, we're spinning madly around.

We're in a full-out flat spin, one I don't know if we'll be able to recover from. I try to turn around, try to see if the princess is okay, but we're spinning, spinning, spinning and the force is too great for me to even turn my head.

The screaming gets louder, but over it, I hear another sound. It's Beckett—and she's fucking laughing.

That's when I know for sure that we're doomed.

CHAPTER 16

Kali

It's been two days since we ended up on this ship, and honestly, it feels like a lifetime.

And definitely not a good lifetime.

I thought life at the palace could be a minefield with all the intrigue and backbiting, but living in close quarters with six of the strangest—and, in some cases, the most dangerous—people I've ever met is something else entirely.

It doesn't help that I feel like a total and complete mess. Not just in looks, but in knowing how to do…anything. The only things I've ever really been trained in are diplomacy and leadership, and this group has no interest in either one of those.

Then again, it's nearly impossible for me to take *myself* seriously, looking like this. Is it any wonder that they don't take me seriously, either?

My slogg dress is unraveling. It's at mid-thigh now, and it won't be long before it's completely indecent. I'm still barefoot, and my hair more closely resembles a drokaray's nest than the coronet braid it was originally styled in. All in all, I'm a disaster.

You would think that would help me fit in with this group—every one of them is a calamity—but somehow it just sets me further apart.

Not that I care. A few more days and I'll never have to see any of them again. Thank fuck.

My lower lip wobbles, and I bite it, hard, to stop the trembling. Then immediately regret it because the taste of blood just reminds me that I've got nothing to wash it away with.

We finished the last of the water an hour ago, and, knowing it's gone, I'm thirstier than ever. I feel completely pathetic next to everyone else. They seem just fine, and all I can think about is how hungry and sad I am. Instead of Gage and Max, I decided to share a room with Rain last night, while Merrick stood guard over us both. He clearly cares for her a lot, and it reminded me of how Arik used to hover over me. Which made me think of Lara and the fact that there's a good chance she's dead. She's the only friend I've ever had, and I left her there on the *Caelestis* to die.

Yeah, the bulkhead slammed down between us, but I should have tried another way. There had to be another way—

"Are you okay, Princess?"

I glance up to see Max smiling down at me. He's so much kinder than Ian that, even after two days of prolonged exposure to both of them, I still can't figure out why they're friends.

I wince at his use of my title—I've never been particularly fond of it, but the way Ian uses it so sardonically has made me despise it. "Never better," I tell him.

He grins. "I thought princesses weren't supposed to lie."

Hah. Just proves he really doesn't know anything about royalty, considering lying is the first thing we *are* taught to do. Back at the palace, it's practically survival 101.

"They teach us a lot of things." I give him a grin I'm far from feeling. "None of which are particularly useful at the moment."

He lifts his brows in a *good point* kind of way. "To be fair, I'm not sure anything is useful inside this flying ablinit can."

"Hey, now. No need to diss the ride," Beckett tells him as she leans back in the pilot's seat I don't think she's left in two days. "She's gotten us this far."

"I'm not sure that's exactly a recommendation," Gage comments, looking up from where he's sketching on one of the old notepads Merrick found in the storage area.

"Sure it is. Askkandia's coming up." Beckett shoots me a look that can only be described as condescending. "Wave to Mummy, Princess."

I ignore her, getting up and wandering across the bridge to the front.

Through the right viewing screen, I can see my home planet, still too distant to make out any details but getting closer all the time. From up here, it's hard to imagine my mother down there in the palace, going about the day-to-day responsibilities of running an empire. Is she worried about me? Or has she already decided that I'm dead? Maybe she's too busy doing damage control on the destruction of the *Caelestis* to spend much time thinking about me at all.

It sounds self-pitying to say that, but it's not. It comes with the job description. Senestris is in serious trouble, and the *Caelestis* was our best hope of surviving that trouble. Now that it's gone, I'm sure she and the Council are scrambling as fast as they can to come up with a new plan. There's no time for her to grieve for me right now.

"Do you think she misses you?" Beckett asks me. "Maybe we can stop by and she can kiss your boo-boos."

"Knock it off," Ian tells her as he walks in, rubbing a hand through his short hair so it stands on end.

It makes me see red. "I don't need you to fight my battles for me."

"Good, because I wasn't planning on it." He doesn't look at me, but that's nothing new. He's been all but ignoring me since I warned him not to touch me—and Rain followed up with information that it was punishable by death.

I'm sure he thinks it's too high a risk. Not that I care. Things are a lot more peaceful without him constantly telling me what to do.

But I can't help surreptitiously watching him as he strolls across the floor. He moves like a predator, all sleek lines and leashed brutal power. He glances toward me as he passes, and I look away—two can play at the ignoring game. But that doesn't stop a shiver from running through me.

He comes to a halt behind Beckett and bends down to study the screen in front of her. With their heads close together, it's hard to miss the similarities between them—the edge of violence that permeates the air around them, as though the veneer of civilization is just a thin coating over their more primitive selves.

Across the room, I notice Rain is watching them, too, and I can't quite decipher her expression. Longing, maybe? Or something a little darker. Needier. Does the priestess have a hankering for bad boys?

I ignore the not-so-pleasant feeling that thought causes, choosing to focus on Ian instead as he turns to face the room.

"Okay, people, here's what's going to happen. We're heading down to the planet and making landfall in Rangar."

It takes all my royal training to hide my shock. "Rangar?" I ask. "You're kidding."

"Now, why would I want to do that?" he answers with a smirk.

"Rangar is…dangerous." Not that I've ever been, but if there's a dead-end place on Askkandia, it's the port city of Rangar. My mother keeps threatening to raze it to the ground, then deciding that at least she currently knows where to find the bad elements.

"And how would you know that, Princess? You been slumming it?"

"No, but I've heard."

"Yeah, Rangar is dangerous, but that's the point. It's likely the only place on Askkandia where we can get what we need with no questions asked."

"Yeah, but—" I break off when I realize Beckett is watching me with disgust.

"Looks like the princess is scared of all the little people," she taunts.

"It's not that I'm scared," I tell her. See, I know how to lie. "I know my mother can be ruthless, but she has to be. It's not easy running Senestris. But she also loves me. And she *will* be grateful if you take me back. *Very* grateful."

"How grateful?" Gage asks, just as Ian says, "No."

No discussion. No explanation. Just *no*. The jerk.

"Doesn't anyone else get a say in this?" I try to sound reasonable despite my annoyance. "Maybe we should go for a vote?"

"I vote you shut up," Beckett snarls.

Big shock there. "I'm just saying, there are other ways besides negotiating with thieves and renegades."

"And here I thought you said you wanted us to go to the palace," Beckett shoots back.

"Enough—"

Ian talks right over me. "Our main requirements are food and water. Now, it's not essential, but it would make things easier if we could pay for what we need. So, does anyone have any money on them? Any way to access planeta credits?"

"You were the ones about to get on a prison ship bound for who knows where," Merrick comments. "You didn't think to bring any planetas with you?"

"We gave pretty much everything we had to Gage to get this far." Max looks at him. "Where's all the money we gave you?"

Gage gives a casual shrug. "Back in my cabin on the *Caelestis*."

"You came on board with nothing?" Ian doesn't sound convinced. But then, he has a suspicious nature.

Gage rolls his eyes. "In case you've forgotten, we left in kind of a hurry."

Ian studies him with narrowed eyes for several seconds, then shrugs and turns to look at the rest of us. But no one speaks up.

"What about you Sisterhood people?" he asks. "Or do they send you out penniless into the world?"

"We had money," Merrick answers. "But it was on the shuttle."

This isn't looking good. Ian must be thinking the same thing, because he looks straight at me. You know he's scraping the bottom of the barrel if he's actually looking to me for help. For a second, I actually wish I could—even though I have no desire to go to Rangar. It would be nice not to feel useless. But I've never actually carried money. Fuck, I've never even been inside a *store*.

He meanders over and stands looking down at me. I resist the urge to tug at the hem of my dress.

"I don't have any money," I say. "I mean, where would I put it in this dress?"

His gaze wanders over me, and a small smile tugs at his full lips. Which irritates the shit out of me. Why is it that when he smiles at me it's because he needs something? "Tell me, Princess, are those real?" He waves a hand at the row of jeweled buttons that runs down my dress.

Of course they're real. A princess of Senestris does not go out in public wearing fake jewels.

"They're real," Beckett asserts. "Only the best for the princess."

Ian reaches out and plucks one of the buttons from the dress, and I slap at his hand. "Hey. Stop that."

He holds up the rare black malinniten, and it glints in the light. "Very pretty," he comments. "Looks like we're sorted."

Except I'm already nearly naked and those buttons are all that's holding me together. "It may have escaped your notice," I snap, "but I didn't exactly pack an extra dress, so you can't have this one."

His eyes gleam with amusement and something else. Something that has my skin prickling and my stomach hollowing out as his gaze wanders down the tight dress to my bare legs. "Give me the dress, Princess, and I'll buy you a new one."

"With my money, I suppose?"

He shrugs. Merrick gets to his feet. "You can borrow my robe," he says.

"So you can be naked instead?" I ask. "You don't have to do that."

The corners of his lips curl up just the tiniest bit in the closest thing to a smile I've seen from him. "I won't be naked."

He drags the robe over his head. Beneath it, he's wearing black body armor—probably part of the reason he looked so big.

My father used to wear something similar. He told me it was because of the lower gravity of Serati, which means their bones aren't as dense and can break much more easily. The armor is strengthened along the arms and legs to provide extra protection. Apparently, everyone from Serati wears something similar when they're off-planet.

Once out of the robe, Merrick looks nothing like a priest. Instead, he looks like a warrior. His body is all hard muscle, and I wonder if

I've misjudged who the biggest threat on this ship is.

"Stop staring, Princess, you'll embarrass the man."

I ignore Ian because I'm not the only one staring. Rain is looking at him as well—I assume because she's never seen Merrick without his robe, either.

He tosses it to me, and I catch it. It's made of some sort of rough natural fiber, no doubt bleached, the only adornment the emblem of the Dying Sun on the upper left of the chest. It's grimy and dirty and smells of smoke, but I'll take it.

"Ten minutes to landfall," Beckett says. Gage managed to spoof legitimate landing credentials to pass through the Askkandian atmosphere, though in fairness, I don't know how difficult that is—especially going into Rangar, which, if you believe my mother, lets any space trash in with a hearty welcome. The countdown to landfall is now visible on Beckett's dash as well as the main console.

"Come on, Princess. Let's have the dress. We don't want to stick around this place longer than we have to."

I heave a huge sigh and give in to the inevitable, but that doesn't mean I'm changing in front of all of them. Clutching the robe, I head out but hesitate at the door as something occurs to me. I turn back to Ian, who raises a brow.

"Give me your knife," I tell him.

Now both brows shoot up. "Excuse me?"

"Your knife. Don't worry, I won't stab you with it—at least not today. But there's no way I'm getting out of this dress without that knife."

He frowns. "How did you get into it?"

"Lara—my companion-in-waiting—dressed me."

Beckett snorts. "'Cause she can't dress herself."

"I probably could if I was wearing a prison jumpsuit," I shoot back, tired of being her verbal punching bag. "The Imperial Regalia isn't quite so easy."

Ian slides the wicked-looking blade from the sheath at the small of his back and hands it to me. I take it without another word and walk off the bridge, down the corridor toward the room I'm sharing with Rain. As I pass the closed-off area in the center of the ship that we haven't been able to access, I pause and rest my palm against the warm metal. For some reason, it gives me comfort, and doing so has become a habit every time I pass.

Once in the room, I pull the material of the dress away from my skin and slice the knife through the front. I almost sigh with relief as the dress parts and I can breathe freely for the first time in days. I make a few more strategic cuts and then manage to wriggle out of what's left of my slogg dress.

I want to take a few seconds to relish being free, but we'll be landing any minute. So I drag the robe over my head and try really hard not to breathe in the stench of smoke and the underlying scent of man. I've never worn somebody else's clothes before. First time for everything, I guess.

I head back to the bridge and toss the dress to Ian. There's amusement but also something else in his eyes—like he knows that there's no room for underwear beneath the Imperial Regalia and I'm naked under this loose robe. He doesn't say anything, though. Just bites on his lower lip as he shakes his head and sinks into the captain's chair. Then he pulls another knife from who knows where and starts slicing off the buttons and other jewels.

"Do you know what these are worth?" he asks.

I shake my head. I don't have a clue.

The thought causes something to warm my skin—shame, I think. Have I really lived in such a rarified world?

I feel like I'm on the edge of a precipice. Like I'm teetering on the brink of everything I've always believed is true and I'm about to fall into the unknown. It's terrifying, but part of me wants to fall anyway.

"Let me see," Beckett tells him.

Ian crosses the bridge and holds out his hand, and she paws through the stones. "If legit, ten thousand planetas at least." Ian whistles. I guess that's a lot. But Beckett continues, "Black market, ten percent of that."

"That will still be enough to get us provisions," Gage says.

"We should probably get something for Beckett to wear, just in case she has to go out in public," I suggest. "Having *Prisoner 826* stamped on your back is probably a big sign saying—" I break off as I realize I'm being undiplomatic—the first cardinal sin for royalty.

But Beckett just grins. "Aw. Didn't know you cared, Princess."

I don't. Or maybe I do. I don't know anymore.

Rain stands up and looks at me. "Can you get me something to wear as well?"

Beside her, Merrick stiffens. But he doesn't say anything, and neither do I. I don't know why she's asking me—I'm not going on this little shopping trip. I doubt they'll even let me off the ship.

At that moment, something beeps, and Beckett turns back.

"Through the atmosphere and approaching Rangar," she says. "External comms are still down, but they got us with a local check. Spoofed credentials worked. And with an assigned spot for landing, no logs required, no questions asked. Hey, I like this place already."

My heart rate kicks up. We're about to land on Askkandia. I just need to find a way to contact the palace without involving the others. Maybe ask Gage to teach me a few techy things, and I can try to get the comms going? Then the others can just go about their business and I can go home.

Which is what I want.

Isn't it?

We've slowed down, and the ship is sort of vibrating, like it's not happy.

"You do know how to land this thing, don't you?" Ian asks.

Beckett twirls in the pilot's seat. "Not a clue."

Fan-fucking-tastic.

The planet is approaching really fast now, and we don't seem to be slowing down. I suspect Beckett has a death wish. Or maybe not an actual death wish but definitely an I-don't-care wish. So, I slide into the nearest chair and strap in. It's hard to believe that only two days ago I was nearly puking as we approached the *Caelestis*. Look at me now.

I grin to myself, then glance up to find Ian watching me. He looks away.

At the last moment, the ship almost screeches to a halt. I brace myself and hold on tight, somehow managing to keep my eyes open. Seconds later, the ship lowers gently to the landing slot.

"Good job," Ian tells her as he peels himself from the captain's chair and starts brushing himself off.

"Not sure what you consider a bad job," Gage mutters as he, too, climbs to his feet.

"Dying," Max answers from his spot on the ground. Strapping into a seat was definitely the right call. Maybe I do have some spaceflight instincts in me.

"It wasn't me," Beckett tells him. "The ship gets all the credit."

"You mean she switched herself to autopilot and landed on her own?" I ask. "Can ships do that?"

"Obviously, or we wouldn't be having this conversation," she sneers back.

I don't even bother coming up with a retort. Not when we've finally landed on Askkandia.

I don't know how it is that I can be back on my home planet and still be as far from home as ever. It feels like the worst kind of failure. But also strangely freeing. I glance down at my grimy, too-long white robe, bare toes peeking out, and a giggle escapes me. Definitely not how I planned on returning from my first official off-planet royal duty.

Ian casts me a weird look, as though he's worried something's wrong with me, which makes me giggle again. I'll go back to worrying about what he thinks of me—what they all think of me—soon. But for right now, I'm just going to stand here and enjoy the sight of Askkandia's bright blue dirt.

And wait for whatever clusterfuck comes next.

CHAPTER 17

Ian

"Okay," I say to Kali as the landing gear locks click. "You're coming with me."

She's still laughing under her breath, which isn't concerning at all. I'm afraid there really is something wrong with her—and can't help thinking I should be around if she ends up freaking out or something.

But as soon as I have the thought, I try to forget it. The princess isn't my responsibility. But I *am* the captain of this ship—for now, at least—which technically means everyone on board is my responsibility. Fuck. I'm not *not* responsible for her, either. Fuck.

This captain shit is a lot harder than I thought it'd be.

"Are you serious?" she asks. "What happened to the whole I-don't-trust-you-not-to-go-running-to-Mummy thing?"

"No joke. It's *because* I don't trust you that I'm taking you with me."

"I won't try to contact anyone. I promise." She actually bats her eyelashes at me like she thinks that will work.

I roll my eyes in response, then say, "Up."

"Oh, come on," she needles, gesturing a hand down over herself. "How can I go out there looking like this?"

I don't see what the problem is. She actually looks sort of cute, like a really grubby ghost at a fancy-dress party. I do miss the bare legs, though. "Easy. People will just think you're a nun."

"I'm a high priestess, not a nun," Rain volunteers.

"I didn't ask," I answer. But I smile to soften it because snapping at her feels a lot like kicking a small, cute prupple. Then I turn back to Kali. "People find nuns nonthreatening, even here. You'll be totally safe."

I can almost see her mind working as she considers it. Or, more likely, considers a bunch of plots to give me the slip and run home to Mommy. But the last thing we need is the Empire on our asses, so I'm going to have to make sure she stays next to me.

Eventually she nods, though, which saves me from having to force the issue. I address Max in my head. "*You stay here and watch the ship.*"

"*Already planned on it.*"

"*Good.*" I look at Gage, who is studying the ship's now blank console like he's trying to figure out how and why it worked. I should probably spend some time doing that, too, while we're on the ground, but the truth is I don't give a fuck. As long as it gets me to Milla, the ship can fly upside down and backward and I won't care.

"I need you to arrange for the water tanks to be filled," I tell him. "Go and talk to the port authority—they pump from the lake."

Rangar is a port city on the edge of a huge freshwater lake, though *lake* is a bit of an understatement, considering it's bigger than other planets' oceans. At least water is one thing there will be no shortage of here—half of Askkandia is covered with it. They ship it out to the inner planets and sell it at an exorbitant price to the poor sods who live there—most of whom can't afford to buy enough to quench their thirsts. One of the few things I remember about my early childhood is always being thirsty.

"They'll want payment," I continue, pulling out what little planetas I have from my pocket and handing them over. "If it's more, tell them I'll pay when I get back." He looks more than happy to take the orange strips of composite carbon and tuck them into his Corporation suit pockets. Typical.

I look around and spot Merrick hovering over his little priestess. Without the white robe, he looks seriously intimidating—which is exactly what I need right now. "You go with Gage. If anyone gets difficult—sort it out."

He raises a brow but then nods.

Good.

"And what will you be doing?" Merrick asks.

I consider telling him to mind his own business. This guy rubs me the wrong way. Probably because I suspect we may have trouble with him once the more pressing issues of dying of thirst or starvation are sorted.

I decide to play it nice—for now. "The princess and I are going to go turn her buttons into cash and buy some provisions. We'll see you back here in a couple of hours."

"*Call if you need me,*" Max says in my head.

"*I won't need you.*"

"*That's what you always say.*"

"*And I'm always right,*" I tell him.

He snorts. "*If that's the story you've got to tell yourself…*"

"Are we going to have to go down that ladder to get out?" Kali asks.

Beckett pushes a button on the console in front of her. "For you, Princess, only the best."

Every time she talks to Kali, there's something in her voice that sets me on edge. On the surface, it's just regular snark, but underneath I sense this deep, burning rage. Max thinks she's a rebel, not just because of her attitude but also because she was Doc V's prisoner.

Kali and I head out of the ship without another word. As Beckett indicated, there's a ramp leading to the ground from the triangular exit door. Of course it's triangular on this weird fucking ship. I peer out. It's late afternoon, and the sun is still high overhead in the cloudless sky. We're on the edge of the space port, and it's quiet here. It usually is, since most of the spacecraft in the system are controlled by the Corporation and Rangar isn't sanctioned.

There's no such thing as a pleasure craft in the system anymore.

Anything not flown by the Corporation is illegal—like us. If we raise any eyebrows, I plan on saying we escaped from the *Caelestis*.

That's one of the reasons I brought the princess—if worse comes to worst, I can trot her out and say I saved her life. I doubt, even if they're skeptical, that anyone will actually risk harming the Empress's daughter.

Looks like I knew what I was doing when I decided to bring her after all—not altruism, just pragmatism. And a strong sense of self-preservation.

No wonder I didn't recognize it at first—it's not usually my strong suit. But until we get Milla out of whatever hellhole she's in, I'm going to be more careful than I've ever been in my life. If something happens to Max and me, she'll be stuck there forever, and that, I cannot allow to happen.

I head down the ramp, with Kali close behind me and Gage and Merrick bringing up the rear.

"There's something different about the ship," she says as we step off the ramp and onto that fucking ridiculous blue Askkandian soil. I turn to look, and she's right.

When we left the *Caelestis*, she was a grimy gray color. Now, the dirt has cleared away, and she's an almost luminescent silver in the bright sunlight. The same color as Kali's eyes.

"Wow," Kali murmurs. "She's beautiful."

I don't disagree.

She walks slowly around the ship, trailing her finger over the surface. Then halts at the nose end, a frown pulling her dark brows together. I come to stand beside her.

"What?" I ask.

"Look at that." She points a finger at the side of the ship just in front of the forward screens. There's an image depicted on the side of it. Covered by grime before, now it's clear to see. A star with rays of light shooting from it and a circle around it.

I've definitely seen that image before. So has Kali, and it's obvious she remembers.

"It's the same as on the heptosphere," she murmurs. "The same as in my—" She breaks off abruptly, and I look at her, wondering what she was about to say.

But when she continues, she's focused on more pragmatic matters. "The ship must be from the Ancients. No wonder none of us have ever seen anything like her before. She's an alien artifact."

She says the last with a startled sort of reverence that's a little concerning.

"Of course she's an alien artifact," Gage says from behind me. "I thought you knew that."

Bastard. "How the fuck would I know that?" I ask, even though it's beginning to make a scary sort of sense now.

"Everyone knows," he answers, which isn't actually an answer at all.

I glare at him. "Well, clearly not everyone."

"Where did she come from?" Kali asks. She reaches out and strokes the ship, and as her fingers connect with the metal, a slight shiver runs through her.

I have a sudden urge for her to touch me the same way, which I deliberately ignore. We're in enough trouble without adding sex into the mix. Especially since sex with me tends to be…complicated, and the princess doesn't seem the type to like complications, even though she is one.

"The same place as the heptosphere," Gage answers. "Doc V brought them in as a package deal."

"Well, that doesn't exactly make me feel all warm and fuzzy," I growl. "That thing was evil."

"No," Kali corrects me. "Not evil, just misunderstood."

I strongly disagree. "We need to go."

She steps back and looks up at the ship. "We should give her a name."

I want to ask why when we won't be hanging on to her, but I keep my mouth shut.

"Let's call her the *Starlight*," she continues. "That's what she looks like. And the image… It's lovely."

Sure, lovely. That's probably why there's a big ball of something nasty coagulating in my belly.

We've been flying on an *alien artifact*.

An alien artifact the Corporation is going to want returned…and fast.

An alien artifact that—most concerning of all—seems to have a mind of her own.

CHAPTER 18

Ian

"Come on," I say to Kali, who ignores me as she continues staring at the ancient spaceship.

I'm just starting to think I might have to drag her away from her new toy when she gives the ship one last look and hurries after me.

Good. The less time we spend on Askkandia, the better.

On the surface, it's the most attractive of the planets—which is why the Empress and her Council live here. It's certainly a hell of a lot nicer than Kridacus, where I was born, but that's not hard. That place is a complete shithole.

Here, there are lots of trees, and I can see blue and green rolling hills in the distance. The air is warm but not fry-your-lungs warm, and once we leave the actual port, it smells clean.

Rangar might be the dirtiest place on Askkandia, but it still beats the other planets, hands down. I don't know what the hell Kali was complaining about.

I head for the town, and soon we're walking among buildings. Fancy it isn't, but it never has been. That's not the problem. I just can't believe how much it's declined since the last time I was here.

As we walk through the streets, there's an air of desperation—and despair—to the place and the people that wasn't here before. It feels familiar—I've been to a lot of planets, and this is the norm, not the exception—but it still makes me wonder about the Empress and her Council. How bad are things in Senestris that they've allowed their home planet to fall into this state?

I'm not the only one surprised. Kali keeps looking around, taking everything in with wide eyes and a deep frown. Everyone we run into hurries past without making eye contact. I figure that's got more to do with the laser pistol at my waist than the fact that I'm walking with the princess—who I sincerely hope is unrecognizable in that dirty white robe. Weapons aren't allowed for the working classes, so the fact that I'm carrying one labels me as something else. And I'm guessing that they're not sure what.

I'd thought about leaving it behind, but from past experience with this place, it's a hell of a lot better to be armed. Plus, I'm dressed in black, which would—if I was a law-abiding citizen—make me Corporation, and most people steer clear of them.

"Who are all these people?" Kali whispers as we turn a corner.

"Mostly port workers, I guess."

"So they have jobs?" She sounds astounded.

It gets my back up a little. "Not everyone can sit around a palace all day, Princess."

"That's not what I meant." She doesn't get mad like she normally would. Just quieter as she continues to look around. "If they are working, I presume they get a salary. So why do they all look so…"

"Poor?" I fill in the blank for her.

"Broken," she replies softly.

"Because that's the way the Empire likes them," I shoot back. I know she's been sheltered, but how out of touch she is with what's going on in the system she's supposed to rule one day still makes me a little sick.

Her frown grows deeper. "That's not true. We want all of our people to prosper."

"If that's the case, why do the people here on Askkandia—even here in Rangar—have the best lives of anyone in the system?" I ask as we skirt a man sitting in the street in a dirty brown robe.

The princess looks horrified—though I don't know if it's by him or my words.

"That can't be true," she tells me, looking around at the trash on the street and the people dressed in rags.

I shrug. "Your dear mama raised taxes a few years back, and it squeezed the last bit of life out of a lot of these places. Most people were already at the poverty level, so it hit hard. Add into that the grain rationing, and everyone's fucked right now. If all they can afford is bread and now that's not available, what do you think is going to happen to them?"

"But we needed the *Caelestis*. She's our one hope of saving the system. We all have to make sacrifices." Her conviction might be more believable if I hadn't just peeled a bunch of jewels off her damn dress.

"Yeah? How about you, Princess? What sacrifices have you been making? You ever gone hungry?"

"I'm hungry now."

"Not the same thing—you know we're going to solve that problem as soon as we find a place to buy food. But what if this was your everyday life?" I don't wait for an answer. "Just imagine we didn't have a pocket full of shiny gems you used to decorate your dress. Imagine you had to live here in Rangar forever, with no way out except death. And then consider that just one of your shiny buttons could probably feed a family for a year."

She narrows her eyes at me. "So, you're going to sell them and give the money away?"

She's got me there. "No. But at least I don't pretend to be acting for anyone but myself." And Max and Milla, though I leave that unsaid. "I don't go around pretending that I'm taxing the ordinary people into starvation for their own good while I sit in my gold-plated palace and look down on them all."

"It's not *gold*. And I don't look down on them." She nibbles at her bottom lip in that way she does when she's nervous—or thinking deeply about something. "I feel pity for them."

I grunt. "It's pretty much the same thing, isn't it?"

She doesn't answer for a long time. Then, as we turn down a

particularly dismal looking street, she whispers, "You really hate the Ruling Families, don't you?"

I do, but telling her that right now feels a lot like kicking her while she's down. "Don't take it personally. I hate a lot of people." Like anyone who tries to tell me what to do. "I've always had a problem with authority figures."

"But someone needs to be in charge; otherwise, it would be chaos and anarchy."

"Yeah, but they don't have to get super-rich at the expense of everyone else—that's gross. And they should be elected by the people." I say the last just to wind her up. I mean, I sort of think it, but I've never had any real interest in politics. You look after yourself, and everyone else—if they've got any sense—does the same.

I stop walking as I realize I've left her behind. She's stopped in the center of the street, and she's staring at me, face eerily blank.

"That's…" She obviously can't think of a word bad enough.

"Seditious?" I suggest. "You'd be surprised how many people think the same thing."

"Are you a rebel?" she asks, and she sounds genuinely horrified.

"Hell no. I'm just trying to make a living any way I can."

Her shoulders slump. "But you hate everyone, and you don't hate the rebels, even though they're evil."

"Nah. Your mother is evil. Dr. Veragelen is evil. The rebels are just trying to free the peasants from the yoke of oppression and all that shit."

"They murdered my father."

I didn't know that, and I can hear the echo of pain in her voice, but lots of people die. My mother was murdered right in front of me when I was eleven—and that wasn't even the worst thing that happened to me that year. Or some years since.

"What about me?" she asks after we walk a couple of blocks in silence. "Do you think I'm evil?"

"Not yet. But I do think you're willfully ignorant, and it's a slippery slope from there into the abyss."

"Wow." She reels back. "Glad your opinion of me is so high."

Maybe I shouldn't be talking to her like this, but life's too short to waste it on lies. Especially when she's literally in a position to do something about all these things that seem to horrify her so much.

"Come on, Princess. You're supposed to be heir to all this, and yet you know nothing about how 'your people' live. I bet you never question your mother or the decisions she makes."

"I do question her, but it doesn't matter. She has to do the right thing for everyone, and sometimes those are tough decisions. I didn't realize how tough."

I laugh, but it's got no humor in it. "And you wonder why the rebels exist."

"That's not fair." She narrows her eyes at me.

"News flash, Princess: Life's not fair. But if you want things to change, you just have to change them." At least that's the way I've lived my life—the way Max and Milla have, too. "All you have to do is say—hey Mom, do you think we should do something about the abysmal infant mortality rate on Kridacus? Or should we buy me another dress instead, or maybe a fancy-ass cloak so I can look like a fucking fool when I go out to see the peasants?"

She's staring at me like I'm the fool. Then she blinks. "Is the infant mortality rate on Kridacus abysmal?"

"I had two younger sisters. They both died before they were three."

Fuck. I can't believe I told her that. I never talk about Amelia and Farrah. I sure as shit don't want to talk about them with the princess so she thinks I'm looking for sympathy or something.

I haven't let myself think of them in so long, but now that I've started, I can't stop. Amelia with the little red bow she loved more than anything. Little Farrah, who used to beg me to play rocks with her. I was young when they died, and some days I can't even remember what they looked like beyond every other sick kid on Kridacus.

The high radiation levels from the sun can weaken the immune system if you're susceptible. Which means if you get ill, you don't pull through. It gets a lot of them young—close to fifty percent.

"I'm sorry," she says, and she sounds like she means it. "But at least you and Max made it out."

That's a shit fucking answer, and she doesn't even know enough about the world to know that. She also doesn't have a clue what she's talking about when it comes to Max and me, but that's hardly surprising. My relationship with him and Milla is not something we discuss with anyone. Ever. Likely, no one would believe us if we tried.

"One day, when I'm Empress, I can make changes."

She sounds sincere, but how long will that last once she gets back to her shiny palace? "Nice dream, Princess. But hey, there's a good chance we're all going to burn in the not-too-distant future anyway, so why worry about a few little kiddies dying?"

"Ian." She reaches a hand out and wraps it around my wrist, drawing both of us to a stop.

I look down at her, surprised, then want to kick myself when I realize her lower lip is wobbling and those shiny silver eyes of hers have turned a dull and murky gray.

Fuck. I said too much. But diplomacy's never been my strong suit, and she was asking.

"*Maybe so, but did you really have to do it so harshly?*" Max's voice is back in my head.

Probably not. I sigh and rub a hand over my face as I try to figure out what to say to make things better. Besides *sorry*, which I can't bring myself to say—not when we're surrounded by people who have a lot more hurting than just their feelings. Plus, she needed to hear it.

But enough's enough. I pull my wrist out of her death-penalty grip and look down the street, away from her. I think I've burst my share of her shiny bubbles for today.

"*More than your share,*" Max says wryly.

"Come on," I snarl as I start walking again. I don't glance back, but I don't relax again until I hear her bare feet slapping the pavement beside me.

We're moving through what passes for the business district now. I know exactly where I'm going to try first. There are more people here, and among the browns and grays is the occasional flash of color—proof that this place really is an outlaw town.

Something occurs to me, and I turn to Kali. "Put your hood up."

"I won't be able to see if I do that."

"Maybe not, but more to the point, people won't be able to see you." I doubt anyone will look at a barefoot girl in a dirty robe and think she's Princess Kalinda—experience has taught me people tend to see what they expect to see—but it's better to be careful. Even dressed like this, with her dark-red hair a mess, she's beautiful. More, she's striking, and people *do* tend to remember beauty.

She scowls but doesn't argue anymore as she pulls the hood up, covering her hair and face. "I really can't see," she mutters, her voice muffled through the heavy cloth.

I grin and reach for her hand. She yanks it away. I grab it back, and we start walking. Last thing I need is for her to trip and make a spectacle of herself.

"Do they really kill people if they touch you?" I ask as we walk.

"Not so far, but perhaps they'll make an exception for you." She pauses, then adds, "If I ask them nicely."

That makes me laugh—something I realize I do with her more than with anyone else, even Milla and Max.

I've never been one for hand holding, but it feels sort of nice to walk with her like this. Her hand fits really well in mine, and her skin is soft and warm. "Where are we going, exactly?" she asks.

"Here." I stop in front of a tavern.

"The Drunken Drokaray," she reads from the sign hanging above the door. "I love drokarays!"

"You do? Don't they eat people?" I'm no wildlife expert, but if I remember correctly, they're a sort of carnivorous four-legged work animal indigenous to Askkandia.

"Only bad people." She smiles at some memory, but then the smile fades. "When I was little, I wanted one for a pet. My dad was always the type to show rather than tell, so instead of trying to dissuade me, he took me to a farm and introduced me to a baby drokaray. It nearly bit my nose off."

"Cute."

She rolls her eyes at my sarcasm. "After that, we used to make up swear words with drokarays in them. And whenever I was being bad, my dad would remind me that a drokaray would bite me."

Now she looks sad. I don't like it—I'd rather have her pissed off at me. "Look," I tell her. "It's probably best you keep your mouth shut in here, okay?"

"Why?" She slips her hand out of mine. "Do you think I'm going to ask for help?"

Actually, that hadn't even occurred to me, but now that she mentions it, I consider gagging her.

She must figure out what I'm thinking, because I can suddenly feel her glare, even if I can't actually see it, courtesy of the hood.

"Don't even think about it, you drokaray dropping," she snaps, but there's no real bite in it. "And yes, I'll keep my mouth shut. Now, can we get on with this? I'd kill for a sandwich right now."

I try not to smile as I pull her in. But then it's easy enough to wipe it off, considering what we're walking into.

CHAPTER 19

Ian

It's dark in the bar after the bright sunlight, and it takes a moment for my eyes to adjust. Even in the afternoon, the bar is busy and there's the beat of some music blasting out. I glance around to see if I can spot anyone I recognize, but there's no one—which could be a good thing or a bad one, depending on the person.

I take Kali's elbow to lead her in, and all eyes turn to us.

The patrons are mostly locals, from their appearances and dress, but I spot a group of wealthy-looking Permunians drinking at a table— probably merchants negotiating a deal for the Stellenium they mine for the Corporation. Their yellow eyes follow us as we pass.

"They're all staring," Kali whispers.

"I doubt they get many nuns in here."

"I'm not a nun—and neither is Rain. No one is a nun!" She sounds exasperated. "And what is this music? I've never heard anything like it."

"You need to go slumming more often. And what happened to keeping your mouth shut?"

"Stop saying things that make me open it." But she shuts up; I'll give her that.

I rest my free hand on my pistol and ignore the looks. At that moment, a young woman in a tight dress that hugs her very abundant curves enters from the door at the back. She sees me straightaway, and a smile flashes across her face as she bounds over.

It takes me a second to recognize her as the person Max had a thing with the last time we were here. Well, one of the people. He likes a lot of variety. And she's also the daughter of the owner of this not-so-fine establishment. Because Max really is a big enough cliché that he actually tapped a barmaid. I just manage to get her name before she reaches us.

"Ian, where have you been?" Ella asks warmly. Probably more warmly than I deserve, considering how things ended with the two of them. "We've missed you."

I shrug that off—she probably says it to everyone. "Around."

"Max not with you?" She looks disappointed.

"Not this time."

"And who's this?" She glances at Kali, her expression curious.

"Just a job." I feel Kali stiffen beside me and hope she remembers our discussion about staying quiet. "Some nun the Sisterhood wants transported off-planet." I lean closer, lowering my voice. "Between you and me, I think they're glad to be rid of her for a while. She's a little difficult, if you get my meaning." I can almost feel Kali bristling. Whoever thought winding up a princess would be so much fun? I should be keeping score—see how many times I can piss her off in an hour or less.

"But she doesn't talk?"

"Mute. Or maybe they cut out her tongue 'cause she never stopped demanding things. Who knows?" Kali full-on twitches beside me at that one, so I figure that means I get an extra point.

"Those Sisterhood people are a weird lot."

"You have no idea. Hey, is your da around? I have some business he might be interested in."

"He's in the back. Just go on through."

I take Kali's arm again and urge her in the direction I want her to go. I'd prefer her not to meet Dylan McBride at all, but I'm not leaving her out here alone, which means she's coming with me.

I push open the wooden door—must be nice to have enough trees lying around to have wood doors inside; fucking Askkandia—and usher her into the little room. There's a desk and a chair and not much space for anything else. A man is seated in the chair, booted feet up on the table, eyes closed. Dylan is a native Askkandian, with green eyes, copper skin, and a penchant for gossip that means he knows everything going on in this port town.

"You're back," he says, opening one eye. "Decided to work for me after all, have you?"

"Nope. You know I don't work for anyone but myself."

"I know you should."

He takes his boots off the table and straightens, then glances at Kali but doesn't ask any questions—that's not the way Dylan works. "So, what are you doing here? I would have thought things would be too hot for you in these parts after that last stunt you pulled."

"I didn't have a lot of choices. Look, Dylan, I need cash, and I need it fast."

"And what have you got for me?" He lifts a brow. "I'm fond of you, lad, but I'm no charity."

I reach into my pocket and pull out the drawstring bag with the jeweled buttons. I tip them onto the table and watch as his eyes light up. He stirs the little pile with a finger, then picks one up and studies it. Pulling a magnifying glass from the desk drawer, he examines it more closely, then looks me in the eye.

"Where exactly did you get these?" he asks.

I fake a laugh. "You know I'm not going to tell you that."

He purses his lips as he looks back and forth between Kali and me. "You might want to take a look at this." He pulls a piece of paper— paper flyers? Again, *fucking* Askkandia—from his desk and hands it to me. I glance down, then turn slightly so Kali can't see.

It's a detailed picture of her in the purple dress with all the sparkly little buttons in plain sight. Reward for any information regarding the whereabouts of Princess Kalinda. Missing from the ISS *Caelestis*. There's some other stuff, but I don't read it, just screw the paper up and toss it in the bin with a quick glance at Kali. Her face is completely covered, so I have no clue what she's thinking, but her arms are crossed beneath the robe and her foot is tapping in a way I'm pretty sure doesn't bode well for either of us.

"Nothing to do with me," I tell Dylan with a smile. "Now, are you interested or not? Because I have other people I can go to."

"Maybe I'm interested." He gives me a sly look. "Those are gonna be hot for a long while—too hot to sell, especially on Askkandia. Depends on the asking price. It'll need to be worth the heat."

I give him the number that Beckett said they were worth, and he laughs. Glad I'm making someone's day. He counters with a number twenty times smaller. I work my way up, and we finish exactly where Beckett said we would. She might be a little strange, but she definitely knows her stuff.

The planetas change hands, and I watch as Dylan picks up one of the jewels and kisses it before slipping it back in the bag along with the others. Then he once again looks back and forth between Kali and me.

"I'd get off-planet as fast as you can. This place will be crawling with the Imperial forces any moment now."

Good advice, made doubly good by the fact that I don't trust him not to turn me in. Sure, we're friends of a sort. But that was a damn big reward on that flyer he showed me, and Dylan loves nothing as much as he loves money. Not even his daughter.

I give a nod and hustle Kali out of the room. I can feel a lot of eyes on us as we pass the bar. I can also feel the cash burning in my pocket. As soon as we're out on the street, she turns to me. "What was that piece of paper?"

"Nothing."

"Why would he show you a paper with nothing on it? It was about me, wasn't it?"

I snort. "Don't worry about it. Everything's fine."

"That's not a no. And what did he mean about the Imperial forces?"

"Nothing to do with us."

I glance around. On the corner of the street is a food vendor selling the local spicy buns. I buy a couple and hold one in front of her face. Maybe if her mouth is full she'll stop asking so many questions.

She scoffs. "I know what you're doing." But she's leaning toward it, breathing in the warm, yeasty smell.

"Is it working?"

She doesn't answer, but her stomach rumbles—which is an answer all in itself. Then she reaches out from beneath the robe and snatches the bun out of my hand.

It disappears beneath the hood, and seconds later, her hand reemerges, empty. Amazing—she had to have eaten it in record time.

I take a more leisurely bite of the other bun—I'm hungry as well, but unlike the princess, I'm used to it—and start walking. She falls in behind me.

"Why don't you just leave me here?" she says. "You obviously don't like me—wouldn't you like to get rid of me? And if the security forces are on their way, I can just hand myself over."

Not for the first time, I think about it. She really does seem insistent that her mom would take care of us, but my gut is saying the Empress can't be trusted. Once we've got Milla and can make ourselves scarce, then sure. But now? Not a chance.

Not that I plan on telling her any of that. Instead, I change the subject. "Who blew up the *Caelestis*?" I ask.

"What? How would I know?" She sounds confused and more than a little offended.

I don't answer. There's a garment shop on the corner, and I enter with Kali close behind me. "Later," I tell her. "Pick some clothes. And be quick."

"We have enough for me to get something, too?" There's surprise in her tone.

"You didn't think I was going to leave you in that dirty robe, did you?"

It's her turn to evade the question, which means she did. I'm not sure if I should be insulted or pat myself on the back. She obviously thinks I'm as big an asshole as I wanted her to.

"Just pick something out before I change my mind." I walk toward the back of the store, where they keep the boots.

"Are you always this bossy?" she demands, following me.

"Yes. Are you always this slow-moving?"

She growls a little at me, which makes me grin for no reason I can understand. Then she moves to the center of the store and turns around in a full circle. The shopkeeper is watching, of course, but Kali clearly isn't the first questionable character to do questionable things in her store. From her bored expression, she's probably not even the first one today.

"I'm not sure what I'm supposed to do here," the princess says in a whisper.

"Choose what you want, pay for it, leave. What's the problem?"

"I've never done that before."

I wonder for a second how she got all the fancy clothes I have no doubt that she wears. Then decide I don't want to know because it's probably too infuriating. "Just pick something."

She sighs. "It's all so…dull."

"You're not going to a goddamn ball. It doesn't have to be shiny," I growl, annoyed because now the shop assistant is looking at *me*.

I get the impression she would like us to leave but is put off from suggesting it by the laser pistol at my waist. I head on over. "Do you have anything with a little more…color?" I ask her.

"Not purple," Kali adds.

The shop assistant's eyes widen.

"I don't think that will be an issue," I tell Kali in a what-the-fuck voice. "Only the Ruling Families wear purple."

I get out a wad of planetas and wave it at the assistant, hoping it will make her forget Kali's faux pas.

It works. She perks up immediately.

"The better stuff is through here," she says, leading us into a smaller room. I've never been shopping with a woman before—except Milla, and she doesn't count—but I'm guessing Kali isn't behaving in a typical manner, even before she stands in the middle and does a twirl.

The shopkeeper comes back with a pile of garments over her arm. "These were ordered, but the customers never came back to collect them." She drops the garments on the counter along the back of the room. "See if there's something here you might like."

Kali paws through them, pulling out a few black ones.

"That works," I say. "Matches the color of your heart."

She just rolls her eyes and keeps shopping.

"I'm not looking for me," she finally clarifies. "I'm looking for Rain."

"She spends all her days in a white robe. So…white jumpsuit?" But Kali looks up at me like I've sprouted a second head. Women are weird. "Just get what you need and hurry up."

She actually does as I say for once, and we're out of there and back on the street ten minutes later. Kali is laden with bags under the robe, and she's wearing the new boots I picked out for her. We just need provisions now, and then we can head back.

I take care of that easily enough, picking up provisions to last us for a few weeks, including enough first-aid supplies to cover the group should we inevitably get into some scrapes. Fresh food for the next few days, a shitload of bottled water, toiletries, protein bars, some dehydrated meals that are years out of date but should be okay, and a sack of mealie-meal flour—the staple of Kridacus. But mostly sacks of dried fishgalen.

I hate dried fishgalen, the tiny freshwater fish abundant in the lakes on Askkandia. It's what poor people eat, and it tastes like shit and smells even worse. But it's high in protein and will keep us alive and there isn't anything else. Most of the shelves in the store were empty—another sign that things are going to shit fast.

To make up for all the fishgalen, I add a few bottles of gerjgin, a strong Askkandian alcohol—actually, more than a few, but who knows how long they need to last? I pay in cash and promise another ten if they deliver to the ship right now. It's time to get the fuck out of here.

As we step out of the shop, I take us on the quickest route back to the port. But we're only about halfway when I become aware of a problem. Someone is following us.

Maybe Dylan sent them to get his money back—honestly, the man's a crook.

Or maybe he sussed out who Kali was and decided to go for the reward.

Or maybe some random stranger just picked up on the fact that we seem to have a lot of cash. In Rangar, it can be any—or all—of those things and more to boot.

There are only three people at the moment, so I'm not overly worried, but the princess is likely going to get in the way if it comes to a fight. Which I'm guessing it will, as there's a lean, hungry look about all three of them.

But the first step is to alert Kali to the problem, so I lean over and quietly say, "We're being followed. Don't look—"

But it's too late. She's already rubbernecking.

"Fuck," I mutter. "You should give a class on how *not* to be inconspicuous."

"Shouldn't we get help?" she asks, her expression carefully blank again.

Oh, to live the life of a princess. "From where? Besides, there's only three of them."

"Exactly," she answers. "There's three of them!"

I try not to be insulted as I search the area for an escape route. The last thing I want is to lead them back to the ship. They might have friends, and it could get messy—plus that alien abomination isn't exactly what I'd call low-key.

I finally spot an alley that cuts off from the main thoroughfare, and I usher Kali toward it.

"Where are we going? I can't see. I don't think—"

"Stop distracting me." I search the alley, then guide her toward a wide doorway. The damn white robe shows up even in the shadows, but it's the best I can do right now. I consider drawing the pistol but decide to leave it as a last resort. Laser blasts aren't exactly commonplace, and I don't want to draw attention to us. Or, rather, *more* attention.

I hurry away from Kali and crouch down, pretending to examine something on the ground, making myself as big a target as I possibly can.

It isn't long before I hear the first one coming for me. I straighten, then in one fluid motion whirl around and kick out, taking him in the chest. He flies backward just as the second one reaches me. I turn to him, and we circle each other slowly. I give him a look that says I've got all the time in the world, which has his eyes narrowing.

It's a good tell, and I'm more than ready for him when he lunges. He's lean and wiry and strong, and we grapple for a few seconds before I let him swipe my legs out from under me and take me down.

I roll as I hit the ground so he's beneath me, then slam a fist into his face.

Oxygen-rich red blood spurts from his nose, but it doesn't faze him. Instead, he reaches up and wraps his hands around my neck like he thinks he's going to choke me to death or something. In a different situation, I'd be impressed with his resilience, but the other two guys are roaming the alley, and there's no way I'm letting them get their hands on Kali.

So instead of letting this fucker have his moment, I let go of the hold I have on his chest. Ignoring his triumphant smile—maybe he's a fucking loser after all—I ram my thumbs straight into his eyeballs as hard as I can.

He screams loud enough to probably be heard back at the *Starlight*, and I focus on that instead of the disgusting squelch of his eyeballs popping beneath my thumbs. He releases my throat as he reaches for his eye sockets.

He's already down, but I need him out, so I slam my fist into his face again. He passes out before I've even pulled my hand back.

Finally, I take a deep breath, relishing the feel of air hitting my greedy lungs.

Then I push myself to my feet.

Right before someone hits me in the head from behind.

Fucking coward.

I'm back on all fours, head ringing, but I manage to roll over just as he leaps for me. I kick up, catching him square in the balls. He stumbles back with a curse, but then he's coming at me again, a knife gleaming in his hand.

I need to finish this.

I draw my own knife from its sheath, the blade gleaming in the sunlight. The moment he spots it, he tries to slow his momentum, but he's moving too fast. Reaching forward, I grab his jacket with one hand, dodging his knife as I pull him close and thrust my blade between his ribs and into his heart.

He's dead before I yank it free.

I turn around, hoping the third man has taken the hint and is on his way out of the alley. Instead, he's walking straight toward where I hid Kali, the sudden purpose in his step convincing me he's spotted her.

Something like fear slams through me, and, acting on instinct, I hurl the knife straight at him.

It hits him in the center of his back. He falls to his knees, his hand grappling in his pocket. I don't wait to see if he's got a gun. Instead, I yank the knife out of his flesh, grab his hair to pull his head back, and slice his throat in one clean swipe.

The hot, coppery smell of blood fills the air. I wipe the knife clean on his jacket before doing the same for my hands—they're covered in exploded eyeballs.

Then I hunker down beside him and run my hands over his torso in case he's carrying anything of value—though I doubt it. These three don't seem like the type.

I don't find anything except a piece of paper tucked in his pocket.

It's a flyer. I see the word *reward*, and at first I think it's the same one Dylan showed me about the princess. But it's not. It's much worse.

It's a picture of me. A good one—obviously recent, since I'm wearing the guard uniform from the *Caelestis*.

No wonder these three picked me up. Below the picture, it reads, *Wanted dead or alive*. Apparently, I'm armed and dangerous. The reward is a wicked amount of money—so much that I'm tempted to turn myself in.

Well, shit. This is fucked.

It's definitely past time to get the fuck out of here.

But when I straighten up and head toward Kali, I realize that the princess is gone.

CHAPTER 20

Rain

I take a deep breath of fresh air. It's warm and smells of fuel and water and smoke drifting in from the city, which I can see in the distance. The sky is clear, and I stare up at the dark blue of it arching overhead.

It seems unbelievable to be here when a few short days ago I was certain I'd never see anything but the monastery on Serati ever again.

And now I'm sitting on a wall on Askkandia, facing the biggest, clearest lake I've ever seen. There are lights glinting on the smooth expanse of water, fishermen setting out huge nets to catch the abundant fishgalen.

It's beautiful here and so different from anything I've ever known. There are no lakes or seas on Serati. In fact, there's very little water at all. Some days it's so hot that it's hard to breathe outside, each painful inhalation searing your windpipe and blistering your lungs if you don't have something to use as a filter.

A faction within the Sisterhood wants to relocate to one of the outer planets, but Serati was the main home of the Ancients, and most of the conclave doesn't believe that anything too bad will happen. They believe that we'll save the world before we burn and that relocating will send out the wrong message to our followers.

I'm more of the mind that a worse message would be to let our followers die, but it's not up to me to make law. I am but an instrument of faith for the Sisterhood, even though some days it's hard for me to have any kind of faith myself.

When I was younger, it used to bother me that I had questions. But then one of the sisters—Sister Luz, who died in her sleep soon after our talk—told me that it's okay to question. That a high priestess must have faith, but she also has a duty to her people to question the Sisterhood's beliefs to make sure that the path they are on remains the true one.

A movement off to the left catches my eye. I know right away that it's Beckett—I've spent enough time studying her over the last couple of days to recognize the way she moves, even from the corner of my eye.

As she gets closer, I immediately have a flashback to the feel of her lips on mine. I shouldn't have let her kiss me—but I wanted her to.

Lately, I seem to be wanting a whole lot of things I shouldn't even be thinking about. Like the fact that I want her to kiss me again.

She comes to a halt beside me, then sits down, and I turn so I can see her face; she's staring at my hair. "Beautiful," she murmurs. "Like sunshine and starlight."

No one has ever said anything like that to me before, and warmth steals through me. For a moment, I imagine what it would be like if I didn't wait for her to touch me. If I reached out for her instead.

I'd take her shoulders in my hands, stroking my fingers over the sharpness of her collarbone that's in such dichotomy to the softness of her skin. Then I'd lean forward and trail my lips along the edge of her jaw, being careful not to brush against the painful-looking scar beneath her ear. The last thing I want is to cause her pain, especially not when I'm dying to drown her in pleasure.

She'll arch into my touch, her body quivering with the same need that will be running through mine. And when our lips meet, she'll—

"Whatever you're thinking about looks good on you," she says.

Her words—and the slightly teasing voice she uses to deliver them—bring me back to reality with a thud. I don't know how to respond, so I just stare at her, eyes wide and heart thumping hard in my chest.

"Nothing to say?" she asks softly.

I shake my head, then immediately feel bad for lying. Because the truth is, it's not that I have nothing to say. It's that I have *so much* to say that I don't know where to start.

Nobody's ever wanted to listen before.

"What were you thinking about?" she asks as she reaches out to run her fingers through my hair.

"You." I blurt it out, because it's true. And because I don't want to hide it. It's not the same as reaching out and kissing her, but as her yellow eyes gleam, I can't help but think it's a start.

"Oh yeah?" Her fingers dig deeper until they're skating against my skull and my whole body goes tight. And then she starts to rub, and the tenseness just oozes from my body.

"That feels so good," I murmur. "I don't think anyone has ever touched my hair before you." I frown, trying to remember back. "I suppose they probably did when I was little, but I can't remember."

She considers me, head cocked to one side. "What about Merrick?" she asks. "Isn't he your lady's maid?"

I giggle. "I think you're mistaking me for Kali. She had a companion-in-waiting to help her dress." I frown. "But then, her dress was way more complicated than my robe is." I pluck at the ugly thing and sigh.

"So, you and Merrick," she asks after a second. "Lovers?"

I gasp and turn to stare at her. "Oh, no! Merrick would never... Even if he wanted to—which I'm sure he doesn't—he takes his duties way too seriously. I think he'd believe a personal relationship would compromise his ability to do his job."

"Which is?"

"To keep me safe."

She smiles. "Except here you are. All alone."

"No, I'm not. I'm with you. Merrick actually told me to stay on the ship and keep out of trouble, but I needed some fresh air. I was restless, and I wanted to see this place and the water."

She nods, those arresting eyes of hers staring straight at me in a way that makes my skin prick. But then she very deliberately looks away, and everything inside me deflates.

At least until she says, "You didn't say anything about yourself."

"What do you mean?"

"You said Merrick would never compromise his duty by being with you. But you never said anything about how you feel about that. Or him."

"Oh! Not like that! Merrick is my—" Protector. Guide. Friend? I finally settle on, "Merrick takes care of me, and that's all either of us wants."

She doesn't say anything to that, and I watch her out of the corner of my eye for a couple of minutes, until I finally give up and look back toward the lake.

We're quiet for a while then, staring out over the still water. The sun is sinking in the sky, the day bleeding into night, casting a faint pink glow over the water; dusk is not far away.

The silence is peaceful. For once, Beckett's almost manic energy is subdued. And her face is clear of the pain that so often fills her eyes. Like this, I find her…disturbing. Striking. Compelling.

I've never met anyone quite like her.

Just like that, I'm filled with a sudden restlessness, like I need to do something. I need to move, to run… I glance at the water again. "Do you want to swim?"

She turns to look at me, and for a moment her eyes are blank, like she's a thousand kilometers away. Then she blinks. "I don't know how."

"Neither do I."

"I thought you were born on Askkandia?" Beckett asks.

She was there when Max, Gage, and I idly chatted in the bridge. I thought she wasn't listening, but she was paying attention. To me. My heart leaps. "Oh, I was, but I was brought to Serati when I was still a baby," I clarify. "No real memories of this place. But hey"—I grin—"we could learn to swim together."

"Or drown," she says and doesn't sound too bothered by the idea.

"Maybe we could just paddle for a little. Or dip our feet in."

She jumps off the wall and holds out her hand to me. And the pricking along my skin comes back with a vengeance.

What am I doing?

Part of me knows that this is wrong. And dangerous. But there's something damaged about Beckett, and I sense that I can help her.

I smile and slide my hand into hers, and a shiver runs through me.

And that's when I know I'm lying to myself. Again. It's becoming an unfortunate habit. Because while I would definitely like to help Beckett, that's not why I asked her to swim with me. And it's definitely not why I took her hand.

I remember the feel of her lips on mine, and longing fills me, seeping into all those little nooks and crannies inside me that I didn't even know were empty. I want her to kiss me again so that I can warm myself in her heat as I stroke the lines of pain from her forehead and make her forget all the bad things. Even if it's just for a little while.

We walk quietly toward the water's edge, until she winces slightly.

"How is your head?" I ask.

"It's okay."

"Yeah?" I prompt because I don't believe her. I can feel the tenseness in her body, the pain that seems to radiate from her.

She shrugs. "It's actually pretty messed up in there. Sometimes I can't seem to hold on to a thought no matter how hard I try. Other times I know what I want to say, but I can't make the words come out right. Everything is out of focus. The past and the present. Sometimes it's better than others. Now is good." She gives me a searching look. "You make everything clearer."

"I'm glad." I squeeze her hand. "It will get better with time."

"Or it won't." She shrugs. "Either way, I'll cope."

"You shouldn't have to cope," I say fiercely, then sigh, because getting angry never helps. "Maybe we should take you to a doctor while we're here."

"Maybe," she agrees. But I sense she's just trying to placate me.

I look around and realize we're the only two people in sight. The sun has nearly disappeared now, just a shimmer of color on the horizon.

"This is so magical," I say.

"I don't think anyone has ever called Askkandia magical before," she answers.

"I don't just mean the planet. I mean…" I pause, struggling to explain what I'm thinking. What I'm feeling. "Back in the monastery, every day was just the same. Sometimes I thought I would die from boredom. But I haven't been bored since the moment I stepped foot on the *Caelestis*."

Her brows go up. "You really think terror beats boredom?"

"Definitely!" And then I realize what I'm saying—and how I must sound to a girl who has been through what Beckett has—and I sigh again. "Goodness, that was terrible. I know there are lots of people with much less than me. And I have a role in life, maybe a chance to help all those people. But that doesn't mean I don't struggle sometimes. I just want so much more than to stare at the same walls, the same desert, for the rest of my life."

There's a narrow beach, and I drop to the beautiful cerulean sand and tug off my boots. Then sit for a moment staring up at her. "I can't believe I'm doing this. That I'm here with you right now. You're different than anyone I've ever met."

"I'm not sure that's a good thing." She looks down at me curiously. "Aren't you interested in why I was on that prison ship? What I did to get there?"

"Of course I am. I'm interested in absolutely *everything*. All my questions irritate Merrick endlessly."

"So why haven't you asked?"

"Because what you did in the past doesn't matter to me." I smile gently at her. "Besides, you'll talk about it when you're ready."

"Maybe I will." The *maybe I won't* hangs in the air between us, but I don't push. I don't want to ruin the magic happening right now. She smiles at me. "Now, let's get in the water."

I jump to my feet, and this time I'm the one who holds out my hand to her. It's not a kiss like in my daydream, but it's not nothing, either. It's a step. One that makes me happy, especially when she reaches out and links her fingers with mine. Together, we walk slowly toward the water.

The water is warmer than I expected, and it feels like silk against my skin—or what I imagine silk would feel like. It seduces me, makes me wade deeper.

I think that at any moment I'll stop and we'll turn back. But I keep walking, and so does she.

When the water is up to my waist, I turn to look at her. Then I grin, release her hand, and fall over backward into the water with a squeal. I go under and come up spluttering and laughing, wet hair plastered to my cheeks and chest.

She looks at me as if I've lost my mind. And maybe I have. Then she laughs as well and dunks under. I follow her down, holding my breath as long as I can, then come up, gasping, into the air.

"I'll remember this when I'm back in the monastery," I say. "This might be the best day of my life."

She shakes her head. "And I thought *I* was sad."

I know she doesn't mean them, so I ignore the words. "I want to float, but I suspect I'll sink in this ridiculous robe. It feels like it weighs a tonne."

"Then take it off. I certainly won't mind."

I peer at her in the dusky purple light, and suddenly the air between us is charged with something new. I remember the taste of her from that brief kiss. The sweetness.

I tell myself to live out my daydream. To move to her and kiss her so I can feel like that again. But my legs are frozen, and so is my courage.

Thankfully, Beckett isn't having the same problem.

Taking a step closer, she reaches out and strokes the hair from my face. Electricity sizzles between us, even before she leans forward and licks the water from my lips.

My knees tremble, and every nerve in my body sparks to life. I take a shaky breath, and she pulls away, her eyes questioning. I start to beg her to come back, to do that again, but I've forgotten how to form words. All that comes out is a quiet moan that smacks of the desperation—the need—that's racing through my blood.

Beckett's eyes go dark, her lips curving in a grin that looks as wicked as I feel. And then she's leaning in again, though this time she doesn't just lick my lips. She presses her mouth to mine, and it feels like my heart is going to stop in the very best possible way.

I moan again, and her lips curve against mine. "I like that sound," she whispers.

"I like you," I answer because it's true. And because I want her to stop talking and kiss me, really kiss me, like in every great love story I've ever heard or daydreamed.

This time, when she leans in to kiss me, I can't help but notice that her lips are cool. Or mine are hot. I can't tell. All the feelings are mixed up inside me. The coolness of the water and the softness of her skin and the fire in my blood. I want her like I've never wanted anything.

I press myself closer, opening my lips under hers just as a shot shatters the night air.

CHAPTER 21

Kali

My new boots are a little uncomfortable and not great to run in, but I do it anyway. I run as far as I can, as fast as I can, until my lungs are burning and there's a sharp pain in my side.

Finally, I spot a doorway close by. I duck into it and bend over, catching my breath.

Don't fucking puke.

I can taste the bile, bitter in the back of my throat.

Ian gouged that man's eyes out, and then he killed the others. Three on one, and he just dove right in like it was nothing.

Maybe to him it *was* nothing.

It's a terrifying thought. From the beginning, I sensed that he was dangerous. That he wouldn't let anything stand in his way. But there's a difference between being dangerous and being a cold-blooded killer. The last man was turned away from him, not even going for him anymore, but Ian killed him anyway. Sliced his throat even after the guy was already down from the knife in the back.

I can still smell the sickly-sweet stench of the blood—so much blood—clogging my nostrils.

I can't live like this, can't be like this.

For a little while, I got caught up in the excitement of everything and forgot who and what I was. I forgot my duty. But that fight was a wake-up call I won't soon forget.

I swallow and wrap my arms around myself. I don't belong here. With him. With any of them. I have nothing to give any of them and could never truly live in this world.

I have to get away. The only problem is I've only got one other place to go—and I'm no longer sure I want to go there. I've seen too much here in Rangar: poverty, desperation, violence. And my mother knows about it all? More, she might be responsible for it?

Calm down. Make a plan.

But what can I do, who can I trust, other than myself? I'm the first to admit I'm completely out of my element here in Rangar. Where would I even go, if not back to the palace or the ship?

I take another deep breath and try to quiet my rioting mind. And decide that I should probably start by getting out of this doorway.

Except, when I peer at the street, my heart sinks. I seem to have run from bad to worse. This area looks run-down, with many of the buildings boarded up and falling apart. Plus the streets are empty of people, and the setting sun is casting eerie shadows. Now that I know just how dangerous this system is, every shadow seems like a threat.

I push my hood up—just enough to see without uncovering my whole head—then, when the area seems clear, I step out.

I pass some sort of notice board with flyers pinned to it. I almost walk straight past it without looking, but then I remember the paper the man in the bar showed Ian. I scan the board and stare at the poster right in the middle.

Wanted dead or alive. The words are written underneath a picture of Gage.

Which doesn't make sense. Why would anyone want Gage dead?

Or Max? Or Merrick or Rain or Ian? There are posters with each of their faces on them, rewards offered for every single one of them whether they're brought in dead or alive.

But it's the one at the bottom that holds my attention.

I reach out and tear it down. Look at it closely. There's no mistaking who the picture is of—me, dressed in the Imperial Regalia.

I'm guessing the picture was taken on the *Caelestis*, before the explosions. But why am I on a poster? More importantly, why am I *wanted dead or alive*?

My mind is whirling.

I scan down and read the small print. I'm wanted for impersonating a princess of the Ruling Families? But…but I am a princess. I'm *the* princess.

It's like the world has gone upside down. And, somehow, I'm not even me anymore. Impersonating a princess? Dead or alive? Who would do this—and why?

A door opens across the street, and light spills out as four men exit.

I go still, like a drokaray caught in a beam of light. I don't know whether to run or to act normally. The last thing I want is to bring attention to myself—no, actually, the last thing I want is to get caught. I try to shrink back, but the white robe makes blending in more than a little difficult.

They're strolling toward me now, and I decide I can't wait around to see what they're going to do. Not if I'm going to have a fighting chance.

I put my head down and hurry forward, cursing myself for pushing the hood up earlier.

My stomach is churning, and my legs are shaking with every step I take toward them. They don't say anything as we draw close together, and I'm just beginning to think everything is going to be okay…

"What's your hurry, sweetheart?" one of the men asks. The syllables are slurred, run together, and my fast-beating heart explodes into flight when he blocks my path.

"Excuse me," I say to two of the others, who are now standing next to him. When they don't move, I make the mistake of looking up for a second, and I lock gazes with the fourth man, who hasn't said a word so far.

But as our eyes meet, his widen. And then they dart to the notice board behind me.

"Hey!" he shouts a little drunkenly. "It's the girl. The one they're looking for, who's impersonating the princess."

"Nah. Can't be," one of the others replies. But he pulls a familiar-looking paper from his pocket.

Done being polite, I try to push past them, but they spread out to block every avenue of escape.

Panic floods me like cold water. "Let me past," I say, summoning every ounce of false bravado I have inside me as I deliver the words.

"Shit, she even sounds like a princess!" one of the others crows. "We're going to be rich!"

Forget reasoning with them. I whirl around and try to run, but one of them grabs my arm before I can get more than a couple of steps. He pulls me backward, against him, until my back is flush with his chest.

Adrenaline is tearing through me now, and my chest is heaving with tears and terror I refuse to give in to. Instead, I drop the bags and try to fight back, kicking my heels against his shin and punching back over my head.

He just laughs and swings me around.

"It's dead or alive, and I don't really care which," he says, the cheap alcohol on his breath making my eyes water. Or at least that's the story I'm sticking to as he continues. "Do you?"

I do, yes. I really, really do.

Lowering my head, I bite the hand that's holding me so hard that my teeth break through dirty flesh. Blood and who knows what other nastiness flood my mouth and I nearly gag. But I hang on, at least until he lets me go with a shout and a curse.

I take off running, pulling my robe up so I don't trip on it as I race down the sidewalk.

But I don't get far before a fist punches me in the back, and I lurch forward, losing my balance. I sprawl to the ground, hitting my face on the pavement so hard that my own blood fills my mouth this time.

Still, I try to scramble to my feet, but a boot covers my back, pressing me into the ground so firmly I can almost hear my ribs crack. The pain is sharp and sudden. I can't breathe, can't draw air into my lungs, and the panic is rising in me. I'm going to die. Here on this dirty street, surrounded by strangers who just want a big payday.

And there's absolutely nothing I can do about it.

CHAPTER 22

Kali

"Let her go."

The voice, quiet and authoritative, comes from in front of me. Ian.

I close my eyes as relief floods my pain-racked body. I've never been so pleased to hear anyone's voice in my life.

"Piss off," snarls the one whose foot is currently digging into my back.

"I can't do that," Ian returns. "And you've got about three seconds to take your fucking boot off the princess before I blow your fucking head off."

"That's no princess. Haven't you seen the posters? Maybe we'll cut you in after—"

"One," Ian says. There's a sudden flash of light, and the pressure is gone. I roll over, gasping for breath, and my lungs fill with the stench of burning cloth and…meat. Roasting meat. Ugh…

"I suggest the rest of you leave. Now."

There's another flash and the sound of running feet.

I blink my eyes open to see Ian looming over me. "You really shouldn't wander off, Princess."

I just stare up at him, trying to find my voice in the swirl of pain and relief.

"Are you all right?" He's starting to sound worried. "Can you move? We have to go because they'll be back. Probably with a shitload of reinforcements."

"Y-You didn't count to three," I tell him. It's the only thing I can think of to say that doesn't have me blubbering all over him.

At first he doesn't seem to get what I'm referring to, but then he lifts an eyebrow. "Yeah, well, they weren't playing fair. Why should *I*?"

It's a good point, so I simply push myself up into a sitting position, then let out a little squeak of surprise and revulsion.

There's a dead man next to me. A laser blast has taken out half of his chest, and it's still smoking. I swallow down the newest round of bile, scooting back as fast as my still-shaking legs can push me.

Part of me thinks I should be sorry—death is a terrible thing—but the truth is, I'm not. He was a truly horrible man. I can still hear his creepy laughter, can still feel his boot pressing down on my back as he hinted at some seriously sinister plans for me.

"Come on now, Princess. Give me a bit of that attitude. That stiff royal backbone you're so proud of." Ian still sounds worried as he holds out a hand to help me up.

I stare at it for a second, not sure if I should take it. But then I remember he spent all afternoon leading me around by the hand. It seems ridiculous to worry about the rules now. Especially because: "Apparently, I'm not a princess after all. I'm just pretending."

He snorts as I grasp his hand and let him pull me to my feet. "Can you run?"

I want to tell him that of course I can, but my back is still throbbing. I release his hand and say, "I think so."

He's picking up the bags I dropped when they attacked me. "Good. Then let's go."

The first couple of steps are agony, but I grit my teeth and take it, because the alternative is still being here when they come back, and I quite strongly don't want that to happen. But as we turn the corner, I hear a shout from behind us.

It only takes a few seconds before other people join in, until the whole street sounds like a pack of baying prupples.

"Shit," Ian growls. He picks up speed, and I grab the skirt of my robe and run like my life depends on it, ignoring the pain that continues to shoot through me. It's nothing compared to what I'll feel if they catch us, and I know it.

Ian rockets down an alley, then hesitates. "Fuck," he growls, and it's not hard to figure out why he's upset. The shouts are getting louder.

"Onto the roof," he orders.

I repeat the words in my head, but they make no sense. *Onto the roof.* How does he expect us to get up there? Fly? "I'm sorry?"

"We have to get on the roof." He looks around. "You can climb on that refuse bin, then swing up."

"I—I can't." I shake my head vehemently. Climbing has never been my thing. My physical education tutors couldn't bribe or punish me into the simplest wall-climbing exercise as a child. Plus, my ribs hurt so badly, I'm almost sobbing. "I'll never make it that high."

"Never say never, Princess." He wraps his hands around my waist and pretty much lifts me on top of the bin before levering himself up next to me.

I take a deep breath, then immediately regret it. The bin stinks like nothing I've ever smelled before. Ian doesn't seem to notice as he tosses the bags onto the roof, then grips the edge and swings himself up. He makes it look so easy. But he's taller than me and I suspect a good deal stronger.

"Come on," he says. "You can do it."

But I can't. I try several times, and I can't even reach the edge, my blood pulsing in my head with each throb of my midsection. "Just go," I tell him. "You're running out of time."

For a moment, I fully expect him to disappear and leave me—it's what I did to him earlier, after all. But then he drops to his stomach and hangs over the edge, holding his right arm out to me.

He's giving me a literal lifeline, and I don't have to be asked twice. I grab onto his hand and jump as Ian heaves. For a second, I'm dangling over the bin, feet kicking wildly in all directions. Then the roof is right there in front of me. I grab the edge with my free hand while he grips the back of my robe with his. Then we're both pulling up, up, up, and then I'm over. I land on my face, then quickly roll over to my back, my entire body throbbing with pain.

"Thank—"

"Shhh," he interrupts, flattening himself against the dark blue roof.

I clamp my lips together and lie very still as I stare up at the rapidly darkening sky. The moon is rising. My heart slams against my chest loudly enough that I'm sure our pursuers can hear.

Below us, footsteps enter the alley. They get about halfway into it before they slow down, and my stomach churns sickly. They're going to find us and kill us, and…I don't want to die.

It's not the first time I've had that thought tonight—all for different reasons. Which is bizarre. Four days ago, the most dangerous thing I'd ever done was help my mother host a conciliatory dinner while the Council was feuding and threatening to implode at any second.

The murmur of voices floats up from below, but they're talking so quietly that I can't make out the words.

Beside me, Ian is breathing slowly and evenly, and I try to match my breaths to his. But waiting on them feels like an eternity.

Finally, the footsteps move away. They're leaving.

I'm shaking with relief and pain as I start to sit up, but Ian stops me with a hand on my arm that has me lying still. We wait just like that for another five minutes or so, maybe seven, until he's sure they're gone. Then he sits up.

I can see his face in the dim light, the sharp angles of his cheekbones. His dark eyes are gleaming. "You're a hell of a lot of trouble, Princess."

I know. And I don't really understand why he keeps helping me. I'm just glad he does.

Tears prick at my eyes at the thought, but I blink them away. I'm fed up with feeling pathetic. I sit and hug my knees to my chest.

"Why the fuck did you run?" he asks.

For a moment, I don't know what he means. I'd somehow forgotten about the men he killed. Now it all floods back. "You gouged that man's eyes out. It was horrible."

"He would have done the same to me. And probably worse to you."

I shudder at that. After the last half hour, I believe him. "That final man was running away. You killed him anyway."

"He wasn't running away. He was trying to find you." He gives me a look, but I'm not sure what he's trying to convey. Pity, maybe. "You're not in the palace anymore, Princess. You're out in the real world, and it's not a nice place. You adapt or you die."

I consider his words. After everything I've seen, I know he's right. But how can someone who's lived her whole life in the darkness adapt overnight to the light?

"Ian. If we get back to the *Starlight*, will you teach me to fight?"

Shock flashes across his face. "You want to be able to fight?"

"I do. And maybe Gage can teach me a few things about computers?"

He rolls his eyes at that. "That man may be a genius, but a teacher he is not."

"Look," I continue. "I obviously can't rely on you being there every time I get into trouble. Those men would have killed me with pleasure, and there was nothing I could do to stop them, even though I tried."

He looks like he wants to say no, but in the end he just shrugs. "I guess I could have a go at it. But my training won't come cheap."

"Well, you've taken all my valuables already. Consider yourself paid."

"Nah. That money was for all of us. Don't worry; I'll think of something." He blows out his breath and runs a hand through his hair. "We'll wait five more minutes and then make a move. What shall we do in the meantime?"

I try to lean back on my arms but wince at the pain.

"Are you hurt?" He reaches out and gently touches a finger to my lower lip. A shiver runs through me. "There's blood on your mouth."

"I banged it into the ground." Not for the first time, it occurs to me just how few people have actually touched me in my life. And never like this.

I feel strange—weepy and weird—totally unlike myself. Maybe that's because I don't know who I am anymore—if I ever did.

Ian brushes his thumb over my cheek, and I try not to flinch. I like the gentle way he's touching me, like even more the way his hand makes me feel as it softly strokes over my skin. But it's scary, too, to be touched when I almost never am. Scarier still for it to feel so good.

"Don't cry, Princess," Ian murmurs. "I don't do crying women."

What a surprise. "Do they scare the big, bad Ian?"

I expect him to laugh, not answer with an earnest, "Fuck yes."

It makes me smile, but that hurts my lip, and I wince again.

"I hate that he hurt you," Ian says, then frowns. "And I don't understand why it matters so much. In my world, everyone gets hurt."

He leans in closer then, and I go entirely still. There's a look in his eyes, half calculating, half fascinated. And all of a sudden I have this bizarre idea that he's going to kiss me.

My breath wedges in my throat as I tell myself that I'm mistaken. That I'm absolutely, positively misjudging his intent. After all, I've never been kissed before. How would I know what a guy looks like before he does it?

But then Ian's rough palm is sliding around the back of my neck, and I decide that, never kissed or not, at this point his intent is pretty hard to mix up. Even before he tilts my head up so I'm gazing into his dark eyes and I can see the intent plainly written there.

But there's a reason I've never been kissed. People do not just kiss a princess of Senestris.

Unless you're Ian, in which case you do anything you want. And as unbelievable as it might seem, it appears that what Ian wants is to kiss me.

This close, I breathe in the scent of him, hot and rich and like nothing I've ever experienced in my life. For just a second, his gaze goes vacant, almost like he's thinking about something a million kilometers away from here. Then he's back as he lowers his head until his lips touch mine, and all rational thought vanishes.

I close my eyes and lean into him, hoping that he'll kiss me again. Harder and more thoroughly this time.

Except he's already pulling away.

I blink, fighting the urge to drag him back to me. But there's a little frown line between his eyes that says he wouldn't come even if I tried.

"You act like you've never been kissed, Princess."

Seriously? That's what he's hung up on? "Obviously," I tell him. "You do remember the no-touching rule, right? Well, believe me, it makes kissing pretty fucking impossible."

For a second, a hint of understanding glimmers in his eyes. "Sure. I get it," he says.

I shake my head. "Absolutely no way you could."

"Story for another day, Princess." For once, the title doesn't sound like an insult when he says it. Maybe because he's so close that I can feel his heart beating against my own, even before he lowers his head. And then his lips are right there, about to meet mine, and he whispers, "Open your mouth."

Trust Ian to be giving orders even now. But where it normally irritates me to no end, at the moment it just gets me…hot. Maybe that's why I do what he asks, parting my lips on a soft, tiny gasp.

When his hands wrap around my biceps, his touch is different. Harder.

And then he presses his open mouth to mine, and heat washes through me like a waterfall.

I drown in it for a beat—drown in him—but a few seconds later, his tongue pushes inside my mouth and I start to panic. Because a part of him is inside me now, and I don't know what to think about that, how to feel about it. His tongue is *touching mine*.

But then his hands slide into my hair, and he angles my head so he can deepen the kiss, and the waterfall becomes an avalanche of sensation. Of need, sizzling over my skin and burning along my every nerve ending.

And then I'm kissing him back, thrusting my tongue into his mouth so I can taste him. Feel him. Explore him.

And still it's not enough. I want more of him, more of the heat pulsing through my body. I'm out of control and acting purely on instinct as I press myself even more tightly against him. I didn't know kissing would be like this, and now I can't believe I waited so long to try it.

When every part of my body is trembling and I'm running out of oxygen, he finally lifts his head. "Fuck, Princess. If you take to fighting like you took to kissing, we'd better all watch out."

I'm not quite lucid enough to unravel what he means, but I think there's a compliment in there somewhere. Maybe.

I want to kiss him some more, but he's pulling away and getting to his feet. He stares down at me. "Stop looking at me like that."

"Like what?"

He smirks. "Like you want to get into my pants, Princess."

I sniff. "You're delirious."

"Maybe. But I'll warn you now—I don't do relationships. So, if you're looking for more than a quick fuck, you're out of luck."

Fuck! Trust Ian to ruin everything. "Totally delirious. Did you bang your head back there while you were gleefully committing murders?"

He ignores me and continues. "I've been looking out for one person for as long as I can remember, and one person only."

I frown because that doesn't sound right. "What about Max and Milla?"

Something flashes across his face before he shrugs. "Yeah, well, they don't count." And suddenly he's all business again as he gathers up the bags and makes his way to the edge. "All looks quiet. Let's get back to the ship. Hopefully Gage will have taken care of the rest of the supplies and we can get the fuck out of here."

He jumps lightly onto the refuse bin, making it look easy. I stare, trying to work out how to get down with minimal pain. I sit on the edge, then turn around and start lowering myself as gently as I can.

My already aching back screams at the movement, but I ignore it—and my shaking biceps. But then Ian's big, calloused hands circle my waist, and I let out a squeak.

They glide up and over me as he lowers me to the metal surface, and I'm sure I'm about to go up in flames. But then he turns me around and lets me go.

"Do you have anything on under that thing?" he asks, looking me up and down. And though I know the robe doesn't show anything, I suddenly feel very, very exposed—in the best possible way.

I think about prevaricating, but I figure he already knows the answer. His hands were just all over me. "No." My voice catches in my throat at the sudden gleam in his eyes. "Remember the very, very tight dress? There wasn't room for anything but me under there."

At first, he doesn't say anything, but eventually he blows out a long breath as he runs a hand through his hair. "Fuck. You really are messing with my head, Princess. Not to mention other parts of me." He takes a reluctant step back. "Let's go."

CHAPTER 23

Rain

After we heard the shot, Beckett and I raced back to the ship—not easy in a water-logged floor-length robe. No one else was in sight, but we heard more gunshots coming from the main port area. Beckett dove right into the pilot's seat and had the engines running before I even sat down along the left wall of the triangle-shaped bridge, where I'm now trying to calm my racing heart.

"Buckle up," she tosses over her shoulder. "This might get rough." There's a grin on her face, like she likes it rough, and that sends a frisson of *something* shivering through me.

Or maybe it's just the wet robe.

My hands are trembling, and I'm fumbling with the harness as Merrick runs through the door, closely followed by Gage. Merrick stops dead at the sight of me, relief flashing across his features. He looks so different without his robe, sort of tough and dangerous and…admittedly very handsome. I've never thought of him like that before—I've never thought of *anyone* like that before.

It's as if this whole trip, from the moment I first saw Kali and especially now, thanks to my time with Beckett, has awakened something new inside me—something that makes me think about a lot of things I never did before.

"You're wet," Merrick says, giving me a funny look.

"I went for a swim."

"You don't swim," he deadpans.

"I was born on Askkandia, remember?" I tease. "It must be in my blood."

Merrick just huffs, then glances at Beckett and frowns, probably because of her wet hair.

There's nothing in the Book of the Dying Sun against priests and priestesses having relationships, even with those outside the faith. Though, from what I've gathered, it is unusual for a high priestess to have a relationship with an outsider—unusual for her to have any relationships, actually—because usually we don't leave the monastery and it's hard to meet interesting people stuck in there. Not that I'm saying those of us in the Sisterhood are boring, but Merrick's pretty much the most interesting person in there, and he's a verified stick in the mud.

I glance at Beckett. "Boring" is definitely not the first adjective that comes to mind when I think of her.

Sexy. Smart. Fascinating. Definitely not boring.

I clear my throat. "Where are the others? Are they okay?"

At that moment, Kali races in, still dressed in Merrick's robe and clutching a bunch of bags to her chest. She drops them on the floor and runs to where Beckett is prepping the ship for takeoff.

"Where are the others?" I ask.

"They're coming. Max is picking up the final supplies, and Ian went to meet up with him to help."

I let out a sigh of relief that no one's been shot. But then I take in Kali's expression. "What's wrong, then?" Because clearly something is—she looks like she's in shock.

"There was a solar flare behind us," Kali says, breathing hard. "Just as I got on the ship. And I'd swear it came straight from the *Starlight*."

Beckett glances over her shoulder and frowns. "Unlikely."

"I thought so as well, at first," Kali says. "But I know what I saw. Can we see what's happening behind us? Ian and Max are in trouble."

"I'm yours to command, Princess," Beckett replies in that snarky tone she always uses with Kali. It's obvious she doesn't like her, but then again, Beckett is an admitted member of the Rebellion, so I guess it makes sense. Kali's family would be her number-one enemy.

A screen above Beckett's head lights up—I didn't even know there were screens on the ceiling, and from their expressions, no one else did, either—and then it flickers to reveal the view from the back of the ship. I lean forward against my harness to get a better look.

"Holy crap," Beckett mutters. But she's grinning again. "Looks like you might have been right about the flare. Though I really don't think it came from here. A ship can't do that."

I don't want to doubt Kali, but I'm kind of with Beckett on this one. We might be on the far edge of the spaceship docking area, but the screen zooms in enough to show that the whole town of Rangar is suddenly on fire. The buildings are a mass of flames reaching up to the sky with people running everywhere. I watch in pure horror as townspeople run out of burning buildings, carrying children, pets, their life's possessions.

And then, from the middle of the conflagration, emerge Ian and Max. They're running as if their lives depend on them getting to this ship.

Then again, they probably do. I watch as one of the buildings collapses behind them, sending waves of sparks and flames shooting across the lake.

"We have to help those people!" I start, but Merrick stops me with a light hand on my shoulder.

"This is Askkandia," he says, then clarifies: "They have plenty of water. They'll be able to put out their own fires."

We watch, our hearts in our throats, as the two guys leap for the ship's ramp. Beckett doesn't even wait for them to make it to the top of the ramp before she presses a button. And then we're rising, the ship shuddering violently as she lifts away from the planet.

My heart rate slows a bit as I see people working large hoses full of water, shooting toward the buildings and starting to put out the flames, before the ship shoots forward without Beckett touching anything else—almost like the ship was waiting for the men to get on board.

It moves so fast and hard that I'm flung back in my seat. Kali goes slamming against the wall, and Merrick just topples over, crashing to the floor with a resounding, "Fuck!"

I don't think I've ever heard him swear before. I don't think I even knew he *could* swear.

Beckett just laughs, so wildly and freely that it gives my heart wings to hear it.

A minute later, Ian appears in the doorway, a grin on his face. "That was...something."

"You're horrible," Kali tells him. "You burned the place down."

"We had nothing to do with that." Max appears behind him. "It was an act of fate. Or, more likely, an act of the Dying Sun. Did you pray for us, Rain?"

"It doesn't work like that," I answer. Though every once in a while, I wish it did.

"Were you worried about us, Princess?" Ian teases.

She looks straight at him as she answers, "Yes."

His eyes widen, and his mouth goes slack. And then the shock is gone, just as quickly as it came. "Get used to it, sweetheart. There's never a dull moment when I'm around."

She shakes her head, sinks into the nearest chair, and closes her eyes. "Just tell me the food got here," she says to the room in general. "I'm famished."

"It did," Max answers with a grin. "I'll go sort it out. I think we could all do with a little something."

"A big something," Kali mutters. "Huge."

He smiles at her, then puts a hand on her shoulder and murmurs something quietly to her that I can't quite hear. Whatever it is, it has a wide, surprised grin flashing across her face.

He winks at her in response, then walks out of the bridge, whistling a song I don't recognize under his breath.

And now I'm really, really curious about what he said. I'm not supposed to be—high priestesses aren't supposed to care about anything as mundane as simple human interactions—but I've never been a very good high priestess. At least not on the inside. And the longer I'm out of the monastery, the more I think I might not want to be a good one on the outside, either. If being good was in the Light's will, then why would I have such a strong urge to be bad?

"Do you think anyone will follow us?" Merrick asks, and maybe I don't know him as well as I think I do, but I'd swear he sounds hopeful.

"Not a chance," Ian replies. "The port doesn't have any aerial support. They might get a message out to the capital—there are ships stationed there. But we'll be long gone before they manage to get in the air." He moves to stand beside Beckett. "Set a course for Vistenia."

"Vistenia coming up, Captain," she replies in her usual snarky tone. It lacks the sharpness she uses with Kali, though.

Max returns a lot sooner than I expect him to, especially since he's carrying a box that smells divine. "The provisions are mostly dehydrated crap, stuff that will keep longer than a few days. But there was some fresh food as well." He places the box on the floor between us.

My stomach rumbles and my body acts on autopilot as I get out of my chair and shift as close to the source of those amazing aromas as I can get.

"How did you make that so fast?" I ask Max. "You were only gone a few minutes."

Gage enters carrying plates and cutlery. "I've been cooking since the supplies got here," he answers. "But I figured we'd all prefer to eat in here, where we can keep an eye on things." He starts handing out the plates while I crouch down and stare at the bounty before us.

"Stop looking at it and eat," Kali suggests. I was so intent on the food that I hadn't even noticed her standing beside me.

I know I should wait, should let everyone else fill their plates first—it's the way of the Sisterhood—but I'm so hungry, I can't do it. Instead, I start piling my plate with a still-warm roll, some green fishgalen-based dish I don't recognize, and a couple of scoops of roasted vegetables and yellow rice.

Beckett is still in the pilot's seat, so I make a plate for her, too. I add an extra roll and an extra serving of fishgalen because she looks like she needs it, then carry it over to where she's fiddling with the console in front of her.

She glances between me and the plate, and her eyes widen. "For me?"

I nod. She's so surprised when someone does something for her—it makes me think that it's been quite a while since anyone's taken care of her. It also makes me want to shower her with every kindness I can.

"Thanks," she mutters a few seconds later, already shoving a forkful of rice in her mouth.

I turn back to retrieve my own plate and find Merrick watching me. His eyes are narrowed in that way he gets when he's thinking hard about something he doesn't particularly like.

In this case, I'm afraid what he doesn't particularly like is Beckett. I know it's probably just because he's worried about my safety—Beckett just came off a prison ship, after all. But the more I get to know her, the less that matters to me. She's a good person. Different, yes. Hurt, for sure. Maybe even confused. But I can see she's decent. Really decent.

I give Merrick a serene smile—one that tells him he has nothing to worry about. Somehow, though, it backfires, because he looks even more concerned.

But I'm too hungry to worry about it right now, so I grab my plate and sit down cross-legged on the floor to eat.

We don't have fishgalen on Serati for an obvious reason—no water, no fishgalen. So the colorful chunks of green flesh coated in some sort of creamy sauce I've never tasted before are extra delicious. The rice—also something that isn't served in the monastery—is incredible, too. I savor every mouthful and don't stop until my stomach is about to burst.

"Good?" Kali says with a smile.

"So good," I agree.

"You know, I think food tastes better when you're hungry," she says. "I don't think I've ever noticed that before."

"I'm pretty sure that's because you've never been hungry before,"

Beckett tells her in a snide tone.

Kali bites her lip but doesn't respond, and Beckett goes back to eating.

Ian disappears and comes back a minute later with two bottles dangling from his fingers. He hands one to Max and then pulls the stopper and takes a long sip. "Fuck, I needed that. It's been a long few days."

"Are you going to tell us what happened down there?" Merrick asks.

"Yes, just not yet, because I'm fucked and I need a drink." He takes another long pull and then holds the bottle out to Kali. "You want some gerjgin, Princess?"

"Can I have it in a glass?"

He smirks. "Scared you're going to catch something?"

"I think it's probably too late to worry about that," she mutters. Then her eyes widen as if she's just realized what she said.

Ian laughs. "Don't worry, Princess. I won't tell anyone you kissed me on a rooftop under the setting sun."

All of us are watching them now. It's like watching a story play out in real time.

"Is that how you remember it?" Kali glares at him.

He lifts a brow. "We can try it again. See how you remember it the second time."

"Third," she mutters, which only makes him laugh harder.

She growls deep in her throat, then snatches the bottle from him and takes a really big gulp. Her eyes widen, but she swallows and hands it back as if it's a challenge.

"That's my girl," Ian says with a smirk.

She narrows her eyes at him. "You're a jerk. You know that?"

"Never pretended to be anything else, Princess." He tilts the bottle to his lips, but not before giving her a wink that makes her snarl a string of uncomplimentary things (almost) under her breath.

I can hear them, and I'm pretty sure Ian can, too, but he doesn't look the least bit upset. Which doesn't make any sense to me. If Beckett said something mean about me now that we've kissed, I'm pretty sure I wouldn't be able to stop myself from crying.

But Ian just takes another pull of gerjgin before passing the bottle to Merrick while Gage hands around glasses. I take one, and Max pours some amber liquid into it from his bottle. I've had fruit liquor in the monastery but never gerjgin, which I believe is alcohol distilled from some sort of grain.

I sniff it. It has a warm, musky smell that isn't the least bit unpleasant.

I take a small sip and roll it on my tongue. It's hot and harsh, but I like it. I swallow and take another sip. Almost immediately, I can feel the heat in my belly. I *definitely* like it.

I empty the glass in one swallow, then look up to find Max watching me, a small smile on his face.

"Can I have another?"

He grins and tops off my glass with a waggle of his brows.

I scoot back to lean against Merrick's chair, then peer around me. These people are all so different. So vibrant and alive, even their bad parts. And I know it's a really wrong thought, but if the *Caelestis* hadn't gone down, I wouldn't be right here, right now, with them. People probably died on the space station, and I hate that so much, but since I'm here, I want to notice everything. Do everything. Feel everything. One day soon, I'll be back in the monastery, where I'll spend the rest of my life locked away forever.

But for now, I'm on a spaceship headed to Vistenia, flown by the girl who gave me my very first kiss. And my second, as well. How could I possibly regret a moment of this?

"Hey, you ready to try out some new clothes?" I look up at the sound of Kali's voice. "Because I'm more than ready to ditch my outfit—no offense, Merrick."

"None taken," he answers, sounding surprisingly mellow as he takes another sip of gerjgin. And I have to say, now that I know how much it chills him out, I think I'm going to keep a flask on my person at all times.

"You found some clothes?" I ask, leaning forward.

"Yeah, let's go see if they fit. I hope so, because I somehow don't think we'll be welcome at the shop again." She thinks for a moment. "Or anywhere else on Askkandia, for that matter."

It's still hard to read her expressions, but I don't think she looks sad when she says it, just pensive, and I wonder what could possibly have happened to her and Ian out there. Yes, the fire was bad, but Askkandia is her home planet. She lives at the palace, for the Light's sake. How can she possibly think she won't be welcomed back there?

And if that's actually true, how can she sound so nearly okay with it? She's talking about her mother. I'd do anything for a chance to know my parents.

I get up to follow her and find myself swaying a bit. My head feels weird, and I'm a little dizzy.

Kali leads the way, and I follow. I can feel a lot of eyes on us, but I don't look back. I've never had clothes other than my high priestess robes, and part of me knows I shouldn't be excited about the idea. But I am.

Please, please, please don't let them be white.

We head to the room we've been sharing. When Kali hands me the bottle as she starts tipping out the contents of the bags onto the beds, I take a gulp of gerjgin.

"I got two each," she says. "In case of disasters. And I had to guess the sizes, so I hope they fit."

The first is an all-black jumpsuit. My excitement fizzles a little, even as I tell myself that black is technically better than white. Or at least different, which is nice.

But Kali tosses it aside, along with another similar outfit. "Those are for Beckett," she tells me. "She seems like the sort of person who'd appreciate black."

I can't help smiling at that. Partly because she's right—Beckett does seem like someone who likes black, a lot—and partly because Kali thought of her even though they don't get along. If someone was as mean to me as Beckett is to Kali, I'm not sure I'd go out of my way to buy this person two new jumpsuits. But Kali did, because she's really sweet. I just wish Beckett could see that instead of whatever bad things she thinks she sees.

"These are for you," Kali says, handing me a bag.

Not white, not white, please not white.

I give her back the bottle and peer inside. Then squeal with delight when I catch sight of what's inside.

CHAPTER 24

Rain

I reach in greedily, desperate to touch what I see.
The first jumpsuit is a gorgeous cobalt blue with shocking pink piping, and it's the most beautiful thing I've ever seen. It's definitely the most beautiful thing I'll ever wear. I stare at it for several seconds, and then I burst into loud, wild tears.

"You don't like it?" Kali asks, serene voice tinged with panic. "I'm sorry. I thought you'd prefer color after all the white, but if you want the black ones instead, I'm totally okay with Beckett having to walk around with a bunch of pink on her jumpsuit."

That makes me laugh, but it doesn't stop the tears. So now I'm crying and laughing at the same time, which I think alarms Kali even more. "It's okay," I tell her when I can finally talk again. "I love it. And I love you. You're the best princess *ever*."

"I'm pretty certain my mother would disagree with you, but thanks. How about the other? And there should be some underwear in the bottom, as well."

I pull out the second jumpsuit, which is green with orange piping. I sink to the bed and clutch it to my chest. "Thank you, thank you, thank you."

"You're welcome, though you should probably thank Ian, too."

She gives a small, unconscious smile at his name. "Anyway, I thought I'd get similar clothes for all of us—sort of like a uniform for the crew of the *Starlight*."

"The *Starlight*?"

"Oh, I forgot. That's what we called the ship, because she has this little design on her and because she's the color of starlight. Also, she's an alien artifact."

Shock hits me in the chest at this revelation. "How do you know?"

"The design is the same one that was on the heptosphere. And apparently Gage knew all about it."

I don't know what to say to that, or to the fact that we are actually flying on an alien spaceship right now. Here I am, the High Priestess of the Sisterhood of the Light, standing on a ship built by the Ancients 400,000 years ago. Maybe I *was* meant to be here all along?

It's incredible.

"Get changed, then, and we'll head back to the bridge," Kali is urging me. "I'm getting hungry again." She takes a swig from the bottle, then puts it down and turns her back. "Hurry. I can't wait to see which one you pick."

I take a deep breath and kick off my mid-calf black boots before tugging the robe over my head. Once it's off, I drop it onto the floor at my feet, and somehow it feels like I'm shedding something.

Which doesn't make sense. Me being the high priestess doesn't change just because I'm not dressed like one anymore. It just means I'm making the best of the situation.

All I have on underneath the robe is a pair of white panties, and I strip these off as well. I pull a black pair from the bag, along with a black sleeveless top with support seams, and put them on before climbing into the blue jumpsuit. The pink piping is my favorite.

I can hear Kali changing behind me as I fasten the closures on the jumpsuit. I've never worn anything so formfitting before, and it feels strange, like a second skin.

But oh, the color makes my stomach jump with joy. I know that it shouldn't matter, know that caring about things like this means I'm so, so shallow. But it's hard to worry about that when I feel so good.

Kali included two pairs of rainbow-colored socks in the bag as well, and I nearly start crying all over again. Instead, I slide a pair on my feet before putting my boots back on. I realize no one else will know I'm wearing rainbow socks, but I will, and that's all that matters.

When I'm finished getting dressed, I stare down at myself, trying to reconcile the Rain I've been for so long with the person I look like right now. It's a lot to take in, but it's great. I'm High Priestess of the Sisterhood of the Light, but I have never felt as powerful as I do in this moment, standing here in this tiny cabin, aboard a renegade spaceship, dressed like a space pirate in colors the Sisterhood would never allow.

I reach for the nearly empty bottle and take a big gulp for courage. Then I turn around.

Kali is just pulling on her boots. She's wearing a gray-and-silver jumpsuit that makes her silver eyes—and her curves—really stand out. "You look amazing," I murmur.

She stands up with a grin. "So do you. Pink suits you."

"I think so, too."

Her smile fades into her placid princess face. "Do you mind if I ask you something?"

"Why would I?" After bringing me this jumpsuit, she could ask anything and I would answer it.

"Why don't you look like the other Seratians? I mean, you're beautiful, and so is Merrick, but…"

My heart soars at the compliment, even as I know I pale in comparison to the princess. "I don't have the beautiful skin swirls of most Seratians because my parents are Askkandian."

"Really? So that's why you don't have to wear body armor under your robe like Merrick?"

"Exactly. I do struggle with Askkandian gravity, after all my years on Serati, but not as much as people whose ancestors have lived with Seratian gravity for millennia."

"You'll have to tell me how you ended up there sometime, but right now we should get back and show everyone the results of my first-ever shopping trip."

She grabs the rest of the bags—and her nearly empty gerjgin bottle—and steps into the hallway.

"I've never been shopping, either," I tell her as we make our way back to the bridge. "I never left the monastery before this trip."

"And I hardly ever left the palace," she says wistfully. She takes a look at me. "Seems like we've both grown up with all these expectations. How we're supposed to behave, how people are relying on us, blah, blah, blah…"

Boy, have we ever. I grin. "But at least you got to wear nicer clothes."

"Ugh! You can't mean the slogg dress. It was so unbelievably uncomfortable." She does a little twirl in front of me. "This is much better. I can actually move. I couldn't open my legs in the other one."

Something about that sounds weird, but it just makes me giggle. "It suits you," I say, and it's true. She's so statuesque. Imposing. Curvaceous, even. I glance down at my own much slighter curves. Blue and pink. I sigh happily.

"Ian picked mine—he said it matched my eyes."

I press a hand to my heart. "How romantic!" Maybe it's not so strange that he kissed her if he's paying attention to the color of her eyes.

"Hah. Not even vaguely."

Though her expression has turned a little wistful.

As we continue walking, Kali lifts the gerjgin bottle to her lips and drains it. "I could get a taste for this stuff."

"Something else we have in common," I tell her with a smile. But when we finally make it back to the bridge, I pause in the doorway as nerves twist in my stomach. I've been High Priestess Rain in the cloying white robe for as long as I can remember. I'm not sure I'm ready for anyone else to see me like this.

"Go on." Kali must have figured out what I'm worried about, because she whispers, "Get in there and wow them. You look amazing."

I smile my thanks at her, then take a deep breath and decide there won't be a better time than right now. But as the door to the bridge slides open and I walk in, I'm glad of the alcohol buzz in my brain.

Someone whistles—I'm not sure who, but it definitely isn't Merrick, because he's staring at me with shock stamped all over his features. And for some strange reason that makes me feel *really good*.

I waggle my fingers in his direction as I pass by.

He doesn't wave back. But he does finally manage to pick his jaw up off the floor.

Beckett is still seated in the pilot's chair, facing the console like she wants to keep herself separate from the rest of us. But as we walk farther onto the bridge, she twirls the chair around and her eyes almost pop out of her head. I grin and saunter over, liking the feel of her eyes on me. A lot. And for once, they're clear of pain—a double success, if you ask me.

I hand her the bag with the black jumpsuits. "Your new clothes," I tell her.

She frowns. "When did you—"

"Kali bought them for you."

She glances behind me—presumably at the princess—and her frown deepens. "I don't think so."

"Oh, come on—she picked the perfect color for you." I nudge her playfully.

I can tell that Beckett wants to look inside the bag...badly. But the distrust festering in her eyes when she looks at Kali again seems to be winning out.

"Why don't you go get changed? Won't it be a relief to get out of that thing?"

"I...I guess." She still seems a little shell-shocked. But she clutches the bag as she heads out of the room. "Don't fuck with my ship," she snarls at Ian on her way out the door.

"No promises," he shoots back. But he makes no move toward her pilot's chair, so I sit in it and twirl around a few times, feeling like I just won something significant. Again, I remember that I'm sitting in a pilot's chair...on an alien artifact...flying through space. What even is this life?

The spinning makes my head swim, which isn't a bad thing. But then someone grabs the back and stops me mid-twirl.

"Merrick," I murmur, knowing who it is without even turning around. "Don't you think I look..." I try to come up with a word.

He studies me with half-closed eyes. "Extremely secular? Yes, I do. Is that really what you want?"

"Don't be a spoilsport, Merrick. My robe was wet and dirty and... *white*." I squint up at him. "Anyway, you're not wearing your robe anymore, either."

"That was a little different," he tells me.

"Was it?" I gently remove his hands from the chair and spin around again. "Why did I never notice before that you were so handsome, Merrick?"

He just frowns at me while he shakes his head. "I think you've had enough to drink."

"Oh, no, I haven't. Not *nearly* enough. I like gerjgin. When we get back to Serati, I'm going to ask Sister Grinor if we can have it in the monastery."

His lips actually twitch. "I will look forward to that conversation."

"And I'm *hungry*, Merrick. How am I hungry again?"

"There are cookies," he tells me with a small smile. Apparently, his shock over the jumpsuit has faded.

"No! Really?"

I'm up and out of my seat in a flash. My sweet tooth is a well-known weakness, and Merrick often sneaks sweets into the monastery for me. I sniff out the cookies straightaway—not that it's hard, as they're sitting on the chair next to Max.

I don't even ask if I can have one—I just help myself to a handful. Then sit on the floor with my back against the wall to eat them. Delicious.

"I like the new look," Max tells me. He hands me another glass of gerjgin, and I swallow the whole lot before Merrick can confiscate it. No way am I giving up any cookies or any gerjgin if I can help it.

Max sits down on one side of me, while Gage sits on his other side. Ian and Kali sit across from us—after Ian snags the box of cookies. One more reason I like that guy.

"What's with your friend?" Max asks, nodding toward Merrick, who is still standing. "He doesn't look happy."

"Merrick never looks happy. Merrick," I call to him. "Come and sit down." I pat the empty spot beside me. "I saved you a cookie."

He shakes his head in exasperation, but to my surprise, he comes over anyway. He even grabs the last full bottle of gerjgin as he passes the table before slumping down beside me.

Without saying a word, he cracks open the bottle and takes a long pull. Then another and another.

I'm guessing he's drowning his sorrows.

Also known as me.

CHAPTER 25

Beckett

I smooth the material down over my hips. I think I've always been thin, but now I'm positively scrawny. My hip bones jut out like I haven't eaten a proper meal in… Well, tonight's dinner was the best fucking thing I remember ever eating.

But the jumpsuit fits well, and I suspect—though there are gaps in my memories, so I might be mistaken—it's the nicest thing I've ever owned.

Though Princess Kalinda bought it for me. For *me*.

It's a lot to get my head around. Maybe that's what's giving me a headache. Or more likely it's whatever they did to me on the *Caelestis*. My thoughts are whirling, and I have to concentrate really hard or they get away from me. Sometimes it's like pushing through fog. Though it's cleared a little in the days since I escaped. Rain helps. So does the flying. In my cell, I longed for the freedom of space.

Fly Free.

It's the rebel call.

I remember now.

I return to the bridge but hesitate just outside. Someone is laughing. It's weird; I almost don't recognize the sound. I glance inside. They're sitting on the floor in a sort of circle, passing a bottle around, and they all look more than a little drunk. My eyes are drawn to Rain. She's sitting cross-legged and looks amazing in the tight-fitting jumpsuit. It hugs her slender curves, while the color makes her eyes shine and her hair gleam like strands of sunlight against the dark material.

She's smiling at something Max says to her. Next to her, her big friend is glowering. He's clearly not too happy with the change, but then, if his job is to look out for her, then it probably just got a whole lot more difficult. She looks nothing like a priestess.

I remember the taste of her, like warm honey. The softness of her skin. The silky feel of her hair. The memories are like clearings in the fog.

She's good. Maybe the only truly good person I've ever met. It shines from her.

Is that why I'm drawn to Rain? Am I hoping a little of that goodness will wear off on me?

I've no right to tarnish that goodness. Just because I can.

I tear my gaze from her, and it locks with another. Princess Kalinda's. She raises a brow as she sees me hovering. Is she expecting a thank-you? Not happening. I barely even wanted to take the thing once I realized it was charity from the princess.

Hate. Hate. Hate.

The emotion pounds through my head.

I can't forget everything she's responsible for.

And that reminds me—I don't belong here.

Not with these laughing, happy, *whole* people.

I back away and disappear into the shadows.

Where I belong.

CHAPTER 26

Ian

I drink straight from the bottle, enjoying the feeling as the heat slides down my throat. Not to mention the buzz in my head. It's been a few hours since we started drinking, and though I'd never admit it out loud...I'm having fun.

Beside me, Kali holds out her hand for the bottle. I hesitate—her eyes are already glazing over—but then, it's not my job to control her. She's an adult; she can decide how much she drinks. Besides, she's a cute drunk.

I hand her the bottle and let my gaze wander over her.

She looks seriously hot in that outfit. Like the dress I first saw her in, the jumpsuit accentuates her considerable charms, but it looks a hell of a lot easier to get her out of.

Not that I'm going there.

She leans in. This close, I can see the black circles around her silver irises. They're sort of mesmerizing, like the color of starlight.

She takes a deep pull from the bottle—I'm guessing she's going to have a hell of a headache when she wakes up. Then she waves the bottle at me, gerjgin sloshing over her fingers. "You know, the first time I saw you, I thought..." She trails off.

Seriously? That's when she decides to remember her inhibitions?

I tell myself whatever she was going to say doesn't matter, but I last about fifteen seconds before I prompt, "What did you think?"

"*Desperate, much?*" Max teases me.

"*Fuck off*," I shoot back before turning my attention to Kali again.

She grins. "That you have a really nice ass."

For better or worse, our conversation is drowned out by singing—the unrobed High Priestess of the Sisterhood of the Light is in the middle of learning a truly (and I mean *truly*) raunchy song from Gage, so no one else hears Kali's statement. Or so I thought.

"*I mean, she's not wrong*," Max comments. "*I've heard a lot of people say that to you throughout the years*."

I'm too busy trying not to laugh to answer him. Kali is so going to regret this in the morning. If she remembers. "Are you objectifying me, Princess?"

"I guess I am. Sorry."

She doesn't sound sorry, but hey, neither am I. I like this side of her. Then again, I'm beginning to like every side of her. And that's a problem.

"So?" she says before taking another drink.

"So what?" I ask, mystified.

"*She wants to know what you think of her. Obviously*," Max tells me.

"I want to know what you think of me. Obviously," Kali says at the exact same time.

I don't have to look at Max to know he's grinning at me.

I try to remember. "I think the cloak made the biggest impression."

Her eyes widen. "You liked it?"

"Hell, no. It made you look like a clown."

She sighs heavily. "Apparently, I am a clown." She stares at the bottle a moment, then places it gently on the floor. "And right now, I think perhaps this clown had better go to bed before she becomes a whole circus all by herself."

"Very sensible decision," I tell her, ignoring the disappointment I feel at the thought of this conversation ending.

"Sensible is my middle name." She sounds depressed at the thought.

I have a flashback to how she looked at me after that kiss. Like she wanted more. "Oh, I don't know. I suspect under all that etiquette training, there's an impulsive woman trying to break out."

She sighs again. "You might be right. In which case, it's definitively time to go to bed." She gets to her feet and sways, balances herself with a hand on the wall, and peers down at me. "You killed those men like it was nothing. Would you kill me as easily?"

"If you stand in my way." But I know it's a lie.

"*Do you want her to hate you?*" Max sounds exasperated.

"*Yes.*"

He snorts. "*Liar.*"

She nods. "I'll do my best not to." She turns and walks toward the door.

"Kali, I—" I break off, unsure of what I want to say to her. I just know I hate seeing her look so sad.

But when she swings back around to face me, I've got nothing. So I just rub a hand over my face and say, "Go to bed, Princess."

"Already on it."

I watch as she sways over to the door, banging into every obstacle on the way. My turn to sigh—she's a problem I don't need right now. I have to focus on finding Milla. I can't let anything distract me from that.

"Here, Kali, wait up." Max springs to his feet, briefly interrupting Rain and Gage's noisy chorus. "I'll walk you to your room."

"*What the fuck?*" I demand.

He holds an arm out to her. "*One of us needs to be chivalrous, and it's obviously not going to be you.*"

"Thank you," she says, looping her arm through his after untangling herself from a chair.

"I'll come with you," Gage says, climbing off the floor as well. He shepherds Rain and Merrick down the corridor toward the cabins, though I notice Merrick takes the bottle with him.

I watch them go, and then I'm alone on the bridge. Exactly as I like it. For a second, I imagine what would happen if I was the one walking Kali to her room instead of Max. Not that I'd let anything serious happen when she's drunk, but if she wanted to kiss me one more time, I wouldn't say no. Which is exactly why I didn't offer to walk her. Neither of us is completely in our right minds tonight.

The only problem is, I'm not sure I've been in my right mind since I saw her. It sure as shit doesn't feel like it.

One more reason it's for the best that I didn't walk her to her room.

Fuck it. I'm not going to think about this—about her—anymore. Nothing good will come of it. Nothing good is going to come of getting too close to a woman who comes with a death penalty attached.

CHAPTER 27

Ian

I wake up sprawled on the floor several hours later with a crick in my neck and a raging hard-on.

Which makes me think of the princess. And that kiss. Or kisses, as she reminded me last night. Neither of which is ever going to be repeated.

She'd be way too much trouble. Fuck — truth be told, she already is.

Not to mention there might be some tough decisions to make in the not-too-distant future, and I don't want my judgment clouded by sex. Which means hands — and everything else — off the princess.

So, it looks like it's just me and my hand. Again.

I ignore the disappointment niggling at the back of my mind as I push myself up. My mouth tastes revolting, but then, too much cheap gerjgin has a way of doing that to a person. It was worth it, though, just to see the princess all pink-cheeked and loose-lipped. Especially in that silver outfit I bought her.

Talk about hot.

But thinking about that — about her — isn't going to make my problem any better, so I shove her out of my mind and prepare to start the day.

"You're awake," a voice says from above me. I squint up at whoever it is. Shit, who made that light so fucking bright?

"I thought you were dead," the voice adds. "So I kicked you—sorry—but I wanted to be sure."

My scrambled brain finally puts the voice with the image my aching eyes are seeing in the pilot's chair. Beckett. Because going a round with her is exactly what I want to do when I'm too hungover to hold my own.

"No worries. Never felt a thing," I tell her in an effort to keep things amicable. "Did you want me for something?"

"Not moving," she answers.

I realize she's right. The ship *is* stationary. What the fuck?

I push to my feet and stumble over to the captain's chair. "Do we know why?"

She points to the screen to her left. A woman of few words, Beckett is.

But the screen shows an external view of the ship—exactly what I need to see. Because the *Starlight* has grown...wings?

I check the other side of the ship, and it's the same—two more wings coming off at angles that must make her look like a star now. I peer at them a little closer, and it's a testament to just how much alcohol I had last night that it takes me a full sixty seconds to realize they aren't wings. At least not for flying.

The *Starlight* has angled herself toward the sun. Which means they're actually... "Retractable solar wings," I murmur. "She's powering up."

"Yep," Beckett agrees.

Make that *very* few words.

At least now we know what's powering her—I've been wondering that since the first day. But how the hell long is this going to take? I'm guessing a long time, which fucking sucks, but spaceships use a fuckload of energy.

I scrub a hand over my face and try to get the last of my wits about me. "I'm going to rinse off real quick. Let me know if anything—"

I stop talking as a beam of light shoots from the sun straight at us, momentarily blinding me.

"Fuck!" Another goddamn solar flare. And I'm pretty sure this time we're the ones who are about to go up in flames.

Except...several seconds pass and nothing happens. What the fuck?

I squint at the screen to avoid burning my eyes out. Looks like the beam has narrowed to about two meters and takes turns hitting the center of each wing for a few seconds apiece. Then, as quickly as it began, it's over. The wings are drawn in, the engine starts, and we're moving once more.

Beckett grins.

"Fucking cool," I say, because it is. Alien technology sure is a piece of work.

Since we're back on course, I find the nearest bathroom and shove my head under the tap. At least we've got water again, so yesterday's trip wasn't a total clusterfuck.

I grab a towel and scrub the water from my hair. I want coffee, but I have no clue how anything in the galley functions and my brain isn't up to working it out just yet. I'll get there. In the meantime...

"*Max?*"

"*What? I'm sleeping.*"

"*Kick Gage awake, will you? Tell him to get that amazing mind he's always telling us about but we never actually see working on how to make me a cup of coffee.*" Gage might be a lazy bastard, but he did manage to make dinner last night. He's gotta know his way around the galley by now.

"*You woke me up to tell me that? Do it yourself.*"

"*Don't make me beg.*"

Max heaves a long-suffering sigh.

I grin. Mission fucking accomplished.

I fill a glass with water from the purifier and head back to the bridge. The place is a goddamn mess. Empty bottles and food cartons litter the floor. Someone needs to clean up around here.

Since Beckett is busy scrolling through the *Starlight*'s screens, it looks like the job falls to me. A captain's work is never done.

Especially since we also need to decide what to do next—and discuss the little matter that someone has offered a lot of money for us all and they don't care if we're dead or alive.

What's with that, anyway? I ponder as I shove all the dirty dishes and empty gerjgin bottles back in the box they were carried here in. Not a perfect fix, but at least it no longer looks like someone went on a three-day bender in here.

As I bend down to pick up yet another pile of used plates, I notice a small bag of brightly colored items discarded near them. *What do we have here?* The bag is full of bean-like things in all the colors of Askkandia. *Looks like some kind of kid's treat.* Certainly nothing I ever ate before growing up. Figuring this is my reward for cleaning up those ungrateful assholes' mess, I pocket the candy.

After I'm done picking up everything and bringing it into the galley, I move back to my chair.

Beckett is still seated, but now she's twiddling with a bunch of knobs and pressing buttons.

Does she know what she's doing? Does she care? Somehow, I doubt it.

"Did you know the ship is an alien artifact?" I mention as casually as I can. I want to add, *So pressing random buttons might not be such a good idea because who the fuck knows what will happen*—but I don't want to set her off. Some (rhetorical) buttons even I know not to push.

"Cool." She keeps right on fiddling.

Not taking the hint, then. "Where the hell is everyone?" I mutter. Complaining about the others seems a much safer route to take than questioning her piloting prowess.

"Bed."

"Yeah, well, if I'm awake, then they should be, too."

"I doubt they see it like that."

"I *am* the captain."

"Of course you are." She says it like it's a pat on the head, but I'm still too hungover to take offense. Especially when she adds, "You want me to wake the others up?"

"Hell, yeah." I appreciate the offer—and the time alone to regroup.

Except she doesn't head out to get them. Instead, she just presses another button.

"Rise and shine, everyone." I hear her voice, but simultaneously it comes through some sort of comms system. It's really loud, and it echoes all over the ship. "Your captain has called a meeting on the bridge in ten minutes. Be here or..." She gives a shrug.

"So you're getting the hang of flying this thing, then?" I ask.

She considers the question for a moment; I can see her trying to concentrate. She presses a finger to her forehead, then gives a quick nod. "Sort of. Mostly, she does it herself—who do you think flew her all night? And so far, when I've put in coordinates, she's followed them. But I'm just waiting for us to have a difference of opinion. I'm pretty sure I'll come out on the losing side."

"You think the ship might have an opinion?" That's seriously screwed up. Is she having me on?

"Well, you did just point out she's an alien artifact."

"You think that makes her sentient?" I ask.

She snorts. "I think that makes her something we don't understand."

I consider that for a second. "Good point."

"And there's another thing. That solar flare that took out an entire town but saved your ass back on Askkandia? The princess seems convinced it came from the *Starlight*."

I dismiss the idea right away. "That's impossible."

"That's what I said, but after what we just saw..." She shrugs. "I'm willing to keep an open mind."

That's because she still has one. I'm pretty sure mine was pickled last night, along with the rest of me.

Before I can get my aching head to think about anything else, Rain appears, looking as bright and chirpy as ever.

Her gaze goes directly to Beckett, and she hurries over, totally ignoring me. "You didn't come back last night and hang out with us," she says. "I missed you."

I whistle under my breath. Sooo that's how things are. Interesting. The little priestess is obviously braver than me.

Beckett shrugs. "I was tired."

Rain frowns but doesn't say anything else.

"Don't you have a headache?" I ask Rain. She put away an awful lot of gerjgin last night for such a little thing.

"Oh, sorry, Ian. I didn't see you there."

Of course not. Because, apparently, I'm fucking invisible as long as Beckett is around.

She smiles like a little ray of fucking sunshine. "My head is fine, thank you. In fact, I feel really good."

But before I can ask anything else, like how that's humanly possible, Merrick appears in the doorway. "I'm glad one of us does."

He's squinting out of bloodshot eyes, and he looks a little green around the gills.

Good. I hate suffering alone.

"Are you all right?" Rain asks him.

"I'll live." He doesn't sound as though that's necessarily a good thing.

Max and Gage appear next, Max carrying a tray with a steaming jug of something I hope is coffee and a bunch of mugs. He puts it on the floor, and we all help ourselves. Except Merrick, who looks like he's seriously contemplating puking.

"The head's that way," I tell him, pointing to the nearest bathroom as I lean against the console behind me and breathe in the steaming coffee. A few cups of this, and I might actually feel human again. Maybe.

I give it a couple more minutes—and another cup of coffee—before I ask, "Anyone know where Kali is?" I try to sound unconcerned.

"She's still asleep," Rain replies. "She woke up briefly, rolled over, said it was too early, and went back to snoring. You want me to get her?"

"I'll go."

I swallow the last of my coffee, then pour a fresh cup and head out. But I can feel everyone's gazes on me, so I turn and give them my best don't-fuck-with-me stare.

No one looks impressed, which doesn't surprise me. "What?" I growl.

Everyone else has the good sense to look away—even Max. But

not Beckett. She just lifts a brow before commenting, "We're all just wondering what the princess did to deserve coffee in bed."

Max sniggers.

I ignore them both and head for the room the princess and priestess are sharing. The door is open, but there's no sign of Kali, except for one foot sticking out from beneath a mound of blankets.

I clear my throat. Nothing.

I knock on the open door.

Still nothing.

"Kali!"

"Go away."

"I've brought coffee." I move closer to the bed and wave it near where I think her nose—and the rest of her face—might be.

Not that I know if she even likes coffee. I realize I don't know anything about Kali except that she's a princess and has a lot more gumption than I originally gave her credit for. Well, that and the fact that she is absolutely, positively not like me—or anyone else I've met before.

Eventually, she lowers the blanket and peers up at me, silver eyes gleaming. "Put it on the table and go," she tells me in full princess mode.

At first, it annoyed the crap out of me every time she used that tone, but now I kind of like it. Whenever it comes out, it means I get to mess with her.

Which is why I stroll toward the bed instead of doing what she said.

"If you want it," I tell her, "you'll have to come and get it."

"I can't," she whines. "My head hurts."

"Yeah, well, you shouldn't have drunk so much of my gerjgin, then."

"*Your* gerjgin?" She snorts and then groans. "Paid for with *my* buttons."

She's got a point. But not a very good one. "If you want any say in what we do next"—not that it's up for discussion—"then you'll be at that meeting. Two minutes."

I turn and walk away, taking the coffee with me. She had her chance at it, and now it's mine.

But my last comment must have worked, because there's a scrambling from the bed. I slow down and glance over my shoulder, then immediately regret it.

She obviously slept in her new clothes, and she's currently pulling on her boots. Her dark red hair is loose and tousled around her shoulders, and she looks rumpled and beautiful and far too good, considering she's got a hangover.

"What?" she asks as she finally stands up. "You're looking at me funny."

No, I'm not. Am I? I don't answer, just hold out the coffee, and she hurries over and grabs it, then takes a sip.

"It's cold and bitter."

I snort. "Would you like me to run and get you a fresh cup, Your Highness?"

A smile quirks the corner of her mouth, and then it's gone. "That won't be necessary. Lead the way." She sounds just like a princess.

As we head back to the bridge, she pauses around the center of the ship and places her hand on the metal of the inner walls. Then she closes her eyes for a moment, a soft smile curling her lips.

"What are you doing?" I ask when she finally opens her eyes. Somehow, she looks significantly better than she did a few seconds ago.

But she just shrugs. "Saying hello. I get the feeling this is the heart of the ship. It almost feels alive to me."

I don't know what to say to that, especially after Beckett and I just had our *is it sentient or not* conversation. So I shake my head and keep walking. I've got a meeting to run.

Back on the bridge, Kali helps herself to another cup of coffee before slumping down in one of the seats. I take what is objectively now *my* captain's chair, stretch out my legs, and survey my crew. They're a sorry lot at the best of times. Right now, they look like every one of them has at least one foot in the grave.

Except for Rain, who is way too fucking cheery. She must have the constitution of a giant drokaray.

Kali smothers a yawn. "Are you going to tell us why we're here so we can go back to bed?"

I give her a cool stare. She doesn't look impressed, just yawns again. "I thought you'd be interested in discussing the fact that someone wants you dead and they're willing to pay a lot of money to make that happen."

She sits up straight. "Those damn flyers."

"What flyers?" Merrick asks, sounding wary.

I pull some out from where they were folded in my pocket and hold them out to him. He gets up—slowly—and takes them, a frown forming between his eyes as he reads.

He turns to Rain. "It says we're dangerous criminals masquerading as officials from the Sisterhood of the Light."

Her eyes brighten. "Really? How exciting."

I don't even know what to say to that.

Thankfully, Merrick doesn't have the same problem. "I wouldn't exactly say it's exciting that they're offering a lot of money in exchange for what is essentially your corpse."

Rain shrugs, but she doesn't look fazed. "Maybe that's not quite as exciting."

"Apparently, I'm wanted for masquerading as the Princess Kalinda," Kali says. She looks at me. "What are they saying about you?" She gets to her feet and shuffles to where Merrick stands still clutching the flyers and holds out her hand. He passes her a paper, and she glances down at what is presumably the flyer for me. If I remember right, it's a pretty good picture.

"You're a mercenary impersonating a Corporation security officer, and you're wanted for the sabotage of the Imperial Space Station *Caelestis*," she reads, then turns to look at me. "You didn't—did you? Oh Light, please tell me that wasn't all because of you."

"Of course it wasn't me." At least I don't think so. I never did ask Max about the diversion thing.

I do now, and he actually laughs. "*No, man. I didn't bring down an entire space station and our best shot at getting to Milla.*"

Then he nods toward the pile of flyers and says aloud, "I think we can assume that everything in there is a pack of lies."

"So, you're not a mercenary?"

"I wouldn't go as far as to say that," I hedge. Max, Milla, and I have been mercenaries for nearly ten years. We'll do most jobs if the money is right and it doesn't involve killing prupples or baby varlens—Milla is very fond of both.

I'm not ashamed of what we do—if I was, we would have found some other way to survive. But we've always had to rely on ourselves, and it turns out we're pretty fucking good at merc work. Which is a good thing, because a lot of times, it was that or starve.

But Kali's judgmental look is pissing me off. "We weren't all born with a fucking silver spoon in our mouths, Princess."

She looks away.

"What about me?" Gage asks.

"You're our accomplice," I reply. "Apparently, you betrayed your own people. In fact, yours is the only one based on anything closely resembling the truth."

"Accomplice?" He looks offended. "Pretty sure we wouldn't be here at all if it wasn't for me."

"I don't know if you should sound so proud of that fact," Max tells him dryly.

"Is there one for me?" Beckett asks quietly.

"Actually, no. There isn't," I say. There's one for all of us *except* Beckett. I'm not sure why—except maybe no one knows she's on board the *Starlight*.

"So we have to figure they don't know you're with us," I continue. "Maybe you were reported dead on the *Reformer*, though I doubt there was ever a record of you being on the *Caelestis* to begin with. The experiments were hardly legal, even if they were sanctioned."

"We don't know that they were sanctioned," Kali says, but her tone lacks conviction.

Beckett turns to look at her, a sneer curling up the corner of her lip and her fingers twitching in her lap. "You're either extremely naive, extremely stupid, or an extremely great liar, Princess."

Enough. I don't want this descending into a fight. Not before

I give Kali some of those lessons she asked for, anyway. It never occurred to me at the time, but they might come in handy on board the ship, never mind off it.

"Okay, crew, listen up. I want you all to rack your brains for reasons why someone—anyone—might want you dead. And I need to hear them now."

CHAPTER 28

Kali

Well, Beckett certainly hates me. And I'm pretty sure Merrick does as well. But Beckett doesn't have the resources to pay a reward, and Merrick could have killed me in my sleep any night so far—so I figure I can cross them off the list.

Which leaves…literally everyone else? The rebels. All enemies of the Empire. The Sisterhood, since I represent the Empire that's trying to stop the sun from dying. Oh, and Dr. Veragelen didn't seem too fond of me. If she's still alive.

So, in other words, the list of people who might want me dead is quite long. Lucky, lucky me.

Determined not to let anyone see how much this fact stings, I sink into my chair and close my eyes. I don't want to know if anyone else is looking at me the same way Beckett always is. Or even worse, if they're looking at me with pity.

They can't all think I'm stupid and naive, like Beckett said, can they? I know Ian does. He thinks I'm useless. And Merrick. I haven't spent enough time with Max and Gage to know how they feel about me, but it's not like they're sticking up for me right now, is it?

"Princess, are you still with us, or have you decided now's the perfect time for a nap?" Ian asks. I open my eyes just long enough to shoot him a glare, which he completely ignores. But it's not like I can tell him I'm over here having a private pity party.

"You haven't answered the question. Can you think of anyone who wants you dead?" he asks.

"The better question would be if I can think of anyone who *doesn't* want me dead," I start. "When you're in power and richer than everyone else, there are always people who want you dead. My father was assassinated when I was fifteen. It's one of the many reasons my mother has kept me so sheltered from public view. I live with that possibility every day of my life."

"Who arranged for you to be on the *Caelestis*?" Max asks.

"My mother. And no, she did *not* send me there to be assassinated. Believe me, if she wanted me dead, she wouldn't have had to send me all that way to do it."

Ian's face says he agrees with me, though he doesn't want to. He turns to Merrick.

"What about the High Priestess? Anyone want her dead?"

"Of course not. Everyone loves her," Merrick insists.

"Do *you* agree with that?" Ian asks Rain.

Her eyes are wide, and she blinks a couple of times. I actually think she's enjoying this. "Well, admittedly the Sisterhood isn't popular with everyone in Senestris. Certainly climate activists may not *love* me and what I represent. We're often at odds with the Empire. So sure, I guess there could be lots of reasons someone would want me dead. But I mean, if I die, I'll just be reborn again, so what would be the point?"

I can't help wondering if she actually believes that. That every high priestess is really just the same soul reincarnated over and over again. It seems impossible to me.

But something does occur to me. "Why were you on the *Caelestis*?" I ask. "I know you stepped in for Ambassador Frellen, but why *you*? You don't seem…" I search for a way to say this without hurting her feelings, because I genuinely like Rain. I think she might be the nicest person I've ever met.

"Very diplomatic?" Merrick suggests dryly. "Believe me, I've been thinking about the same thing myself. I think maybe the Sisterhood had gotten word about the heptosphere and wanted to see if Rain reacted to it."

Rain and I look at each other. Suddenly, her appearance on the *Caelestis* seems even more mysterious.

"Why would she?" I ask.

He gives a shrug. "There are many stories in our scriptures connecting the high priestess with alien artifacts."

I'd never heard that before, but the Sisterhood is a secretive lot. "And did you?" I ask Rain.

"I don't think so. But I only touched it briefly."

"Okay, so 'everyone' for Kali and 'everyone' for Rain. Cool." Ian rolls his eyes before turning to Merrick. "What about you? You piss anyone off recently?"

"Probably," Merrick answers with a shrug.

"Fucking great," Ian snarls, sounding increasingly frustrated. "Gage?"

"I work for the Corporation," Gage says matter-of-factly. "We aren't exactly popular."

"Fuck!" Ian is pacing now, pulling at the ends of his short hair.

I lock eyes with him. "Well, what about you? I mean, you did kidnap a princess, and you're keeping her here against her will now. It's probably the Empire looking for my safe return."

"That doesn't explain why your face is plastered on those wanted ads right alongside ours, sweetheart," Ian argues. "And for someone who's here against her will, you sure don't seem to be protesting very much."

I let out a huff. "Fine. But I'm sure you've annoyed *someone* to the point of murder recently."

He smirks. "You mean other than you? Sure, every day."

I throw my hands in the air. "So we're no closer to narrowing down who's after us than we were before. *Anyone* could be chasing us, wanting us dead. We're all guilty—which means we're all innocent," I reason.

"Look, I don't know about you, Princess, but no one even knew who Max and I really were on the *Caelestis*," Ian argues. "We just got caught up in someone else's shit."

"Why *were* you on board?" I ask. "I know you're looking for Milla, but what made you think she was on the *Caelestis*?"

For a moment, I don't think he's going to answer. But then he glances at Max, who shrugs.

"Milla was captured about three months ago, while we were on what should have been a straightforward job. But when we broke into the prison she was supposed to have been remanded to so we could rescue her, she was already gone, with no obvious trail as to where she'd been transferred."

"Maybe she's dead," Beckett says, though she at least has the sense to look contrite about it. "They often execute prisoners quickly. I know it's what I expected."

"But what about a trial?" I ask. "People aren't just executed in the Senestris justice system."

Beckett gives a contemptuous roll of her eyes, but she doesn't answer my question.

"She's not dead," Max tells her. "We'd know if she was."

I want to ask him how they can be so certain, but Ian is talking again. "Anyway, we found her after the prison. It took us a little while—we had to get some money together for bribes—but we found out she'd been transferred to the *Caelestis*, though as far as we could tell, there was no official paperwork to back it up. With a few more bribes, we got taken on as guards—their security is actually pretty lax, like they think they're too fucking important for anyone to mess with. But by the time we got there, she was already gone."

"When was this?" Beckett asks.

"About two months ago. We figured she was transferred, so we got our very expensive *accomplice* here"—he waves a hand in Gage's direction—"to break into the records and learned that she was taken off the *Caelestis* and onto the *Reformer*. An illegal prison ship run by raiders out of Vistenia. But there was no record of where she'd been shipped to."

"So we hung around until the *Reformer* was due again," Max continues. "We planned to stow away and find out where the prisoners are taken after Doc V has finished with them. We did manage to figure out that they're not taken back to the prisons."

"Maybe she just dumps them in space," Beckett suggests helpfully. "Problem solved. She really is a miserable fuck."

"Max told you," Ian growls. "Milla is alive."

He seems so sure, but how?

"Anyway," Max continues, "we all know how well that plan went down."

Ian scowls. "Yeah, so now all we can do is make a visit to the *Reformer*'s home port on Vistenia and hope we can bribe or otherwise coerce someone into telling us where she was headed."

"We don't need to go to Vistenia," Beckett says.

Ian's eyes narrow to slits. "If you say Milla is dead one more time, I'll…"

Beckett raises an eyebrow but seems in no way intimidated. "Chill the fuck out, Captain. We don't need to go to Vistenia because I know where the *Reformer* was heading. At least her first stop."

"Why the hell didn't you say something earlier?"

It's Beckett's turn to narrow her eyes. "Because I didn't know you wanted to know. Communication is a two-way street, Captain."

Ian closes his eyes for a moment and takes a deep breath. And when he opens them again, he's smiling—with all of his teeth. "So, could you tell me, oh wise Beckett, where the fucking *Reformer* was fucking heading after it left the fucking *Caelestis*. Pretty please."

"Glacea."

Glacea? Seriously?

"And you know this how?" For the first time, Max sounds as annoyed as Ian.

Beckett shrugs. "When we were taken on board, one of the guards asked. Apparently, they were just refueling on Glacea, but it's likely someone would know where they were heading afterward."

Glacea is the outermost planet of the system. Where could they be heading after that? There's nowhere to go.

"Then set a course for Glacea," Ian says with a wide grin that matches the one on Max's face. "And now would be good."

Blame the hangover-induced insanity, but I can't help smiling along with them. I'm glad he's got a real lead—it's made him happier than I've ever seen him. Again, I wonder who she is to him, to them, but can't bring myself to ask. Not because I'm afraid of the answer but because… I sigh. I'm totally afraid of the answer. Which is ridiculous, considering we've only ever shared a couple of kisses on a rooftop when we were waiting to be sure we weren't going to die.

That doesn't count for anything.

But when he crosses to Max and the two of them start talking excitedly, I suddenly need to be alone.

I get up and walk out, and I don't think anyone even notices me going.

I go to the galley for some water. My head is pounding, my stomach gurgling, and no matter how much I tell myself not to puke, I'm not sure it's actually going to work this time.

Hangovers are as bad as everyone at the palace always said they were.

I'd like to say I've learned my lesson and that I'll never indulge in alcohol again. But the truth is, I liked the way it made me feel. Like someone else—someone free to say whatever I want. I wonder if that's what it feels like to be Beckett, who doesn't need false courage to say what she thinks—or to stand up for herself.

Once I'm in the galley, I notice a huge box of dirty dishes and glasses just sitting on a counter. Clearly, someone started cleaning up but didn't bother to finish the job. *How hard could it be to wash a few dishes?* I think. *Nobody else is going to do it—why* not *me? I can be useful.*

I run some water in the sink and roll up my sleeves. As the crumbs drift down the drain, I think about our next steps. I don't want to go to Glacea. I want to go home and get this whole imposter-princess thing sorted out. Or at least that's what I think I want, before digging a little deeper into how I'm feeling.

The truth is, Ian wasn't too far off when he said I wasn't exactly protesting being on the *Starlight*. These last few days have made me see my life—and the entire Empire of Senestris—in a whole new way.

I mean, here I am with my sleeves rolled up, *washing a dish*.

And sure, I've always known the Empire wasn't perfect. Always known my mother would choose her kingdom over everything else, including my father. And me. She's my mother, and she cares about Senestris. It's why she's been so hard on me.

But it's a far cry from that to everything these people are accusing her of. Or, worse, not accusing her of. Just speaking about it like it's no big deal. Like it's accepted truth.

And I think what scares me the most is that I'm beginning to like these people. Beginning to maybe even trust them a little bit, though I can't say they're affording me the same. So what does it say when everyone except Rain—who's been locked up in a monastery for practically her entire life—thinks my mother is capable of all kinds of terrible things? Even worse, what does it mean when I'm starting to believe it, too?

Rangar was horrible. And I know she is aware of what's going on there—she had a study done on Rangar just last year. But apparently she did absolutely nothing with the results. And I just took her word and the word of the Council that everything was fine.

That the people of Senestris look up to the Ruling Families. That they respect us. That the assassination attempts we worry about are just from jealous people who want that respect and power for themselves.

If any of that's the case, I haven't seen a shred of evidence of it yet.

As for the rest...I don't know what I want. More to the point, I don't know who I want to be. All I know is it's not the perfect little princess my mother's been training me to be. The one who accepts that the way things are is the way things have to be. Maybe I need this—here and now, a chance to see the system as it really is, and then I can formulate a plan for how it should really be and how to get there.

Or maybe I just want to stick around so I can kiss Ian again.

Ugh.

He's another whole story that I don't want to get into right now, I think as I look down and realize I've finished cleaning the entire box of dishes. Huh. Maybe I have actually found something I could be good at—

A giant crash echoes through the ship. It's followed by a scream and another crash—and it all seems to be coming from the bridge.

I'm out the door and running before the second scream rips through the air.

CHAPTER 29

Rain

Ian and Merrick have been arguing the merits of heading to Glacea versus Serati for the past twenty minutes, and if they aren't calmed down soon, someone is bound to get hurt. The air is charged between the two men, noticeably so, as Max looks at Merrick and says, "Stand down."

"I'm not afraid of you," Merrick sneers at Max. "Or you, either."

"Merrick, please stop," I beg. "I'll be good, honest. I'll wear the robe. I won't drink any more alcohol. Please don't fight because of me."

"I'm fighting because it's the right thing to do. What I'm supposed to do. Keep you safe."

"Even if he shoots you?"

"Some things are worth dying for," Merrick answers, his eyes locked with Ian's dark ones.

"Maybe so, but not this." I turn my gaze to Ian and Max. "Please, don't—"

"You don't ask them for anything!" Merrick snaps so meanly that I rear back in shock.

But underneath the shock is an anger I almost don't recognize. It's such a rare emotion for me that it takes me a second to realize what the burning in my blood is. By the time I do, I'm half ready to shoot Merrick myself—or at least punch him in the nose.

But by the time I come around to that, Ian is already unbuckling the holster from his waist. "I don't have to shoot him to make my point." He tosses the holster—and the weapon—to Max and then holds up his hands. "So now what?"

"If I win, we go to Serati?" Merrick asks, studying Ian carefully.

Ian shrugs like it's the most obvious thing in the world. "Of course."

It occurs to me that Merrick isn't exactly on his game if he believes Ian—I mean, he is a self-professed mercenary and killer. He's hardly going to balk at telling a lie.

Merrick stiffens his shoulders. "Last chance. You—"

But Ian doesn't wait for him to finish. He dives for Merrick, and they both crash to the ground. I let out a little scream and then clamp my hands over my mouth as I scramble to get out of the way.

I glance around the room; surely, someone will stop them. But Max hardly seems interested. He's chatting with Gage like this is no big deal while Beckett is watching them as they roll on the floor, her eyes gleaming with amusement. I really like her—like, really, really like her—but she has a weird sense of humor.

I've seen Merrick fight in tournaments, and it's a beautiful thing, like a choreographed dance. This is not at all like dancing. It's messy and bloody. And I'm worried that Merrick can't move as fast as he should because of the higher gravity. Though I don't think speed is important here—they're grappling on the floor, both getting in punches. I scream at the spurt of blood that comes with the crunch of Ian's fist on Merrick's nose. But then Merrick rams his fist into Ian's mouth, and he spits out blood.

It's horrible. So, so horrible I can barely watch. But I'm afraid not to. What if one of them gets carried away and—

Kali storms into the room with a bit less regality than usual. "What's going on?" she demands. Then jerks to a halt as she sees exactly what's happening.

"They're fighting," Beckett says unnecessarily. She's come up on my other side.

"Shocking." Kali snorts. "I never would have guessed. But why?" She looks at me, but I don't want to admit this mess is about me.

Beckett has no such qualms. "Merrick wants to take Rain home, thinks she might be having too good a time here. He demanded Ian take us to Serati so he can lock her back up in the monastery and…" She waves a hand at the two men. "Ian didn't agree."

The two men are on their feet now. Merrick whirls, kicking Ian in the stomach. He grunts but doesn't go down. Seconds later, he punches Merrick in the chest so hard he stumbles backward. Then they're grappling again, gripping each other's shoulders and jockeying for position. They come crashing toward us, and we move away. Merrick forces Ian back, and he slams into the wall.

I wince. I don't want Merrick to get hurt. But a part of me—the dark little part that I didn't know even existed until now—doesn't want him to win, either.

But then Ian head butts him in the face and blood spurts from his already broken nose.

"Ouch," Kali murmurs, assessing. "They're both good, but I think Ian is meaner."

"It's because he learned in the real world," Beckett says without moving her gaze away from the fight. "Win or die."

I don't know what to say to that, and judging by the look on her face, neither does Kali.

"He said he's going to teach me," Kali adds.

Beckett peels her eyes away from the fight to give Kali an appraising stare. But for once, it's not openly hateful. Or at least not *only* openly hateful. There's respect in there, too, I think.

"Teach you what?" I ask as once again the men come crashing toward us and we have to skitter out of the way. This time even Max and Gage have to move to avoid getting slammed into.

Kali grins. "How to fight."

"God help us all," Beckett mutters, but she flashes Kali the slightest of slight smiles.

The men grapple some more, crashing into the console. A yellow light starts flashing, and then a shrill beeping begins.

"Hey, watch the fucking spaceship," Beckett yells, hurrying over. As they both crash to the floor at her feet, she presses something, and the light stops.

I glance at Max, who's still talking to Gage like he's at some kind of social event and not witnessing a bloody fight between his best friend and someone else. But then I realize he is paying attention to the fight, his hand unconsciously rubbing his stomach and his eyes following the action on the ground even while he talks to Gage about the last time he and Ian were on Glacea.

Knowing he does care a lot more than he's letting on makes me like him more.

"So…how long do you think this is going to go on?" I ask nervously.

Kali shrugs. "Who knows? I do wish I had some chobwa bites, though. This is getting good."

Merrick rushes Ian, but he sticks out a foot and trips him, sending Merrick slamming to the ground.

"You're not bad for a priest," Ian tells him with a grin. "But you're just playing. Show me what you've really got."

Merrick, who's back on his feet, lunges for him, but Ian laughs as he spins out of reach. Then he stops and seems to look over Merrick's shoulder to where I'm standing. Merrick has his back to me; I can't see his expression. But shock flashes across Ian's face, his eyes widening. I glance around, but there's nothing. Suddenly, he shouts, "No, Rain, don't do it!"

Do what? I look at Kali, confused, but it's obvious she has no clue what he's talking about, either.

But Merrick takes the bait, whirling around to see just what it is I'm doing, and that's when Ian leaps for him. He sweeps out with a leg and swipes Merrick's feet out from under him. Then drops him down on his back and smashes his head to the floor.

"No! Don't kill him." I run forward, grabbing Ian by the shoulder and trying to pull him back. He doesn't budge, but that doesn't stop me from yelling, "Get off him."

"Don't worry—he's not dead. Far from it." Ian stands up and wipes the blood from his cheek. Max tosses him his weapon, and he straps it on.

Merrick is lying facedown, and I gently roll him over. For a second, I think Ian was lying and he is dead, but then his eyes flutter open.

And I sag. All the strength goes out of me.

Merrick pushes himself up so he's sitting. His hand goes to his face, and he gently touches his broken nose. Then he looks past me to where Ian is standing with an amused expression on his face.

"You don't fight fair," Merrick growls.

Ian shrugs. "That's what you get for picking a fight with a mercenary. Besides, I was getting bored. And we need to be on our way." He gives Merrick a pointed look. "To Glacea." He turns away and says something to Beckett, who sits down in the pilot's seat and starts pressing buttons.

Despite the fact that Merrick is currently bleeding all over the place, I can't help wondering if maybe she'll teach me how to fly. Ian kissed Kali, and now he's going to teach her to fight. It only seems fair that Beckett teaches me something as well.

"Bastard," Merrick mutters as he once again climbs to his feet. But he actually looks quite impressed.

Ian turns back. "You didn't even ask Rain if she wants to go home."

"It doesn't matter," Merrick replies. "We all have duties in this life."

"Not all of us," Ian tells him. "Some of us do whatever the hell we want. So go ahead. Ask her."

I hold my breath because I don't want him to ask. The answer should be easy.

"Rain?"

And it *is* easy, I realize. But it's not the one Merrick is looking for.

CHAPTER 30

Ian

Well, that went better than I expected.

I figured from the start that eventually Merrick and I were going to have to go a round or two. He's the type to want things his own way. The only problem is, so am I. And when it comes to finding Milla, I'm not prepared to compromise.

Despite that, I actually like the guy. More, I feel sorry for him. He has a mission to protect a girl who clearly does not want to be protected. Even though she dodges his question and says they'll talk later, we all know what her answer was going to be.

Good for her.

"Do you always solve things with your fists?"

I glance up at Kali's voice. She's standing beside me, hands on her hips, looking judgy as all hell. What now?

"Mostly," I answer, because why lie when you don't need to? I'm not ashamed of who I am. I've had to fight for every scrap of joy in my life, and I'm fucking good at it. It's why Max and Milla and I have made it out of scrapes on every one of the seven planets. "Sometimes with my fists. Often with my knife. Occasionally with my pistol, and once with—"

"I get it," she snaps, giving me an eye roll before she whirls around and strides away.

Why the fuck's she rolling her eyes at me, anyway? My proclivity for fighting saved us from those guys last night. Twice. Two separate groups of assholes. Making me doubly awesome.

And didn't she ask me to teach her to fight? What's the point of that if she doesn't expect to ever use it?

Besides, she has no clue what it's like to struggle for every single thing you own. For every single thing you eat and for every single breath you take. I decide I need to point that out to her. Right now.

I follow her off the bridge and can't help noticing just how hot her ass looks in that jumpsuit. And her legs. Not to mention her—

Max casts me a glance as I pass. "*Really?*" he says. "*You're going there? Right now?*"

"*No, I'm not. I just need to set the princess straight on one or two small things.*"

"*You ever think that maybe she needs to set* you *straight on one or two small things?*"

"*Fuck that. And fuck you.*"

He grins. "*If you say so.*"

"*We're just going to talk,*" I tell him.

"*Of course you are.*"

I don't appreciate the sarcasm, but that's Max for you. The trouble is that he knows me as well, if not better—he has the advantage of a little distance—than I know myself. Which is why his comments should be enough to stop me in my tracks or at least give me pause. But my feet keep right on moving.

I find the princess in her room. The door is open, so I take that as an unspoken "come on in." If she'd wanted me to stay out, she would have closed the damn door.

But the second I catch sight of her standing with her back to me, arms wrapped around her waist, my anger dissolves. "Kali, are you okay?" She's hugging herself like she's cold—or hurt.

She turns slowly. "As good as can be expected, I guess."

"What the hell does that mean?"

"I'm on a goddamn spaceship going who the fuck knows where—"

"Glacea," I put in helpfully, and she rolls her eyes at me. Again.

"I should be going home. My mother will be frantic. The Council will be furious, and…" She takes a deep breath and sort of sags. "I actually enjoyed watching you fight."

The change in subject makes me frown. It also makes me feel all twisted up inside. I want to say that I'll fight for her anytime, but I don't think she's saying that like it's a good thing. So I keep my mouth shut and wait for her to continue.

She doesn't say anything else for several seconds, and then she shrugs. "I'm not sure what that says about me, but it's nothing good."

"There's nothing wrong with fighting for what you need. Or what you believe in."

"Is that what you were doing in there?" she asks, sounding more restrained than I've ever heard her. "Fighting for what you need?"

"Fuck yeah. I was fighting for Milla." I give her a what-are-you-getting-at look.

"So you need Milla?"

"I—" I freeze mid-sentence, partly because I don't know what I want to say to that and partly because my brain is suddenly flashing a giant warning sign at me, telling me there's danger down the path she's leading me on. "I mean, Max and I—Milla—we—"

She holds up a hand to stop me, which I'll always be grateful for. Especially since Max is currently laughing at all my floundering.

"*Smooth,*" he tells me. "*Is this the part where you tell her a couple of things? Or is that going to come later?*"

I flip him off mentally. "*Shut the fuck up.*"

"*So you have no problem telling me off.*" He's still snickering.

"*Stop distracting me, will you? I need to pay attention to Kali—*"

And now he's full-blown laughing again. But at least he's stopped talking, so I'll take the win. And later I'll beat his ass for fucking with me right now.

"*You can try,*" he taunts.

I focus back on her. "Kali—"

"I'm not upset about going to Glacea, Ian. Even though maybe I should be. And I liked watching you fight. A lot." Her eyes light up briefly before she sinks down onto the bed, and for the first time since I met her, she looks defeated. I don't like it. Yeah, I always complained about her fighting me, but I'll take that a million times over if the choice is between that and this sadness that's pulling at her.

"What do you want, Kali?"

"That's just it. I don't know." She runs a hand through her hair, and I can't help but notice the way the light moves through the dark red locks. "Do you know how much that trip to the *Caelestis* meant to me?"

I don't have a clue, but she continues before I can say that.

"It was my first official duty—the first time my mother went against the Council and trusted me enough to let me represent her. I wanted so much to impress her."

I frown. "Why?"

"Because she's the Empress of Senestris, the most important person in the system, *and* she's my mother."

"I never knew my father, and my mother was murdered when I was eleven," I find myself saying. I can't believe I admitted that. I never talk about my mother.

Her eyes widen. "I'm so sorry, Ian. That must have been so hard." She reaches out and touches my arm, and my skin burns beneath her touch.

Chemistry is so fucked up. Usually, I don't mind that fact—hard to mind when you don't spend more than a couple of days in any port and you can fly away from all your problems—but it sucks right now. Especially since every time I think she's as big a monster as the rest of the Ruling Families, Kali proves me wrong.

"My father was murdered, too."

I don't answer. I just reach out and stroke her hand.

She grabs onto my fingers. "He was a good man, and I loved him. I want to be the kind of ruler that would make him proud."

"Isn't that the same kind that would make your mother proud?" I ask.

It doesn't seem like a hard question, but she thinks about it for a long time. So long that I start to think she isn't going to answer at all.

But then she says, "I used to think so. But after the last few days, I'm not so sure. My dad hated for anyone to suffer."

Then he really picked the wrong woman to fall in love with, didn't he?

I manage to stop myself from blurting it out, but something about the look in Kali's eyes tells me she's already thinking the same thing.

Her hand is still in mine, and I stare down at it, feeling the warmth from our touch seep through my body. At least until she realizes we're basically holding hands and snatches hers back.

I stand up. This conversation is clearly done.

"As soon as we find Milla, we'll make sure you get home safe. Okay?" Just saying it fills me with a weird queasy feeling, but I've always known that had to be the endgame. No use getting bent out of shape about it now.

"I can wait." She smiles a little. "I know how devoted you are to finding Milla. It's admirable, really."

Her words give me a little stab of…something. Guilt, maybe. Because my saving Milla isn't really altruistic—at least not the way she makes it sound. I hate keeping secrets, and I hate feeling guilty even more—I just haven't had enough practice for it to come naturally—which tends to make me mean.

Maybe that's why I lash out.

"So, yeah, let me do what I need to do, and then we'll get you back to being a sheltered princess. And just forget about any more kissing," I throw in.

A hurt look flashes in her eyes, and there's that goddamn guilt again, stabbing me in the gut. Even her eyes harden.

"What kissing?" She sniffs. "Hey, looks like I've already forgotten it." Her eyes gleam.

And suddenly, the air in the room charges and we're both thinking about kissing each other.

I take a step closer. "And just so you know, it's never going to happen again."

"What isn't? The kiss that was so unremarkable that I've already forgotten it?"

My lips twitch. The really sad thing is, I like her. Besides Milla—and that's very different—I've never actually liked a woman before. Maybe because I've never allowed myself to know them well enough to get to that stage, or maybe because none of them were as fascinating as Kali.

The problem is that she makes me feel like the world might not be such a bad place after all. Which makes no sense, considering her family is a big part of the reason this system of ours is such a shitty mess.

Not to mention she just agreed to let me bring her back so she can help Mommy make it even shittier.

I mean, sure, I know everyone says the world is going to end unless we do something drastic and that's why we all have to suffer—and by all, they mean everyone who isn't in the Ruling Families—but I've always believed it's just another ploy to try and keep us down. As for the Sisterhood saving us by embracing the Dying Sun or whatever, that's just a big steaming pile of shit, no matter how genuine Rain seems to be.

"You sure are thinking awfully hard," Kali says, breaking into my cheerful thoughts.

"Just contemplating the shitty state of the world."

"And here I was, thinking you must be remembering the kiss. But then I remembered there is no kiss, because we've both forgotten it already."

She swipes her tongue over her lower lip, biting it with sharp white teeth. Obscenely hot.

I pull her up so that we're standing face-to-face, so close together that she has to tilt her head to look into my eyes. So close I can see the black rings around her silver irises.

Her eyes draw me in, just like they always do when I look at them. I even see something in them before she gives a little shake of her head and they go blank.

"Back off, Ian." She slaps a hand on my chest and pushes. "You're right. We should forget the kiss. This—you and me—isn't going to happen. It can't."

That's exactly what I've been telling myself, but the problem is—I've never been very good at following orders.

I lean down, and this time she doesn't back away. "I hate it when somebody tells me I *can't* do something," I whisper close to her face. "It makes me want to prove them wrong."

"And how would you do that?" she murmurs, her head tilting up to me so that her warm breath caresses my cheek. At the same time, her breasts brush against my chest, and I'm not sure which one of us sucks in our breath harder and faster.

I slip one hand around the back of her neck, beneath the silk of her hair, and tilt her face up farther. Every muscle in my body clenches.

I touch my lips to hers and—

Something slams into the ship. It lurches to the side, sending us flying. We land on the bed with Kali on top of me.

Then there's a loud crash and the lights go out and the ship lurches again, and we're on the floor and Kali is beneath me.

"What just happened?" she whispers in the dark.

I have no fucking clue. But I have a really bad feeling. Which becomes ten times worse when Beckett's voice breaks through the comms.

"Captain, report in. I repeat, report in. We're being attacked."

CHAPTER 31

Kali

As I follow Ian out the door, another blast hits the ship and we both collide with the wall. For a second, I wonder if this is it—the end—and my body clenches, waiting for another hit. But then the ship seems to drop, and we crash to the floor.

"Stay still for a minute," Ian whispers.

I'm more than happy to oblige. Beckett said we're under attack, but from whom?

And fuck it, if we're about to die, I would have actually liked to have that kiss.

Maybe kissing me isn't a big deal for Ian, but for me? Every time he gets close to me, it just makes me more desperate for him—for the feel and smell and taste of him.

Sometimes I feel like if he doesn't kiss me again, I'll implode, like a star that's burned itself out.

I've never felt this way before. Not for any of the people my mother paraded in front of me in the hopes that I'd make an appropriate choice for my royal Askkandian consort. And not for any of the ambassadors' and Councilors' kids I've had crushes on through the years.

Maybe it's because Ian was the first person to truly touch me. Or maybe it's because Ian is a man, not a boy. Sure, he isn't more than a couple of years older than me, but age isn't everything. All I have to do is look in his dark eyes to know that he hasn't been a boy for a very long time. And when Ian touches me, he makes me feel like a woman who can match him kiss for kiss, adventure for adventure.

I like being that woman—probably a lot more than I should.

Several seconds pass without another crash before Ian jumps to his feet. "Come on. Let's get to the bridge and see who's attacking my ship."

I don't bother to correct him, even though I know in my bones the *Starlight* is mine.

Ian holds out a hand to me and I take it, letting him pull me up.

When we make it to the bridge, everyone is strapped into their seats, even Beckett, who normally never uses her harness.

Ian heads straight for her. I stay close, even though he doesn't need me for this. But I'll be honest with myself: If I'm going to die, I'd prefer Ian to be within reach.

"Status report," Ian demands.

Beckett casts him a blank look. "Do you mean you want to know what's happening?"

Sometimes I think I could actually like her.

"That would be a status report." When she still doesn't say anything, Ian sighs. "Just tell me."

"Like I said, we're being attacked," she deadpans.

"Seriously? That's it?" He looks ready to explode.

But Beckett just seems baffled. "There's nothing I can say that you can't see for yourself." She waves at one of the screens. And there it is. A ship directly in front of us.

"Do we know who she is?" I ask, straining to see any markings. Part of my royal training included memorizing every official insignia being used in the Senestris system. Fun times.

"No," Beckett answers. "No markings and no name. Like we said before—could be anyone trying to kill us."

A laser blast shoots out from the ship. Terror rips through me as I clutch Ian's arm.

"Are you going to try to avoid that?" he asks Beckett in an impressively calm voice, considering I want to scream at her to do something.

"Don't need to," Beckett replies. She turns to look at us with a grin. "Just watch for a second."

I want to, but I can't. My eyes screw up, and I clutch Ian's arm like he alone can stop me from being obliterated into space dust.

Then the ship is dropping again, fast and hard. At least this time Ian and I both manage to stay on our feet. When I open my eyes, the screen is filled with light. But then it disappears, and, somehow, we're still here.

"What the fuck?" Ian demands.

Beckett grins. "I know. Amazing, right? She's the most mind-boggling ship *ever*. I think I might be in love." She turns back to the console. "And here they come again."

This time, I keep my eyes open. I see the blast leave the ship; then, when it's about halfway to us, we just…drop. And the blast shoots off somewhere above our heads.

"So, you're not doing *anything*?" Ian asks.

"*Nothing*." As if to prove it, Beckett holds her hands up with a laugh.

"It took her a couple of shots to realize we were under attack," Gage says. "So, if we could find a way to give her an advance warning, that would be great. Or maybe there's some sort of monitoring system we can turn on. I'll take a dig around when this is over."

We drop again. This time, I didn't even notice the blast.

"That is sort of cool," Ian says, still sounding less than impressed. "But maybe we should get the hell out of here before whoever that is gets lucky."

"Aw," Beckett says. "Why do you always got to ruin my fun? But I suppose you *are* the captain."

She presses a couple of buttons and swirls her hand on the console in front of her, and we're pulling a one-eighty. As soon as we're facing away from the attacking ship, Beckett slams her hand down on the console and we shoot forward at a truly alarming speed.

I crash to the floor again, with Ian right beside me—which makes me feel a little better. I start to get up, but after a moment's reflection I decide I'm better off where I am.

Even before Beckett screams, "Yee-haw! I fucking love this ship."

CHAPTER 32

Beckett

This might be the first time I've ever admitted to loving anything in my entire life, but I truly love this ship.

We've left our attackers—whoever they were—far behind. The *Starlight* is superfast. I've never known a ship so quick. It makes me wonder about the aliens who built it. Maybe Rain is right—maybe they were gods after all. All I know is they certainly knew how to build kick-ass tech.

Now that we've left that other ship in the dust, I touch the speed control and the *Starlight* slows. I wasn't sure she would listen to me, but it seems she only takes over when she thinks I'm not going to manage on my own. Which is insulting. And also freaky.

Do I really believe the ship can think for herself on that level? Those capabilities are so far beyond anything we've got, unless the Ruling Families are holding out. Which they probably are. Who cares. My head hurts.

I recheck our course for Glacea—but the *Starlight* has already adjusted her flight plan—then sit back with a sigh to take stock. My mind is getting clearer, the gaps in my memories shrinking, and I'm feeling more lucid than I have since I was drugged and taken on board the *Caelestis*. But I suspect it's a temporary reprieve.

My head always hurts. It varies from a dull throbbing in the base of my neck, like now, to a pain so intense it's as though someone is drilling into my skull. I wish I remembered what they did to me on that shithole space station. The not knowing—it's another violation, one more on top of the many the Empire of Senestris has been serving me my entire life.

Part of me thinks I shouldn't try to remember. That I'm better off not knowing what they did. But then I take off this jumpsuit for bed and can't help but see the fresh scars and healing injuries all over my body. And the horror of not knowing takes over, making it impossible for me to sleep. Impossible for me to think.

The only thing that helps is sitting in this pilot's chair—and Rain. It's impossible to feel trapped when I'm sitting here, the endless expanse of space spread out at my fingertips, mine for the taking.

I can go anywhere, fast. And while, yeah, Ian would probably have something to say about that, it doesn't matter. Because the knowledge that I *can* go anywhere makes the need to do so shrink.

As for Rain…I can feel myself blushing when I think about her, and I never blush. I'm usually as stone-cold as they come—it's how my mother raised me—but there's nothing cold about my feelings for her. Which is freaky, too.

Not freaky enough for me to stop wanting to hold her, kiss her, *touch* her. But freaky enough to have me wondering what happened to me. What's happening to me still.

My body aches. A bonus gift from my time on the *Caelestis*. I shift position, stretch out my back and legs a little. Tamp down the newest wave of rage at what they did to me.

I used to be able to go for hours, for days, without feeling so much as a twinge. My family conditioned me since birth to make sure of it. Now, I can't even sit in a fucking chair for longer than half an hour without some part of my body cramping up.

As the shock and fear from the attack fade, the others start to talk around me. I let their voices wash over me without paying too much attention to their words. The more my head hurts, the harder it is to comprehend the words being spoken, so these last few days I've gotten in the habit of hearing without listening.

I twirl my chair around and grin. Rain is seated on the closest chair on my left, and Merrick is sprawled out next to her. His broken nose is swollen to twice its usual size, which probably explains the surly expression. Rain looks a little subdued but gives me a wan smile when she catches my eye.

Ian and the princess are still on the floor. Probably thought it was the safest place. He's sitting up, arms wrapped around his legs while she's still lying flat out, eyes open, staring at the ceiling.

Even I have to admit Ian is a fine specimen of a man. I'd be tempted myself if I liked that sort of thing, which I don't. Probably just as well. I've seen the way he watches the princess when he thinks she isn't looking. I wish him all the luck with that.

Though I have to admit, her asking him to teach her to fight was… unexpected. And actually kinda cool. Which pisses me off.

My back is still bothering me, so I get up and stretch. "So," I say. "After what just happened, should we renew the conversation about who wants the lot of you dead?"

"I thought we already went over this," Rain says, sitting up straighter.

"Yeah, well, that was a whole new murder attempt we just lived through, so I think the sentiment bears repeating."

Kali gets to her feet. "You don't think it's just people after the bounty?" she comments as she brushes herself down.

I roll my eyes. "The flyers said dead or alive, but even dead, they'd need bodies to prove it's you all. And whoever that was, they were doing their best to vaporize us. No bodies, no bounty."

"She's right," Ian says. "Whoever was in that ship wasn't after the bounty. But it could still be whoever put out the flyers in the first place." He shrugs as he gets to his feet before pulling a flask from his pocket and taking a gulp. "Or it could be someone completely different."

"Popular lot, aren't you," I say. But it's an intriguing mystery. One we need to find a few more pieces of if we actually hope to solve it.

If I'm being logical, I know it's highly possible that it could be my group. Except, unless things have changed drastically since I've been away, we didn't have the resources to take on a job as big as attacking the *Caelestis*. At least not without a lot of help.

"Maybe we just need to think it through," Gage says.

"Don't hurt yourself, big guy," Max snarks back.

He just shoots Max a winning smile, then continues. "Who would want the princess dead?"

"Just about everyone in the system with a brain," I offer.

Aw. She almost looks hurt. Which almost makes me feel bad.

Which, in turn, makes me lash out more. Because what the fuck does she have to be hurt about?

"What? You control the food and, through the Corporation, the technology. Where people live. What they do. How they die—which is miserably, by the way. The whole system is built around your time zones, your orbits, your years. Is it any wonder they hate you?"

She opens her mouth to argue, then shuts it again.

"Hey, the fact that the sun is failing isn't Kali's fault," Max defends her. "Everyone is suffering."

"You saw that dress she was wearing." I turn to Kali. "You ever know what it's like to think about drinking your own urine because you're so desperate for water? Except you've got nothing to pee because it's been so long since you drank anything."

She looks away. Yeah, as much as I am coming to not full-on despise Kali, I hit a chord there. And it feels good. If she's not all bad yet, I'm sure the Empress will guarantee that happens soon.

"So, you think it could have been the rebels?" Gage asks.

I shrug. "Who knows?"

Ian snorts. "Come on, Beckett. It's not as though you wouldn't have a good idea. *Fly Free* and all that."

So, he knows. I did wonder. "How?"

"You talk in your sleep. Or yell, more like it."

"Wait. You're a rebel?" Kali demands. She's got her hands clenched into fists now, and her face is suffused with rage. Or as much rage as a little princess like her can manage.

I narrow my eyes. Take off the mask I wear that hides my own rage. Which could bury her little candle of anger in one fell swoop, if I ever let it loose.

"You murdered my father," she snarls.

"I didn't, no. But I wish I had." It's a shit thing to say, but I don't care. I'm sick of this little fuck always playing the victim.

Kali lets out a screech of anger and lunges for me. "We should have left you on the *Caelestis* to burn."

Oh, goody, a fight. Even injured and recovering from who knows what, I'm more than up for kicking her candy ass.

I brace myself for a hit that never lands. Ian grabs her before she can get to me and holds her back.

"Spoilsport," I tell him.

He rolls his eyes.

"The rebels blew my father up," Kali cries out. "They killed him for their own selfish reasons—"

"And the Empress's forces killed my father, just because they could," I shoot back, getting in her face the way I've been dying to since the very first day. "Even though he wasn't a rebel. Even though he had never *been* a rebel. They came for him in the middle of the night, tortured him to death right in front of me and my baby brother. And a few years later, they came back for Jarved. They kidnapped and killed him, too." Or at least I've always believed they did. Now that I've been on the *Caelestis*, I can't help wondering if he's out there somewhere, locked up with Ian and Max's Milla.

All I know is that I have to find out, so yeah, I'm down with following Ian's lead here. If he finds Milla, maybe I'll find Jarved.

"Okay, can we all just take a deep breath—" Max starts.

"I'm not done," I snap at him before turning back to Kali. "You may want to keep living in your little fantasy land, but I'm sick as fuck of indulging you. Take a look around, Princess, at the people you're traveling with. The people who have saved your life more than once in the last few days. Every single one of them, except maybe Rain over there, has suffered—badly—at the hands of your family. You think because we don't whine about it all the time, it doesn't count. That we haven't been hurt just as badly or worse than you. But you're wrong. The only difference between us and you is that we chose to save you anyway.

"You think I didn't have the spaceship ready to go before you and Ian returned from your little adventure the other night? I could have left you to burn." I deliberately use the same word she did a couple of minutes ago. "But I didn't do it, and neither did they. Outlaw, murderer, thief, rebel. Looks like we're all better than you and yours."

Even though I know I should stop, even though part of me wants to, in this moment, I can't.

"So fuck you, Princess, and fuck your whole evil little Empire."

CHAPTER 33

Beckett

"Enough!" Ian roars in a voice that echoes through the bridge. I contemplate not listening to him. But for once Ian looks like he means business. Besides, I've already said everything I wanted to, and now that it's all out, I actually feel calm. Calmer than I have in ages.

"Is that true?" Kali whispers, looking between Ian, Max, and me.

"Kali—" he starts.

"Don't lie," I interrupt.

"Look, we have important things to figure out right now, and none of this is making it any easier," Ian says through gritted teeth. "Beckett, get back to your chair and get us to Glacea."

I touch a finger to my forehead in a mock salute. "Your wish is my command, Captain."

"If only," he growls.

The bridge is quiet for several minutes, which might be a record. Eventually, though, Rain sits on the floor next to my chair.

"You okay?" she whispers.

"I'm fine," I answer in a normal tone, because I'm not ashamed of anything I said or did.

She smiles gently. "I'm glad." Her hand rests on my knee for just a few seconds.

I wish she had left it longer, but I get why she didn't. Merrick still doesn't look happy, and there've been enough fights on this bridge today.

Several more minutes pass before Ian starts, "Maybe the rebels—"

I shake my head, because I already know where he's going. "I don't think so. We just don't have the resources to attack the *Caelestis* like that."

"Maybe one of the other Ruling Families, then?" Merrick suggests, looking to Kali for confirmation. "We've all heard rumors of unrest."

"And it's a known fact that none of them have any real loyalty to the Empress," Max adds.

"That's because she's a crap leader who's in bed with the Corporation. And no one wants to go against them and be cut off."

"Enough, Beckett." Ian runs a hand over his tired eyes, then looks at Kali. "Do you agree? Could this be some sort of power play?"

She considers for a second, then shrugs slightly. "Maybe. There's always some unrest among the families, someone who wants more power. But it doesn't make sense—they would never willingly destroy the *Caelestis*. She was our one hope of saving the system. Without her, we're all likely to burn."

"But again, maybe whoever blew up the *Caelestis* is different from whoever is trying to kill us now," Merrick points out. "Maybe whoever that is is taking advantage of the fact that Kali is vulnerable away from home."

"So, maybe we really do need to take you home?" Gage asks Kali. "It's what you want, right, and it'll also get rid of the threat."

"Or we could just shove her out of the airlock," I suggest helpfully. "Take a picture of her floating in space as evidence. We'd lose the dead weight, and hey, maybe they'd even send us the reward. Win-win."

Ian looks like he's about to explode all over me, but it's Kali herself who looks like she's been punched. For the first time, I actually do feel a little guilty at the look on her face.

"Is that how you all still see me?" she asks quietly. "Dead weight?"

"Kali—" Ian starts, but before he can figure out what to say next, she's gone.

CHAPTER 34

Kali

I don't know what to do or what to think.

I've spent years hating the rebels because of what they did to my father. And even now, after everything Beckett said, I still hate them. Or at least, I want to hate them. How can I not? My father was a good man. He didn't deserve to die.

But how can I hate Beckett when her father is dead, too? And her brother, if she was telling me the truth. And I think she was—her pain seemed too real.

She said their deaths are my mother's fault. The Empire's fault. If that's true, I can understand why she became a rebel. The amount of hate I had for the people who killed my father has made me think terrible things through the years. If I'd had the chance, I might have done terrible things to get revenge if I could.

But is she right? Is my mother somehow responsible for what happened to her father? Even worse, is she responsible for what's happened to everyone on the *Starlight*? I keep seeing Ian's face when Beckett said that everyone on board had suffered because of my mother.

His eyes went blank, and his whole face closed down. Not in his typical "I'm in charge and not in the mood to explain myself to you" way, but in a way that all but screamed that she was right. That something really terrible happened to him to make him the way he is.

I've always known my mother was ruthless, always knew she would do anything in the name of the Empire. And she's only gotten harder since my father left her—then was murdered before he could come back.

At the same time, we're facing an existential threat right now. I don't agree that there's ever a reason to hurt people, even in the name of progress. But maybe she doesn't see it that way. Maybe she and Dr. Veragelen believe they have to take harsh steps to make sure everyone in Senestris doesn't die.

But at what point does sacrificing your humanity become acceptable? At what point does the sacrifice exceed the goal?

Not to mention…the words "dead weight" are still ringing in my ears. I knew I was useless when I first boarded the *Starlight*, but I've been working so hard, learning so much. I thought the others were starting to see it, but clearly not.

My mind is spinning as I'm trying to think through all these questions, all this pain, when there is a knock on my door.

"Come in," I call, and my heart is suddenly in my throat. Because if it's Ian, I don't know what I'm going to say to him. I don't even know if I'll be able to face him after what Beckett said. Shame burns in my belly.

But when the door slides open, it's not Ian standing there. It's Max; two glasses of gerjgin in his hands. "I thought you could use a drink," he tells me, extending one of the glasses out to me.

I hadn't planned on drinking any gerjgin for a while—I'm still feeling the aftereffects from last night—but I'm shaking from the confrontation with Beckett, not to mention everything I've been thinking about my mother.

"How'd you know?" I ask as I take the drink.

He gives a rueful laugh. "Because I need one, too."

"Fair enough." I lift the glass in a silent toast and then take a sip, relishing the way the sharp burn of it cuts through the chill deep inside me.

He settles down on the bed next to me. "You okay?"

I don't even know how to answer that. So I take another sip. "Is it true?"

"Is what true?" His gaze turns wary.

Even the Council would be proud of the imperial blankness of my face as I raise an eyebrow at him. "Don't be like that."

"Everyone's got a story, Kali."

"I know." I take another sip of gerjgin. Fake courage and all that. "What's your and Ian's story?"

"I—umm—"

"Never mind. That's all the answer I need."

He shrugs, and it's his turn to take another sip. "It's complicated."

"As complicated as turning into collateral damage in someone's assassination plot?"

"Don't count me out yet—I'm not that easy to kill. And don't jump too fast into putting all the blame on yourself. Each of us has enemies out there, and Ian is particularly good at pissing people off." He grins. "I've thought about offing him myself once or twice."

"Only once or twice?" My brow lifts again.

"Today. Once or twice today."

This time, we both laugh. "You're close, aren't you?" I ask, because I have a ton of questions when it comes to Ian. And because Max is a really nice guy—and very easy to talk to.

Something flashes across his face—maybe amusement. "More than you can imagine." Then he shrugs. "We've had to be. The three of us have been alone since we were eleven years old. We look out for one another."

I frown. "Three of you?"

"Yeah. Me, Ian, and Milla."

I think about that for a second. "So Milla is your sister?" Why hadn't I realized that before? Max and Ian do have similarly dark skin and dark hair, but so do a lot of people. The two never struck me as siblings before now.

There's that flash of something again. But I'm too caught up in the conversation to analyze it too closely. "Who did you think she was?" he asks, studying me.

I hadn't thought about it too much. Clearly, she's someone Ian cares about a lot, and maybe I hadn't wanted to know the gory details.

He grins. "Did you think she was his girlfriend?"

"I didn't think at all." I sniff. "And why would I care if she was?"

"Oh, I think you care, Princess. A lot more than you want me—or him—to know. But for your information and absolutely no other reason, Ian has never had a serious partner."

As if that means anything to me. The warm, fuzzy feeling deep inside me is just because of the alcohol. "So, tell me about Milla. Obviously, Ian is the obnoxious asshole; you're the nice, goofy one. What's Milla like?"

Max's smile flashes as bright as a solar flare. "She's the clever one. She got all the brains."

"I don't believe that. You seem pretty smart yourself."

He laughs. Hard. "I notice you don't say the same about Ian."

"He's smart, too. He's just…"

"Impulsive," Max fills in. "Pugilistic. Completely without common sense."

"All of the above." I study him closely. "So Milla's not like that?"

"Well, the pugilistic part is something they have in common." He gives an amused shake of his head, like he's remembering some funny thing that happened in the past. "But the rest, no."

"She sounds…" I search for a word and settle on, "amazing."

"She is," he tells me, sounding sadder than I've ever heard him. "She's everything."

I reach over and squeeze his hand. "I really hope you find her."

"We will." I can hear the conviction in his voice, and the last thing I want to do is put any doubt in his mind. But how can he even be sure she's alive? It's been months since she was taken, and the Senestris system is a dangerous place. I've learned that over the last few days.

He pats my leg. "Anyway, try not to worry too much. Once we've found Milla, we'll get you home."

"And if I don't want to go home?" I ask.

His eyes turn watchful. "Don't you?"

"Beckett sprung a lot on me today. I don't know what I want. I just know I don't want to be dead weight. I want—" I want my mom to not be a monster. I want there to be an explanation for the things Beckett said. The things I saw on Rangar. But what explanation could there possibly be?

My head is whirling with a million questions that I don't know the answers to. Questions that I'm not sure there even *are* answers to.

I don't say that, though. I can't. So instead I ask, "Why are you so much nicer than Ian?"

But Max just grins. "I'm not. But you can feel free to tell him that the next time you see him."

"So he can hit you, too? No, thank you." I shudder.

"Ian and I've gone a round more than a few times," he answers. "It always works itself out."

"Before anyone ended up needing medical attention?" I ask archly.

"Now, where's the fun in that?" He stands up. "Speaking of which, I'm going to head back to the bridge before Ian comes looking for both of us."

"You don't actually think he'd be jealous if he found you here, do you?"

He flashes me a grin. "Nah, of course not. Ian knows I would never try anything with *his* girl."

I grit my teeth. "I am not *his* girl. In fact, he specifically told me that he does not do relationships. So, I'm reliably informed that it's *never* going to happen."

"He's running scared."

"He doesn't look scared. And he doesn't act scared. And he's not actually running anywhere." I sigh. Why are we even talking about this? It's not as though I want to be Ian's "girl" anyway. Despite the fact that he does have a nice ass. A really nice ass, actually, and a face to die for.

All the same, I can't help but ask, "So, say—just as a matter of academic interest—I did want to make Ian jealous. Which obviously I don't. But how would I go about it?"

"You wouldn't," he answers dryly. "Not if you want to avoid bloodshed."

CHAPTER 35

Rain

I watch Beckett as she works at the console. She's a rebel—not *used to be* a rebel or *was* a rebel, which I already knew—it's not like *I was forced to be a rebel*, or even *I used to support the Rebellion but I've changed my mind*. She actively *is* a rebel. Right now. Someone intent on destroying the order of things, who doesn't care who they kill or hurt in the process.

In other words, she's everything the Sisterhood is not.

I should want nothing to do with her. But the truth is, when I'm near her, none of that matters. Nothing does but talking to her. Touching her. Kissing her.

I want to do all those things with her right now. But I don't know where to start. Those things she said to Kali earlier—about her father and her brother? She's suffered so much. Losing them and then getting captured and tortured herself?

Is it any wonder she's a rebel? Any wonder she wants nothing to do with the Empire or the Corporation? I wouldn't, either, if I'd had her life.

The fact that she's still as kind as she is—and she *is* kind, no matter what the others think—is a testament to just how good a person she is.

I can see the soft curve of her cheek, framed by the glossy black curls. The purse of her full lips as she considers something on the screen in front of her. The long, slender line of her back as she arches, stretching it out.

Then she rubs at the back of her skull, and I know she's in pain. I'm filled with a need to help her. I tell myself it's because I'm a member of the Sisterhood and that's what we're all about. But deep inside, I know it's so much more than that.

"There can't be anything between you. You know that, don't you?"

Merrick's voice is soft, and I can hear the pity in his tone. It hurts more than his anger and more than his disappointment.

I know he feels like I've let him down, and I hate that. But at the same time, I feel the stirring of my own rebellion deep inside. The part of me that has lived my life for other people knows I should shove it down and lock it up tight. But the other part...the other part of me wants to take it out for a spin and see where it goes.

Beckett gets to her feet and stretches, raising her arms above her head so the material of her jumpsuit is pulled taut, showing the lean lines of her figure and her small breasts. She needs to eat. But still, the sight of her sends warmth through every part of me. And my skin suddenly feels so sensitive.

"I'm getting coffee," she announces. "Anyone else want some?"

She didn't have to offer. It's just one more sign that she's a good person who's had a lot of bad things happen to her. No one can condemn her for that.

As she passes, I jump to my feet. I carefully don't look at Merrick, though I can feel him stiffening beside me. "I'll help you."

"Yeah, 'cause I can't make coffee on my own." But she smiles to let me know she's teasing.

Or at least I think she's teasing. It's not as though I have any experience with this...whatever this is.

I'm aware of everyone's eyes on us as I follow her out of the room. But I don't look at any of them, because I have enough trouble figuring out what I'm thinking at the moment without trying to puzzle everyone else out as well.

We don't talk on the way to the galley, and I have to wipe my sweaty hands down my thighs a couple of times. But once we're inside, Beckett shuts the door and turns to me.

I nearly jump out of my skin. My heart is racing. My head is spinning. And my lungs feel like someone just set a giant narthompalus on my chest.

What am I doing?

It's not too late to back out, to just turn around and go back to the bridge. If I do that, then everything will return to normal. Merrick will stop being so disapproving and getting into fights. Beckett will move on to someone else. And soon we'll be back in the safety of the monastery and I can—

The narthompalus turns into a full-grown drokaray, and all of a sudden I can't breathe. The walls are closing in on me, and I feel myself getting smaller, smaller, small—

"Rain!" I blink as Beckett brings me out of my daydream.

I blink again, and she comes back into focus. Her eyes are wide and worried as she studies me.

I take a step toward her, closing the distance between us.

Her eyes grow wary, and for a second I think I've made a calamitous mistake. But then she leans into me so that her body rests against mine, and nothing has ever felt so good.

I wrap my arms around her waist, pulling her even closer, and then tilt my head up in an obvious invitation.

But she doesn't kiss me. She doesn't even lean down to brush my cheek with her lips. Instead, she just stands there, her long, soft, beautiful body pressed against mine, and waits for something I can't quite figure out.

"Beckett?" I want to ask what the matter is, but I can't quite force the words out of my too-tight throat.

She just smiles. "You started this," she whispers. "How are you going to finish it?"

And that's the problem, isn't it? I don't have a clue. But I know that I don't want her to back away, just like I know that I want to feel her mouth on mine.

Nerves are jumping in my stomach, and my hands are shaking. But some things are worth doing anyway, no matter how scared you are. Everything inside me tells me this is one of those things.

So instead of wishing and waiting for her to make the move, I take a deep breath and slide my hands along her spine until I'm gently—so, so gently—cupping the back of her head in my palms.

Her breath catches in her throat, and those beautiful yellow eyes of hers turn to molten gold in a moment. Seeing her, hearing her, feeling her tremble against me gives me the courage to keep going. To take the next step.

So I slowly push up onto my tiptoes and press my trembling mouth to hers.

And then we're kissing and it's easy and it's right. So right.

So perfect.

Her lips move against mine, softly at first and then harder and harder, until it feels like we're fused together, one person in two bodies.

Fire burns through me—dancing along my nerves, roaring through my veins. And somehow still leaving me hungering for more.

I clutch at her hair, trying to be careful of her injuries even as heat consumes me from all directions. But Beckett just laughs—a low, throaty sound that only fans the flames inside me. She nips at my lower lip, traces her tongue along the seam of my lips, licks at the corners of my mouth until I open for her. And then she darts inside, her tongue stroking slowly, softly, sensually, against mine.

And out of nowhere I'm drowning in her, dying for her, desperate for this kiss to go on and on and on.

And even more desperate for whatever comes next.

I've never felt like this before, never imagined that I *could* feel like this. Like every beat of my heart is her name, like every breath I take is a way to draw her deeper inside myself.

She makes a sound low in her throat and starts to pull away. But I'm not yet ready to let her go, not yet ready to give this feeling up. And so I clutch at her, my fingers tangling in her hair, my body wrapping itself around her as I kiss her and kiss her and kiss her.

She responds with a moan, her hands sliding down to cup my bottom. And then she's boosting me up.

My eyes go wide, and I make a startled sound deep in my throat, but Beckett laughs that sexy laugh of hers again. It sends shivers down my spine, even before she coaxes me to wrap my legs around her waist. And then she's turning us, bracing my bottom against the counter as she grabs my hair in her hand and pulls my head back hard enough to make me squeak.

"Okay?" she asks.

But I'm already diving back in, my hands cupping her cheeks as I bite and kiss and lick my way inside her mouth.

She smells like the searing wind on Serati, tastes like the sweetly sour little berries I love to pick from the bushes that grow along the edges of the monastery's greenhouse. Feels like every dream of home I've ever had. And I never want to let her go.

We kiss until our mouths are bruised. Until our lungs burn for oxygen and our bodies burn for each other. And then we kiss some more.

Eventually, Beckett slides me gently down the cabinet until my feet hit the floor once more. My knees buckle, and she grabs onto me with a little laugh, and I bury my face in her chest as she holds me against her until my legs can once again support my weight.

Only then does she pull away just far enough that she can slide a finger under my chin and tilt my face up to hers. Her cheeks are flushed, her mouth is soft, and her eyes are a warm pool of amber that it feels like I can fall straight into.

I want to fall into them. No, I want to dive into them—into her—and then wrap myself around her and keep her safe from all the terrible tragedies that haunt her.

"You're sure?" she murmurs, tucking a strand of my hair behind my ear.

I know what she's asking, and I nod—I'm not certain I can speak. Still, I force myself to say the words, because she deserves them. "You know when Merrick was fighting with Ian earlier? I didn't want Merrick to get hurt, but I also didn't want him to win."

I didn't think it was possible, but her eyes soften even more. "You needn't have worried. Ian would never have honored that particular bet."

"You don't think so?"

"Fuck, no." She smiles gently. "You know if we do this, you're going to piss a few people off? And not only Merrick. I'm used to that, but I'm guessing you're not. You can walk away now. I'll understand."

Will she? And how could she let me go so easily, when the thought of leaving her is a physical ache inside me? Maybe I was wrong and she doesn't want me after all. Or not enough.

"Will you?" I ask, and my tone is curt.

Her lips twitch. And I glare, because I don't see anything funny about this at all.

She laughs and then touches a finger to my cheek. "I've never met anyone like you," she murmurs.

"Is that good or bad?" My voice is still stiff—she hasn't answered my question yet.

"I don't know." She looks away for a moment, and when she glances back at me, the laughter is gone from her eyes. "You're so... perfect. So kind. And I'm anything but."

"That's not true—" I start, but she cuts me off.

"Oh, it is. You're too good for me, and everyone on that bridge knows it. Even I know it, just like I know you'll be tainted by our association. And I can't help but wonder if that's part of the reason why I want you so badly. Because I can't stand to see someone so good in the world and I want them to turn bad."

I'm not sure what she even means, but I think she's wrong. No, I know she's wrong. "You're underestimating both of us," I whisper. "And you've got it the wrong way around. You're not going to turn me bad. We're going to make each other good."

She looks shocked—just for a second, and then back to suspicion. "You think you're *that* good?"

"I know we're making something good together. Nothing that feels this good can be against the Light's will."

"High Priestess," she mutters under her breath as she shakes her head. "Did I mention the bit where I've never met anyone like you?"

I nod.

"Look at me," she says.

I do. She's beautiful. Even the darkness in her eyes and the scar that snakes down her neck. I reach up and touch it. Then I trace the dark stain around her yellow eyes, and my fingertips drift over her long lashes. All signs of her heritage, of the life she's lived up until now.

I want to know everything about her.

"What was it like?" I ask. "Growing up on Permuna, I mean."

"Hard. Like most places." Then she gives a shrug. "But not all bad."

"What do you miss?"

She looks away for a second, remembering. "I miss the desert. In some ways it's like space—so vast and empty. And I miss the starburst cacti." She closes her eyes for a moment. "Even thinking about them makes my mouth water."

"I've never tasted one. Maybe you can feed me one someday."

The smile fades from her face. "Maybe."

I hate to see the joy fall from her eyes. Maybe all we have are these stolen moments on the *Starlight*.

Only now.

I trail my hand down her cheek, dance my fingers lightly across her lips. She draws in a sharp breath, and I have to press my lips together to keep from grinning. The oh-so-snarky Beckett isn't nearly as cool as she pretends to be.

I slide lower, across her jaw and down her throat, where I can feel the pulse of her blood flutter against my fingertips. Then lower still, to the sharp edges of her collarbone and the soft neckline of her black jumpsuit. I slide my fingers along the edges, but I don't quite have the nerve to go any farther.

She takes pity on me, her hands skimming my shoulders and down my arms before coming to rest on my waist. The heat from her palms sinks into my skin. She slides them up to cup my breasts, and my nipples go hard, pressing against the soft material of my camisole. She circles one with the pad of her thumb, and pleasure sings through me.

Then she lowers her head and I raise mine and we meet in the middle for one more kiss.

It's sweet and soft and not what I was expecting at all. Tears prick the backs of my eyes, so I close them and take a deep, shuddering breath.

Beckett steps back, pointing to a pot that seems to have magically brewed itself. "They'll be waiting for their coffee."

For a second, I have no clue what she's talking about. Then my hands tighten on her arm and I whisper fiercely, "I don't care."

"Yes you do, good girl." She takes a step back and smirks. "Besides, I'm taking this slowly. One of us has to be the sensible one in this relationship. And fuck us both—it looks like it's going to have to be me."

CHAPTER 36

Ian

I hate it when I don't know what's going on. And right now, I've got no fucking clue.

Anyone in the Senestris System could be after us. Except every time we think about the flyers and now the ship, too, Max and I come back to Kali.

I hate to say it, but I have to finally admit that we might all be a hell of a lot safer with her gone. Because maybe she's right—maybe she *would* be able to ensure our protection. I've been underestimating her for way too long.

All I have to do is take her home—but it's the one thing I can't seem to make myself do.

This is *not* who I am. I protect Max, Milla, and myself. That's it.

I glance over to where Kali is talking to Max, their heads close together. They've been sitting like that since he brought her back to the bridge a couple of hours ago. The fact that he went after her is weird. What's even weirder is that he likes her, and he doesn't like many people. Or any people, really.

Outsiders always think he's the nice one of the two of us, but that's just 'cause they don't know what's in his head. He doesn't open up easily. It's all surface stuff with him. All smiles and laughs and whatever, but few get to see the real Max. Probably just as well.

"Hey, Captain, you might want to take a look at this," Beckett shoots over her shoulder. She has this really sarcastic way of saying *Captain*, but I let it go for now. She's a fucking good pilot, even if the *Starlight* is doing all the hard stuff on its own. And what's with that, anyway? Just add *sentient ship* to my list of shit to figure out.

I need to spend some time and learn how to fly the ship myself. Just in case, because although Beckett appears better than she was when she first came on board, there's still something not right with her. She's tough, so she hides it, but she's clearly in a lot of pain. And I can't afford to not know what to do if something happens to her.

Maybe she could give me lessons, and maybe another backup as well. Gage? He seems like the logical choice, but while he's got a brilliant mind for technical stuff, flying is more of an intuitive thing, and he's flat out of intuition. He likes facts too much to listen to his gut. Remember the red fucking button?

I look around the room, and my gaze settles on the high priestess. Maybe she'd like to learn to fly and spend more time with Beckett. Don't think I didn't notice the heat between them when they came back to the bridge half an hour ago. Plus, that would have the added advantage of pissing Merrick off. I may like the guy, but I'm not above getting a rise out of him whenever I can.

I'll run it by Max, see what he thinks before I decide anything.

I open my mouth to ask Beckett for a status report, but I can't get the words out of my mouth. It's what Milla used to say whenever we were planning or doing a job.

"Time for a status report, boys."

I push the memory away. One thing at a time.

"What's happening?" I ask instead.

Beckett tosses me a grin. "Company."

"Are you fucking kidding me? Not again." And why does she always seem so happy in the face of impending disaster? I'm about ready to push the big red button Gage tried earlier myself if it'll just make all this shit stop.

I mutter a few of my favorite curses as I head over to study the screen. Sure enough, there's a blip right in the middle. "Are you sure it's not just some sort of space debris?" I ask hopefully.

"If so, that's pretty big space debris." Beckett presses a button, and we zoom in. "And it's shaped just like a ship."

"A big one," Gage adds helpfully as he comes up behind us.

"It's not the same one, is it?" I ask, squinting at the screen as if I can vaporize it with sheer will alone. But I've tried that more than once before, and it never works. "Could it have followed us somehow?"

"It could. But it didn't. This one's bigger and faster." She blows up the screen even more. "And more dangerous."

"It's a frigate, and she's well-armed." Gage points to the ship's undercarriage. "Look at those rocket boosters. And this one has markings."

He leans forward and taps the console, and we zoom in closer. I can make out writing on the side but can't read it.

"It's Corporation," Beckett says.

Fuck, fuck, fuck. I squint, trying to get a better look. "You sure about that?"

"Completely sure. It's the *Archer*."

"The *Archer*?" I've never heard of her.

"She's a hunter/seeker. A high-tech surveillance ship."

"A surveillance ship that just happens to be equipped with enough weapons to wipe us out completely?" I ask skeptically.

Gage snorts. "Look at you, so optimistic. That ship's equipped with enough weapons to wipe out half a planet. We won't even slow her down."

"Maybe she's not looking for us," I offer up. But as much as I like that idea, all three of us know it's a pipe dream. Why else would the *Archer* show up so soon after our encounter with a different laser-happy ship?

"They could be looking for someone else—or some*thing* else," Kali suggests from behind us. "How about a recon mission for their alien artifact? I bet they're pretty pissed someone stole it."

"I'd hardly say we *stole* it," I retort.

She lets out a little sigh. "What would you call it, considering we're currently flying it halfway across the system?"

I think for a moment. "We appropriated it in a life-or-death situation in order to save the heir to the Empire. We're not thieves; we're herocs. We deserve a fucking medal."

She snorts. "Good luck with that."

I glance back at the ship. Corporation. Corporation leads to the Empire. The Empire would get Kali back home safely. Even though every cell in my body is pushing me not to do it, I still say, "Maybe we should try to communicate with them. See if they can get the princess home safely."

"No way," Beckett says with so much force that we all turn to stare at her. "I've been a guest of the Corporation before—it's not happening again. They will have to shoot me out of dead fucking space first."

I can see her point. But still...

"Maybe we should put it to a vote," Rain says.

Beckett lets out a harsh laugh. "Since when has this ship been a democracy?"

It's another good point, and even Rain seems to know it, but she still isn't daunted. "This affects all of us. We should all have a say."

I'm not particularly into this democracy thing on board my ship, but I am interested in which way everyone will vote. If nothing else, it will help push me to make the right decision.

I turn to face the majority of my crew. "Raise your hand if you want to stick around and talk with the nice people from the Corporation."

I raise my hand. And absolutely no one else.

Max doesn't for obvious reasons.

Gage is smart enough to figure out he's finished if he goes back to his wayward employer.

Beckett was never going to agree.

Rain clearly wants to help her new girlfriend stay free.

I understand their reasoning, but Merrick surprises me. I would have expected him to vote to stay for no other reason than he's desperate to get Rain back to Serati. But when I look over at him, his face is expressionless and both his arms are firmly down.

Yeah, there's definitely something there. Some reason he doesn't trust the Corporation. It makes me wonder what secrets he's keeping.

Then I turn to Kali, look at her crossed arms. "Really? Even you?"

But all she says is, "Let's get the fuck out of here."

Before anyone can stop her—or even say a word—Kali's at the control panel, and with more force than I thought possible, she slams her hand down on the button we've all seen Beckett push a hundred times. The one we all know means "Go, Go, Go."

There's a scramble for seats. We're all getting to know how the *Starlight* tends to fly when that button is pushed.

This time, I'm ready for it, and boy, is it a rush when you're sitting down and not tumbling ass over elbow.

Within seconds, we leave the *Archer* far behind.

"Eat our dust, you fucking drokaray shit," Kali yells.

And I find myself laughing. Half in amusement. Half in relief.

CHAPTER 37

Kali

That felt fucking *good*.

With the push of one button, not only did I send a big ol' fuck-you to the Corporation *and* my mother, I made my own decision about my fate and stuck with it. I'm on the *Starlight* now because I want to be. Because I need to be. And because I've earned my spot here, and fuck anyone who says otherwise.

Who's dead weight now?

"Well, that was unexpected," Ian says. Then he grins at me. "Welcome to the *Starlight*, Kali."

The others send huge smiles my way, too. Even Beckett looks less hostile, and you know what? I'll take it. It feels amazing to be useful for something besides ensuring there's always a fresh pot of coffee.

"Set a course for Glacea again, please," Ian says to Beckett, and she does, no snarky comment added in.

I head over to take a seat next to Rain, blowing out a long, deep breath. Now that the adrenaline has started to wear off, I feel wiped.

Rain gives me an encouraging smile. "That was amazing," she says. "Well done."

"Thanks," I say. Then: "Looks like we're officially off to Glacea."

"I know." She says it with her usual brand of enthusiasm. "I've never been. I can't wait. It's supposed to be beautiful."

"And cold."

"How absolutely amazing! Do you think we'll get to see some snow?"

I think on it. I've never actually seen snow, and surely Rain hasn't, either.

"You know what—I hope so. What do you think it feels like?"

"I've read that it can be lots of different textures. Sometimes light and fluffy, other times heavy and super wet. But always the most pristine shade of white." She's talking faster now. "Oh! And! Did you know it's made up of all these tiny flakes, and I read each one of them is completely unique? No two flakes are alike. What must *that* look like?"

Her enthusiasm is infectious. I try to imagine it. "I once read a story about catching them on your tongue. How amazing would it be if it was *snowing* when we get there, like actually falling from the sky, and we could give that a try?"

She sighs. "A real-life run-in with snow. How divine."

Our eyes meet, and we both giggle at the sacrilege.

"You know what I mean," she adds, then sighs again before meeting my eyes. "You know, in some ways, we've got the same problem," she says. "We've both been brought up with strict views on who and what we are. Our place in the world. I'd never questioned it before—it's just the way things are. But these few days have made me realize that things don't have to be that way."

"You'd turn your back on the Sisterhood?" From everything I learned about the high priestess's role, just the idea is unthinkable. Her eternal lives awaiting the Dying Sun is the spiritual center of the Sisterhood.

"No. I believe as high priestess, I have an important role to play and a chance to do good in the world. But I hope that doesn't mean I have to have a closed mind and live my life how others believe I should. I hope I can find a way to balance what they want me to be with who I'm discovering I really am."

"That'd be nice, wouldn't it?" I don't even try to keep the

wistfulness out of my tone.

"Very nice." She smiles. "Though Merrick doesn't see it that way. He's finding this very hard. I'm really not supposed to have a mind of my own. It makes his job far more difficult."

I glance across to where Merrick is seated, long legs stretched out, a brooding expression on his face. He's developing an impressive black eye, and his nose is completely swollen. "Maybe you should lay off a little. Just until he can see out of both eyes again."

"Right?" She makes a face, scrunching up her nose. "To be fair, I don't think it's all my fault. I suspect Merrick is going through a crisis of faith."

"Aren't we all?" I add.

"Of course. It happens to most everyone at some point. His father died recently—he never talked about his family, but I think they were close—and it's hit him hard. Made him confront his mortality and question his role in life, even before we ended up on the *Caelestis*."

Her words have me looking at Merrick again, maybe even seeing him in a different light. "It's funny, isn't it? We see people and we make judgments and believe we know who they really are, but mostly, we're wrong. We can never truly understand what someone else is going through. I mean, it's hard enough working out what *I'm* going through, never mind anyone else."

Rain smiles. "Remember that when you think of Beckett. She's had a hard life. She seems tough, but it's a mask she wears to hide the pain."

"Tough" seems like an understatement, but she's not wrong. And after everything Beckett said earlier, it's not hard to understand why she is the way she is. Who wouldn't be hard after everything she's gone through?

But thinking on that is chasing away the high of my earlier actions, so instead, I change the subject. "What do you think snow tastes like?"

"Sugar," Rain breathes out, and we both sigh this time. "If it's snowing when we get to Glacea, promise me we'll catch some snowflakes on our tongues."

"You got it," I say with a grin, and this has officially become my favorite day ever.

So of course it's at that moment that Ian claps his hands. "I hate to bring more bad news, but I really think we've got another problem. And this one we can't outrun."

CHAPTER 38

Kali

"I've been thinking," Ian starts.

"Well, that's terrifying," Gage comments in an acerbic voice.

Ian just flips him off in a non-heated way and continues, "The bad guys—and right now, I consider that pretty much everyone who's not on this ship—keep finding us. And while I'm willing to believe it happened once out of shit luck, twice feels like we should be paying better attention.

"What we need to figure out is—how? How the fuck are the bastards chasing us?" He looks around at each of us in turn, his gaze pausing just a little longer on mine, and I give him my most innocent smile. Which is easy because I really have no idea.

"What's your theory?" Merrick asks, though it comes out sounding a little funny, considering his lower lip is still swollen from Ian's fist.

"While I'm willing to believe the first ship picked up our trajectory from Askkandia and tracked us that way, with the second, we were way too far off-planet for that to have worked. So, I'm thinking that maybe we've got a bug."

"What sort of bug are you talking about?" Rain asks, looking totally disgusted.

At least until I lean over and whisper, "Electronic. So they can trace us—and maybe listen to us."

"That sounds even worse than I'd imagined," she whispers back, her eyes wide.

"Why don't we ask our resident technical expert. Gage? Are bugs a possibility? Could someone have bugged the *Starlight* while she was docked on the *Caelestis*?" Ian asks.

Gage frowns while he thinks about it. "It's not impossible, but it is unlikely. I doubt it ever occurred to anyone that the *Starlight* was going anywhere, so why bother with a bug? Fuck, from what I understand, they'd been trying to get her to function for years and gotten nowhere."

"Yeah, but say she *was* bugged," Ian continues. "You used bug finders on the *Caelestis* for your Corporation work in the docking bay, right? Could you rig one for us to use here?"

Gage looks thoughtful for a moment, then nods. "Yeah, okay. I think I can do that."

"Well, what are you waiting for?" Ian looks at him like he can't believe Gage is still just sitting there.

Gage mumbles something uncomplimentary, but he's already up and shuffling out of the room. Seconds later, Max gets up and follows him.

I think about sticking around to see what else Ian has to say, but at that moment my stomach rumbles. I figure there isn't anything I can do to help right now anyway, so I head to the galley to find something to eat instead. Maybe I can get a head start on cooking us all up some dinner.

There's still a bit of the fresh food left, and I help myself to a piece of bread and some sort of fishgalen paste from the refrigeration cabinet, along with a glass of water from the purifier. After my first few days on board the *Starlight*, I'll never take the chance to drink water for granted again.

I sit at the big table while I eat, because there's something really appealing about being alone right now. On the plus side, I find that I actually like the paste. My mother refers to fishgalen as food for the poor, and ever since my dad passed away, the palace chef stopped serving it, focusing mostly on proteins imported from all over the system. No expense spared.

I sigh. Everything they say about me is true. I really have been terribly spoiled.

But I'm not about to let myself sink back into self-pity. Instead, I start cutting up pieces of the loaf of bread, maybe to put together some fishgalen sandwiches for the crew, while I try to unravel what I know and don't know about current technology in the hope of getting some answers.

The Corporation has always been secretive about what they can do. And they control all the tech. The vast majority of the population live in a virtually technology-free world, though the Ruling Families have access to some. We have comm units that allow communication between ourselves and also between planets. We have motorized vehicles and access to ships for inter-planetary travel. But everything comes from the Corporation. It's a convoluted exchange between the Ruling Families and the Corporation, in which we sort of control their activity but they possess and delegate all resources. And I wonder now, for the first time, just what we have to give them in return for those resources.

I remember Ian saying that he'd heard of prisoners on the *Caelestis* dying after being forced to touch the heptosphere. And yet, when the delegates were in the lab, Dr. Veragelen was encouraging all of us to touch it. Why would she even do that, knowing we might die? And how did she plan to explain it if Rain or I did? We were the two highest-ranking officials on the *Caelestis* when it exploded.

The more I think about things, the more nothing makes sense. Or maybe it's that I don't want to untangle the muddled strands because then I would see clearly and I might not like what comes into focus. In fact, my entire belief system might unravel. It already feels like my life has.

Exhausted and still a little hungover—maybe even buzzed again from my drink with Max—I rest my head on the table and try to clear my mind. But the second my eyes close, I'm dozing.

I'm not sure what wakes me up.

But when I open my eyes, I hear voices, so I head out of the galley to see what's going on and almost bang into Gage and Max. They're laughing hysterically at something, and Gage is waving some kind of wand around.

"What are you up to?" I ask as they pass right by me.

"Casting spells," Gage answers, pointing the sleek wand straight at me. "Surrender or I'll turn you into a slogg."

I turn to look at Max, brows raised.

He shakes his head with a grin. "We're checking the ship for bugs. But Gage, here, was inspired to cast spells by some old fairy tale he read."

"Yes, well, surely there's someone else on board who would benefit from being turned into a slogg much more than I would," I tell him in my poshest princess voice. Because if you've got it, why not flaunt it at a time like this?

"Yeah, but Ian fights dirty," Gage comments. "As evidenced by the state of Merrick's face."

Well, I certainly can't argue with him about that one. "How much have you done?" I ask, thinking about volunteering to take over, as the two of them seem a little punch-drunk.

"We've done the airlock and the cabins and…well, everywhere except the galley and the bridge."

I shake my head but lean in the doorway and watch as Gage methodically walks the corridor, waving the wand slowly up and down the walls.

"I assume you've repurposed some hunter/seeker sensor, but where did you get enough aluminum alloy for the base?" I ask. "I haven't seen any on the *Starlight* until now. I've been trying to figure out what she's made of, and it's definitely not an alloy I know."

Gage narrows his eyes at me. "I liberated some parts from a *Caelestis* drone that happened to fall into my toolkit. Why do you ask?"

I shrug, but my cheeks heat. "I like science."

"Noted," Gage says. "But this isn't science—it's magic."

He whips the wand into Max's face, and—credit where credit is due—Max does a pretty perfect imitation of a man turning into a slogg. Even I can't help laughing.

"I take it you haven't found anything yet?" I ask.

"Not a thing," Gage replies. "Not that I expect to. No way someone bugged this ship. But Ian won't believe me until I search every single centimeter of it."

He walks into the galley, wielding the wand like a sword. In the meantime, I look at Max, who is still smiling. "Looks like you two were having fun," I tell him.

He shrugs. "Gage does an amazing impression of—" Then he breaks off, like he just remembered who he's talking to.

Which, of course, only makes me want to know more who Gage was impersonating. "Of?" I prompt.

But Max just shakes his head. Unlike Ian, he really does know when to keep his mouth shut.

I glance into the galley just in time to see Gage finish up his sweep. "Come on, just the rest of this hallway and the bridge to go," he says.

I follow them back. And watch as they repeat the process in the bridge while everyone looks on. No beeps. No alarms. Not even a blinking light to indicate a problem.

Gage puts the wand on the back console and slumps into a seat. "I did say it was unlikely," he mutters. But he still seems annoyed that he couldn't find something.

"Damn." Ian runs a hand over his face. "So how the fuck did they find us, then?"

"Maybe they've developed a way to track alien artifacts," Gage tries. "I know they were working on some sort of prototype."

"Well, let's hope that's not the case, or we'll never lose them again."

Max picks up the wand for himself, tosses it in the air, catches it, then points it at Gage's head. "Prepare to be—"

It beeps.

Everyone goes still and turns to look at Gage.

Max moves closer, waving the wand over Gage's head. The beeping gets louder.

Gage frowns. Then his expression clears. "That's not a bug," he says, brushing the wand away. "It's my neural chip. We all have them in the Corporation. They're implanted when we join up." He glances around and frowns. "Why are you all looking at me like that?"

"You have a chip in your head?" Ian asks. "A neural chip?"

"Yeah. What's the big deal? I told you—we all have them."

"And what do these chips do, exactly?"

"All sorts of cool stuff, but you don't get access to most of that until the higher levels. Initially, they just use them for keeping track…" He trails off, his eyes widening. "Oh shit."

"Oh shit, indeed," Ian mutters. "And you're supposed to be the intelligent one in this little group. Fucking *fuck*, man." He runs a hand over the top of his short hair—I've noticed it's a habit of his when he's thinking or pissed off about something. "So, you have a neural chip in your head that they can use to track you?"

"Yeah, but I don't know how far away it can be picked up."

"Let me take a wild stab in the dark—*pretty fucking far*." He shakes his head. "So, what do we do now?" His eyes narrow on Gage. "My vote is toss the fucker out of the airlock along with his neural chip."

Beckett raises a hand. "I second the motion."

Bloodthirsty drokarays—both of them.

Gage tugs on his earring, then glances at Max, who shrugs like he doesn't care one way or the other.

And now Gage is starting to turn a little green.

"Don't be silly," Rain says. She crosses to Gage and pats him on the arm. "Of course we're not going to toss you into space and leave you to die."

"Pity." Ian shoves his hands in his pockets and eyes the other man. "I could use a little something to break up the monotony. Maybe just his head, then, and we'll keep the rest of him around for old times' sake?"

My lips twitch, and I almost laugh—except I'm not totally sure he's joking. That's the thing with Ian: I've seen how easily he kills. And once seen, that sort of thing cannot be forgotten.

"Could we remove it?" I suggest tentatively. "Do you even know exactly where it is, Gage?"

Gage looks more than a little alarmed at the suggestion. "Not a chance. It's inside my skull. No way are any of you goons digging around in my head. No way." He jumps to his feet and starts pacing. "Look, I'll kill it," he says quickly. "I heard there's a way they can be deactivated. It just needs an electromagnetic pulse. A big one, but I'm sure I can rig something up to do it. Just give me a little time."

"That does sound painful," Ian said. "Maybe the airlock is the better option. I heard it's real quick."

Again, I think he's teasing. But again, this is Ian I'm talking about, so who really knows?

Gage's eyes widen. "Come on, Ian. Seriously? I can do this. You have to at least give me the chance. You need me in order to find Milla."

"I don't have to do anything." Ian takes a step toward him. "But for Milla's sake, you can go ahead and try—before your fucking friends find us again. Or I really will toss you out of the airlock, and I won't even feel bad about doing it."

CHAPTER 39

Kali

Gage comes back an hour or so later, eyes watery and bright with pain. Max enters behind him, looking shaken. When I give him a what-in-the-system-happened look, he just shrugs. Still, when we try the wand on Gage's head, it doesn't beep anymore, so I'd call it a win.

Once Gage is "deactivated," no more ships come after us, and the rest of our journey to Glacea goes by uneventfully. Ian is a pretty fucking good captain. He generally keeps the peace, making sure there are two people on the bridge at all times, but I've noticed that I'm never alone with Beckett. Most days are spent traveling, arguing, and with a few small moments when Ian is actually willing to teach me a couple of simple self-defense maneuvers. I'm now the proud wielder of a kick-to-the-groin move that honestly isn't half bad.

Usually, Ian assigns me to the bridge with Max or Rain—both of whom work just fine as partners for me. Max makes me laugh all the time, and Rain makes me feel like the system might not be the horrible place I'm beginning to suspect it is.

Ian has also set up a roster for cooking and cleaning. He's actually amazingly organized, for an obnoxious thief and murderer. My first time in the galley, they all waited with bated breath to see what sort of disaster I was going to produce. Hah. My dad taught me to cook in the palace kitchens—fare from around the Senestris System—and our favorite was a delicious dish playing on Seratian cuisine but using Askkandian protein: the dreaded fishgalen that everyone but Merrick hates so much.

I reconstituted it, made a sauce from dried onions and fungi, and served it with maize porridge, a staple of Kridacus. Rain said she loved it, that it made her feel like she was back home, and for once she actually seemed to be comforted by that thought. Even Ian ate two portions, and he'd said beforehand that just the smell of fishgalen made him hurl. I'm sure my mother would call it peasant food, but I don't care.

And neither did my dad. He believed everyone should be able to cook at least well enough to look after themselves, so he taught me. He said just because we were royalty didn't mean we had to be useless. Though he never said anything like that where my mother could hear.

Anyway, it was fun to cook for everyone, and I don't mind the cleaning, either. I feel almost blissfully exhausted at the end of each day, a kind of satisfied ache throughout my shoulders that tells me I did something that day. Something that mattered and that makes me a part of a community.

A part of this team.

So, yeah, I've been happy.

That's all about to change, though, because we're approaching Glacea. There aren't any checks to pass on entering the atmosphere, but that's because the planet is basically inhospitable outside protected ports—hopefully the spoofed credentials from Askkandia will work once we approach civilization. Maybe we'll find Milla. Maybe we won't. But I have a strong feeling it's not going to be easy.

First, though, I start to smile as I hear Ian say, "Five minutes," to Rain for the twentieth time. "You have five minutes to get back on the ship, or we're leaving without you."

Rain stands on tiptoe and kisses him on the cheek. "You're the best captain ever," she says. He looks a little bemused.

Our ultimate goal is the sky port of Rodos, but Beckett has made a slight detour to the Herodios Mountains way toward the northern pole. Because Rain has convinced our captain that the two of us need to see snow.

We had to fly deep into the vast mountain range—Glacea is the least affected of the planets by the current situation, as it's the farthest from the sun, but even here the effects of system warming are clear to see. But we finally found some snow in the end, and the view from the viewing screens is completely white. Plenty of snow on the ground in all directions, but, disappointingly, none falling.

Rain holds a hand out to me. "You have to come with," she says.

"Obviously," I agree, only hesitating slightly before putting my palm against hers.

"Beckett?" she asks hopefully.

For a moment, I think Beckett is going to stay put, but then she gets up and crosses the bridge to stand on Rain's other side and grabs her other hand.

"Merrick?" Rain says. "You want to come?"

"I'll pass," he mutters. His face has healed a lot in the last two weeks, but he still looks unhappy. And distracted. Something is definitely bothering him, and I suspect it's more than just Rain. Then again, I know how distracted I was, how much I hurt, after my father died. Is there any wonder Merrick doesn't seem like he's on his game?

Rain, Beckett, and I start to wander from the bridge. To my surprise, Ian follows us. Before I can even get fully down the ramp, Rain is running like a child while Beckett follows bemusedly behind her.

I wrap my arms about myself as I shiver, but I keep pressing forward. It's too fun to watch Rain experience her first snow.

She's twirling in the stuff. Slowly, because she's clearly finding the higher gravity of Glacea harder to maneuver in. She's in her blue-and-pink jumpsuit, and it stands out brightly against the whiteness. It makes me glad she's not still in her priestess robes—there's no way I'd even be able to see her out there.

But all of a sudden, the sweet little high priestess stops, leans down, and makes a snowball—which she promptly hurls in Beckett's unsuspecting face.

"I bet three hundred planetas that Beckett won't throw one back," Ian murmurs from his position at my shoulder. We haven't been this close since our last near kiss.

"You don't have three hundred planetas," I shoot back. "And if you do, they're likely mine anyway. Remember the buttons?" It's only a few seconds before Beckett balls up a handful of snow herself and hurls it straight at Rain. "Looks like you would have lost."

"Wonders will never cease." He shakes his head. And I understand the slight grin teasing his lips. Beckett, while still surly toward me, has seemed a lot lighter, for lack of a better word, the last couple of days. I don't know if it's Rain or if she's finally starting to feel better after being away from the *Caelestis* for so many days.

I guess I hope it's both.

Suddenly, as if from an unseen force, a few little flecks of white start drifting down from the sky. Rain squeals like I've never heard from her before. "Kali! Get your beautiful ass over here right now! *It's snowing!*"

A herd of rabid drokarays couldn't keep me from this. I run forward, my tongue already out, trying to catch the few tiny specks of white as they drift toward the ground. Somewhere to my left, Rain is laughing, yelling, chasing Beckett as they both try to beat the other to their first taste of snowflake.

I probably never actually catch one. But maybe I do.

Either way, I'm alive. This is living.

I turn to grin at Ian and find him watching me with a curious look on his face. The feeling of his eyes on me is heady, intoxicating, and suddenly my heart is beating fast for a whole new reason. I go back to chasing flakes but add a little swish to my hips for good measure, and even with my back to him, I continue to feel him watching me. I feel my face redden.

"Hey, kids," Ian eventually shouts. "Time's up. Back to work."

Rain turns, raises both arms in the air, and throws herself backward, almost disappearing in a drift of snow. "Please, Daddy? Just one more snow Ancient before we go?"

Laughing, Beckett drags her up, and they stumble back toward the ship, arm in arm and laughing like the kids Ian just accused them of being.

They're still laughing as they hurry past Ian, brushing off the last remnants of snow and leaving a watery trail in their wake as they head for the bridge. I reluctantly follow, though not before I nudge Ian with a snow-covered shoulder as I brush past him.

"Think I caught my first flake," I murmur, darting my tongue out to the corner of my mouth.

He groans. And it's fucking *amazing*.

A couple of minutes later, Beckett is back at her post. Then we're in the air again, flying toward the sky port of Rodos.

It's close to Glacea's capital city, Lanberu, and in a highly populated area. We could be recognized, and that likely wouldn't be ideal, considering the dead-or-alive-flyer thing. But Rodos is where the *Reformer* was heading, so that's where we're going, too.

"What's the plan?" I ask as Ian and I stroll back to the bridge at a more leisurely pace.

"Gage and I are going to ask a few questions."

"And what if you don't get the answers you're looking for?" I really hope he does, but I'm doubtful. And worried about what he'll do next if he doesn't find Milla here.

"Gage is Corporation, remember? He'll have the ins we need to get the answers." He shrugs. "And if not, he'll see if he can break into their systems. The *Reformer* likely had a flight plan filed—even if it's not accurate, it will at least give us a next move. And the security in these places is usually crap. Not many people have a clue how to hack into a spaceflight management network. Most have never even seen one."

That's a lot easier for me to imagine after our stop in Rangar. But all I say is, "You're lucky to have Gage, then."

"Yeah, even if tossing him out of the airlock still seems like a good idea now and then." He grins.

"What about the rest of us?"

"I only thought about tossing you out of the airlock a couple times," he teases, but then he gets serious when he sees my look.

"You stay here. Beckett is going to take off so the *Starlight* isn't a sitting varlen in port, but she'll keep close. We don't know if there are any reports out about the ship, but best not to risk it. Then we'll rendezvous back here in a couple of hours."

"I think I should go with you and Gage."

He turns to study me, one eyebrow raised.

"I'm not going to contact my mother," I protest. "Surely you believe me by now?"

He looks pained, but he says, "I do."

"I'm just thinking that if you do get into any trouble, then having me along might make a difference. You could use me—or rather pretend to use me—as a hostage. Or I could persuade them not to shoot you. The possibilities are endless."

"I think you've forgotten that you are also wanted dead or alive."

"I absolutely haven't. But I'm convinced that there's more than one lot of people after us. One group might want us all dead." And I really wish I knew why. "But the other—the Corporation—I think likely just wants to get me back. And then there's also a chance we might run into the security forces. My mom is bound to have everyone she can out looking for us."

He's considering it; I can all but see the thoughts flickering through his mind as he studies me, and I cross my fingers behind my back.

"You might have a point," he says eventually, but then his lips twitch. "Hmm. Just give me a minute. I might have an idea." He disappears in the direction of his room, then reappears a few moments later, looking way too pleased with himself. "Hold out your right hand," he says.

I frown but do as he asks.

Then quickly regret it as, quick as a bug jumping off a dead drokaray, he grabs my wrist and slaps a silver cuff on it. I'm still staring at it in disbelief when he fastens the other half of the set to his left wrist, officially binding us together.

"What the actual fuck?" I screech, tugging at my wrist. "I thought you said you trusted me!"

"I said I believed you, and that is not the same thing," he points out. "And anyway, this just proves your little hostage story. We're making it believable."

I scoff. "Sure, sure. And what sort of pervert actually carries handcuffs around with him?"

"One who's prepared for anything."

Merrick appears in the doorway to the bridge. He sees us, and his eyes widen, then narrow almost immediately. "Am I interrupting something?" The disapproval in his voice would be hilarious if I wasn't freaking out so much at this newest turn of events.

"Just preparing to disembark," Ian says with a grin, holding up our joined wrists. "The princess wants to come along—apparently, she can't bear for us to be apart. So I'm just making sure we've got our stories straight."

Merrick turns to me. "Are you okay with this?"

What am I supposed to say? No, I'm not okay with this—not even close. But the last thing I want right now is to instigate another fight between Merrick and Ian—Merrick's black eye is only just fading.

I do want to go down to this planet, too. I actually do think I can be of some use if things go wrong. And while I'm furious with Ian, I'm also a little bit impressed. The man's well of dirty tricks never ceases to amaze me.

So, I give a resigned smile. "I wouldn't say okay, exactly, but I'll be fine. At least he won't leave me behind."

"I do have a key," Ian murmurs.

"If I'm so slippery, aren't you worried I'll knock you out, steal the key, and leave your bleeding corpse behind?"

"Bloodthirsty, isn't she?" he says to Merrick. "But you have a point." He pulls a small silver key out of his pocket and tosses it to Merrick. "Look after this until we get back."

Merrick catches it, then says, "Beckett asked me to tell you we'll be setting down at Rodos in five minutes. Be ready to disembark; the *Starlight* will be taking off again immediately. They cleared us for drop-off, not landfall."

Ian nods. "Where's that tosser Gage?"

"Here," Max says from behind us. I turn. Gage is with him. He's wearing a blanket over his lab suit like a poncho. Good move.

"Nice bracelet, Kali." Max grins. "If I'd known you were into the kinky stuff, I would have obliged."

"Ha-ha. It was a present from Ian."

"Yeah, he pinched them from my bag."

So, Ian isn't the kinky one, after all. I'm sort of disappointed. Max tosses a blanket to Ian and then one to me. Mine's gray, and Ian's is black.

How did Max know I'd need a blanket? That I was going on this little trip? His prescience is a bit spooky.

He's already cut a hole for my head, and I slip it on. It has the added advantage of hiding the cuffs, which might have otherwise inspired some difficult questions.

I feel the moment the *Starlight* touches down, light as a doklen's feather.

"Looks like we're on," Ian says and heads toward the exit, tugging me along with him. Gage gives Max a peck on the cheek and falls in behind us.

The ramp is already lowering, bringing a wave of icy air into the ship, so I wrap my poncho closer around me. As I come to a halt beside Ian, I can't help but gawk at Glacea's sky port.

The sky is gray shading to white, the landscape bleached of color. It's a bleak, desolate view, causing me to shiver, and not only from the cold. A sense of foreboding washes over me.

Now, when it's too late, I wouldn't mind staying on the ship.

CHAPTER 40

Ian

Kali comes to a full-on stop, and I give a little tug on her arm. I admit, it's hardly the most welcoming of views, and already I can feel the icy cold seeping into my bones. But loitering here won't make the view better. And it sure as fuck won't get the job done.

I reach out with my mind *again*, but, like all the other times I've tried it, all I find is Max.

"*Don't worry*," he tells me. "*We'll find her.*"

"*I know. But could you try to sound a little more confident when you say that?*" I ask.

"*I'm doing the best I can here.*"

"*Yeah, I know.*" We both are. So far, it hasn't been close to enough.

And I'm beginning to suspect this leg of the trip isn't going to have the happy ending I've been hoping for. If Milla were here, my sense of her would be sharper. But there's nothing. No glimmer at all of her warmth or her wry sense of humor. Which means, if she is still here on Glacea, then she's currently out of reach. Or she's already gone, taken off-planet to who the fuck knows where.

I suspect the latter. But I live in hope. The eternal optimist — that's me.

Right.

"Come on. Let's get this done."

I head down the ramp, and Kali comes with me—it's not like she has a lot of choices. The handcuffs were a great idea. Though they might make things a little awkward if we have to run—or fight. Hopefully, it won't come to that.

As soon as we reach the bottom of the ramp, Beckett starts drawing it in and I hear the change in the *Starlight*'s engines. Then she's lifting off, and we all watch as she shoots away into space. The plan is that they return in two hours. If we're not here, they take off and return an hour after that. And so on, until we're done.

"What if they don't come back?" Kali asks.

That *had* occurred to me. It's why I left Max on board. Not that I don't trust the others, but…yeah, I totally don't trust them.

"They'll come back. Max will make sure of it." Then I glance at her, because I can't not when she's this close. It's impossible to ignore her when I can smell the clean water and sweet berry scent of her. Considering we all share the same shower—and body wash—I don't understand how she can smell so different than the rest of us. So much more appealing. I'm beginning to think it's just Kali who's so appealing, which isn't a problem at all.

She's biting on her lower lip so hard I'm afraid she's going to make it bleed, and I want to tell her everything's going to be all right. But I don't know if it will be. In fact, I'm pretty certain it won't.

Everything is fucked up. It has been for a long time, and I mean more than just Milla. Because if the Corporation doesn't get us here, someone else will at the next stop. And if, by some miracle, we manage to avoid whoever is gunning for us, the fucking sun is just waiting to finish the job.

I've never really thought much about the whole dying-sun thing. And when I did, I guess I just figured it was one more way for the ruling classes to fuck us all over. You know, they've been telling everyone that things are so tight because they need all the resources they can get to fight this thing. And I was just like—yeah, more likely just to line their own pockets.

But now, after all I've seen and heard—on the *Caelestis*, in Rangar,

and now from Kali—I'm starting to believe that there's something to
it after all. Maybe they are all telling the truth and the whole system
is on the brink of burning if they don't figure out what to do about it.

I hate thinking like that, mostly because I really hate thinking
that Kali might have a point—that the Empress has had to make
some tough decisions in pursuit of the greater good. And now that
the *Caelestis* is gone—according to Kali, the one hope of salvation
our whole shithole of a system had—it looks like we're well and truly
fucked.

Kali jiggles my arm. "You're staring into space as though the end
of the system is coming," she says.

"Isn't it?" I blow out my breath, then turn to Gage. "You studied
the maps. Where to?"

"The port supervisor's office. He might talk to me. Do you have
any money left if we need it?"

"A little," I reply, which isn't quite true. I've actually got a lot left
over from selling Kali's buttons, but I'm not telling Gage that. He
goes a little funny in the presence of large sums of money.

We start walking, and every step takes twice as much energy as
normal due to Glacea's extremely high gravity—higher, even, than
that of Kridacus, where just walking to the end of the street is enough
to give you a cardiovascular workout.

Add in the fact that the air seems really thin here, as though you
have to work twice as hard to get enough oxygen, and it's hard to
think of Glacea as anything but a shithole. I definitely don't envy the
poor sods who live here.

"This city is horrible." Kali is obviously on my same wavelength
as we struggle across the open space, blasted by the freezing wind
that seems to be picking up a little more speed with each second that
passes. The good part of coming into a sky port is that there are fewer
laymen around with time to connect our faces to wanted posters; the
bad part is that sky ports are always at high elevation and designed
for loading and off-loading, so really fucking hard to navigate on
foot. A perfect storm of freezing cold, out of the way, and hostile to
outsiders. Fucking terrific.

"Why would anyone live here?" Kali asks as if she can hear my grouching.

"It's not as though they have a choice," I say. "If you're born here, then you live here and you die here. That's the way it is on all the planets."

It feels like her silver eyes slice right through me. "Not for you, though?"

"Sometimes the system's a terrible place, Princess."

"I know that!" she exclaims, sounding offended.

I lift a brow. "I guess you do now."

Gage stops in front of a dilapidated gray building. "We're here," he says, then looks at Kali. "It's not all bad, actually. Some of us have a chance to get out, to better ourselves. My family were farm laborers on Vistenia. You want to know what hard work is, try digging up root vegetables for a thirty-five-hour day. I was given an Imperial sanction to change categories and a place in the Corporation."

"That's because you've got a brain as big as a space station," I say. I've always wondered about Gage's background, and hearing it now, I can't say I'm surprised. No wonder he's so obsessed with money— when you're born literally dirt poor, you have to farm a shitload of vegetables to make one-tenth of what I paid him to help us out on the *Caelestis*. "Though I do question whether joining the Corporation is 'bettering yourself.'"

Gage grimaces. "Yeah, me too. Especially lately."

Then he pushes open the building's front door and waves us inside.

The room is slightly warmer than outside, but not a lot. A single meager fire burns in a grate at the far side of the large room. There's a desk close to the fire, and a man in beige coveralls sits behind it, wrapped in a dirty gray fur. Even seated, he's clearly short—Glaceans tend to be short because of the gravity—and his pale face is mostly obscured by a mat of black beard. He glances up as we enter, his little round eyes narrowing.

"Who are you?" he demands, and not in a good way.

I step forward, which has Kali shooting me a nasty glare. She'd been edging toward the fire, and when I moved, I dragged her along with me. Oh, well. *Better cold than dead* is my motto.

Gage gives me a let-me-handle-this look, so I don't butt my nose in. I do, however, rest my hand on the pistol at my hip, just in case things turn bad.

The first thing Gage does is turn his head so the bearded man can see the CT tattooed on his neck—the sign of the Corporation. The man purses his lips but doesn't look particularly happy—not that I blame him. A visit from the Corporation isn't usually a reason for joyous celebration.

"We're looking for information on the *Reformer*," Gage says.

"Yeah, you and me both." He snorts. "All I know about that ship is she was supposed to show up on our extra-atmosphere radar two days ago, and we still haven't caught sight of her. She never even pinged Vistenia."

Well, that's interesting. Looks like the Corporation hasn't told anybody about what happened to the ship. Does that mean no one knows about the *Caelestis* at all?

I glance at Kali, who looks as surprised as I feel. "That's not possible," she whispers to me. "There's no way they could hide—" She breaks off when I shake my head sharply.

Now isn't the time or place to talk about that.

"We're more interested in the last time she was here," Gage tells him. "Where did she ship out to? And did she drop off any…cargo?"

"How the fuck would I know? I don't keep track of everything the Corporation does."

Gage nods to the terminal on the desk. "Look it up."

The man sits back in his seat and stares at us. I suspect *he's* beginning to suspect that we're not legit. "Now why would I do that?" he asks.

Pretty sure that's my cue to join the conversation. "Because we're asking nicely?" I suggest.

"Maybe you could ask a little more nicely."

Now we're getting somewhere. I reach into my pocket and pull out a handful of planetas. As I hold them out to him, an avaricious gleam shows in his eyes. *Gotcha.*

I drop the strips on the desk in front of him, but when he reaches out to take them, I slam my hand down over them. "Information first."

He switches on the terminal and scrolls through logs. "After this, the *Reformer* was heading to Askkandia. It was just a refuel. And nothing was off-loaded here." He checks again. "Or loaded."

No fucking way.

Fury rips through me, and I don't even try to tamp it down. We just came from fucking Askkandia. It took weeks. *Weeks.* And I'd bet my blade that the *Starlight* is faster than any prison ship. No fucking way does the *Reformer* fly all the way out here from the *Caelestis* to "refuel," only to turn around and go back to Askkandia without losing something or picking something up.

No fucking way.

I already knew Milla wasn't here—I could feel it, and so could Max. But this shit about Askkandia means we've got nothing. No clue to go on at all.

Because the *Reformer* didn't leave here for Askkandia. It makes no sense, logically or fiscally. And while the Corporation might not always be logical, they always, *always* err on the side of money.

Rage mingles with the disappointment washing through me, and it takes every ounce of self-control I have not to punch the nearest wall—or the nearest asshole.

But then a hand slides into mine and squeezes. I don't look at Kali; I can't. But as her thumb strokes the back of my hand, a little of the rage leaks from me so I can think again.

"That makes no sense," I say. "They wouldn't come all the way out here for no reason. So what were they doing, if they weren't loading or off-loading?" Because they sure as shit weren't refueling, no matter what this guy's terminal says.

He licks his lips and looks at the money still in front of him. "Any more where that came from?"

I shrug. "Could be. It depends on what you've got to tell me."

He sniffs, then glances at Gage like he's looking for permission. Even out here, the Corporation holds sway.

"Go ahead," Gage tells him.

"Look, everyone knows the *Reformer* isn't legit. But no one does anything about it because she has Corporation backing and no one messes with the Corporation." He pauses and flashes another look at Gage.

"I'm beginning to think I should take a few of these planetas back," I murmur.

"Wait, wait!" He holds up both hands in a chill-out gesture. "I don't know where she goes after she leaves here. Or what her manifest is."

"Did I say a few?" I start to gather the money. "Maybe I should take it all back."

He runs a nervous finger under the rough-sewn neck of his furs. Then says quickly, like he's afraid of changing his mind if he doesn't get it out fast, "There's a man staying in town. He's crew on the *Reformer*—done a number of trips. But he was injured in a fight the last time the *Reformer* was in port. They left him here until the next trip."

Now that sounds a lot more promising. If this man has done the trip before, odds are high that he was on board at the same time as Milla and will know where she was taken. I feel the first spark of hope, though I do my best to tamp it down. Low expectations and all that.

"Where is he?" I ask.

He swallows hard. "Staying at the boardinghouse near dock C3."

"In the center of this level, then," Gage clarifies. "Near the bars."

"Yeah. Popular place," the guy drawls with a sleaziness that puts my back up.

Time to go. I pull out another handful of planetas and drop them on the desk. "Thanks. You've been very helpful." Then I give him the smile Max always says looks like a threat. "But if you tell anyone about this visit, I'll shoot you. And if I'm dead, I'll get my friends to shoot you."

"Who the fuck would I tell, anyway?" The man rolls his eyes. "I don't even know who you are."

"Keep it that way," Gage tells him, since I'm already heading toward the door, tugging Kali along with me.

"There's a storm coming," the man says, coming out from around his desk and heading toward us.

Out of an abundance of caution—and years of being fucked over—my hand goes to the pistol on my hip.

I turn back to look at him. "So?"

"So you might want to get yourself to shelter before that happens. Or ride it out here…for a price. I'll even throw in some coffee to warm you up."

"Coffee sounds amazing," Kali sighs. "With sugar?"

"Sugar?" the man and I repeat at the same time. But when I glance over at him, his eyes are narrowed on Kali.

Kali just looks confused. "For the coffee?"

I shake my head as I exchange a look with Gage. Only a *princess* would think they had sugar way out here in Glacea. And definitely only a *princess* would think a stranger would share it if he did have it. We need to get out of here. *Now*.

"We're fine," I tell the man curtly, but my heart is starting to pound. "Let's go."

Again, I pull her by the cuff toward the door. But this time, she digs her heels in, refusing to move.

"It's about to start storming out there," she says, glancing back and forth between Gage and myself. "Shouldn't we just wait here until the worst is over—"

"We're not waiting," I tell her through clenched teeth. The last thing we should be doing is having a coffee date with this guy, who I'm pretty sure would sell his left hand if it meant a quick profit and who is starting to look at Kali like she's made of pure gold.

"Are you sure?" the guy asks again. There's something in his voice that has every cell in my body going on red alert.

"Move, Kali," I order in a voice much calmer than I'm feeling.

When she looks like she's about to argue again, I decide to hell with trying to be polite and drag her to the door. Gage must be getting the same vibes I am, because he's right on our heels as I throw open the door.

And run straight into the business end of a very large gun.

CHAPTER 41

Ian

"Dammit!" I start to slam the door, but the asshole with the laser gun shoves a boot in the jamb to keep it from closing.

I yank out my own laser pistol, whirling around to point it at the guy behind the desk, and the next thing I know, I hear a loud male grunt and Kali is slamming the door shut again.

"I did it!" she yells. "I kicked him in the groin!"

"Lock the fucking door!" I shout at her, even as I fire at the bastard I just paid a shitload of money.

But he's already got a gun in his hand and is firing right back. His shot goes wide, missing both Kali and me. Mine, however, hits him straight in the chest, and he falls over, dead.

"Come on!" I yell at Kali and Gage. "We need to get behind the desk—now!"

It's not great protection, but neither is that door. I can hear the guy outside firing at the lock and know it's only a matter of seconds before he's inside.

Kali is with me—not like she has much of a choice with the handcuffs—and I expect Gage to be right there, too. But he's not. When I turn back to look for him, it's to find him slumped on the floor, clutching his side. Motherfucker.

"Why are we stopping?" Kali screeches. But then she looks over her shoulder, too. And screams. Right in my fucking ear.

"How bad is it?" I growl, racing back to Gage's side.

He's already struggling to his feet. "Just a graze," he mutters, but his face is pale and he looks like he's about to pass out.

I go to grab him, but Kali's arm moves with me. Goddamn handcuffs suddenly seem like a much less good idea. I need to get us out of these damn things, but there's no time. That last shot at the lock sounded like the planeta-maker.

"Work with me!" I snarl at Kali as I reach for Gage again.

But he's finally on his feet and hauling ass for the desk. Maybe it is just a graze after all.

"Come on!" I yell to Kali, and we dive over the top of the desk — sending the terminal crashing to the ground on top of its dead owner — just as the door slams open.

Laser blasts hit the wall just above our heads. I drop a hand on Kali's hair and shove her down just as another blast comes straight at where she was.

"There's three of them," Gage assesses. He's on his stomach peering through the crack where the desk ends and the floor begins.

Fuck, fuck, fuck. "Yeah, well, at least we're not outnumbered," I say to encourage them. Except one of us is injured and one of us is a princess. No offense to either of them, but let's be honest, that's as outnumbered as it gets.

They're racing toward the desk, lasers blasting. And while the thing is thick wood and surprisingly good quality for where it's located, it's no match for lasers. We've got one chance to get out of this alive.

"Grab his gun!" I shout to Gage, nodding at the dead man's pistol, which has fallen a few feet from his dead body. "Then count to three and fire at whoever is coming over this desk."

I don't wait to see if he's going to be able to get it. Instead, I hiss, "Close your eyes," then shoot out the overhead lights.

It's not night outside, but the storm has turned the sky a dark, dismal gray. Add in the fact that there's only one window in this shithole, and the whole room plunges into a twilight shade of darkness. Then I grab the dead asshole's coffee cup and pitch it at one of the side walls as hard as I can.

As soon as it hits, the fuckers on the other side of the desk whirl toward the noise, guns blaring. It's only for a second or two, but it's the break I've been waiting for. I pop up just enough to fire a laser blast at the guy closest to us.

I aim for the head, and what's left of him hits the ground in an instant. I whip toward the second guy, sending a stream straight at him, too. But he crouches to the ground fast, and the white-hot blast goes right over his head.

"Did you get the gun?" I shout at Gage.

"I did!" Kali tells me, and she waves the thing in the air like it's some kind of toy.

"Don't do that!" I shout, giving Gage a what-the-fuck eye roll.

But he's looking a little green as he gives me a what-could-I-do shrug, and I tell myself I shouldn't kick an injured man's ass. But fuck is it tempting.

"You're the one who said to get the gun!" Kali shouts back.

"Yeah, to point at *them*, not me."

I peer around the side of the desk, just to see what's going on. But it's too late. One of them is already here, leaping over the top and landing right on Gage, who yells as the guy's weight crashes into his injured side.

I grab the guy with my free hand and yank him off Gage just as the second one comes barreling around the desk. I send his friend flying into him and then take aim. But Kali beats me to it, waving her gun in their general direction before pulling the trigger several times in quick succession.

Most of her shots go wide—really wide—but they give me the cover I need to fire as well. Mine don't miss. And seconds later, they're both on the floor, as dead as their two friends, and I'm slumping down against the desk, taking a deep breath and trying to figure out what the fuck to do next.

CHAPTER 42

Kali

"Well fucking done, Princess," Ian says as he yanks my cuffed hand toward his so he can give me the most sarcastic slow clap in the history of Senestris.

"What?" I ask, affronted. "Those guys are dead, aren't they?"

"No thanks to you." He reaches over and rips the gun out of my hand. "Have you ever even fired one of these?"

"I have now," I tell him, and I can't help feeling a little proud that I played a part in defending us. I'm also happy that I didn't actually kill anyone. I'm not sure how well I'd handle that—there's a wide gulf between pulling my weight and murdering people.

"I don't even know what I'm supposed to say to that." Ian rolls his eyes, but a small smile plays along his mouth, and I can't help but grin just the tiniest bit, too. Then he turns to Gage. "How are you holding up?"

"I told you. It's just a graze." But his pained haughtiness says otherwise.

"Yeah, well, we need to get the fuck out of here. Who knows how many reinforcements this bastard called in." He bends down and gathers the planetas that scattered on the floor during the fight and shoves them in his pocket, then turns to me. "Just do me a favor and don't shoot at anything else, will you? I don't think Gage and I will survive a second time."

I can't help but laugh. "Hey, I was shooting with my *left* hand! Because *someone* handcuffed my right! And look, I did a number on that wall over there. Crushed it."

"Oh, you crushed it all right. You showed that plaster who's boss." We're both laughing now, and I kinda can't believe it when there are four dead people at our feet.

"I think you did great, Kali," Gage says with a weak smile. "You kept them busy until Ian could take them out. It's a super important job."

His words warm my belly, but they also remind me that he's the one who was shot here. "What can I do to help?" I ask Ian.

"Get the door. We're leaving—now."

"What about Gage?" I ask, worried by just how nauseous he's looking. "I don't think he can go very far—"

"If it's a choice between staying here and dying and getting the fuck out of here and living, I'm pretty sure he'll take the second choice." Ian starts moving more quickly, half helping, half dragging Gage along.

"I will, definitely." Gage hobbles faster in an effort to keep up. And since I know exactly what that feels like, I deliberately drag my feet so that Ian has to slow down a little.

At least until I scoot past them to push open the door and step out into what is already a full-blown storm. Like, a textbook storm—the kind I doubted in geography lessons with my tutors on Askkandia. Within seconds, the wind and snow are slapping us in our faces so hard that there's no need for me to slow Ian down. Nature is more than taking care of that for all three of us.

Suddenly, the concept of snow falling from the sky isn't as sweet and innocent as it felt earlier. And I've got more of it in my mouth than I ever could have asked for.

I really don't want to go out there—Glacea has turned into a frozen nightmare. But as Ian so graphically explained, the other option is staying here and waiting for the dead men's backup to arrive and kill us.

Frozen nightmare it is.

The second we're outside, another gust of wind whips up and snatches the door from my hand, slamming it shut. For a minute, we stand in the small shelter provided by the building, getting our bearings as we try to figure out what we can possibly do next.

I tremble as the wind cuts through me and icy rain lashes at my face. "Which way do we go?" Gage asks in a much more subdued voice than I'm used to hearing from him.

"We just need to put a little distance between this place and us," Ian answers as he starts striding down the level, Gage—and me—in tow. "Max will be here any minute to take you back to the ship."

"How do you know?" I ask. "Has it really been long enough—"

"Is it safe for him?" Gage cuts me off, his voice filled with a concern that has me looking over at him to read his expression. It's... one I don't recognize, twisted with pain.

"Is anything on this shithole safe?" Ian shoots back.

The answer is no—nothing on Glacea feels safe right now, especially not the elements. "We should all go back—" I start but break off when Ian gives me the fiercest, angriest look I've ever seen.

"You wanted to come on this trip, Princess. Now you're here. So chin up and let's get this done."

He continues walking quickly, forcing me to scramble to keep up despite the icy wind and snow slapping at every millimeter of exposed flesh. He doesn't stop until we ride an elevator down to a courtyard with a giant iron fence. We slip inside the narrow entrance.

"What is this place?" I ask.

"Doesn't matter," he answers.

I'm about to ask him why not when the gate clangs behind us. I whirl around, heart in my throat, only to find Max standing there.

He doesn't say anything, and neither does Ian, but they stand there staring at each other for several seconds before Max slips a hand under Gage's arms and says, "Be careful."

Ian snorts.

He and I watch as the silhouettes of Max and Gage fade into the swirling white of the storm. I hope the *Starlight* is right around the corner, ready to get him first aid, but I can't see a thing.

I start to duck back into the street and the wind, but Ian grabs me at the last second and yanks me against his chest.

It's the last thing I expect, and I squawk as he pulls me off balance. I have one second to register hard thighs, a flat stomach, and an even harder chest pressed against me before his free hand is sliding over my mouth.

What the fuck?

I struggle, but his hold keeps me completely immobile. "Chill, Princess!" he hisses at me just as five large men walk by, fully armed.

I stop struggling as I realize Ian thinks they're looking for us.

Once they pass, he lets me go slowly with the warning, "Keep quiet."

"Got it," I shoot back. The fact that I can still feel the imprint of his body from my neck to my knees is something nobody else needs to know. "Next time, just tell me," I offer, trying to push the sensation away.

"Next time I'm saving your life, I'll keep that in mind. Now let's get going. We need to get to the boardinghouse."

"Are you serious?" I demand. "We just killed four people—"

"We?" he asks, brows raised.

"I was trying to be a team player and not assign blame."

"When it comes to saving your life, you can blame me anytime, Princess."

I roll my eyes. "Okay, fine, *you* just killed four people who attacked us. And more are looking for us. And we're still sticking with Plan A?"

"We have to find Milla," he says simply.

I want to argue with him—if he really thinks people are looking for us, then it's a recipe for disaster for us to go anywhere in this sky port, let alone into the heart of it to ask questions about someone who may or may not have disappeared from here several months ago—but one look at his intractable face tells me to save my breath.

And though I may disagree with him, I understand where he's coming from. He's searched the entire system for Milla. Now that we're this close, there's no way Ian is leaving until he gets information on her.

So instead of arguing, I say, "Let's move, then. We're running out of time."

He looks surprised, like me being supportive of what very well might turn into a suicide mission surprises him completely. It makes me sad; he's clearly had so few people support him like this in his life.

Ian steps out from the shelter of the building, and I follow him. As soon as we do, I'm hit with a face full of snowflakes, courtesy of the brutal wind.

Why, why, why did I think I wanted to come to this fucking place? I should have stayed on the Starlight *where I belong.* But then again, nobody said anything about sub-zero storms, high gravity that makes every step a battle, and low oxygen that makes every breath feel like my last. Not to mention dealing with all that *and* being handcuffed to a man currently showing absolutely no sense of self-preservation.

Which is interesting, considering Ian is usually all about saving his own skin. But once Milla's in the mix, all that falls by the wayside. Everything does, except trying to find her.

I push on because I have to, fighting the high gravity to keep up with Ian. Buffeted by a particularly strong gust of wind, I stumble, and Ian tightens his grip on my arm, pulling me closer.

I blank my mind and concentrate on putting one foot in front of the other. It can't be much farther, right? The light is fading, and it will be night soon, and then I'm guessing it will get even colder, if that's possible. *Please, please don't let it be possible.*

Our walk is silent and solitary, except for the howling wind. No one else is ridiculous enough to be out in this mess, so at least we don't have to worry about being recognized.

When I think I can't go any farther, Ian taps my arm. "That's it," he says, nodding toward a ramshackle building to our right.

My relief is so keen that I nearly cry. I hope they've got a fire.

I speed up a little so I'm actually pulling Ian for the first time and even manage to get to the door before him. I push it open and then pause as it occurs to me that I have no idea what I'm about to walk into. What if, somehow, whoever is after us realizes where we were going and beat us to it? What if there is a whole contingent of people inside, just waiting to kill us?

I can tell Ian's having the same thought. His pistol is in his hand, and his eyes are scanning everything and everywhere as we step inside. *Please, please, please don't let anyone be in there. Please, please, please.*

The door opens into some sort of bar area. The light is dim, just a couple of naked bulbs hanging from the low ceiling. But relief floods me as I realize it's completely empty. There's not even anyone behind the bar.

More relief hits me as my eyes fix on the one thing I've been begging the universe for. Using strength I didn't even know I had, I drag Ian toward the fire burning in the huge grate opposite the entrance. I can feel the heat from here, and I groan at how good it feels.

For once, he doesn't try to stop me and get his own way. Probably because he's just as cold as I am but wants to pretend he's some sort of tough guy impervious to the elements. For several minutes, we stand in front of the fire, hands held out as the warmth of it slowly seeps in. Eventually, when I'm finally convinced I'm not in imminent danger of dying of frostbite, I glance around and take in my surroundings.

The whole room is about the size of the bridge on the *Starlight*. In other words, not very big at all. There's a bar running down one wall and three tables, each with four rickety chairs. Ian nods to the one nearest the fire, and I gladly sink down into it. My legs are shaking. Actually, all of me is shaking. I don't think I'll ever be truly warm again.

A man appears from a door behind the bar. Like the port supervisor, he's really short and broad, but his bushy beard is a bright coppery red. What little skin I can see is red, too, no doubt from exposure to the elements.

He heads toward us with a curious look, but there's no malice in it. And, as far as I can tell, absolutely no sign of recognition. He's probably wondering what kind of people are foolish enough to be walking around in this mess. But all he says is, "Can I get you folks something?"

"Gerjgin," Ian replies. He gets a planeta out of his pocket and tosses it to the man, who glances at it, raises a brow, and slides it in his apron.

"Coming up."

"Wait a second." Ian stops him as he starts to walk away. "Do you have a crew member from the *Reformer* staying here?"

"Who's asking?" The barkeep looks immediately suspicious. "And why?"

"We just want to ask him a few questions. If he's willing to speak to us, there'll be something in it for both of you," Ian tells him.

The man studies both of us for a few seconds before giving a curt nod. "Brent's upstairs. I'll let him know you're looking for him."

We don't speak while we wait. I've got nothing to say—nothing polite, anyway. Though I know I can't really blame this one on Ian. He didn't want me to come, even tried to talk me out of it. And I can also understand why he's pushing so hard. In fact, the way he's putting everything he has into this search for Milla actually makes me feel a little better. Anyone who will search an entire solar system and risk everything that he's risked can't be nearly as bad as Ian says he is.

The bartender reappears with a bottle of gerjgin and three glasses. "Brent is on his way," he tells me, placing them on the table in front of us.

Ian pours us both a glass. I swallow mine in one go, relishing the burn in my throat and the warmth in my stomach, before holding the glass out for more. He gives me a dubious look but refills it.

"I'm not carrying you back," he tells me. "So don't drink too much."

I sit back and sip this one, though I really want to gulp it down, too. But Ian has a point. Getting here was hard enough sober. I can't imagine what it will be like to fight that wind after a few glasses.

Suddenly, the door in the back of the room swings open and a man appears. He's middle aged, mid-height, pretty much mid-everything. His skin is gray, but his hair is black and lank, and when he licks his lips, I see a flash of red teeth. So he's from Ellindan, then. That's interesting to know.

He looks us over, face wary, before finally shuffling up to our table,

Ian pours gerjgin into the third glass and nods to the seat opposite him.

Brent sits. "I don't know you."

"Never said you did," Ian answers.

His eyes narrow. "Sam said you wanted to talk to me. I don't talk to strangers."

"Even strangers who will pay for the honor?" Ian slaps a couple planetas on the table in front of him.

Brent takes a sip of his drink. "Maybe I can make an exception."

"We appreciate it." Ian flashes him a smile that somehow manages to feel more like a threat. "You're a crew member on the *Reformer*?"

"So what if I am?"

Ian answers with another question. "You were on the last trip here? What was the cargo?"

The man shrugs and gives an obnoxious smile. "Just some old junk. Nothing of any value."

Despite the high gravity, Ian moves so fast I nearly miss it. What I don't miss is the result—his knife stabbing straight down through Brent's hand, pinning it to the table.

CHAPTER 43

Kali

I let out a little yelp of surprise.

Brent, on the other hand (no pun intended), lets out a piercing scream.

"Fuck! Shit! What the fucking Light?" Brent's trying to pull his hand free, but Ian just presses down harder. I risk a quick glance at his face, then wish I hadn't. His eyes are cold, deadly—vicious in a way I've never seen from him before, even when he was killing those men in the alley.

Brent's turning green, sweat rolling down his forehead as he looks frantically between his hand and Ian's face.

The bartender appeared in the doorway at the first scream. He takes one look and moves right back through the door.

"We need to hurry!" I urge, even as I can't believe the words are coming out of my mouth. If anyone had told me a month ago that I'd be sitting at a bar on Glacea while the only person I've ever kissed casually stabs a stranger, I would have laughed them out of the palace. But here we are. And the chance that the bartender comes back with help gets higher every second we waste.

Ian must realize the same thing, because instead of trying to reason with the now bleeding, sweating Brent, he just twists the knife, opening up the wound so blood glugs onto the table.

Brent screams once more, but Ian ignores him.

"Shall we try again?" he asks in a reasonable tone. "What exactly was the cargo on the *Reformer*?"

"P-prisoners," Brent stammers. "Just prisoners from that space station. Nobody important."

I hear Ian's indrawn breath, and suddenly his rage makes a lot more sense. "And where were you taking them?"

"Back to Askkandia. Ask the port supervisor. Our flight plan was filed. I'm telling you the truth."

"No, you're not." He twists the knife again, back the other way this time, and I hear a sickening squelch as muscles and ligaments are severed.

Don't puke. Don't puke. Don't fucking puke.

"Okay, okay. Stop. Please stop." Brent's full-on crying now, and I'm pretty close myself. I'd get up and leave, but I'm stuck here, chained to Ian for the foreseeable future, whatever that may bring. "We were taking them to the Wilds. We sell them out there. That's the truth. Honest. Please. You've got to believe me."

"Oh, I do," Ian says. His face has gone pale. "Are you raiders?"

"No! No. I mean, yes, some of them—but not me, man. I don't do that shit. I just fix comms. You gotta believe me."

Ian's expression doesn't change. "Which asteroid?"

This time, Brent doesn't hesitate. "Delta V47."

"Come on. We've got what we need." Ian pulls the knife free and stands up. "Just one more thing," he says, then plunges the knife into Brent's throat.

He makes a gargling noise, his hands scrambling to his neck as though he can hold in the blood that's spurting everywhere. Ian pulls the knife free, calmly wipes it on Brent's jacket, and slips it into the sheath at his thigh. Then he turns and walks away, grabbing the bottle and pulling me along.

And I have no choice but to go right along with him.

As we pass the bar, I see a flickering screen that's got to be a century old embedded into the wall, right below the VIOLENCE NOT

TOLERATED INDOORS sign. And that flickering screen has a message that's becoming all too familiar. *Crap.* It's one of the dead-or-alive postings, in digital form because getting paper flyers onto treeless Glacea would probably be even more expensive than the reward they're offering. This one is of Ian, and he's clearly identifiable, even on the low-quality tech. Things just keep getting better and better.

As I step outside, I welcome the icy cold, because my stomach is churning and I feel hot all over. Why did Ian's actions surprise me? I've seen him kill before—fuck, I just watched him kill four people, and it barely registered on my radar. I know exactly who and what he is. I just hadn't expected it this time. Not when there was no reason for killing that man when he'd given us everything we asked for.

I need to know.

Ian is ahead of me, almost dragging me along through the gravity and the biting wind that's slamming us straight in our faces over and over again.

But this time I dig my feet in and refuse to move. Short of carrying me, his only option is to stop. Which he does with a glare. "What?" he growls.

"You didn't have to kill him."

"Yes, I fucking did." His voice is filled with so much rage and pain that I take an instinctive step back.

The handcuffs strain, locking me in place.

Then Ian takes a deep breath and blows it out slowly. "I don't have to explain shit to you, but just this once, I will. There was a good chance he would have sent a message, warned his bosses we were coming. I couldn't risk it." He shakes his head. "But that's not the only reason I killed him. He's a human trafficker, Kali. A raider. Absolute scum. He fucking sold Milla and who knows how many other people into whatever the fuck is out there in the asteroid belt and beyond. That's a death sentence—not to mention a life of torture. And when the people that man in there sold for a quick payday kill themselves or they die from abuse or neglect or straight-up murder, the assholes out there just buy more from the Corporation whenever they need them. So, no, maybe I didn't have to kill him—but I fucking wanted to. Any other questions?"

I shake my head, my face the perfect passive royal mask as his words whirl through my mind.

I know there is business along the inner edge of the Wilds, but I've never thought much about it before. I certainly never thought about how they got people to work all the way out there.

And suddenly the sickness churning in my belly kicks up several notches, and this time no amount of *don't puke*-ing is going to stop me. I turn away, bend over, and throw up on the wet, ice-slicked street.

There's nothing in there but alcohol. Still, I stay bent over, dry heaving for a solid minute, before my stomach finally calms a little. My thoughts do anything but, whirling as they settle on one clear truth. I've been so naive. About everything.

I straighten to find Ian staring at me like he knows exactly what I'm thinking.

Rather than say a word, he holds out the bottle like a peace offering, and I grab it because even cheap gerjgin has to taste better than my mouth right now. I take a pull and swallow quickly, hoping it will stay down this time. It does, and I hand the bottle back. Ian takes a swig before jamming the stopper back in.

Then we start walking. Fast. Luckily, the wind drops a little, and we make good time. I'm horrified, devastated, and so far past emotional and physical exhaustion that it takes every ounce of energy I have to keep going.

Snowflakes swirl in the air but don't settle, and an occasional gust of wind still slams into us, making us slip and slide on the icy road. It's fully dark now, but for the occasional dull glow from the docked frigates, starships, and shuttles waiting to be loaded or off-loaded when the storm has passed. We've reached the edge of the dock where we're meeting the *Starlight* when Ian stops.

"What is it?" I ask.

He raises his head, tilting it to one side as if listening to something. "There's someone coming. Lots of someones." He grabs my hand. "Run!"

I run, but it's like moving through glue. But then, I don't have a lot of choice in the matter—the story of my life. I can hear them now. The sound of boots crashing through the ice. They're coming fast.

"Stop," a man shouts from the right of us. "Stop or we'll shoot."

We keep going, though I can feel my muscles tensing in anticipation. I know I'm slowing us down. Ian's taller and fitter, and my breath is already coming in huffs that still can't get enough oxygen into my lungs. He should leave me, but of course he can't. I bet he's cursing these cuffs now.

I hear a bang from behind us, and Ian swears. Then something slams into my left thigh, and I'm hurled to the ground so hard and fast that my momentum pulls Ian down with me. For a second, I'm completely numb; then, a red-hot spike of pain shoots through my leg, and I whimper.

"Are you all right?" Ian shouts, stopping to kneel at my side. "Kali, talk to me. Are you okay? For fuck's sake—answer."

No, I'm not all right. I've been shot. "I'm alive," I manage through clenched teeth. That's as good as I can offer right now.

"Can you walk?" He glances behind us. "Fuck." He starts to rise as more shots come from behind, then rolls to the side as a bullet hits the ground close to us. *Bullets*, my addled brain supplies in a mist of pain. *That's weird. Real bullets.* He pulls his laser pistol and shoots toward them. There's a lull in the shots, and he's up, pulling me along with him. He slings me over his shoulder, wrenching everything from our wrists to our shoulders in the process, thanks to the cuffs.

I barely feel it as pain obliterates everything else, my whole world shrinking to the agony shooting through my leg. My vision dims. I'm pretty sure this is it. Then he's running, zigzagging to avoid the bullets, but I can almost feel them whizzing by. Then he hurls us both over a low wall made of Glacea's signature weathering steel. I crash to the ground, and for a moment I black out. When I come to, Ian is crouched near me, peering over the wall. He must sense I'm awake because he turns briefly to look at me.

"Thank fuck. I thought you were dead."

"No, still here." *Just.* "Have they gone?"

"Yeah, they decided to go home for a sing-along." Then he shakes his head. "Sorry, this is no time for sarcasm. Yep, unfortunately, they're still there."

I reach out and touch his arm above the silver cuff. "In the bar. I saw a dead-or-alive posting for you on a screen. I spotted it as we left. I bet it's part of every digital bulletin cycle in the port."

He stares at where my fingers make contact with his wrist. "Great. So these could be backup from the first four guys or they could be bounty hunters. Regardless, it looks like they've definitely decided on the *dead* part."

He shifts his focus down to my leg. "Any chance you can walk?"

I follow his gaze and wince. There's a hole in the material of my lovely new jumpsuit, and through it, I can see another hole. In my leg. I'm going to hurl again. Blood is oozing out. A wave of nausea washes over me. "Not an iota of a chance," I say.

On the plus side, I'm still alive, which means the bullet missed an artery. Or maybe that's a negative, considering what's about to happen to us. At this point, I can't actually tell.

"Thought as much. Looks like we're fucked, Princess." A barrage of bullets comes flying over our heads as he speaks, as if to underscore his words.

Not that I needed the extra evidence—I pretty much figured that out on my own.

Ian reaches his laser pistol over the wall and lets off a few blasts. Then he tosses me the bottle of gerjgin.

But when I go to take a drink, he says, "It's for the wound. It will clean it."

"It will?"

Is there any point if we're just going to die? I start to ask him, because it's not like someone is going to be like, wow, she died with such a clean wound. But Ian is looking at me with a "get on with it" expression, so, taking a deep breath, I trickle some of the alcohol over my leg. Then scream as fire streaks through me.

"Fuck! Fuck, fuck, fuck, fuck!" I squeeze my eyes closed as the agony threatens to overwhelm me.

Just as the pain is slightly ebbing, another round of bullets comes crashing into and over the wall.

Don't puke, don't puke, don't fucking puke.

Ian fires off a few more blasts of his laser pistol in response, and judging by the two screams that sound in quick succession, he actually hits a couple of people. Which I might be happier about if there weren't so many of them. And if I could actually think past the agony tearing through me.

I take a couple more deep breaths, and finally the pain abates enough for me to open my eyes and meet Ian's worried gaze.

"Now you can take a drink," he tells me.

"I'm beginning to think I should have done that first," I tell him before taking a long swallow.

At least the pain is taking my mind off the cold. I hold the bottle out to him with a trembling hand. But before he can reach out and take it, another volley of shots come at us, and the accompanying shouts sound closer, like the mercenaries who are after us are getting braver.

Even Ian spinning around and firing several blasts off above the barrier doesn't seem to make them retreat. Which makes me wonder how much longer it's going to take before they decide the risk is worth the reward and just rush us.

How much longer before it's all over.

CHAPTER 44

Kali

"I'm still glad you came along, Princess," he says, holding up our wrists.

"I thought I could help," I say, wondering what I was thinking. "I bet you wish you didn't give Merrick the key right about now."

"Probably," he says with a face that's hard to read as he reaches into his pocket and pulls out a silver key. "Except I do happen to have a spare."

I stare at it and grit my teeth, not sure if I want to laugh or cry. "Then why didn't you use it when we first left the boardinghouse?" I growl. "Or before that, when we were hiking through the storm?"

"Maybe I was enjoying your company."

"Yeah, like I believe that." I take a deep breath and shake my wrist. "Well, Ian, it's been grand, but maybe it's time to part company."

He slides the key into the lock, and the cuffs click and spring open.

I force back a sniffle.

I guess this really is goodbye.

Ian is uninjured. He's got a gun. He can get himself out of here and get back to the *Starlight*. Me, not so much.

I try to push myself up, and a little sob escapes my throat at the pain. But I refuse to die lying on my back.

Ian looks bewildered at first, but when he finally realizes what I'm doing, he leans over me and helps me lever myself into a sitting position so that I'm propped up against the steel with my legs stretched out in front of me.

I have a much better view of my leg in this position, so I pull down the poncho so I don't have to look at the hole in it—or the blood that continues to ooze out of it.

Another volley of shots come at us, and the accompanying shouts sound closer still.

There's a part of me that wants to beg him not to leave me. I don't want to die. And I especially don't want to die all alone on this freezing, shitty planet. Maybe, if he's feeling generous, he'll leave me the booze and I can just drink myself into oblivion before they get to me.

Considering how close they are, I don't think that's going to happen. And I don't want to be incapacitated when I die, either. I just don't want to be scared and alone, and honestly, I don't think there's anything I can do about either of those things.

Besides, as much as I don't want to be alone, I don't want Ian to stay about a hundred times more. Because if he stays, he'll die, too. And Ian is the most alive person I've ever met. The thought of him dying hurts worse than my leg does and way worse than the thought of dying myself does.

Besides, Ian needs to live to rescue Milla from the Wilds where she's being held against her will and forced to do truly terrible things.

"You're looking pretty sorry for yourself, there, Princess," Ian says. "Chin up."

He's right. I raise my chin. Time to end this pity party—for good this time. "You'd better go," I tell him. "Maybe if you leave me your pistol, I can hold them back while you get away."

"Like I'm going to leave you my pistol." He snorts. "So you can take out a couple more walls before you die?"

"Hey, haven't we been over this already? *First time* holding a gun and all that?"

There's another barrage of bullets, and he blasts back at them one more time. But again, their voices are closer, and it's only a matter of time before they decide to do a full-on attack and take us out.

"Fine," I tell him. "Take your stupid pistol and get out of here before it's too late."

"I don't know. I'm pretty comfortable here—I like this wall—so I think I'm going to stay."

"You can't stay!" I tell him. "You'll die."

He lifts his brows. "There you go underestimating me again."

"It's not underestimating you if it's the truth. And there's no need for us both to die. You have to go!"

He smirks. "Princess Kalinda, the martyr. Not sure the look suits you. Besides, I've always been a sucker for a damsel in distress."

"No, you haven't!" I tell him, and the desperation is growing inside me. Because time is running out.

"Okay, you're right, I haven't." He blasts some more laser fire in their direction, then looks at me, his expression serious for once.

"Just go, Ian! Please. Go."

He studies my face for several seconds, like he's trying to decide what or how much he wants to say. But in the end, he just shrugs and says, "I can't do it."

"Yes you can! The cuffs are gone. You can totally—"

"It's not that kind of *can't*, Princess." He shakes his head. "The truth is, part of me is screaming at me to run. But I can't do it. I don't know what the fuck it is about you, but pretty much from the first moment I saw you, I've had this really inconvenient urge to keep you safe. I hate it, but it's not going away, so neither am I."

"Well, you're doing a great job so far," I tell him with a roll of my eyes. But even as I give him a hard time, his words fascinate me. They also make me feel warm and fuzzy inside—or at least as warm and fuzzy as I can feel when blood is leaking out of my leg at an alarming rate and any second a mob is going to attack us with the express purpose of making us dead.

So maybe it's not warm and fuzzy at all. Maybe it's more like cold and sad and a little bit grateful. Because he's staying. I would have sworn he'd have been the first one to vanish on me, and yet, here he is.

Tears prick the backs of my eyes, and I blink. If I'm going to die, I'm not going to do it bawling my eyes out just because some hot guy says something nice. I'm tougher than that. Anyway, it's probably the gerjgin.

Another barrage of bullets with a bunch of shouts intermingled. Ian blasts with his laser gun, then peeks over the barrier.

"Shit," he mutters, reaching out to squeeze my hand. "It looks like this is it, Princess."

CHAPTER 45

Ian

I never thought it would end like this.

Actually, I never thought much about it ending at all.

I have a moment of regret for Max and Milla. Max keeps trying to talk to me, but I'm blocking him out when I can and ignoring him when I can't. Because I know this choice is unfair to him, to both of them. But it's the choice I have to make.

"*Get your head out of your fucking ass, Ian, and tell me where you are!*" There he is again, his voice blasting through my skull. Max has gone from joking to concerned to angry to wheedling in the past few minutes, trying to get me to respond to him. Now, apparently, he's back to angry.

I don't blame him. But it's not like I'm going to ask him to bring that incompetent crew down here to die with me. There's nothing they could do, even if he *could* get here in time. No use giving him a front row seat to everything falling apart.

I don't look at Kali again. I can't bear to when it's all my fault that she's here. I should have let her go home when she first asked to. But I've never been particularly altruistic. And I didn't want to let her go.

Funny how I can admit that now that it's too fucking late.

Shit, I really am as big an ass as she thinks I am.

The bullets are coming in a constant bombardment now, which means they're getting braver. More brazen. I risk a quick peek over the metal wall thing, and sure enough, they've spread out and are heading this way. There are about twenty of them, and while they're coming in combat formation to evade getting shot by my laser gun, it's not going to take them long to get to the wall. A few minutes, maybe.

And there's no way I can take them all out. I'll go down shooting—so much better than the alternative. But what about Kali?

The fear that comes with that thought cuts through the guilt and has me turning to her. She's pale, her eyes shadowed, and she's biting her lip—probably to stop herself from screaming. That leg's got to hurt bad. She's being amazingly brave for a princess.

What will happen to her once I'm dead? There's a good chance that they'll kill her straightaway—the poster does say wanted dead or alive. But what if they don't? What if they take her alive? I try to convince myself that they'll just hand her back to her mother. But I don't believe it for a moment.

For some reason, these people really want her dead. Which means, if they take her alive, there's a good chance they'll torture her for information and then they'll kill her. Or worse, they'll traffic her like they did Milla. Just the thought makes me want to hurl. I can't let it happen.

"What?" she demands all of a sudden. "You're looking at me funny."

The words feel disgusting in my mouth. "I can't save you, Kali."

"Oh fuck, this must be serious. You're not calling me princess."

"You don't want them taking you alive." I take a deep breath and then say the last thing I ever wanted to say to her. "I can make sure that doesn't happen."

I see the moment my words sink in. Her face goes scarily blank, and she swallows as she glances from my face to the gun in my hand. Then she shakes her head. Emphatically. "No fucking way." She shakes her head again even more vehemently. "What are you going to do?"

"I'm going down shooting."

"Then so will I. You'll just have to help me up." She clenches her jaw. "Give me the other gun."

I realize what she means, and I admit I'm relieved. I'm not sure I could shoot her, however much it needs to be done. Though it's not like I'd need to live with the guilt for long.

"You're sure?" I ask.

She nods and holds out her hand. It's shaking. I want to comfort her, but time's nearly up.

There's another shooting lull. They're probably discussing strategy right now.

"*Goodbye, Max. I'm sorry.*" It's the first time I've spoken to him since this began. "*I'm so sorry.*"

"*Fuck that, Ian. And fuck you! Tell me where you are. Tell me—*" His voice breaks.

I don't answer him. Instead, I do my best to block him out as I grab hold of Kali's hand and squeeze. Then I slide the gun she nearly killed all of us with into her hand and take a deep breath before reaching for her.

I wrap my arm around her shoulder to support her and because if we're going to die, I want to be holding her when it happens. Then I use my other hand to reach into my pocket. Pull out the little bag that's been in there for what feels like ages, which I was going to save for myself when this little adventure was all over.

I take a rueful look at the little rainbow beans. Then I pass the bag to Kali.

"Sugar," I say. "For you."

For a second, she says nothing, just looks at the bag with a reverence I've only seen on her face once before—the first time she saw snow falling from the sky.

"Thank you," she whispers. "This means…everything."

She puts the pistol down next to her and takes the bag, twisting the tie to open it and taking out a few different-colored treats. Then she pops them into her mouth, closing her eyes as she savors each one.

I've never seen her look more beautiful.

When she opens her eyes, she holds the bag out to me. "Have you ever had jelly beans before?"

"Never," I admit. "But now seems like a really great first time."

She pours a few into my hand, and we both chew in silence for a beat. The candy is sticky and gets caught in my teeth, and honestly, I'm not sure what the big deal about sugar even is. But I'll remember the taste for as long as I'm alive.

"Hey," Kali says suddenly, looking at me with a small smile. "At least I got to kick a man in the groin once before I died."

I chuckle. "You sure as shit did, Princess."

"It felt pretty great. Thank you for teaching me."

Before I can respond, the shooting begins anew, and it's closer than ever before. I kneel forward and send a continuous laser blast over at the oncoming men. Kali finishes with a few shots of her own. *Attagirl.*

All of a sudden, there's a new lull in the barrage of shots, which I wasn't expecting. They were prepared for the blasts, shouldn't have been affected by them at all.

I peer through the smoke and realize they're all staring at the sky. Then, out of nowhere, they break ranks and flee for cover.

I look upward, too. I have one second to realize what's happening, and then I'm yelling, "Get down!"

But I don't wait for Kali to act. Instead, I just shove her to the ground and hurl myself on top of her, covering as much of her as I can with my body.

A piercing ray of bright white light shines down from above. It looks a lot like a concentrated solar flare, and seconds later, high-pitched screams fill the air—followed by the smell of burning flesh.

It seems to go on forever, and I don't chance looking up in case I get caught in the blast. Kali is still beneath me, and in the middle of all hell breaking loose, I realize she's not moving. At all.

What if she took another bullet? What if she's dead? I lift myself slightly off her, trying to see what's going on. What if—

She takes a huge breath and lets it out slowly. So, not dead, then. Just being suffocated by me.

I get my knees under myself so that I can still cover her but not crush her. It seems to take forever for the last of the screams to die away. Once they do, I roll off Kali but can't seem to get the strength up to move any farther.

"Is this it?" Kali murmurs. "Am I dead?"

"Not a chance, Princess."

"So, what just happened?"

"*IAN?!*" It's Max yelling in my head. And he sounds more than a little panicked. Also more than a little pissed, but that's something for us to deal with later.

"*I'm alive*," I tell him as I sit up. "We aren't dying today after all, Princess. Our lift is here," I say to Kali. "Time to move your ass."

"Are we back to Princess again?" she asks.

"I think so, yeah." It's for the best.

I can't believe how close we both just came to dying. And just how much I didn't want her to die, just how much I hated that I couldn't save her.

Now that the threat is over, none of those feelings make sense. That's not who I am. And it's sure as shit not who I want to be. I have responsibilities—a lot of responsibilities—and Princess Kalinda isn't one of them.

I need to remember that. And I will. Just maybe not right now.

I push myself to my feet, and the first thing I see is the *Starlight* coming in to land just behind us. I've never been so happy to see anyone or anything in my life.

As I wait for the ramp to lower, I look around. There's a circle of burned ground all around us and the charred remains of what had been our attackers on the other side of the wall.

The devastation is complete.

I've never seen anything like it. Not only did the *Starlight*'s beam of light take out all the attackers, but it did so with a precision I've never encountered anywhere before. So Kali was right about the solar flare. I feel fucking ridiculous. If I'd have known the *Starlight* had attack capabilities, I would've called for backup a long time ago. The charred ground comes to within a meter of where I was lying with her. One slight miscalculation, and we would have been toast, too.

We should have been toast, and yet, somehow, here we are.

"What is this?" she asks, and now she's looking around as well.

"I don't know," I tell her honestly. "I have no fucking idea. But I'm starting to think we should've been more scared of the sentient ship we've stolen and what she's capable of."

CHAPTER 46

Kali

I bite back a whimper as Ian carries me toward the ship. Now that the adrenaline is wearing off, everything hurts again, and I can't stop trembling. The ramp lowers as we approach, and then Max is running down it. Merrick, Rain, and a bandaged but smiling Gage stand at the top, watching us, and Beckett is nowhere to be seen. I'm assuming, gladly, that she's on the bridge ready to get us the fuck out of here.

"We're almost there, Princess," Ian tells me, and his voice is so much softer than how he normally talks to me that I can't help blinking. I'm either dying or delirious, and right now I'm not sure which is worse.

Max comes to a halt in front of us and looks us up and down. "Good to see you," he says. Then, "Is she alive?" He sounds dubious as he stares at me.

I raise my head a little and waggle my fingers. "Mostly alive," I answer. "Thanks for saving us, by the way. I thought for sure it was over."

"We didn't save you," Max replies as we keep walking. "We were coming in for the second rendezvous when we saw what was happening, but we couldn't get here fast enough." He runs a hand through his hair. "I thought you were dead for sure."

"So, why aren't we?" Ian asks.

"The *Starlight* took over. Completely. Beckett didn't have to do anything. The ship flew us over here, and then she just started blasting. It was amazing—like a concentrated solar flare, just like Kali saw on Rangar. I thought for sure you were caught up in the middle of it and fried to a crisp."

As soon as we make it to the top, the ramp rises behind us, and the ship lifts off. Then we're flying away from this nightmare of a planet. Despite just surviving what should have been certain death more than once, I can't help a slight feeling of foreboding at Max's words.

Who's in charge of this little adventure—us or the *Starlight*?

And if it really is the *Starlight*, then what's her agenda?

I can't think on it too much as we start walking through the ship; the pain is too distracting, and my consciousness floats in and out. I assume we're going to my room—where else would we go—but when Ian turns the wrong way down one of the *Starlight*'s hallways, all the others following behind us, I don't argue with him. I can't.

My leg is throbbing but also aching. Plus, a sharp pain runs through it every few seconds that has me pressing my lips together and trying not to scream.

So I close my eyes and rest my head against Ian's chest. He smells of smoke and blood and something uniquely Ian. It's becoming familiar and strangely comforting for such a hard-assed guy.

The others are following him, and I can hear them talking, but trying to assign meanings to words is too hard, so I just let the conversation flow over me.

If I'm honest, everything feels like too much work now. My whole body feels strange, like I'm floating and detached from everything and everyone around me. Except Ian. Him, I can feel. Him, I can hear and see and smell. I hold on to that, on to him, as the world once again shifts and realigns beneath my feet.

I'd thought I was going to die—had resigned myself to it, if not accepted it. And now that I'm coming back from that edge, everything feels strange. Different. Like nothing will ever be the same again—in my life or in me.

I'm sure Ian would tell me I'm just being dramatic, but I don't care. If I can't be dramatic after I nearly die, when can I be?

I hear the *swish* of a door, and then Ian is lowering me to a bed as everyone crowds around me.

"Come on, Princess. Lean forward for me." He's tugging the wet poncho over my head.

I open my eyes to an unfamiliar ceiling. Definitely not my quarters.

"Welcome to the sick bay," Max says, wrapping a blanket around my shoulders. "You're only our second patient."

I'm lying on a wide bed. It's higher than my own bed and covered in some sort of white, nonporous material—probably so they can wipe off the blood.

"How are you feeling?" Ian asks as he slips off my blood-covered boots.

I stare at him. "Like I've been shot."

Gage laughs. "Nice to see you haven't lost your sense of humor."

"Nice to see you haven't lost yours," I answer right back.

"Is that what we're calling it?" Max has propped the back of the bed up so I can sit, and I lean back against it with a grateful sigh.

"Are you okay?" I ask Gage. He looks okay, but I'm not exactly tracking right now, so I want to hear it from him.

"Almost as good as new," he tells me. "Nothing but rave reviews for the sick bay. And on the plus side, I'm on some really great painkillers at the moment. So just think what you have to look forward to."

"Painkillers are definitely something I can get behind right now," I say. My leg feels like it's on fire, and I just want to cry.

Which I'm absolutely not going to do, since everyone, even Beckett, is here now, looking like they want to help but are unsure how.

Ian has his back to me. He's rummaging through the first-aid supplies we got in Rangar. Then he turns and gives me a forced smile. "Let's get you fixed up." He steps closer.

"Have you ever stitched up a bullet wound?" Rain asks, sounding as worried as she looks.

"Not technically," Ian replies. "But I've certainly experienced more of them than your average medic."

I don't ask why that is. Mostly because I've seen him in action.

He has a pair of scissors in one hand, and he's brandishing a hypodermic needle in the other. My eyes are fixed on the needle—not because I'm scared of them, but because I'm not sure Ian is the one I want stabbing me with it.

"I'm an excellent seamstress," Rain says with conviction, coming up next to Ian now. "I spend a lot of time doing needlework at the monastery. Why don't you let me handle the stitching-up part?"

"And why don't I take that huge needle off your hands," Beckett adds, joining her. "I've certainly seen my share of those while on the *Caelestis*." She gives me a wink, and I'm sure I'm delirious now, because did Beckett really just *wink at me*?

Ian steps back, and then the dream team of Beckett and Rain is hard at work. I barely feel the prick of the needle—Beckett is better at this than I imagined—but within seconds, blissful numbness is running through my leg.

My whole body relaxes. "That's so lovely."

"Okay, then. Let's get that bullet out," Ian says. "Bullet retrieval is definitely my specialty."

"Can I sit up a little more?" Now that the pain is fading, I want to see just how badly I'm wounded. Max presses a button close to my head, and the top half of the bed raises so I'm half sitting.

Turns out I can't actually see much, currently, as the wound—and my beloved jumpsuit—is covered in blackish coagulating blood.

Ian presses a finger to my leg. "Can you feel that?"

I shake my head. "No." Thankfully.

"Let's do this, then."

As he works, the others crowd around me, keeping my focus off what Ian is doing by telling me how brave I am, how worried they were, and how amazing the *Starlight* was with its odd solar flare.

"Hey, Kali," Gage pipes up. "You ever hear the one about the drokaray crossing the solar system?"

I know exactly what he's doing, but I take the bait anyway. "No,

Gage. Why don't you tell me?"

"Why did the drokaray cross the solar system?"

We all look at him, patiently awaiting the answer.

"To get to the other side!"

Rain giggles, but the rest of us sort of stare at one another, and Ian lets out a snort. "That's terrible, man," he says.

"I know," Gage admits, "but it's still funny to me. The other side. Ha."

Ian rolls his eyes at me, but he's smiling. "Bullet's out, Princess."

I take a peek. Ian is holding up the bullet. It's black and quite small and really doesn't look capable of causing nearly as much pain as it has.

My leg is bleeding freely now, though. Max swoops in and wipes away the blood, then holds the wound together as Rain does her thing with the needle. She really is quite good at it, and it's only a few minutes before she steps away and Max wraps a bandage around it.

My stomach settles once everything is covered, but it still hurts. A lot. Max hands me some painkillers and a glass of water while Ian gives me another jab—in the arm this time. "To stop any infection," he tells me.

Then I'm done.

He goes to the bottom of the bed and covers me with a blanket. At least the shivering has stopped, but as soon as I'm alone, I'm going to get out of what remains of my wet jumpsuit.

He tucks me in. Aw. We really have come a long way.

"Why don't you try and rest," he says. "While we go and work out what the fuck we're supposed to do next."

It's a good suggestion, but I don't want to be alone right now. "I can't rest yet. My head is whirling. And I want to help figure out what to do. As the one who's come closest to dying—twice—I think I have a pretty high stake in this."

Surprisingly, Ian doesn't argue with me. Instead, he shrugs and says, "Fair enough."

"Make yourselves comfortable, people." Max looks at Beckett. "Is there anything you need to do?"

She shakes her head. "No, we're in orbit. Too high to be picked up from the planet. So, we're good for now." She turns to Ian. "I take it you didn't find your friend?"

"No. She's gone." His voice is as empty as his eyes. "She's in the Wilds. Trafficked to one of the asteroids."

"Shit. That's not good. You want me to set a new course?"

"Not yet."

Ian blows out his breath and moves away from me. There's a counter along the opposite wall, and he leans against that, then looks around. "Before we do anything else, we've got to come up with a plan."

CHAPTER 47

Kali

"You mean besides not dying?" Max says. "Because that's pretty much my plan at this point."

"It's a good plan," Beckett agrees. "Completely solid."

"Yeah, well, the odds that we make it out of this are going down fast." Ian runs a tired hand down his face. "Which is why we need an actual plan."

"I think that plan should involve heading to Serati," Merrick suggests, and I kinda can't believe he still thinks anyone will agree with him at this point. "The monastery offers sanctuary and protection."

"Yeah, because it would be so hard for professional mercenaries to raid a building full of sisters," Gage drawls. It's the most confrontational thing I've ever heard him say, but he does seem a little high on pain meds right now. I should know. I'm getting there myself pretty quickly.

I'm starting to feel all kinds of floaty, and I can't say it's a bad thing. My toes are tingling, and so are my lips. Still, when nobody else has anything more to say, I decide to ask the question I've been wondering about since we tried to bribe that guy on Glacea.

"How much do mercenaries cost?"

"Why? You thinking about hiring one?" Beckett asks, brows raised.

"If I did, I know who I'd ask them to kill first." The second the words leave my mouth, I feel bad. "I'm sorry. I didn't mean that."

But she just grins, and for once it seems to be reflected in her eyes. "Don't back down now, Princess. Looks like getting shot agrees with you."

I grimace. "I don't think I'd go that far." But the floaty feeling is spreading fast, and a lot more than my toes are tingling right now.

"More like the pain medication," Max says wryly.

No arguments from me on that front. This feeling is totally bizarre—and also pretty wonderful at the same time. Part of me wants it to go away so I can think, and part of me is grateful to be free of pain.

That doesn't mean I don't owe Beckett an apology, though. Human decency is human decency. "I am sorry. It was a terrible thing to say, and I didn't mean it."

And I may have butted heads with Beckett, but I finally feel as though I understand her. Plus, now that I've learned what the Corporation does with its prisoners, it's a small silver lining that it's only because the *Caelestis* blew up that Beckett isn't already on her way to the Wilds.

The thought almost makes the lovely floatiness disappear.

"What made you ask about mercenaries?" Rain prompts.

"I don't know much about them, obviously." Apparently, I don't know much about a great many things. "But I assume they aren't cheap—especially that many. There were at least twenty guys, and they seemed like they knew what they were doing. Which means whoever is currently trying to kill us not only has the money to chase us through the system, they also have the money to hire a lot of mercenaries."

"A lot a lot," Rain comments.

"A lot a lot," Ian agrees grimly. "But that's probably not the Corporation. The only thing they like more than their money is keeping their money."

"Exactly," I add. And even though it's the last thing I want to say, I finish with, "This smells like the Empire to me now."

"Fuck," Ian says. "One more someone to add to the list of people on our ass."

My head is starting to spin now as well as float, but at least I've made my point. "Can we keep talking about this tomorrow?" I ask. "After Gage and I have gotten some rest?"

"What did you give her?" Rain asks, her face coming very close to mine. I can see her eyelashes and the worried look in her eyes. "She's slurring her words."

"The painkillers *are* pretty heavy-duty," Max concedes.

Merrick snorts. "That's one way to put it."

As if to prove his words, Gage sways a little on his feet. Or maybe that's me swaying. I can't really tell anymore.

I yawn at the same time my stomach growls. Loudly.

"Hungry, Princess?" Ian smirks, but I don't care—he saved my life, so he can smirk as much as he likes. Just for today.

"Starving." I haven't eaten all day, and now that the pain is almost gone—as are my inhibitions, thanks to the medicine—all I can think about is food and sleep.

"Okay, I'm calling it," Beckett announces to the room in general. "I say we let Gage and the princess get some dinner and then sleep it off. We'll reconvene tomorrow, and hopefully we'll all have had some time to process shit and have some new ideas."

"Sounds good. I'll go sort out some food." Ian looks around. "The rest of you go do something useful."

"I'm always useful," Gage says, sounding insulted. And then promptly walks face-first into the sick-bay wall.

"What the hell was in that syringe?" Beckett laughs as she hooks her arm through Gage's. "Come on, gearhead, I'll tuck you in."

"I always liked you, Beckett," he says as she guides him toward the door.

"Yeah, yeah, yeah. I've always liked you, too." Her tone is long-suffering, but the look she has on her face is…something. Affectionate, maybe?

It's such a strange word to apply to Beckett that I'm sure my drugged-out mind must be playing tricks on me. But there's definitely something there. I just can't figure it out right now. Maybe later, when I don't feel so tired and I can actually see straight.

As they're walking, something shiny slips out of his pocket and hits the floor at her feet. "Oops!" he says, giggling a little. Which isn't like Gage—he's definitely not a giggler. If we're on the same pain meds, apparently I've got that to look forward to next.

"I'll get it," Max volunteers, bending down to pick up whatever Gage dropped. But something must be weird about it, because he freezes the second he does. "Where did you get this? It's got blood on it."

"My blood," Gage says, and he sounds very far away. I don't know if that's because of his voice or my ears, though. "It fell off one of the guys in the office. After Ian killed him, I saw it and grabbed it."

"It's a Sisterhood medal," Max announces grimly.

"What is a Sisterhood medal doing on the floor of a place like that? In Glacea, no less?" Ian asks.

He's looking straight at Merrick when he asks the question, but Rain is the one who answers. "Maybe the soldier was a believer."

"Gotta love believers." Beckett snorts. "Especially the murdering kind."

"We do have a small force on each planet," Merrick says quietly.

"A force?" Rain asks, her voice rising.

"There's been a lot of unrest the last several years," he explains. "Ever since the sun started dying. Our followers were in danger, so we've had to put a small fighting force on each planet to protect them."

"Protect them?" Ian asks. "Or act as mercenaries?"

"Protection only," Merrick tells him, his voice firm.

Ian narrows his eyes. "You sure about that?"

"I am, yes." Merrick sounds very confident.

"So now we've got proof that the Corporation tried to take us out, a hunch that the Empire was next, and we round it out with the Sisterhood. Fucking fantastic," Ian says. "It's not just someone on our ass anymore. It's *everyone*."

Right then, my stomach growls again, even more loudly this time, and I can see the second he decides to table this problem.

"I'll be back with food in a few," he tells me as he heads through the door.

Everyone else files out behind him, except Rain, who bustles around for a couple of minutes, cleaning up the last of the supplies the crew used to fix up my leg. I watch her with my eyes half closed, which is the best I can do.

Part of me wants to just roll over and go to sleep, but it seems rude. Also, I'm exhausted but restless, my brain going over and over the fact that Ian, Gage, and I almost died today. My mind is too fuzzy to put much more than that together, but the echoes of the fear—and regret—are definitely floating around in there. So much so that I'm having a really hard time just closing my eyes and letting go.

"You're okay, Kali." Rain's soothing voice washes over me as she moves the room's only chair over to sit next to my bed. "You're safe now."

"I know," I whisper to her through dry lips.

"Oh!" She jumps back up and rushes over to the sink. "Let me get you some water. You must be so thirsty."

I take the cup she offers me and drain it before she even sits back down. She takes it from me with a soft smile and fills it up again. This time, while I drink it more slowly, she wets a clean cloth and brings it over to me.

"I thought you might want to wash your face and hands," she tells me, holding out the cloth. "Or I can do it for you—"

"I think I've got it," I answer. I take the cloth and wipe my face and neck, then my hands and wrists. It's such a simple thing, but I can't believe how much better it makes me feel.

"Thank you," I say again, after she's disposed of the cloth and is sitting down.

She smiles sweetly—typical Rain. "You don't have to keep thanking me. You know we're in this together."

"A princess and a high priestess careening through space on an ancient ship filled with people who don't believe in law or order?" I ask. And though I'm slurring my words so badly that even I can barely understand what I'm saying, Rain laughs.

"It's wild, isn't it? I've never done anything in my whole life, and now—"

"Now you've got a girlfriend."

"I do." Her smile fades. "And a friend who's been shot. Two friends, really."

"Is that what we all are?" Normally I'd never ask such a blunt question, but the painkillers are firmly in control of my tongue now. "Friends?"

"I don't know. I've never had a real friend before. But I think that's what this is. Isn't it?"

Sadness settles over me as her question makes me think of Lara. "I've only ever had one friend before. She died on the *Caelestis*."

"I'm sorry." Rain squeezes my hand.

"Me too. But I like the idea of being friends, Rain. I like you, even if you do have shit taste in women."

"I like you, too, Kali. And Beckett's actually pretty great when you get to know her."

"I'm going to have to take your word on that." My eyelids keep getting heavier, until it becomes a real struggle to keep them open. "You don't have to stay. I'll be okay by myself."

"Of course you will. I mean, you did just fight off a pack of professional mercenaries."

I grin at the description even as I give up the fight to keep my eyes open. "Pretty sure that was Ian and the Starlight. But I helped a little. I actually kicked a guy in the groin."

"That…is so badass," she tells me, then squeezes my hand again. "Go to sleep, Kali. You'll feel better after some rest."

I struggle to say something else—something important that's floating around the edges of my mind—but sleep is coming fast. So I settle for squeezing Rain's hand back and give myself up to the darkness washing over me.

CHAPTER 48

Ian

"**N**ext time you decide to take on a pack of pro mercs, you might give me a little more warning," Max says as we enter the galley.

"I'd say there won't be a next time, but I think we both know that's a load of drokaray shit."

"True fucking statement," he agrees, pouring us two glasses of gerjgin. He slides one to me, then downs his in a couple of swallows.

I drink my own the same way. It's been an absolute shit day from start to finish.

I hadn't really expected to find Milla on Glacea, but hope springs fucking eternal. Of course, I'd also hoped to get off-planet without getting Kali shot, so...

"*You're not dead*," Max tells me, like he thinks it will sink in more if he says it directly in my head. "*And neither are Kali or Gage. That's got to count for something.*"

"Maybe." I nod at him. "At least we know where she is."

"Yeah, and it's not going to be easy to get her out. All the shit out there is heavily guarded."

"We'll find a way. We always do."

I don't know about that. Maybe I'm feeling particularly pessimistic because I did just offer to kill Kali to keep her from falling into the hands of who the fuck knows. Nothing like the threat of having to carry out a mercy killing on the woman you spend entirely too much time thinking about to put you in a foul fucking mood.

"You spend too much time thinking about her, huh?" Max asks slyly.

I don't bother to answer, considering he knows—firsthand—just how much space Kali's taking up in my brain these days. Not that I have any intention of talking about that.

"You eat yet?"

"Yeah, absolutely." Max rolls his eyes. "I kicked back with some noodles and had a grand old time watching you and Kali fight for your lives."

"Keep it up, and you can make your own food." I rummage through the cabinet and find the least objectionable of the dehydrated food— so, *not* fishgalen—and place it in the processor.

When it's ready, I hand it to Max, then quickly make two more packets for Kali and me and throw them on a sheet pan that can double as a tray. I add some silverware, another drink for me, and the last of the planzina juice for Kali. She needs the calories after all that blood loss.

"You okay to keep watch on the bridge tonight?" I ask. "I'd planned on relieving Beckett, but..."

"I've got you covered," he answers.

I pick up the tray with a nod, then make a quick detour to my room to get changed—and grab a clean shirt from Max's stash— before heading back to the sick bay.

As I walk, I realize just how fucked I am—and wonder why Max was so tolerant. If I'd been in his shoes, I would have threatened to kick my ass for the stunt I pulled today.

I could have left. And Max could totally make the argument that I *should* have left. He won't, because he's not that kind of guy. But he should be. We're doing all this to get to Milla and she never would have survived it if I was killed. I already know—we all know—that we can't live without one another. No drama; that's just how it is.

I've always put them first—always made sure to save my own skin because it means I'm saving theirs, too—and today I walked away from a lifetime of that. Because of Kali. Not to save her life but just because I couldn't stand the idea of her dying alone.

Which would have been fine, if I only had me to think about. But I made the choice for Max and Milla, too, and that can't happen again.

Kali's eyes are closed as I step into the sick bay, and I consider just leaving and letting her sleep. But what if she doesn't feel good in the middle of the night? What if she needs more painkillers or has to go to the bathroom and can't manage without help?

And yes, I'm aware that I sound like a complete candy-ass now.

"Not a complete one," Max teases. *"But definitely half. At least."*

I mentally flip him off as I drop the tray on the counter and grab my food off of it. I sit down in the chair that someone pulled close to the bed—Rain, I guess—and eat quickly as I watch Kali sleep.

She looks like she's been through a war. Her face is pale, and she's got dark circles under her eyes. Her full, purple-red lips are chapped from the cold, and her skin is drawn tight over her cheeks. Her red hair is a mess around her face, and her jumpsuit looks like it's hanging on by a thread. And still I can't take my eyes off of her.

Which is precisely the damn problem.

Some people look totally different when they sleep. I figure it's because their masks drop and you get to see the real them in a way they never let you see when they're awake. But it's not like that with Kali. Oh, she had a mask that first day on the *Caelestis*—I recognized it the second I laid eyes on her. But since then? On the *Starlight*? It's been slipping more and more. At first I thought it was because she thought we didn't care enough—that she saves her princess persona for people that matter—but the more I've gotten to know her, the more I realize this is just who she is.

She's not wearing her mask because she doesn't have to with us. I don't know what that says—about her or about the rest of us.

She shivers in her sleep—I hate that we didn't even get that damn jumpsuit off her—but I don't have the heart to wake her now that she's sleeping so well. So I set my empty plate aside and grab an extra blanket from the supply cabinet to drape over her before dimming the lights.

Then I settle down in the rigid chair and close my eyes as I stretch my legs out in front of me. I'm not sure what it says about my life that this isn't even close to being the most uncomfortable place I've ever slept.

A noise gets my attention a few hours later, and I spring up, hand on my gun even before I blink the sleep out of my eyes. It takes a second to register where the noise is coming from, but once I realize it's Kali, I relax.

"I'm sorry," she tells me from where she's sitting upright on the edge of the bed. "I didn't mean to wake you."

I shrug. "What are you doing awake?"

"My leg hurts. I woke up, and then I realized—" She breaks off, ducking her head.

"You've got to pee?" I guess, moving closer to the bed.

"Yeah, but my leg isn't exactly cooperating."

"We'll figure out what to do about mobility aids in the morning," I tell her. "For now, I'll get you there."

But when I lean down to pick her up, she swats at me. "You are not carrying me to the bathroom!"

"I carried you onto the ship. How is this any different?" I ask, brows raised.

"It just is." But when she tries to push off the bed, she cries out in pain and ends up right back on her butt. Which, I'm now realizing, is exactly what woke me up.

A more gentlemanly guy would probably offer to help her over there with an arm around her waist or something. But I sense that Kali needs to do this for herself, so I'm willing to stand aside to let her get there on her own.

But it turns out I underestimated her stubbornness—and overestimated my ability to watch her hurt herself. She tries two more times to get off the bed and fails each time, and on the third try, my patience fails along with her.

"Okay, Princess, I know the Imperial bladder is probably not supposed to be acknowledged, let alone spoken of so specifically, but you're going to be there all day if someone doesn't step in." So I do, scooping her into my arms and striding across the sick bay to the bathroom. The fact that she doesn't even argue this time tells me she's hurting—and running out of steam.

I deposit her in the bathroom and let her kick me out, though I keep an ear out for her falling as I wipe down the plastic on the bed she was laying on—there were a few spots of blood from earlier—and put a blanket down to make it more comfortable for her.

The toilet flushes, and then I hear water running, but when a couple more minutes pass and the door doesn't open, I can't resist calling out, "You okay in there?"

"Fine!" she answers. But she doesn't sound fine. She sounds frustrated as hell.

"I'm coming in," I say, and the fact that she doesn't argue with me tells me everything I need to know.

I cross the room in a couple of strides, and when I open the door, she's slumped against the sink in frustration, what's left of her jumpsuit around her ankles. She's not naked—she's got on a thin tank-top thingy and a pair of panties—but that doesn't keep me from noticing a whole lot of things I feel like a creep for noticing, considering she's hurt and obviously in pain.

"I can't pull it up," she says, sounding defeated. "It's still damp and it's clinging and—"

"I've got you," I answer as I squat down and, instead of pulling it up, gently finish peeling the jumpsuit over her feet.

She sighs. "I still need that." But, again, the fact that she isn't arguing tells me just how tired she is—and how much she's hurting.

"I brought you a shirt. Sorry I didn't think about giving it to you when you came in here." Then, ignoring all the pretty parts of her I refuse to be thinking about right now, I give her a look that asks permission. Once she nods, I sweep her back up into my arms and carry her to bed.

After getting her settled on the bed again, I grab the shirt and help her into it before tucking her back under the blanket.

"I'm sorry," she says, voice loaded with frustration and—I think— tears. Which…shit. I can handle four guys coming at me with blasters without blinking an eye, but women who cry? I can practically feel my hands shaking already. I've told her before. I don't do crying women.

"Why are you crying? Are you hurting? I'll get you more pain meds. Just don't cry." I practically leap for the medication cabinet.

"I'm sorry I'm so useless," she says, and there are more tears—in her voice, on her cheeks.

"You were shot," I tell her. "That's not the same as useless."

"It kind of feels the same."

I shove another painkiller into her hands, along with the glass of juice I brought for her earlier. "Trust me, I've seen useless. This isn't it."

"I don't believe you."

"So don't believe me." I shrug. "No skin off my ass. But take your damn pain meds so you can feel better."

She narrows her eyes at me, but she's not crying anymore and she's taking her meds, so mission fucking accomplished. "You should eat, too," I tell her.

"You should be careful, Ian, or someone's going to think you actually like me."

"Yeah, well, I think my rep can take it." I grab the tray of food and bring it over to her.

"You brought me dinner?" She makes grabby hands at the tray. "I'll love you forever."

A weird little shiver goes through me at her words. I ignore it— she was only fooling around—but what I can't ignore is the wide smile she gives me as she forks up a bite of the not-very-good mash I brought her. It's a good look on her, and as she continues eating, I can't help realizing that I've never seen a genuine smile from her before.

I've seen princess smiles, polite smiles—even don't-mess-with-me smiles. But the smile she just gave me… Maybe it's time for that *I don't do relationships* conversation again. With myself, this time.

"This is delicious!" she says, holding a forkful out to me. "Do you want some?"

I shake my head. "I ate a few hours ago."

She shrugs as if to say my loss. For the first time, I can't help wondering if she's right—and I'm not talking about the mash.

Fuck, this is ridiculous. Nearly dying today must have really messed with my head. There's no other reason for me to be thinking like this.

"Are you done?" Her plate isn't empty, but she's put her fork down and leaned back against the bed.

"Yeah, I'm stuffed."

I take the tray to the small counter and come back with some wound-wash and new bandages. "This shouldn't hurt," I tell her as I start unwrapping the bloody gauze. "We just need to clean it up a little."

"I'm not worried." She glances down at the wound. "Will I have a scar?"

"None of us are medics, so probably."

"Good." She gives me another one of those smiles. "It was a solid joint effort. Plus, now I'll look mysterious and dangerous."

"Only if people can see your legs." I rinse away the newly dried blood with the wound-wash.

"Good point." She winces a little. "Maybe I'll get in a few more battles before this trip is over. Aim to get shot or stabbed in somewhere more noticeable this time."

I smile. "Let's get you through this battle scar first, okay?" I dry the wound and cover it with bandages to absorb any more leaking while she finishes off the last of her juice.

Concentrating on that keeps me from noticing how good she looks in Max's shirt, eyes bright and hair wild around her shoulders. But I don't take advantage of injured women or women under the influence, so it doesn't matter how good she looks. Only that her wound is clean and taken care of.

"So, are we heading for the Wilds to rescue Milla?" she asks after I get the blanket pulled over her. She doesn't sound scared, like so many people would be. Just curious.

"Yeah. But first I need to work out exactly how we're going to get her out of there. The Wilds are a dangerous place, and anyone we might come across out there is not someone we want to be fucking with."

"Like who?"

"Wilders run the gamut. Space pirates. Raiders. There's a black market for everything if you know the right people. And it's pretty lawless out there."

"Is that how they get away with human trafficking?" she asks, sounding aghast.

"Probably. Growing up on Kridacus, there were stories parents would use to frighten children. Be good or we'll send you to the Wilds."

"I keep thinking about those people on the *Caelestis*. People like Beckett and Milla, experimented on and then dumped like they're worthless. It's unconscionable—and it has to stop."

I don't disagree. But I also know things have been going on like this for a very long time. Change won't come easy, if it ever comes at all. "And who's going to stop it?"

Kali doesn't say anything else. It's clear this trip is opening her eyes to what the system—and her mother—is really like. I knew she was an idealist who lived in a gilded bubble. But now that bubble has well and truly burst.

Even beyond that, though, I suspect there's a core of steel inside her that's being revealed. And one day, if she gets the chance, she could become a good leader—exactly what this system needs. If we don't all burn before she gets that chance. And if we can keep her—and everyone else on this ship—alive long enough to see it through.

Fuck. I sink down into the chair, running a hand over my face. How did I ever find myself in the role of protector? That's never been my thing.

I'm exhausted. And not a little overwhelmed. I have to keep everyone alive and find a way to rescue Milla from the asteroid belt and make sure this damn ship with a mind of its own doesn't do anything too outrageous and Kali—

I cut myself off before I can go there. Kali and the weird feeling inside me when I think of her are going to have to wait. Because I have a shitload more important things to figure out right now than anything as nebulous as feelings.

But before I can so much as think about solutions, I have to get some sleep.

Kali reaches out and grabs my hand. She swallows, and her lower lip trembles in that way that means she's trying to be brave but is also really scared or sad. And I'm a fucking goner. Even before she asks, "Will you stay with me?"

It's a bad idea. No question about it.

I know it, and maybe another night I would care. But after the day we've both had, I don't want to leave her here any more than she wants to be left.

So I shrug out of my jacket. Kick off my boots. Unfasten the holster at my waist.

She watches my every movement, a faint flush across her cheekbones. She wants me. I've always known that. Maybe because I'm something she can't have.

Maybe I want her for the same reason.

Who the fuck knows?

But we're both safe tonight. The painkillers have already turned her eyes glassy.

I move to the other side of the bed, where her good leg is, and lift the blanket. "Shift over, Princess."

She scoots to the far side, and I slide in beside her, doing my best not to jostle her. But there's not a lot of room, and I can feel the warmth of her body as I move as little as possible, trying to get comfortable. I'm never going to sleep like this.

Beside me, her breathing has already slowed. I match mine to hers. And when her slumbering body relaxes, the curve of her side melding to mine, I finally fall asleep.

CHAPTER 49

Rain

I sit on the edge of my bed in the cabin I usually share with Kali. And technically Beckett, though she never seems to sleep here. I'm not sure where she sleeps. Maybe she doesn't.

It's late, really late, but I haven't been able to sleep.

Because Ian, Kali, and Gage nearly died today.

When I close my eyes, I can still see Kali and Ian hiding behind that wall. We were so close, but I was sure we wouldn't get there in time. Max was freaking out behind me, yelling at Beckett to go faster, and it was all so scary.

Sure, before now, being in a little bit of danger was fun, exciting. But not this time.

And then the two of them stood up and every bone in my body dissolved at the same instant.

Being on the *Starlight* has been full of tragedy, like watching the *Caelestis* implode and knowing how many lives were lost, or when the solar flare set Rangar on fire. And scary, like when the ships attacked us. But for me, a girl who has lived her whole life sheltered away for a cause that maybe never felt fully real to me, it's still felt full of life. Both the good and the bad.

And there has been good—so much of it. Making friends with

Kali, Ian, Gage, Max. Wearing color. Eating snow. And Beckett. Beckett most of all.

But today, when it looked like Ian and Kali were going to die, and we could do absolutely nothing about it, it all slammed into me like the frequent meteor showers on Serati. I realized just how much I'd come to care for all of them.

I've never had friends before, and now that I do…now, it matters so much more if we don't get out of this alive. Reincarnation or not, I don't want any of us to die. But how do I prevent that from happening when someone is definitely trying to kill us?

Maybe I should talk to Merrick. He's always been so level, and I usually know what he's thinking. But now, he's not talking to me at all. Maybe it's because he's so disappointed in me, but I don't think that's it. Something else is going on too. I just wish I knew what it was.

Is there more to know about the Sisterhood medal Gage found? More to know about our security forces on Glacea?

I need to know. There's no way I'm going to sleep with my thoughts whirling around like this.

I jump to my feet and head for the door. He's not outside like he was the first few nights—like me, I think he's come to believe that he can trust the others on this ship. Or at least trust them not to kill me.

On my way to the bridge, I pass the galley, and there he is, sitting at the table, a mug of what smells like coffee in front of him and a brooding expression on his handsome face. I still can't get over how different he looks without his robes.

He glances up as I hover in the door. "You should be sleeping," he comments before looking back at his coffee.

"I can't. My mind is going round and round." I slip into the room, sliding into the chair opposite him, and realize that the coffee odor must be coming from somewhere else, because his mug definitely smells like it's filled with gerjgin.

"Can I have some?" I ask.

He pulls a bottle from beneath the table, and I grab a mug. He pours a few centimeters of amber liquid, and I take a sip. We sit in silence for a while.

"You seem different since the *Caelestis*," I say.

He raises an eyebrow. "*I* seem different? Have *you* looked in a mirror recently?"

I reach across the table and touch his arm. "Please talk to me, Merrick," I beseech. "Maybe I can help."

He shrugs. "I don't know."

He looks so casual that I can feel my anger rising. It's not an emotion I experience very often, but I recognize it now. He's lying to me about something—I'm just not sure what. "I'm having a few doubts, Merrick. I need help."

"Everyone has doubts occasionally, Rain."

"Do you? Is that what's going on? You're doubting your faith?"

He sips his drink. The brooding expression is back, and it doesn't seem like he's going to answer. Then, he exhales. "I told you—everyone has doubts at some point." He pauses like he's weighing his next words. "Mine have just been going on longer than most."

I blink a couple of times. Did he just admit that he doesn't believe anymore? That he hasn't for a while? And if *he* doesn't, what am *I* supposed to do?

A smile flashes briefly across his face and then is gone just as suddenly. "Don't worry. We wouldn't be human if we didn't question."

"I hope so," I tell him. I hate to think about him hurting. And I hate even more to think of losing him.

And there's that brief smile again. "You're a good person, High Priestess. I always knew that."

This is all going to take some processing. But he's talking, and this might be my best chance to get to the bottom of what's been bugging him. It sounds like his doubts have been in place a long time, but he's changed since the trip to the *Caelestis*. So, what triggered that change?

"Why do you think they made me temporary ambassador?" I ask.

His face closes up, and I know I've made a mistake. He knows something, but he's not ready to share. I try again. "Why do you think the Sisterhood attacked Kali and Ian today?"

"I don't know. And we don't know for sure it was the Sisterhood."

"Come on, Merrick, I know you know more than you're saying."

He purses his lips as he considers me before he says calmly, "Kali and I are cousins."

For a moment, the words make no sense. "You and Princess Kalinda? Cousins? What? How?"

He nods. "Her father and mine were brothers."

I knew Kali's father was a Seratian priest—it's common knowledge. But how did I not know my bodyguard was related to her? "I don't understand. Why did you never mention it before?"

"It's not something we ever talk about. When my uncle married the Empress, he turned his back on the Sisterhood and his family. There were a lot of hard feelings, and that led to him being estranged from my father and his. Then he was assassinated, and any chance of reconciliation was lost forever. I never met Kali. Not until that day on the *Caelestis*."

Wow. I mean, I'd known something was bothering him, but I would never have guessed something like this. I scrutinize his face, trying to see some sort of similarities. And they're there when you know to look. They have the same skin swirls, though Kali's is bronzer. The same high cheekbones and strong chin. "Does Kali know?"

"No."

"Are you going to tell her?"

"No."

"But you're family. That must mean something." I never knew my own family. They gave me up to the Sisterhood when I was a baby and renounced all ties with me for the greater good.

I try not to let that hurt.

It was an honor for them, though I'm guessing money also changed hands. They were apparently very poor.

"Family is…often complicated," Merrick says. "And love even more so. My uncle was caught in between both."

"Maybe he had no choice? His love was just too strong?"

He shakes his head. "You are such a good person. But there's *always* a choice. You just have to accept the consequences." He stands up. "Time for bed."

Something tells me that he has a lot more secrets than he's letting on. That he gave me the Kali-and-I-are-cousins thing to deflect my questions from the ones he doesn't want to answer. Part of me wants to push for more, but I know he's done talking for today.

"Okay, but I think you should tell her," I say.

He inclines his head. "I'll consider it."

And he walks out, leaving me more confused than ever. I sit there long after he's gone, even pour myself another drink and ponder what he's told me and what it means.

Merrick and Kali are related. Could that have any connection to what's happening to us all?

And I weigh in my mind how I feel about the fact that Merrick is not a true believer.

Where does that leave me?

More confused than ever.

Suddenly, I have the urge to be near the one person on this ship who I know will tell me the truth. The one person who sees me as I am.

Not as a high priestess. As a woman.

CHAPTER 50

Rain

My heart is beating out of control as I lead Beckett down the hallway to my room. Our room, though she's never once slept in it.

After my talk with Merrick, I found her sitting in her pilot's seat, dozing lightly. The second I walked up, she opened her eyes, immediately on high alert. But they softened when she saw it was me.

I took her hand and pulled her to standing without a single word.

As we walk now, I imagine what will happen when we finally get there. I'm oddly grateful that Kali is sleeping in the sick bay tonight, that the room will be empty when we get there. I imagine wrapping my arms around Beckett's waist, pulling her long, powerful body against mine, kissing her lips and her neck and her shoulders before sliding lower and lower, until I've touched and tasted and licked every single part of her.

I imagine being bold. Being confident. Being sexy and desirable and everything Beckett could want in a partner.

And I realize in this instant that I don't need my imagination anymore—my silly, childish fantasies. Because no fantasy could ever be better than the reality of this moment.

It's right there waiting for me. I just have to reach out and take it.

Except my stomach grows tighter with every step we take, and my breath grows shallower. Because no matter what I imagine—no matter how I want tonight to go—the truth is, I'm none of those things when it comes to sex. Not bold, not confident, and definitely not sexy.

I'm just me. Rain. A girl who's spent her entire life in a monastery. How could I possibly have thought I could do this?

But I want to. I really, really want to.

By the time we get to the cabin, I'm a nervous, flustered wreck. I try to hide it from Beckett, but as the door closes behind us, I can feel the weight of her yellow eyes on me.

"Hey," she whispers, sliding her arms around me and pulling me against her, my back to her front. I've always hated being short, but as she wraps herself around me, I have to admit it feels nice to be so completely enveloped by her. More than nice. It feels *sexy*.

"We don't have to do anything," she whispers against my ear. "If you're having second thoughts, it's okay. We could just sleep."

"No!" I tell her so forcefully that it's embarrassing. I can feel my cheeks burning, and for a second I think about agreeing with her. But then this will be just like everything else in my life—a fantasy that I imagined and dreamed about but was never brave enough to reach out and take. And I don't want that. Not with Beckett.

Not with us.

And so I swallow back every ounce of fear and embarrassment as I turn to face her. After searching for the right words to no avail, I settle for telling the truth. "I've never done this before. Slept with someone, I mean. Or…anything else. The Book of the Dying Sun doesn't forbid relationships, but I've never found anyone I wanted to… But I want to. With you." I reach up and cup her sad, tired, beautiful face in my palms. "I really, really want to."

She studies my eyes for several seconds, and I don't know what she sees in them, but it must be enough. Because she whispers, "Okay."

"Okay?" I repeat, and it suddenly feels like my heart has skipped a few beats.

Beckett smiles softly. "Turn around."

"Turn—"

"Around." When I don't immediately move, she presses her hands gently into my shoulders and moves me until I'm once again facing the bed. But instead of wrapping herself around me this time, she takes the band off the bottom of my braid and starts to slowly unplait my hair.

It doesn't seem like a sexy thing. But when Beckett does it...when Beckett does it, nothing in the world could possibly feel better.

She takes her time unraveling the braid, takes her time stroking her strong, calloused fingers through my hair until it falls around my shoulders and tumbles down my back. And then she takes her time rubbing those same fingers against my scalp, my neck, my shoulders, until every ounce of tension and worry slides right out of my body and all I can think about is her.

All I can want is her.

"Like sunshine," she murmurs, running strands of my hair through her fingers. "My own personal sunshine."

"It's so boring compared to your curls." I whisper because I don't want to break the spell.

"Nothing about you could ever be boring, Rain," she whispers back. Then she sweeps my hair over my shoulder and leans forward to press her mouth against the nape of my neck.

I gasp as shivers run through me, and she laughs a little, not *at* me but like she's delighted with me. It's the first time I've ever heard her laugh like this, and I like the sound of it. Warm and soft and open. So unlike the Beckett she shows to the world. So like the Beckett she shows to me.

"Do that again," I tell her, tilting my head to the side so she can have better access.

This time when she laughs, it's a little darker, a little more wicked. And I like the sound of it even better.

Instead of kissing me like I requested, she nips at the sensitive skin where my neck meets my shoulder, and my entire body spins out of my control. My knees tremble, my hands clench, and for several impossible seconds, my lungs forget how to breathe.

She does it again, and the tremble becomes a full-blown shake. It's all I can do to stay upright as pleasure courses through my body.

"Do you trust me?" she whispers, once again smoothing her hands over my shoulders.

With my life. The words tremble on my lips, but I don't say them. Not because I don't mean them—I do; very much—but because Beckett doesn't trust herself that much. Not even close. And the last thing I want to do right now is get her thinking about all the reasons she isn't sure we should be doing this.

"Yes," I finally tell her, leaning back against her so she knows it's true.

Her mouth is still pressed to my skin, and I can feel her smile as she slides her hands around my waist. She leaves them there for a second, stroking my stomach and the top of my hips until my body starts moving restlessly against her of its own volition.

I tell myself to stay still, to wait for whatever she wants to do next. But it's so hard to do that when I'm on fire. When my every nerve ending is screaming for more. Screaming for her.

There's an ache in my belly, a hollowness deep inside me that's begging for something I never imagined I'd need. Not like this. And that's before she slides her hands up my ribcage to cup my breasts in her palms.

"Oh!" I gasp, and the first press of her fingers against the underside of my breasts has me moving restlessly against her. "Beckett!"

She stills. "Do you want me to stop?"

"No!" The word bursts from me like an explosion. "Please don't."

There's that laugh again. "I won't." And then her thumbs are sliding back and forth against my nipples, the edges of her nails flicking at them through the thin fabric of my jumpsuit.

"Oh my—" A shudder works its way through me. "Beckett!"

"Oh my Beckett." She grins against my neck, presses soft kisses all the way up and down it. "I like that."

"I like it, too," I gasp out. I'm shuddering now, shaking, my whole body aching for hers in a way I've never felt before.

"Good." Her hands slide up past my breasts, and I whimper a

little at the loss. But she just hushes me and slowly, carefully begins removing my jumpsuit.

As her fingers brush against my naked skin, I've never been so happy in my life that I didn't have a clean camisole to wear this morning. And when she finally—finally—peels the jumpsuit off my shoulders and rolls it down my back to my waist, I nearly cry out with joy.

"You have a tattoo," she says after a moment, tracing the design on my left shoulder with a fingertip. "It's pretty. Reminds me of the motif on the *Starlight*."

"It's a birthmark," I tell her of the star surrounded by the rays of light. "All the high priestesses have them. It's one of the ways they recognize us from birth."

Beckett is quiet, her fingers trailing the mark. "Interesting," she finally says. "I like it." She leans forward and presses hot, open-mouthed kisses to my shoulder before her tongue sneaks out to trace the lines of my birthmark.

My knees nearly go out from under me then, and I swear the only thing that keeps me upright is the strong arm Beckett wraps around my waist. "Still okay?" she murmurs as she licks and kisses and bites her way down my spine.

"Not even remotely," I manage to gasp out.

She pauses about halfway down my back. "In a good way?"

"In the *best* way."

"The best way," she murmurs as she drops to her knees behind me. "You're good for my ego."

"Yeah, well, you're good for my everything." It's not even an exaggeration.

She laughs, then moves to unclasp my boots. I kick them off as she tugs on my jumpsuit, drawing the material over my bottom and down my legs so that I can step out of it. And then I'm standing there in nothing but the pair of black panties Kali got me on Askkandia what feels like a lifetime ago.

Suddenly, I'm nervous. What if Beckett doesn't like the way I look? My skin is so pale next to the rich olive of hers, my small curves so different than her long, lean angles. It's hard to stand here like this without seeing her face, without being able to judge if she likes what she sees.

But then she lets out a low, shuddering exhalation that fans across my lower back as she slides reverent hands over my hips and down my thighs. "You're so beautiful," she breathes, her voice rough.

"So are you," I tell her.

But she's not listening, her hands and her focus moving to the edges of my panties. She skims a finger along the edges of the legs, moving back and forth several times before dipping inside to stroke my mons, the edges of my sex.

I whimper at the first touch, my already shaky knees turning completely useless in a moment. She moves quickly, sliding around until she's kneeling in front of me, her arms wrapped around my thighs to steady me.

"Brace your hands on my shoulders," she tells me in between the soft, tickling kisses she presses to my abdomen.

I do as she says, unable and unwilling to even think of saying no. As soon as I do, she hooks her fingers inside the waistband of my panties and slides them down, down, down my legs. As soon as I step out of them, she leans forward and presses a long, wet kiss just at the top of my mons.

I'm trembling now, a shaking, sobbing mess of want and need and fire—so much fire licking its way over my skin, along my veins, through the very heart of me. "Please," I whimper as she traces designs on my skin with her tongue. Over my hip, around my belly button, and then down along the seam where my legs meet my torso. "Beckett, please."

She laughs again—this time, it's definitely a wild, wicked sound—and stands, her mouth moving straight up the center of my body—from my navel to my heart to the hollow of my throat. She tastes all the different parts of me before finally taking a step back.

I reach for her with desperate hands. I don't want her to stop, don't want this feeling to ever go away. "I just need a moment," she whispers, bending forward so she can nibble her way along my collarbone.

Then she's stripping off her own boots and jumpsuit, leaving them in a jumbled pile on the floor that is totally unlike the obsessively tidy Beckett. The fact that she doesn't care tells me she's as into this as I am, and I feel a strong wave of gratitude.

For tonight.

For this moment.

But most of all for Beckett. Always for Beckett.

It's my turn to take a step back as she shimmies her panties down her legs. And I'm glad I did because I have the most glorious view—her rosy brown nipples; her long, lean body; the soft curls between her legs.

"I'm not beautiful like you," she says, gesturing to her scars, and for the first time I realize she's as self-conscious as I am. Maybe even more, though she has no reason to be.

I take her hands, holding them tightly as I bring them to my heart. "You have nothing to be self-conscious about," I tell her fiercely.

"I know what I am," she says.

"Good," I answer. "I'm glad you know that you are beautiful and powerful and strong—" My voice breaks as I look at the scars—the many, many scars—marking her warrior's body. "So, so strong. Not to mention the sexiest person I have ever seen in my life."

"I think you're mistaken," she teases. "That title belongs to you."

"It doesn't, no. But I'm glad you think so. That's all that matters to me."

Beckett smiles as she slides a finger beneath my chin. She tilts my head up and then slowly, carefully, *perfectly*, lowers her mouth to mine.

The moment our lips meet, my body sinks into hers. She tastes like the sweetest berries from the monastery garden, like cream and sugar and just a hint of gerjgin.

She feels even better, the dips and valleys of her body magic beneath my questing palms.

And when she leads us toward the bed, when she lays me down across it, every particle in my body yearns for more. For everything. For her.

She follows me down, and her mouth finds mine again as I wrap my arms around her and stroke my hands down her warm back. My fingers run into scars, and a part of me wants to linger, wants to explore each one with my hands, my eyes, my mouth. But I'm afraid doing so will only push her away from me—at least for now—so I ignore the badges of courage, of survival, that she carries on her body and focus on all the other things that make Beckett Beckett.

I toy with the coarse curls that frame her face.

Trace a finger along her full lower lip.

Rest my hand over her big, strong heart.

She whispers my name every time I touch a new place, until the sound of it falls around us over and over again, like the softest droplets in a summer storm.

She gives me a few minutes to explore her—to taste and touch and smell all the beautiful pieces of her. And then she takes over, kissing my throat, my jaw, the pulse point beneath my ear.

Heat licks through me as she moves lower, kissing and sucking her way over my collarbone to the hollow of my throat to the upper curve of my breast. My head spins, my heart races, and my hands clutch at her shoulders, her arms, her waist.

I've never felt like this before, never imagined that I could feel so much at one time without crying—without dying. And still, somehow, want more.

My body arches off the bed, a desperate plea for something I don't know how to ask for. Beckett understands, though—she always understands—and she slides lower, lower, lower, until her mouth is on my thighs and her fingers are dancing over my mons to the edges of my sex.

Need explodes through me as she eases my legs apart and presses light kisses to my inner thighs. When I whimper low in my throat, my hips moving against her, she grows bolder. Surer. More devastating.

Her fingers slide along my sex, stroking, petting, circling, and I can't stay still. My hips come off the bed, my hands clutch at her hair, my legs wrap around her as I urge her, "Hurry, hurry, hurry."

But Beckett won't be rushed as she kisses her way inside my lips to my clit. She flicks her tongue back and forth across it as her fingers slide deep inside me, and nothing in my life has ever come close to feeling as good.

She's stroking me over and over again, sucking my clit into her mouth, sliding her tongue along the lips of my sex as my breaths get harsher and my movements wilder.

I feel myself spiraling up, up, up, my body balanced on a precipice of pleasure so intense that I can barely process it. I'm close, so close, to something I don't understand, and all I can think is *more*. I need more. I need everything.

Beckett gives it to me, her fingers twisting deep inside me as she circles my clit with hard little lashes of her tongue. And then I'm flying, my body shooting off the bed and flying straight into oblivion as pleasure washes over me, through me, around me, inside me.

Beckett rides me through it, with her fingers and her lips and her tongue, until nothing else matters but her and me and the ecstasy burning so brightly between us. And then, when it's over, she does it again. And again. And again.

Until I forget how to breathe, how to think.

Until I forget what it was like to exist without this endless well of pleasure.

Until I forget what it was like to be me without her. Without Beckett.

When it's over, she slides her way back up my body and I reach for her. I'm exhausted, wrung out, but I'm determined to bring her at least a fraction of what she's just given me.

"I want to make you feel like that," I whisper, my fingers toying with her wild curls as my other hand creeps slowly down her body.

But she just drops a kiss on my mouth, lets me taste myself lingering on her lips. "When we wake up," she murmurs, and I want to argue, but my eyes are already closing and so are hers.

I drift into sleep with the sound of her soft breathing in my ear, and I wake up the same way. And when she moves restlessly on the bed, I do what I've been wanting to do all along.

I kiss my way down her body until her hands clutch in my hair and her hips arch against my mouth, and the sweetness of her release flows over me like a river.

And nothing has ever felt so right.

CHAPTER 51

Beckett

Six days later, and we're still in orbit around Glacea. The *Starlight* won't move.

I've done everything to try to convince her otherwise, as has Gage, but nothing has worked. This is definitely one of those times when the ship has a mind of her own and she won't be dissuaded.

Ian, of course, is losing it. With every hour that passes, he's getting grumpier and more pissed off. Even Kali and Max can't calm him down—and I know, because I've broken all my rules about asking for help and begged them to try. Because if he comes onto my bridge one more time and starts harping at me about getting the *Starlight* to go, I'm not sure I won't gut him. Or at least punch the hell out of him. After all, he's not the only one desperate to get to the Wilds.

The only thing that's saved him so far is the fact that I've been a little…preoccupied with Rain. Kali is back in the bedroom, so I don't get to hold her every night like I want to. But since things have been completely dead around here flying-wise, we've spent more than a few hours locked in the cabin together. And every time is somehow better than the last.

Not that we spend all our time in bed. We've also spent hours talking about her life in the monastery and mine with the rebels.

Talking about stories we've read, places we want to go, and anything else that strikes our fancy.

Rain has told me so many stories about the different people at the monastery that I feel like I know them. I particularly want to meet Sister Malconi, who has the biggest flower hothouse in the monastery, underground to protect it from the heat, and treats everyone like criminals just trying to get their hands on her blooms.

Every day, Rain tells me another story about her. We laugh and laugh. I don't know, because I have nothing to compare it to, but I think it's happiness I'm feeling.

I've also been teaching her about the *Starlight* and—theoretically— how to fly her. A few times, Kali has even joined us, and I've taught her, too. She seems to have a serious thirst for knowledge, and fuck it, who am I to deny her?

Yet for some reason, when I woke up today, it was with a black cloud pressing down on me. I'm tense, impatient, and the rage that's been my companion since my father died is riding me hard.

Jarved would have been nineteen today.

Nineteen.

He was still a boy when I saw him last. He'd be a man now, the same age as Rain.

So much rage.

If there's even the smallest chance that he's alive, I have to go look for him.

A pain stabs at the back of my skull, threatening a migraine, just to make my fucking day complete.

I stride onto the bridge, hoping for a little solitude before I have to face everyone else at lunch in the galley. And come to an immediate standstill, because everyone is here. Everyone. In my bridge at the time I most want to be alone.

Merrick and Rain are seated together along the right wall. She glances up and does a double take. Apparently she's picked up on my black mood. Max is sitting in the captain's chair while Gage stands behind him, leaning against the seat. And they're all watching Ian and Kali, who are standing in the center of the space.

Uncontrollable rage surges through me as I stare at the princess. Sometimes I manage to forget who she is, that her family is responsible for every terrible thing that's happened to me in my life, and in those moments I swear I could actually like her. But other times, like right now, on Jarved's nineteenth birthday, I can't.

Her mother's forces had my father tortured and killed.

The same forces took my brother several years later and more than likely did the same to him.

Then those forces came back for me, taking me to the *Caelestis* to be tortured and experimented on before they tried to ship me off to the most terrifying place in the system.

And here she stands, smiling like she doesn't have a care in the world. She's looking up at Ian, teasing him about something, with a wide grin on her face. I have to fist my hands at my sides to stop myself from crossing the room and punching her in that smiling mouth.

It works for now, but I know it's a quick, cheap fix. One that won't last forever—or even for the next few minutes.

CHAPTER 52

Kali

I'm aware of Beckett as soon as she steps onto the bridge.

I'm pretty sure we all are, considering she looks like a black hole, just waiting to pull all of us into the overwhelming gravity of her fury. It's strange to see her like this, all stone-faced and angry, when for the last week she's seemed so different than usual. Softer. More relaxed, despite the fact that Ian has been hounding her nonstop.

Something's definitely changed that today, considering she's nearly incandescent with hostility. Her eyes are a cold and gleaming yellow, while the scar on her neck shows up in stark definition against her skin. And her lips are a tight line as she stares directly at me in a way I can't ignore, no matter how much I want to.

Who pissed in her Moon Mallows this morning?

"Are you paying attention?" Ian demands, his voice sharp as he stares at me impatiently. He's as impatient and combustible in his way as Beckett is in hers. Which should make today extra fun.

Lucky, lucky me.

I drag my gaze away from Beckett to focus on him, though part of me thinks I'd be better off keeping a close watch on her. She really does look ready to explode.

"Of course," I answer. In between bugging Gage to teach me

more about the inner workings of the *Starlight* and bugging Max
to give me more cooking lessons so I can help out with meals, I've
been trying to get Ian to give me another fighting lesson for days.
He's held out until this morning, saying that I need to let the bullet
wound heal up. But it's fine—I've always been a fast healer, though
admittedly my childhood scrapes weren't anywhere near this. It still
twinges, obviously, but compared to where it was a week ago, I'm in
great shape.

Now that everyone—including Beckett—is staring at us, I'm
thinking that maybe we should have gone somewhere more private
for this lesson. But this is the biggest space on the ship.

"To win a fight," Ian is saying, "you have to recognize your
opponent's weakness. You're tall but still thinner than most people,
and so you're unlikely to ever win on strength alone. And skill takes
time to develop. So, you need to use your brain. Find their weak
spot. Piss them off. Do whatever it is you need to give yourself an
advantage."

"Cheat, you mean?" Merrick says. Looks like he's still smarting
from their fight—and the dirty trick Ian pulled to end it.

"There's no such thing as cheating in real fighting," Ian answers.
But he doesn't sound put out by the accusation. "There's just winning
and losing. Living and dying. Doing what you have to do to survive."

Out of the corner of my eye, I see Beckett slide into the chair next
to Rain. As that should keep her occupied for a little while, I relax a
little and give Ian my full attention.

He's frowning again. "Are you sure you're ready for this, Princess?"

"Of course." I flex my leg, and it only hurts a little. "I think I'm
even ready to get my stitches out."

"Okay, then we'll start with a few more basic defensive moves."

That doesn't sound like much fun. I've already mastered the groin
kick, after all, so I was hoping for something more advanced. "Can I
have a laser pistol?"

"Hell no." He actually blanches.

I hadn't actually expected him to say yes. "How about a knife?" I
tease. After what happened on Glacea, I suspect the idea of me with

any sort of weapon makes Ian extremely nervous.

"Maybe later." He winces. "A lot later."

"I'll give you a weapon, Kali," Max calls to me.

I shoot him a wide grin, which he responds to with a wink and a smile of his own.

"Spoilsport," I tease Ian. "So how do I defend myself without a weapon?"

"You need to strategically pick where you hit." I have a flashback to Ian sticking his thumbs in that man's eyes on Askkandia. The horrible wet noise they made as they popped. Ugh. I'll never forget it, but I'm not sure I could ever do that. Even if my life depended on it. Surely there are other places to try.

"Okay, so show me where you're vulnerable," I tell him.

He smirks. "No such place. But in general, throat, solar plexus, and eyes, in addition to your favorite, the crotch. A hard hit in any of those areas might give you the chance to run away."

"I don't want to run away. I want to be able to stop them."

"You mean kill them?" He studies me for a moment, head cocked to one side. "I'm not sure you have it in you to be a killer, Princess."

I hear a snort from the edge of the room. Beckett. I ignore her.

"Not necessarily kill," I say, because I'm not sure I've got that in me, either. "But incapacitate, so they can't chase after me or anyone who's with me."

"Let's concentrate on keeping you alive first," Ian answers. "Then we'll worry about you 'stopping' people. So, if I come at you from the front—"

He moves toward me and grabs my shoulders. I twist away, and he lets me go, just like that.

"Good—" he starts, but I cut him off with a frown.

"Why do I get the feeling that you're not giving this all you've got?" I ask. "Come on, Ian. How can I learn if you don't take it seriously?"

"If I give it all I've got, then you're dead, Princess."

He makes a fair point. "Okay, then. How about we start by you taking off the kid gloves? I'm not so fragile that you have to worry about breaking me."

"Says the woman who just got shot," he mutters to himself. But he must take my words to heart, because the next time he comes for me, he moves superfast.

He grabs my arm, pulling me toward him with a quick spin that ends with his arm around my throat. Panic crawls through me as his grip tightens and my air supply becomes a lot more restricted.

Part of me knows very well that he won't hurt me—but it's not the same part that has a vise around her throat. That part is freaking out, my hand coming up to claw at his arm in an effort to give myself just a little more space.

"Come on, Princess," he taunts. "You've got maybe thirty seconds before you pass out. What are you going to do?"

I try to pull away, but he's not budging. I stamp on his foot, and he laughs close to my ear.

"Ten seconds," he murmurs. My vision is going dark.

I try to stab him in the solar plexus with my elbow, but it hardly even connects.

Finally, he releases me and steps back. "That's the problem. You'll never be a match for someone bigger and stronger who wants to hurt you."

The smug look on his face makes me want to wipe it off.

"That's not necessarily true," Max tells him. "I've seen Milla take on guys nearly twice her size and beat the shit out of them."

"Yeah, but Milla has been fighting all her life. The princess has never lifted a finger against anyone."

"No, she just pays people to kill for her," Beckett mutters.

Max ignores the interruption. "Kali just needs to start with someone smaller. She needs to get the feeling of what works and what doesn't. She can't get that sparring with you because there's no give in you."

Ian lifts a brow. "Are you volunteering?"

"I'm not that much smaller than you." Max snorts. "And neither is Merrick. But maybe Gage—"

Gage squawks. "No, thank you. I'm a thinker, not a fighter."

Out of the corner of my eye, I see Beckett rise to her feet. I have a bad feeling about this.

"You want to fight, Princess?" she queries, a malicious look in her eyes. "Because I'll fight you."

Oh, fuck, no. I turn slowly to face her. She has the temperament of a rabid faconal and the coiled energy of a rattlez. No way am I going near her or the insolent sneer on her face. Besides, I'm pretty sure she's also been fighting all her life. She didn't get that scar by being nice and friendly.

"Sit down, Beckett," Ian growls. He must feel the same way I do.

"Why not let the princess decide?" Beckett suggests.

My stomach drops. Beckett hates me again today, sure. But I have some of my own rage built up inside me. Because she isn't the only one who lost a father. And while I've been telling myself for days now that it isn't her fault, there's a part of me that blames her anyway.

The Empire killed her father, but the Rebellion killed mine.

"I'll fight her." I know even as the words come out that I'm making a big mistake. Huge. She's likely going to kill me.

"That's not a good idea, Kali." Ian looks worried. But I need training. And truthfully, we need to resolve something between us.

"We're just going to spar," I tell him with what I hope is a reassuring smile. "Right, Beckett?"

"Right," she agrees, and even though we're on different sides, we're on exactly the same page.

But when I look into her eyes, a shiver runs through me. Because I see absolute, abject rage. It's the most terrifying thing I've ever seen—because it's personal.

Max gets to his feet and takes several steps toward me. His mouth is tight. Our gazes collide, and I shake my head at him.

The fact that he's right there, willing to stand for me against Beckett if I ask him to, means so much to me. More to me than I ever imagined.

Rain moves to stand beside Max, a worried look in her eyes as she glances back and forth between Beckett and me. And Ian—Ian looks pissed as his gaze, too, shifts between Beckett and me. For a second, I think he's going to pull rank as captain and refuse to let it happen. I can see that he wants to—it's written all over his powerful face.

His gaze slams into mine so hard that it almost has me taking a step back. But if I can't stand up to a look from him, how can I possibly expect to stand up to a full-blown attack from Beckett? So I stand my ground and put all my own frustration, my own anger, my own need to have the conflict between us over and done with, into my eyes.

It must be enough, because Ian blinks and looks away. Right before he takes a step back and gestures for us to take our places at the center of the bridge.

"Remember, this is a training exercise only," he says as he walks toward the captain's chair.

As my friends gather around, I know that yes, that's true. But something more is also going to be settled today, if I have anything to do with it.

Beckett approaches slowly but gracefully. By the time she gets to me, she's balanced on the balls of her feet.

I cast my mind for what Ian told me in our training sessions—find their weakness and piss them off.

But I'm not sure Beckett has a weakness, except for Rain. And I'm sure as fuck not going to go for her.

I move on to the balls of my feet, too, and start mirroring her movements so that we're circling each other. She grins like she can't wait to take a swing at me. I dance back a little bit, just in case.

Her only other weakness, as far as I can tell, is underestimating me. Except she's not really doing that either, is she? She thinks I'm a crap fighter—and she's absolutely right.

She moves a little closer, and I move a little farther back—and to the right. She follows me, and I do the same thing again. It's not the most impressive move, but hey, we've been in a fight for a full thirty seconds and I'm not dead yet, so it can't be all bad, either.

She lunges for me, and I let out a startled squeak as I jump back. Then immediately hate myself because she's laughing at me now—and I don't even blame her. Especially since I realize that was a mock attempt on her part anyway. She was just trying to shake me up.

Like I need to be more shaken up?

She moves like lightning to the left this time, and I circle just as quickly to the right. I have one second to congratulate myself for lasting another thirty seconds when she lashes out again. This time, convinced she's just messing with me, I don't jump back nearly as far. And she whirls, kicking out with one leg.

The next thing I know, I'm flat on my back and she's above me, a terrifying darkness in her eyes as her knee presses into my chest.

The air leaves my lungs in a whoosh.

"This is for my father. And Jarved," she snarls, and her knee presses down even harder.

And suddenly, I'm furiously angry as well. What right does she have to think she has the monopoly on bad shit?

I go limp and close my eyes like I'm all weak and pathetic—which I am honest enough to admit that I am. I sense the moment she thinks I've passed out, her body relaxing, and I sweep up with my arm as hard as I can.

My fist connects with her nose, and blood spurts everywhere. Beckett actually has the gall to look slightly impressed before she lets out a bloodcurdling cry. She straddles my hips and presses my shoulders into the floor with both her hands. And I'm sure I'm going to die, but I'm still too angry to be worried. Her blood drips on my face.

"That was for *my* father," I yell at her. "Your people killed him, and he didn't deserve that. He was the best person I've ever known."

At first, she doesn't react. But then I see the moment she comes back to herself, the darkness fading from her eyes. She swings her leg over so she's no longer on me and sits, knees bent, looking at me as though she can't quite believe she didn't kill me. The rage is gone, and now she just looks…sad.

I lick my lips and taste the sharp, metallic tang of blood. I'm not sure if it's mine or hers.

"We didn't kill your father," she tells me as she puts her hands on either side of her nose and jerks it back into place.

"Maybe you didn't, but the rebels did."

"That's what I'm saying. The rebels had nothing to do with his death."

"I don't believe you."

Beckett gives me a pitying look. "Believe me—it's not something I'd deny if we *had* done it. I'm not always proud of the things we do, but I never back down from admitting them. And guess what. The Rebellion did not kill your father."

I don't want to believe her, but there's a ring of truth in her voice that's hard to ignore. It's also hard to ignore the fact that my mother has lied to me before. Is it really so hard to believe that she lied about this, too?

But if so, why? And if the Rebellion didn't kill my father, then who did?

CHAPTER 53

Kali

An hour later, I'm lying in bed, drinking a glass of water, staring at the weird alien metal of the ceiling, and still trying to work out the answer to the question of my father's death.

But I've got nothing. My mother sold me such a bill of goods on the Rebellion being responsible for my father's death that I never thought to dig any deeper when I was at the palace. And now that I want to dig, I'm out here at the edge of the system with absolutely nothing to go on but the word of a rebel who wants me dead most of the time.

It sucks. Everything just sucks.

Maybe one of the other Ruling Families decided to kill my father. Or maybe it was someone within the Council—the desire for power is a dangerous thing at the best of times. In a solar system on the brink of extinction, it's more than dangerous. It's downright apocalyptic.

So is it such a stretch to imagine that one of the power-hungry councilors decided to do my father in? I don't know what they would have hoped to gain from it—except to destabilize my mother so badly that they could launch a coup? If so, it didn't work.

It's also common knowledge that there were many within our

family and the Council who were unhappy about my mother and father's union. Maybe his death was a byproduct of that.

Or maybe the Sisterhood did it. Maybe they harbored a grudge that he'd left them for my mother. I used to think that the Sisterhood was basically peaceful. Now I'm not so sure—they have a freaking army stationed on every planet. And Merrick is definitely not what I would call a pacifist...

If not the rebels or the Council or my family or the Sisterhood, then who?

My mind is whirling, and all I can think about is my mother lying to me about my father's death. Lying to the entire Senestris System about it as she and her Imperial forces enacted a purge designed to wipe the rebels from existence. All those people dead for no reason.

All those people imprisoned and tortured for no reason.

Don't puke, don't puke, don't fucking puke.

The warning to myself comes too late—or maybe it never stood a chance against all the things I'm thinking about. Either way, I end up rushing to the bathroom and vomiting the water Ian insisted I drink after the fight right back up.

There's nothing else in my stomach—which makes for a delightful vomiting experience—so I brush my teeth before heading back into the bedroom, only to find Rain sitting on the bed.

"Are you okay?" she asks.

"I have a lot to process," I admit. "I'm just lucky Beckett didn't decide to kill me."

Rain looks sad. "She's hurting, Kali. She's been hurting for a long time. And she blames your family."

"She blames me."

"At first, maybe. Now, not so much. I think she's beginning to understand that we're all products of our circumstances. You, me, her, Ian, Max, Gage. Even Merrick. We are who we are because we've been taught to be that way. And, except for Gage, we've never tried to be more than that."

"I don't think I even knew there was more than that," I tell her.

"Yeah." She smiles a little sadly. "Me neither."

But I do now. And ignorance isn't something I can hide behind anymore.

"Beckett's also in a lot of pain," Rain says after we sit in silence for a few minutes. "I mean physical pain. She hides it because she doesn't want anyone to know, but I can see it. Whatever they did to her on the *Caelestis* did more than mess with her mind. It damaged her physically."

"I know, and I feel terrible about it," I say honestly. "I wish I could help her."

"We're actually helping her right now—or we would be, if we could get the *Starlight* moving again," Rain says. "She believes her brother might be in the same place Milla was sent to. If he's alive. She thinks Jarved might have been sent to the *Caelestis* four years ago like she was and ended up thrown away out there like all the other prisoners who were taken on the *Reformer*."

It makes a lot of sense. Ian said they use people up out on the asteroids. That they die pretty quickly and the companies just get an influx of more. But then, how could Jarved have lasted this long? If he even survived the *Caelestis*. I remember Ian's belief that prisoners had died touching the heptosphere—and with the shape Beckett's in, I wouldn't be surprised if they died in other fucked-up experiments, too.

At that moment, Beckett's voice comes over the comms.

"All crew members to the bridge. Captain's orders."

Beckett's the only one who refers to Ian as Captain—well, besides Ian himself. Rain and I roll our eyes at each other before I sigh and push myself up. Everything aches like I've been tossed around and sat on, which I suppose I have.

We're the last to arrive, and as we walk in, I realize everyone is strapped in. Well, everyone but Gage, who is currently on the ground, messing with some of the *Starlight*'s controls. Apparently, Ian's already thin patience has worn out completely.

"Is the *Starlight* ready to move again?" I ask, taking a seat and getting to work on the harness.

"Not yet," Ian says grimly.

"Then why are we—"

I break off as I suddenly realize what everyone is looking at. The *Starlight*'s front viewing screens are unshielded for the first time in days, revealing three ships cruising directly toward us. They're still a good distance away, but that doesn't mean anything. Weapons travel far and fast in space.

"What do we know?" I ask.

"Not much," Ian answers impatiently, "but we'd know more if we had a working comm system and could communicate with them."

"Fuck off," Gage mutters.

"Can't we just outrun them again?" Rain asks.

"Maybe we could." Ian sounds even more bitter now. "If we had a pilot who could get the ship she's supposed to be flying to actually, I don't know, *fly*."

"Fuck *right* off," Beckett snarls as she continues to press buttons and levers, all to no avail.

"So what is the plan?" I ask, because those ships are getting *closer*.

"There is no plan," Max answers grimly. "I think that's why everyone is freaking out right now."

"So, now's a good time for me to be freaking out, too?" Because I have been since I sat down.

"Oh, yeah," Merrick intones. He's leaning forward, his forehead resting on his elbow in an I-can't-believe-this-shit-is-happening-again pose. "It's an excellent time for that."

All of a sudden, the *Starlight* jumps about fifteen meters. A torpedo bigger than a drokaray flies right by on our airlock side.

"She's awake!" Beckett calls.

"Yeah, no shit," Ian growls. "Now can you get her to move?"

"I'm trying," she answers testily. But nothing happens.

"They're using torpedoes," I point out. "That's a violation of space-debris procedure. That's illegal."

"I'll be sure to let them know," Ian says snidely.

Another torpedo comes at us, and this time the *Starlight* shoots up about ten meters so it can pass below.

"On the plus side, at least these ships don't seem any better at hitting her than the other ones did," Gage says, getting up and dusting himself off.

"Yes, but what if—" Rain breaks off as three torpedoes come at us at the same time, followed by three more, followed by three more—all simultaneously.

"Get her moving, Beckett!" Ian snarls.

"I'm trying. She's not—"

The *Starlight* does an arcing spin through space that ends with a full three-hundred-and-sixty-degree vertical circle that flings Gage across the bridge and has the rest of us yelling.

But the first three torpedoes miss us, and so do the next—

All of a sudden, the *Starlight* shudders, the entire ship groaning and buckling as a torpedo slams straight into her left side.

CHAPTER 54

Ian

"Beckett!" I bark as two more torpedoes slam into the *Starlight*'s hull. "Run a status report now!"

"I'm trying, but she's not cooperating, Ian." The fact that she calls me *Ian* and not her preferred *Captain* tells me just how frazzled she is.

"Gage, can you get in there? See what you can make happen before we get blown right out of the sky?" I shove a hand through my hair.

Gage doesn't answer. I whirl around to find him passed out several feet from the bridge door with Kali kneeling at his side.

"Get back in your seat!" I roar, unfastening my harness and running across the bridge to her.

"He needs—"

"He needs to be strapped in, and so do you, or you're going to end up with the next concussion." I sling him over my shoulder and carry him to the nearest open chair. Max is already there, waiting to fasten him in.

"*You get back to your seat as well,*" I snarl as the *Starlight* zips to the right to avoid more projectiles.

The jump is effective, but it's not nearly as smooth as it was the first time, and I nearly end up going ass-over-ankles myself.

"*Maybe you should take your own advice*," Max shoots back with a raised brow.

Before I can tell him to fuck straight off, the *Starlight* jumps again—and this time I end up taking a header straight into Max. We land in a heap on the floor while Gage lolls about, blissfully unconscious, strapped into his chair.

"We need to stop fucking around and get out of here," Merrick growls as I try to stand up and nearly go flying again as the *Starlight* does yet another fancy maneuver.

I land on the floor next to Rain this time, and fuck it. Just fuck it. I start crawling to the captain's chair, determined to get there before who the fuck knows what else happens.

But the torpedoes are coming so fast and furious now, one after the other, that even crawling is difficult as the *Starlight* does the most bizarre evasive maneuvers I have ever been witness to in an attempt to avoid them.

"Why isn't she flying away?" Rain asks, sounding like she's going to cry.

"Because those are Corporation catamarans bearing down on us," Max answers grimly. "The fastest ships ever made. No way we can outrun them."

"Yeah, well we should at least try," I shoot back. "This damn sentient spaceship and her fucking agenda. I knew she was going to be trouble. I just fucking knew it."

"What about her solar-flare-beam thing?" Kali asks. "Can we fire that?"

"Which part of 'we're not in control of this fucking ship' do you not understand?" Beckett snarls at her. "We can't do anything!"

"Yeah, well, we better start doing something, or we're all gonna die." Max looks over at me. "Any suggestions?"

"Besides blasting them out of the whole fucking system, which she seems incapable of doing?" I growl. "No, I've got nothing."

Another torpedo slams into us, just to the right of the nose, and the whole fucking ship shudders like it's about to collapse in on itself. An alarm goes off—the same one from our first day on board, when

Gage pressed the big red button. Something tells me pressing it now isn't going to turn the alarm back off this time.

"We need to know what that is," I shout to Beckett to be heard over the alarm. "Can you pull up the video feed—" I break off because she's already doing it.

"Is anything vital breached?" I ask as she whizzes through the pictures.

"It doesn't look like it, but that alarm means something." She blows out a long breath. "And if this keeps up, it's only a matter of time. We have to—"

The *Starlight* emits a sound that can only be described as a high-pitched, mechanical scream. It chills me to my bones and has all of us whipping around, trying to figure out where it came from.

"What the hell was that?" Merrick demands.

I turn to the pilot. "Beckett?"

"I don't know." She sounds frantic. "I don't fucking know. This ship isn't telling me anything, and it's not doing anything I want it to do. I don't know what—"

Another high screech echoes through the bridge. And then the *Starlight* finally—*finally*—starts to fly.

CHAPTER 55

Beckett

"No, no, no, no, no!" I shout as I realize what's happening. The relief I felt when the *Starlight* started to fly dies an instant death as I realize she's not trying to outrun the ships after all. No, she's flying straight toward them.

"Umm, shouldn't we be turning around?" Rain asks in what is probably the politest voice used on this bridge since this whole clusterfuck began. "Why are we flying toward the scary spaceships when we should be flying away from them?"

"Good fucking question," I mutter as I do the same thing I always do to make the *Starlight* turn. It doesn't work.

I try again. Still doesn't work.

"Beckett?" Ian asks in his best captain voice. "What the hell is going on?"

"I don't know." I push the buttons that help with turn maneuverability. Nothing. I pull back on the control that handles her speed, trying to slow her down. It makes her go faster.

As does pushing on the control.

As does leaving it alone.

"I think she's angry," Kali volunteers.

"Spaceships don't get angry!" Ian barks at her.

"Yeah, well, she's hurt," Kali points out. "She's acting just like Beckett did when I punched her in the nose. Hurt equals angry equals *make them pay.*"

"But she's just a—" He breaks off as the *Starlight* lets out what can only be described as a full-on, bloodcurdling war cry.

I've gone into battle dozens of times. Never have I heard anything that sent ice down my spine as quickly as this scream does.

"Oh, yeah." Ian changes his tune pretty fast. "She is fucking pissed off."

"Oh, really?" I drawl. "I never would have guessed."

More torpedoes are firing at us now, and I brace myself for the one that blows us into a million different pieces. But before that happens, the *Starlight* throws out some kind of pulsing green beam that makes every single torpedo veer off in different directions away from us.

"Wait! She could do that the whole time?" Merrick yells. "Why did she let us get hit at all?"

I don't have an answer for him, about any of it. The *Starlight* has gone rogue, and there is nothing I can do to change that fact. So for now, I'm just going to sit back, watch the show, and hope we don't all die.

We're getting very close to the other ships now—uncomfortably close—and they must feel it, too, because they switch from torpedoes to laser blast after laser blast. One after another after another.

There's no way the *Starlight*'s going to be able to evade them all unless she's got another pulsing green beam up her sleeve. If she does, she doesn't fire it, and as the first blasts approach our hull, I brace for impact.

Except we're not there anymore. Out of nowhere, the *Starlight* pulls the coolest maneuver I've ever seen, doing a vertical somersault over the three spaceships before coming in behind them.

The second she does, the blaring alarm stops, and so do the random screams—because she's not there anymore. I don't mean like she's gone into stealth mode and cloaked herself from the other ships.

I mean she fucking disappears from us, too.

We're still strapped in—I can feel the pilot's seat beneath me and the harness holding me in place—but I can't see either of them. And I can't see anything else on the ship, either. No console. No walls. No floor. It's like I'm sitting in an invisible chair floating through space while six other people, one of whom is still passed out, are doing the exact same thing.

No, make that five other people, because Kali, too, has vanished.

"What the fuck is happening?" Ian demands, whirling around.

I can see the moment he realizes Kali is gone, because his jaw goes tense and his eyes practically pop out of his head. "Kali!" he yells. "Kali, where the fuck are you?"

"I'm right here?" she answers from the general vicinity of where she'd been sitting. "Why are you freaking out?"

"What. The. Fuck?" Max says, and his eyes are pretty wide, too. All of ours are.

Because this is the most bizarre thing I think any of us have ever experienced.

The ships in front of us must be panicking, too, because they decide to bug out. Is it because they think we've disappeared? Or because they see five people just floating in space like it's the most natural thing in the world?

Which it isn't. At all. Not even a little bit.

"Are we going to go after them?" Rain asks. "Or just let them go?"

"You say that like you think I've got any control over what's happening here right now. And I absolutely don't." I'm trying not to let that fact freak me out to the millionth degree.

Before I can say anything else, the *Starlight* shimmies beneath us. And then shoots a giant solar flare straight at the three ships. It's like the ones she used on Askkandia and Glacea, except it's a lot longer, a lot wider, and I'm guessing a lot stronger, because it vaporizes all three of the catamarans.

One second, they're there. The next, they're gone. Just like that.

"Holy. Shit." Max sounds almost reverent.

Before anyone else can say something, the *Starlight* shimmies again. And the most truly bizarre stealth mode ever created turns

off and everything goes back to how it was. She's still damaged—
something we'll definitely need to deal with once Gage wakes up—
but it seems like she's still operational.

"Kali!" Ian turns around, frantic, only to find Kali sitting right
where she's been since this little adventure started.

She looks as weirded out as the rest of us felt. "What was that?"

"Are you all right?" Ian asks, throwing off his harness and
bounding across the bridge to her under all of our watchful eyes.

As he rips her out of her seat and wraps her up in a hug that has
her feet dangling off the floor, it pretty much proves what all of us
but Kali and Ian have suspected all along—that the captain has fallen
head over heels for the princess.

Since the thought makes me want to throw up a little in my mouth,
I look back at the controls in front of me. And, with the *Starlight*'s
permission, set a course straight for the Wilds, plan or no plan.

CHAPTER 56

Ian

"Are you all right?" I demand as I lower Kali's feet back to the ground and reluctantly let her go.

"I'm fine," she assures me, but she looks a little pale.

Rain moves to hug her next. "Are you sure, Kali? You disappeared!"

"Disappeared how?" she asks, sounding mystified. "I was here the whole time."

"Yeah, well, we sure as shit couldn't see you. We were all just sitting there in space, no ship, no helmets, no nothing. Scariest moments of my life, and that's saying something." Max wraps an arm around her shoulders. "Don't ever do that again, okay?"

"I'd say okay if I knew what it is I supposedly did," she assures him. "But at least we're safe, right?"

"For now," I say grimly. "But I'm damn sure going to—"

I break off as Gage groans. "Why does my head feel like it's the size of a narthompalus?"

"There's so much to tell you!" Rain says, and she sounds almost excited. That makes one of us. "Come on. Let's go down to the sick bay and get you looked at. I'll fill you in on everything that happened."

Gage lifts his brows. "We're not under attack anymore. Does that mean the *Starlight* finally got it together?"

"The *Starlight* did something," I tell him with a clap on the back. "Not sure it was getting it together. But we're definitely going to figure it out."

Because there is no fucking way I'm going through that again. Not just the attack I couldn't fight off, but watching Kali disappear like that? I may never be the same again.

"Well, I say we celebrate," Max tells the room at large.

"Celebrate the fact that we nearly died?" Merrick growls as he finally unfastens his restraints and stands up.

"I'm pretty sure he means celebrate the fact that we didn't," Kali says with a grin. "And I think that's a fabulous idea."

She loops an arm through Max's and walks him toward the door. "Come on. Let's go down to the galley and make a feast for the party tonight. Or as big a feast as fishgalen will allow."

While the others prepare for Kali's celebration, I settle down with Beckett and an obviously concussed, now medicated Gage and try to figure out what the hell happened back there. But considering none of us have an actual clue, it's not what I would call a productive meeting. Though we do make a game plan for Gage to start fixing her damage as soon as his head feels better.

Still, when it's done, we go over every damn millimeter of the *Starlight*'s controls. The Ancients were an incredibly advanced race— that becomes more obvious with every day we spend on this ship. So you can't convince me that they just turned everything over to some sentient ship with anger issues and let her have her way. Not when that way was as likely to get them killed as it was to save them.

And since the best we can come up with about Kali's disappearance is that it had something to do with the chair—it does look different than the others in here, slightly larger and with a lighter gray harness, and I've never paid attention to that fact—I do the only thing I can think of to make sure it doesn't happen again. I rip the damn thing up so it's unusable. We're down to seven seats now, but I consider it a fair fucking exchange.

Those minutes when Kali just up and disappeared were some of the scariest of my life. No way am I going to chance that happening again. No fucking way.

"*Me too, man. Me too*," Max tells me as I make my way back to the bridge.

"*I don't want to talk about it.*"

He laughs, but there's not a lot of humor in it. "*Tell me something I don't know.*" There's a pause. "*We're headed toward the Wilds?*"

"*Yeah.*"

"*What do you think—*"

"*We'll find her*," I tell him, because nothing else is an option. Not now. Not ever. What state we'll find her in is something else entirely. But at least she's alive. We can come back from everything else. "*You got alcohol?*"

Because the not knowing is worse than the knowing, and it's going to be a long fucking flight to the asteroid belt. For both of us.

"*I'm already three shots in.*"

"*Sounds like a party to me. I'll be right there.*"

CHAPTER 57

Kali

Ian and the others walk in just as Max and I put the finishing touches on the fishgalen casserole recipe Gage taught me the other day. It's not the most delicious thing in the world, but compared to eating the things straight from a dehydration packet, it's pretty damn good. Plus, Max used up the last of the fresh root vegetables and herbs in a roasted side dish that looks amazing. I can't wait to dig in.

Something about being under attack and surviving has made me absolutely ravenous.

Max told me it's the adrenaline, and he's probably right. But I can't help wondering if it has something to do with whatever weird thing that seat did when it disappeared me.

I was there the whole time—I could hear everything, see everything—but at the same time, it's like I wasn't. Not just to everyone else but to myself, too. I couldn't feel my body, couldn't reach out and touch anything.

It was the strangest experience in a trip full of strange experiences. And I have to admit I'm not the least bit sad when Ian mentions he ripped up that seat. I don't think I could ever sit in it again.

Speaking of Ian, he heads straight for the gerjgin when he walks through the door—and then straight toward me. My stomach jumps a little as he stands over me, his dark eyes filled with a concern I don't usually see from him.

"You okay?" he asks, his gaze roaming over me from head to toe, like he's looking for something to fix.

But I'm not broken. At least not on the outside. "I'm good." I nod toward the dishes Max is just now pulling out of the processor. "Get something to eat."

He holds up his glass. "I've got everything I need right here."

"Because what we need right now is a captain who's completely drunk off his butt," I tell him as I make a plate and then shove it into his hands. "Here, eat this. It'll sop up some of that gerjgin."

"I'll eat if you have something, too," he answers.

"Oh, I intend to."

He continues to watch me as I make a plate for myself, and there's something different in his eyes—something I've never seen there before. I wouldn't call it predatory, exactly, but I wouldn't not call it that, either. All I know is, as I sit down, my entire body feels like it's gone on red alert—and not because of what happened earlier.

No, the feelings currently bouncing around inside me are all because of Ian.

It doesn't take long before we're all seated around one of the thin tables in the galley, eating fishgalen casserole and drinking gerjgin. It's a far cry from the parties I used to attend at the palace—where one glass of fiznachi was my allotted limit and the finest food in the system flowed like water—but that's okay, because this is so much better.

Ian and Max are telling stories of other strange things that have happened to them in their years flying around the system. Rain is peppering them with a million questions, while Beckett hangs back and watches with darting eyes. Gage and Merrick have their heads together and are riffing off each other. Merrick's drunk enough gerjgin to make him almost as hilarious as Ian and Max.

As for me, I'm nursing the same glass of alcohol Ian slid into my hand when we sat down. I still remember my hangover from the night of our trip to Rangar, and I have no desire to repeat it.

Ian, who is sitting next to me and hasn't left my side since he walked into the galley, surprisingly isn't hitting the booze as hard as I expected him to, either. Instead, he keeps asking me if I need anything and running to get me water or more food or an extra napkin even though I keep telling him I don't need anything.

Max, on the other hand, is sitting across from me and downing shots like his life depends on it. It surprises me, because he's usually not like that, while Ian totally is. They've both come close to dying on this trip—Ian more than once—and I've never seen either of them react like this. Maybe it's because this time it was out of their hands. The other times, they were in control of what they were doing, but this time the *Starlight* took it from them and they were at her mercy.

Considering they both seem like control freaks in their own ways, I can see how that would freak them out.

Max finishes telling a hilarious and slightly slurred story about the time they got roped into smuggling Askkandian seeds onto Vistenia and ended up with a giant borgameloon growing in their cargo hold that ended up feeding them for months as it resisted all their efforts to uproot it.

"So, is that what you'd be doing now if Milla hadn't been captured?" Rain asks as she puts another serving of casserole on her plate. "Smuggling things from planet to planet?"

"Maybe." Max shrugs. "Or maybe we'd be fighting in someone else's skirmish. Merc work usually pays the best."

"And doesn't leave us with a rogue plant taking over the cargo hold," Ian says, tossing back the last of his gerjgin in a quick swallow.

"Did you ever work for the rebels?" Beckett asks. It sounds like a casual question, until I see the way she's watching them.

"Not since early days, when we escaped from the work camps."

"Work camps?" I ask, because I've never heard of them.

An awkward silence descends over the table, and I realize I've said something wrong—or, more likely, done something wrong in not knowing about the camps. Even Rain looks uncomfortable, and usually she's as clueless as I am when it comes to these types of things.

I turn to Ian. "Tell me." If it's one more horrible thing my mother and the Council have done, I want to know about it. How can I ever hope to fix things if I don't know what's broken?

"The Corporation raids all seven of the functioning planets for resources several times a year," Beckett says matter-of-factly. "It's supposedly a sweep for illegal activity, but people die in the raids, defending their homes and their families, and the Corporation scoops up whatever they had—including any kids they left behind. They take them to the camps under the auspice of caring for the orphans and teaching them a trade so they can have successful lives, but there's not a lot of success that comes out of those camps."

My stomach clenches at just the thought of what she's suggesting.

"How old were you when your parents died?" Gage asks. He's got a bag of ice on his head, but he's not slurring his words or nauseous, so I think he's okay.

Max doesn't answer, just pours himself another drink. So Ian finally says, "We were eleven when we got to the camps. Still just kids ourselves."

"You were eleven?" I ask, bile rising in my throat. I don't know what happens at these camps, but based on Beckett's description, I'm guessing nothing good.

"Milla, Max, and I met in the camps," Ian says. "And we escaped together when we were twelve."

There's a wealth of things he's not saying in that statement. A wealth of things I don't know, though my imagination is running wild with all kinds of scenarios, none of which are good. And if my imagination isn't enough to convince me, the expressions on everyone else's faces certainly do.

"And you've been on your own ever since?" I ask, appalled at the idea of three twelve-year-olds negotiating life on the seven planets entirely on their own. I'm almost twenty, and this is the first time in my life I've been on my own. And while I acknowledge that my situation isn't exactly normal, either, it's a lot more normal than what Ian and Max are saying.

My heart breaks for them. No wonder they're so intent on finding Milla. The three of them were forged in the fires together.

"You make it sound so bad, Princess." Ian gives me the rakish grin that never quite reaches his eyes. "Twelve-year-olds in charge of their own destiny is the stuff child fantasies are made out of."

Yeah, until they're actually on their own.

Instead of saying that, I reach under the table and squeeze Ian's knee in sympathy. He jumps a little, and when I look across the table it's to find Max watching me with wide eyes.

I smile at him, and he shakes his head, but not before I see his lips curve in a tiny grin.

"What about you?" I ask Gage, determined to shift the focus off Ian and Max and onto someone else. "What would you be doing if you weren't here?"

"I'd probably have gone down with the *Caelestis*, so—concussion or not—this is looking pretty good to me right now." He shrugs.

"We'd be getting ready for the festival of the Light," Rain volunteers, and I shoot her a grateful look. "It's my favorite festival."

Merrick smiles briefly. "Mine too."

"What about you, Kali?" Gage asks as he eats the last of his casserole. "What would you be doing right now back at the palace?"

"Trying to convince my mother to let me *leave* the palace, probably."

Beckett looks confused. "What does that mean? You didn't want to live there anymore?"

I laugh. "Oh, that definitely wasn't a choice I could make. I just meant getting off the palace grounds. My mom's not exactly big on letting me roam free."

"Yeah, but you were on the *Caelestis*," Gage says. "That's pretty far afield from the royal palace."

"It is," I agree. "A four-hour shuttle ride. The first time I left the palace. My first and, I'm fairly certain, last royal duty, considering how spectacularly it failed."

"That's one way to put it," Max says with a laugh. "A spectacular failure."

"It was spectacular," Rain agrees, and she's giggling, too.

It doesn't take long for everyone else to join in. We've all been looking at the *Caelestis*'s explosion from our own points of view, and it's kind of nice to step outside that. To look at what it means to everyone else. So much so that I don't even mind that they're all laughing at me right now. Because I am, too, and after the last few weeks of terror and confusion, it feels really, really good.

At least until I glance over at Ian and realize he's staring at me with an intensity that seems to cut right through the amusement to the scared, confused heart of me.

CHAPTER 58

Ian

I can't stop staring at Kali. Can't stop brushing my arm up against hers or handing her something just to feel the warmth of her fingers as they slide over my own.

She's alive. After spending the last few weeks convincing myself that I didn't give a shit—that I couldn't give a shit—she went and snuck under my defenses anyway.

And now I don't want to let her out of my sight.

Tomorrow, things will go back to normal. I'll put the distance between us that so clearly needs to be there. But don't ask me to do it tonight, because I won't. I can't.

I reach for the gerjgin bottle and pour myself a second glass as everyone else around me gets drunker and drunker. Especially Max. He was as terrified as I was today, and he's handling it about as badly as I am. Differently, mind you, but equally as bad.

It's another hour before people start passing out on the table—nice one, Max and Merrick—or heading off to their cabins to do the same, until Kali, Gage, and I are the last two conscious people on board.

"You two can head to bed," she says as she carries an armful of dishes to the sink. "I'm just going to wash these before I go to sleep."

Gage glances across the table, brows raised. I get what he's asking, and I appreciate it, though I'm not sure how tonight is going to end. I give a little affirmative shrug anyway, because whatever happens, I want to spend some time alone with Kali, even if it's just to assure myself she's all right.

"I think I'm going to head up to the bridge," Gage says a little too loudly. "There are a few things I want to check on."

"Okay, well, let us know if your head starts to hurt again," Kali tells him with a warm smile. "Or if you need any help."

He smiles back, a little charmed by her, I think—which I get, even though I don't want to—and he says, "I think I've got it, but thanks."

He grabs another glass of water—no drinking after a concussion—and heads out.

I wait until the door closes behind him before telling Kali, "You really don't have to wash all the dishes. It's Merrick's night on the rotation."

"Merrick's drunk off his ass, in case you didn't notice," she says. "And it's not fair to leave Rain with these in the morning, when her rotation starts. Besides, I don't mind. Doing dishes relaxes me."

"I never imagined I'd hear you say that," I tell her as I start gathering what's left of the plates and glasses, being careful not to bump Max and Merrick, who are passed out on separate ends of the long table.

"Me neither," she says with a giggle. "But a lot has changed in the last few weeks."

"You can say that again." I scrape the last of the food scraps into the disposal chute.

"Oh, I can get those!" she says. "It'll only take me a few minutes. Go on to bed."

I lift a brow. "Are you trying to get rid of me, Princess?"

"Of course not." Her cheeks flush that dusky rose color I like so much. "I just figured you were probably tired."

"I think I can handle scraping a few plates."

Kali looks like she wants to argue some more, but in the end she just shrugs in a suit-yourself kind of way.

I resist the urge to tell her I always do.

We work in silence as we set the galley to rights. It only takes about ten minutes, and when it's done, we leave Max and Merrick to their drunken snores and head down the hallway toward the cabins.

We get to Kali's cabin first, and I know I should keep walking. I even *tell* myself to keep walking. But somehow my feet stay exactly where they are. Right in front of her door.

"Are you tired?" she asks, hesitant in a way I'm not used to from her. She's been pulling the princess act on me from the very beginning, and I admit, it used to get my back up, but now, seeing her suddenly shy and uncertain, I have to admit that I much prefer her when she's bossing me around.

"I don't have to be," I answer.

She gives me a funny look. "I don't know what that means."

"It means if you want a tour of my room, I'd love to give it to you."

Her eyes go wide, and I wonder if I was a little too forward. But that's who I am, and it seems pretty absurd to try to change it now. Besides, when it comes to this one thing, I want to make sure Kali knows she's the one in charge of if and when.

I wait for her to say something, and when she doesn't, I take a step back. Sure, tonight is especially convenient, since Max is completely out of it, but there will be other nights when she feels more comfortable with this. With us.

Except then Kali's lower lip wobbles in that way it does that drives me wild—when she's nervous and she wants to work up the courage to do something but she isn't sure she'll be able to. I really hope, this time, she'll be able to.

So I wait another moment, just to see what she decides. Just to see if that lip is going to wobble again—if it does, I don't know if I'll be able to stop myself from nibbling at it.

Kali takes a breath and starts to open her door, and I'd be lying if I said that wasn't a major fucking disappointment. At least until I hear her say to Rain, "I'm going to be late tonight, so feel free to take advantage of my absence." Female giggles follow the announcement, followed by a low murmur that makes it sound like Rain and Beckett might be just as glad regarding Kali's absence as I am with Gage's and Max's.

Even before Kali turns back to face me and says, "I'd love a tour of your room."

CHAPTER 59

Kali

I'm nervous.

I know I shouldn't be, know that it is just Ian who is currently staring at me with that look in his eyes like he wants to eat me up. Ian, the same guy I spend most of my time on this ship arguing with—not because he's always wrong, but because it's always fun to wind him up.

He's not the first man to look at me like that—I'm nearly twenty years old. He is, however, the first one I've looked back at the exact same way—with a definite interest I don't even try to hide.

As Ian opens his door and ushers me inside his surprisingly clean cabin—neither he nor Gage nor Max strike me as the uber-clean type; then again, it's not like there's so much lying around for them to make a mess with. None of us are exactly drowning in possessions. Normally, I'd be totally okay with that, but right now, when I'm casting around for something to say or something to do, I could really get behind him having a collection of space rocks I could ask about.

Once he ushers me into his room, Ian closes the door behind us. And for a second, I think about running. Not because I don't want this, but because I do. The truth is, I've wanted it for a very long time, though I've gone out of my way not to admit it to myself, let alone anyone else. But now that the time is finally here, all I can think is that this is a bad idea.

A very, very bad idea.

What if I make a fool of myself? What if I can't do what he wants me to do? What if I'm just really, really bad at it?

"You okay?" Ian asks as he walks across the room toward me. "I could run back to the galley and get you some water, if you'd like."

It's not a bad idea—all of a sudden, my mouth is desert dry. But I don't think all the water in the world will change that. Not when Ian will still be standing in front of me, looking tall and dark and sexy. So very sexy.

"I don't need water," I finally tell him when I can finally get my mouth to cooperate.

His eyes somehow go even darker—or maybe it's just that the pupils dilate until they're so blown out that his beautiful, brown irises are just thin rings of color around them. "What do you need?"

"I—" I break off, my voice cracking. "I don't know."

He stops his forward prowl at the words, and for a second I'm terrified he's going to send me on my way. But then he smiles and holds out a hand for me, and I relax.

I just need to work up the courage to slide my hand against his, and everything will be okay.

When the alternative is going back to my room without feeling his lips cover mine and his body move against me, it's easy to forget the nerves. Easy to forget everything but Ian and the way he looks at me. The way he makes me feel.

Like—for this moment, anyway—I'm the most desirable woman in the system.

When our palms finally meet and our fingers lock together, he gives a little tug, and I flow smoothly from my place at the end of his bed to a place in his strong, powerful arms.

He feels good. More, he feels safe. And when I look up, it's to find that his mouth is only a few centimeters from mine.

"I'm going to kiss you now," he says, and it's the first time he's ever felt the need to announce it like that. It makes me wonder just how nervous I look. "Is that okay with you?"

More than okay. I start to give him an enthusiastic yes, but my tongue hasn't completely untied itself yet. So I settle for a nod and then wait, heart beating out of my chest, for him to finally lower his mouth to mine.

This isn't our first kiss, but with the amount of sensation that runs through me the moment our lips meet, it might as well be. I learned before that Ian knows how to kiss, but as his lips slowly, carefully move against mine, I can't help thinking that he *really* knows how to kiss. And that I want him to go on kissing me for a very, very long time.

His hands slide up my arms to my shoulders, from my shoulders to my cheeks. As he cups my face in his palms, I expect the nerves to return. But there is no nervousness, no awkwardness, no fear of looking like I'm out of my depth. No, as his mouth claims mine, the only thing I feel is desire. Pleasure. Need.

So much need as his tongue sweeps along the seam of my lips. As it toys with the sensitive corners of my mouth. As it delves slowly, sweetly inside of me.

"You taste so good," he murmurs, sucking my lower lip gently between his teeth. "You've always tasted so good."

"So do you," I answer, licking my lips in an attempt to get more of him. He tastes like warm gerjgin, bittersweet coffee, and pure, warm man. From the moment he poured me my first gerjgin, I've been drawn to the taste of it, relishing the warm heat of it on my tongue, the burn as it makes its way down my throat, the fire it brings to my belly. As I relish the taste of him now—smooth and sharp and delicious all at the same time—I can't help wondering if the reason I like gerjgin so much is because it reminds me of Ian.

I don't know the answer to that question, but I do know that I'll never be able to drink the liquor again without thinking of him. Without thinking of this moment when his fingers tangle in my hair and his mouth tangles with mine.

As his fingers tighten in my hair—not enough to hurt but more than enough to have more sensations spinning through me—I follow his unspoken request and tilt my head back to give him better access.

And then his mouth is on mine again, and nothing has ever felt so good. So perfect. So real.

He bites down on my lip—softly, this time—and sensations claw through me. Shivers run down my spine, heat pools low in my belly, and a hollowness I've never felt before takes up residence at the very heart of me. Then he soothes the tiny little hurt with his tongue, dancing it over the inside of my lip until my hands are shaking and so are my knees.

Ian is really good at this. Really, really good.

It makes me want to be good, too.

So when he moves to pull away from me, I don't let him. Instead, I nip him back, sinking my teeth into his upper lip before pulling it into my mouth and sucking away the hurt.

Ian groans low in his throat at the tiny prick of pain, and the sound gets me hotter than it has any right to. I slide my hands up his back so that I can tangle my fingers in the short curls at the nape of his neck.

They feel surprisingly good slipping back and forth against my palms, sliding over my skin, wrapping themselves around my fingers. I wish we could live right here—right fucking here—in this moment of possibility forever.

But then he tilts my head back even more, and there's a new moment for me to live in as his mouth devours mine. As he bites and sucks and licks his way inside my mouth, his tongue sweeping against my own until all I can think about is him. Until all I can see or hear or taste is him.

I moan low in my throat, and this time when my fingers tug on his hair, there's no gentleness in it. How can there be, when Ian is driving me slowly, inexorably, out of my mind? And making sure that I love every second of it.

It's my turn now, to nibble at his lips, to run my tongue over his teeth and the sensitive skin between his gum and his upper lip. He groans when I lick inside him, capturing my tongue and sucking it even deeper inside his mouth.

I've never been kissed like this before, never even imagined that a kiss like this could exist, and I want to hold onto this feeling for as long as I possibly can. For as long as Ian will let me.

But then he's moving on, his lips tracing a hot trail across my cheek to my ear. He pauses there, nibbling at my lobe before moving on to press hot, open-mouthed kisses into the sensitive spot just below my ear.

I gasp when he licks his way across my skin, pausing for a moment to suck his way along my throat in a move that I'm fairly certain will leave me with the best kind of bruises tomorrow—the kind that will remind me that this isn't a dream after all.

"Is this okay?" he murmurs as he delves even lower, his fingers dancing across the zipper of my jumpsuit and dragging it down to the center of my breasts.

I'm too busy arching my back, too busy grabbing onto his hair to hold his mouth in place against my skin to do much more than nod.

Thankfully, a nod is all he needs, and his fingers skim lower, tracing the curves of my breasts before delving inside my camisole to glance across my nipples. Once, twice, then again and again until I can't breathe, can't think, can't do anything but drown in the sensations Ian pulls from me so easily.

"I want to see you," he murmurs as he kisses his way over my collarbone and down the center of my body to the spot just between my breasts.

"Yes. Please." I arch against his mouth to give him better access, and he laughs—a dark, seductive sound that shoots all the way through me.

Then he's lowering the zipper on my jumpsuit completely, peeling it down my arms and body until it pools around my waist. He pauses then, sliding warm, calloused fingers along the sensitive skin at my waist, stroking his way under my camisole and up, up, up my ribs until he's cupping the weight of my breasts in his hands.

He's moving his mouth lower at the same time, nibbling his way down my neck to the spot where my neck meets my shoulder. And then he's sucking gently there, too, and my entire body lights up like a meteor shower, sensation dancing along my nerve endings in every direction possible.

He spends a few minutes in that one spot before sliding lower over my shoulder to the round scar I've had as long as I can remember.

"What's this?" he asks, pressing hot, open-mouthed kisses to the slightly slick skin.

"I fell when I was little, got impaled on one of the sharp wrought-iron spindles at the palace. I don't remember it, but my mother says I screamed and screamed."

"I bet. That's a pretty big area to be hurt on a little kid." He kisses it again—several times—before moving on.

"Ian," I gasp, hand cupping his head as he moves even lower and my entire world narrows down to this moment. To this man and the way he makes me feel just by touching me.

I need to be touching him, too.

But I'm not nearly as skilled as he is, and my fingers fumble a little as they dance along the warm, resilient skin of his waist and burrow under his shirt to stroke his lower back, his sides, the smooth, taut skin of his abdomen. He's lean and muscular and so, so warm, and I don't think I've ever felt anything better in my life—at least not until he does the same to me and I forget how to breathe. How to think. How to do anything but just be.

And then he's peeling my jumpsuit down, over my hips and down my legs as his fingers stroke each newly revealed centimeter of skin. It gets caught on my boots, and for a second my cheeks burn with embarrassment at forgetting to kick them off.

But he just laughs and drops to his knees in front of me so that he can pull them off and then slip my jumpsuit off as well.

"Lift up your foot," he murmurs, and so I do, clutching at his shoulders as my trembling knees threaten to collapse.

He laughs again as he wraps a strong arm around my hips to help steady me before licking his way along the edge of my panties and then delving lower, lower, lower until he presses his mouth against the damp cotton at the very heart of me.

My legs go out from under me completely then, and I fall backward onto his bed.

"I like the way you think," he teases as he follows me down. And then his mouth—his wicked, wild, wonderful mouth—is everywhere. Everywhere.

Kissing its way over my stomach.

Nibbling its way along the curves of my legs.

Sucking a path across my breasts.

And nothing has ever felt so good.

But it's not enough—it's not close to being enough. Not when every single part of me is aching for every single part of him.

And so it's my turn to pull his shirt off.

My turn to slide to my knees in front of him as I fumble his boots off and his pants down his legs.

My turn to kiss a slow, hot trail right down the center of his body.

Ian groans, low and deep. And then he's pulling me up, up, up and over his body, spreading my thighs so that I'm straddling him, a knee on either side of his head.

For a second, embarrassment floods me—I'm so open, so exposed—but then he's groaning deep in his throat, ripping off my panties, and burying his face against my sex.

"Ian!" I gasp out at the first feel of his mouth on me, but his hands move to my hips, anchoring me in place. And then he's kissing me everywhere—everywhere—and nothing has ever felt so good.

"Please," I moan as heat continues to build inside of me. "Please, please, please."

I don't even know what I'm asking for, but Ian does, and he gives it to me, one long, deliberate lick at a time. And then he's pulling my clit into his mouth, his hands holding me in place as he sucks so, so gently.

Heat turns to need, need turns to ecstasy, and just like that, my body explodes like a supernova. I call his name again and again as I drown in a maelstrom of sensation so intense that it would have terrified me if Ian wasn't there with me, holding me, kissing me, loving me through every powerful, overwhelming second of it.

And when it's over, when the pleasure finally stops racing through me like a shooting star, he rolls me over and settles between my thighs. Then he starts all over again, his hands cupping my breasts, his mouth gliding over my shoulder, his body sliding against mine. And somehow, somehow, the heat rekindles deep inside of me, and it isn't long before I'm wrapping myself around him and pleading for more.

He takes his time stoking the flames inside of me until I'm nearly out of my mind with need. Only then, when I'm arching and shuddering and writhing against him, does he finally slide inside of me.

And this time when he takes me up and over, he joins me. And nothing in my life has ever felt so good.

CHAPTER 60

Kali

W hen I wake up, Ian is gone.

I start to feel bad—what girl wouldn't, when she wakes up to find that the man she had sex with the night before has disappeared?—but then I see the cup of coffee on the small shelf built into the wall next to Ian's bed and remember him dropping kisses on my face as he set it there.

Gage had needed him on the bridge—something about fixing the *Starlight*'s damage—and though I offered to get up, he'd told me to sleep in. That he'd come back as soon as he could.

Apparently, whatever Gage was doing was more time-consuming than he thought, because it's now late morning and Ian still hasn't returned.

I reach for the coffee and take a long swallow, not minding that it's lukewarm. The second the bitter liquid hits my insides, the cobwebs around my brain—a side effect, I'm pretty sure, of mind-blowing pleasure—start to disappear.

Which is a good thing, because I can't spend the whole day in bed, no matter how tempting the thought is—especially if Ian's in the bed with me. So I put my jumpsuit back on and head out to find everyone else.

The closer I get to the bridge, however, the shyer I get. Ian and I had a great time last night, and judging from the way he held me this morning—and the coffee he brought me—he's not regretting it. I'm not regretting it, either. But I still don't know what I'm supposed to do when I see him, especially since it will be in front of the rest of the crew.

Am I supposed to pretend last night didn't happen? Not forever, but just in front of everyone else?

Or am I supposed to pretend last night didn't happen forever? Like, it was just a one-off, never to be repeated?

Or am I supposed to just acknowledge it like it's no big deal?

The worst part is, I'm not sure which one of the above choices makes my stomach hurt more.

I guess it doesn't matter, because the walk from Ian's cabin to the bridge isn't long enough for many more recriminations. Besides, if I'm learning nothing else on this trip, it's that if you don't like what things look like at the moment, wait five minutes. They will change.

I take a deep breath and another long sip of coffee and then walk through the open door to the bridge.

Shockingly, I'm the last one here. Again.

I take a second to take stock—Gage is holding court at the front of the bridge, with Ian standing right next to him, listening closely to what he has to say. Beckett is right there, too, looking as blasé as usual, while Rain looks downright unhappy, which isn't normal for her.

Merrick looks as blasé as Beckett, a surefire tip-off that something is going down. And Max—Max looks up and notices me before anyone else.

His smile is broad and immediate, despite the fact that he was passed out drunk in the middle of the galley less than ten hours ago. Apparently, he and Rain are really living right.

I give him a wave and a little smile, and he immediately gets up to make his way over to me. To break the news of what's going on up front? Or to run interference between Ian and me?

Something tells me it's the latter, and my stomach does an extra flip—even before Ian's head shoots up. Across the bridge, he turns around to see what's up—and his eyes lock immediately with mine. My heart jumps to my throat, and I don't know what to do. But then he smiles. Not the usual, sarcastic, *thanks for joining us, Princess* smile that I'm used to, but his real smile. The one I saw for the first time last night in bed.

I find myself smiling back before I even make the decision to do so. But how can I not? A smiling Ian is a gorgeous sight to behold.

As is a smiling Max, if I'm being honest—though not quite the same way. "You're looking good," I tell him as he approaches me.

"Considering how I woke up this morning, I view my quick recovery as no less than a miracle," he replies.

"If that's the case, could you maybe ask for a couple more? Because things are getting really strange around here." Ian has gone back to talking to Gage, but that doesn't stop me from sneaking glances at him every thirty seconds or so.

"Isn't that the truth?" He, too, looks toward Ian.

"What's happening?" I ask. "Why does everyone look either happy or like they're one short step from freaking out completely?"

"Gage got the comms working."

The words are so unexpected that for a second they don't register. "He did?" I finally exclaim once they sink in. "When?"

"He says he woke up in the middle of the night with a brainstorm and has been working in here ever since. Guess concussions are good for ideas?"

No wonder Rain looks so sad. Operational external comms means contacting home planets, telling people we're okay. Setting up rendezvous for safe returns. It doesn't take a genius to figure out she has no interest in returning to the monastery—especially not if Beckett can't come with her.

I try my best not to think about what this means for me. I'm not ready to go back to the palace yet. I'm definitely not ready to go back to my mother's iron rule. There's still too much I need to learn about in the system. Things like the camps Ian and Max and Milla were sent to. And the assassination of my father, which was blamed on people who didn't do it.

There's no way my mother will tell me the truth about either. Or anything else, for that matter. For the good of Senestris, my ass.

But I should at least call her, let her know I'm okay. Find out if she's the one who keeps trying to blow the *Starlight*—and everyone on her—to pieces.

"You can't, Kali," Ian says, clearly reading my mind as he comes to stand beside me. "At least not yet."

He's standing so close to me that I can feel the heat of his body from my shoulders to my toes. And he called me Kali, not Princess. "I know. Milla comes first." For me, too, though I don't tell him that.

He nods. "Yeah. Then we'll get you home."

His voice is devoid of emotion as he says it, and I don't know if that's a good thing or a bad one. Is he dying to get rid of me after last night, or does he actually want me to stick around?

I hate that I'm thinking like this, hate that I don't know how to act around him now. I hate even more that I'm waiting to take my cue from him, as if his feelings are so much more important than mine—and I also hate that today of all days is when Gage figured out how to fix the comms. Couldn't it have waited just another couple days, until Ian and I figured out what, if anything, is going on between us?

Basically, I hate everything this morning, which I would have said was impossible, considering how good I felt when I woke up. How could the energy from four fantastic orgasms turn into this emotional maelstrom?

"So, what's the first thing you want to do with the working comms?" I ask Ian. He's been on Gage's ass about getting them up and running since the beginning.

"Yeah, I'm sick of not knowing what the fuck is going on or why it's going on. I want to put out feelers to a few people I know, see if anyone's figured out what happened with the *Caelestis*. And then I want to ID the ships that have been on our ass—all Corporation? Or are some actually the Sisterhood, like that medal Gage found implies? And if so, why the hell are they willing to shoot the high priestess out of the fucking air?"

"I already told you," Rain says quietly. "I'll just be reincarnated, so it's not a problem for them."

"Yeah, well, it's a major fucking problem for me," Beckett snarls. And for once, I agree with her, though not for the exact same reasons. Obviously.

"Well, if you want to know who's after us," Gage pipes up from the back wall, where he's been fiddling with the comms, "you could start by checking out who's been trying to contact *us*."

CHAPTER 61

Ian

"Someone's been calling us?" I demand. "Why didn't you mention that?"

"Because I just found the log about thirty seconds ago," Gage says. "There are twenty-two calls logged. All with the same origin point."

I shoot him a narrow-eyed glare. "And that would be?"

"Askkandia. And not just Askkandia—the royal palace."

Well, fuck. Of course it's the palace. And I'd bet my last planeta that it's the Empress herself who's been reaching out.

"Just because the palace is trying to get in touch with us doesn't mean they know who's got the ship," Max argues.

"True. But they've probably got a pretty good idea of at least a couple of the passengers." Beckett looks pointedly at Rain and Kali.

She's right. I know she's right. Otherwise, why would the Empire give a fuck about this ship? Ancient artifact or not.

"Yeah, well, I'm not giving her either of them," I say. Handing Rain over to that woman would be like taking a kanadoo to the slaughter. As for Kali—no way. I just found her. There's no fucking way I'm giving her up to that woman.

No fucking way.

"Will she be able to tell our location if we talk to her?" Max asks

Gage.

"No. I should be able to scramble it."

"Should be able to or can?" I demand in a voice that warns him not to fuck with me.

"Can," he says after several seconds of further tinkering.

I still think it's a bad idea. But maybe if we talk to the Empress, we'll have an idea of who blew up the *Caelestis*. And why everyone in the fucking solar system seems to have a hard-on for us right now.

"*Why don't you ask Kali?*" Max says. "*This isn't a decision you have to make by yourself. It affects her most of all.*"

"*Because if she ends up hurt because of it, I don't want to spend the rest of my life feeling guilty.*" Fuck, I miss the old Ian who did what was best for Milla, Max, and himself and damn everyone else. This worrying-about-other-people thing fucking sucks.

"*Exactly. So let her have agency in the decision.*"

"*Agency?*" I repeat, arching a brow.

"*Self help books are a thing,*" he answers defensively. "*You might want to try a few.*"

It shows just how much I've changed that I don't take the time to make fun of him for that. "*What if she wants Kali?*"

"*Well, she can't fucking have her,*" he growls.

Yeah, that's pretty much how I feel, too.

I turn to the others. "I hate the idea of talking to her, but maybe the Empress can give us some clue as to what the hell is going on. All those in favor of having a lovely little chat with a royal, raise your hands."

CHAPTER 62

Kali

I look around the room, but everyone is standing frozen, looking at me. And I have no idea what I want to do.

I turn and look at Ian.

He looks like he wants to say no. But instead, he blows out a breath and asks me, "Do *you* want to talk to her?"

I think on that for a moment. "No—"

"Okay, then," he interrupts immediately, looking very relieved, "let's—"

"But I think I should." My heart is pounding as nerves get the better of me. But just because something is hard—and maybe a little terrifying—doesn't mean I shouldn't do it. "She *is* my mother. She must have been worried about me."

To emphasize my point, I raise my hand, then look around the room as everyone else slowly raises theirs, too. Except for Ian, but that's to be expected.

Looks like we're going to be talking to my mom.

Bile rises in my throat at the thought. Not about letting her know I'm alive—but about what it means once that happens. Ian and I finally had a real moment, and now I'm terrified I'm going to have to leave without ever knowing what might happen next.

Ian nods, like this was the decision he expected all along. Then he asks, "So when should we do it?" He sounds as resigned as he looks.

"I don't see any reason to draw it out," Max replies. "Let's get it over with."

I slide into one of the side seats as Gage taps a few keys on the main console.

The projection beams out in front of my chair, and I'm glad Gage has rigged it so the rest of them won't be visible on the comms. Because when the screen lights up, my mom is sitting there, eyes narrowed and fingers tapping impatiently on the marble desk in front of her. For one tiny moment, the little girl inside me is thrilled to see her. She is my mother, after all. But then everything I've learned about her in the last few weeks overwhelms me, and the excitement fades in a wave of chest-tightening disappointment and fear.

I close my eyes for just a second, take a breath to center myself. And when I open them again, I'm ready for anything. Even the Empress.

We have the same coloring—light-brown skin with dark red hair that was passed down to the Empress from her mother and grandmother. I have my father's eyes, though, and I take after him in the height department, too, as I'm much taller than my mother. Except for the squinty eyes, her face is expressionless, but I can see a tic jumping in her cheek—a sure sign that she's not happy.

My stomach plummets at the realization, and I can feel my entire body tense up. It's been weeks since I've seen her—weeks in which a whole host of new and shocking things have happened to me—so I don't know how one look at her face can so quickly have me feeling like a child waiting to be chastised.

Her eyes widen as she catches sight of me, then narrow down to slits. At first, I don't know what I've done to upset her, until I realize she's staring at my silver jumpsuit. Apparently even with all the problems in the solar system, having her daughter not dressed in Imperial Regalia is high on her list of complaints.

Still, I force a neutral expression. "Hello, Mother."

"Kalinda, I'm glad to see that you're well. Now give me your coordinates," she orders in the voice she uses for misbehaving children and recalcitrant councilors. "I'll dispatch a force immediately to get you."

"I can't do that."

Her fingers stop tapping—her anger has just ratcheted up another notch.

"I can't come back yet, Mother. There's something I need to do first."

"Nonsense. You need to get home where you belong."

"Not yet."

Her eyes narrow, and I realize that I've never actually said no to my mother in my whole life. It feels good. Liberating.

"Kalinda, if you won't come home because your mother asks you to, then come because it's an order from your Empress."

She's bringing out the big guns. And I'm not impressed. "What are you going to do—lock me in a cell?"

"I will think of a suitable punishment." Then her face softens. "Is this because of these people you're with? I've heard they are outlaws, murderers…"

Friends, I think. They're my friends, and I won't let her take that from me just because she doesn't understand.

"They saved my life on the *Caelestis*."

"Sometimes people can attach inappropriate feelings to their captors. They can even fall in love with them. Is that what's happening here, Kalinda?"

I can feel my cheeks heating, and I force myself not to look at Ian. "No one is a captor here, and I don't love anyone."

Beckett snorts while Max clutches a hand over his heart and pretends to be devastated. I ignore them both, my expression perfectly smooth.

My mother plows ahead. "We have strong reason to believe that the attack on the *Caelestis* was a deliberate attempt by the Rebellion to assassinate you."

Beckett snorts again. And this time I want to snort right along with her.

My mother has been using the Rebellion as a boogeyman against me since I was a child. She became even more adamant after my father was murdered, convincing me they were the ones responsible. But if that was a lie, why should I believe this is any more true?

"Our intel strongly suggests that they are still coming after you," my mom says. "That they know you're out there and vulnerable and they are not going to stop until they hunt you down and kill you."

I don't doubt that—someone is definitely trying to kill us, and it makes sense that I'm the target. But she's not providing any new information, so if she wants to scare me, she's doing a lousy job. We've survived five assassination attempts—three on the *Starlight* and two on Ian and me. Telling me someone is out to get us isn't exactly news.

I glance sideways at Ian, where he's leaning against the pilot's console. A little frown has formed between his eyes, and he looks worried. I give him a tiny reassuring nod before turning back to my mother.

If she's so concerned, I do have something she might be able to help with. "I've noticed there are bulletins all over the system declaring I'm an imposter and offering a reward for my capture. Have you seen them?"

Her lips pinch tight. "The intelligence service has made me aware of this, but we haven't been able to get to the bottom of them yet. We will, I can assure you, and those responsible will be brought to justice. But Kali, my darling, that's just one more indication that I can't keep you safe out there."

"Maybe I don't need you to keep me safe," I tell her.

"What about your new friends?" she asks. "Do you need me to keep them safe?"

"They're fine," I tell her.

"Are they?" She arches a brow. "You clearly care for them. Whether you want to believe me or not, someone is trying to kill you. Do you really want to put your friends at risk? Are you willing to let them die with you? Because that's what will happen. Whoever is after you will find you, and you will *all* die, and it will be your fault. Do you really want their blood on your hands?"

For the first time, her words get through to me. My stomach clenches, and I feel sick. We've been trying to figure out who's trying to kill us for weeks—and who the intended target is. Now my mother is saying that she knows. That it's me and that I'm putting everyone in danger by being here.

I don't want it to be true, but there's a part of me that's known all along that it had to be me. I think back to Gage getting shot. Think back to Ian staying with me when he should have run back to the ship. To the *Starlight* racing straight at those battleships and nearly getting us all killed. If my mother is right and the people who are trying to kill us are after me and not Rain or any of the others, then I truly am putting them in danger.

As if sensing her advantage—the Empress is nothing if not a prudent observer of weakness in others—she goes in for the kill. "Think about what I'm telling you, Kali. But not for long, or it will be too late. Send your coordinates, and I will come and collect you. As soon as we can show that you're safely back in the palace, there will be no point in going after them. They will be safe. It's the only way."

And then the screen goes blank.

She's gone.

And all I can think about is my friends dying because of me. It's one thing to know someone is trying to kill you and your friends; it's another to know they're trying to kill *you* and the people you care about are just collateral damage.

A shiver runs through me as my mind churns with nightmare scenarios. All of them ending with my friends dead. All of them ending with Ian dead.

Just the thought has tears burning the backs of my eyes. What if my mother's not just trying to get what she wants? What if she's actually telling the truth for once and my being here is doing nothing but hurting all these people I've come to care about?

Ian moves in next to me, rests a hand on my shoulder. Before I even know I'm going to do it, I swing around and wrap my arms around him, holding him as tightly as I can as the truth creeps through me.

I'm going to lose him before I ever really get the chance to have him.

I tell myself he's never really been mine to lose—that this is just an exciting little interlude for both of us and that it ending was always inevitable. But it doesn't feel like an interlude—not to my heart. And not to me.

"You don't believe her, do you?" Ian asks.

I take a deep breath and hold it inside until the urge to cry dissipates. Because I do believe her. Not necessarily about the Rebellion—Beckett says they don't have the kind of resources necessary to pull off the explosions on the *Caelestis*, and I'm willing to believe her—but about the rest.

It only makes sense.

All along, I knew I was the target. Why else would they wait until I was aboard the *Caelestis* to blow it up? It's one thing to take down the premier space station in the system. It's another thing altogether to take it down with the crown princess on board.

One is murder and destruction of property. The other is those things and full-blown treason. No one does that accidentally, especially not with all the extra safety protocols in place for my arrival. It had to be deliberate, which means it really was aimed at me all along.

"Hey, Kali." Ian pulls back just enough to slide a finger under my chin and tilt my face up to his. "We've done okay so far, haven't we?"

We have. But for how long? At what cost? And how much longer can we keep it up?

"I just—" I break off as Ian stiffens against me. I start to ask him what's wrong, but before I can, across the bridge, Max screams and falls to his knees.

CHAPTER 63

Ian

A shrill scream pierces my skull.

At first, I think it's coming from Rain or Beckett—it's definitely female, and Kali's right in front of me, perfectly fine—but then I realize it can't be them. Because the sound is coming *from inside my head.*

The pain is unbearable, slicing along my every nerve ending and taking over my entire body until it feels like I'm being ripped apart. I've never felt anything like this before, never even imagined anything like this could exist, and I try to fight it as I struggle to understand what's happening.

"Ian?" Kali's eyes go wide, and she stands in a rush, her hands moving to my shoulders. "Ian, what's wrong?"

I try to answer her, but I can't. I can't talk, I can't think, I can't do anything but endure. The agony is overwhelming, all-consuming, utterly devastating.

I fall to my knees, nearly taking Kali out with me, and through the red haze of agony I see Max on his knees a few feet behind me, his hands clamped on the sides of his head like he can somehow shut out the pain.

And I know what's happening.

Milla.

I call out to her in my mind, yelling her name over and over again. Seconds later, Max joins me, his voice hoarse and pained as he, too, screams for her.

At first, there's nothing—only the yawning blackness that's been there for months every time we try to reach for her. But then I hear it, so faint that I can't be sure my mind isn't playing tricks on me.

"*Help me. Please help me. Please, please, please. Help me.*"

"*Milla!*" I scream.

"*Ian, please.*" The impression of tears pouring down gaunt cheeks. "*Please help me.*"

"*I'm coming, Milla! I'm coming right now!*"

But it's too late. The pain—and with it, my connection to Milla—vanishes as quickly as it came.

I turn to Max, who—like me—is still on his knees. He's staring back, eyes wide with horror.

"*You heard?*" I ask. Even in my head, my voice sounds hoarse.

"*I heard.*" If possible, he sounds even worse than I feel.

"Ian, what's the matter?" Kali drops to her knees beside me. She's searching my face, panic filling her eyes as her hands race over my head and chest like she's looking for a wound. "What hurts?"

I don't even know where to start.

I've been wanting to talk to her about this for a few days now, but this isn't how I'd planned to do it.

"*You okay?*" I ask Max.

"*Are you?*" he shoots back.

Not even close. After what I just heard, I'm not sure I'll ever be okay again.

"What's going on?" Merrick asks as he strides onto the bridge, Rain right behind him and Gage after her. "We heard screams."

Max doesn't answer, just shakes his head as he stumbles to his feet.

He's a better man than me, because I don't think I can get up yet. I'm shaking too badly, and all I can hear—all I can think about—is Milla.

Max crosses the room on unsteady legs before collapsing into a chair along the right wall. Then he pulls out a half-empty bottle of gerjgin from underneath it and takes a long drink before holding it out to me.

I take it with hands that are still trembling like an amateur's, but I'm still too fucked up to be embarrassed. I take a couple of long swallows and feel the alcohol do its work. My heart rate slows, and I finally stop shaking enough to drag myself up and into the captain's chair.

I blow out a breath and take another swallow before handing the bottle back to Max. What the fuck just happened—and more importantly, what does it mean?

"*How could we have heard her?*" he asks. "*Do you think she's close?*"

That makes the most sense—usually we can only transmit our thoughts to each other over short distances—but I shake my head. "*We're nowhere near the Wilds yet.*"

"*You sure that's where she is?*"

I think back to my conversation with that bastard on Glacea. I'd bet everything I have—which isn't much, but it's the thought that counts—that he was telling me the truth. "*Yeah.*"

"*She's got to be in agony, then.*" Max runs a still-unsteady hand down his face.

Pain ups the range we can transmit, but we're talking about an impossible distance here. We're still way far out from the Wilds, in deep space, but maybe that means we're moving in the right direction? This is only the second time we've sensed her since she disappeared, and the first time was right after—when she was, presumably, still close.

It wasn't as intense as this, though. To be fair, nothing's ever been this intense before. Which means Milla's going through hell.

"*But at least she's still alive,*" I tell him. "*She has to be.*" Because we're still here.

"Does someone want to explain what the fuck just happened?" Kali says in a tone that isn't actually a question. She looks from Max to me. Everyone is staring at the both of us in confusion. "And by someone, I mean you." She gives me a pointed look.

"*Tell them*," Max says in my head.

"*We've never told anyone*," I reply. "*I never thought we would.*"

"*That's because we've never had anyone to tell before. It's different now.*"

He's right. And for a moment, the thought scares the shit out of me. I take another swig of gerjgin and look around the group. Merrick and Rain, Kali, Gage, Beckett. They're all watching us with varying levels of concern. We might have our differences, and in other circumstances we might have actively tried to kill one another, but it's obvious that here—now—they really do care.

The trouble is, we're not actually that easy to explain. In fact, we're fucking unbelievable. Hell, sometimes I don't believe it.

I look at Max. He gives a one-shouldered shrug.

I take a deep breath. Then hesitate.

"Come on, Ian," Beckett says. "Spit it out. How hard can it be?"

"Really fucking hard, actually."

"Yeah, well, I'm making up my own stories about what just happened, and most of them end with us having to toss you out of an airlock because of homicidal psychosis, so it's probably better than that, right?" She gives me the same pointed look Kali did a few minutes ago, and it almost makes me laugh. Those two have more in common than either would ever want to admit.

I run a hand through my hair, trying to figure out what words to use to explain something that can't be explained.

"*Fuck it, I'll tell them*," Max says. "*You're going to hurt yourself over there.*"

I flip him off. "*Feel free.*"

I don't want to be the one to tell Kali anyway. I don't want to be looking at her when everything changes—and it will. How could it not?

"I know some of you are wondering about the relationship between Ian, Milla, and me," Max starts.

"*Strong start*," I interject.

"*Seriously?*" He gives me a what-the-fuck look. "*You want to do this?*"

"*Not even a little bit.*"

"*Then butt the fuck out,*" he snarls.

"Until I was eleven years old," I butt the fuck in, "Max and Milla didn't exist. Then I went through a…traumatic experience, and somehow I…" I run a hand through my hair again.

"*Just say it,*" Max urges. "*It's not going to get any easier.*"

"I split into three." My words are met with silence. I look around, and now everyone is frowning. Except Merrick, who has a dawning understanding on his face.

Does that mean he knows something about what we are? If so, how?

"Like three personalities?" Beckett asks, eyes narrowed in thought.

I have a flashback to that day. Of finishing my chores early and wandering through a hole in the fence at the children's refugee camp where I'd been taken when my mother was murdered. There were several holes we liked to sneak out of—no one at the camp paid too much attention to our comings and goings as there was nowhere for us to go, nothing in any direction but barren desert for hundreds of miles.

A sandstorm came up, and I dug deep into a dune to try to shelter myself. I hid there for an hour, maybe two. Something happened in that dune—something painful and terrifying and unlike anything I'd ever felt before. And when I tunneled out after the storm, I was three instead of one.

"Like three people," I tell her. "I was me, and then I was we. Me, Max, and Milla. They were just there, and I didn't understand, but at the same time I did. They were me. I was them."

"We," Max says quietly. "We can hear one another's thoughts. Feel what the others are feeling. Know what the others are going to do before they do it. I'm Ian. He's me. We're both Milla."

"Like a gestalt or a hive mind," I put in. We'd done a lot of research over the years before we even ran across those terms and understood that they were the closest explanation. Years of research before we were able to even accept what we are.

Now, we wouldn't want it any other way.

"But how?" Kali says. She doesn't look disgusted, thankfully. Just very confused. Which is understandable, considering what we're talking about is fucking confusing. "I've never heard of such a thing, and I thought the Imperial libraries held knowledge about everything."

"I have," Merrick says. Apparently I was right about the look on his face earlier. "It's called tripartition. When a single entity—in this case, Ian—splits into three and forms a triplex."

"But still—how? Giving it a name doesn't make it make any more sense." Kali doesn't look at me when she says it. I don't know if that means she's disgusted by us or just that she doesn't want to make me uncomfortable while she tries to understand. I'm hoping it's the second, but I doubt it.

"The Sisterhood believes in lingering DNA from the Ancients," Merrick says. "We've been collecting records for millennia. Some people, especially Seratians, have traces of DNA strains that survive from before humanity evolved in Senestris. We think of these genetic anomalies as blessings from the Light, and they often come with side effects that we study—visions, foresight, longevity. There are also side effects when people who *don't* have alien DNA come in contact with it. Tripartition is one of those side effects, though it's very rare. I've only heard of one other case in the last hundred years, and they died when…"

Sure. Exposure to Ancient DNA. Makes as much sense as anything else we've read about what happened in that dune.

"When what?" Rain asks. She's leaning forward, fascinated in a way that Kali doesn't seem to be at all.

Is that good or bad? Then again, it doesn't really matter, does it? We are what we are. I can't change it and wouldn't change it if I could, so it's no use worrying about whether Kali thinks we're okay or not.

"When one of them was killed in an accident," Merrick answers reluctantly. "They all died."

And there it is. The one big—and I mean huge—downside to our little gestalt. "Yeah," I say. "One of us dies, and we all die." We discovered that little gem in our early research. We never found an explanation like the one Merrick just gave me, but we did come across stories and legends that could only be the same thing.

Kali backs away from me and sinks down into a chair behind her. Her eyes are wide. "So, what just happened?" she asks, and her voice quivers.

"We felt Milla. She was in pain. That's the only way we can feel her over large distances."

"Is she dead?" Beckett asks, and for a second she looks like she's just waiting for Max and me to keel over.

Max rolls his eyes at her. "Which part about *if she dies, we die* was not clear?"

She shrugs. "I'm just making sure we weren't going to have to prepare for you to go down any second."

"Beckett!" Rain looks horrified.

Beckett throws her hands up. "I'm just saying, this is some really weird shit. I'm just trying to figure it out."

"I'm glad you're not dead," Kali says softly.

"Us too," Max says.

"So, how does it work?" Kali asks Merrick. "This tripartition thing. I mean, if one person becomes three, there has to be some kind of biological explanation. I mean, at bare bones, physics is a thing, and mass occupies a certain amount of space. Not to mention things like organs and nervous systems and blood."

"Like I said, we have the knowledge on Serati but not a lot of practical application of said knowledge," Merrick clarifies. "To the best of our understanding, the alien DNA acts like a virus in the host it comes in contact with. Over a very short time—I don't know how long, but accounts in the Sisterhood's records say an hour or two—normal, healthy cells begin to split at a really fast rate. So fast that other cells don't have time to die out like they normally would."

"Hold up," Gage says. "All the cells split? Brain, organ, everything?"

"Again, no medical professional has ever witnessed it happening—to my knowledge, anyway—but that is the supposition. When the cells become too much for one body to handle, it splits."

"So kind of like cloning," Gage says. "But with one consciousness."

"And—in Ian's case—enough female alien DNA to create at least one female in the triplex," Merrick finishes, and he's studying me like I'm some sort of curiosity.

They all are—even Kali. Which is the other reason we never tell anyone what we are. Just think what would happen if someone like Dr. Veragelen got hold of the information.

"The Sisterhood consider those altered by Ancient DNA children of the gods," Rain says. "We call you the Gifted."

"I don't feel particularly fucking gifted right now."

"No, she's right," Merrick adds. "Likely, you'd be considered a miracle back on Serati and revered for your holiness." He sounds amused by the idea.

Beckett smirks. "Holy Ian and Max. Somehow I doubt it would stick."

Me too.

"So, we have to find Milla," Kali says abruptly. "Not just because she's obviously suffering, which is bad enough. But if we don't …"

She trails off like she doesn't want to say it. But it's a reality Max and I live with every day—and why I felt so selfish when I stayed on Glacea with Kali when she was shot. Because that decision by me doomed all of us.

"If we don't," Max finishes for her, "Ian and I don't have much time left, either."

CHAPTER 64

Kali

Two hours later, I'm still reeling from everything I've learned today.

I'm in the galley using all the tricks Gage has taught me about making reconstituted food taste better to try to put together a decent meal for everyone, but I'm not sure how well it's going to turn out. I keep getting distracted by what my mother said about how I'm the target of all these attacks. That they aren't trying to kill all of us—just me.

Which means I'm the reason ships keep trying to blow us out of open space.

I'm the reason Gage got shot.

And I'm the reason Ian has nearly died twice.

Don't puke, don't puke, don't fucking puke.

I take a deep breath to settle my suddenly churning stomach, but it doesn't work. Maybe the old Kali who first got here and thought everyone lived to serve the Empire could have handled the thought of people dying to protect the crown princess.

But the woman I've become since the *Caelestis*? The last thing I want is *anyone* sacrificing for an empire that apparently doesn't give a shit about them. And I definitely, definitely don't want anything happening to the people on this ship because of who I am or decisions that I make.

Because we're not out of danger yet—we could be attacked again, if they can find us. And now that we know Milla is running out of time, it's so much worse. Because if we're too late and she dies, then Ian and Max die, too.

I can't let that happen. I *won't* let it happen. Not to them, and not to anyone on the *Starlight*.

We may have started out strangers and enemies, but that's not what we are anymore. It feels like we've lived a lifetime in a couple of weeks, and now I can barely remember what it felt like not to have their backs—or what it felt like for them not to have mine.

I don't know if I'd say we're all exactly friends—Merrick and Beckett are hard to get a read on sometimes—but we're definitely not enemies. And I do care about them all so, so much. Way too much to sit by and let them be collateral damage in the machinations of the Empire. They've already suffered enough for Senestris. No way am I going to be the reason these smart, funny, courageous people die.

Just the thought of a world without them makes me sick.

A world without Rain, whose love and joy is so incredibly inspiring?

Or Max, who always has a smile and an understanding ear to lend? And who's taught me so much in my time on the *Starlight*?

Or Merrick and Gage, who are so completely different but still manage to both come through for us when we need them most?

Even Beckett, with her darkness and sarcasm and hatred of me. She's suffered so much and has had such a terrible life, and yet she's so incredibly resilient. Somehow, someway, she always bounces back. How could I not admire that?

And finally, Ian—what can I even say about Ian? I was supposed to hate him, smug, arrogant, controlling asshole that he is. And somehow, someway, I fell for him hardest of all. Not just because we slept together, but because inside all that I-don't-care-about-anyone-but-me grumpiness is a guy who cares too much. About everyone and everything.

Since we left the *Caelestis*, they've been taking care of me in so many ways. Stitching me up. Telling me jokes. Calling me brave. Teaching me to fight—and literally kicking my ass. Now it's my turn to take care of them the only way I can. No matter how much it hurts. Because losing them would hurt so much worse.

Ever since I got here, the only thing I wanted was to be useful. To be so much more than dead weight. I've tinkered with tech. I've cleaned toilets. I've cooked food. But maybe all along, the best, most useful thing I could do...was leave.

"Hey, can I talk to you for a minute?"

I freeze at the voice, my stomach clenching and my heart fluttering with nerves in my chest. Because I've known this moment was coming since I walked off the bridge. But it's not like I've got a choice. The conversation has to be had.

"Sure." I keep my voice casual as I start to fill up the sink with soapy water so I can wash the bowls I used to put together the casserole that's now being finalized in the processor. "What do you need?"

"Is that how you want to play it?" Ian asks as he strides across the room toward me. "Like you didn't run from the bridge the second you could?"

I plunge my hands into the soapy water so he can't see how badly they're trembling. "I didn't run. I just wanted to get started on a meal."

"So, we're lying to each other now?" he asks, leaning a hip against the cabinet next to me like he's got all the time in the world to have this argument. And suddenly I'm as angry as I am nervous. Because he's got some nerve, accusing me of lying.

"Oh, I don't think we're just starting now, do you?" I shoot back.

He goes pale at the implication, but he doesn't step back—or away—like I'd hoped he would. Then again, this is Ian, and I've yet to see him back down from a fight. But instead of coming at me with one of the biting comments I know so well, he just shakes his head as if to clear it and says, "It wasn't only my secret to tell."

My tiny little flare of righteous indignation—brought on by my own guilt and sadness; I'm aware—dies a terrible death. "I know. I didn't mean to accuse you of anything."

"Sure you did," he says easily, the tension leaking from his shoulders. "But I don't blame you for that. What I am is hard to talk about and even harder to understand."

He's not wrong there. "It doesn't change anything for me, except…" I break off, unsure of how to ask what I'm thinking.

But Ian knows—I can see the knowledge in his eyes even before he says, "He was passed out drunk, Kali. He didn't feel or witness anything—I swear. I never would have made love to you without you knowing what I was if there was any chance it would be more than just the two of us."

Relief sweeps through me at his words. And at his understanding that it freaked me out completely, thinking that I'd slept with both of them without knowing it. It's not that I don't like Max, and it's not that this gestalt thing upsets me so much that it makes me not want to be with Ian. It just felt strange to think that someone had seen me like that—so vulnerable emotionally and physically—while I didn't know anything about it.

"Thank you for explaining that," I tell him. "It means a lot to me that you made sure."

He nods.

An awkward silence descends on the galley, and I can't stand it. Ian and I have fought, laughed, snarked, made love, and none of it has ever been awkward. But now…now it feels like everything is a little bit off, like a picture that's just a tiny bit out of focus.

I hate it. I'd much rather be fighting with him than have this awkward politeness between us for one minute longer.

Maybe that's why I choose this moment to say, "I'm going to call the Empress back and tell her I'll come home."

CHAPTER 65

Kali

H e freezes in the act of running a hand over his hair. "No, you are not."

I lift a brow. "Is that Ian the captain speaking or—"

"That's the man you're sleeping with speaking," he growls. "And you don't just get to walk away when things become a little uncomfortable for you."

"I don't know because I've never tried it, but I'm pretty sure dying is a *lot* uncomfortable, thank you very much. And I would prefer none of us do it for a very long time."

Ian doesn't look impressed. "And you expect me to believe that's the reason you're running away?"

"I'm not running away!" I tell him. "I'm leaving so that whoever's trying to kill me will stop coming after the *Starlight*. You'll be safe—all of you will be—and I'll—"

"Be back home with Mommy?" he finishes. "And what if the person trying to kill you is at the palace?"

"Well, then, you'll still be safe. And my mother may not be a good leader—" He snorts, but I ignore him and keep talking. "But there's no way she's going to let anyone kill the only heir to her throne. So I'm safer there than I am here. And you guys are much safer, too."

"And that's the only reason you want to go?" he asks again. "To protect us?"

"Of course. Why else would I want to leave? I love being on the *Starlight*."

Ian folds his arms over his chest. "I don't know, Kali. Why else would you want to leave?"

"That's what I'm asking you!" I tell him, exasperated.

But he doesn't answer. He just continues to look at me with a blank face that really isn't blank at all because it's so freaking obnoxious. Part of me wants to say to hell with it and walk away right now, but I don't. Because the longer I stare at him, the more I realize there is something there after all—a strange hurt buried so well in the depths of his eyes that I almost didn't notice it.

But what does he have to be hurt about? I'm the one leaving the *Starlight* and the only real almost-friends I've ever had. He gets to stay here with everyone, and he and Max get to go after Milla and—

And it hits me. Why he's so angry—and so hurt. "Oh, Ian." I reach for him then, resting a hand on his biceps as I close the distance between us. "You can't think it's because of the gestalt."

His ridiculously chiseled jaw clenches so tightly that I'm afraid he's going to break a molar or three. "Pretty hard to think it's anything else, considering you just found out about it and you can't get off this ship fast enough."

"I also just found out that I'm the target of the assassination attempts," I say, exasperated. "Literally just minutes before I found out about you, Max, and Milla! So maybe you could cut me a little slack here, okay? I really am trying to do what's best for everyone."

He doesn't say anything to that, but I can tell he's thinking about it. Trying to weigh out if he wants to believe me or not. And maybe I'd be angry about that—I don't lie, and I definitely don't lie to him—except it's so obviously coming from a place of his deepest insecurities that I can't be mad.

"It doesn't feel like it's what's best," Ian finally says.

And he's not wrong. Because it doesn't feel like that at all. It feels awful and gross and like I'm making the worst mistake of my life even thinking about walking away from the *Starlight*. But I can't think of anything else to do that will keep them safe from the Empire.

I don't say that, though. I can't. Not if I have any hope of getting through this conversation without crying. And not if I'm going to have a chance to prove to him that he has nothing to be insecure about.

It's so strange to think of him like that—big, tough Ian who always has an answer and is happy to run over whoever he needs to to get his own way. But that's only part of who he is—and I don't mean the gestalt. I mean he's also the guy who's obviously spent a lifetime avoiding any kind of emotional intimacy with anyone but Max and Milla because he can't imagine anyone accepting them for who they are.

Accepting him for who—and what—he is.

I've spent my life living that way, convinced that if anyone ever saw the small, simple human behind the princess, they'd be disappointed.

I wouldn't wish that feeling on anyone. And I definitely wouldn't wish it on the man I'm starting to fall in—

I stop before I can even think such a thing. Because what's the point of acknowledging it when it will only hurt more when I leave?

Instead, I concentrate on Ian. On the way he looks, all big and tough and sexier than he has any right to. And give myself permission to indulge one last time.

I have a few misgivings—the gestalt fascinates me, but it also makes me a little nervous—so I choose not to focus on it. I focus on Ian instead, just Ian, and not the sorrow that feels like a giant meteor in my stomach, weighing me down and burning me to a crisp all at the same time.

Stepping forward, I close the space he's so carefully left between us. His dark eyes narrow, like he's trying to figure out just what I'm up to, but I don't bother to clue him in. He's a smart guy. I'm pretty sure he'll figure it out.

We're so close that I can feel the heat emanating from him now, and it's such a contrast to the cold that's taken up residence deep inside me that I can't resist it. Can't resist him.

I reach out and press my hands to his chest, relishing the strength of Ian's powerful muscles beneath my fingers. His eyes turn black, the pupils blowing out even before I move higher and dance my fingertips along his throat to play with the hair at the back of his neck. It's cool and soft, and I love the way it slides against my skin.

I love even more the way his breath catches in his throat, his hot, hard body crowding against me as I cup the back of his head in my hands. I go up on tiptoes and slowly, carefully, pull his mouth down to mine.

Ian groans before our lips even touch—a dark, hungry sound that shoots straight through me as I close the very last of the distance between us. And then my lips are on his, his lips are on mine, and nothing has ever felt so good.

Like the twinkling lights that crowd the ceiling of my room back at home combined with the effervescence of the jelly beans he gave me back on Glacea.

I nip at his lower lip, and he groans again, deep in his throat this time. I take instant advantage, sucking his lower lip straight between my teeth. He stiffens for a second, and then a shudder runs through him and his arms snake around me.

He pulls me even closer, plastering our bodies together so I can feel all of him against all of me. He's taking over now, his tongue stealing into my mouth to stroke against my teeth, my tongue, the roof of my mouth. Pleasure slams through me, frissons of need lighting me up from the inside.

I'm the one making noise now, a low, keening whine coming from deep inside me as Ian slides his hands down my back. He cups my ass in his palms and in one effortless motion lifts me up so that he's carrying me. My arms wrap around his shoulders. My legs wrap around his waist.

He feels good, so good, and I whimper as he spins us so that my back is against the wall. And then I'm arching against him, my body taking over as I press myself against his dick over and over and over again.

The heat grows inside me, and so does the emptiness, until all I can think about is Ian and the feel of him inside me. "Please," I murmur to him as I trail hot kisses along his jaw, his throat, the sensitive spot behind his ear that makes him growl.

"Please, please, please." It's a litany inside me now, a breathless plea falling from my lips over and over again.

And then he's sliding my legs back down his body until my feet are once again on the floor. He still holds me tightly against him—which is a good thing, considering I'm not sure my trembling knees can support me right now.

But then he's dropping to his knees in front of me, pulling my zipper down as he goes. "You're so beautiful," he mutters as his lips race down the center of my body, over my breastbone and my belly button and then lower, to the very heart of me.

He keeps my jumpsuit mostly on even as he angles us so that the majority of my body is hidden by the powerful width of his—we are still in the back of the galley, after all. And while everyone else is busy, the chance that one of them might walk in here is unlikely but not unheard of.

There's something sexy about that thought, something forbidden and hot and desperation-inducing, especially when I think about Max being the one to walk in on us.

Or can he see us already?

But then Ian's fingers are sliding over my mons, pulling down my panties and dancing along the slit of my sex before dipping gently inside.

My whole body lights up then, a strangled scream coming from deep in my core as he thrusts two strong, thick fingers inside me. He fills me up, has me riding his fingers like my life and my sanity depend on it. And then he's leaning forward, pressing kisses to my abdomen before trailing his lips lower and lower.

His tongue snakes out, strokes a circle over my clit. I lose myself then, my hands clutching at his hair as my body arches and trembles and bucks against him.

Ian just laughs, and his hands come up to hold my hips against the wall as he continues to lick and suck and nuzzle me until all that matters is him and this moment and the inferno burning inside of me.

"Ian, please," I beg, the ache growing until it's painful. Until I'm balanced on a precipice of need, teetering on the edge but unable to tip over because he won't let me. Because he's determined to keep me there—right there—edging toward ecstasy as long as he can. "I need...I need..."

His breath is hot against my core, his tongue wicked and wild and wonderful as it glides over me. I whimper again—the longer this goes on, the less control I have over my body—and then he's lifting one of my legs, draping it over his shoulder as his fingers burrow even deeper.

They find a spot that lights me up from the inside, that has every nerve ending on red alert and every other part of me begging for release.

I let out a high, keening cry then, and his free hand comes up to silence me with a finger against my lips. But I'm too far gone to care who hears me, and I bite down hard on his fingertip before sucking his finger deep inside my mouth.

It's Ian's turn to groan now, his mouth and fingers growing more insistent, more desperate, more determined.

Another stroke of his tongue against my clit, another twist of his fingers deep inside me, and I'm shooting straight over the edge. Pleasure explodes through me like a supernova, burning me alive from the inside out, racing along my veins and nerves and skin and pouring out of me in waves I can't hope to contain.

"Ian, Ian, Ian." My orgasm goes on and on, and his name is a prayer on my lips, a benediction and a cry for mercy all at once.

But Ian's not backing off and he's not backing down, because the next thing I know his fingers are replaced with his tongue, licking its way deep inside the very heart of me. And just like that, I'm going over again, one release on top of the other as my body spins completely out of my control.

When it's over, when I can finally think and feel and breathe again, Ian slides my leg back onto the floor and carefully stands up, one hand on my hip to support me just in case my trembling, wobbly legs have trouble working on their own. And then he's sliding my panties back into place, pulling up the zipper of my jumpsuit, and making me presentable again.

As long as you don't count the flush in my cheeks and what I'm sure is the pleasure-glazed look in my eyes.

I reach for him, my hands sliding over his hard, hot dick. A shudder runs through him, and I start to unbuckle his belt, to unfasten his pants so that I can give him the same pleasure that he's just given me. But Ian stops me with a kiss, his fingers tangling with mine as he pulls my hand away from his body.

"Don't you want—" I start, but he nips at my lower lip before pulling reluctantly away.

"Later," he murmurs. "They'll be coming in for food any minute."

"Yes, but—" I try again, stroking the hard length of him through his pants.

Ian shudders, thrusts helplessly against my caress. But then he's pulling away, straightening up the collar of my jumpsuit and his own state of dishevelment.

Just in time, it turns out, because about a minute later, Rain and Merrick come striding into the galley.

Ian and I are both decent—but it's a close one as Ian washes his hands and dries them before moving to the processor to pull out the casserole. He's cool and collected, and if anyone was looking at only him, they'd have no idea what just happened here. Me, on the other hand? There's no mirror in here, so I can't see myself, but I'm pretty sure it looks like I just got fucked in the galley. And I can't even bring myself to care.

Especially when Max walks in thirty seconds later. His gaze meets mine across the room, and I can see it in the depths of his eyes—the knowledge and the heat and the interest.

It should embarrass me, but it doesn't. Instead, it rekindles the fire inside of me, my heart going wild and my nipples going hard. Max notices, and so does Ian—and suddenly the air around us seems charged with an electricity I can't explain and am not sure I'd want to if I could.

But then Max smiles and breaks eye contact and the moment

dissipates like so much vapor.

Beckett and Gage wander in soon after, and then we're all sitting down for a meal at the table I set. And as the conversation flows back and forth between them all, I can't help thinking that this is what I want. This perfect moment of laughter and camaraderie and satisfaction—so much satisfaction—all rolled into one. It's taken us a while to get here, but now that we have, I can't help wanting it to last forever.

But moments are fleeting. No matter how hard we try to capture them, they disappear as easily as they come. And as Gage and Merrick clear the dishes, I know what I have to do.

I just hope I have the strength to do it.

CHAPTER 66

Kali

I wait until Rain has fallen asleep, and then I creep out of our
room and down the hall to the bridge. It's the dead of night, and
everyone is sleeping except me—and, I hope, Beckett. I really need
to speak with her.

Thankfully, she's sitting in her pilot's chair, per usual, munching
on a protein bar and doing something I can't quite make out on the
screen in front of her.

"Hey," I say from the door in an attempt not to startle her. She's
jumpy at the best of times—for obvious reasons—and we've all
learned it's better to give her a warning than end up at the business
end of whatever object she turns into a weapon when she's startled.

She stiffens, but she doesn't reach for anything to throw at me, so
I'll consider it a win. "What are you doing here?" she demands. I can
tell she tried to inject her tone with the same vitriol she usually has
when she speaks to me, but it just isn't there. I think I'm growing on
her like one of the fungi from Ellindan.

"I was hoping to speak with you. I have a favor to ask." I cross the
bridge, and she rushes to close her screen, but not before I see what's
on it. "Are you playing stirobi? Against who?"

"You're sure asking a lot of questions for someone who wants a favor," she snarls before leaning back in her chair and kicking her feet up on the console in front of her.

I sit down in the chair next to her. "It's a game. I didn't realize the answer was top secret."

"I'm playing against the *Starlight*. She always wins, but I'm getting better." She takes a big bite of her protein bar and gives me an are-you-happy-now look. "So what do you want? I thought you'd be off boning the captain and his other half or something."

"Wow, classy." I roll my eyes as she laughs.

"Yep, that's me." She takes a swig of water. "So lay this favor on me so I can tell you no and you can get the fuck off my bridge."

"You know, Beckett, the thing I'm going to miss the most about being on this ship is your incredible graciousness. It's always so heartwarming."

"Yeah, well—" she starts, then freezes. "Going to miss?"

"That's what I want to talk to you about. Are we close to anywhere with a breathable atmosphere?"

She narrows her eyes. "Define close."

"Under three hours away from?" I'd like to get this done before anybody else wakes up.

For several seconds, she just stares at me. Not like she's in shock—like she's trying to figure out if I'm for real. Whatever she sees in my face must convince her that I am serious, because she doesn't say another word. She just turns back to the *Starlight* and presses some buttons.

Seconds later, a huge map of the system around us comes up on the viewing screens. "Turns out we're about two hours away from one of Glacea's outer moons and about four hours from another." She gestures to their relative positions on the screens.

"Is there anything on the closest moon?" I ask.

"Not a lot. But it is a military outpost, so you shouldn't have any problems finding a ride home—if that's where you're planning on going."

"It is."

"I figured." She fiddles with the *Starlight*'s controls for a few seconds. "You want me to set course for it?"

Do I want her to? Not even a little bit. Am I going to have her do it anyway? "Yes, please."

She doesn't say anything else, just enters the coordinates of the moon and then, after another long glance my way, goes back to playing her game.

It's why I asked for her help. She's the only one on board, besides maybe Merrick, who won't try to talk me out of this. And since I really, really don't want to leave, I'm afraid it won't be that hard to convince me not to—especially if Ian is the one doing the convincing.

We sit in silence for over an hour, Beckett playing her game and me using the paper I found in the storage bay to write out a message to Ian, trying to explain to him what I barely understand myself.

"He's going to be pissed. You know that, right?" Beckett says as Glacea's moon fills up the screen in front of us.

"Better angry than dead," I answer. It's what I need to hear, too, to get rid of the ball of tension in my stomach and the index of regrets in my head. Because I'd rather everyone on board be angry instead of dead—even Beckett—and if there's any way I can save them, I have to take it.

"You really think your mother was telling the truth?" she asks. Coming from anyone else, her tone would be one of total boredom, but for Beckett, any mild interest is the equivalent of burning curiosity.

"About the assassination attempts being aimed at me? I do," I tell her. "It never felt right it could be the Corporation—they're really just all about profits and my family keeps them profitable. The Sisterhood would never risk harming their high priestess by shooting us down. It can't be the rebels; you've already vouched for them. And I trust you."

She lifts a brow at that but doesn't say anything.

I shove a shaking hand through my hair, because saying it out loud just makes me even more convinced. "The Empire is the only other entity with the money to command that many ships and the reach to distribute all those flyers. If you disagree, I'm all ears. But I've been giving it a lot of thought, and nothing else makes sense to me."

"Me either, but this way I can tell Ian I tried to change your mind."

I give her a rueful grin. "Saving your own skin, huh?"

"No one else is going to," she answers with a shrug.

She's not wrong, except— "That's what I'm trying to do right now, Beckett. I'm not just leaving because of Ian, you know. I'm leaving because of all of you."

She doesn't say anything to that, but she does turn back to the console and start fidgeting with some of the switches there, a surefire sign that she's uncomfortable. Which is fair, but it doesn't stop me from telling her, "There's something else I want to say to you. I hope you don't mind."

She shrugs, but her hands still and it almost seems like she's holding her breath.

I try to get my thoughts in order because I'll only have one chance to say what needs to be said. "In my time on the *Starlight*, I don't think it's any secret that we've had massively separate agendas. And while we were born on very different sides of the conflict currently rocking Senestris, I need you to know that I'm sorry. The crown princess of the Empire that has abused you and hurt you and done you very wrong is sorry. You should never have been treated how you were treated. You should never have had to suffer what you've suffered. And I promise you that I will spend every day that I'm alive while my family is in power working to make sure that no one suffers at our hands ever again the way that you have."

A powerful shudder runs through her too-thin body, and she bows her head so that her black curls cover her face. Another shudder, followed by one harsh, indrawn breath. And then she whispers, "I'm glad I didn't try as hard as I could have to kill you."

I almost laugh, but I can hear the sincerity in her voice. And honestly, it's probably more of a concession than I deserve. "Me too," I tell her. And while a part of me wants to reach out and hug her, another part of me wants to keep my hands and arms attached to my body. Also, I'm afraid I'll cry, and if I start, I don't think I'll ever stop.

The *Starlight*'s command center beeps, and Beckett takes over the controls. "Landfall initiating," she says. "Huh. Military outpost waved us through without asking for credentials. We'll be landing in about four minutes, if the *Starlight* here is correct."

The *Starlight*'s always correct, and we both know it. So I pick up the bag I packed earlier with a blanket and a few packets of dried fishgalen and sling it over my shoulder. Then I put the letter I wrote Ian on top of the captain's chair he so loves and make my way to the bridge door.

"You'll call the Empress once you're away from here? Tell her where to pick me up?"

"I will." Beckett does look at me then. "Although I don't know why you're trusting me with that task. What if I decide to leave you on some broken-down old moon outpost forever?"

"Because if that happens, the Empress will make a big fuss about not having her precious daughter home. And someone, sometime soon, will bring enough firepower to take down the *Starlight*—and you."

Beckett considers my words as she sets the ship down on a patch of purple dirt. "You make a compelling argument."

"Nice of you to notice." I smile at her, and for once she smiles back—or at least she only snarls a little bit, which is definite progress. And she doesn't comment on the fact that my lip is wobbling, which I also appreciate.

She punches a button, and the landing gear goes down. "You sure about this?" she asks.

No. "Absolutely." I force my feet to start walking, when what they really want to do is stay exactly where they are. As does the rest of me.

"I'll call your mom as soon as we get some distance from here."

"Thank you, Beckett." I hold out a hand to shake, and she takes it. Then—to both of our shock—she reaches over and gives me an awkward half back pat, half hug thing that is a lot more comforting than it should be.

I start walking down the ramp, stomach in knots and tears burning the backs of my eyes. I'm about halfway down when Beckett calls my name again, and I turn to find her standing at the top of the ramp.

"Thank you for not being as big an asshole as I thought you

were," she says.

"Right back at you," I tell her. And then I make my way fully down the ramp.

I watch as Beckett raises the ramp again. Watch as she starts up the *Starlight*. Watch as she takes off and flies into the night. And then I watch some more, until the ship looks like little more than a comet streaking through the pitch-black sky.

Only then do I sit down in the middle of the purple dirt and sob. Because I'm pretty sure my entire heart is on that ship, and I just watched it fly away.

CHAPTER 67

Kali

When I finally finish crying, I wipe my face on the blanket I borrowed from the *Starlight*. It's freezing here—not snowy like on Glacea but still very, very cold—so I wrap the blanket around myself as tightly as I can. Then stand up and look around for the first time.

Serai has risen over the horizon, and the atmosphere on this moon has her looking blue as she does—not a great sign for my long-term survival in open air, if the radiation scattering is so different through this atmosphere's particles than it is on Askkandia, but the *Starlight* indicated I'd be safe here for at least a few hours after landfall, and I trust her. The world around me has become light enough for me to see a giant purple mountain range in the distance. I also notice five large, industrial-looking buildings to my left, as well as a silver-and-black military pod racing straight toward me.

After everything that happened in Rangar and Rodos, I'm more than a little nervous about what'll go down when they get to me. But I remind myself this is a military outpost, presumably loyal to the Empress, and I am the princess. I just have to remember that and act like one—at least for now.

I take a second to tie back my hair, smoothing it as best I can.

Then I straighten my shoulders, put on the placid princess face I've fallen out of the practice of wearing—though I do have to admit, it *does* help me feel more in control—and wait for whatever comes next.

Whatever comes next is three soldiers pouring out of the large pod that hovers right in front of me. All three of them are carrying laser rifles, and all three of them level those laser rifles at me.

"Hands up!" the first one yells. She's a stern-looking woman with a grumpy face, and the insignia on her heavy rust-colored uniform tell me she's the highest-ranking of the three. I'd guess she's from Kridacus, judging by her sturdy build and her velvety peach skin—wherever she's from, this is a long way from home for any Inner, so the fact she's out here means she probably did something the Empire didn't like.

Which kind of makes me like her automatically.

While a part of me wants nothing more than to throw my hands up—I really don't want to have done all this just to die out here on some distant outpost—I know there's no way my mother would ever do such a thing. So I focus all of my attention on the lieutenant and give her my most disapproving face—one I've channeled directly from the Empress herself.

"Put those guns down," I order in a voice as cold as a Glacean storm. "I am Princess Kalinda, daughter of the Empress Violatta of the Senestris System, and I am in need of your assistance. Please take me to your base so that I may speak with my mother."

All three of them look confused at my words, but their weapons don't so much as waver. My heart is beating out of control now. "I will give you three seconds to lower those weapons before I have you arrested and tried for treason."

I would never—they really are just doing their jobs. Besides, I don't even know if that's a thing anymore. But I really don't want to get shot, so this is what I've got to work with.

The laser rifles waver and then finally lower. "Princess Kalinda?" The lieutenant steps forward. "What are you doing out here?"

"With help, I escaped from the *Caelestis* after the unfortunate incident a couple of weeks ago. I've been on a ship since then. It is time for me to go home." My lip wants to wobble at the thought, but sheer will alone keeps it steady. "I assume you can help me with that?"

"Of course, Your Highness. My name is Belinda, and my men are Jakob and Vincen. We'll take good care of you. Welcome to Espia."

Once they accept who I am, things happen quite quickly. I get bundled into the front passenger seat of their pod, an extra blanket wrapped around my shoulders. A thermos filled with hot coffee is thrust into my hands by one of the male soldiers—Jakob, I think—and then we're speeding off toward the buildings in the distance.

Within an hour, I've been given access to soldier's quarters—with many apologies from Lieutenant Belinda for the unimpressive accommodations. I think they're great, though—especially since they come with a hot shower and a comfortable bed.

I've just finished brushing out my hair and changing into the heavy soldier uniform Belinda left for me when there's a knock on my door.

"Coming!" I call.

I open the door to find two female soldiers standing there—Julia and Dominique were the names they gave me when we were introduced. One is carrying a pile of bedding, and the other has a food tray.

"Come in, come in," I tell them, ushering them inside. "Thank you so much for everything."

"Where would you like me to put your breakfast?" Dominique asks. She's tall and thin, with friendly eyes, brown skin, and the short-cropped hair of all soldiers in the Empire's military units.

"The counter is fine," I tell her, gesturing to the small kitchen area.

"May I make your bed, Your Highness?" Julia asks, holding up the bedding in her hands.

"Oh, you don't have to do that! I can make my bed myself."

They both recoil, and I'm not sure if it's from shock or horror. Either way, I mentally kick myself. How could I forget that princesses don't make their own beds? Rain had to show me the first day on the *Starlight*, but since then it's become habit.

One I apparently have to unlearn if I'm going back to my mother's palace. "Yes, you can make it for me."

Julia nods, and her friendly look is back in place.

"How long have you been stationed here?" I ask Dominique as Julia moves toward the bed in the corner and begins making it up.

"Two years, Your Highness," she answers, shuffling her feet a little like she's nervous. "Julia and I came together, right out of training."

"Do you like it?"

They exchange a look that tells me everything I want to know. But all Dominique says is, "It's a quiet post, Your Highness. You're definitely the most exciting thing to happen on Espia in the two years I've been here."

"To be fair, having the princess show up out of nowhere would be exciting for anyone, not just us," Julia adds.

"You're right," Dominique agrees. "We'll definitely have something to brag about at our next post."

"Dom!" Julia hisses, and the other soldier flushes as she just realizes what she said.

I laugh, though, because they remind me that there are nice people in the world who work for the Empire—something it was easy to forget on the *Starlight*, when nearly all of my traveling companions had been treated so badly by them.

I start to ask them more questions, but before I can think of anything, there's another knock on my door.

Dominique rushes to open it, and Lieutenant Belinda is standing there. She salutes when I come to the door, touching her finger to her forehead. "I wanted to let you know that we've contacted the palace, Your Highness. We've been told that there are several shuttles already deployed nearby, as they've been looking for you. The closest one has already set course for Espia and will be here before lunch tomorrow."

Relief sweeps through me at the news. I thank the lieutenant, who offers to show me around the base. I want to say no—I'm emotionally drained and miserable, and the cold weather reminds me of walking through the docks of Rodos with Ian—but I'm not sure sitting in this room on my own will do me any good, either.

So in the end I agree. How long could a tour of Espia take, anyway?

The answer is way more hours than I anticipated, because there is a lot more out here than there looked to be when I first landed. Yes, the base is small, but I didn't realize that there was so much beyond the mountains.

We drive through a tunnel cut into the base of the mountain, with Lieutenant Belinda explaining to me how the tunnel was made to streamline access to the facilities on the other side.

She adds that Espia was settled a long time ago, when the Corporation had wanted to explore Tybris and Nabroch, the two dead planets in the system.

They're at the edge of the system, right before the Wilds. Almost none of Serai's warmth makes it out here—one of the reasons the planets died so long ago. But when we found nothing usable, exploration halted, and nothing's been out here since.

Or so I was taught.

Now, however, I think that's not quite the case. Otherwise, why would the *Reformer* have brought Milla all the way out here, into the Wilds? And why would Ian know how horrible it was and that no one ever comes back?

Something is out there, obviously. Maybe a prison filled with people like Milla and Beckett, who are set to be experimented on? A child camp like the kind Ian grew up in? Something even worse?

It turns out that Espia has none of those things. Just an industrial park much bigger than the base, filled with identical-looking buildings—all painted Corporation black.

My suspicions grow. Something doesn't feel right about this. What is the Corporation doing with an active presence on Espia? But when I ask for a tour of the facilities, Lieutenant Belinda shakes her head.

"The military is discouraged from interrupting operations over here," she tells me stiffly, and I can tell it's a sore spot with her.

I start to ask her why she even brought me over here, and then I realize. It's because she's as suspicious of it as I am, and this is her way of letting her leadership know. That little laser gun incident this morning notwithstanding, Lieutenant Belinda is growing on me.

I will be checking up on this after I get home. And if I need to take another shuttle out here in a few months, then that's what I'll do. My mother and the Corporation aren't going to control me anymore.

We're almost back to the tunnel when I spot someone coming down the side of the mountain. The lieutenant must spot him, too, because she slows our pod down to a crawl.

It's a large man—taller even than Merrick, I think—and he's wearing some kind of mechanical device on his right leg, probably to help him climb the mountain. It doesn't seem so unusual, though, and definitely not the smoking gun I was hoping for. The Corporation is in charge of technology for the entire system, and they're always researching and developing something new.

Tech to help people negotiate rough terrain seems like a really great project, actually, considering what some of the planets are starting to look like as the sun dies.

Eventually, he disappears from sight and we speed up again. Once we get back to the base, I excuse myself to my room and spend the rest of the day doing exactly what I told myself I wouldn't do. I wallow in my own misery. On the plus side, the base has a fairly extensive digital library, and after I have dinner with the soldiers, I stop and check out a tablet.

I read until I fall asleep in the middle of the night, and when I wake up, it's almost time to go. I dress in the uniform they gave me yesterday, then pack my dirty jumpsuit into my backpack. I know I should just get rid of it—I've been wearing it so long that I'm sure it's unsalvageable—but I can't bring myself to do it. So I just shove it to the bottom of my bag and tell myself I'll deal with it when I get home.

After having lunch with the soldiers, I walk around and thank each of them individually for their service. Dominique gets overly excited and nearly throws her arms around me—which horrifies her lieutenant but makes me really happy. When I get home, I'm abolishing the no-touching rule anyway.

By then a ship has been spotted beyond our atmosphere, so I walk out beyond the base's perimeter and wait for my ride. Ten minutes later, the shuttle sets down. It's a mid-range transport ship with my mother's insignia of a star-studded diamond on the side. Dread settles in my stomach the second I see it, but I ignore it. I never thought it would be easy going home to Askkandia, but it's the decision I made. Now I've got to own it.

I watch as the engines settle to a low rumble, the external door opens, and the ramp slowly lowers. The moment the ramp is fully extended, a man dressed in the black-and-purple body armor of the Imperial security forces appears at the top. The second I see him, the tension oozes out of me, because he's not just any Imperial soldier but a personal favorite of mine.

I race for the spaceship as he strides down the ramp toward me. "Arik!" I shout.

"Princess Kali!" Relief floods his face as he realizes that I'm okay. The second I reach him, I hurl myself into his arms, and his eyes widen with alarm.

He catches me, and after the initial shock of me touching him, he allows his arms to wrap around me.

I give myself a few seconds to hold on tight—he smells like home—and then reluctantly release my death grip on his shoulders.

"It's good to see you, Your Highness," he tells me once we both step back. "Though I almost didn't recognize you."

Considering I'm currently in a soldier's uniform, I can only imagine. "You look exactly the same, Arik."

"You don't." He studies me a moment longer. "You remind me of your father."

"That's the nicest thing you've ever said to me. It's so good to see you."

"And you. We feared the worst when you disappeared from the *Caelestis*."

"I was terrified for all of you." I take a deep breath, then ask the question that's haunted me for weeks. "Did Lara make it?"

He nods. "She did. She suffered a broken arm, but she's back on Askkandia now. Waiting for you."

The relief is palpable. Whatever else happens, at least I'll see her again. "And Vance?"

"He didn't make it." His eyes are sad. "Over a hundred people died in the aftermath of the explosions, including Ambassadors Terra and Holdren."

"I'm so sorry." I didn't know Vance so well, but all the same, the thought of his death—especially while protecting me—fills me with sorrow. "It shouldn't have happened."

"No, Your Highness. But we're doing everything we can to find those responsible and bring them to justice."

I wonder if that's true. Or if—like with my father's death—my mother will wait a couple more weeks and then come out with "evidence" against the Rebellion. Another rout of the rebels' hideaways sounds exactly like something she'd be interested in.

I don't say that, though. Instead, I settle for a simple, "I hope so. A lot of innocent people died, and we need to find out why so we can make sure it doesn't happen again."

"Now you're sounding just like your father as well. You've grown up, Your Highness."

His words make me feel warm and...hopeful. My father was a good man. I hope I can be like him.

"Let's get you home. Is this bag all you have?"

I nod, even as I recoil at his words. Because the palace no longer feels like home. The *Starlight* does, and she's far away from us by now. *Which is exactly what I wanted*, I remind myself. Even though it feels like shit.

Then again, so does having to face my mother. Thankfully, I've got time to prepare myself. Because something tells me it's not going to go well.

CHAPTER 68

Kali

The ship lands lightly on the docking pad of the palace, and I take a deep breath. My chest hurts, my stomach is in knots, and there's a part of me that thinks I've made the wrong decision. But what choice did I have? Let my friends—let Ian—get killed because of me?

I never could have lived with myself.

It's taken a few weeks to get back here, weeks in which I've had plenty of time to think—with nothing else to do. And I've come to the conclusion that I have to put what happened on the *Starlight* behind me. At least for now. Senestris is still facing the biggest existential threat it ever has—a system-wide killer—and that has to be our priority. *My* priority. If I learned anything on this journey, it should be that. I can make a difference.

Arik clears his throat. "We're cleared to disembark, Your Highness."

That's when I realize they're waiting for me. I don't know how long I've been sitting frozen in my seat, harness still fastened, but it's long enough that whatever protocols they normally take to land at the palace are already complete.

My heart hurts as I remember Gage teaching me a few things about how a ship's mechanics help it take off and land. How I listened in on Beckett's lessons to Rain about flying, and how even though Beckett never acknowledged my presence, she never told me to fuck off, either. I've learned so much.

And now I'm back home.

I take a deep breath and put my princess face on again. "Thank you, Arik."

I've waited so long, the ramp is already lowered. As I get to the outer door, I look down. And there she is, looking just like my mom always looks.

Beautiful—way more beautiful than me.

Commanding—even standing here, waiting on her only daughter to return, it's obvious she's the one in charge.

Tiny—I get my height from my father and my Serati heritage. My mom only comes up to my chin, but she has such a big presence, I don't think anyone notices how small she is.

I think that everything I learned about her while on the *Starlight* had me building her up in my head into some kind of monster. And in some ways, she definitely is. But in others, she's just my mom, with all her good points and her bad.

I need to remember that when it's time to plead my case.

I straighten my shoulders—posture is nearly as important as your facial expression when you're a princess—and paste on my best regal serenity. Then I glide down the ramp toward my past and my future, making sure to keep my chin up the whole time.

I can't tell anything from my mother's expression, but that's to be expected. I did get my princess face from her, after all. Still, the last thing I expect when I come to a halt in front of her is for her to hug me.

But she does, pulling me to her and holding me close for several seconds. At first, I'm so surprised that I don't know what to do—she's never hugged me in my life—but eventually I figure it out and wrap my arms around her, too.

She smells like flowers, like the big bushes in the garden filled with purple and red blooms. It's a comforting scent, and I take a deep breath, soaking it in as I try to figure out how I feel.

Weird. Awkward. But also like maybe this was the right thing to do after all.

My mother loves me. Whatever she's done, whatever she's planning to do in the future, I know my mother loves me.

I just need to remember that through whatever comes next.

Eventually, she steps back and holds me at arm's length, her nose wrinkling as though she's smelled something bad. Probably me—my weeks-long pity party on the trip home didn't exactly translate into frequent showers. The Imperial transport had all the amenities a princess could dream of, of course, but every luxury just drove a new, painful splinter into my heart, because it wasn't the *Starlight*.

"Kalinda," she says, and there's real emotion in her voice. "I thought I'd lost you. I thought you were dead." Her gaze drops down over me. "And what in the system are you wearing?"

"I missed you too, Mom. And I thought you'd recognize it. It's an Imperial military uniform."

"I know what it is." Her nostrils flare. "The question is why it's on my daughter's body."

Well, the choices were this, my ratty old jumpsuit, or Arik's clothes, which are uncomfortably large on me. But I merely settle on, "It's been a wild ride."

Her gaze sharpens on me. "You've changed."

I have. But I'm certainly not about to apologize for that—or make excuses. "I had to adapt to life on the *Starlight*, but now I'm home."

"You need to put that period behind you. And those *people* you were with."

Never. "They saved my life."

"I've seen the reports. They're murderers and outlaws, the whole group of them."

"What about the High Priestess of the Sisterhood of the Light—and her bodyguard?"

"You know how I feel about the Sisterhood." She sniffs. "But I see they've influenced you in some way. You always did have a fondness for the underdogs of the system. We'll have to work on that."

I don't think that's going to happen. But I nod. "I'm already over it. But I would be dead if it wasn't for them." This is important, so I look her square in the eye. "Please promise me you won't go after them. Promise, Mom."

She pats my arm. "Of course not. No reason to think of them further. And I'll always be grateful to them for saving you."

"Thank you so much." I knew she would see reason. But that doesn't mean Ian's words aren't still echoing in my head, telling me the Empress can't be trusted. Just in case, I'll talk to Arik after this, put a few fail-safes in place separate from Mom.

There is one question I can't wait to ask. "Mother, do you know what happened? Who attacked the *Caelestis* and why?"

"Not yet, and this discussion will have to wait, Kalinda. First, we need to get you cleaned up; then, we will reveal you to the world. We must show everyone that you are back safely where you belong, that any plan against your life has failed, and that those involved will be hunted down and punished. I've already instigated an order that any known rebel sympathizers be brought in for questioning."

"But you said you didn't know who launched the attack."

"Maybe not, but this will do nicely to slow down the rebels. They're like sloggs breeding in the sewers. Every now and then, they need to be eradicated."

I go cold at her words. That's exactly what I was afraid she would do, but hearing her say it like that—so easily—is absolutely terrifying. And infuriating. As is the thought that she used my father's death as an attempt to do the same thing instead of going after his real killer.

I bite my lip, tell myself not to say anything that will upset her quite yet—there are so many things I have to say to her—but it's hard. Really hard.

Thankfully, she takes that moment to start walking. "Come inside," she tells me. "There's someone who's been waiting to see you."

Lara? I wonder, excitement racing through me for the first time in days. It's all I can do not to run into the palace. But I've worked too hard not to let my mother know how much I care about her to blow it now. The Empress tends to take away whatever I care about, and if I don't want the same thing to happen with Lara, I need to keep up the facade.

One of my mother's personal bodyguards holds open the door for us, and I can't help the small grin that comes to my face as I walk inside. At least until I realize that I've miscalculated—horribly. Because it's not Lara waiting for me inside the palace.

It's Dr. Veragelen. She's alive. She's here. And she's smiling.

Freaking steaming drokaray droppings.

CHAPTER 69

Kali

My feet are glued to the floor.

There's a part of me that wants to run, but where would I even go? There's nowhere to go except forward. *Shit, shit, shit.*

I square my shoulders. Because it doesn't matter why Dr. Veragelen is here—I'm going to convince my mother to help those who need it, and she can't stop me.

It's that thought that gives me the strength to walk forward, to force my feet to carry me—one step at a time—straight toward her.

Don't puke, don't puke, don't fucking puke.

Play it cool, and everything will be fine.

She gets my best regal nod—the one I reserve for people I despise. "Dr. Veragelen, how good to see you. I was so glad to hear you survived the...trouble...on the *Caelestis*."

"I feel the same way about you, Your Highness, though I fear you had a much more difficult time of things than I did."

I think about the attack in Rangar.

About the ships tracking us across the system.

About Ian and I both nearly dying on Glacea. How Milla and Max nearly died that day, too.

"I'm sure it was...difficult for both of us," I tell her graciously. "But

I am glad to be home."

"As am I. And now we can put it all behind us and move on to a much brighter future."

I really don't like the sound of that.

My mother gestures to the group of seats around a small, ornate table where fiznachi and crystal glasses have been set out, and I have a sudden craving for the burning taste of gerjgin.

Dr. Veragelen and my mother sit on one side of the table while I sit on the other—as far from the doctor as I can manage and still be polite.

The lines have definitely been drawn.

I pick up my glass of fiznachi and swallow it in one gulp before pouring another.

My mother glares at me, and part of me wants nothing more than to raise the glass to her in a toast to the people. A small shock might do her personality good.

"So," Dr. Veragelen starts without so much as touching her drink. "Now that you've returned to us, Kalinda, there's something you need to know. The heptosphere—"

"It wasn't destroyed in the explosions?" I ask. I was sure it would have been.

"Of course not. As far as we can tell, it's impervious to any and all damage, thankfully, since it is vitally important in our strategy to save the system."

Its supposedly pivotal importance is nothing new—it's the same story she was selling when we were aboard the *Caelestis*. I give her my most unimpressed look.

"But so far," Dr. Veragelen continues, "we have been unable to… activate it."

"I'm not sure what that has to do with me," I tell her.

"That day in the laboratory. You woke it up."

"Me? I didn't have anything to do with those whirling lights."

"Perhaps not on purpose. But you were close to it after the explosion, and I saw it come alive with my own eyes. You, Princess Kalinda, are exactly what we've been searching for for so long. You are the one person who can save the system."

For a second, shock flashes through me, but then I realize she's laying it on a bit thick. "I'm sure there are a lot of people who—"

"There aren't," she interrupts. "We've been trying for years to find the one person it responds to. You are definitely that person." She must realize how strident she sounds, because her voice softens immediately. "Together, we can solve all the issues caused by the dying sun. Make the system a place of peace and prosperity once more."

My thoughts are whirling. Normally I wouldn't believe something like this, but her eyes are filled with the fervor of a zealot, and I have trouble believing she doesn't mean every word she's saying.

What if I really am the only person who can save the system?

What if I can finally make good on my promise to save those who need me most—and more, to save everyone?

CHAPTER 70

Ian

"What the hell happened to you?" I growl as Gage walks onto the bridge. He's got a black eye and a cut on his left temple. His eyes widen at my tone, and he takes a few steps back. Not surprising—everyone's been giving me a wide berth since we found out Kali snuck out in the middle of the night like a damn thief. I haven't seen Merrick at all this morning, and this is the first time Gage has had the nerve to poke his head in here to see what's going on.

"I fell," he says after a minute. "Lost my balance during the *Starlight*'s last acceleration and took a header into the galley sink. *Loving* the head-injury pattern I've got going on."

"Ouch," Beckett says, not unsympathetically. "It looks bad. You should wrap it."

"Already have, but I'll do it again in a while." He flops down in the chair farthest away from me. Probably afraid I'll blacken his other eye.

Which isn't an unfounded fear. I've torn into Beckett half a dozen times in the last several hours over stupid shit—and that's after I ripped her a new one over dropping Kali on some fucking moon in the middle of fucking nowhere late last night.

I get that Kali made her own decision and—as Beckett reminded me—she wasn't a prisoner. But a little heads-up would have been fucking nice. A chance for me to change her mind. Instead, I slept through the whole thing like a fucking asshole.

I don't know if I'm madder that she left or that she played me for a fool. If she wanted to leave so fucking bad, why didn't she just tell me? Yeah, I would have had a fucking fit, but I wouldn't have stopped her. I'm not in the habit of holding anyone against their will—usually.

"*She did what she had to do.*" Max's calm voice barely infiltrates the haze of betrayed fury that is currently my brain.

"*Drokaray shit. She didn't have to leave. She chose to leave.*"

"*To protect us,*" he reminds me.

"*Or because she couldn't handle us,*" I mutter, and there it is. The root of my anger—and the hurt buried just below it. "*She found out about the gestalt and checked the fuck out, Max. That's what she did.*"

"*You don't really believe that.*"

"*Damn straight I believe it. What the fuck else would make her go running like that?*"

He sighs. "*Exactly what she said. She didn't want to be responsible for getting us killed.*"

"*I wouldn't have let that happen.*" I run a hand down my face, telling myself that I've got to calm down. That I can't go into the asteroid belt like this—not if I'm going to have any chance of getting Milla out alive.

I can't believe she left. I cannot fucking believe she left. She left me. I thought— I don't know what I thought. Whatever it was, it was ridiculous, though. I didn't really think a princess would actually fall for me, did I? A poor kid from Kridacus with more red flags than one of the Corporation's secret labs?

Of course I didn't. I just forgot for a minute, and now I'm here. All fucked up with no one to fight. It's a bad situation for all of us.

"*We'll see her again, Ian.*" Max sounds so confident. "*When this is over and we've got Milla—*"

"*I don't ever want to see Kali again,*" I tell him. And because I want him to hear the absolute fucking truth in those words, I don't even growl them.

It must work, because he doesn't try to talk anymore. He just leaves me to brood and plot the princess's downfall. Not that there will be a downfall, because I'm never going to see her again. But if I was, I'd definitely make sure to—

"Ian." It's Merrick, standing in the doorway, looking rumpled from sleeping late but also like he ran here at top speed. "Rain just told me Kali left?"

"She sure as shit did," I snarl. "And she's never coming back."

"We have to find her," he snarls right back at me. *"Now."*

Over my dead body. "Yeah, well, that's not going to happen, so you should probably come up with another wish for your fairy godmother."

"That isn't a wish. It's a necessity—we have to get to her before it's too late."

"Oh, well. That sounds nice and dire, but she's not my problem anymore," I tell him, doing my best to sound as unconcerned as I feel. "She's on her own now."

"What do you mean?" Beckett asks. "Is Kali in danger?"

I want to ask her when she started to care, but I'm too busy listening for Merrick's answer. Not that I give a fuck what happens to her—she could fall into a black hole for all the shits I give—but I probably should know what's going on. Just in case it affects the rest of us. Or Milla.

"The whole system's in danger," Merrick says.

"I should go get Rain," Beckett adds, standing. "Everyone should be here for this together." She rushes out toward the bedrooms.

"Merrick, you're going to have to give me more than that," I prod.

"The heptosphere," he says. "It's a weapon. The heptosphere is a weapon—"

"I don't give a shit about that hunk of metal," I retort. Then nearly kick myself. I'm not even supposed to be listening, let alone caring what he's saying. I busy myself with studying the buttons on the captain's chair that I have never once figured out—might as well start now.

Merrick sighs. "It's a weapon—one they think is powerful enough to revitalize the dying sun."

"Well that sounds convenient," Max tells him. "Isn't that what we need?"

"Yes and no," Merrick answers. "Do you know why a sun dies?"

"No," I say. "Why don't you educate me."

Merrick looks at me dubiously, but when I narrow my eyes, he starts talking.

"I think to understand how a sun dies, we need to go back to how they're formed," he says. "At its simplest, stars are formed when clouds of dust—nebulas—get dense enough to have a gravitational pull. Under pressure, the temperature inside the nebula increases until it's millions of degrees, and at that point nuclear fusion occurs."

"And that's what makes the sun burn," I clarify. "And it keeps happening over and over again, right?"

"Yeah, that's what keeps the star alive," Max adds.

I nod. "So it dies because there's no more nuclear fusion?" When Merrick agrees, I continue. "What makes the nuclear fusion stop?"

"Stars are in balance—gravity pulling inward, energy pushing outward," Merrick explains. "But as the nuclear fusion continues, helium is turned into carbon, oxygen, neon, and so on. Finally, the core turns to iron.

"When that happens, there's no more hydrogen. No more hydrogen, no more fusion, no more energy. Gravity takes over, pulling it inward, so the core becomes denser, but at the same time the outer layers expand. The star becomes unstable and pulsates, sending out energy."

"Which is where we are now?" I ask.

"Yes. The Dying Sun is unstable, shooting out flares, the core getting hotter and the outer layers expanding—soon they'll engulf the inner planets completely." He frowns. "The thing is, usually this takes millions of years, but for some reason our sun is going through an accelerated process. And it's taking decades instead.

"And at some point," he continues, "in the not-too-distant future, the core will shrink further, the temperature will rise, and the whole thing will explode."

"Boom," Gage says from his seat in the corner. "That's when a star goes supernova."

"And we all go up in flames," I add.

Merrick nods. "Has anyone here ever heard of the Star Bringer?"

We all look at each other, most faces appearing confused. But Gage sits up a little straighter. Suddenly he looks nervous, like he wants to be anywhere but here. Still, he comes over to where the rest of us are sitting. "I wasn't actually working on the heptosphere on the *Caelestis*. But I know a woman who was, and she told me Dr. Veragelen believed that the heptosphere is powerful enough to send a blast of energy into the sun and reignite the core. That she referred to it as the Star Bringer."

"The Star Bringer?" I rack my brain, trying to remember if I ever heard anything like that in my travels, but nothing comes to mind.

"This still sounds like exactly what we need," Max says again. "Did the doctor really think it would work?"

"Who knows?" Gage shrugs. "But according to the projections, whether it works or not, the planets of Serati, Kridacus, and Permuna will be completely destroyed in the blast."

"Destroyed?" I repeat, waiting for him to correct me. Because I knew the Empire was evil, but murder-the-entire-population-of-three-whole-planets evil? What the fuck?

But he doesn't tell me I'm wrong. Instead, he says, "Yes, destroyed. Dr. Veragelen plans on using the heptosphere to help her destroy three planets and everyone on them."

"That's not possible. Even if she could do it—"

"The models say she can. She hasn't been able to so far, because the heptosphere hasn't ever worked for her. But if she could…"

Merrick looks like he's about to explode. "That's what I came here to tell you all. The heptosphere isn't the Star Bringer. A person is. *Kali is.* Which means if she activates it, we're all in serious danger."

CHAPTER 71

Ian

All I hear is *Kali*.

Kali is in danger.

"Why her?" I urge, my heart pounding inside my throat. "Why do you think she's this Star Bringer person?"

"Alien DNA." Merrick and Gage say it at the exact same time.

I look at them like they're both confused. Very, very confused. "I'm sorry, what now?"

Gage rubs his hands together. "I've heard Dr. Veragelen has been searching for someone with alien DNA who can awaken the heptosphere—"

"Alien DNA." This has to be a joke. "You mean like the Ancients?"

"I don't understand it totally, either," Gage says. "But that's what a lot of the experiments were about. Why the prisoners were brought to the *Caelestis*. I'm not sure how it happened, but a good number of people in the Senestris System, especially people from the inner planets, have alien DNA incorporated in their own. Some of them can cause the alien artifacts to wake up and do things. And for those without alien DNA, sometimes the artifacts have...adverse side effects."

"Like getting burned to a crisp?" I ask, and it's all starting to make a weird sort of sense. There were a lot of hushed-up deaths while I was working on board the *Caelestis*.

"Yeah. Or so I've heard. Bottom line, Doc V's not been able to activate the heptosphere without the Star Bringer."

"But I still don't get why it's Kali specifically," I say, turning to Merrick. "How do you know for sure she's the Star Bringer?"

Beckett and Rain choose that moment to come back to the bridge, sounding a little breathless. Merrick suddenly looks like he could get sucked out the airlock and be less uncomfortable.

"Beckett told me about the plan to blow up the Inners," Rain says, a grim look on her face. Then she must see something else in all our expressions because she adds, "What? What'd I miss?"

CHAPTER 72

Rain

"We were just discussing something called the Star Bringer," Ian says.

Shock hits me in the gut, and I choke a bit on air. Beckett is kind enough to thump me on the back a few times until I can breathe again.

Merrick fidgets with his fingers and studies the rest of us for a minute. Finally, he asks Ian, "What do you know about the Sisterhood of the Light?"

"Not a lot," Ian admits.

"The Sisterhood of the Light was born on Serati, because it was the home of the Ancients—we have many of their artifacts, as well as remains of their civilization. Deciphering some of those remains has taught us much about their civilization, and we came to learn that the Ancients were the architects and creators of the system. That they had the power to create suns and planets with the assistance of an orb known as the heptosphere."

Merrick sounds so comfortable as he speaks of our belief system, as if all those doubts we talked about earlier have been resolved in him. But maybe this is the easy part. I can speak just as eloquently of our history—I've studied it since I was a small child—but that doesn't mean I don't have doubts that any of it is true.

It also doesn't mean that I don't wonder why I was chosen by the universe to be the high priestess when I feel just as confused and doubtful as everyone else. Especially now that I've met Beckett.

Maybe that's the point—it's not a choice if it's easy. I just wish it didn't have to be this hard. I've been trying to convince myself that anything I want must be the will of the Light—but every day, it feels less like I'm following the Light, and more like it's just me, alone in a dark, enormous system, making harder and harder choices.

"So it's not a weapon, then, like Gage was told?" Ian asks.

"That's not its primary purpose," Merrick answers, "but like all things of great power, likely it can be used for destruction as well as creation."

"And the alien DNA?" Max says. "Is that true?"

Merrick smiles. "It is. At least for some of us. No one knows what happened to the Ancients and why they vanished. But once we found the artifacts, we did research and uncovered much of what I'm telling you."

"And it looks like the Corporation was doing the same sort of research," Gage says.

Merrick frowns. "Yes, I wasn't aware of that. But these secrets were bound to come out in the end."

I feel sick. All these years, the Sisterhood saw our doctrine as a way to spread the word, and now, all these years later, people are being tortured—and murdered—by the Corporation because of something they have absolutely no control over: their DNA. It's disgusting. And terrifying. And even worse than I imagined.

"Which is your way of saying that anyone could have alien DNA." Max looks a little green and I understand his unease. The possibility of being from the Ancients is something I've lived with my entire life. I believe it makes us special, believe that we hold a part of the Light inside us. But I imagine being a part of a gestalt could make someone question a lot of what the Sisterhood believes.

"According to the Book of the Dying Sun," I say, "when a high priestess dies, a new one is reborn. Sometimes it takes a while, but it always happens. And that person has the power to activate and control alien artifacts like the heptosphere. Essentially, the high priestess is the Star Bringer. *I'm* the Star Bringer."

Most everyone is looking at me at this point—except Ian. He's glaring at Merrick like he puked on his good shoes.

"So have you…ever activated an alien artifact?" Beckett asks me. Thankfully, she seems fascinated and not disgusted.

"No. But then none of the high priestesses who came before me have either. Our scriptures say that our powers will manifest when the time is right."

Ian is still looking at Merrick when he says, "The Star Bringer is the high priestess, Merrick?"

Merrick sighs, and the weight of the entire system is in the sound. It stops the blood in my veins for a second.

"Yes," Merrick says. He looks right at me. "The high priestess is the Star Bringer. And the Star Bringer…is *Kali*."

CHAPTER 73

Rain

For a second, I'm sure that I've heard incorrectly. Merrick can't possibly be saying what I think he's saying. Not only is Kali the Star Bringer, she's also the high priestess? But that's impossible. That's what I am.

Before I can say anything, though, Ian whirls around and stalks toward Merrick like he wants to kill him—or at least punch the stuffing out of him. Max must think so, too—and of course he does, I realize; he's *inside Ian's head*—because suddenly he's there, between the two men.

He slams a hand down on Ian's chest. "Back up," he tells him, but Ian doesn't look like he's in the mood to listen. To be fair, he hasn't been in the mood to listen to anything or anyone since we woke up to find Kali gone.

"Not until he tells me what the fuck he's talking about," Ian growls. "How are the Star Bringer and High Priestess of the Sisterhood of the Light connected?"

"They're one and the same," Merrick clarifies. "The Sisterhood seeks out the high priestess specifically because she's the one who interacts with alien technology. Because she's the Star Bringer."

"What the fuck?" Ian says what I bet we're all thinking. "How could everyone think Rain's the high priestess if you're saying it's actually Kali?"

"Because the Sisterhood faked it," Merrick says. "And everything's gone to absolute shit since."

"Faked it?" I gasp as everything inside me reels from the knowledge. "How is that possible?" And why? I've spent my whole life locked up in that monastery thinking that something was really wrong with me because I didn't feel things the way they said that I should, the way other high priestesses always have. And now I find out it's because it was all a lie? I'm just…a regular person?

Why would someone do that to Kali? And why would someone do that to me?

For a second, I can't breathe.

I know it's selfish, know I shouldn't be thinking about myself right now when so much else is at stake. Including Kali's safety, plus the safety of the three inner planets, *and* the safety of the entire system. And I do care about all of those things. I do. But I still need a minute, because this is bad. This is really bad.

"How long have you known?" I ask Merrick hoarsely.

He shakes his head. "I've suspected for a while. But I knew for sure when I saw Kali wake up the heptosphere."

"It was her?" I ask, and now my heart is beating out of control. "You know for sure she did it and not me?"

"I was watching," he said. "Very closely, because I wanted it to be you. I wanted to be wrong. But I wasn't. It was definitely Kali."

"Why didn't you say something, then, when Kali was so sure?" I demand.

"I've spent my whole life being loyal to the Sisterhood," he answers. "Was I really supposed to just give all that up to a bunch of people I barely know? Besides, I thought she was staying on the ship, at least until we made it to the Wilds. I thought I had more time to get confirmation and figure out what to do."

I've known something was wrong with him ever since the *Caelestis*. I thought it was because of me and the fact that I wasn't behaving as a high priestess should. But it turns out he really was having a crisis of faith. Over this, not over me.

"You should have said something," I tell him, an unfamiliar feeling burning in the pit of my stomach. It's so rare for me that it takes me a few seconds to recognize it as anger. "If not to them, to me. You know everything I've been struggling with. And now I know it's because I'm nothing but a fake."

"Rain—" he starts, but I cut him off with a shake of my head.

"You should have told me."

Ian has finally calmed down enough that he doesn't look like he's going to kill Merrick, but I figure that can change at any time. Max must think so, too, because I notice he doesn't move from between them.

"Why did you first start to have suspicions?" I ask.

"I had a vision five years ago of what I thought was my father's death," he answers. I wait for him to say more, but he doesn't.

"Your father just died a few months ago," I say gently, because I know it's something that hurts him greatly. And no matter how angry I am at Merrick right now, I could never want to cause him pain.

"I know. Because it wasn't a vision of his death at all. It was a vision of his brother's."

I remember what he told me in the galley when neither of us could sleep. "Kali's father," I murmur.

"Kali and Merrick are cousins?" Max asks.

At the same time, Ian says, "That's some fucked-up shit."

"This whole thing is fucked up," Beckett growls. I realize that she's standing behind me, that she's got her hands on my waist and is bearing a lot of my weight. I've been so in shock I didn't realize she was even there, let alone how heavily I've been leaning on her.

"When Kali's father married her mother, he renounced his connection with my family and cut off all contact. It nearly broke my father—they were so similar in age, looked alike, had done everything together their entire lives. So when I had the vision of the assassination, he realized it wasn't his. It was his brother's, so he traveled in secret to Askkandia to warn him."

"You knew about Kali's father's assassination before it happened?"

I ask. This just keeps getting worse and worse.

Merrick nods grimly. "Yes. The visions don't always come to pass exactly as we see them. But this one did, even though he was warned. My father begged him to return to Serati, but he refused to leave Kali. And the Empress would never have allowed him to take her with him, so he remained where he was."

"And you didn't tell Kali?" Beckett asks. "She blamed the rebels for her father's death, and you saw the whole thing—"

"I don't know who's responsible for his death. I didn't see that— only that he died. But on that trip, he told my father something that changed everything."

I want to scream at him to tell me what it is, but high priestesses don't scream. Except I'm not a high priestess anymore, according to Merrick. All those rules I've lived my life by don't apply anymore.

"What did he say?" Ian growls, and there's something in his eyes that tells me he's already figured it out.

"The Empress didn't want to lose her daughter to the Sisterhood," Max says. "So when Kali was born, she refused the portents, right?"

"Worse than that," Merrick tells him. "My uncle said he knew right away what Kali was. But the Empress wouldn't let him contact the Sisterhood. She removed the birthmark Kali was born with—"

"Birthmark?" Ian asks. "Where was it?"

"On her left shoulder," I murmur. Because that's where mine is.

Ian's eyes narrow. "She has a scar there. I saw it when—" He breaks off, but we can all fill in the blanks.

"What about mine?" I ask, my knees shaking so badly that I know Beckett is the only thing keeping me upright right now. "How did I get mine?"

Merrick looks devastated for me when he answers. "From what my father told me at the end, you were just a baby, born at the right— or wrong—time. The Empress paid off your mother, and when the Sisterhood came looking, they found you. They tattooed a birthmark on you identical to Kali's, bribed people so it appeared you were the real high priestess. All of the tests to confirm your reincarnated soul were faked. No one from the Sisterhood questioned it."

I'm drowning in a sense of betrayal. And I need to lash out. I whirl on Beckett. "Did you know?"

"Of course not!" But her eyes look unsure. "I mean, when I first saw your birthmark, it looked slightly artificial to me, but how could I be sure?"

I let out a low moan. *Everyone* suspected but me. I have been so, so naive.

"I can't believe parents would do that to their child." And I can't believe Merrick wouldn't tell me as soon as he knew. "Who knows about this?" I ask, my mind reeling.

"No one," Merrick answers. "Kali's father swore mine to secrecy. Dad only told me when he was on his deathbed."

"And you never told me," I say, my voice breaking. "You've known for months, and you never said a word."

"Suspected, Rain. Not known. I didn't want to believe it." He looks at me pleadingly. "My father was old and broken at the end. I wanted it to be just the incoherent nightmare of a man whose mind was fleeing more with each day that passed. And like I said, I had no proof, only what he told me. It wasn't until that day on the *Caelestis* that I had to admit to myself that what he said was true."

That makes sense. I probably wouldn't have told him, either, until I had proof. But it still hurts so much that I can barely breathe. Everything about my life has been a lie, from the moment my parents sold me—*sold me*—to the Sisterhood. And the only person I ever really trusted, besides the crew of the *Starlight*, helped perpetuate the lie.

My whole life is a lie. I'm a lie.

Fuck. The Light itself is probably a *fucking* lie.

The room starts to spin around me. "I don't feel good," I gasp out. "I think—"

The next thing, I know I'm on the floor, a pillow under my head and Beckett sitting cross-legged beside me, yellow eyes anxious as she studies my face.

I sit up, only to find Merrick seated a meter away from me, looking as devastated as I feel. "So what happens now?" I ask.

I'm thinking about the Sisterhood, about the fact that I can't go back there and pretend to be the high priestess. It's sacrilegious. Wrong. And also, I want a life as far away from the people who did this to me and Kali as I can get.

It's Beckett who answers, and it's not what I expect. "Captain's ordered a course correction. Milla will have to wait a little bit longer. We're going after Kali."

CHAPTER 74

Kali

"I was just telling your mother that the heptosphere is being brought down from the remains of the *Caelestis* as we speak," Dr. Veragelen says. "It should be here in the morning if all goes well."

Already? That's certainly faster than I was anticipating. But the sooner I can help halt the Dying Sun and protect everyone, the better.

"Annora," Mom says, turning to Dr. Veragelen, "perhaps you'll explain for Kalinda's benefit just what is expected of her when it comes to the heptosphere." My mother's cultured tones slide down my spine like a shiver.

Dr. Veragelen smiles again, a twist of her thin lips that does nothing but creep me out. "Of course, Your Majesty. It's actually quite simple, Your Highness. When the heptosphere arrives, you will be taken to it. You will lay your hands upon it, and when you do, it will activate."

I can't help but ask, "There were a lot of people in the lab that day. All the delegates touched it. Have you ever considered it could be one of them who activated it?"

"I know what I saw, Your Highness." She gives me a steely look. "You should consider yourself a very special lady."

"She's the crown princess of the Senestris System," my mother says, as if that explains everything. "She's already very special."

There's an edge to her voice that wasn't there a minute ago, and it's my first clue that maybe she isn't as happy with this situation as she's making herself out to be. On the surface it appears that the Ruling Families are in charge of everything, but in truth, it's a very delicate, very tense balance of power between us and the Corporation. Without their access to the technology, we'd all be totally isolated. Cut off from each other on our own little planets, with no communication between them at all.

"Of course she is special," Dr. Veragelen attempts to soothe. "But what I'm talking about is another sort of special altogether."

I take a slow, deep breath and look Dr. Veragelen right in the eye. "And once the heptosphere is activated, then what?"

She finally takes a sip of her fiznachi. "Hopefully, your part in the proceedings will be over. Of course, you'll be required to stay around in case you're needed again. But I believe we'll be able to take over from there and fire a blast of pure hydrogen into the sun, which will cause a reverse fusion reaction and halt the decay of Serai so that things will go back to normal."

"Halt the decay of Serai," I confirm. But something is niggling at me. Something that makes my heart start to pound. "If Serai is fired on by pure hydrogen, what will happen to the planets closest to it?"

Dr. Veragelen's cheek tics furiously, but when she finally answers, her voice is as composed as usual. "Unfortunately, the inner planets will be destroyed in the explosion. But as you know, these are hard times, and sacrifices have to be made."

No.

I feel sick as I watch my mother's face while Dr. Veragelen speaks, searching for some sign of reluctance, of revulsion. But there's nothing except a hint of relief that chills me to my core.

She knew this was Dr. Veragelen's plan all along, and she doesn't have any compunctions about it. How is that possible? And how could I have never seen it before?

"I cannot abide sacrificing three whole planets' worth of people," I tell them. "Why can't you relocate the people from the inner planets first, get them to safety before I activate the heptosphere?"

"Unfortunately, that's not an option," Dr. Veragelen tells me in a voice that says she doesn't think it's unfortunate at all.

"You can't honestly support this, can you?" I ask, pleading with my mother for some sign of remorse. Some sign that she isn't as horrible as I'm afraid she is.

Her spine is ramrod straight. "The Corporation has provided me with the reports and information I need to make the decision. Leaders have to make hard choices, Kalinda. If we didn't do anything, then *everyone* would die. This is the only option we have."

"Then evacuate," I say. "There's still time. We have years before the system reaches danger levels."

"You're wrong. We've been keeping things quiet to avoid panic, but the Corporation believes we have months, not years, before Serai dies and takes all of us with her."

Months? Shock holds me rigid for several seconds. It doesn't seem possible that in months we could all be dead. Not that it matters for me. Murdering millions of people to save others isn't the answer. It can't be.

Dr. Veragelen continues. "Maybe if you hadn't taken your little… *detour*, we could have evacuated the inner planets in time. But with you presumed dead, we were exploring other avenues. It really was thoughtless of you to not contact us for so long."

She's trying to say it's *my* fault? I fight to keep my outrage from showing on my face.

"If we work quickly," Dr. Veragelen says, "we might have time to remove any alien artifacts of interest from Serati. But that's it."

"Then work quickly and take the fucking people off first." My voice is rising. I'm losing the cool I've worked so hard to maintain.

"Language, Kalinda. And where would you propose we put these people?" my mother asks, brows arched. "No planet is equipped for that kind of immigrant influx. We can barely keep them fed as it is."

Dr. Veragelen chooses that moment to get to her feet, brushing an imaginary speck of dust from her immaculate black lab suit. "I fear I must leave you two alone to discuss this. I have preparations to make. I *will* see you tomorrow, Your Highness," she finishes with a pointed look.

I don't even glance her way or acknowledge her comment. I'm staring at my mother. There's a slight flush on her cheeks, and her mouth is a pinched line. She doesn't say anything until the door closes behind the doctor.

But as soon as we hear the snick of it closing, she turns to me. "Are you out of your mind to question me like this?" she says. "What has come over you, Kali? You're acting like you're some sort of... rebel."

"Why? Just because I don't believe we should kill millions of people?"

"No. Because you are questioning your Empress." Her voice is like steel, the look in her eyes beyond dangerous.

And while I want nothing more than to ask why people shouldn't question her—if she's doing the right thing, she'll have nothing to fear from questions about it—I'm smart enough to figure out that doing so will send her completely over the edge. And since I don't want to totally push her away tonight, I grit my teeth and take a large rhetorical step back.

"I apologize, Mother. You always taught me that I need to understand the decisions we make. And I still don't understand this one. It seems..." Words fail me.

She reaches across the table and fills my glass with fiznachi—a big concession for her. "You know what's at stake here, Kalinda—we've shared the timeline with you now. Surely you can see the impossible situation we're in. We're balancing on a knife's edge, and any little thing will send us spinning toward certain disaster. I'm doing this to save as many people as possible. But I can't save everyone."

I want to believe the sadness I see in her eyes, but I can't. Because I know she doesn't care about the lives of the people on the inner planets. She just cares that she has her perfect life here in the palace. Shit, we could probably fit a few hundred refugees in our empty rooms alone.

But then she shrugs. "Plus, think about this rationally. The

reduction in population will mean the resources will last longer—
we'll no longer have to supply grain to the Inners. And, of course,
there's the added advantage that with the destruction of Serati, we'll
eliminate the threat from the Sisterhood of the Light, who are getting
too powerful for their own good. And with Permuna gone, we'll wipe
out most of the Rebellion supporters and stop their endless uprisings."

The thought sickens me, has my stomach twisting itself into knots
and my lungs tightening to the point of pain.

My mother is a sociopath. There's no other explanation for what
she's saying, what I'm hearing. She wants to murder millions of people
because it will make things more convenient for her, and what's not
to like about that?

"And what about Kridacus?" I ask in an amazingly calm tone,
considering it's taking every ounce of self-control I have not to
scream at her. Or puke all over her fancy white couch.

She waves a careless hand. "They're parasites, sucking the
resources from the other planets and giving nothing back. Can't you
see it's a win-win, Kali? We'll actually be helping so many people if
we do this."

Win-win? This is a nightmare.

"Don't look at me like that," she suddenly snaps, and all attempts
at civility are gone from her tone.

"Like what?" I ask.

"Like your father used to when he was disappointed in me. In me!
His Empress."

He obviously didn't look at her like that enough. If he had, maybe
we wouldn't be here.

"What if I won't do it?" I ask.

Her eyes narrow. "Well, we can always have you dragged to the
thing in shackles and force your hand—literally. But I don't think that
will be necessary. Will it?"

"I won't do it, Mother. I won't have anything to do with killing all
those people."

She considers me for a moment, her head tilted to one side like
she always does when she's thinking. "You know, Dr. Veragelen isn't

the only person to have survived the *Caelestis* aside from your group of outlaws. Your companion-in-waiting and bodyguard are still here as well. I considered having them executed as examples of what happens when someone fails in their duty to the Ruling Families. I changed my mind when I received news that you were alive. But, Kali, cross me in this, and they will suffer. Make no mistake."

Bile burns the back of my throat as my heart threatens to beat out of my chest. Lara and Arik. How can I lose them now, when I've just found them again? But I don't say anything else—even I can figure out that the time for talking to her is through…if it ever existed at all.

She gets to her feet. "But it won't come to that."

Silently, I shake my head.

"Good. Now, drink your fiznachi. You need to get cleaned up. You have a public appearance in an hour, and I don't think I need to remind you that you must make me proud." She leaves.

I don't move until the door closes behind her. Then I pick up the bottle of fiznachi and take a long pull. It doesn't touch the horror cycling inside me. Then again, I don't think anything will—not even a bottle of Ian's gerjgin.

I think I made a terrible mistake leaving the *Starlight*.

CHAPTER 75

Kali

"Your Highness." Lara greets me with a little curtsy when I walk into my rooms a few minutes later.

Even with my mother's threat hanging in the air, the joy at seeing Lara here, alive if not safe, is overwhelming. I hug her like I hugged Arik, and she responds much the same way—with shock, followed by a hug nearly as desperate as mine. "I'm so glad you're okay," I whisper, holding her close.

"I'm so glad *you're* okay." She pulls away. "Though you do stink, if you don't mind me saying so."

"I've been told."

"I'll run you a bath." She starts toward my bathroom, which is nearly as big as all of the *Starlight*. The thought shames me.

"You don't have to do that. I'll just grab a quick shower."

She shakes her head adamantly. "It's my job to run your bath."

"Yeah, well, after everything my mother has put you through, I think you deserve a break. Or ten." I don't want to panic Lara—yet— but my mother's threat *is* echoing in my ears. I can't allow them to kill three planets' worth of people, but how can I sacrifice my earliest friend?

When she looks down at her shoes, my chest tightens. "Was it horrible?" I ask. I'm afraid of the answer, but I'm not going to hide from it, either.

My days of hiding are done.

"Nowhere near as horrible as what happened to you, I'm sure," she finally answers. "What did that guard do to you?"

She's talking about Ian. "He saved my life." It's not the only thing he did to me, but that's all Lara needs to know, at least right now.

She studies me for a second. "You care about him, don't you?"

That she can read me so easily takes me aback for a second, but then I'm smiling. There's no point in denying it. "I did, yes. But I had to leave, and I'm sure he'll never forgive me for it. Still, I did what I had to."

Lara studies me for a second, and I can see the same realization in her eyes that my mother had. Even before she says, "You've changed, Your Highness." But from her, it doesn't sound like a crime.

"What did my mother do to you and Arik?" I look at her closely now, at her bruised skin and the shadows under her eyes.

"It's not important."

I want to push her, but it's obvious the subject is making her uncomfortable. It reminds me that trust is a terrifying thing at the palace, and not something any of us are very practiced in. After my weeks on the *Starlight*, it's hard to imagine how I lived like this for so long, watching my back every second of the day, waiting for a blade to slip between my ribs.

"Hey, Lara. I'm back now, and you're safe. Whatever she did to you, I won't ever let her do it again."

Lara nods, her throat working before she turns and heads toward the bathroom. "I will turn the shower on for you."

"You don't have to—" I start, but she's already gone.

After I scrub my hair and every millimeter of my body, I step out of the shower and reach for a towel. But Lara is already there, ready to dry me off and rub scented lotion into my skin.

I wave her away. I've been taking care of myself for weeks. I think I can manage to dry off without any extra help.

Again, Lara looks shocked and a little sad, but she sets herself to pulling my clothes for the public appearance out of my wardrobe. I have a flashback to standing in that store in Rangar with Ian, watching him haggle for the clothes I picked out for Beckett, Rain, and myself. I've come a long way from that moment, but the sensation in my heart remains the same. It was fun and exciting. It was real.

Suddenly, I have the most intense longing for Ian. I hadn't realized how safe he made me feel. How protected, even when he was mad at me. Now I'm here with Lara and Arik, and it's my turn to do the looking after.

My turn to keep them safe.

I don't mind it—I'd do anything for them. But a reassuring hug from Rain or a growl from Ian would go a long way to making my stomach—and my heart—feel steadier.

Lara's patience with my newfound independence runs out right about the time I slip into my undergarments. She hands me a robe, which I put on, and then she points me toward my dressing table. While part of me wants to argue, another part of me doesn't give a shit what I look like.

Which probably means I should let her take over.

"Your mother had this dress made for you once Arik picked you up on that Glacean moon," Lara tells me as she pulls it out. "Isn't it beautiful?"

It is, but it's also ostentatious and a massive reminder of just how grossly the Empire treats its people. The dress is, of course, royal purple, not quite as elaborate as the Imperial Regalia I wore on the *Caelestis*, but it's more than fancy enough to make my stomach roll. Even before I see the elaborate pattern made by the tiny stones embedded in the velvet. Stones that I know could feed a lot of people for a very long time.

Don't fucking puke.

It's like I've never been away. Nothing has changed at all—except me.

I stand perfectly still, as a princess should, while Lara buttons me into the elaborate dress and fixes the royal cloak over my shoulders.

As she swishes it around, making sure it falls properly, I can't help but think of Ian. Again. On the *Caelestis*, he said I looked ridiculous. What I wouldn't give for him to tell me I look ridiculous again, just one more time.

"Well, that's as good"—*or as bad*—"as it gets," I say when she finally stops fussing.

"You look beautiful."

"I look hideous, but who cares. Let's get this over with."

Lara looks like she wants to say something, but in the end she just shakes her head and holds the door open for me.

Let the shit show begin.

CHAPTER 76

Ian

"A re we there yet?" I ask Beckett for what I'm guessing is the thousandth time, judging by the way she rolls her eyes. And doesn't answer me.

"*Chill out,*" Max tells me. But he's not the one about to jump out of his skin.

"*You don't think I'm just as worried?*" he asks archly. "*You got us into this mess. The least you can do is acknowledge that you aren't the only one who cares about her.*"

I stop pacing long enough to glare at him, because he's right. Except for the part about me caring about her. Because I don't. Not anymore.

He laughs. "*Yeah. Keep on telling yourself that.*"

"*I plan to.*" Then I turn back to Beckett. "Can this thing go any faster?"

She growls deep in her throat—a warning if I've ever heard one. And maybe if I wasn't so far gone, I would care. As it is, I'm more than ready to growl back—

"*Bugging the fuck out of Beckett isn't going to get us to Askkandia any faster.*"

No, but it makes me feel like I'm doing something. If I have to just sit here wondering what's happening to Kali for one more minute, I'll go out of my fucking mind.

I've had a bad feeling for days now, something inside telling me that everything's not okay with her. I know we're only three days or so behind her—besides one short, extremely necessary supply run, Beckett's been pushing the *Starlight* as fast as she can possibly go, which is probably why she growled at me just now—but a lot can happen to someone in a couple of days.

Where I come from, a lot can happen to them in an instant. One second, you're alive, and the next, you're dead. Just like that.

Please don't let Kali be dead.

"*Not that you give a shit, right?*" Max is laughing in my head now.

I snarl at him. "*Just because I don't want her to be dead doesn't mean I'm in love with her.*"

"*No, but the fact that you think about her pretty much every second of the day is a clue that you might be.*" He holds up his hands. "*No judgment here. I'm thinking about her, too. We all are.*"

"*I just don't want her to be dead. Without her, there's nothing to keep the Empress in check.*"

Max rolls his eyes again, and I know that he doesn't believe what I'm selling. But I don't care. I don't need him to believe me. I just need Kali to be okay so that I can yell at her for sneaking out on me in the middle of the night. And then ignore her forever, because no way am I giving her another chance to—

I break off, but not before Max shoots me a superior look. "*Another chance to do what? Break your heart?*"

"*Fuck you.*"

"*I think you should wait for Kali on that front,*" he shoots back.

"Kali's fine, Ian." Rain's voice comes from behind me, where she's curled up in her chair, a blanket wrapped around her, but clearly reading the expressions on my and Max's faces. "We'll be there soon."

She looks exhausted, the dark circles under her normally bright eyes testament to the fact that she hasn't been sleeping. Then again, how do you sleep when you find out your whole life has been a lie? My early life wasn't fun—no father, dead mother, child camp, terrifying escape, life of crime to survive. Not to mention the whole tripartition thing to deal with. But I don't think I would trade it, knowing what things look like for the other side.

Sure, Rain and Kali always had enough to eat. They lived in safe places and had beds to sleep in every night. But the betrayals they've both faced...at least I've always seen the knife headed for my solar plexus. Those two keep getting stabbed in the back.

I settle into the captain's chair—not because I want to sit, but because I figure if I'm so untethered that I'm even bugging the shit out of Rain, then I've got about two minutes before Beckett tries to shove me out the airlock. And while I might be stronger than her, I don't like my odds against her.

To keep myself busy, I press the keys that light up the HUD on my captain's chair. Just one of the really useful gadgets Gage has been working on the last few days. It can give me a readout from all the available data on the ship, and it lets me access any of the systems from right here.

Or at least all the ones we know about. Gage thinks there are a bunch more that we don't know about yet. But he's getting an understanding of how the *Starlight* works and uncovering all sorts of things I've never encountered on a ship before. I thought it was because I'd only ever flown on crap ships, but Gage says no. Some of this stuff, *he's* never even heard of.

Suffice it to say, he's having a blast.

The HUD shows Askkandia another several hours away. Which isn't bad, I try to tell myself. A few more hours, and I'll know for sure that Kali's okay. And I'll be able to get her out of that nightmare of a palace, once and for all.

Which reminds me... "We're heading straight for the palace, right?"

"No," Beckett snarls. "I'm taking us to a little restaurant I know in the city. I thought we could have dinner first."

I know she's messing with me. But I still glare at her.

She flips me off in response.

A gentle hand rests on my shoulder, and I whirl around to see

Rain. She's still got her blanket draped around her shoulders, and up close, she somehow looks even worse. "I know she's fine," Rain says again. "She's probably wrapped in some jewel-encrusted cloak, eating fancy cakes or something. She's probably already forgotten us."

Nobody bothers to argue, though I'm sure we all see that for the lie it is.

"Have we decided what we're going to do when we get there?" Merrick asks from his spot at the back of the bridge.

Rain stiffens at his voice, but she doesn't say anything. She also doesn't so much as turn around to look at him—something that bothers him, judging by the way his jaw clenches.

"Yeah, what's the plan, Captain?" Beckett asks. It's payback for the fact that I've been bugging the shit out of her—she knows better than anyone that I don't have a plan.

"Thank you for asking, Beckett. I would *love* to make a plan with the huge wealth of information I have," I reply. "Can you have the *Starlight* pull up the schematics of the palace, please?"

Yeah, as if the Imperial Palace would just have schematics available to passing vessels. The *Starlight* might have some cool tricks, but the Empire doesn't leave classified information lying around. I'm just being a dick to stall.

And Beckett knows it, too. "Why don't you ask her?" she suggests with a shrug.

Oh, yeah, lots of payback coming my way. She knows I hate talking to the fucking ship. And that my suggestion was a fucking deflection.

"*Starlight*, can you bring up the plans for the palace on Askkandia?" Max comes to my rescue.

Seconds later, the plans pop up on my HUD, and I whistle.

"No way," Gage exclaims. "She must've cut through every level of security Askkandia has to get those plans. Doc V would *kill* to be able to do what this ship just did."

Beckett is the only one who seems unimpressed as she levels her gaze at me. "Maybe she deserves a little more respect from her captain," she says.

Point to Beckett, but I'm not going to give her the satisfaction. Instead, I focus in on my HUD. "That's a big fucking palace."

"Better for us," Merrick comments. "More places of entry."

He's not wrong. "Okay, then, any guesses as to which of these areas might be Kali's room?" I haven't lived in a house since I was eleven years old, and when I did, it looked nothing like this palace. And since none of the rooms are labeled, I haven't got a fucking clue about which section is which.

Beckett frowns as she leans in to get a better look. "My guess is one of these two suites of rooms," she says after studying the drawings for a couple of minutes.

"What makes you so sure?"

"Because they're the biggest." She points to the smaller of the two. "And they're obviously bedroom suites." She points at the different boxes on the drawing. "Sitting room, bathroom, bedroom, dressing room, closet."

I'm as horrified as I am fascinated. No wonder Kali felt like she was slumming it on the *Starlight*. "Who needs five fucking rooms? Or a closet that's bigger than this fucking ship?"

All of a sudden, the *Starlight* shudders.

"I don't think she liked you calling her a fucking ship," Gage pipes up from his spot under the dash, where he's messing with who knows what.

"Or maybe you messed something up," I shoot back. "Be careful what you fuck around with under there. And you'd better be making sure our landing credentials aren't going to be flagged crossing into Imperial airspace."

He flips me off—there seems to be a lot of that going around right now.

"So, assuming our *genius* over there doesn't fuck up the credentials, we need to figure out how to get in there without getting noticed," I say. "That seems like it's going to be difficult, considering her rooms are literally in the center of the palace."

"More proof that they're hers," Merrick says. "Easier to protect her and the Empress that way."

"Yeah, that's kind of the problem," I tell him. "Easier for them to protect her. Harder for us to sneak her out." I look at the others. "Any of you have any suggestions?"

I'm usually a wing-it kind of guy. But storming the royal palace doesn't seem like a wing-it kind of situation.

Beckett leans over my shoulder and points to an entrance at the back of the palace. "That might be the best place to try to get in."

I'd already thought of it, but my experience in breaking into shit is that the most vulnerable-looking entrances are rarely the most vulnerable in reality. Guards tend to compensate for the weakness with extra personnel.

But when I say as much, she throws up her hands. "Well, then, if you think we can do better, why don't you ask the *Starlight* for a plan?"

"Not a bad idea," I say, just to humor her. "Hey, *Starlight*, we need to rescue Kalinda from the clutches of the evil Empress before she unwittingly kills three planets' worth of people. Any ideas?"

I don't expect anything to happen. I mean, it's a spaceship. She might be able to defend herself from attack, but she doesn't have actual *ideas*. That requires a kind of tech wizardry that hasn't been invented yet.

Except I feel another shudder run through her. And then we're speeding up, the map in front of us revealing a slight change in trajectory. I watch the new coordinates flash up on my HUD, along with a new schematic of the palace.

"Holy shit," Beckett says. "She's doing it. She's really fucking doing it. I love this ship."

I'm starting to see why. A little uneasy, I settle back in my chair and study the new schematic she just threw up—complete with her projections for the easiest door to hit to get in.

"Isn't she great?" Beckett crows.

She kind of is. Not that I'm about to admit that.

I do, however, memorize every place she points out as vulnerable. Just in case the *Starlight* really is as smart as Beckett thinks she is.

CHAPTER 77

Kali

The public meeting was excruciating. My jaw aches from holding it in precise position. But the feed went out to all the Ruling Families, and at least the news will filter out and the world will soon know that I'm back in the palace. That, combined with the one-on-one I just had with Arik, finally makes me feel like Ian and the others will be safe. And that makes all the very bad lying I just did worth it. Or at least that's what I'm telling myself.

Now I'm sitting on the bed in my palatial bedroom, but I feel claustrophobic. Like the silk-lined walls are closing in on me. I'm still wearing the purple dress, and I can't get up the energy to change. Lara offered to help, but I need a few minutes alone to think. And to just be.

But I can't sit still. I stand and start pacing back and forth, trying to come up with a better way to protect all the people on the Inner planets. But I've got nothing. As long as I'm here in the palace, my mother and Dr. Veragelen will find a way to make me.

Which means I've done all the good I can by having come here and protecting my friends on the *Starlight*. If I can convince Lara and Arik to come with me, then I have to get out. Now.

Before I can figure out how to do that, however, there's a light tap on my door. I scramble to open it and find Lara on the other side, carrying a tray of food. There is a guard on either side of her, obviously stationed outside my door.

For your safety, I can practically hear my mother say. *Not because you're a prisoner, but because someone is trying to kill you, and now they know where you are.*

Too bad I don't believe for a second that all she wants to do is protect me. I am very much a prisoner in this palace. I should have listened to Ian. It's galling to admit that, but the truth is the truth.

I never should have come back.

"Are you all right, Your Highness?" Lara asks. "You look seriously freaked out."

"I am seriously freaked out. There are guards by my door."

"I know. It's terrible." She sighs. "But you need to sit down and eat, Your Highness. You've had nothing substantial since you arrived. You have to keep your strength up."

I allow her into the room, figuring once we're alone, I can level with her and make a plan of escape for us. She enters and closes the door softly behind her, then puts my tray down on the small dining table in the corner of my sitting room. I dig in—it's delicious, but I was kind of craving fishgalen casserole.

"Would you like me to pour you some coffee, Your Highness?" Lara asks.

I nod because it's easier than telling her I'll do it myself. But then I nearly burst into tears when she mixes one and a half spoons of sugar into the mug—exactly how I like it.

At one point, I thought I'd never have sugar again. And I was truly okay with that.

As she settles down in the chair opposite me, hands folded primly in her lap, I think of the best way to start, to convince her she's in danger and that she needs to leave with me. But as I study her, I notice she's worrying her lip back and forth between her teeth. I've known Lara a long time, and that's a surefire tell that she's afraid whatever she has to say is going to upset me.

Which only makes me want to know what's going on even more.

"Spit it out, Lara," I finally say.

Her eyes widen at my less-than-royal words, but she finally starts talking. "I wasn't sure I should tell you," she begins. "I mean, I didn't think you would care one way or another. But then earlier you said that those people were your friends. And I've been thinking about it ever since. It was something I overheard while your mother was talking to the dressmaker about your dress for today. She was also having a conversation with Mikhaela."

I nod, because that's not unusual. Mikhaela is my mother's chief advisor on policy within the Senestris System.

"Just after Arik confirmed he collected you," Lara says, "your mother apparently contacted the Corporation and arranged for a whole load of ships to mobilize around Glacea. She thought that your…friends would stick nearby until after you were collected, and she's hoping to run them to ground." She pauses. "They haven't been found yet, but now that you're here, she's ordered them all to be killed, not just captured. Every ship from Serai to Glacea is searching for them. Apparently, they know too much."

She says the last in a rush, like she can't get the words out fast enough.

I have to say, I really wish I hadn't downed that coffee, considering I'm pretty sure I'm going to puke.

Don't puke, don't puke, don't fucking puke.

Some things even the mantra can't stop. I can feel my dinner crawling back up, and I race to the bathroom.

I barely make it in time.

When I'm finally done, Lara brings me a cool cloth and some mouthwash. I rinse my face and my mouth, then stumble back into my bedroom to think about what Lara told me.

The worst thing is, I'm not even surprised. Horrified, yes. But surprised, not even a little bit. Disposing of threats is pretty much my mother's modus operandi.

Every new thing I learn is designed to teach me that my mother is not a woman of honor.

I sit very still while I think over what Lara has told me. My mind is whirling. I can't breathe, and sweat is trickling down my spine. Sure, Arik and I made a plan, but only about an hour ago—and he must not be in on my mother's plans. My mom's execution order has apparently been out since I made landfall.

My friends could be dying at this very moment.

The *Starlight* could have been blown out of the sky.

Ian could be dead, and so could Rain. Max. Gage. Merrick. Beckett.

My already shaky stomach threatens to revolt again, but I refuse to give in to it.

The *Starlight* is too good at evasive maneuvers to just be brought down like that. She's gotten us out of scrape after scrape. I have to believe she'll do it again.

They're probably already in the Wilds, picking up Milla beyond the reach of Corporation ships. Nothing else makes any sense.

But what if my mother's right?

What if they didn't take my leaving as well as I thought they would?

What if something went wrong with their plan and they're flying right into my mother's evil trap?

Once the thought occurs to me, I can't unthink it, no matter how hard I try.

I thought I was keeping them safe by leaving. In reality, I signed all their death warrants.

So what should I do? What *can* I do?

I have to find a way to save them. I have to. I just don't know how.

"Your Highness, talk to me. Tell me what you're thinking. What do you want me to do?"

At her words, I go still, tell myself to calm down. Panicking never helped anyone.

"I've made a mess of everything," I finally tell her. "I never should have come back."

"Whatever you need to fix it, you can count on me. I'll help any way I can. And there are others in the palace who will help as well."

She doesn't use his name, but I know she means Arik. "You know what will happen if you go against my mother?"

"I know." She gives a short, humorless laugh. "That has been made very clear to me over the last weeks. But I'm tired of being afraid of her."

"Me too," I tell her. "The weeks on the *Starlight*, when I wasn't afraid? When I was just me? They were the best of my whole life." I reach out across the table and take her hand. "I'll take you with me, this time. You and Arik. You won't have to stay here any longer."

"Arik and I already talked it over, before I brought you your food. And we swore if you wanted to escape, we'd find a way to help you."

"*And* come with me."

"And come with you," she agrees.

"Thank you," I whisper, squeezing her hand.

"You're welcome," she answers.

We're both quiet for a moment, contemplating the enormity of the task ahead of us.

"How?" I finally ask. "The guards at the door aren't going to let me just walk away."

"Arik and I will take care of them. You just be ready to go."

"When?"

"An hour, maybe two." She stands up and straightens her skirts. "I'll be back as soon as we've put everything into place."

And then she's gone.

Terror rolls through me at the thought of what we're about to do—and what will happen if we get caught. But some things are worth fighting for. And so are some people.

Ian and the others have already fought for me so many times.

Here, tonight, it's my turn to fight for them.

CHAPTER 78

Kali

Every second is an eternity as I wait for Lara and Arik to return for me. I think about packing a bag, but if I get caught skulking through the palace at night, I'll look a lot less conspicuous if I'm not carrying anything with me.

I'll also look a lot less conspicuous in my fancy dress. And at least this one isn't so tight that I can't run in it.

Still, I'm not totally unpractical, so I grab as many of my fancy gemstone earrings and necklaces as I can fit into my pockets. Currency, while I search for the *Starlight*. And maybe a present for Ian afterward, to help with fuel and food and anything else we'll need. They'll have Milla by now—she'll probably need new clothes. Maybe we can stock up with her favorite foods. I wonder if she hates dried fishgalen, like Ian.

That only takes a few minutes, and after that, I sit down on my bed and wait.

Twenty seconds later, I'm back up, pacing the floor again. This is torture, pure and simple. I wish Lara and Arik would just hurry up and get here already.

It's two lonely, excruciating hours before I hear the light tap on my door again. I resist the urge to throw it open and demand answers.

But it opens on its own, and there's Lara again. Arik is with her, and he's dragging what looks like a dead or unconscious Imperial guard.

He lugs him into my suite and closes the door. Then pulls some cuffs from his pocket—they remind me of Ian, tugging painfully at my heart—and fastens the guy to the metal poster of my bed, then ties some sort of gag around his mouth before turning to give me a small bow. So, unconscious, then. That's good.

"Your Highness."

I realize I haven't so much as breathed since they came in the room, and I do so now, dragging oxygen into my starving lungs.

I have one moment of terror—this is it; this is really it—but then I let the breath out, and the fear goes with it. Because it's already too late to turn back.

"Thank you," I tell him. "You didn't have to—"

"Pardon me for interrupting, but I promised your father I would look after you. Tonight, I get to keep that promise. Are you ready to go?"

As ready as I'll ever be. "What's the plan?"

"There's a short-range shuttle waiting on the roof. The pilot will take us to Luna. I've arranged for a longer-range ship to meet us there."

"How did you arrange everything so quickly? It seems—"

"I've suspected for a long time that one day we might need a way out."

"But why?"

He starts to say something, then must think better of it, because he just gives an awkward shake of his head. "I believe that's a long conversation for another time. But I'm glad I did, and I'm glad I can be of service."

"Me too. Arik, I will always appreciate this."

"Just turn into the sort of person your father would have been proud of," Arik says. "And that will be better than any gratitude."

I blink back tears. I'm turning into a crybaby. "I'll do my best."

"Good. Then let's go."

The guard is still out cold as we leave the suite. Arik locks the door behind us, and then I lead the way, Lara behind me, with Arik bringing up the rear. We want it to look as normal as possible, like I'm just heading up to the roof for a night stroll, the way my father and I used to all the time.

But we don't see anyone. And as we pause at the door leading to the roof and the shuttle landing dock, I start to think that this is actually going to work.

Arik opens the door to the roof, and I peer outside. It's a beautiful night—clear and filled with stars.

For a moment, I can't help thinking about the *Starlight* out there somewhere. I hope she's okay, hope the people on board her are safe and comfortable and free in the Wilds. Once I get away from here, I'll find a way to get a message to them somehow and warn them of what's coming.

"It's clear," Arik murmurs.

I take a deep breath and step out onto the rooftop. The shuttle is at the far side of the landing platform, the hum of its engines the only sound in the tranquil night.

It's so close—we're so close. Just a little bit farther, and we'll be free.

A little bit farther, and I never have to see this palace again.

My stomach clenches at the thought—it was my home for a very long time.

My house, actually, I realize as I think about my time on the *Starlight*. This place hasn't been a home to me since my father died.

We race across the roof, keeping to the edge overlooking the city. I can't help but think about the people in the city spread out below us—I used to come up here all the time when I was sad or frustrated or simply overwhelmed. I'd look out over the edge of the palace and make up stories about the people in the city down below or the stars blanketing the sky above.

Stories of adventure, of fun, of a life beyond the loneliness of the palace. It's only now, as I'm trying to leave the palace behind, that I realize that, for a short while, those stories came true. For a short while, I lived a life of adventure in the stars.

I only hope I'll get to do so again. I only hope I'm not too late.

The ramp to the shuttle is already down, and I can taste my freedom. We're halfway there when Arik suddenly stops and raises his head. Then he turns to look at me, and I see the sadness in his face. "I'm so sorry," he murmurs. "I did my best."

A group of guards, weapons drawn and pointed straight at us, appears from behind the shelter of a building at the edge of the landing pad. They're wearing the black-and-gray body armor of the Corporation security forces. Behind the soldiers are my mother and Dr. Veragelen.

My heart stops. The escape is over. And while I don't think my mother will hurt me, I've put Arik and Lara in terrible danger.

I rush out to greet them, my hands held in front of me in obvious surrender. "Mother, please. This is all—"

"Kill him," my mother interrupts in a voice completely devoid of emotion. It's so empty, in fact, that it takes me a moment to register what she said.

But when it does, I scream "No!" and hurl myself to the side, desperate to protect Arik no matter what.

Lara grabs onto me, her arms looping through mine as she holds me in place. The guards fire, and Arik doesn't even cry out when he gets shot. He just crashes to the ground at my feet, his eyes forever open and staring into the void.

"Get the servant," my mother demands. "My daughter appears fond of her, and she may prove useful."

One of the soldiers steps toward Lara, and she backs away.

"I'm sorry," I whisper. "I'll find a way to help you. I'll—"

I break off as she jumps up on the low parapet that surrounds the roof. "I won't let them use me against you," she cries out. "Don't give up, Kali. Don't ever give up."

Horror slams through me as I realize what's happening, and I race for her, throwing myself toward her feet. But I'm one second too late, my hands clutching at the air where she used to be as she throws herself backward and falls, falls, falls.

For a moment, I'm so devastated that I'm tempted to follow her over—there's nothing but misery left for me here. But without me, there's no one left to warn my friends, and I didn't come this far to let them all die.

A dozen hands are clutching at me as I stare down at Lara's bruised and broken body. I shake them off as I turn around, and though my knees are wobbling, I lock them in place. Princesses of the Empire do not collapse in a heap just because their life is over. We're made of sterner stuff.

So, I stiffen my legs, straighten my shoulders, and let the rage burning inside me rise to the surface.

"I'll never forgive you for this," I tell my mother.

"Me?" she asks, brows raised. "You're the one who brought all this about. It's your fault that they're dead, not mine."

I want to argue with her—she gave the order that killed Arik—but the truth is that I *am* the one who got them into this. The one who swore to protect them and then instead let them die. Their deaths are on both our hands.

"You didn't have to do this," I tell her.

"Oh, don't be so overdramatic, Kalinda. They were only servants, and you must have known you were putting their lives at risk by involving them in your little escape plan." She steps toward me. "I mean, where did you think you were going? And why? I never would have believed it if Annora hadn't come to me with her suspicions."

I look at Dr. Veragelen. She returns my look with a small smile. "We ran the possible scenarios through the algorithms, and they all came up with the same answer. You would run."

"Kalinda," my mother says, "you know what's at stake here. I can't believe you would jeopardize the future of the whole system. For what?"

"You told me my friends were safe. You lied—you sent out system-wide orders to execute them."

The smallest of frowns forms between her eyes, and I can almost see her mind working. She clearly didn't expect me to know that. "It was better in the long run. You would have come to realize that. They weren't our sort of people. They were Inners. Scum."

"What about my father?" I yell. "Was he Inner scum as well?"

Her eyes go icy cold. "We will not discuss your father." Then she sighs. "Kali, I didn't want it to come to this. But I suppose I must force your hand."

She's unbelievable. I turn my face away from her. But that only brings my gaze to rest on Arik. So, I turn back. "You can't make me do anything. You have nothing to hold over me anymore."

"Maybe not, but that won't be needed. Apparently, Annora has been working on some drugs that will make you a little more… compliant. And that—hopefully—will not have any long-term side effects."

I don't like the sound of that. Not one little bit. I think of Beckett. She's never talked about what went on in the labs on the *Caelestis*, but I know it was horrible.

"In the meantime, I think we'll make sure you don't wander away again. And give you a little time to consider your choices." She turns to the guards. "Take her…somewhere safe." Then she walks away from me. Dr. Veragelen follows, and they head off the rooftop and disappear from sight.

Hands take my arms, and I know it's over.

CHAPTER 79

Kali

The guards drag me from the roof, my princess face forgotten as tears roll silently down my cheeks.

It's over. Everything is over, and there's nothing I can do about it.

I try to glance behind me, to get one last glimpse of Arik before they shove me through the door to the palace. But there are too many guards between him and me, and all I can see is a sea of black and gray.

What am I going to do? The thought haunts me as they drag me down the stairs and through the halls. What am I going to do? Lara is dead. Arik is dead. And my friends on the *Starlight*…if they aren't dead already, they will be soon.

The pain of it drives me to my knees.

I hit the ground despite the hands propelling me forward, and sobs rack my body. I did this. With my selfish, reckless determination, I did all of this.

Beckett tried to warn me. Dark and confused as she is, she knew my mother was evil, and she tried to tell me. I didn't believe her, and now it's too late. My willful ignorance has doomed us all.

"Get up!" one of the guards holding me shouts.

I don't move. I can't. My legs have turned to water beneath me.

What did I do?

What did I do?

The words are a mantra in my head, guilt a pounding, burning devastation in my blood. I want to go back in time, want to change all of this. But I can't. It's done. Arik and Lara are dead, and there is nothing I can do about it.

"Get up!" the guard growls again, and this time he yanks me up so hard that I feel a wrenching in my shoulder.

I barely notice the physical pain through the emotional agony bearing down on me from all directions. My legs are still weak, my entire body trembling so badly that I can barely stay on my feet. Which only pisses the guards off more.

They start to drag me through the hallway, one of them on each side of me. Normally, I would fight them, but I have no fight left in me. All I can think about is Arik's crumpled body and Lara's broken one. All I can think of are their sightless stares. And then I can't stop myself from imagining those same looks on Ian's face. On Max's face. On Rain's and Merrick's and Beckett's and Gage's faces.

No, no, no.

Please let them be okay.

Please don't let them be dead.

I don't even know who I'm pleading with. The universe? Rain's nebulous higher power? Fate itself?

Please, please, please don't let my mother have killed them.

The guards drag me down another flight of stairs and then down the hallway that leads to my room. I have one moment to wonder if my mother has changed her mind. But then they're half pushing, half pulling me past my door, and I know that my mother hasn't changed anything.

It's a holding cell for me. Before today, I had no idea we even had holding cells within the palace.

We turn another corner and then another and another, and I'm crying so hard I can't even see the floor beneath my feet. I have no idea where we are at this point, no idea what part of the palace they've dragged me to, and a tiny part of my brain—the part focused almost entirely on vengeance—urges me to pay attention. To figure out where I am so that I have a clue what to do if I escape.

But escape is such an impossible concept that I can barely wrap my head around it. Not when sorrow is crushing in on me from every side, weighing me down, turning my insides into a dark and endless void.

We're only halfway there when a commotion sounds behind us. I don't bother to even try to turn my head. Whatever it is, it won't bring Lara and Arik back, and right now that's all that matters to me.

All of a sudden, the guards holding me shove me face-first into the ground. Laser cannons fire all around me, their yellow streams bouncing off the walls and ceilings and even the floor a few centimeters in front of me.

Beside me, the guards are falling one after another. Whoever's attacking them is smart—they waited until they were in the long, narrow corridor so there was no escape. And no chance for them to really fight back.

Another guard falls, dead, at my feet, and I smother a scream. A modicum of self-preservation squeaks through the grief, and I push myself up to my hands and knees, start crawling down the hallway, through the blood and the burned flesh littering the floor in all directions.

I don't know what's going on here, don't have a clue who has found their way into the palace to take on my mother's and Dr. Veragelen's guards. And I don't care, as long as they don't kill me, too. Because I'm not going down unless I can destroy my mother and Dr. Veragelen in the process. They deserve to lose everything for what they've done.

But first, I have to escape. Laser fire and screams continue to fly around me, so I stay as low to the ground as I can, remembering what Ian taught me. There's a corner up ahead, a hallway that leads away from this one, and it's my present goal. Get there and get out of the line of fire. For now. Everything else can wait.

I'm almost there—maybe three meters away—when a pair of worn boots appears right in front of me. At first, I don't realize what

I'm looking at, but then the shooting stops. And the person attached
to the boots squats down.

"Looks like you got yourself in a real jam this time," a familiar
voice says. "What do you say we blow this place, Princess?"

Ian. It's Ian. He's still alive, and—despite everything—he's come
to get me.

CHAPTER 80

Ian

"Everything clear?" I call to Merrick, who's at the other end of the hallway, laser gun still drawn as he peers around a corner.

"Looks like it," he calls back.

Good. It only took us mowing down about twenty Imperial guards to do it—maybe some Corporation security guys—but that's no skin off my nose. I've wanted to shoot more than a few of these guys for a long time now.

"Okay, then, Princess." I pull her into my arms and then stand back up. "Ready to go?"

"You're alive," she whispers, one trembling hand reaching out to touch my cheek like she can't believe it.

And fuck. I've been so mad at her for what feels like ages now. I'm still mad at her. But when she looks at me like that, all wide-eyed and tear-stained, it's hard to remember why I'm angry. Hard to remember anything but the way it feels when she's in my arms.

"*Sorry to bust up this happy little reunion.*" Max's sarcastic voice floods my head. "*But Beckett and I are holding off another thirty guards or so up here on our own. If you'd like to help.*"

"*You act like it's hard,*" I say, but I'm already striding down the hall, stepping over dead bodies as I go.

Merrick's ahead of us, racing down the hallway to our access point, laser gun tracking back and forth as he looks for threats. I've got to say, for a priest he's pretty damn good with that thing. No wonder they picked him to be Rain's bodyguard.

"You think you can walk?" I ask Kali as we get closer to the door. I don't know what's waiting for us out there, and I need my hands free.

She nods against my chest where she's curled up, and I reluctantly let her go. Her curves feel pretty fucking amazing sliding down my body, but I've got no time to concentrate on that right now. Instead, I bark, "Stay right behind me," as I step past her.

Then the two of us are hauling ass to join Merrick, who's waiting for us at the door, two strangled guards at his feet. We got them on our way in.

"Ready?" he asks, then glances at Kali with a smile bigger than I've ever seen from him. "Good to see you," he tells her.

"Not as good as it is to see you," she answers, and I try not to get annoyed. All I got was a *You're alive.*

"As we'll ever be," I snarl, then push the door open.

We walk straight into pandemonium, gunfire flying in all directions as Max and Beckett do their best to take out a whole slew of Corporation security and Imperial guards. When Max said thirty of them, he was obviously being conservative. Or maybe he was just counting the dead ones—with all the smoke floating around from our distraction grenades, it's hard to tell.

"Where's the ship?" Kali shouts to be heard over the gunshots.

"Right in front of us," I tell her as we wade into the fray.

Two guards pop up from behind a huge planter box, guns leveled straight at the princess and me. Merrick takes one down while I take the other, but then three more come racing toward us.

"Give me a gun," Kali shouts.

"Don't have an extra one," I shout back.

She sighs like I'm an utter disappointment, which pisses me right off, considering I'm here rescuing her ass. But what the fuck else do I expect from this woman? She's been busting my balls from the day we met.

All of a sudden, another whole influx of guards comes running across the Empress's previously well-kept garden at us. "There's too many!" I shout at Merrick. "We need to move, now!"

He nods his agreement as a whole slew of gunfire comes their way from the *Starlight*. Several guards go down, and the others dive for cover.

"Thanks," I tell Max.

"Thank Beckett," he answers. "That woman can shoot."

"Let's go, Princess! The *Starlight* is waiting!"

"Where?" she yells again. "I can't see her."

"That's because she's cloaked," Merrick tells her as he shoots a guard directly over my shoulder.

I return the favor by shooting the two bearing down on him.

And then we're running straight toward the steady, nonstop blasts that are spraying the ground between the guards and us.

Out of nowhere, a guard jumps out and grabs onto Kali, wrapping one hand around her neck and another around her waist as he pulls her backward.

I level my laser pistol on him, but he's using her as much as a shield as a hostage and I can't get a bead on him. At least not one that won't also get Kali. And I didn't come this far just to lose her now.

Kali must feel the same way about dying, though, because she leans forward and then rears back as hard as she can, head-butting the guard straight in the nose. He screams as blood spurts everywhere, but the princess has no mercy in her. She stamps down on his foot as hard as she can, and when he loosens his grip, she spins away and then kicks him right in the balls.

"Found a few vulnerable bits," she deadpans.

I grunt. But damn if I'm not proud of her.

"Looks like those lessons Ian gave you are really starting to pay off," Merrick tells her as I grab onto her wrist and pull her toward me.

"I learned most of that just from watching him fight," she answers. "He fights dirty."

Only because I've spent my whole life having to level the playing field. The only good fight is one you get to walk away from.

I level my pistol at the soldier who had the nerve to touch Kali, but he looks so miserable I decide to leave him alone. A blast through the brain would put him out of that misery way too easily.

We're almost at the ship now, and though the guards keep coming, my anxiety levels go way down. Because once we get on board, I know there's no way they can touch us.

"Incoming!" I yell to Max as I whirl around and shoot a guy coming at us right between the eyes.

He falls down dead at our feet, and Kali jumps over him like an old pro. She's gotten tougher since that first fight in Rangar. Much tougher.

"How much farther?" she asks.

I aim right above her shoulder and take out two more guards.

"*Tell Gage to lower the ramp!*" I tell Max.

"*Already on it,*" he says.

Without a sound, the *Starlight* uncloaks herself right in the middle of what I understand is the Empress's prize garden. Looks like she'll be needing some new Verbosnia bushes.

Merrick's in the lead as we race up the ramp in a hail of laser fire. I grab Kali and push her in front of me so that I take any shots coming her way. The second I clear the top of the ramp, the *Starlight* takes off, shooting straight into the sky before the ramp is even fully retracted.

"Way to go, Captain!" Beckett slaps me on the back.

"You okay?" I ask Kali, visually checking her over for any damage. Miraculously, short of a few bumps and bruises, she seems to have gotten through that whole debacle okay. We all have.

"Kali!" Rain shouts, running into the tiny loading bay and throwing her arms around the princess. "Don't ever do that to us again! Sneaking away in the middle of the night is a really awful thing to do."

Yeah, I want to say. *It was a really fucking awful thing to do.* But if I say that, she'll think I care more than I do. And I don't give a shit. If she wants to leave, she can have at it. She just can't go back to the damn Empress and bring down half the solar system with her.

Suddenly, the *Starlight* shudders, nearly knocking us off our feet.

"What was that?" I demand, racing for the bridge.

Beckett's right behind me. "What did you do?" she demands of Gage, who's standing next to the pilot's chair like he doesn't have a care in the world.

"I didn't do anything." He points at the *Starlight*'s front console. "She did."

"Beckett," I say warningly. It's one thing for the ship to fly us out of here on her own. It's another thing for her to decide to take matters into her own hands.

I slide into the captain's chair. "Get control of this ship," I bark at Beckett.

"Thanks for the suggestion," she snarls back as she jams her hand down on the controls.

The *Starlight* doesn't so much as acknowledge her presence. It's like autopilot on steroids. But you can switch off an autopilot.

I glance at Gage. "Can we do anything?"

He just shrugs.

"Thanks," I tell him.

Another shrug. Useless bastard.

"Everyone get to your seats!" I order. "Now."

Because something tells me things are about to get ugly. And with the *Starlight* in control, there's nothing I can do about it.

"I thought Gage fixed this," Max grumbles as he buckles himself into the nearest seat.

"So did I," Gage answers.

"You mean you don't know?" What the hell am I supposed to do with this guy? So glad Max thinks he's a freaking genius.

Gage rolls his eyes at me. "Well, she hasn't gone into autopilot since I thought I fixed her. Hence, I assumed she was fixed."

"Yeah, well, you might want to try again. She—" I break off as a message pops up on my HUD.

SHORT-RANGE BALLISTIC MISSILE ATTACK. EVASIVE ACTIONS IMMINENT.

"The fuck?" I demand, right before the *Starlight* jerks us several meters to the left.

"That was close," Merrick comments as we watch a missile fly right by on the viewing screens.

Not this again. "Gage!" I yell. "Get your ass under that console and figure this out!"

"I'm on it—" he starts, but then *Starlight* starts to spin and he's hurled halfway across the bridge.

"Everyone okay?" Beckett shouts from the pilot's seat. Apparently, she and Max were the only two smart enough to buckle up (yes, fucking including me), because everyone else is on the floor with me.

The *Starlight* finally calms down and pulls herself out of the spin, so I take advantage of the quiet and crawl my way back to my chair. I click the harness into place just as the ship spins in the opposite direction. And then we're upside down. Then we're right side up. Then we're upside down again.

There's a lot more screaming and a few more crashes and bangs. My stomach—usually made of iron—lurches, and I swallow down the sick. No way am I puking in the middle of this. Beckett would never let me hear the end of it.

We flip right side up again, and I dare to dream that the *Starlight* has finally calmed the fuck down.

EVASIVE ACTIONS SUCCESSFUL. MISSILES AVOIDED. NO FURTHER ACTION REQUIRED.

Fuck yeah! That sounds promising.

I glance around at the bridge. Beckett is in the pilot's seat grinning like she's just been on the most kick-ass ride of her life. Rain, Merrick, and Max are all looking a little green despite being seated and buckled in, while Gage and Kali are still picking themselves up off the floor. I give Gage a cursory once-over and Kali a more thorough inspection, but neither seem damaged.

Maybe they'll be quicker to follow my advice in the future.

On the plus side, once they're up, they both lunge for their seats and buckle in. Just as well, as another message comes up on my HUD.

LASER ATTACK. EVASIVE ACTION IMMINENT.

Fuck me. This ship is determined to kill us all in her efforts to keep us alive.

Except I can see the lasers now, coming one after the other. Beams of yellow light blasting up from the planet's surface, strong enough to follow us out of the atmosphere, which I think we're just about to pass through. I grip the arms of my seat, prepared for the worst. But all that happens is some sort of shield comes up that covers the outside of the ship. The screens at the nose end of the ship reflect what's going on, and I brace myself as the laser blasts come straight for us, filling the whole screen with white light.

A faint shudder runs through the ship as they hit, followed by a couple of bigger shudders that have Rain gasping and Max swearing.

But we're still here at the end of them, so whatever damage the attack caused I'll still call a win.

TARGETS ACQUIRED.

"Oh shit." Beckett slams her hand down on the control panel, pressing button after button in an effort to stop what's about to happen. "Stop, stop, stop!"

"Let her go," I tell her.

"What do you mean, let her go?" Beckett demands. "She's about to destroy the Empress's palace. I'm pretty sure that's an act of war."

"Like killing dozens of her guards and stealing off into the night isn't?" I ask, brows raised. "Besides, better to know what the *Starlight*'s going to do now instead of later, when she might get us in a whole heaping pile of drokaray shit."

I'm in the mood to live dangerously. Not to mention completely fucking pissed off that the Empress is apparently okay with firing on a craft she knows her daughter is on. That's some cold-blooded shit if I've ever heard it.

Especially when I glance back at Kali's face and realize she's figured it out, too. The guards aren't firing on us on their own. They obviously had permission to do so, considering the Empire's crown princess is on board.

My HUD shows the *Starlight*'s acceleration out of the Askkandian atmosphere has slowed. We're centered over the Imperial Palace.

TARGETS LOCKED.

A bright white light that looks a lot like what she fired at Kali's and my attackers on Glacea shoots out from the front of the *Starlight*, straight at the bank of anti-spacecraft weaponry that's been shooting at us since we took off.

I see flashes as she hits something—what, I have no clue. At least not until...

ENEMY WEAPONS ELIMINATED flashes across my HUD.

The shields lift, and through the viewing screens I can make out the rooftop of the palace. There's a lot more smoke, now, and guards are scrambling—for safety or weapons, I don't know.

INDIVIDUAL TARGETS ACQUIRED.

"Get us out of here, Beckett!" I order. The last thing I need Kali to see is the *Starlight* opening fire on her mother's entire battalion of guards in zoomed-in high-def.

"I'm trying!" she shoots back as she messes with the control panel.

INDIVIDUAL TARGETS LOCKED.

"Now, Beckett!" I growl.

"I'm—" She puts her hand on the velocity control for what has to be the tenth time. But this time it actually works, and the *Starlight* shoots backward and up, up, up. Ninety seconds later, we're leaving Askkandia's atmosphere and soaring straight into space.

"Set a course for the Wilds," I tell Beckett as I lean back in my chair.

Because now that our crew is back together, time is running out, and nothing is going to keep me from getting to Milla before it's too late.

CHAPTER 81

Kali

As soon as we're safely past Askkandia's atmosphere, I fumble my way out of my harness and race out of the room. Grief and horror and shame are pressing in on me from all sides until I can't think. Can't breathe.

Thankfully, I make it to the head before anyone can stop me to check on me, and I lock myself in. Water isn't unlimited on a spaceship—not even close—but I can't think about that right now. Instead, I turn the tap on and let the water run over my wrists for a couple of minutes. The chill of it calms me down, giving me something to focus on besides the frantic beating of my heart and the instant replay that my brain wants to do of everything that just happened.

Every time I close my eyes, I see Lara flinging herself off that parapet. I see Arik going down under that guard's fire. I see my mother watching the whole thing with satisfaction in her eyes. Satisfaction. Two people she has known for years are dead because of her, and she looks satisfied.

Just knowing that messes me up deep inside. It makes me angry, but even more, it makes me sad. Sad for Lara and Arik. Sad for myself. Sad for my mother.

It's that last one that messes me up so much. My mother is a horrible, horrible woman. She doesn't deserve anyone feeling sad for her. And yet, here I am, hands shaking and tears burning the backs of my eyes as I try to figure out what I'm supposed to do now. And how I'm supposed to feel.

But I can't hide in the bathroom forever, no matter how much I want to. So I cup water in my hands and splash it over my face until all the makeup that makes me look like Princess Kalinda is gone and all that's left is me. Kali.

I'm still learning who she is, and I probably will be for a while. But at least I know who I don't want her to be.

No matter what happens, no matter how much I get hurt or how afraid I am, I'll never be like my mother. More concerned with myself than with the people I'm supposed to care about. The people I'm responsible for.

When I've finally managed to get all the elaborate makeup off, I grab a towel and dry my face before heading to my cabin. I know I should probably return to the bridge and thank everyone for coming back for me, but I'm exhausted and miserable and all I really want to do is lay down in my bed and cry. Just for a little while. Then I'll figure out what to do, how to save the system without killing millions of people.

But I barely make the turn into the hallway near my bedroom before I run into Ian. He's coming out of his room, looking as exhausted as I feel, with some extra grumpiness.

Our eyes lock, and I wait for him to say something to me. This is the first chance we've had to say something to each other when we're not being shot at or flung around by the *Starlight*. But he doesn't say anything at all. He just turns and walks away without so much as a nod.

And suddenly, my exhaustion disappears. Anger takes its place, and before I know I'm going to do it, I take off after him. "What's wrong with you?" I ask as I chase him down the corridor toward the galley.

He doesn't answer, which just makes me angrier. I've spent my life being ignored by my mother, either being told that my questions and opinions don't matter or just not being answered at all. No way am I going to let Ian treat me the same way.

"Hey!" I grab his arm. "I'm trying to talk to you."

He shakes me off and walks into the galley, where he pours himself a glass of water and drinks it with his back to me.

"Seriously? You're going to pretend I don't exist? I don't deserve that."

"You don't deserve it?" he snarls, finally whirling around to face me. "You didn't want to talk when you had Beckett drop you on fucking Espia like you were running away. You didn't want to talk when you decided to go back to your mother and your fancy dresses." He sneers as his eyes run over my clothing. "And you sure as fuck didn't want to talk when you crept out of my fucking ship in the middle of the night and disappeared from my life like what we were didn't matter at all. So why the fuck do you want to talk right now?"

For the first time since he showed up on Askkandia, I realize that Ian is furious. Not just angry, not just enraged, but deeply, coldly furious in a way I don't think I've ever seen him. Sure, he's been annoyed or mad or frustrated before, but not like this. Not like he really wants nothing to do with me. Or worse, like he's disgusted by me.

Tears burn my eyes and tighten up my throat, but I swallow them back down and keep my expression as controlled as possible. No way am I going to cry in front of him when he's looking at me like that. No way I'm going to try to do anything with him.

I step back, hands up in a gesture of surrender, and back out of the galley, more determined than ever to hide in my room until I can get my feet back under me.

But this time, Ian's the one who follows me. "Nothing to say now, Kali?" he sneers. "Why am I even surprised? Seems pretty typical to me."

He moves to brush past me, and suddenly the tears are gone and I'm back to being angry—as angry as he is. "I left when you were asleep because I knew you'd try to talk me out of it!" I shout at his back.

"Like that's an excuse?" He whirls around. "You literally fled the ship like I was some kind of abusive asshole. How do you think that made me feel? Oh, wait, you didn't worry about that, did you? I mean, why should you? It's not like I'm a normal person with normal feelings, right? I'm just some weirdo you couldn't get away from fast enough!"

I freeze, blinking in confusion. "What do you mean, some kind of weirdo?" I demand.

His eyes narrow. "Don't play naive with me. If that's the way you feel, it's fine. I just wish you'd said something to me instead of running away."

Now I'm not only confused—I'm baffled. "Said something to you about what?"

"The gestalt, Kali," he roars. "The hive mind between Milla, Max, and me. Once you heard about it, you couldn't get away fast enough."

I recoil in horror. "You can't actually believe that, Ian. You can't actually believe I left the ship because I was…" I trail off, not even sure what word to use at this point.

"Disgusted," he fills in. "Go ahead and say it. You were disgusted by me. By us."

"No."

"Fuck, Kali, it's even worse when you deny it. If that's how you feel, fine. I get it—it's not like you're the only one in Senestris who would feel uncomfortable being with me knowing what I am. I know it's a lot; we all do. It's why we keep that shit close and don't tell anyone. But you could have been honest with me. You could have just said how you felt. I wouldn't have held it against you."

"Just like you're not holding my leaving against me?" I ask archly.

"Oh, no, I'm definitely holding that shit against you. It was a dick move, and if you can't even figure out why that is, then I don't know what to say to you."

Again, he starts to move past me, and again I get in his way. Because it's occurring to me what's really going on here. Ian isn't angry with me at all—he's hurt. I hurt him, and he's not going to forgive me for it easily.

Still, when you hurt someone, you should apologize to them. It's one of the first things I learned from Lara when we were just children. She knocked me down accidentally, and she apologized to me for it.

It was the first time in my whole life that I'd ever heard someone use the word *sorry*, and I remember how it made me feel. Like I was important. Like I mattered—not because I was a princess, but because I was me.

Somehow, I made Ian feel like he didn't matter. And that really sucks, considering people have been making him feel like that his entire life.

"I'm sorry," I whisper to him, resting a hand on his muscular forearm. "The last thing I ever meant to make you feel is like you disgusted me."

"Forget it, Kali." Again, he goes to shrug me off. But this time, I'm hanging on.

"Look at me," I whisper, and I don't let go until he does. "I have a lot of feelings about you, Ian. But the one thing I definitely don't feel—the one thing I could never feel—is disgust."

"Princess—"

"No." I press two fingers to his lips. "It's my turn to talk and your turn to listen. I didn't leave the ship because I found out about you being a gestalt. Did it surprise me? Yeah, it absolutely did. Did it make me not want you anymore?" I blush as I think about the last time we were together, in the galley. "Not even a little bit.

"I've never wanted anyone in my life the way that I want you. And finding out about Milla and Max didn't change that. If I'm being honest, I don't think anything could change it." To prove it to him, I move closer, until my body is pressed against his. And though I know this is a bad idea, though I know it's the last thing I should be doing right now, I thread my hands through his short, coarse hair and pull his mouth to mine.

For one perfect second, heat explodes between us. But then he's stepping back, ripping his mouth away from mine. "Why'd you leave like that, then? Why'd you sneak away in the middle of the night if it wasn't because you couldn't wait to get away from me?"

I consider lying to him. Not to protect him—to protect me. It's been a really shit day, and already I'm feeling more vulnerable than I ever want to feel again. But he's feeling vulnerable, too. For Ian, a guy who'd much rather punch something than talk to it, to bare his emotions to me like this is no small thing. Lying to him now, or ever, feels like a really terrible thing to do.

So I don't lie. Instead, I take a deep breath and admit the truth. "Because I knew I had to go in order to protect everyone. And if you were awake and watching me, there was no way I'd ever be able to walk away. Not when I want you the way that I do."

It's his turn to take a deep breath. His turn to blow it out slowly. And his turn to show just how vulnerable he is when he whispers, "And how do you want me, Kali?"

"Too much," I whisper back. "I want you too much."

Ian's eyes go dark, the chasm of want that opens up in them threatening to swallow me whole. But before he can reach for me, Max comes barreling around the corner. He doesn't even blink when he sees us standing so close together, but then, why would he? If he and Ian share a mind, he probably knows everything that just happened here.

Or does he? I realize I don't know. And that maybe I should find out.

"You need something?" Ian asks after a second.

"Beckett told me to get you. There's something important you need to see on the bridge, right away."

CHAPTER 82

Ian

"What does that mean?" I demand, pissed off that I'm being interrupted just as I was making some headway with Kali. Then again, maybe it's a good thing. We sure as shit have a lot to talk about, and maybe clouding it with sex isn't the way to get that done. Especially since shortly after the last time we hooked up, she up and ran away in the middle of the night.

Maybe it wasn't because of the gestalt. Maybe it was because she was overwhelmed by everything she was feeling. But it seems like we should probably have another conversation or five before we end up right back there again.

"I think it means get your ass to the bridge," Max tells me, obviously exasperated. "If I knew more than that, I would have told you."

Mentally, I flip him off. But I turn to Kali, who says, "Let's go. We can talk later."

"You wanna talk about it?" Max says as we make our way back to the bridge.

"Not if you want to keep your head attached to your body."

He laughs. *"So the talk went well then, hmm?"*

"I'm glad you think this is funny."

"*Falling in love at the worst possible time with the worst possible woman?*" Max's snort doesn't have a lot of humor in it. "*Yeah, I don't think there's a lot that's funny about that.*"

"*Who said anything about love?*" I snarl.

Now he laughs, a full-blown belly laugh that makes me want to punch him in his smug face. But that would just mean we both had a headache later.

I don't wait around for his answer, mostly because I know what it's going to be. Instead, I speed up so that I swing into the bridge several steps in front of Max and Kali. "What's wrong?" I demand of Beckett, who's staring at her console like it holds the secrets to the damn universe.

"The *Starlight* is heading in the wrong direction," she answers. "And I think it's because of this," she adds, popping a graphic up on the main screen.

"Now that's something you don't see very often," Max mutters from behind me.

"What is it?" I demand. "A black blob?"

"By not very often, I assume you mean never," Merrick says.

"Never say never," Gage singsongs as even he sits up to watch what's happening.

"Never minus one?" Rain says quietly, and I realize it's the first time she's spoken in a long time. I shoot her a quick look, just to make sure she's okay, but she's sitting up like everyone else, her attention completely focused on what's directly in front of us.

Namely, a huge, dark orb.

It's the heptosphere.

It's nearly pitch-black, like the first time I set eyes on it. And it's currently being towed behind two ships like a broken-down satellite. Only much, much bigger.

Kali suddenly moves all the way to the nose end of the bridge as she reaches a hand out as if she can actually touch the thing. As she stands there, transfixed by the ancient artifact, I can't help thinking that Merrick is right.

Kali might really be the Star Bringer.

And we need to tell her the truth.

"What are they doing with it?" Rain asks.

"They're taking it down to the palace," Kali answers. "They planned on me destroying a few planets in the morning."

"So you know?" I ask.

"That I can activate the heptosphere? Yeah, Dr. Veragelen was pretty adamant," Kali says. I glance over at Rain, who gives a small, sad head shake. We'll get to the rest of it—the Star Bringer, all the deception, her role as the true high priestess—later.

"But why are we here, watching it?" I ask, since it seems pretty clear to me that this is what has the ship going off course. "What does the *Starlight* want with the heptosphere?"

The others shrug and shake their heads.

"I'm assuming we're about to find out." Max moves to wrap a comforting arm around Kali's shoulders. When she sags against him, I wonder if maybe she's okay with me after all. That maybe I really did misread the situation between us. It wouldn't be the first time.

The *Starlight* slows to a stop—right in the path of the two shuttles towing the heptosphere. On the plus side, they're short-range passenger shuttles with no weapons.

"What's she doing?" Gage asks, and he doesn't sound impressed.

"I don't—" I break off as, with absolutely no warning, two beams blast out from the *Starlight*.

They hit the shuttles simultaneously, and seconds later, both ships explode into nothingness. They just disappear.

"Holy shit," Beckett whispers.

"I really don't think those were normal lasers," Gage contributes.

"Thanks, tech genius," I drawl, but he's not wrong. The *Starlight*, quite literally, vaporized two ships in an instant.

With the ships gone, the heptosphere is free of its restraints now. They've fallen away, and it's drifting in space. At least until the *Starlight* makes a beeline for it.

"Can you stop her?" I ask.

Beckett shakes her head. "Not a chance. I'm guessing this is what the detour was for."

"But how did the ship even know it was here?" Rain asks. She looks as fascinated and as horrified as I feel.

"They're both alien artifacts," Merrick suggests. "Maybe they have some kind of common signal that lets them talk to each other."

Yeah, or maybe there's something more going on here. Something we don't have a fucking clue about.

Either way, we're level with the heptosphere now, staring straight at it as we fly closer and closer.

"She needs to get closer," Kali answers, and again her hand is on the display, like she's dying to reach out and touch the giant black orb as the *Starlight* circles it once before turning around and flying away.

"That's it?" Max asks. "She just wanted to see it?"

"Nope, that's definitely not it." Beckett presses a couple of buttons on her console, and the right viewing screen switches to show the rear of the ship.

To where the heptosphere is now following us through space.

CHAPTER 83

Kali

"So we've got a heptosphere on our ass now, too. Because we didn't have enough shit going on already," Max comments from beside me. "You okay, Kali?"

I have no idea. I don't feel okay, but I don't think that has anything to do with the heptosphere. I haven't felt okay since I watched Arik and Lara die, and everything that's happened since has only made it worse. Including the fact that I'm drawn to that giant black orb in a way I've never been drawn to anything ever before.

Except maybe Ian. But that's something else I don't want to talk about right now. Max interrupted our talk earlier, and I have no idea where we left off.

I don't know if he believes me when I say the gestalt had nothing to do with me leaving.

I don't know if he's still mad at me.

Basically, I have no idea where we stand, and right now I can't bring myself to care. Not when it feels like the entire system is about to implode around us.

"I have control back," Beckett announces. "Looks like the *Starlight* did what she came to do."

"Then let's get out of here," Ian answers. "And hope we don't have any more unwelcome company on our way to the Wilds."

Going to the Wilds, finally rescuing Milla, is the only thing I truly want to do right now. After everything we've been through, everything that's been sacrificed, at least Ian and Max should get to reunite with her. And she should get to be safe.

But what about the dying sun? If we really only have a few weeks left—not years, as I thought—how can I just run off and leave that problem for another day? Because if the sun implodes, nothing else matters.

"I can't go to the Wilds, Ian," I tell him quietly. "We have a bigger problem. Serai might be dying a lot quicker than we thought, and I still have to help protect the whole system."

He looks at me with fire in his gaze, and not the good kind. "I couldn't give two shits about the dying sun, Princess. We've come too far to not get Milla back now. I'm sure your mom will figure something out."

"This is what she figured out. What Dr. Veragelen and all the smartest minds in the system figured out. We don't have any other options. We're out of time."

"Well, time is just going to have to wait a little longer," Ian growls. "Your mom and Doc V and their fucked-up plan are why Milla is where she is. So pardon me if I don't give a shit about doing things on their fucking timeline."

I sigh, because I really do understand what he's saying—more, what he's feeling. But that doesn't negate the fact that if the sun implodes, Milla won't be alive anyway. None of us will.

"Do you even know how to work the heptosphere?" Merrick asks suddenly. "Everyone—including you—seems to have bought into the fact that you can fix everything with it. But do you even know what to do?"

"I guess I thought it'd be kind of self-explanatory," I answer.

He raises a brow. "Like it was in the lab on the *Caelestis*?"

I pause. He's not wrong.

"All of this is superfluous," Ian says, "because we're going after Milla right now."

An idea starts to formulate in my mind. Merrick is right when he says I have no idea how to control the heptosphere. But if I have any hope of actually using it to save the sun, then I need to learn. The only problem is, I have to assume the learning curve is really steep—that thing is dangerous, and who knows what will happen if I just start trying to figure it out near the most populated planets.

No, much better to rescue Milla and then test out the heptosphere at the edges of the system, where there's nothing but a few asteroids and two dead planets around. Talk about killing two varmaks with one rock.

"Okay," I say, meeting Ian's very annoyed eyes. "Let's go to the Wilds. And while we're out there, I'll see just what this hunk of metal and I can do together."

Beckett looks impressed. "You're getting more diabolical in your old age, Kali. I think I like it."

Now I know the universe has turned upside down. My mother is a stone-cold killer. A rebel says she likes something about me. And I've just turned my back on everything I've ever known to hop on a sentient ship headed straight for the Wilds.

There's no turning back now.

CHAPTER 84

Beckett

I feel like shit, but I drag myself back to the bridge anyway. The only other option is going to bed, and the last thing I want to do is pretend everything's okay when Rain comes to check on me.

With me. With her. With us.

I want to help her, but she's still too hurt by everything Merrick said to be able to accept that help. Even if I knew how to offer it. Which I don't.

She wants to help me just as much, but the truth is, I'm beyond help. I'm nothing but darkness, and I just can't ruin her light any more.

Rain thinks time will cure everything, but that's a pipe dream. Time isn't curing me. It's making me worse. Yes, the blankness and missing pieces have gotten a little better since I've been on the *Starlight*, but the pain has gotten so much worse. It feels like a drill digging into my brain all the time, a chisel chipping away at everything that is me until all that's left is a mound of screaming, desperate rage.

I don't want that for her, and I definitely don't want that for us.

I reach under my chair and pull out the bottle of painkillers I nabbed from the sick bay. I dry swallow a handful, then look up to find Ian watching me.

When our eyes meet, he raises a brow. I shrug in return. Then I lean back against the pilot's chair and wait for the pain to get better. It never goes away, but the painkillers make it so I can at least think. For a while, anyway.

I wonder for the millionth time what they did to my head on the *Caelestis*. Whatever it is, it's broken something inside of me. I can feel myself changing, becoming...something. I don't know what it is, and I don't know that I want to know. But something tells me that the end is going to be a race between insanity and death, and I have to get away from here before either happens. Rain doesn't deserve to see that. Better she thinks I'm just gone because I want to go.

I don't want to go, but I can't stay here.

I've never really felt like I belonged anywhere before. Even with the Rebellion, I was on the outside looking in. Trying to get my mother's approval. Trying to be what she and the rebels needed me to be. Sometimes, late at night—like now—I acknowledge that our relationship isn't all that different from Kali's and her mom's. Before the *Starlight*, I never would have seen it or believed it, but now...it's hard to miss the parallels in our lives.

Both our fathers died in tragic circumstances.

We both have controlling mothers—though I don't think it's a stretch to say hers is worse than mine.

We both think our way is the right way.

And, most pathetic of all, we both had the lack of foresight to join a ship full of misfits. Even worse, we both fell in love with one of them.

Oh, Kali will deny it. But then, so will I, if anyone asks. It doesn't make it any less true.

That's the other reason I know it's time to go. Because lately, I've been getting these ridiculous feelings of belonging.

I love this ship. The *Starlight* feels like the home I haven't had since my father died. But it's not just the ship. It's the people—not only Rain, but all of them. I've never had friends before, so I could be totally off base. But I think they might actually care about me. I know that I care about them. Even Kali, with her purple dresses and privileged attitude. She's a pain, but she's our pain.

And a tiny, optimistic part of me thinks that might be all that matters.

And that's why I have to leave. Because it's that kind of thinking that gets people hurt. I don't care about me so much, but I can't stand the idea of something happening to one of them. Especially Rain.

But before I go, I have to find out about my brother. I have to know if he went the same route as Milla. If he did, is there some way to find him, too?

It's a lot to ask of one sentient ship and seven people who are just beginning to learn how to trust one another. But I've been playing with an idea of how to manage it. It's not a good one, but it won't leave me alone.

I look around. Everyone is a little subdued right now, but I think that's to be expected. Ian is sitting, brooding, in his captain's chair. I would have thought he'd be happier now that we've got the princess back. But obviously not. It's been maybe two hours since she went to bed, and he keeps looking at the door like some lovesick prupple.

I check the screens. There's no one following, just that giant creepy orb keeping pace behind us.

Should I broach my idea? Or should I just forget about it? I mean, there's a good chance they won't agree to it anyway, since there are several risks involved. But at the same time, it might be the best chance that we've got, and shouldn't we take it? Don't Milla and Jarved deserve it?

Before I can decide, the comms unit buzzes with an incoming call. Ian jumps to his feet and heads over. "Who is it?" he asks.

Gage taps a few keys. "That merc you asked me to contact in the Wilds. Looks like he got the information."

"Great. Can you put it up on the other screens?" Ian asks.

A stream of data flashes across the screen. I start reading. It's a map of the building where Milla is hopefully being kept, considering it's the largest structure on Delta V47, where the *Reformer* was headed. The exact location of the asteroid itself. And numbers of guards and their shifts and changeover times. It's a lot of great information, but it's also really bad news.

At least there's no long-range surveillance system, but there are between fifty and a hundred guards on duty at any time, plus we have to presume the off-duty guards will join in if there's an attack. We'll never be able to take that many. Not with just the seven of us, only four of whom are fighters.

Judging by the expression on Ian's face, he's thinking the same thing. "Fuck," he mutters. "How the hell are we going to do this?"

"We're not," I answer. "Not alone."

Kali chooses that moment to appear. She doesn't look much better than when she went to sleep.

"What's going on?" she asks.

Ian takes a step toward her and then stops himself. Probably put off by her closed expression and general air of leave-me-alone-ness. "We just got the intel from the Wilds. It's not good."

"Too many guards," Max puts in. "We're going to need help."

"And where are we supposed to get that kind of help? It's not like there are so many people we can trust. And it's not like that many people are jumping at the idea of flying straight into the Wilds. Not with the shit that goes on down there." Ian is pacing the bridge now, freaking out. The man can't stay still when he's tense. I'm pretty sure he wore a new groove in the days before we liberated Kali from the palace.

Which means there won't be a more ideal time to toss my idea into the pot and see just how desperate they are.

But before I can speak, Kali moves forward. "Could we hire people? Mercenaries, maybe?"

Ian shakes his head. "We don't have any money."

"Would this help?" She reaches into her pocket and pulls out a handful of jewelry, all pretty and sparkly. She pushes it into Ian's hands. "I brought whatever I could. I thought it might be useful."

Ian stares at his hands for a moment, like he can't believe what he's seeing.

"And there's the dress as well." She waves a hand down at the purple dress she came back to us with, its hem encrusted with gemstones.

Ian looks at Max, and I guess they're doing that mind-talking thing, because Max shakes his head. Honestly, I can't believe I didn't pick up on it earlier. It's not that subtle.

"Thanks, Princess. But it won't work. It's too dangerous. I don't know of anyone who will go into the Wilds, even for this." He tries to hand the jewels back to her, but she shakes her head, and he shoves them in his pocket.

"I do," I tell him.

Everyone turns to look at me. "You do what?" Ian asks, a frown on his face.

"I know someone who will go wherever we need them to go. Or at least maybe make a diversion and keep a good number of those guards occupied while we go in and find Milla and…"

I trail off. Like I'll curse the whole thing if I say my brother's name out loud.

"Who?" Ian asks.

"The Rebellion, of course."

He frowns like he's missing something. "And why would they help us?"

"Because I'll ask them to."

"And they'll listen?" Ian doesn't sound convinced. "Why?"

"Because my mother is Marlina Orsgood."

His eyes widen, and he doesn't respond. I almost pat myself on the back—it's not easy to render him speechless.

"Who's Marlina Orsgood?" Rain asks.

"The leader of the Rebellion," Merrick says slowly. He's studying me as though I've grown an extra head. "The most ruthless leader they've ever had."

Max frowns. "Isn't she known as the Butcher of Narreth?"

"An exaggeration," I say, fingers crossed behind my back. She slaughtered a whole garrison of Imperial troops at Narreth.

"And the Slayer of Snolmek?" Merrick adds.

"It didn't happen quite the way the stories say it did." Because it was so much worse.

"And what about—" Gage starts, but I cut him off.

"Do you want her help or not?"

"I don't know," Ian answers, looking doubtful.

"Yeah, well, it's not like you've got so many other offers. And it's not like she'll be gunning for you."

Ian sits in his big chair, which means he's thinking about it. I give him time. If I push this, he'll back off. But really, it's the only way, and it won't take him long to figure that out.

"Why?" he says after five minutes of intense thought. "Walk me through it. Why would she help? Why would you ask her to help?"

I lick my lips and consider how much to reveal. "I'm going in anyway. There's a small chance I might find my brother. Or at least find out what happened to him."

Kali looks at me with renewed interest. "I thought you said your brother was dead?"

"He is. Well, he probably is. But all this talk about Milla has got me wondering—I mean, she's made it through. Why not Jarved, too? Which means I have a vested interest in the success of this mission, and so will my mother, for the same reason. She might be ruthless, but she loves us."

My head is starting to throb again—the painkillers don't last very long anymore—but I have to persuade them. Because I really do think it's the only way we can succeed. And it will be my way out of here, whether I want a way out or not.

"Plus a blow to the Wilds is a blow to the Corporation—and the Empire. Which she's always up for. And if you think the rebels need an added incentive, you can throw in the jewels. They're always in need of funds."

"Will you tell her Kali's on board?" Max asks.

"Not if she doesn't want me to."

Kali shrugs. "I don't care. I'm not scared of the Rebellion."

"You should be." Still, I respect her for not hiding. At some point, we have to live our lives, and fuck everyone else.

"Not to mention Rain and Merrick," Max says. "The Rebellion is hardly fond of the Sisterhood. Or the Corporation, for that matter. Which includes Gage."

"She won't touch them if I ask her not to." I hope. You never can tell who's going to show up—my mother or the Butcher of Narreth. But now doesn't exactly seem like the time to bring that up. "I'll tell her that you all saved my life. That will mean something to her."

"Do you have a way to contact her?" Ian asks.

"I do." We've always had a private line of communication for emergencies. Considering both her children are missing, I'm sure she hasn't changed that.

Ian looks around the room. "What does everyone think? Do we risk it?"

"Do we have a choice?" Max answers. "Beckett's right. We're not exactly swimming in options."

"You really think we can trust these people?" Merrick asks. He turns to me. "You know her better than anyone—will she honor an agreement?"

"Yes. It's getting the agreement that might be hard. But once she's committed, she won't betray you. She has her own code of honor that she won't break."

"Look," Ian says to Merrick, "there's no reason for you and Rain to come with us. We can drop you off somewhere close to one of the Sisterhood's headquarters, and you can go home."

I hold my breath as Merrick and Rain exchange a glance. I don't want her to go. I'm not ready yet. I know I said I have to go, but not yet. Please.

She gives a small shake of her head—I think she feels the same way—and I expect him to argue. But he doesn't. It's one more thing in a long line that makes me believe something else is going on with that man. I just don't know what.

"We'll stay," he finally says.

"Good." Ian turns to Gage. "What about you?"

"I say go for it. But maybe don't give her *all* the jewels."

Big shock, Gage. I've never seen anyone more obsessed with money in my life.

Ian must feel the same way, because he snorts but doesn't comment. Finally, he looks at Kali. "How about you, Princess? You think we should join forces with the rebels?"

She shrugs. "I trust Beckett. If she says that it will work, then I believe her."

That actually is a shocker—one that makes me feel a little strange. Sure, she said she trusted me before she left the last time, but that was one-on-one. Now, in front of everyone… I want to say something soppy like *I won't let you down* or—

I cut off the thought as a stab of pain pierces my skull. This needs to be sooner rather than later. "So, are we doing this?" I ask.

"Hell, why not," Ian says, throwing up his hands. "It can't be worse than any of the other decisions we've made lately. Go ahead. Call Mommy."

I get up. I should feel happier about this. It will get me what I need.

I glance at Rain, and she gives me a smile.

If not what I want.

CHAPTER 85

Kali

I can't sleep. I've been back on board the *Starlight* for three days, and I haven't been able to sleep at all. Every time I close my eyes, all I can see is Arik collapsing right in front of me—alive one moment and dead the next. And Lara's face as she falls off the parapet, her mouth wide open as she screams.

They died for me. Because of me. If I'd stayed put and just did what I was told, they would be alive. And millions of other people would be dead.

If this is what it means to be a princess, I'm ready to give the job back. Right now, I'd rather be anything but.

"Hey," Ian says as he walks into the galley, where I'm making yet another cup of tea. The crew grabbed some on a supply trip on their way to save me, and I couldn't be gladder for it. My churning stomach makes it impossible for me to keep anything else down right now, so I've been carrying a cup around with me wherever I go.

"Want one?" I ask, holding up my mug.

"Coffee?" he asks hopefully.

"Tea."

"Pass, thanks." He wrinkles his nose and pours himself a water instead. "You got a few minutes to talk?"

Considering we're just sitting around waiting to get to the Wilds—and waiting for Beckett's mother to call back—it seems like a ridiculous question. It's not like there are so many other things to be doing right now. But all I say is, "Sure," even though my stomach leaps at the thought.

We haven't been alone together since I first got back on the *Starlight* and we talked about why I left. I thought I'd convinced him that I didn't leave because of Milla and Max, but now I'm not so sure. Especially since he hasn't tried to kiss me even once.

I finish steeping my tea and sit down at the table. I expect Ian to sit across from me, but instead he settles into the chair next to mine. "You okay?" he asks.

"Fine," I tell him. As long as I don't close my eyes. "Why?"

"Because you've been through a lot?"

I shrug. "We've all been through a lot. You're fine, aren't you?"

"Not even close." He laughs.

I roll my eyes and take a sip of tea. "You know what I mean."

He doesn't answer right away, and I don't have anything to say, so we sit in silence for a little while. Eventually, though, Ian asks, "So you're solid? Even with everything that happened with your friend and your bodyguard?"

I jerk in surprise. Hearing it come out of his mouth makes it real in a way I'm not ready to hear. "How did you know about that? I thought you hadn't arrived yet."

Ian's face is soft, and it's more than I can bear. "We were close enough that the *Starlight* gave us a view of what was happening on the roof. I'm sorry. I would've done more if I could, but we were too far away and it happened too fast."

I look away. There's no point wishing he arrived sooner. It's done. "Did Max put you up to this?" He's been checking on me regularly, waiting for me to break down, I think. But even crying seems like too much effort right now.

"He didn't. But I know he's worried, too. We all are."

I change the subject. "Why did you come back for me?" I ask, because I've been wondering ever since my first night back on the *Starlight*.

"Did you not want us to?" he asks, watching me closely. I don't know if it's because he has something to hide or if he's still feeling insecure about the way I left.

"Of course I did. I'd be dead or imprisoned now, if you hadn't." I don't flinch from saying the words. I've spent the last few days trying to come to grips with who my mother really is. "But that still doesn't tell me what made you decide to come find me."

"That's actually one of the things I wanted to discuss with you. I thought maybe it'd be better coming from Rain, but she thinks I should be the one to talk to you."

I don't like the sound of that. What could he possibly have to tell me that is so bad they had to debate who was going to break the news to me? "Is my mother dead?" It's the only thing I can think of.

"What? No!" He sounds so genuinely shocked that I believe him.

"So what do you want to talk about, then?" I ask, getting a little annoyed with the prevaricating. "Just spit it out."

"It's not a spit-it-out kind of thing." He blows out a long breath. "You know how Rain is the High Priestess of the Sisterhood of the Light?"

I give him a what-the-fuck look. "Obviously, I do."

"Well, something came out after you left."

"Came out?" My stomach starts to jump, though I don't know why. Maybe because he's so hesitant to talk about this, and Ian is never hesitant. "What do you mean?"

"It turns out that you and Merrick are related. Your fathers were brothers."

Shock holds me immobile for several seconds. "That's not possible," I tell him.

"Why not? I thought your father was from Serati." He's watching me closely now, and that just freaks me out more.

"He was. But he didn't have any family; he never talked about them—"

"Because he cut himself off from them when he married your mother. I get the impression they didn't approve."

I want to argue with that, but after what I just went through at her hands, it's not that hard to believe. "And Merrick told you this?"

"He told us a lot of things. Including the fact that your fathers made up not long before your dad died. And that your father told his father something that…might be difficult for you to hear."

The nerves twisting in my stomach turn to something darker, uglier. Fear crawls up my throat, and there's a part of me that wants to scream at him to stop. Not to tell me any more. That I can't take it—not with everything else I'm trying to deal with right now.

But it's only been a few days since I promised myself that I would never choose ignorance again, so I don't say any of the things running through my head. Instead, I whisper, "Just tell me. Whatever it is, just get it over with fast."

"Your father told Merrick's father that when you were born, all the signs pointed to you being the high priestess. But your mother refused to give her daughter—the heir to the Empire—to the Sisterhood. So she burned off your birthmark and paid another couple—and the Sisterhood—to pretend that their child was the high priestess instead."

His words are so unexpected that for a second I don't even comprehend them. But when I do, I start to laugh. Because: "There's no way I'm a high priestess. That's absurd, Ian."

"Not just a high priestess, Kali. *The* high priestess."

"That's just completely ridiculous. Rain is a much better person than I am. Plus, she has faith, and I don't. There's no way I'm *the* high priestess." I start to laugh again, but then something else occurs to me—something that gives me pause. "What does this have to do with you coming to find me?"

The watchful look in his eyes only makes my heart pound faster.

"Does being the high priestess have something to do with activating the heptosphere?"

He nods. "It's not just about the high priestess, Kali. Activating the heptosphere means you have alien DNA. You're what the Sisterhood calls the Star Bringer."

"So you came after me because you decided I was this…Star Bringer? And if I touched the heptosphere—" I break off as the truth slams into me, powerful and undeniable. My stomach burns, and my lungs tighten so much that it's hard to draw a breath.

I've always felt an undeniable connection to this ship. It's given me comfort in a way I've never been able to explain. Drawn to the heptosphere, too, so strongly sometimes that it almost consumes me.

And...when the *Starlight* disappeared, they said I disappeared, too.

Not Rain. Me.

Ian pulls me into his chest then, his strong arms wrapping around me. And though I know I should pull away, know that things are so strange between us that I shouldn't be taking comfort from him right now, I can't help it. He feels so good, so big and strong and solid, that it's impossible to pull away from him. Instead, I curl into him, my hands clutching at his shirt as I bury my face in his chest and breathe in the warm coffee-and-gerjgin scent of him.

The tears I haven't been able to shed since Lara and Arik died burn in the back of my eyes, mixing with the grief over my father and the anger over my mother, until I can't breathe. Can't think. Until all I can do is sob, my entire body shaking against his as I cry and cry and cry.

He holds me the whole time, his hands stroking down my hair, rubbing my back, holding me tightly against him. And I know things are messed up between us, but right now, he feels like the only solid thing in my life. The only thing that's not shifting in a world that's suddenly gone completely topsy-turvy on me.

Eventually, I cry myself out, and Ian's here for that, too. He sweeps me into his arms and carries me down the hall to his cabin. Gage and Max are still in the bridge, so it's just the two of us as he pulls back the sheets on his bed and lays me gently beneath them.

I'm exhausted, physically and emotionally, and all I want to do is sleep. But I don't want to be alone. Not yet. Not right now. "Please," I tell him as he starts to back away. "Please don't leave me."

"I'm not going anywhere, Princess," he whispers. And then he kicks off his boots and crawls into bed beside me, wrapping me back up in his arms. "Sleep. I'll be here when you wake up."

I nod, burrowing against him as he turns off the light. And only then, when we're in the dark, do I finally work up the nerve to say what I've been thinking ever since he told me about what my mother did to Rain and me.

"She killed my father, didn't she?" I whisper, the words burning away all the sorrow inside of me and filling my heart with rage. "She couldn't afford for what she did to get out, so when he told Merrick's father, she had him assassinated."

Ian shifts in the darkness. "I don't know about that," he says. But I can hear in his voice that he thinks it's possible, too.

"I do," I tell him as the rage coalesces deep inside me into a powerful need for justice. "She killed him to keep her secret and then used it as an excuse to capture and torture hundreds of rebels. People like Beckett and her brother."

"Maybe." He nods.

"There's no maybe about it," I tell him as the need to sleep finally creeps through me. "And I'm going to find a way to prove it."

CHAPTER 86

Beckett

Everyone else is asleep, and once again I'm sitting on the bridge alone. Rain came in earlier, tried to convince me to come to bed. And I wanted to—I really wanted to. The days that I have left to hold her and kiss her and press her sweet, soft body against mine are running out.

But I put in the call to my mother's emergency number nearly twenty-four hours ago. Which means I should be hearing back very soon. We've always had a twenty-four-hour rule about returning calls on that channel, and I have to believe that hasn't changed.

Everything else certainly has.

A sharp pain rips through my skull, and for a second it takes me over so completely that I can't do anything but endure it. Even breathing is impossible. It goes on longer than the last one, which was longer than the one before it. Just another sign that something is wrong. Just another sign that my time is running out.

I stare at the comms link, willing it to ring. I have to get this done. I have to make sure Rain and the others are safe before I go. The thought of leaving when they're still in danger makes the pain, and everything else, so much worse.

I reach below my chair and pull out the painkillers. I'm almost out, and to be honest, I'm not sure why I take them anymore. They barely touch the agony. Hope springs eternal, I suppose, which seems ridiculous—I thought I lost my ability to hope right around the time I lost my father.

I swallow a couple of the painkillers because taking them is better than not taking them, then start fiddling with the *Starlight*'s commands. Every day, I learn something new about this ship, something that blows my hair back and makes me wonder what the hell kind of technology the Ancients had access to. I've flown a lot of ships in my life, and none of them—*none* of them—come close to doing what the *Starlight* can do.

She's the strangest and most kick-ass ship I've ever seen. I think I'm going to miss her almost as much as I'm going to miss Rain.

I yawn as I glance at the clock on the *Starlight*'s dash. Seventeen more minutes until the twenty-four hours have come and gone. Seventeen more minutes until I can crawl into bed with Rain and pretend, for just a little while longer, that everything is okay.

At eight minutes to go—just when I've convinced myself that she isn't going to call—the comms link starts to ring. It could be any number of people, but I know even before I pick it up that it's my mom.

Sure enough, the moment I hit accept, her familiar face fills the screen. She looks older than she did the last time I saw her. But a lot has happened in the last ten months, so I guess that's to be expected.

"Beckett!" Her yellow eyes light up when she realizes who she's speaking with. "You're alive! I thought—"

Her voice breaks. She clears her throat, tries again. "All the reports I could glean together said that you disappeared from the prison compound months ago and that the Empire was reporting you as deceased."

"Fuck the Empire," I answer, and she laughs merrily. No one can say I don't know my audience.

"Tell me where you are, baby, and I'll send someone to get you." Now that her happiness at finding I'm still alive has leveled out, she looks me over with critical eyes. "What did they do to you?"

"Does it matter?" I ask. "I'm free now."

For a second, I think she's going to push on my health. While a part of me wants somebody to, that's not what I need to talk about right now. "I have a lead, Mom. To Jarved."

"Your brother is dead." Her tone is final, with absolutely no room for argument. And I get it. For a long time I couldn't bring myself to even think about Jarved, either. I missed him so much.

I still miss him that much, but I've gone over and over the Milla thing in my head. Gone over and over the fact that I almost ended up in the exact same place. No matter how hard I try to resist imagining that my brother might be alive, the thought has taken root. And nothing will make me let it go except knowing for sure.

I fill my mother in on what happened to me—the capture, the jailing, the experiments on the *Caelestis*. And then I tell her all the reasons I think Jarved is still alive.

When I'm done, her cheeks are drained of color and her eyes have lost their spark of joy. In its place is a fury I'm all too familiar with. Like mother, like daughter, after all.

"This is what they did to you?" she asks. "Experiments? Torture? To what end?"

"I don't know," I answer. "I have holes in my memory—I don't remember a lot of it. Just…"

"Just what?" she asks in a voice as cold as Glacea's moons.

"The pain." It feels good to admit it to someone. And while a part of me worries I'm weak for saying it, I figure if I can't tell my mother, who can I tell? Even if she is known as a butcher.

"Tell me where you are," she urges again. "And I'll come for you myself."

"That's actually why I was calling. I have a proposition for you."

"For me?" she repeats, sounding wary.

"For the Rebellion." I fill her in on the details—the Wilds, the *Reformer*, the raiders and human traffickers. And some other stuff, too—the heptosphere, the *Starlight*. Maybe more than I should, but it feels nice to talk to my mom. To see her nod. I finish with, "The people I'm with have money. We can pay for your help."

"You're talking about a chance to strike back at the bastards who tortured my daughter and more than likely murdered my son. I'd do it for free." My brows go up—my mother doesn't do anything for free.

Before I can even ask her about it, she gives me a rueful smile. "I'm glad I don't have to, mind you, but I would."

Now that sounds much more like my mother.

"We're going to need weapons. And someone to cause a diversion so we can sneak in and find Milla and Jarved."

"What kind of weapons are you thinking about?" she asks, all business now.

I pull up the list Merrick, Ian, and I put together this morning and rattle off what we need.

She whistles. "That's a lot of firepower, baby girl."

"Our information tells us there are a lot of guards. And a lot of security."

She nods her understanding. "Are you sure you want to get yourself involved in this? It seems like there's a lot of potential to get captured again—"

"He's my brother," I tell her. "I have to check."

Her smile is sad but proud. "You wouldn't be my daughter if you didn't." She glances down at the list she typed on her own console. "It's going to take me a few days to get this together."

"That's okay. We're several days away from Glacea."

"How do you know I'm still there?" she asks. "I could be anywhere."

"You could," I agree. "But I recognize the wall behind you. It's from the rebel base on Glacea."

"You never did miss a trick," she answers with a smile that doesn't quite reach her sad eyes. "I'll see you soon, my darling."

"I'll see you soon, Mom."

"Before you go," she says. "Who are these people you're with? Just so I know what to expect."

This is where it gets tricky. Do I tell her everything?

In the end, I settle for the truth that isn't actually the whole truth. "Just some people from when the *Caelestis* exploded," I say vaguely. "They were escaping the wreck and let me come along with them."

"The *Caelestis*?" Her eyes sharpen, lose the softness reserved for me and my brother, and become the cold, dead eyes of a woman who looks like she actually deserves the nickname Butcher of Narreth.

"The crown princess went missing from the space station," she mentions in a pondering tone. "Along with the high priestess from Serati."

"Seems like you know a lot about it," I say.

"It's my job to know about it." She gives me a hard look through the screen. "Are you traveling with Princess Kalinda?"

And now I'm cornered. "I'm not sure she's a princess anymore," I hedge. "She and the Empress had a huge blowout."

"Their types always do." My mother waves a careless hand. "But when it comes down to it, they're always loyal to each other. The Empire above all else—even human decency. We've seen it a million times."

Normally, she's right. But I still don't think Kali will go back. I saw her face on that roof, when she was fleeing from her mother's soldiers. And I've seen her since, when she's trying not to think about all the terrible, terrible things her mother has done. But I'm not naive enough to say something as incendiary as *Kali's different, Mom*. Partly because I'm still getting used to the idea that she is and partly because my mother won't care. She's very clear about what her mission statement is, and *Death to the Empire* is a big start.

Which is why I'm not even surprised when she gives me a speculative look. She says, "Kill the princess, and you can tell your friends that I'll give them the weapons—and the aerial support—for free. Choose to keep her alive, and the deal will cost them. Probably more than they have to give."

Of that, I have no doubt. My mother has a way of making people wish they'd never been born—including me, on occasion. It's not the way I like to live, but I get that sometimes it's a necessity.

"I'll see you soon, baby," my mother says as she signs off. "And don't worry. We'll figure out how to get the princess, and we'll see if your brother's alive. No matter what it takes."

The screen goes dark, and I lay my head down on the dash in front of me and try not to cry. Normally, it's not that hard, but right now, finally beating the tears back feels like a miracle.

CHAPTER 87

Rain

I wake up to find the bed next to me empty. Again. A quick glance at the clock above the door tells me it's the middle of the night. Beckett promised she would come to bed tonight, just like she promised she would come to bed every one of the last few nights. It hasn't happened yet.

Most nights I just lay here and wait for her, heart breaking a little bit more with each hour that goes by. But tonight I don't have it in me to just wait around for a woman who's never going to come. Maybe that's because I don't have any more heart left to break.

Merrick's announcement about the Sisterhood certainly broke a big chunk of it, and Beckett has been taking care of the rest every night for the last week. What's the point of having a girlfriend you love if that girlfriend won't even talk to you? Or worse, if she lies straight to your face and tells you she's fine when it's obvious that she's barely holding on?

When it's almost as obvious that *you're* barely holding on.

Every day since Merrick's life-shattering announcement—thanks for that, by the way—I spend hours wondering what to do. Wondering who I am. Wondering how either of us are ever supposed to go back to our lives on Serati.

And the answer is, I'm not. How can I when everything about my life, from infancy, has been a carefully cultivated lie? I was trapped in a monastery and told I could do nothing, be nothing, except the object of salvation for millions of people. Told that I needed to try harder, be better, live up to what it means to be a high priestess.

And it turns out I never had a chance.

No matter how hard I tried, no matter what I did, the task in front of me was always an impossible one. I couldn't be a good high priestess, because I was never meant to be a high priestess at all.

I've spent a lot of hours over the last few days thinking about this—and thinking about the fact that a lot of people had to be in on this lie for it to work.

Kali's parents.

My parents—whoever they are.

The Sisterhood elders.

The sisters who cared for me as a baby and beyond. Maybe most of them didn't know, but surely there was some gossip, some speculation.

They all knew about the lie being perpetuated, and they didn't care. They just kept telling it, until it got bigger and bigger and harder and harder to control. Until it stole my life, Merrick's life, Kali's life—maybe even Kali's father's life.

Because I've been thinking about that, too. And I realized that an organization that would do all this—that would lie and betray and steal—wouldn't draw the line at murder. To keep their secret, they would do whatever it took. They would have to, because if the secret got out, they would lose everything.

No wonder Merrick was having such a crisis of faith.

If they can just fake things, if they can just substitute a fake high priestess for the real one, how can anything about the Sisterhood be real? In which case, we're just as screwed as everyone else when it comes to the Dying Sun. Even though no one on Serati wants to admit it.

If the Sisterhood isn't real, maybe the Light itself isn't real.

Unable to lay in the dark for one more second—not when these thoughts are roiling around in my head from all directions—I throw back my covers and pull on my blue-and-pink jumpsuit, then prepare to spend the night roaming the ship.

But tonight, my feet don't roam. Instead, they carry me to the bridge—to Beckett.

I want a hug from her. More, I want her to wrap her arms around me and tell me everything is going to be all right—with my life, with her life, with our lives together. I don't believe it's true, but it would be nice to hear it just this once.

Except, once I get to the bridge, it's to find that Beckett isn't draped over her pilot's chair, contemplating the universe outside of the *Starlight*, like she usually is at this hour. Instead, she's sitting at the comms unit, her head in her hands and her entire body shaking.

My own discontent abandons me the second I lay eyes on her. Because it's obvious, especially to someone who's spent as much time studying her as I have, that something is very, very wrong.

I don't call her name as I race across the distance between us—I think it's better if she has no time to compose herself. No time to pretend that I'm seeing things and that she's just fine. Not because she wants to lie, I don't think, but because she's never had anyone to worry about her before and she doesn't know what to do about it.

"Beckett." I put a soft hand on her shoulder, and she jumps up so fast that I'm a little surprised she didn't knock me over—or land on her butt.

"How long have you been there?" she asks.

I search her face, wondering what has her in such a state. And I'm absolutely astonished to realize she has tears trembling on her eyelashes. In all the days I've known Beckett—and in all the situations—I've never seen her cry before.

"What's wrong?" I ask, my own problems forgotten.

She shakes her head, and I know what she's going to say even before she says it. "Nothing."

"It doesn't look like nothing," I say. And while part of me wants to yell at her until she's honest with me, I've never yelled at anyone in my life. I don't have a clue how to even go about doing it.

"I'm fine," she says, shrugging off my concern yet again. "You should go back to bed."

I try not to let it hurt me, this incessant need she has to push me away. But it's getting a little harder with every day that passes.

Still, I have to try. I can't just leave her like this, suffering. It's not in my nature. More, it's not who I want to be. Not because of the high-priestess thing, but because of me. Rain. The last thing I ever want to do is deliberately turn my back on someone who's hurting.

Especially not Beckett.

So I put my arm around her waist, bolstered by the fact that she only fights me a little as I guide her away from the comms link and out the bridge door.

I'd like to take her to our bedroom—she has a much harder time lying to me the fewer clothes I'm wearing—but Kali is sleeping there at the moment. So I take her to our storage room, and after getting her situated on the cot we put up inside there, I start to gently, gently massage her head with my fingertips.

"What are you doing?" she asks hoarsely.

"Loving you," I answer as honestly as I can. "The only way you'll let me."

"Rain—"

"Hush," I tell her, deepening the massage just a little. I'm careful to avoid the scars on her head—I know them as well as I know my own body these days—but I dig a little deeper into the muscles at the top of her head, over her temples, and along the back of her neck on either side of the scar along her spine.

Beckett holds herself rigid for most of it, but as I hit the muscles at the base of her skull, her whole body arches off the cot. "Did I hurt you?" I gasp, immediately lightening up on the pressure.

She shakes her head, and her voice is hoarse when she says, "Please. Do that again."

I can no more turn that down than I could cut off my own hand. So I carefully dig deeper, running my fingers in steady, deliberate circles over the back of her head and up the sides.

By the time I get to the crown of her head, her entire body seems to have collapsed in on itself, but in a good way. So I keep going until she finally asks me to stop.

"Thank you," she whispers, wrapping an arm around my waist and pulling me down until I'm sitting in her lap.

"You don't have to thank me for that," I whisper. "I hate that you're in pain. And I hate even more that you so rarely let me help you with it."

"I don't want—" She breaks off.

She tries to look away, but I slide a finger under her chin and gently turn her face toward mine so that I can search those gorgeous eyes of hers. Tonight, they look like molten gold—hot, endless, dangerous—and I have to fight from falling into them.

Falling into her.

"What don't you want?" I ask in a tone that tells her I'm not going to move on from this until she talks to me, no matter how much she wishes I would.

"I don't want you to see me as less," she finally answers.

I nearly laugh out loud. "Less?" I ask incredulously. "Beckett, how can you not see that you're everything? That there's nothing about you that's anything but incredible?"

She shakes her head, and her glorious black curls bounce over her forehead and her shoulders. "I'm messed up, Rain. You know I'm messed up."

"We're all messed up," I shoot back at her. "Haven't you figured that out yet?"

"You're not." Her arms are around my waist now, holding me in place, and her fingers are tracing little patterns on my back that send shivers up my spine—even through the jumpsuit.

This time, I do laugh, because that's the most absurd thing I've ever heard. "I'm the most messed up of everyone here!" I tell her.

"That's not true," she answers.

"Isn't it? My entire life has been a lie, from the very beginning. I have no idea who I am or where I come from. More, I have no idea where I'm going. At least you know all of those things."

"Yeah, but I have no idea where I've been. And—" She gestures to her head.

"The headaches are getting worse?" I ask.

She shrugs, which from Beckett is basically a firm yes.

I don't like the sound of that. I was hoping they'd get a little better the longer she was away from that evil facility. "What can I do to help?" I ask.

"That's just it. I don't want your help. Not with this—not with anything."

Her words hit like the knives Ian carries with him at all times, the sharp little points pricking my skin before digging themselves deeper and making me bleed.

"What *do* you want?" I ask, then hold my breath, because for the first time I'm truly afraid of the answer. For the first time, I'm afraid of her. She won't physically hurt me; I know that. But emotionally? She's already gutting me, and she hasn't even left me yet.

But looking at her now, I know she will. No matter how tightly she holds me—or how closely—I can see the truth in the depths of her eyes. I've already lost her to the demons she has inside. Everything else is just timing.

CHAPTER 88

Ian

Thanks to some truly unreal speed from the *Starlight*—like, speeds spaceships shouldn't be able to achieve, especially dragging a giant heptosphere; whatever the Ancients were up to, they were clearly doing it fucking fast—we're about to land back on Glacea, which puts me in a foul mood. I hate this fucking place, and not just because Kali nearly died here. Though, if I'm honest, that's definitely one of the lowlights.

"You ready for this?" Beckett asks me as she straps on the knife she asked to borrow from me.

"I'm pretty sure I should be asking you that question," I answer. "You *are* the one who feels the need to arm herself before a meeting with her mother."

Her grin is a little bit wild and more than a little bit reckless. Looking at her now, she reminds me of the Beckett from the beginning of our time on the *Starlight*, which doesn't concern me at all.

She just shrugs. "It's for show. My mother would never respect anyone who didn't come armed to a meeting. If she saw me without a weapon, she'd be convinced I was going soft. That's not good for anyone right now—least of all me."

I can't argue with that. Not when every experience I've ever had in the Nine Planets has proven to me that weakness gets you killed. And softness gets you killed faster. The system is a fucked-up place, and there are a lot of people only too willing to take advantage of that fact.

"So, where exactly are we going?" I ask as Beckett slides into the pilot's seat and sets the *Starlight* down just outside the limits of a little town called Sorcha that I've never heard of. Apparently, the rebels have a base here and Beckett has arranged for us to meet her mom and exchange jewels for weapons.

"You'll see," she answers. Max and I exchange a look. It's one thing to put our lives in the hands of rebels—that's a calculated risk. One we need to take if we have any chance at all of getting Milla back.

But it's another thing to put our lives in Beckett's hands when her eyes are shining with an odd kind of brightness that looks a lot like chaos—and maybe something even worse. I glance at Rain, hoping maybe she knows what's up with her girlfriend, but she just looks away, which is pretty much the worst thing she could do.

"*Fuck.*"

"*Looks like there's trouble in paradise,*" Max tells me.

"*That's because we're in a nightmare,*" I snap back.

"*You still think this is a good idea?*"

I snort. "*Hell, no. We're walking into a rebel stronghold with the prodigal daughter, who looks like she's on the edge of something really fucking bad, and we've got nothing to protect ourselves with but a couple measly weapons. Add in the fact that if we fuck this up, we lose Milla forever, and no. I definitely don't think it's a good idea. But then, it never was.*"

Ideas born in desperation are rarely good ones, even if everyone involved has their shit together. When people don't—I look from Rain to Beckett and back again—bad ideas tend to become really fucking bad ideas.

Lucky, lucky us.

"You ready?" Kali asks.

Not even close. But I grin. Never let 'em see how fucked you are. That's my motto. "I was born ready, Princess."

She rolls her eyes, but she's grinning when she says, "I swear, some days you're nothing but a walking cliché."

"And here I thought I was a lot of things." To prove it to her, I yank her against me and drop a kiss down on her perfect pink lips. I mean for it to just be a quick peck, but when she opens to me, I can't resist going for it.

"Seriously?" Beckett says, sounding bored. "Do I have to remind you that the Butcher of Narreth hates it when people are late?"

"You said that was an exaggeration," I answer when I finally let Kali go. Damn, I like the way she tastes. I like even more the way she feels against my body, but that's for later. When the conquering heroes return.

"Maybe I was exaggerating when I said it was an exaggeration," Beckett says as she shrugs into one of the ponchos we made from extra blankets on board the ship.

"Are you *trying* to mess with their heads?" Gage asks as he and Kali walk us to the outer door.

"Better me than my mother," she answers as she presses the button to lower the *Starlight*'s ramp.

Fuck. This day just keeps getting better and better.

I head down the ramp. "Let's get this over with."

"Stay safe!" Kali calls after us.

It's the first time anyone's ever said that to me, and it feels good. I can't help grinning as I set foot on Glacea—something I never thought would happen. But knowing Kali's waiting for me back on the ship is kind of nice, even if we still have some shit left to work out.

"*A lot of shit,*" Max comments.

I snort. "*Why do you have to rain on my parade?*"

"*Oh, it's a parade now, is it?*"

"*Better than the shitshow we're used to.*"

"*Isn't that the truth?*" He claps me on the back as our boots hit the ice and snow that perpetually line the streets of this frozen shithole.

It's early morning, so it's especially cold, the weak sun illuminating the ice and snow around us but doing nothing to actually warm us up. I pull my jacket more tightly around me as we set off through the town, Beckett in the lead, since she knows where we're going.

I've tried to get the location out of her, just so I could scout it a little from the *Starlight* and make sure it's safe. But once a rebel, always a rebel, and there's no way she was giving the exact coordinates of their stronghold to me.

Which makes sense, I guess. But I still hate going into this thing not knowing. Beckett may trust her mother, but that doesn't mean I do. There are a lot of stories out there about Marlina Orsgood, and none of them are good.

But time is running out, and right now, this is the best option we've got. Fuck, even if we do get the rebels to help, there's no guarantee we'll actually succeed at this. We could all die in the attack, though I am working on a plan that should at least keep Kali and Rain safe. If it all looks like it's going to shit, they'll take the *Starlight* and evacuate as fast as they can. Gage as well, probably. He's a lot of things, but he's definitely not a fighter. The guy is basically a walking head injury, for fuck's sake.

Obviously, I haven't actually broached this with any of them yet—something tells me Kali will be particularly ornery about it. Doesn't mean I'll care, but I think I'll leave the conversation until I absolutely have to.

Beckett slips a little on the ice in front of us, and I speed up so I can grab her arm and keep her from falling on her ass. She of course repays the favor by snarling at me and shrugging me off. But not before I get a good look at her face.

She's pale, and despite the cold, there's a sheen of sweat on her forehead. I make a mental note to stock up on the painkillers she's been popping like candy lately, but the truth is, I don't think they'll fix whatever this is.

"You're sure this is the right thing to do?" I ask for maybe the hundredth time in the last few days. But Milla's life depends on us not fucking up, so we have to get it right.

Beckett blinks at me like my words are taking a second to register. When they finally do, she says, "No. Actually, I think we should all get back on the *Starlight* and go visit Kali's mother instead. See if she'll help us."

I do hate sarcasm. In anyone else.

Max chuckles, and I send him a fuck-off look, which only makes him laugh harder.

I don't know what he's got to be so happy about. Except for the fact that Beckett has given us a real chance.

I've always suspected saving Milla is a suicide mission, but now, I think we may actually have a possibility of succeeding. But only if we can convince the rebels to help us.

We're walking through the town now, and though it's still closed up—it's early yet—the place actually seems quite prosperous, especially compared to the other side of the planet, where everything is shit.

The houses are brick and solid-looking. There are a lot of stores that seem to carry pretty impressive goods. And there are even stores selling some decent-looking food.

Definitely one of the richer towns in the system.

Makes me wonder if that's a rebel thing or if there's something else going on here that I don't know about. It doesn't matter, I guess, but I don't like mysteries. And I especially don't like mysteries that involved unexplained money, because it usually means there's more to worry about than I thought.

For most of the Senestris System, the Sisterhood of the Light isn't the organized religion. Greed is, and people will do anything for a buck.

I make a mental note to dig a little deeper into Sorcha when we make it back to the *Starlight*.

If we make it back.

The wind kicks up again—there's nothing money can do about the fact that Glacea is a meteorological shithole—and I hunch against the chill as we traverse several more streets, winding our way deeper and deeper into the center of the town.

I don't like how far away we are from the edge of town and the *Starlight*. But I'm not calling the shots here; Beckett is.

She finally stops in front of a tavern called the Dancing Varnook.

"We're here," she announces, and for the first time, she looks a little nervous.

"You good?" I ask. Maybe her paleness has more to do with

meeting her mother than her actual sickness.

"Worry about yourself," she snarls before pushing through the heavy double doors. Max and I exchange a look—here goes nothing— then follow her inside. It's dark after the sunlight, and I take a moment to let my eyes adjust.

The room is bigger than I expected, with numerous tables—all empty at the moment—and fires already built in the fireplaces at both ends. I gravitate toward one of them, but Beckett coughs and nods toward a door at the side of the bar.

A tall man with a black beard stands in front of it, a gun on either hip and a scowl on his face. Beckett heads over, with Max and me right behind her.

"*It will work,*" he tells me.

"*It had better.*"

The man, who's clearly Permunian like most of the rebels, doesn't speak. He looks us over, his face expressionless, before opening the door and nodding at us to enter.

The room beyond is much smaller, with a second door opposite and no windows. But there is a fire, and I can feel the warmth sinking into my bones. I really, really, really hate this fucking planet.

There's another problem, though. There's no one here but us. Maybe Beckett's mother isn't coming after all. Maybe she's decided she doesn't trust us.

"*She'll come.*"

Max is being annoyingly optimistic. "*And you're being a miserable bastard.*"

I lift a brow. "*You mean a realist?*"

At that moment, the door at the back of the room opens and a man enters. This one isn't Permunian. At a guess, he's from Serati. He's tall and broad and just big in every direction. His skin is swirled, his eyes are a dark blue, and he has a head of bushy black hair that looks an awful lot like Max's when he doesn't get near a barber for a while.

Beside me, Beckett makes a little shocked sound. My hand goes automatically to my own weapon, but then she's running forward.

The giant opens his arms, and she leaps right into them. Then he swings her into the air with a belly laugh that fills the room.

"*Well, that's something you don't see every day,*" I tell Max.

"*A giant?*"

"*Beckett looking happy.*"

He shrugs in a live-and-let-live way.

Finally, the man puts her down and pats her cheek—and she doesn't even try to bite his hand off. Surreal.

"It's so good to see you again, Vix!" Beckett says.

Then he turns to Max and me with a frown. "Weapons," he growls.

"I'm good, thank you." I pat the laser pistol at my side. I know exactly what he means, but I don't like handing her over to anyone.

"Weapons," he says again.

"And here I was hoping for a hug."

His eyes narrow in warning.

"I trust him, Ian. Give him the gun," Beckett says. Then she grins. "I promise I'll protect you."

"Shit," I mutter. But I give in to the inevitable and unstrap the holster from my waist. As I hand it over, I see Max is doing the same.

"And the rest," the big guy orders.

I scowl but pull the knife from under my jacket and slam it on the table. He raises an eyebrow—what is this guy, a mind reader? I bend down and pull the blade from my left boot and, without waiting for another request, the last one from the small of my back. I feel naked.

"Now, that wasn't so hard, was it?" he says.

"Fucking near impossible," I reply.

He goes back to the door and taps three times. A few seconds later, it opens, and Beckett's mom walks in. I know it's her because there's a really strong family resemblance. So strong that they look more like sisters than mother and daughter—though her mom definitely looks healthier than Beckett does. She's medium height, with olive skin, curly black hair pulled into a ponytail, and those distinctive yellow eyes you only ever see from Permunians. She's wearing khaki pants tucked into long boots and a matching shirt covered by a long leather duster. It's open, and I can see the laser pistol strapped to her waist and the knife at her thigh.

I'm betting she's also got even more hidden weapons on her person than I usually do.

Overall, she's beautiful, but she also looks as tough as shit—it's easy to see where Beckett gets it. I can't read anything in her eyes, which I don't like. But her expression softens a little bit as she looks at Beckett.

"My daughter." She presses a hand to Beckett's cheek. "I thought you were dead."

Beckett grins. "Pretty sure I was at one point or another."

"I told you that fucking job was too dangerous. But did you listen?"

"No, Mom."

"Calculated risk, always. That's what I taught you. You won't forget next time, will you?"

Beckett shakes her head.

Only then does her mother turn to us. "I'm Marlina Orsgood, and I believe I have you to thank for saving my daughter's life."

I shrug. "While I'd like to take credit, I'm pretty sure she saved herself. You could say she just hitched a ride with us."

"Either way, you have my gratitude."

"That's good to know."

A cagey smile flickers across her face. "Why don't we sit down, and you can tell me just exactly how you'd like me to express that gratitude."

Well, this is going well so far. Maybe too well.

"*Miserable bastard.*" The words echo in my head, but I don't respond. I need to keep my wits about me and concentrate on the matter at hand. This is our best chance of getting Milla out. Plus, there's the fact that if this meeting doesn't go our way, I have a distinct suspicion that we won't get out of this room alive. So, I do what I'm told and sit. Marlina sits across from me with Beckett beside her while Max takes the chair next to me.

The big guy produces a bottle and four glasses, placing them on the table between us before going to stand by the door, arms folded across his chest.

Marlina pours us all a hefty slug of what I'm guessing is blazketty and then raises her glass. "Death to the Empire," she murmurs with a challenge in her voice.

"Freedom for the people," I respond with the second half of the rebel's toast. I've heard it enough on my travels to know when to pull it out. I raise my glass and swallow the shot down in one gulp.

"Okay," Marlina says. "Talk."

I'd expected her to have a catch-up chat with Beckett first, but clearly she's all business.

I hadn't decided how to broach this—I wanted to meet the woman first. But I'm guessing she's the sort of person who doesn't like idle chitchat, so I get straight to the point.

"I need to get someone out of Delta V47. We need weapons to do it, plus Beckett thinks you might be willing to provide a…distraction to help us out."

"Now why would I do that?"

I smile. "Gratitude."

"Much as I love my daughter, I'm not sure I'm that grateful. After all, she did just 'hitch a ride.' And the Corporation keeps the buildings out there heavily guarded. No one enters the Wilds without a really good reason." She takes a sip of her drink. "What else is in it for me?"

"A blow to the Corporation is a blow to the Empire," Max says.

"There is that. And…?"

"You're welcome to anything that we find there."

She thinks for a moment. "No one knows what's in those buildings. It could be nothing."

"Heavily guarded nothing," I remind her.

She doesn't look impressed, so I bring out the last weapon in my arsenal. "My intel tells me that its payroll is six days from now. We could coincide with that. You could snatch it going in."

She's starting to look interested.

"Tell me about the prisoners," she says. "My daughter filled me in a little bit the other night, but I want to hear more."

"Ian and Max's…sister"—Beckett sends us an apologetic look—"was on one of the shipments out here. That's who they're trying to get out. And it occurred to me that maybe…" She swallows. "That maybe Jarved was there before me. We've both seen how he just disappeared from the prison records. And we could never find any evidence of his execution, however many people we bribed."

Her mother has gone completely still. "You say this, but it's impossible. Your brother is dead." She pauses, and we all wait. "Part of me doesn't want to believe it," she admits. "Doesn't want to think that he could have been there. Suffering all these years. I'd killed him off in my heart, and it nearly broke me. But I'm not sure this isn't worse. *Fuck*, we let him down. Gave up on him."

"And we can't do it again," Beckett says, her voice fierce. "What if he is still alive? I know it's a slim chance. But we can't ignore it. At the very least, we might finally discover what happened to him."

Marlina sinks back into her chair. She refills her glass with blazketty and sips it in silence. I'm itching to say something.

"*Don't*," Max says in my head, and I clamp my lips closed. "*Marlina needs to think it through.*"

When the glass is empty, she places it gently on the table. "Tell me what your plan is and how we can help."

I exhale. We're not through this yet, but now that we're this far, I allow myself to think that maybe it will work, that we'll get Milla back and the nightmare will be over.

I spend a few minutes explaining our plan. Beckett's mother listens, interjecting here and there to point out flaws or ask questions.

When I'm finished, Marlina thinks for a few more minutes; then, finally, she gives a curt nod, and I have to hold back my whoop of joy. "Looks like you've got yourself a distraction," she says. I lean across and pour myself another drink, then slump back in my chair. I feel drained. I hadn't realized how tense I was.

"*We're going to get Milla back*," Max says in my head.

"*I know.*"

"There is one more thing to discuss," Marlina says.

I raise a brow. "And that is?"

"Between my daughter and me." She turns to Beckett. "Did you do what I asked?"

All the color drains from Beckett's face, and somehow, I know that we are fucked. Again.

CHAPTER 89

Beckett

I knew that question was coming, and I've been dreading it. Because, no, of course I didn't kill Kali. Maybe I could have weeks ago, when we were first on board together, but now that I know her? Now that we're kind of a team? Now that Rain would never forgive me?

"No, I didn't."

Her mouth tightens. "You had one job. I said I would help you, but you needed to do that one thing for me."

"What thing?" Max looks back and forth between us warily.

I don't answer him. He doesn't need to know.

"I know what I'm doing, Mom," I tell her, even though that's probably the biggest lie I've ever told. I haven't known what I'm doing in a very long time. "You have to trust me."

"I did trust you, and you've disappointed me." She turns to Ian and Max. "The deal's off."

"What the fuck?" Ian leaps to his feet, which has Vix looming threateningly over him. He tends to not like any sudden movements around my mother. "You can't just cancel—"

"I can do whatever I want. You're in my town now." She pushes back from the table.

Ian gives me a look that clearly says, *Fix it.*

I don't know if I can, but I'll try. "Why don't you guys go outside? Let me talk to my mom alone for a few minutes."

Skeptical looks from both of them.

"It's fine," I tell them.

The look my mother gives me—and them—says it's definitely not fine.

But since everything rests on me being able to convince my mother, I don't have much of a choice. And since Ian won't take well to any discussion about murdering Kali, the only way this is going to work is if I get them out of the room.

"Go!" I tell them. "But leave the jewels."

"Jewels?" my mother asks, brows raised. And in no time, she's back in the game. It's what I was hoping for.

Ian looks like he wants to argue, but I give him a just-do-it look. He does, reluctantly, dumping a handful of Kali's necklaces on the table. Not all of them, I notice, but I figure if I was him, I'd hold something back, too. Especially since, in his mind, everything just went to shit for no reason.

After reuniting them with their weapons, Vix shows Ian and Max into the main bar area. And I'm one-on-one with my mother.

"You were alone on that ship with the crown princess, and you didn't kill her?" my mother snarls. "Are you a traitor to the Rebellion or just a coward?"

"Neither. But killing her means nothing, Mom. The Empress has disowned her."

"For now. I told you the other day: royal blood calls to royal blood, Beckett. You'll do well to remember that."

After what went down between Kali and her mother, I seriously doubt that. But maybe I'm wrong—my mother does have more experience with the Ruling Families than I do.

"That's not the only thing, though." I play the last card I've got. "I couldn't kill Kali on the *Starlight*, Mom. Not if I wanted a snowball's chance on Serai of making it back here to you."

"You think some little princess could take you?" She sounds shocked now. "My daughter?"

"Not Kali. Ian. He's in love with her."

My mother's head tilts in surprise. "That big, tough mercenary who was just in here with us is in love with the crown princess?"

"He's completely head over heels for her. If she died with only five other people on the ship, he wouldn't rest until he'd killed whoever was responsible. I wouldn't stand a chance of surviving. Not to mention, we'd lose our best chance to find out if Jarved was ever on Delta V47."

For a long time, my mother doesn't say anything. She studies me like she studied Ian and Max a few minutes ago, as if trying to decide if she can trust me.

"What about when the job is done?" she asks. "When you've gotten onto the asteroid to find your brother? Will you kill the princess then?"

I swallow down the nausea in my stomach. Do my best to ignore the pain that feels like my skull is being split in two. And whisper, "Yes, of course," even though I can't imagine actually doing it.

Again, she studies me. "And you'll come back to us when the job is done? When the princess is dead?"

"Of course," I repeat. I've known it was heading toward this all along, known I was going to have to leave Rain sooner rather than later. But it still makes me ache to hear it out loud, to know just how close we are to the end.

She shifts her attention to the four necklaces on the table in front of us. "These are Kalinda's, I assume?"

"They are."

She holds up one of them—a huge ugly purple pendant surrounded by rondolinite. She studies them closely before holding it up so that the light glints off the jewels. "Definitely real. And definitely part of the Imperial jewels."

She looks back at me. "Go confirm the list of weapons with your friends. I'll have them ready when we meet in the Wilds in six days."

It's better than I expected—almost more than I'd hoped for.

But as I head into the bar, she calls after me, "You will need to keep your end of the bargain. Or there will be consequences."

Ian looks up at her words, his dark eyes meeting mine with a question I have no intention of answering. And a trace of suspicion I have no way to allay.

I turn back to my mother with a nod and a look that tells her I get it. Of course there are consequences. In my world, there are always consequences. And those consequences are usually bad.

Why should this time be any different?

CHAPTER 90

Rain

The Wilds are directly in front of us, and as I watch them through the viewing screens at the front of the *Starlight*, I don't know how I feel about that. Because once we rescue Milla—and maybe Jarved—from the asteroid, there will be nothing left to do. We'll go our separate ways, and I may never see any of these people again.

I may never see Beckett again.

She already said as much to me last week, before we went to see her mother. But hearing it then and knowing just how close it is now are two very different things. Add in the fact that I've decided I'm never going back to the Sisterhood, and I feel completely rudderless.

Ice skates down my nerves, and my stomach churns with terror. So many unknowns. So much pain. This living-out-here-in-the-real-world stuff is a lot harder than it looks. But I wouldn't trade the past few weeks, and everything I've learned—everything I've done—for the safe ignorance of the monastery. Not for anything in the universe.

"Can we talk?" I hear from behind me.

I want to say no. Talking to Beckett right now is the last thing I want to do, but talking or not talking isn't going to change anything, so…I nod.

She takes my hand and leads me from the bridge.

"Do you want something to drink?" she asks as we walk past the galley. "A cup of tea or—"

I grab her then, smushing her cheeks between my hands and pressing my mouth to hers like the fate of the universe depends on this kiss.

And maybe it does. Not the fate of the universe but definitely the fate of my universe.

Beckett stiffens against me, and for a second I think she's going to shove me away. But then she's whirling us around, slamming my back up against the wall, and unzipping my jumpsuit all at the same time.

I yank my mouth from hers. "What are you—" I gasp, trying to tell her that we're not in the storage room or our bedroom. We're in the corridor, where anyone can pass by.

But she doesn't let me speak. Instead, she slams her mouth down on mine again, biting and sucking her way from my upper lip to my lower as harsh sounds of need pour from her chest. Her hand is in my underwear now, her fingers tracing the sudden wetness of my sex before thrusting inside me.

I let out a shocked gasp, but then I forget where we are and just how terrified I am that this might be the last time I ever get to hold her. The last time I ever get to feel her inside me. My deep, dark, beautiful Beckett.

And instead I just drown in sensation.

Heat. Need. Pleasure. They rise up and overwhelm me as completely as Beckett overwhelms me. "Please," I gasp out, my fingers tangling in her curls as my leg wraps around her waist. "Please, please, please."

"I've got you," she whispers, and then her thumb is on my clit, her fingers rubbing against the spot inside me that makes me feel like a shooting star whenever she touches it. "I've got you, my Rain. My sweet, sweet Rain."

The sound of my name on her lips combined with the magic of her fingers on my sex is all I need to go over the edge. I come, gasping out her name, and she slams her mouth down on mine again to swallow the sounds.

"Please," I whimper when she finally pulls her mouth away. Tears are pouring down my face, but I make no attempt to stop them. In my head, I'm begging her not to leave me. Begging her to give us a real chance. Begging her to stay for just a little while longer. But all I can say is, "Please, please, please."

And so she kisses her way down my neck, rubs the fingers of her free hand against my peaked nipple, twists her fingers deep inside of me, and takes me over one more time.

One last time.

By the time she zips me back into my jumpsuit, I've recovered enough to keep the tears from falling. And when she steps away, I know that this is the end. And so I do the only thing I can do—press my lips gently to hers. And though everything inside of me yearns to tell her that I love her, that I'll always love her, I swallow the words back down my impossibly tight throat.

And instead, I whisper, "It's okay."

"Rain—"

"It's okay," I tell her, once again cupping her cheeks in my hand.

"It's okay," I say, pressing one last kiss to her mouth.

"It's okay," I whisper as I turn away and walk back down the hall into a future without her.

CHAPTER 91

Kali

A shiver runs through me as we make landfall on the asteroid for the arranged rendezvous with Beckett's mother. The leader of the Rebellion. It's strange that I'm depending on her to keep my friends and me safe when I've spent so much of my life hating her and everything she stands for.

But that hate was based on a lie, I remind myself. And the future I'm trying to build is going to be based on truth, even the ugly bits of it. And the truth is, I misjudged Beckett, and I've misjudged her mother. I owe them both an apology.

Then again, as Crown Princess of the Senestris System, it seems like I owe a lot of people an apology. Maybe someday, I'll get the chance to fix everything my mother has broken.

If we make it out of the Wilds alive.

If the sun doesn't actually die.

If I find a way bring peace back to Senestris.

But that's a worry for another day—I've got more than enough to freak out about today.

Starting with the fact that the *Starlight* will be lowering the ramp soon and I'll get my first real glimpse of an asteroid. Which is totally not a sentence I ever imagined thinking, let alone living, just a few weeks ago.

Beckett's mom chose this place, apparently, because it's on the edge of the Wilds, has an okay gravity, and is only an hour or so away from Delta V47, where the man Ian killed in Rodos told us the *Reformer* would have taken Milla. Unfortunately, it has no breathable atmosphere—not many of the asteroids do. Except Delta V47, which has apparently been terraformed and is actually bigger than Serati and Kridacus put together.

But Gage found some breathing masks on the ship. We tried them out, and they seem to work—despite being made by, and presumably for, the Ancients. They're big and weird, but as long as they're strapped on tightly, they're functional.

"What are you doing down here?" Beckett asks as she comes up behind me, and I can't help noticing how terrible she looks. I want to ask her what's wrong, but the peace between us is still new and fairly fragile. Pushing at her seems like a good way to fracture it.

"I just wanted a look at the asteroid that doesn't come through a screen." I hold up my breathing mask to show her that I'm prepared.

But she doesn't look impressed. "Yeah, well, you need to stay out of sight. Far out of sight. These are rebels we're dealing with, and reformed princess or not, you aren't exactly everyone's favorite."

I guess I never thought of it like that, but I should have. The last thing I want to do is jeopardize the deal Ian, Beckett, and Max worked so hard to strike.

I step back just as Ian appears in the hallway, followed by Max and Merrick.

"You stay on the ship, out of sight," Ian tells me, and I don't even try not to roll my eyes at him.

"Yes, oh lord and master. Your wish is my command."

"Shit, that's sexy. You should say that to me again later, after all this is done."

"Ian!" My cheeks burn with embarrassment—and maybe a little anticipation—but he just laughs. Right before he lowers his mouth to mine for a kiss that makes my toes curl and my heart beat way too fast.

"Shouldn't you be thinking about what you've got to do down there?" I ask when he finally lets me go. The word comes out a little stilted, as I'm more breathless than I want to admit. For all his faults—of which there are many—the man sure can kiss. And other things, but I have no intention of demonstrating those for our shipmates.

"I am thinking about them. Which is why I need you to promise me you'll stay up here."

"I will. I already promised Beckett."

"Did you?" Ian asks, and the look he gives her is inscrutable. She returns it with interest.

"Okay, are we ready?" Max asks, stepping in front of Beckett and breaking whatever weird eye contact was going on between her and Ian.

I'll ask him about that later, when everything is done. Right now, we all have bigger things to focus on than some new petty conflict.

Everyone but Rain and I slip on breathing masks—apparently, we're the two fragile flowers they don't trust to go out there, besides Gage, who's staying on the bridge in case we need to make a hasty getaway. I get why I'm not allowed out, but what about Rain? I thought she'd want to meet Beckett's mother.

I start to ask, but she doesn't seem in any better of a mood than Beckett. I guess I'm not the only one freaking out about what's going to happen next.

The *Starlight*'s ramp lowers, and the others head down while Rain and I wait in the airlock. But when it comes time to bring the ramp back up, Rain doesn't press the button. Instead, she puts her mask on and steps back through to the top of the ramp. At first, I think she's going to disregard the plan and go down there anyway, but then I realize she's just watching. And that I can, too, without breaking my promise to Ian or Beckett. With the mask on, no one will have any idea who either of us are.

So I slip on my breathing mask as well and then join Rain at the top of the ramp.

This meeting is to pick up the weapons the rebels have brought for us and to make sure we arrive on Delta V47 at the same time.

They've spent hours finalizing the plan over the last days via the comms, and I think everything is finally in place.

I mean, it better be, since it's time to go. And there are no second chances to get this right.

I just hope this meeting goes well. If it does, it will make it so much easier to believe that all the other death-defying steps between us and Milla and Jarved will go well, too.

CHAPTER 92

Beckett

I'm going to throw up. I never get nervous, but right now my palms are sweating and I can't catch my breath. I tell myself it's the oxygen mask—ever since I woke up on the *Caelestis*, I've had a fear of being trapped or closed in, and breathing masks definitely give that feeling.

But I know it's not the mask. It's everything that happened with Rain—and the uncertainty of what's about to happen with my mother. There's a part of me that thinks we'll all be fine. That my mom is going to keep her end of the bargain and we'll get back on the *Starlight* and fly off to the asteroid just like we've planned.

There's another part of me that knows her better than that. Even thinking she's got the better end of the deal here, between the jewelry and her daughter, she's still going to look for an edge. Still going to look for a way to make sure she's the one who comes out on top. After all, she hasn't lived as long as she has as the leader of the Rebellion without being more canny than any opponent she comes up against.

I'm afraid she thinks that includes her own daughter. If that's the case, then I have no idea what she'll do. I just know that a double cross isn't entirely unheard of.

I haven't said anything to the others, but I don't think I have to.

Ian and Max came up in the same school of fucked-up knocks that I did, and they're always prepared for the worst. I just hope this time that preparation is unnecessary, on all our parts.

Once we're on the ground, I glance back up at the ship, and my gaze locks with Rain's. She waves a little when she sees me looking, and the pain in my head—and my stomach—gets a million times worse. I can still smell her on my fingers, can still feel her body moving against mine.

I can't believe that was the last time.

My mother's shuttle has already landed about a hundred meters from the *Starlight*. And as we walk toward it, the door opens and the ramp lowers. Two people appear—Vix and my mother, with translucent breathing masks over their faces.

I step forward to greet them, Merrick on one side of me and Ian on the other. Looks like my mother isn't the only one here with protection. But as we reach them, it's clear their attention is not on us. They're staring at the heptosphere as it floats a few meters off the ground right behind the *Starlight*.

"What the fuck is that?" my mother asks.

"That's the heptosphere," I answer. "I told you about it."

"I didn't think it would be so big." She shakes her head. "We certainly live in strange times, don't we?"

"They're getting stranger by the minute," Ian answers.

I shoot him a look, but he stares at me blandly in response. Then he turns to my mother and says, "Good to see you again, Marlina."

"And you." She nods before nodding at Merrick and Max in turn.

I introduce her to Merrick, and though I don't say he's a member of the Sisterhood, her gaze narrows in on him as if she knows exactly who and what he is. Then again, my mother has been everywhere in Senestris—even the Wilds—and she hears stuff from everywhere. It wouldn't surprise me if she knew Merrick was the high priestess's bodyguard.

"Now that everyone has gotten to know one another, do you have the weapons?" Ian asks. He's really not one for small talk, but I don't blame him. He's been waiting for this day for a long time.

My mother nods to Vix, who walks to the shuttle and enters a code to open the cargo bay doors. Inside are three black metal boxes of what I hope are weapons.

Max and Merrick walk over, pull out the boxes, and bring them to where we're standing. As they do, I notice my mother checking out the *Starlight* again. I turn to look, but I don't see anything amiss.

"Do you mind if we do some inventory?" Ian asks.

My mother's grin is sharp. "I'd be insulted if you didn't."

The guys open the boxes and check the contents. I catalog them, too, from where I'm standing. Laser guns, flash grenades, smoke grenades, explosives—more than we should possibly need. But Ian and Merrick both believe in preparing for any eventuality, and I can't say that I blame them. The only people trickier to deal with than the rebels are the Corporation. No matter how smart and prepared you are, they'll always find a way to screw you over.

I definitely have firsthand experience with that.

"Everything look okay?" my mother asks after they pack the lids back on.

"Looks good," Ian agrees. Then he holds his hand out for my mother to shake.

She takes it, grinning as she looks him right in the eyes. "Pleasure doing business with you," she tells him. And then, as quick as a shooting star, she whips the laser pistol out of her hip holster and fires—straight at the top of the *Starlight*'s ramp.

Straight at Rain…and Kali.

"What the fuck?" Ian exclaims, but I can tell from the look in his eyes that he already knows what's going on.

He tries to rip the gun from my mother's grip, but she kicks him in the balls, then fires up the ramp again and again and again.

I throw myself at her, tackling her around the midsection and taking her down. *Not Rain*, is all I can think as we hit the ground hard. *Not Rain, not Rain, not Rain.*

"You didn't have to do that!" I scream as I try to wrestle the gun away from her.

"Of course I did," she answers, throwing an elbow that catches me in the jaw. "You've already proven that you aren't woman enough to do what had to be done."

Behind me, I can hear Merrick and Ian grappling with Vix, and panic nearly consumes me. Both are good fighters, but Vix is a mountain of a man—the best fighter I've ever seen in my life. Together, they might stand a chance against him, but it isn't a good one.

I start to turn around to warn them, but my mom is rolling on top of me now, her fist pulled back. And I really, really don't want to get in a fistfight with my mother, but I'm not sure I'm going to have a choice. Especially when she brings the fist forward, aimed straight at my nose.

I throw my own fist up, catching her in the mouth. She laughs— cool, Mom—and then rolls off me and fires another several rounds toward the top of the ship.

I'm assuming Kali and Rain aren't ridiculous enough to still be standing there, but that doesn't matter. These are the only people I care about in the whole fucking system, and enough is enough.

I punch my mother full in the face, and when she rears back in shock, I wrench the gun from her hands and level it at Vix—who is more than holding his own against the other two guys.

I don't know where Max went, and right now I don't give a shit. "Back away, Vix!" I yell, firing a blast at his feet to make sure he knows I mean business. I'd never shoot him, but he doesn't need to know that.

"Get the guns and run!" I yell to Merrick and Ian, who are looking at me in shock. I guess this isn't how either thinks a family reunion should go.

My mother rears up, tries to grab the gun from me, and I kick her in the face just hard enough to knock her back down. I don't want to kill her—I just want to keep her out of commission for a few more minutes.

Ian reaches down to grab his gun, but I move so that I'm between him and Vix. No more shots are being fired here today unless I'm the one doing the firing. "Go!" I yell again. This time, I swing the gun around toward them, just so they know I'm an equal-opportunity asshole.

They don't argue again. Instead, they each grab a box of weapons and haul ass up the ramp to the *Starlight* like death herself is after them.

When they get to the top, they turn around and wave at me to join them. But it's too late. I've already made my choice. Besides, if whatever the Corporation did to me ends up killing me, I'm going out alone. No way am I dragging Rain down with me.

But as I watch the *Starlight* fly off into the system without me, I can't help wondering what happens now. And if I'll live long enough to find out.

CHAPTER 93

Ian

"What the Light just happened?" Merrick demands as the *Starlight*'s ramp retracts behind us.

"We got fucked, that's what," I growl. "Beckett's mother fucked us."

I glance around, desperate to lay eyes on Kali. And where the hell is Max?

"*Over here!*" he calls from behind me, and I whirl around to find him and Kali gathered around Rain, who is spread-eagle on the floor. It looks like she just lost a shitload of blood.

I'm ashamed to admit that my first thought is gratitude that it's not Kali, but then I'm leaning over her, trying to get a look at the wound.

"How bad is it?" Merrick asks as he drops to his knees beside her. He looks like shit—nearly as bad as Beckett did as she waved that gun and ordered us to go.

"Not good," Max answers. "It's an arm wound, but she hit an artery."

"We've got to repair it," Merrick says, his eyes lifting to mine. "Do you know how—"

"I could try," I answer grimly. "But Rain was really always the better healer of the two of us."

"I'll get the kit." Kali jumps up and races off toward the sick bay, and I'm struck again by an overwhelming sense of thankfulness that she isn't the one on the ground right now. Doing one surgery on the woman I love is more than enough for me.

That'll be a thought to unpack another day.

"Gage!" I shout. "You're the new pilot now."

"Beckett didn't come after us?" he asks as he emerges from the bridge, then blanches at the sight of Rain. "Where are we going? I know there's a hospital in Rodos—"

"She won't last that long," I tell him. Even though Max has a tourniquet wrapped around her biceps, she's already lost a lot of blood. We need to fix this thing now. "Set course for the asteroid."

"For where?" Merrick growls. "No way are we going after them right now—"

"We don't have a choice. The rebels know our plans. If they trade the information to the Corporation tomorrow or next week, then we're fucked. They'll know we're coming."

"We don't have a distraction," Gage tells me.

"Yeah, well, you're supposed to be the brains of this operation," I say. "You've got just about an hour to figure one out."

Kali comes running back down the corridor, brandishing towels and a bottle of gerjgin in one hand and the large med kit in the other. "I think I got everything," she tells me.

"You did," I answer, then take the bottle of gerjgin and hold it up to Rain's lips. "You're going to want to drink a hell of a lot of this, sweetheart. Because this is going to fucking hurt."

CHAPTER 94

Ian

An hour later, I've got Delta V47 in my sights. The crew is a little tense—between losing Beckett, nearly losing Rain, and then having Gage give a blood transfusion straight from his arm to Rain's, we've all had better afternoons.

And while I don't think Beckett would ever betray us to the Corporation, her mother has proven she can't be trusted. And she knows exactly what our plan is.

Currently, the *Starlight* is situated behind and slightly to the left of the asteroid—which is a huge hulk of gray rock bigger than my home planet—hidden in the lee of another chunk of rock. This place is lethal. There's a good fucking reason it's called the Wilds.

Luckily, the buildings we're aiming for are all on the inner side of the asteroid belt. I don't think the *Starlight* would have survived a journey deeper inside. Even out here, there are chunks of rock flying everywhere that she's constantly having to evade.

This is the part of the plan when the rebel ship would have attacked and created a distraction—but that's gone now. It looks like we're the distraction *and* the rescue operation.

Gage has rigged a kind of computerized bomb that the *Starlight* is supposed to hurl straight at the front of the buildings as we fly on by. It's got a timer that should set it off about two minutes before we reach our chosen extraction zone. It's weak—really weak—but it's all we've got.

Fucking rebels. If we make it out of this alive, I'm not going to forget anytime soon just how badly they screwed us.

But fuck it. It's finally time to move.

My gut tightens, and a zing of excitement sizzles along my nerves. It's happening at last.

I turn to check where Kali is—something I haven't been able to stop doing ever since she nearly got herself shot again, ever since Rain *did* get herself shot—and she's fine, harnessed in and alert and gorgeous, if a little pale.

"I'm firing the distraction," Gage says, pressing one of the weaponry buttons. Seconds later, the bomb deploys.

There goes nothing.

"I'm taking her in," he continues, and I turn my attention back to the HUD on my captain's chair.

We slip out from behind cover. I stare at Delta V47 as it grows bigger on the screen, holding my breath, waiting for the flash of light that would indicate they'd spotted us and are retaliating. Our intel says they don't have any defensive weapons on this side of the asteroid because they don't believe anyone would be reckless enough to venture that far into the Wilds. But then, they haven't met us yet, and intel purchased from shady mercs I worked with years ago has been known to be wrong.

Luckily, there are no shots in our direction.

"Going dark," I say, and the ship's lights go out on approach. Because seeing where we're going when we land on this rock is amateur hour. Obviously.

Would be cool if we could get the *Starlight* to go invisible again, but it's her best-kept secret. Just another perk of captaining a ship with a very stubborn mind of her own.

We descend and hug the surface as we head toward our destination. We're planning on making landfall as close to the building entrances as we can. Hopefully, the guards will all be too busy trying to figure out where the bomb came from to notice the fact that the landscape on this side of the compound has changed.

We're cloaked, obviously, but I can't do anything about the giant orb following us around, so there's only so much hiding we can do.

Our plan is to slip in as quietly as we can and find Milla and Jarved—if he's even here, which I have my doubts about. Part of me thinks we should leave him after that clusterfuck an hour ago, but I can't do that. I can't just leave someone behind. If I could, I'd take everyone in this place—which is a far cry from the old Ian.

But that's not feasible right now, so I'm going to do my best to find Jarved. Even though logic says if he was brought here, he'll be long dead. No one lasts years in the Wilds. No one.

Once we find them, we'll slip out just as quietly as we came in—hopefully before anyone realizes we're here.

But we're ready for a fight. We're all weaponed up, thanks to the two boxes we managed to grab on our way up the ramp. We each have two pistols, and I have the explosives and grenades I asked for in a bag over my shoulder. Just in case we need to blow any doors down.

I can make out the buildings now—the offices, which are squat and hug the gray landscape, and another, darker building that looks a lot like a lab and a prison. My gut tells me that's where Milla will be.

I shudder as it hits me that she's been in this hellhole for three months. Three months.

Gage sets the *Starlight* down gently right beside the lab entrance. I can't see any movement around us, so I'm hoping no one noticed.

He swivels around in the pilot's chair to stare at me with wary eyes. "You ready to go?"

"I will be."

I've been dragging my feet because I'm terrified Milla won't be here—that they've moved her again, and this time we'll never find her—but I can't put it off any longer.

Wiping my clammy palms on the legs of my pants, I take a deep breath and try.

"*Milla?*"

Nothing. I glance across at Max, who's trying as well. He shakes his head.

"*Milla, are you there?*"

Long seconds pass, and my stomach churns.

"*About fucking time.*"

I hear her loud and clear. Max is grinning, so I know he heard it, too.

"*Just don't go anywhere,*" I say. "*We're coming to get you.*"

CHAPTER 95

Kali

"Go!" I hiss, because Ian has stopped halfway down the ramp and he's peering back at me like I'm a recalcitrant child and he's the parent checking to make sure I'm where I should be.

And by should be, I mean where he's ordered me to be.

It's like he's expecting me to do something stupid, like maybe stand at the top of a ramp in plain view of the most wanted woman in the whole system, who's made it her life's mission to annihilate my entire family, and who obviously wasn't opposed to just shooting at anyone on board the *Starlight* on the off chance she turned out to be me.

Rain, who thankfully awoke for a short time, and I have both admitted it wasn't the smartest of moves. But Ian isn't ready to accept our apology.

Still, I'm planning on sticking with him, which is a good thing, considering he's not planning on letting me out of his sight. Max and Merrick will split off to disable the cameras, then head back outside and stop anyone who tries to enter the buildings while we're here. They're both behind us—though Merrick looks like shit. He just got off a last-minute comms call with Serati that I'm sure involved him getting his butt chewed out over Rain's unfortunate near-death experience…

Being Rain's bodyguard isn't nearly as easy as it should be.

And Gage is staying with Rain and the *Starlight*. They'll be ready for a quick getaway if we need it—and I have no doubt we'll need it.

I take a deep breath, then step off the ramp and onto the asteroid. It's like being on a planet, though the air is cold and thin, like I'm at a high elevation.

Ian is beside me in a second. What a surprise. "No handcuffs?" I ask.

"Don't tempt me," he growls.

And I decide to stop messing with him—he's nervous enough without me adding to it.

The ramp lifts behind us, and I turn for a last look at the ship. The heptosphere has settled close by, hovering a few feet off the asteroid's surface. This is the closest I've been to it since the *Caelestis*, and already I can feel its pull.

I ignore it as best I can, but it's not as easy as I'd like.

"Let's go," Ian tells me.

I follow him across the open space to the building entrance. There's a big metal gate, but Max is already there with a laser cutter. At the same time, Merrick uses the handheld device Gage gave him to disable the alarm. It only takes seconds, and the doors swing open.

Once we're inside, we have to move quickly. There are hundreds of cameras, and while we're hoping the guards are distracted by the explosions we can still hear coming from the other side of the compound, that won't last for much longer. Hopefully Merrick and Max will make it to the guard's station, where intel says all the buildings cameras are wired to, and disable them before the entire compound can see our images in high-def.

We get to the end of a hallway, and Ian turns right. He memorized the schematics days ago. But I'm overwhelmed by the sheer number of rooms. We'll never find Jarved in here, if he even is in here.

He pauses for a moment, and I know he's talking to Milla. "To the left, then down four levels," he says quietly. "She's in the single cells reserved for troublemakers."

Yeah, she sounds just like Ian.

Merrick and Max break off to take out the cameras while we find the stairs Milla told him about. The lower we go in the building, the worse the smell gets, a mix between sweat and blood and a strange chemical—something like ammonia? We're heading into the bowels of the asteroid now, and the clean-looking building gives way to jagged rock walls and dark hallways.

There are no cameras on these levels that I can see, and I don't know if it's because the prisoners don't matter or because they think no one would come down here. Or worse—because they don't want what happens down here to be filmed. Either way, I want out. Now. My body is still begging me to go back up, to return to the heptosphere, with a compulsion that has me on the verge of panic.

I ignore the feeling, swallowing my fear as I concentrate on following Ian. The darker it gets, the harder it is to see him—I have to follow the beam of his light as it slices a slim, eerie white line through the shadows. Add in the occasional pain-filled moans, and I'm about to jump out of my skin.

We finally get to the fourth level, and Ian stops at the bottom. Then he heads off, striding purposefully into the darkness that scares the shit out of me.

I tell myself that it's okay, that everything is going to plan. But it doesn't make it any easier to be down here.

The moans are louder, as are the screams of agony, and I want nothing more than to rescue all of them. The fact that this has been going on with my mother's permission—right under my nose— shames me like nothing else ever has.

One way or another, I'm going to end it. No matter what.

Ian stops in front of a heavy wooden door with bolts at the top and bottom. He's still for a minute. I think there must be something wrong—or maybe he's just scared of what he might find behind that door.

But finally, he moves, crouching and wrenching the lower bolt open before straightening and opening the second one as well. Then he pulls the door toward us and flashes the beam of light inside.

A moment later, someone hurls themselves at him. I raise my

pistol, but there's no way I can shoot without hitting Ian.

But judging by his shout of relief, I don't think any shooting will be needed. The light crashes to the ground as Ian wraps his arms around the woman and swings her through the air. She's laughing. I pick up the light and wait for them to finish.

"Whew, you smell," Ian says as they come to a standstill. He puts her gently down, and their foreheads touch as they do the silent-talking thing again.

They both turn to me then, and I get my first good look at Milla. The similarity to Ian is astounding, even more so than with Max. She's tall, maybe five centimeters or so taller than me, and with dark brown skin and eyes that look just like Ian's. Her black hair must have been shaved at some point and is just now growing out.

She also has Ian's sharp cheekbones and passionate mouth—and I'm guessing from the tilt of her chin, she also has Ian's attitude.

Great.

Two assholes to deal with.

But I'm grinning so hard, they can probably see it back on the *Starlight*.

She's wearing a gray jumpsuit, similar to the one Beckett was wearing when we first met, though it's in tatters on her emaciated body. Dark bruises and scars mar her bare arms.

"Who's this?" she asks aloud, giving me a cool look. Even her voice is familiar.

"This is Kali. She's helping out."

Her eyes narrow. "Since when?"

"Since…" He shrugs. "We'll tell you everything later. Right now, we need to move."

"Good idea." She pauses. "How much room do you have for others?"

I step forward. "We should rescue as many as we possibly can. By any chance, do you know a young man named Jarved?"

Milla grins. "Do I ever. And even better—I can lead you to him."

Finally, something has gone our way. For Beckett, we'll get him out.

Milla touches Ian's face. "Thank you. I thought I was going to die in this shithole."

"So did I. And don't thank me yet—a lot has to fall in place before we're out of here." He turns to me. "Kali, lead the way."

So, I do, as fast as I possibly can. Just a little while longer and we can be away from this horrible place.

But there's a lump in my stomach and a horrible feeling that so far, it's been way too easy.

Nothing is going to go wrong, I tell myself. *We planned for everything.*

Too bad I don't believe it.

CHAPTER 96

Ian

We meet up with Max and Merrick on our way down the hallway to the door. Already, I can hear guards' footsteps behind us, and I know it's only a matter of time before they catch up to us.

Milla steps out in front of the group. "Follow me, and we can free the others," she says, and she's speeding ahead, running so fast that I can't keep up, no matter how hard I try.

This is definitely the right next step, but I'm also afraid if we do it, they'll just get slaughtered. That army out there is not fooling around.

I say as much to Milla as we run, but she shakes her head. "*Don't count them out yet.*"

"*They're not even armed,*" I tell her.

"*No, but they aren't completely human anymore, either.*"

"*What does that—*"

She flashes Max and me a mental picture of her legs—or what I think are her legs. I recognize the tattoo on the front of her upper thigh—a three-leaf clover—but the back of her leg...the back of her leg is completely mechanical. No skin, no muscles, just mechanical pieces.

It's horrifying. "What did they do to you?"

"*You're a cyborg?*" Max chimes in. "*A freaking cyborg?*"

"*Experiments to, I quote, improve humanity.*"

I struggle against a new wave of rage. This is what they've been doing out here? This is what those experiments on the *Caelestis* were leading to? Finding people with alien DNA for Doc V's pet heptosphere, and if that didn't work — and they didn't die — she'd send them out here? Make augmented humans, testing tech for the Empire and Corporation to help her torture and kill more innocent people?

I should have killed Dr. Wicked when I had the fucking chance. It's not a mistake I'll make a second time if I ever see that monster again.

"*Are you okay?*" I ask.

"*I'm fast,*" she answers. Which isn't the same thing as okay. At all.

But all those scars on Beckett are starting to make a lot more sense.

Still, now's not the time to get into it, not when I can hear people racing along the corridor behind us. No use getting bogged down in rage when it'll just slow me down. Better to get out of here and figure out how to make them all pay for what they're doing.

We race along the staircase, and Milla stops in front of the first barred cell door. Then she grabs the second pistol out of my belt and shoots out the lock and opens the gates. "Everyone out," she yells. "We're under attack! You can go fight or you can hide until it's over." No one moves. "Out," she shouts.

They start filing forward, and we move on to the next cell. Max, Kali, and I join her in shooting locks open, firing again and again until we hit the last one in the corridor. In it is a young man huddled up in the corner. At first, all I can see is his curly dark hair and dirty gray jumpsuit. But when he lifts his head and sees us, the look of defiance in his yellow eyes is one I immediately recognize. I saw that same look snarking at me from the pilot's chair every day since we found the *Starlight.*

Jarved.

"Let's go, let's go!" Milla is yelling at him, and he slowly gets to his feet. "You can trust them," she continues. "This is Max and Ian."

Recognition hits his wary gaze.

"Your sister sent us," I add. "She gave up everything so we could find you. And we're going to get you back to her now."

Max helps him down the hallway as we make our way forward.

"We need to get to the *Starlight*," I yell as we burst through the door to the outside. "Now!"

I can hear vehicles approaching. Worse, a bunch of shuttles are flying straight for us. I'm guessing they'll be full of troops. And if we don't get out of here fast, then we're well and truly fucked.

We can't fight the guards and the whole Corporation, however much we want to. Live to fight another day and all that shit. Hopefully we gave those people in the cells a chance to fight another day, too—or maybe we doomed them all, but I can't think about that right now. I grab Kali's hand, and we race toward the *Starlight*, which is uncloaked. She shouldn't be uncloaked.

Plus the ramp is up and the door is closed. The heptosphere floats creepily to the side as if it's fucking laughing at me as I press the ramp button again and again. I hit the comms unit on my wrist. "Gage, open the goddamn door." There's no answer, and I swear. "Gage, where the hell are you?"

Still nothing. Bastard. A sick feeling starts in my stomach as I stare at the ship, seething with frustration. She's shut up tight, and there's absolutely no way in.

"Call Rain," Kali suggests.

"No way she's awake yet—she needed to rest," I say. "I drugged the hell out of her."

"Try anyway!" Max tells me. "We can't just stand here waiting to get shot."

I buzz the sick bay. "Rain, Rain are you awake?"

No answer.

I do it again. Still nothing.

I can see the vehicles now. Approaching from the right, they're huge, armored trucks with big wheels for crossing the rocky terrain. Off to the left, the first shuttle hovers just meters above the asteroid's surface, disgorging its content of troops before rising up again. They're dressed in the black-and-purple mecha armor of the Imperial forces. So, this little nightmare is officially a joint venture, then. Good to know.

A sudden shiver runs down my spine, and I turn to check on Kali, then go still as a whole new horror explodes within me. "Where's Kali?"

CHAPTER 97

Kali

"Kali!"

I stop running back through the hallways, where I'd headed to try to find a ladder or something to help us get into the *Starlight* without the use of the locked ramp. Someone is calling my name, though, so I turn and peer into the shadows. Gage is standing in a doorway, gesturing for me to join him.

I hesitate, but he gestures again, and I head over. Maybe he's hurt and needs help.

But when I get to him, he looks perfectly fine.

"What are you doing here, Gage? You were supposed to stay with the *Starlight*. We can't get in. We have to get on board. Now. We've got a lot of freed prisoners to help."

He doesn't answer, and I peer at him in the dim light. There's something up. I take a step closer, and he lunges for me. His hand grasps my wrist, and I pull back.

What the fuck?

Brain clouded with panic, I try to remember what Ian taught me about fighting. I make my muscles relax and let him drag me against him, then raise my knee and jab him in the balls. And miss. His grip tightens, so I reach up and try to claw his face. I have no clue what's going on with Gage, but my instincts tell me it's nothing good. Especially when I remember the closed-up *Starlight*.

Thankfully, he's not a fighter like Ian and we're pretty evenly matched. I can do this. I make a fist and start to plunge it into his side, but before I connect, he presses something against me and a shocking pain shoots through me.

I lose control of my body and crash to the floor. And for a moment, everything goes black.

When I come back, he's dragging me along the corridor upright, his arms around my waist, away from the *Starlight*. I feel as weak as a newborn drokaray.

"What did you do?"

"Stunner. There'll be no permanent damage. I don't want to hurt you, Kali. In fact, I'm here to save you."

"Save me from what?" I snarl.

"There's no chance for the others. They're going to die. But *we* don't need to."

He pauses at the door and peers out.

Panic is clawing at my guts. Where's Ian? Hasn't he realized I'm missing? The man hasn't taken his eyes off of me in days, and he chooses to start now? I have to keep Gage talking, slow him down from whatever he's up to—eventually he'll slip up and I'll find an opportunity to get back to the crew. "Gage, please tell me what's going on. Then I'll go with you quietly."

He licks his lips and shifts nervously. "Dr. Veragelen contacted me just after you all left the ship. She told me she'd reactivated the chip in my head. I didn't know she could do that. That's how she found us. She says she can set it to self-destruct and it will blow up my head. But if I do what I'm told, she promised she'll take me back into the Corporation. And all I have to do is save your life."

Fury fills me, red spots dancing in front of my eyes. "That's not all you had to do. You betrayed us. You locked us out of the *Starlight* so we couldn't escape. How? What did you do?"

"Shut down the systems. Then blew out the door mechanism—just in case she decided to override me."

Bastard. "If the others die, I'll make sure you do as well."

"You don't understand. I don't have a choice."

How many times have I thought that? How many times have I justified my actions—or more likely, my lack of actions—by telling myself I have no choice? But it wasn't true then, and it's not true now.

"You always have a choice," I tell him. "You just have to accept the consequences. Take me back before it's too late."

"I'll die if I do that. So will you. And the others will all die anyway. We can't win against the Corporation."

I glare at him, trying to raise my arms to push him away, but I still have almost no strength. A few more minutes, and I might be able to fight him off again. "Maybe you can't, but—"

"Gage!"

I almost sag to the floor at the sound of Ian's voice. And yeah, saving myself is all well and good, but sometimes it fucking rules to have a crew to back you up.

I stare at Ian. He's not alone. Milla, Max, Jarved, and Merrick are behind him, plus a whole crowd of people in ragged gray jumpsuits. The prisoners.

Ian's face is deadly as he raises his pistol. "Let her go, Gage."

"I can't do that. And I'll kill her if I have to." He presses the weapon into my side.

Ian growls low in his throat. "You harm one hair on her head, and I'll rip off your arms and beat you to death with them."

But I can see the frustration on his face. He won't risk attacking Gage in case he hurts me. And I can't allow Gage to take me out of here. I'm guessing that's the only thing that is delaying the troops from an all-out attack on the others. They're waiting for word that Gage has gotten me free.

It's good to know how much Dr. Veragelen believes she needs me. You never know when you'll need a bargaining chip. But first, I have to get away from Gage.

I take a deep breath. I can do this. I've been trained by the best, after all.

I move as fast as my muscles will let me, jabbing my elbow into

Gage's solar plexus. He gasps and folds over, and I pull my arm forward, punching up. Pain radiates through my hand as I catch him in the jaw. He screams, and I finally jerk my arm free and stumble forward.

Gage reaches for me just as a blast comes from the left of us. It takes him in the chest, and he spins with the impact. His eyes turn sightless, and he's dead before he crashes to the ground.

I turn slowly. Max stands there, arm outstretched, pistol in his hand.

His face is expressionless as he drops his arm to his side, and with a last glance at Gage, he turns away.

Then Ian is on me, wrapping his arms around me and hugging me close.

"Handcuffs," he mutters into my hair. "Fucking handcuffs."

CHAPTER 98

Ian

I'm pretty sure that was the worst moment of my life. Fucking Gage. I never should have trusted him.

"You did great," I tell Kali. Better than I would have expected. She kept her cool and gave us the chance we needed. But I'm still shaking, and I don't want to let her go.

I take a deep breath and step back. We have to get off this asteroid and get everyone to safety. Because once we're safe, I want nothing more than to hear her say she loves me. And then I'm taking her to bed and we're not coming out until the world explodes around us. And maybe not even then.

The prisoners are pouring through the corridor now. I tug Kali to the side as they stream past, dozens of them, heading for the entrance. We told them there's an army out there—I guess they don't care, but only a couple of them are armed.

It's going to be a massacre.

The first of them rushes out into the open. I hear cries and the crash as the body hits the ground. It doesn't deter the others. They're flooding out, and the air fills with a cacophony of blasts.

We were supposed to sneak out the back way. That was the plan.

I grit my teeth, then look at Kali. She nods.

I look at Max, who nods as well.

"We're going out there." We're going to help these people, and we're going to die. I don't want to die. Not before Kali tells me she loves me.

Fuck. When did I become such a fucking sap?

"Anyone got an objection to that?"

No one does.

Looks like it's unanimous, then, although Milla is looking a little confused. Altruism hasn't been a big part of our lives before now. But she draws her weapon with the rest of us. "Let's do this."

I turn to the rest of the people who have been kept prisoner here. "Give us five minutes to clear the way. Then go for it. Grab any weapons you can." I look around at them all, and I feel like I have to say it. "Most of you aren't going to make it. But some of you might."

"Which are better odds than we had before," one of the women says. "No one survives here for very long."

I nod. But Milla did. Jarved did. "If we do get out of here and back to our ship, we'll fit as many of you on board as we can. For the rest of you, we'll call for help and make certain you're safe."

There is one thing I have on my side. I reach into my bag and pull out the grenades I brought along. I expected to be blowing up doors, but they should work just as well with people. I have four. I hope it will be enough to give us an edge. I hand one each to Kali and Max and toss another to Merrick.

I take a deep breath and head for the entrance. Kali is beside me, and Milla and Max are right behind me, with Merrick bringing up the rear.

I peer outside. The light is dim, but I take it all in in a second. A troop of Imperial soldiers is marching our way. The Corporation guards have taken cover behind a row of trucks off to the left. "Kali— aim your grenade for the trucks. The rest of us will go for the troops. Then shoot for their knees. It's the weak point in the mecha armor."

I step outside with all of them beside me. We have to shift around the dead bodies already littering the entrance. At first, the soldiers don't shoot; they seem to be waiting for something, though I don't know what.

Not that it matters, because I'm not waiting. "Now," I yell.

I pull the pin and toss my grenade before diving to the ground as the roar of explosions fills the air. My ears are ringing from the blasts, and the place has descended into chaos, wounded troops and guards screaming. I hear the people from the cells streaming out behind me as I roll to my feet and come up shooting. Kali is beside me, arm outstretched as I taught her. Her eyes are screwed up, but she's doing okay.

I take out one of the soldiers who's still standing. Then another who's trying to get to his feet. There's no room for mercy right now when we're fighting for our lives.

Finally, I'm standing back-to-back with Kali, gun arm outstretched but with no one left to shoot.

We're still alive. I really hadn't expected that.

It all goes silent except for the moans of the dying. Then a huge cheer goes up from the prisoners who are left. I do a quick check of my little group—we're all still standing, though Merrick has taken a shot to the leg. It looks like just a graze, though. He'll survive.

I turn to face Kali. I expect to see triumph, but she's staring around at the devastation, her lower lip wobbling for all it's worth.

"We had to do it," I say. "It was us or them."

"I know. But it's not fair. They were just doing their jobs. They didn't know why."

"They should have asked why," Merrick says.

We can debate later. Right now: "We need to get to the *Starlight*."

"We're going to have to find a way in. Gage sabotaged it."

"That greedy fucking backstabbing bastard."

Before I can figure out what to do, the comms unit on my arm crackles, and then we hear a voice.

"*This is the battle cruiser* Ravenol. *We have a four-thousand-kilogram warhead aimed at your position. Surrender your weapons and yourselves or we will completely annihilate the asteroid. You have five minutes.*"

And then the comms unit goes dead.

CHAPTER 99

Kali

I stare up at the sky where the huge ship floats like some bloated slogg. I can see the weapons launcher situated at the front. It's aimed right at us.

I can't believe we've come so far, done so much, just for it to end like this.

Five minutes.

Less, now.

I don't want to die.

I look around at all the devastation, then at the *Starlight*. It can't end here.

Ian slips his hand into mine. "We can surrender if that's what you want. They probably won't harm you—"

"We're not surrendering," I snarl. Because they may save my life, but all my friends will die. And I could never live with that.

There has to be a way. I just have to think of it.

My gaze settles on the heptosphere. I did say I was going to test it out here in the Wilds, but that idea required *fewer* people. Not dozens of innocent people relying on us for their survival. Still, we need something big. Something drastic.

I didn't want the danger that comes with being the Star Bringer.

But maybe—just maybe—it's time to embrace it.

I take off running toward the heptosphere, glancing back to make sure Ian is still with me. He is—and so is everyone else. They're all behind me.

I skid to a halt in front of the orb where it hovers only a meter from the ground, and I have to rethink my idea. An Ancient artifact with the power to create and destroy suns. Maybe it's not such a great idea to just fire it without knowing what it can do.

But then I look up at the sky and realize the warhead in the *Ravenol*'s weapons launcher is glowing. We really are almost out of time.

"Go ahead, Kali." Merrick is standing next to me, a confidence I'm far from feeling on his face.

But something strange *is* happening inside me. It's like the thing is calling out in my head, asking me to touch it. Before I make the conscious decision to do so, I'm walking over there, my feet moving of their own accord.

And then it's right there in front of me, and every ounce of my body yearns to touch it.

I turn to Ian, one last question in my eyes. But he just nods, and so I raise my hands and press them to the curved side of the heptosphere.

It's warm, and there's a soft vibration deep within it. But that's all I feel, all there is. Until a shudder runs through it—runs through me—and my head is filled with whirling iridescent lights.

It's awake.

But what now?

I don't even know what it does, let alone how to get it to work.

I glance up at the sky and see that the weapons launcher is glowing red now, preparing to fire.

"Do something," I plead with the giant orb. "Please don't let all these people die—"

I break off as another shudder slams through me, bigger than the first. And then the orb is rising and turning slowly on an invisible axis. A beam of light shoots out of it, *but in the opposite direction of the battle cruiser.*

Shit! This is why I wanted a chance to practice! I'm terrified to look, terrified to see what the heptosphere is aiming at.

But then Ian mutters, "Holy shit," behind me, and I have to look.

I glance at him and realize he's staring at the *Starlight*, his eyes wide. The beam from the orb is hitting her straight on, and she's coming to life, lights flashing all around her as she, too, lifts off the ground and turns so that she's facing the sky.

But she's too late. I took too long.

The battle cruiser releases its warhead in a flash of light, and I brace for impact, reaching for Ian.

Except, bolstered by the heptosphere, the *Starlight* blasts a ray of light right back, and this one is so bright that I screw up my eyes to keep from burning them. Seconds later, a huge crash fills my ears, and when I open my eyes, the sky is filled with a burning orange ball. It's all that's left of the battle cruiser. Another blast of light, another explosion, and the shell shatters into a thousand pieces.

"Get under cover," Ian screams. But there isn't any.

But that's okay, because the *Starlight* has thought of everything. A thousand rays of light emanate from the heptosphere and spread out in all directions, and as they hit the debris, the pieces explode, filling the sky with falling stars.

Looks like I really am the Star Bringer.

CHAPTER 100

Kali

The sky above us is clear. The shuttles were either destroyed in the blast or have fled. The lights in the heptosphere are fading as the *Starlight* comes in to land close to where we're standing.

Now we just need to get inside.

We approach the side of the ship, and Ian does what he tends to do. Bang the shit out of the door. Nothing happens.

"Why is that always your answer?" I ask from beside him.

"Because it works sometimes." He shrugs.

Just when he looks like he's about to try again, the hatch on the top of the ship flies open and Rain sticks her head out.

"I can't get the ramp to go down," she shouts to us, her eyes going wide as she looks around. "What'd I miss?"

She looks a little groggy but otherwise pretty good for having just been shot. And I start laughing, because—despite everything—we're alive. And right now, that's all that fucking matters.

"Throw down the ladder and we'll fill you in," I say.

"Her arm—" Merrick starts, but I narrow my eyes at him.

"She can do a lot more than you give her credit for, you know."

As if to prove my words, the ladder comes rolling down the side. Looks like we're back in business after all.

We herd as many people onto the *Starlight* as we can fit. She's not large by any means, and many others will have to wait for us to get a separate ship here to take them home. But we've lost Gage, and we've lost Beckett, and there's no way I'm leaving this shithole without as many others as we can squeeze on board.

Merrick and I get them settled in the galley and storage bay, with Milla guiding the ones who need help. It's not exactly luxury quarters, but it's better than the airlock. And way better than the evil lab we freed them from.

But on our way back to the bridge, I get a strange feeling inside of me—a hollowness in my stomach that gets worse the closer I get to the strange, locked room at the center of the *Starlight*.

As we pass it, I lay a hand on the wall, as I always do. But instead of the comfort I usually feel, the second my fingers touch it, an electric shock shoots through me.

It's strong enough that I yank my hand back with a shudder.

"What's wrong?" Milla asks, suspicious.

"Nothing. I'm just…jumpy, I guess." I start walking quickly, determined to put as much distance between me and that room as I can. But the greater the distance, the worse the hollowness inside me gets.

I do my best to ignore it once Milla, Merrick, and I make it back to the bridge.

Ian is just hanging up with Marlina. And judging from the satisfied look on his face, he convinced her to rescue the people we had to leave behind. The news that we found and saved her son should have helped.

"So, where do you want to go?" Ian asks once Rain gets Jarved settled in our old cabin and Max finishes taking inventory of our existing food supplies. It'll be tight for a while, no doubt, but we'll get more provisions as soon as we can. "The Senestris System is ours for the taking."

"Except for the fact that we're still wanted," Max tells him dryly.

"And we never did figure out who's trying to kill us," Rain adds. "We should probably do that before we go too wild."

"I already know," Merrick says.

"Oh, yeah?" Ian tosses him a questioning look as he fiddles with his HUD, which appears to be stuck in the lowered position. "By all means, fill us in."

"That call I got, right before we went to free Milla—it was from a contact of mine back on Serati. I reached out to him a few days ago for some information, and he finally came through."

"Serati?" Rain says, sounding shocked. "Why am I certain I'm not going to like what you've got to say?"

"Because it's the Sisterhood that's been trying to kill us. And by us, I mean you and Kali."

"Me?" I can't help feeling a little outraged. "What did I ever do to them?"

And then I remember. Much like everything else in my life to date, it's not what I've done. It's what my mother's done. Good thing I'm ready to start changing that, because so far, she's done a pretty crappy job with my life.

"They want to kill us both," Rain says slowly, like the answer is just starting to dawn on her. I lean forward, interested in what she has to say and if it's the same idea percolating in my head now.

"If they kill Kali, the high priestess will be reborn. But the optics of that won't work if I'm still alive." She looks at Merrick. "So they have to kill us both, and that will start everything over again. And they think they'll finally get their Star Bringer."

"Except they've already got her," Merrick says, and he's grinning at me just like a proud cousin would.

"I wouldn't go that far as to say they have me. I'm still not sure I know how to use that thing," I tell him.

"Pretty sure the heptosphere just proved you wrong," Ian replies.

And I can't help remembering what it felt like to touch it, to feel the warmth and power of it pulsing against my palms. Maybe they're right. Too bad I don't have a clue what I'm supposed to do about it.

"I hate to be the harbinger of doom," Max says, "but it occurs to me that we've got another problem."

"No you don't," Milla teases him. "You do love your problems."

"Well, with no Gage and no Beckett…" He trails off and waits for it.

"Well, shit," Ian grumbles from where he is now banging on the console of the captain's chair to no avail. He stops abruptly and turns to look at me with an odd glint in his eye.

"Why are you looking at me?" I ask. And then it dawns on me. "No way. I'm not ready. Beckett didn't really teach me that much. I just sort of listened in while she taught Rain. Maybe she—"

"No way," Rain interrupts with a knowing grin. "I just got shot. No flying for me. Besides, I'm pretty sure I'm going to have to be the new mechanic."

"Can you actually fix things?" Ian asks, sounding skeptical.

"Well, I know better than to just bang on them, so I feel like I'm already a step ahead of you." As if to prove it, she reaches over with her good arm and tightens something under his console. Seconds later, his HUD rises smoothly.

"Point made," Max says.

"Thanks," Ian tells her, then grins at me. "I'm the captain, and the captain's orders are to get your butt in that pilot's chair."

I'll admit I've never been so nervous in my life…but also a little excited as I do as he asks and slide into Beckett's chair.

Once there, I take a moment and press my hand to the yellow hair tie Beckett left wrapped around the armrest. Then I lean forward and press the *Starlight*'s ignition.

The ship comes to life around us, and I grin. "Where to, Captain?"

"Anywhere but this fucking asteroid," Ian answers.

"Yes, sir," I tease, trying to concentrate on him instead of the weird feeling inside me that seems to be getting stronger. Surely it will ease once we're away from this evil place.

Seconds later, we're clearing the atmosphere and flying straight into space, the entire solar system spread out in front of us.

Freedom has never looked so good.

But twenty minutes later, with a long-term course set for Serati—we've got some wanted posters to deal with—the feeling is so bad it's all I can do to stay in my seat. And that's before something else strange happens.

Ian's HUD lights up, and the screen shows a perfect view of the heptosphere, which is still following behind us. But it looks different. It's all lit up, with a red light coming out of the top and a bunch of numbers running across its black center.

"What is that?" I ask, changing the front right viewing screen to show the image so we can all get a better look.

30 – 07 – 10 – 15

As we watch, it changes.

30 – 07 – 10 – 14

30 – 07 – 10 – 13

30 – 07 – 10 – 12

"It's a countdown," Max says.

30 – 07 – 10 – 11

"But to what?" Rain wonders.

"Oh, fuck no," Milla says, coming to stand next to me, her eyes glued to the heptosphere. "Please tell me that isn't what I think it is."

She looks down at me then, and our eyes meet. "Depends on what you think it is?"

"Out in the Wilds, people talk. Lots of it is just rumors, but there was one thing I kept hearing over and over again, and you just don't hear the same story that many times without a little bit of truth. That there was a large device the Empire was trying to use to save us, but in reality it's dangerous. Dangerous to humans in a way we might never fully understand before it's too late."

Something about the way she says it turns all the blood in my veins to ice. Because what could be more dangerous to humans than a sun about to explode?

Before I can ask Milla for an explanation, more lights flash on the heptosphere, all different colors shining into space.

"What the hell is it doing now?" Max asks.

I don't know. But the more those lights flash on the heptosphere, the more impossible the compulsion inside me is to ignore, until finally I can't resist anymore. While everyone else crowds around the screen, waiting to see what happens next, I unbuckle my harness, stand, and walk down the hall.

For the first time since we've been on board the *Starlight*, the locked door is open. Wide open.

"What the hell?" Ian says from behind me. Turns out he and the others have followed me from the bridge. "You finally figured out how to open it?"

I shake my head, because I had nothing to do with this.

"Well, the *Starlight* obviously wants us to see something." Rain gives us an impatient look before squeezing past me and walking in.

Despite the hollowness inside me—and the compulsion all but screaming at me—I don't want to go in that room. But staying out here won't change whatever's in there, so I exchange an oh-shit glance with Ian and then walk inside.

It's not as bad as I feared. I don't know what I was thinking we'd find, but it's not the giant rectangular display that takes up an entire wall of the room.

"What does it do?" Max asks as we get closer to it.

"I don't know," I answer. "Maybe Gage—" I break off as it hits me, really hits me, that he'll never fix another problem on the *Starlight* again.

No matter how angry I am at him for what he did back there on the asteroid, there's a part of me that grieves for him and what could have been, too.

Ian rubs a comforting hand down my back, but before I can tell him I'm okay, a laser shoots out of a tiny device above the display and scans Rain, who is standing closest to it.

"What the—" Max breaks off as it scans him, too.

Nothing happens on the screen, except the laser moves on to Ian. Then Merrick. Then Milla. And then, finally, me.

When it scans me, instead of moving on, it emits one long, high-pitched beep. And then hundreds and hundreds of file names begin rolling across the screen from top to bottom in small blue print— conveniently legible, considering this was made by the Ancients, so maybe the *Starlight* is translating it for me.

"What is all this?" Rain asks.

Max shakes his head. "I don't know. It's scrolling so fast that I can't read it."

"What about you, Kali?" Merrick queries. "Why don't you try touching the screen?"

Everything in me recoils, except...not really. My brain definitely doesn't want to touch the screen, but every other part of my body yearns for it.

"Go ahead," Ian says. "We're all right here."

Something tells me we're never going to get anywhere if I don't touch it, so I finally take a deep breath and reach toward the screen.

The second I touch one of the files, it opens up, information spreading across the wall.

"Moderate success," I read from the central section, as most of the others contain nothing but numerical data. "Two dead planets, Tybris and Nabroch. Life flourishing on other planets."

"Moderate success?" Merrick asks, sounding as bewildered as I feel. "Moderate success at what?"

I swipe the file away and choose another one from the list that continues to scroll by.

This one has a lot of numerical data as well, but it has the same central summary. SENESTRIS BATCH SPECIMENS 77% SUCCESSFUL TO DATE, THOUGH DATA SUGGEST SUCCESS RATE WILL DROP TO 55% BY END OF MILLENNIUM. ASKKANDIA IS THE MOST FRUITFUL PLANET, FOLLOWED BY KRIDACUS AND GLACEA, THOUGH DATA SUGGEST GLACEA MAY DROP OFF SOON. RECOMMENDATION: PRE-EXTINCTION HARVEST.

"Harvest?" Rain whispers. "What do they mean by harvest?"

"Nothing good," I answer grimly. But when I go to swipe on a third file, the display lets out a series of high-pitched beeps. And then numbers begin running across the screen.

The same numbers we saw on the heptosphere a few minutes ago. Except the sequence now reads: 30 – 07 – 03 – 57

We've lost six minutes from whatever it's counting down to.

We wait another couple of minutes, just to see what happens. But no matter where I touch the display, the only thing that changes is the numbers on the countdown sequence as they continue to scroll across the screen.

"I don't like this," Max says.

"Yeah, no shit," Ian replies. "But there's nothing we can do about it from in here."

He walks out of the room, and I follow him, because he's right. Although I can't help but think there's nothing we can do about it anywhere else, either.

And that's before we get back to the bridge and confirm the countdown sequence is still displayed on the heptosphere. Except around the center where it started, there is something new. A sentence that reads:

HUMANOID SPECIMENS OF THE SENESTRIS SYSTEM. WE HAVE FOUND YOU AND ARE ON OUR WAY. OUR HARVEST IS OVERDUE.

"There's that word again," Merrick comments. "Harvest."

The heptosphere emits more flashing lights, and then the phrase running across the center changes again.

POPULATION HARVEST TO COMMENCE IN 30 − 06 − 59 − 12

"Population harvest?" Merrick repeats. "What exactly does that mean?"

"I think you know exactly what that means," Ian answers.

Rain shudders. "Us? Something wants to harvest us?"

"Pre-extinction harvest." I repeat what we read in the locked room.

"But what's going on?" Rain asks, pointing at the heptosphere. "We've had that thing following us for days, and that room never unlocked before."

"Kali must have connected them," Max suggests. "When she did that thing on Delta V47 with the heptosphere and the *Starlight*."

"You think that's what did this?" I ask, horrified. "You think I somehow activated the countdown?"

"Do you have a better suggestion?" He raises a brow at me.

I don't, but before I can say that, the heptosphere changes yet again. The words disappear in an array of colored lights, leaving only the countdown running across the middle of the sphere and a pulsing light that appears at the poles of the orb.

"What do you think those lights are for?" I whisper, though I'm afraid I already know.

"It looks like a beacon," Merrick answers, confirming my worst fears.

"So, let me get this straight." Ian runs a hand down his face. "Not only have we somehow communicated to something out there that we're ready to be harvested, but we've also given them a fucking lodestar to help them on the journey?"

"That's not terrifying at all," Milla drawls.

"That's not even the most terrifying part," I tell her.

"What is?" She looks more curious than horrified, which makes one of us.

Rain answers for me. "What out there is so advanced that they think of us as nothing more than plants to harvest?"

"Exactly," I agree, reaching for Ian's hand as a chill runs through me. "And what are they planning to do with us once the harvest is complete?"

ACKNOWLEDGMENTS

Writing this book has been so exciting, and I am thrilled to have the best team in the world to work on it with me.

Nina Croft, thanks for being a great writing partner.

Stacy Abrams, your patience and enthusiasm are infectious. Thank you for all the late-night phone calls and brilliant ideas.

Emily Sylvan Kim, you are the best agent in the world. Thanks for everything you did to make this book a reality.

Hannah Lindsey, for everything. Sincerely. You are the most wonderful tour companion, copy editor, and all-around support system a girl could ever ask for.

Liz Pelletier, thank you for everything. I've wanted to write a space book forever, and I will always be grateful to you for making that dream a reality. You're amazing!

Molly Majumder, for taking so much time and effort to help this book shine. Thank you for everything.

Thank you to everyone at Entangled and Macmillan for all of your help and support with this book. I am so lucky to be a part of such an amazing team. Special thanks to Veronica Gonzalez, Curtis Svehlak, Toni Kerr, Heather Riccio, Meredith Johnson, Bree Archer, Elizabeth Turner Stokes, Nicole Resciniti, and the Entangled Buddy Read for everything you all did to get this book into the hands of readers.

My family, for all your love and support through all the late nights. I adore you all.

And finally, thank you to my incredible fans. I have the most wonderful fans in the business and I am so, so grateful for every single one of you.

—Tracy

ACKNOWLEDGMENTS

Many thanks to the entire team at Entangled Publishing for their exceptional efforts in bringing *Star Bringer* to life! I'm so in love with the cover. And a special thanks to Liz Pelletier, for inviting me to be part of this amazing book, for her ideas, advice, constant enthusiasm, and for her belief in my abilities. I've loved every moment of working on Star Bringer.

To the wonderful Tracy Wolff, my coauthor, whose collaborative spirit, insights, and creativity have enriched every page of this book.

To Rob, my other and better half, for putting up with me constantly disappearing into worlds of my own making, and for his unwavering support and encouragement.

Lastly, to all the readers, who I hope will have as much fun reading *Star Bringer* as I had writing it. Thank you!

—Nina

Do you love fiction with a supernatural twist?

Want the chance to hear news about your favourite authors (and the chance to win free books)?

Christine Feehan
J.R. Ward
Sherrilyn Kenyon
Charlaine Harris
Jayne Ann Krentz and Jayne Castle
P.C. Cast
Maria Lewis
Darynda Jones
Hayley Edwards
Kristen Callihan
Keri Arthur
Amanda Bouchet
Jacquelyn Frank
Larissa Ione

Then visit the *With Love* website and
sign up to our romance newsletter:
www.yourswithlove.co.uk

And follow us on Facebook for book giveaways,
exclusive romance news and more:
www.facebook.com/yourswithlovex

PIATKUS